英文溝通寫作全技藝

求職、行銷、情書、慰問…
50種工作與生活情境, 面面俱到
的英文書信寫作要點

How
to Say It

Choice Words, Phrases, Sentences, and
Paragraphs for Every Situation

Rosalie Maggio   Jason Lee

鄒詠婷   羅莎莉・瑪吉歐   李佳勳

譯   著   審訂

作者序

《英文溝通寫作全技藝》是本容易使用的實用工具書，它會告訴你該說些什麼，以及該怎麼說。這本書的篇排方式給予讀者很大的使用空間，讓讀者能在短時間內組織出一封鏗鏘有力的信。

在今日，雖然電話、通訊 app、電子郵件或面對面的方式已經成為主流溝通方式，但在商場，把信寫好依然是成功的必要條件，信件亦是人與人之間最強烈的連結之一。

《英文溝通寫作全技藝》一書提供廣泛的單字、詞組、句子與篇章段落，讓你在各種溝通主題上，都能用自己的觀點與風格表達想法。這些清單就像同義詞字典一樣，陳列了與各種主題相關的用語。無論你希望聽起來正式或輕鬆、傳統或現代、專業或休閒、冷淡或親切，無論你想寫的是強勢、令人信服的商業書信，或是溫暖親密的私人信函，都能在本書中找到適合的措詞。

寫信並沒有標準答案，你可以遵循書中的指導，也可以修改、甚至忽略它，因為你比任何一本工具書更了解你寫信的對象與想傳達的訊息。除了拿破崙之外（他一生寫了超過五萬封的信，從來沒有人叫他「做點更有意義的事吧！」），幾乎每個人都能透過這本書，把信件寫得更快、更有個人風格，並從中獲取更多成就以及樂趣！

Rosalie Maggio
羅莎莉・瑪吉歐

中文版推薦序

國立台灣師範大學翻譯研究所教授　廖柏森

隨著全球化腳步的快速進展，國人以英文書信（包括電子郵件和傳真）與外國人士溝通的機會越來越多，內容訊息也越來越複雜。舉凡工作上的協商討論、提案報告、商品訂單、邀約請求、客訴抱怨、求職申請等，乃至於社交的節慶恭賀、弔唁問候、推薦建議等各種情境，都常需要以書面文字傳達訊息，但這也為我們帶來許多英文用字的困難和跨文化溝通的問題。

英文不是我們的母語，大多數人也缺乏於英語系國家生活的經驗，因此在書寫英文書信時經常難以拿捏詞句的正確性、語氣的適切性、語域（register）的正式程度、以及面對各種情境想要達成的功能目的。例如商業書信傾向正式嚴肅、私人信件講求溫馨親密，反映在詞章上就有迥異的文體風格和文字調性，加上中西社會文化的差異，導致我們在撰寫英文書信時備感艱辛。

幸而 EZ 叢書館引進美國經典的書信寫作書《英文溝通寫作全技藝》（*How to Say It*），可以有效解決此種難題。這本書的原文是以美國讀者為對象，九〇年代上市後就受到熱烈歡迎，不僅長年暢銷，還蔚為風潮，進而衍生數十本的系列書籍（如 *How to Say It Best, How to Say It at Work, How to Say It from the Heart, How to Say It to Seniors* 等）和眾多類似的仿作（如 *How to Write It, What to Say & How to Say It* 等），令人目不暇接。筆者於美國留學期間在書店就常看到這些書，連大賣場 Costco 也有特價銷售（是種居家必備工具書的概念），我難免心動購買幾本臨摹學習，對提升英文書信寫作能力的助益極大。同時我也深刻體會到，美國人在使用自己的母語作書面溝通時，其實也是需要學習訓練的，並不是會講英文的人就自然而然會寫好英文書信，溝通過程還包含許多做人處事的眉角訣竅。更何況，台灣讀者的母語是中文，在學習英文書信寫作時更應該取法乎上，以美國人使用的道地英文書信為學習標竿，而不要落入自創中式英文（Chinglish）的陷阱，造成辭不達意，可能還要為溝通錯誤付出慘痛代價。

有別於一般書信範本只是提供範例，這本《英文溝通寫作全技藝》的特色極為鮮明，共收錄多達 50 個不同主題（如求職信、公告通知、表揚信、致謝函、介紹信、拒絕信、慰問信、情書等），並依書信功能分為九大類（如基本禮儀、表達立場、職場交流、維繫情感等），內容豐富詳實，讀者可視個人需求選擇寫作的功能和主題。而每個主題又分為「使用時機」、「該怎麼說」、「什麼不該說」、「寫作訣竅」、「特殊狀況」、「格式」、「單字」、「詞組」、「句子」、「示範段落」、「示範信」，架構清楚而有系統，讓我們知其然，知其所以然，甚至知其不然，也就是了解什麼是不該寫的內容，可說是學到全方位跨文化溝通的精髓。

另外，讀者在使用這本書時會發現，不同主題情境的信件內容當然會有差異，但其詞彙組合和句法型式經常具有固定的慣用搭配。因此讀者寫信時，除了可從書上抄錄套用大量詞組和例句之外，還可由附贈的光碟中複製範例段落和信件，貼上所需的相關內容，方便快速即可完成措詞精確、語氣得體、達成溝通目的之英文書信。

總言之，筆者欣見這本經典工具書能夠引進國內，並譯成清楚流暢的中文版。相信透過此書的協助，英文書信寫作對國內英文學習者而言，不再是遙遠的攻略目標，而是垂手可得的溝通成果。請讀者善加利用，享受省時又輕鬆的書寫過程。

本書使用說明

✉ 目錄依溝通功能分類，加速找到需要的章節

本書目錄依「溝通功能」將 50 種溝通章節分成九大類，這九大溝通功能就像索引一樣，你可以先鎖定溝通功能，就能更快找到需要的書信章節。以下為本書的九大溝通功能：

1. 各種狀況通用	2. 基本禮儀	3. 傳遞訊息
4. 表達立場	5. 求職申請	6. 職場交流
7. 利益相關	8. 維繫情感	9. 安排個人計畫

✉ 各主題章節依內容分成三大部分，依需求隨找隨用

每個章節內容細分成三大部分，分別是「說明篇」，「應用篇」與「範例篇」：

Part 1 說明篇：
先簡單介紹主題、列出此種信件的使用時機，並說明一封信須包含的要素，與應避開的內容。此外，提供特殊狀況下該如何措詞的實用建議，並說明適用的格式。

Part 2 應用篇：
提供可以用來架構該種書信 / 溝通情境的「單字」、「詞組」與「句子」。

Part 3 範例篇：
提供數則範例「段落」與完整「示範信」，讓讀者直接作為範例使用，也能幫助讀者腦力激盪，甚至也能從中找到更多適合的語句與措詞。如需更多範例參考，可以使用書後所附的完整範例文字光碟。

章節內容說明

Chapter 21

接受
Acceptances

> 理智給我們千百種說不的方式，
> 但說「是」的方法只有一種，也就是發自內心。
> ——美國電視主持人蘇西・歐曼（Suze Orman）

一旦你決定接受邀請或請求，不妨直接說出口；這是最簡單的一種信。

如果你的「是」並非發自內心，你的接受函也會看起來冷淡疏離，不久後你甚至可能反悔。下定決心說「是」，比寫接受函本身更難。

✉ **PART 1 說明篇**

接受函的使用時機

同意加入	接受邀請	給予會員身分
學校、俱樂部、組織協會	聚餐、會議、派對	董事會、委員會、組織協會
同意加盟	接受提案	提供工作
接受演講邀請	同意請求	接受婚禮邀請
研討會、工作坊、宴會	答應參與、給予協助	參見：50 婚禮相關信

章節名稱
點出該章節的溝通主題或信件類型

介紹主題
簡單介紹信件或溝通主題

使用時機
此處列出信件使用的時機，讓你寫對信件，也能充分知道如何運用這種信件

相關主題
提供與主題相關的其他章節，供進一步參考

該怎麼說？

依序列出信件該具
備的內容

什麼不該說？

提醒不該提及的內
容與遣詞用字

寫作要點

進一步列出寫信的
要訣

特殊狀況

根據各種狀況，進
一步列出不同狀況
下該如何微調措詞

該怎麼說？

1. 表達接受邀請、提議、出價或請求的喜
   悅。
2. 複述對方提到而你也接受的細節，如會面
   時間、出價金額或你貢獻的程度、提供協
   助的具體方式、或你答應承擔的責任。
3. 提出特定需求：符合免稅標準之捐贈收
   據、邀請人聯絡資訊、演講所需器材、或
   其他相關單位名單。
4. 在結語表達喜悅之情，或提及未來的行
   動，如預計完成的事項、預計採取的行
   動、或回報的方式。

什麼不該說？

勿給太多但書，避免寫出以下句子：「我很
忙，但我應該處理得來」；「我已有兩個行
程，但會試著過去打聲招呼」；「我不會是
個好讀者，但我會試試看」。給一個直截了
當的「是」；如果你猶豫，拒絕是比較好的
選擇。

寫作要點

- 盡快寄出接受函。如果遲寄可以道歉，但不需詳述理由。
- 接受函多半簡短，而且只跟「接受」有關。
- 知名修辭專家魯道夫·傅萊區（Rudolf Flesch）曾說：「如果你對一個請求的回應為
  『是』，那應以『是』作為一封信的開頭，是很不錯的選擇。」
- 展現熱情。直接告訴對方你樂意接受，並複述與邀約相關的細節。如果你能再說一些私人、
  有趣或輕鬆的話題，那你與邀請人、雇主或朋友的關係會更好。
- 收到的邀請函上有一個以上的署名時，請在回覆中提及所有名字。可將接受函寄給信中的聯
  絡人，或第一個署名的人。
- 如果你收到的邀請函寫著「請回覆」（RSVP 或 Please reply.），請立即回覆，這是義務的、
  必要的且重要的。

特殊狀況

- **收到錄取工作通知時**，請寫一封接受函表達你的熱忱與喜悅，並確認工作相關細節。
- **寫接受函通知申請人錄取工作時**，納入以下內容：恭喜申請人獲得錄用的賀詞，並讚賞對方
  資歷、經驗或面試表現；工作相關資訊─職責、薪資、主管姓名與到職日；公司聯絡人姓名

英文溝通寫作全技藝 | **229**

✉ PART 2 應用篇

單字

accept (v.) 接受	gratifying (a.) 滿意的	satisfying (a.) 滿足的	touched (a.) 感動的
approve (v.) 同意	pleased (a.) 樂意的	thoughtful (a.) 體貼周到的	willing (a.) 願意的
welcome (v.) 歡迎	delighted (a.) 高興的	thrilled (a.) 興奮的	pleasure (n.) 喜悅
certainly (adv.) 一定			

單字、詞組與句子

列出該信件或溝通主題之下常用到的單字、詞組與句子

詞組

able to say yes
同意

accept with pleasure
欣然接受

agree to
同意做……

glad to be a[...]
很高興能投贊[...]

happy to let [...]
很高興告訴你[...]

I am pleased[...]
我很高興／開心[...]

it is with gre[...]
樂於……

it was so tho[...]
您做……真體貼[...]

it will be a pleasure to
很樂意能……

pleased to have been invited
很高興能被邀請

thank you for asking me to
謝謝您邀請我……

21
接受

句子

After reviewing your application, we are pleased to be able to offer you the funding requested.
在審查您的申請後,我們很高興提供您所申請的補助金。

I accept with pleasure the position of senior research chemist.
我很榮幸接受這個資深化學研究員的職位。

I am happy to be able to do this.
我很高興能夠這麼做。

I appreciate very much (and accept) your generous apology.
我感謝(並接受)你誠摯的道歉。

I'll be happy to meet with you in your office March 11 at 10:30 to plan this year's All-City Science Fair.
我很樂意於三月十一日上午十點三十分在您辦公室與您會面,一起計畫今年度的全市科學博覽會。

21
接受

In a word, absolutely!
簡而言之,當然願意!

In response to your letter asking for support for the Foscari Children's Home, I'm enclosing a check for $500.
回應您來信詢問資助法斯卡利兒童之家的意願,我在此附上 500 元美金支票。

範例文字光碟

完整的範例文字附
於書後光碟，可以
直接複製使用

範例段落與
示範信

本處節選出數則範
例段落與範例信，
以中英對照呈現

段落

I will be delighted to have dinner with you on Friday, the sixteenth of March, at seven o'clock. Thanks so much for asking me. I can hardly wait to see you and Anders again.

很高興能與你在三月十六日週五七點共用晚餐。非常謝謝你的邀請，我等不及再次見到你與安德斯了。

Thanks for telling me how much the children at St. Joseph's Home liked my storytelling the other night. I'm happy to accept your invitation to become a regular volunteer and tell stories every other Thursday evening. Do you have a CD player so that I could use music with some of the stories?

謝謝您告訴我聖喬瑟夫兒童之家的孩子很喜歡我那晚的說故事活動。我很高興能接受您的邀請成為固定志工，於每隔週週四傍晚為孩子說故事。您是否能提供唱片播放機，方便我幫一些故事搭配音樂呢？

I'm looking forward to your graduation and the reception afterward. Thanks for including me.

我很期待參加你的畢業典禮與接下來的茶會，謝謝你邀請我。

Your bid of $6,780 to wallpaper our reception rooms has been accepted. Please read the enclosed contract and call with any questions. We were impressed with the attention to detail in your proposal and bid, and we are looking forward to our new walls.

書，有任何
我們的新牆

21
接
受

示範信

Dear Selina,

　　Vickers and I accept with pleasure your kind invitation to a celebration of your parents' fiftieth wedding anniversary on Saturday, July 16, at 7:30 p.m.

　　　　　　　　　　　　　　　　　　　　　　Sincerely,

親愛的莎琳娜：

　　於七月十六日下午七點半，維克與我很高興能參加您父母的結婚五十週年慶祝會。

　　　　　　　　　　　　　　　　　　　　　　○○敬上

通寫作全技藝 | 233

Dear Ms. Thirkell,

　　I am pleased to accept your offer of the position of assistant director of the Gilbert Tebben Working Family Center.

　　I enjoyed the discussions with you, and I look forward to being part of this dynamic and important community resource.

　　The salary, hours, responsibilities, and starting date that we discussed during our last meeting are all agreeable to me. I understand that I will receive the standard benefits package, with the addition of two weeks' vacation during my first year.

　　　　　　　　　　　　　　　　　　　　Sincerely yours,
　　　　　　　　　　　　　　　　　　　　Laurence Dean

21
接
受

范杜騰先生您好：

在此答覆您於二月十日的來信。我們很樂意讓您的租期展延兩個月，此期間您可繼續租用展示我們樂團的投影片。

我們很高興能夠協助您；如您所言，望貴公司會讓能因此增添「些許樂趣」。

我們以此展延信向您問候。

勞菈·西蒙斯敬啟

Dear Dr. Cheesewright:

Thank you for inviting me to speak at your county dental society's dinner banquet on October 26 at 7:00. I am happy to accept and will, as you suggested, discuss new patient education strategies.

I'm not sure how much time you have allotted me—will you let me know?

With best wishes,

契斯萊特醫師您好：

謝謝您邀請我於十月二十六日七點在您們州內的牙醫協會晚會進行演講。我很高興能接受您的邀請，並會如您所建議的，在演講中討論新的衛教策略。

我不太確定您安排給我多長時間做這場演講，可以麻煩您告訴我嗎？

○○謹復

21
接受

Mr. Clarence Rochester
accepts with pleasure
William Portlaw and Alida Ascott's
kind invitation to dinner
on the sixteenth of June at 7:30 p.m.
but regrets that
Dr. Maggie Campion
will be absent at that time.

克勞倫斯·羅徹斯特先生
欣然接受
威廉·波洛與愛莉姐·艾絲考特
盛情的晚餐邀約
於六月十六日下午七點半
但遺憾告知
瑪姬·坎朋博士
此次無法到場。

✉ 參見：03 回應、22 拒絕

章節延伸
整理出與本章節相關的其他主題，讓你對書信的架構概念更完整

目錄 Contents

Chapter 01

電子郵件
E-mail

這年頭，承認你沒有電子郵件信箱，
就好像承認你還在聽卡式錄音帶一樣。

——暢銷書作家湯姆‧麥尼可（Tom McNichol）

電子郵件不像電話那樣打擾人，也比寫信簡單迅速，因此在商務與私人交流上受到熱烈歡迎。

我們很難算出正確的數字，但全球每天寄發的電子郵件大約有一千八百多億封，其中差不多有百分之七十是垃圾郵件或廣告郵件（而其中百分之八十的垃圾郵件，都出自同一批寄件者，總人數不到兩百人）。

電子郵件的一大特徵在於，電子郵件與交談很類似。由於問題與答案都可以快速來回寄送，就像在對話一樣，而一般信件則比較像是獨白。相對而言，電子郵件較不花力氣，因此大家變得更願意溝通。多年未寫信的人卻願意使用電子郵件，因為它簡單、直接且快速。而這在商務上省下的時間、郵資與工時是無可計算的。當和在另一時區生活，或生活作息與你迥異的人聯絡時，你不必擔心會吵醒他們。當工作到太晚，你可以將資料寄到電子信箱，對方隔日一早便能處理。需要花上十五分鐘的電話，電子郵件用三十秒就能完成。

人們匆匆寄出電子郵件，因為他們知道，即便犯錯或遺漏資料，仍可以立刻寄另一封郵件。這種立即性有一個缺點：人們開始會寄便條、無聊想法、笑話、瑣事，或是轉寄信件或連鎖信，這些都是以前他們絕不願意花費時間、心力與金錢（郵資）去寄的。現在，我們總能知曉朋友同事心中那些不成熟的念頭與最近的想法。就像有了手機之後，我們才發現自己醒著的時候，總有著「與某人聯絡一下」的需求（「我正在排隊，你在做什麼？」），這是我們以前從未注意過的。電子郵件也是一樣，我們因此產生無時無刻都想保持聯絡的欲望。

不過，只要善加利用，電子郵件會是這幾世紀以來最重要也最有用的溝通工具。

即時訊息（Instant Messaging，簡稱 IM）在某些方面與電子郵件很類似。想知道關於即時通訊的訣竅，請見下面「特殊狀況」的部分。

✉ PART 1 說明篇

哪些訊息可用電子郵件寄發？

簡短的	非正式的	緊急的
同時寄給多人的	有時間限制的	

該怎麼說？

1. 在寄出電子郵件之前，再次確認電子郵件地址是否正確。

2. 用一句話、一個字或一個簡單的詞組寫出主旨，讓讀者立刻了解郵件的主題。絕不要把主旨欄空著。收件人有權立刻知道這封信的主旨。下列是主旨的範例：Re: Welcome back!「關於：歡迎歸來！」；Subject: the check's in the mail「主旨：支票附在信中」

3. 以 Hi、Hello，或收件者的名字起頭，後面加上逗號或破折號。以電子郵件而言，用 Dear 起頭的寫信方式太過正式。

4. 簡述要傳達的訊息。長度盡量不要超過一個螢幕長度，多數人看到過長的信件會選擇晚點處理或忽略。

5. 必要的話，告知對方可採取的行動：打電話、回覆電子郵件、出席會議。如果這封郵件只是為了讓他們知道某些資訊，請明確寫出 FYI（供你參考）。

6. 必要的話，用禮貌用語結尾，正式的結尾祝頌詞（如 Sincerely、Truly yours）並非必要。

7. 結尾打上署名，因為對方的電子郵件系統可能只顯示電郵地址。尤其是在商務場合中，所有的電子郵件都應包含你的全名、職稱、電話號碼與電子信箱；你也可以加入住址，或任何跟公司有關的標記或資訊。這麼做有助對方立刻認出你的身分，而當這封信被轉寄給需要聯絡你的第三方時，這些資訊也相當有用。

什麼不該說？

- 不要用電子郵件來傳達重大消息，如死亡、新任總裁上任、或重病。

- 不要用電子郵件寫任何你不希望全世界都知道的事情。電子郵件一點也不私密，很容易就被轉寄或寄錯地址。它並不是用來傳達機密訊息的。禮儀專家佩姬‧波斯特（Peggy Post）曾說：「工作上的電子郵件就是一種公開文件；如果你不會把這件事寫在備忘錄或貼在公布欄，就不要把它寫進電子郵件。」

- 不要用電子郵件寄發緊急消息，除非你知道對方正在等待消息，或你已經打電話告知對方你會寄信。對方不一定會馬上讀信。雖然有些人會頻繁查看郵件，而且在辦公室中，電腦通常都會通知使用者有新郵件寄達，不過，也有些人幾天才檢查郵件一次。

- 不要在電子郵件中發火；我們太常在發洩怒氣後感到後悔。

- 不要全部都用大寫字母，除非你希望對方知道你正在大吼。

寫作訣竅

- 確認你的電子郵件地址中的代號適合你現在的身分。

- 每封信只講一個主題。若你有三個不同的問題，比起把三個問題放在同一封信中詢問，分別寄三封信會比較容易得到回應。

- 使用日常用語。在一般信件中，你會寫「I will」或更正式的「I shall」；在電子郵件中，你則會寫「I'll」。不過，儘管電子郵件的用語比較不正式，當你寫給上司時，還是要確認標點符號、文法與拼字是標準無誤的。

- 小心使用「回覆所有人」的功能。有時候，你並不希望每個人都收到你的回信。

- 收到電子郵件請立即回覆，尤其在工作上，你也許得在二十四小時內回應。若你無法立刻給予答案或資料，也先讓寄件者知道你已經收到訊息，但你會晚一點回覆。若你有一天或以上不會在辦公室，可先設定好「我不在」的自動回覆。

- 電子郵件使寄發副本變得容易許多，寄出副本前請先思考：對方真的需要收到這封信嗎？

- 如果你將其他收件者納入「bcc」（密件副本），你的主要收件人便不會知道別人也能看見郵件內容。請謹慎小心使用這個功能。

- 電子郵件通訊錄上能設定通訊人群組（如部門同事、壘球隊員、家庭成員），你只需要按下「通訊委員會」或「材料科學小組」，就可以一次寄信給群組內的所有人。請經常更新你的群組清單，並在寄信給群組前再次檢視，也許只有其中的一兩個人需要收到這封信而已。太多人都有著一個叫做「我在這世上認識的每一個人以及更多的人」的群組，並常會把笑話、

評論、新聞等等寄給整個群組。沒有人會喜歡一大疊的紙本信，電子郵件也是一樣的。請謹慎使用群組。

- 直接忽視連鎖信、笑話與請願書，不用覺得自己沒有禮貌。沒禮貌的其實是寄這些信的人。幾乎沒有人會喜歡這種未經篩選的隨機信件，所以請忍住別轉寄。當然，你也可以與有共同興趣的家人朋友一起享受這種文章，只要你確定這是你們的「共同」興趣。

- 轉寄信件之前，先取得原寄件人的同意，並刪去郵件正文以前的部分，以及無關資訊。

- 不要在未經同意下透露他人的電子郵件地址，也千萬不要把你的密碼或帳號提供給你沒有非常非常熟悉的人。

- 有些人很喜歡使用縮寫，有些人則從不使用，甚至覺得縮寫很惱人，像是：

  ASAP：as soon as possible（盡快）

  BTW：by the way（順帶一提）

  FAQ：frequently asked questions（經常詢問的問題）

  FYI：for your information（供你參考）

  LOL：laughed out loud（放聲大笑）

  OCI：oh, I see（喔，我知道了）

  TIA：thanks in advance（提前謝謝）

  TMI：too much information（太多資訊了）

  TY：thank you（謝謝你）

  WTG：way to go（做得好）

  在商務交流上，請避免這些縮寫，除非你跟對方很熟。想知道更多縮寫，可上網找尋，如 www.netlingo.com。

- 表情符號也同樣有人使用、有些人不用。舉例來說，「:-)」指的是高興的表情（請把頭歪一邊看著它），而「:(」則是不開心的表情；「:)」是微笑、「;-)」是眨眼、「:- D」是大笑、「:'(」是哭泣。

- 在寄送很大的檔案時，需考量以下情況：對方郵箱有空間限制；對方的電子信箱空間已滿；對方網速慢，需要很長時間載入；會打斷對方正在進行的工作。

特殊狀況

- **在工作上使用電子郵件**，務必徹底了解公司對於電郵使用、監督、隱私、安全及歸檔的政策。電郵系統是公司的財產，而多數的組織機構都會設定員工使用規範。你必須了解哪些屬於工作範疇、哪些屬於公司允許的個人使用範疇。

- **定期備份電子郵件**，必要時才能回顧當時的細節。刪除舊的商務信件並不是個好主意。請查看公司規定，以了解這些信必須保存多久。

- **電子郵件的附件有風險**。如果你是在大公司工作，而你的電腦有完善保護，不讓你受電腦病毒侵害，那你便可以安心寄送接收附件。但在小公司或家中使用電腦的人，可能因此盡量避免打開附件，以免受到病毒感染。若你非得寄送附件，先向收件者確認願意且能夠（擁有合適的防毒軟體）打開附件。請記得，不是所有東西都該放到附件，你可以把一些內容貼到電郵正文，讓收件人比較容易閱讀。

- 據估計，百分之七十的電子郵件都是**垃圾郵件**。這些不請自來、不受歡迎的垃圾信被寄到上萬個電郵地址，可說是電子形式的廣告信。有些垃圾信同時也是詐騙信，千萬別上當。（可以到 www.snopes.com 及其他終結謠言的網站，了解信箱中有哪些神奇故事是真的、哪些是假的。）目前而言，要完全清除垃圾信仍是不太可能。你可以使用擋信軟體，不過，那些人會創造隨機而無法捉摸的新電郵地址來避開這些限制。要是你回覆他們，要求他們移除你的地址，他們反而會很高興找到了一個「活人」，並繼續寄給你更多的垃圾信。你只須刪掉垃圾信即可；連嘆息的時間都別給它，刪除就好。（某些公司則會允許你將地址從他們的系統中移除，你只需要按下「取消訂閱」即可。）

- 有的**私人信件**會讓你的收件匣塞滿笑話、感人故事、罐頭建議、病毒危害消息，或是某個你一定會造訪的網站公告。前白宮社交祕書蕾蒂莎・鮑德・瑞奇（Letitia Baldrige）曾建議這樣回覆寄件人：「我真的很感謝你想到我，並一直把我放在你的寄信名單中，但我很抱歉，我必須告訴你我真的很忙，我已經無法好好讀那些必要、緊急、沒那麼有趣的信。我想，是時候將我的名字替換成別人，因為時間大人不會允許我閱讀你的信的。」佩姬・波斯特則建議這麼說：「我很高興聽到你的消息，但請別再用電子郵件寄給我笑話。我的工作非常忙碌，沒有時間注意私人信件。」

- **即時訊息**有很多種，隨著硬體、軟體與功能而有所不同，不過內容都跟電子郵件很相像，皆有簡短、迅速、著重單一主題、具即時性的特色。即時訊息大多用於快速詢問問題、澄清內容、安排並協調工作與會議，或聯繫家人朋友。為了節省時間與按鍵次數，人們會使用縮寫、首字母縮略字、俚語與「簡訊專用語」。本章多數的內容也同樣適用於即時訊息，尤其注意以下兩個方面：

  (1) 商務與私人信件之間的嚴格分界；

  (2) 了解公司對於安全、保密、病毒、歸檔與私人使用的規定（美國有超過一萬條法律與條例，用來規範電子訊息與紀錄保存，所以公司會這麼講究即時訊息的使用，是其來有自的）。

格式

- 電子郵件的格式取決於你的伺服器系統，不過你還是可以有一些選擇（每行長度、是否將對方的原文納入你的信裡）。
- 電郵內容可以列印出來，便能像信件或備忘錄一樣永久保存，其法律效力也幾乎相等。

✉ PART 2 應用篇

單字

announce *(v.)* 宣布	inform *(v.)* 通知	thank *(v.)* 謝謝	attachment *(n.)* 附件
answer *(v.)* 回答	inquiry *(v.)* 調查	reply *(v.) & (n.)* 回覆	message *(n.)* 訊息
explain *(v.)* 解釋	notify *(v.)* 通知	following *(a.)* 以下的	reminder *(n.)* 提醒
forward *(v.)* 轉寄	respond *(v.)* 回應		

詞組

alert you to the possibility 通知你注意這個可能性	in answer to your question 為回答你的問題
ask your help 請求你的協助	just a note to let you know 提醒一下讓你知道
do you know 你是否知道	please let me know ASAP 請盡快讓我知道
for your information 供你參考	send me a copy of 寄給我……的副本
here are 這就是	wanted to follow up 想要知道後續情況
information you wanted/requested 你想要／要求的資料	will you please send 可否請你寄送

句子

Are you available to judge a race walk a week from Saturday?
你有空可以來當一場競走比賽的裁判嗎？從週六開始連續一週？

Did you see the article about elder law in today's *New York Times*?
你有沒有看到今天《紐約時報》上那篇關於老年人法的文章？

Feel free to forward the following to anyone who might be interested.
隨意轉寄以下資訊給任何可能有興趣的人。

Forgot to ask—is it their 37th or 38th anniversary?
忘記問了：這是他們第三十七或三十八個紀念日？

Here are this week's airfare bargains.
這是本週的機票優惠。

I had a note from Mrs. Hook Eagles asking about a vacancy in the 1330 building—do we have one, do you know?
我從胡克‧伊格斯太太那邊收到一封信，詢問 1330 號大樓裡有沒有空房。你知道我們還有沒有空房呢？

I'll be gone the next two weeks—if anything comes up, e-mail me and I'll get back to you after the 3rd.
接下來兩週我不在，如有任何事情，請寄電子郵件給我，我會在三號之後回覆你。

I'm trying to round up some people to hike through New England for two weeks this fall—are you interested?
我正在試著召集一些人，在今年秋天花兩週時間一起登山跨越新英格蘭。你有興趣嗎？

I read about the tornado that went through your area—are you OK?
我看到消息，有龍捲風從你們那區經過，你還好嗎？

Is it my bookkeeping or am I missing a check for the last job?
是我記帳有誤，還是我上一份工作少拿了一張支票？

Is there any news about Cressida?
有任何關於葵希妲的消息嗎？

I've just mailed you the material for your presentation—you should have it Monday or Tuesday.
我剛寄給你能用在簡報中的資料，你應該在週一或週二就可以收到。

I've lost Miriam Ephraim's address—do you have it?
我弄丟了米麗安・艾芙蘭的地址，你有嗎？

Just a note to say I enjoyed your op-ed piece on hog confinements—have you had much feedback, so to speak?
只是想告訴你，我很喜歡你在社論對頁版關於肉豬限制的文章。你想必已經得到很多迴響了吧？

Just a reminder about the conference call with Eusabio International Friday at 3 p.m.
只是想提醒你，週五下午三點與尤沙國際有一個電話會議。

New surge protectors are now available for anyone who needs one.
新的斷電保護多孔插座已經到貨了，需要的人都可以購買。

Subject: Nearby houses of worship
主旨：附近的禮拜堂

Tax forms are available in the lobby from now until April 15, thanks to Courtenay Brundit, who obtained them for us.
從現在開始至四月十五日，報稅單可於大廳取得。謝謝科狄內・布朗第幫我們拿來這些表單。

Thanks for forwarding the specs—I'm interested.
謝謝你轉寄給我這些規格，我很感興趣。

This is to let you know that your order (#08554) was received and will be shipped this afternoon.
在此告知您，我們已收到您的訂單（#08554），並會於今日下午出貨。

We've been notified that Highway 36 will be closed from July 9-15; you may want to plan alternate routes to work.
我們收到通知，三十六號高速公路將於七月九至十五日關閉，請各位計畫替代的上班路線。

When you have a minute, will you fax me a copy of your most recent patent application?
如果您有時間，可否將您最近一次的專利申請表傳真給我？

段落

Please mark your calendars. William Denny, industrial engineer at our new high-tech data entry facility in Porter, will explain the latest technology on Thursday, Jan. 21 at 3 p.m. in Building 201B, Room 43. A question-and-answer period will follow.

請在月曆上記下這天：在波特新高科技數據傳輸所擔任工業工程師的威廉‧丹尼，將會解釋最新的科技，時間為一月二十一日（週四）下午三點，地點位於 201B 大樓 43 廳。演講結束後，會有問與答時間。

You wanted to know who keeps my Harley in such great shape? I do! Okay, okay, I know what you mean. The greatest Harley repair and service east of the Mississippi is The Caloveglia Shop on South Douglas.

想知道是什麼讓我的哈雷機車一直保持在最佳狀態嗎？是因為我！好啦、好啦，我知道你的意思。在密西西比河東，最棒的哈雷機車修理保養廠就是南道格拉斯的卡洛佛商店。

Thanks for the new programmable multifunction mouse that you sent over. I'm having a good time with it!

謝謝你寄來的多功能滑鼠。我正在好好使用中！

In response to your question about the community organizer position, yes, benefits are included. In addition, the deadline for applying has been changed to September 30.

此信回答您關於社區幹部一職的問題：是的，福利包含在內。此外，申請截止日期已改為九月三十日。

Would you please let me know the name of the contractor who did your deck? We're inspired enough to get going on ours.

你可不可以告訴我幫你們做甲板的承包商名稱？我們也想處理我們的甲板。

01

電子郵件

示範信

FROM: info@ducksfordinner.com
TO: foxes@email.com
DATE: 20 Nov 2018 14:30:01
SUBJECT: Order confirmation #82654560
This is an automated message acknowledging acceptance of your online order. You may check your order status by writing to: info@ducksfordinner.com

主旨：訂單確認 #82654560
這是自動寄發的信件，確認已收到您的線上訂單。您可以寫信至 info@ducksfordinner.com 查看訂單狀態。

FROM: clubred@aol.com
TO: juliagotrocks@email.com
DATE: Thr, 18 Jan 2018 16:53:31 EST
SUBJECT: Thank you!
Hello, Julia—I received your check. Thanks! I put $30 toward dues, and $50 as a contribution to our latest fundraising drive. You'll be getting a fundraiser letter but it will be fyi only—not to ask you to give again. Netty

主旨：謝謝！
哈囉，茱莉亞，我收到妳的支票了，謝謝！我用 30 元繳了應付帳款，剩下的 50 元則放入我們最近的募款基金。妳會收到一封募款信，但只是供妳參考而已，並不是要妳再捐一次。娜蒂

FROM: sgk@email.com
TO: rmk@email.com
DATE: Thr, 29 Mar 2018 17:02:35 +0400
SUBJECT: Help—April 1
Hello from Russia! I'm planning my April 1 English class around the idea of practical jokes and I'd appreciate your help. (1) Could you describe this tradition as far as you know it from your own experience? (2) Do you remember a really successful April 1 practical joke? (3) In Russia the joke ends with the clichè "Spervym aprelya!" which means "Congratulations on April 1!" What do they say in the circumstances in your part of the world? Thanks!

主旨：救救我——愚人節
來自俄羅斯的哈囉！我正在為我四月一日的英文課想計畫，我想要找一些惡作劇的點子，希望你能幫忙。(1) 你可以就你自己的經驗，盡量為我介紹這個傳統嗎？(2) 有沒有一個非常成功的愚人節惡作劇讓你記憶猶新？(3) 在俄國，惡作劇結束時，大家會說「Spervym aprelya!」，意思是「愚人節快樂！」在你們國家，同樣的情況下你們會說什麼呢？謝謝！

FROM: hcalverly@email.com
TO: thewhitecompany@email.com
DATE: Sat, 29 Jul 2017 17:34:08 (EDT)
SUBJECT: ATTN: Doyle
I received the fax of the essay. It was above and beyond the call of duty, and yes, I still needed it. I owe you one. Best, Hugh

主旨：致：道爾
我收到文章的傳真了。這篇文章的品質完全超越徵文的要求，而且是的，我仍然需要它。我欠你一次人情。祝好，休

FROM: msadlier@email.com
TO: kcairns@email.com
DATE: 07 Apr 2017 13:01:21
SUBJECT: favor
Kitty, would you be willing to spend fifteen minutes or so speaking with a high-school senior in your area who's interested in the Fanny Gaslight School of Design? Thanks!

主旨：需要協助
凱蒂，你是否願意花十五分鐘左右的時間與一名高三生聊聊？他住在你們那區，並對芬妮葛斯萊設計學校有興趣。謝謝！

FROM: gordy@email.com
TO: cary@email.com
DATE: Sat, 30 Sep 2017 11:21:21
RE: amorphous metals symposium
Oct. 16 is fine with me. Sorry to be late with my response—I've been out of town. I hope all's well with you. Gordy

回覆：非晶態金屬專題研討會
十月十六日我可以。很抱歉那麼晚才回應，我之前不在城裡。希望你一切都好。高帝

參見：14 收件通知、17 後續追蹤信、32 備忘錄、47 給親友的信

Chapter 02

傳真信
Faxed Letters

> 人生中唯一能確定的事情就是變化。
> 在日新月異的科技競爭遊戲中，
> 惟有加快速度，才能讓自己跟上時代。
>
> ——美國作家蓋爾・謝（Gail Sheehy）

對很多人與公司來說，傳真機（facsimile machine，簡稱 fax）已經是不可或缺的工具，它加快了溝通速度，讓我們對於「回覆時間」的概念從數日變成了數分鐘。傳真機用來掃描傳送信件或文件，將字與圖片轉化為能透過電話線傳送的訊號，並把訊號傳至電話的另一端。

透過傳真機，你不需要將信件放入信封中，只需要列印出信件並簽名後，直接放在傳真機傳送出去即可，而對方會在幾分鐘以內就收到信件。

然而，傳真信的好處在於速度，而不在於美觀。有些傳真會隨原稿品質與用來寄發的傳真機而異，印出來的內容可能模糊、有墨漬，有時甚至難以辨識。

PART 1 說明篇

何時可以用傳真？

遠距聯繫	難以用電話聯絡	速度是第一考量
文件美觀與否並不重要	對方要求以傳真寄送	

該怎麼說？

- 先確定傳真是否為最好的方式。若你與收件人都同意該文件必須快速傳送，傳真會是最好的選擇。
- 跟寫其他信件一樣，要小心仔細。
- 在傳真文件前加上一張空白頁（稱 cover sheet「封面頁」），或是在傳真第一頁，加上以下訊息：收件人的姓名、部門與傳真號碼；你的名字與聯絡方式（傳真號碼、電子信箱、公司名稱與地址、電話號碼）；傳真的總頁數（計算時要算入封面）。

什麼不該說？

- 別用傳真寄送致謝函，除非你跟對方很熟。因為這麼做會削弱致謝函的意義，而且也不是很溫暖。
- 別用傳真寄送機密或敏感資訊，除非你很確定收件人會在另一端親自收取傳真資料。傳真機印出資料等收件人來領取的期間，人人都可以看到傳真內容。徵才廣告可能會說「傳真履歷會保密」，但是你最好有心理準備，傳真資料不太可能完全保密。

寫作訣竅

- 手寫信或小字條並不適合傳真。能用印表機列印出來的紙張大小才是標準的傳真原稿。
- 使用容易辨識的字體，十號字級大小是下限，十二號更好。
- 如果要傳真的文件很重要，在寄發傳真的同時將原稿郵寄出，這樣對方也能持有一份像樣的原稿。（可以在郵寄信的下方註明，這是用來確認某月某日寄發的傳真。）
- 在發送之前，仔細檢查資料，尤其是具法律約束力的文件。
- 別發送已經傳真多次的文件。每傳送一次，文件清晰度會降低，使文件難以閱讀。若你收到的傳真已經有點模糊，當你再次把它傳真出去，看起來會更模糊。你可以用傳真機上的影印模式將文件影印幾次，出來的結果大致就是收件人會看到的模樣。
- 要傳真的信或文件的字體如果小又密集，將解析度調整為「超高品質」，這樣文件會比較容易閱讀，傳送的時間只會稍微變長而已。
- 請記得，傳真機會讀取紙上的一切。粗體字、圖表、邊界、圖標都會增加傳送的時間，另一端則會消耗更多的墨水。請刪去傳真文件上不必要的東西。
- 如果你很依賴傳真機，就設計一個包含傳真所需資訊的信頭信紙。你可以試驗不同墨水顏色、信頭、字體與商標，找出傳真後看起來最出色的搭配。此後，你就再也不需要替傳真文件增加一張封面，也會為你與你的收件人省下許多時間、紙張與電話費。
- 若想為你的傳真信做出更多調整，可參考：
  《Can I Fax a Thank-You Note?》，作者：Audrey Glassman。

特殊狀況

- **跟不同時區的人聯繫**，傳真很好用。現在許多旅館會請房客以傳真訂房。傳真擁有電話的立即性，又比打電話便宜。
- 傳真很適合用來**處理快速且例行的通訊**，如收取或確認訂單，確認貨運資料、規格、報價及修改處理中的合約或提案。只要確認傳真內容夠清楚，這個方法就是便利又划算。
- **遠距離的商業交易**也因為傳真而變得可能，文件可以傳給某人簽名或簽上字首字母，再傳真回來。雖然最後還是會需要原稿簽名，但傳真縮短了整體交易過程。
- **單向的推銷訊息**並不適合傳真。理論上而言，銷售人員可以把銷售信傳給所有他能找到的傳真號碼；然而，這表示收件人必須為了他們未要求收到的傳真付錢。儘管我們大多都已學會與不請自來的傳單共處，但若是要為此付錢，我們可不會高興。由於收件人收到傳真時必須付費，所以一定要確認對方願意收到這封傳真。
- 很多公司現在接受**以傳真寄送履歷與申請信**，有些還會要求申請人這麼做。在這種情況下，用傳真寄出履歷與申請信是合適的，甚至是必要的，因為其他申請人也都會用傳真的方式寄出資料。不過，請記住傳真的履歷看起來無法像郵寄的原稿一樣專業清晰。
- **沒有傳真機的人**，可以去影印店或便利商店寄發收取傳真。若要寄發，應事先準備好須傳真的信件或文件。不要使用裝訂針，因為傳真時一次只能寄發一頁。若要收取傳真，告知寄件人該影印店或便利商店的傳真號碼，並請對方在第一頁最上方註記你的姓名與電話，這樣在傳真到達時，影印店便能聯絡你。

格式

- 傳真信可以用有信頭（letterhead，指英文信紙上之上端印有發信公司的訊息欄）的標準信紙或備忘錄用紙。
- 可以事先製作小表格填入傳真資訊，將這種小表格貼在信件或備忘錄的第一頁，便不須再加上封面頁。不過，這只適用在第一頁還有空間可貼表格的情況。

PART 2 應用篇

單字

confirm *(v.)* 確認	send *(v.)* 寄送	attached *(a.)* 附加的	speedy *(a.)* 快速的
forward *(v.)* 轉寄	correction *(n.)* 修改	following *(a.)* 下列的	immediately *(adv.)* 立刻地
request *(v.) & (n.)* 請求	instruction *(n.)* 指示	prompt *(a.)* 迅速的	quickly *(adv.)* 快速地
rush *(v.) & (n.)* 匆忙	transmittal *(n.)* 傳送	urgent *(a.)* 緊急的	

詞組

additional instructions 額外指示	please acknowledge receipt 收到請通知
as soon as possible 盡快	price quotation 報價單
as you requested/at your request 按照你的請求	prompt reply 迅速的回覆
because of the tight deadline 由於截止日期緊迫	the information you requested 你要求的資料
by return fax 以傳真回覆	to advise you 以告知你
by this afternoon 在今日下午前	to speed your application 以加速你的申請
happy to be able to send 很高興能夠寄發	transmittal problems 傳送上的問題

I need a response by
我在……之前需要得到回應

via facsimile transmission and U.S. mail
透過傳真與美國郵政服務

pass along
傳閱

句子

Below are the figures you need for the meeting this afternoon.
以下便是你今天下午會議需要的圖表。

Here is the missing paragraph for my newsletter piece.
這裡是我的新聞文章中缺少的段落。

I'd appreciate a call at 661-555-4234 when you receive this.
當您收到此傳真時,請撥打電話至 661-555-4234。

I'm sorry about the rush, but I'd appreciate it if you could look over this press release and let me know by noon if it's all right with you.
我很抱歉如此匆忙,但希望您能仔細看看這篇新聞稿,並在中午之前讓我知道您對內容是否有任何問題。

In response to your ad for an estimator at your headquarters office, I am faxing you my résumé.
為回應您在廣告中徵求的總部辦公室估價師一職,我將我的履歷傳真給您。

Let me know if you have any problems reading this.
若此傳真難以閱讀,請讓我知道。

Please have the current owners and the buyers sign below to indicate that they have received this disclosure, and then fax it back to this office.
請讓目前的所有人與買家在下面簽名表示已收到此聲明書,再將它傳真回本辦公室。

Please read and initial the attached rider to your contract #007945.
請詳閱附件中的合約 #007945 附加條款,並簽上姓名字首字母。

This will confirm the arrangements for delivery of order #C18803 made on the telephone this morning.
謹以此傳真確認今日早上在電話中為訂單 C18803 安排之運送事宜。

We were ready to start printing when Itzik Landsman pointed out that these figures don't make sense—will you check them and get back to us right away?

我們原本已經要交印，但艾奇克‧蘭思曼指出這些圖表有問題。您能否檢查這些圖表，並立即回覆我們？

You may use this form to respond.

您可以使用這張表格回覆。

Your Peterkin Turkeys will be delivered today between 2 p.m. and 4 p.m.

您的彼得金火雞會於今日下午兩點至四點間送達。

Please check the delivery against the attached order, sign to acknowledge receipt, and return the signed order form to us.

請根據附件中的訂單檢查到貨，再簽名確認收到貨品，並將簽名後的訂單寄還給我們。

02

傳真信

段落

Your good faith estimate of closing costs is attached. Please read it and call me with any questions. I'd like to get a final copy typed up this afternoon. Thanks.

附件是您貸款所需費用之誠信估價單。請詳閱,有任何問題請打電話給我。我希望今日下午能收到最終打字版本,謝謝。

Bettina Vanderpoel has provided us with the necessary figures and documents. Please check the attached statement for errors or inconsistencies and fax it back with your corrections as soon as you can. Before 3:00 today would be helpful. Thanks!

貝蒂娜・范德普已經提供我們所需的圖表與文件。請檢查附件中的結算單是否有錯誤或不一致之處,並盡快將您修改的部分傳真給我們。若能在今天三點前回傳最好。謝謝!

O. A. Pardiggle Termite Inc. Wood destroying pests and organisms inspection report for 2405 Cedarwood. Please read, sign, and return ASAP.

O・A・帕狄格白蟻公司針對雪松路 2405 號的樹木害蟲與有機檢驗報告。請詳閱、簽名並盡快回傳。

Please complete the attached Uniform Commercial Loan Application, responding to all fields marked with an X. Sign and return by 9/23.

請完成附件中的統一商業貸款申請表,請回應所有欄位,以 X 符號標示作答。於九月二十三日前簽名回傳。

示範信

Kim Cameron
Fax # 307-555-7777
August 31, 2017
Dear Kim Cameron,
While putting the final touches to our 40th Annual Investment Banking Convention brochure, I realized we don't have a professional bio for you. Will you fax us one (about a paragraph in length) as soon as possible? Thank you.

金‧卡麥隆

傳真號碼 307-555-7777

二〇一七年八月三十一日

金‧卡麥隆您好：

在為我們的第四十屆年度投資銀行大會手冊定稿時，我發現我們沒有您的專業自傳。您可否盡快傳真給我一份呢（大約一段的長度）？謝謝。

TO: Lambert Strether
    Strether Medical Supply
    Fax 612-555-2566
FROM: Chadwick Newsome
      Newsome Mfg. Co. Inc.
      Fax 715-555-2534
RE: Order # LSX-655-12211
DATE: Oct. 12, 2017
The above-referenced shipment should have arrived before noon today and did not. Are we scheduled to receive it this afternoon? Let me know. We were assured we would have it today. Thanks.

收件人：蘭伯特‧史傑瑟
        史傑瑟醫療用品
        傳真 612-555-2566
寄件人：查維‧紐森
        紐森製造公司
        傳真 715-555-2534
關於：訂單 #LSX-655-12211
日期：二〇一七年十月十二日
上述的訂單應於今日中午前到貨，但卻未送達。我們是否安排今天下午到貨？請讓我知道。貴公司當初保證我們今天一定會收到。謝謝。

✉ 參見：32 備忘錄

Chapter 03

回應
Responses

> 我很高興能夠立刻回答：我不知道。
>
> ——馬克・吐溫

收到信件後給予迅速而周到的回應，就跟你辛辛苦苦寫的銷售信一樣，對生意有舉足輕重的影響。迅速回覆私人信件也能為你的私人生活帶來許多好處，電影名人珍妮佛・威廉斯（Jennifer Williams）曾說：「快速的回應，展現的是積極、真切的關心；對收信人來說，沒有什麼比這更討喜、感人的了。」

若你是以直接的「是」或「否」作為回應，請參見：21 接受、22 拒絕。

 PART 1 說明篇

收到以下信件需要回應

公告通知	抱怨信	恭賀信
致歉信	慰問信	致謝函
詢問或請求	邀請函	缺席會議收到的信

1. 第一句說明回應的事項（信件、邀請、備忘錄），這樣對方可立即知道來信目的。有些情況下，可加上參閱訊息，如 Re: Order #2K881「關於：訂單 #2K881」。
2. 簡要提供對方請求的所有資訊。
3. 無法回答對方詢問的所有問題時，轉介給能提供更多資訊的人（提供姓名、地址與電話號碼）。
4. 若無法立即採取行動，至少提供目前處理進度，以及預計獲得結果的時間。
5. 若適合的話，提出進一步協助的意願。
6. 感謝對方來信，且很高興能回信。
7. 結尾時，給予祝福，或期待未來的聯繫。

什麼不該說？

- 不需提供對方沒有詢問的資訊。多數時候，這是不必要且沒有幫助的。
- 不要拼錯對方的姓名。
- 不要顯露不耐，儘管你認為對方的來信很無禮、無知或荒唐。

03

回應

寫作訣竅

- 立即回應。「這應該成為每間公司的目標：每封信都在收到的當天就回覆。」亞歷山大・L・薛弗與愛德娜・英格斯（Alexander L. Sheff and Edna Ingalls）寫於一九四二年的建議，在現代看來或許是不可能的事，但仍不失為一個好目標。
- 回應一封問了許多問題或內容複雜的信時，用編號、項目符號、星號等方式來組織答覆，並預留大量空白空間。
- 如果你的回應簡短而直接，你可以直接在收到的信下方寫下回應、重新折起信紙、在信封寫好地址、直接回寄。這是很省時間的一種方式，但只有在你不需要記錄信件往來時才能使用。

特殊狀況

- **當顧客寫信詢問問題**時，這便是一個可以推銷產品、服務與公司的絕佳機會。要用最恭敬的態度、最快的速度、最好的效率與十足的活力來處理這種信，因為詢問通常就是購買的前兆。回答問題時，越完整越好，並附上相關的清單、文章、報告、書冊、傳單或型錄。要讓顧客很容易就能進行下一步（下訂單、拜訪當地批發商、打電話至免付費服務專線）。

- **回應工作邀請時**，要讓對方知道你很高興能在這間公司工作；說些讚美面試與面試官的話；適當的話，可重述雇用條件；再次強調你與這間公司很適合彼此，你對此很有信心；感謝對方。

  有時候，你的回應是帶有條件的；你想要這個職位，但無法接受某些雇用條件。向對方解釋這個職位是你的第一志願，但對於其中一部分有疑慮；是否有任何解決方法呢？

- **收到標有 RSVP（敬請賜覆）或 Please reply（請回覆）的邀請時**，務必要回信，這是義務的、強制的、必要的、強迫的、有責任的且重要的。如果你不打算參加，也務必要回覆標有 Regrets only（不能出席請回覆）的邀請。要是你收到的邀請函沒有寫 RSVP 或 Regrets only，也沒有附上回覆卡，便沒有必要回應。這種類型的邀請函會用在大型活動上，如政治集會、募款活動、商務雞尾酒派對、組織大會。

- **回覆邀請函的原則：** 在收到的幾日內就回覆；明確說出是否能參加；模仿邀請函，使用相同的格式與幾乎一樣的文字內容。如果你有名片或是私人特製信紙，你也可以直接在你的名字下方寫上 accepts with pleasure the kind invitation of...「很高興接受……的盛情邀請」，並重述活動類型、時間、日期與地點。

- **邀請函**（婚禮、猶太成年禮）**與資訊布達信**（訂婚、畢業、出生、領養）都需要回覆（寫信或寫卡片祝賀，內容要用手寫），但如果你無法參加，也不需寄送禮物。

- **收到慰問信也需要回覆。** 形式有許多種，從手寫的正式致謝函（參見：12 致謝函），到在報紙上發表謝意（參見：15 公告通知），都是可行的。若是公眾人物，可以印製收件通知，一次寄給一大批人，因為這些人與死者家人並無交情（參見：14 收件通知）。回應可以很簡短，在葬禮後的六週內都可寄發，也可以請別人代表與死者最親近的人寫信。

- **回覆募款信時**，不一定要回信，甚至一句話也不用寫。多數機構都只要求你打勾，再放進隨附的信封中寄回。若你要以寫信回應，要提及你捐獻的總金額，也可以要求收據（為了抵稅）。

- **回覆道歉信**，只是為了讓對方知道你收到了；在此之後，你要怎麼做便是你的選擇。作曲家茱莉亞・沃芙（Julia W. Wolfe）曾說：「聽到對方道歉時，願意退不只一步，並好心原諒對方，這樣的人，會讓挑釁者覺得慶幸，因為麻煩已經過去，但同時也明白，下次不能再發生了。這樣的人，有能力維持美麗又長久的友誼。」

- **回應讚美信或是恭賀信時**，首先要說「謝謝」，然後親切地回覆。艾琳諾・漢彌爾頓曾說：「讚美就是一種禮物，不能隨便亂丟，除非你想要傷害到送禮的人。」要將讚美回饋給讚美你的人，如 how nice of you to write「你人真好，寫了這封信」；your letter touched me「你的信感動了我」；how thoughtful of you「你真體貼」。

- 有人問你或你**親近的人想要的禮物時**，請講一個廣泛的禮物類別（例如書，但錢不包含在內），這樣送禮的人便有多種價格的禮物可以選擇。

格式

- 依照收到的信件格式照樣回覆即可。如果原來的信是打字的，你也用打字；若是手寫，你也手寫。如果邀請函是正式的，回信也該用第三人稱的正式格式；若是非正式、以第一人稱寫在私人信紙上，那你的回覆也照做。

- 若你收到一封正式邀請函，上面刻印或印刷著你的名字，那你可以在你的姓名下方寫上 accepts with pleasure（樂意接受）或 declines with regret（遺憾婉拒），作為回應邀請的方式。加上活動的日期，你的收件人才知道你回應的是哪個邀請。

- 回應例行的詢問時，印有表格的制式信或卡片是很有用的。若對方請求提供資訊、材料或樣品，你可以用張印好文字的卡片回覆，上面印著：This comes to you at your request.「按照您的請求寄送。」或 Thank you for your inquiry. Enclosed are informational materials.「謝謝您的詢問，隨信附上資料。」

  你也可以設計一張簡短、能應付多種情況的制式信，信中感謝對方詢問，並寫上你將寄去的資訊類型。附上一張資料清單，這樣你便能指出哪些資料會附在另一封信中或另外郵寄。也可以設計空格供之後填寫：Thank you for your inquiry about _____.「謝謝您關於_____的詢問。」或是上面列出所有想得到的回應方式，回覆時僅須勾選合適的項目，如 Your order has been sent.「您的訂單已寄送。」；We are temporarily out of stock.「暫無存貨。」；Please reorder in _____ days.「請於_____天內再下訂單。」；This is a prepaid item, and your payment has not yet been received.「此商品為預付商品，而我們尚未收到您的帳款。」；Please indicate a second color choice.「請提供商品顏色的第二選擇。」

- 以電子郵件回應電子郵件。如果寄來的紙本信中提供電子郵件地址，而你的回覆很簡短或只是例行公事，那你也可以用電子郵件回信。

✉ PART 2 應用篇

單字

acknowledge *(v.)* 告知收到	enclosed *(a.)* 隨信附上的	inform *(v.)* 通知	respond *(v.)* 回應
appreciate *(v.)* 感激	feedback *(n.)* 回饋意見	notify *(v.)* 通知	return *(v.)* 回寄
confirm *(v.)* 確認	grateful *(a.)* 感謝的	regarding *(prep.)* 關於	send *(v.)* 寄送

詞組

according to your letter 根據你的來信	pleased to be able to send you 很高興能夠寄給你
appreciate your business 感謝你的光顧	thank you for your letter telling us about 謝謝你來信告訴我們關於……的事
appreciate your calling our attention to 感謝你讓我們注意到	to let you know 讓你知道
as mentioned in your letter 如你在信中提到的	under separate cover 以另一封信寄出
delighted to receive 很高興收到	want to reply to your letter 想要回應你的來信
enclosed you will find 在附件中你會看到	we appreciate your interest in 我們很感謝你對於……的興趣
your sympathetic/delightful/ helpful/ comforting/encouraging letter/note 你富有同情心／令人開心／有幫助／撫慰人心／激勵人心的信件／字條	we have carefully/thoughtfully considered your letter 我們已經仔細地／周全地考慮你的來信

happy to hear from you 很高興得到你的回應	for further information 以提供進一步的資訊
I'm sending you 我正要寄給你	in response to your letter of 回應你在……的來信
meant a great deal to me 對我來說很重要	

句子

As requested, we are submitting a budget figure for construction surveillance for the water and sewer line project.
按您的要求,在此寄給您供水與排水道專案的建設監視設備預算報價。

Here is the information you requested about the tank closure.
這是您所要求的儲油槽關閉相關資料。

I have received your apology, and hope you will not give the matter another thought.
我已經收到你的道歉信,希望你不會再擔心這件事了。

I hope this information is useful to you in resolving any remaining title issues.
我希望這份資料能幫助你解決在產權方面的問題。

In response to your request for sealed bids, a bid from Dale Heating and Plumbing is enclosed.
為回應您對於密封投標的請求,在此附上來自達爾供熱管道公司的投標案。

Letters like yours have been a great comfort to us all.
許多如同你寄來的信,對我們全部人來說是一大安慰。

Mary Postgate has asked me to respond to your letter about the settlement agreement dated January 30.
瑪莉‧波士蓋請我回覆您於一月三十日的來信,內容是關於和解協議。

Thank you for sharing with me the lovely memories you have of Father.
謝謝您與我分享您對於家父的美好回憶。

Thank you for taking the time to write, and please excuse my delay in responding to your letter.

謝謝您花時間寫信，請原諒我未能及時回覆您的來信。

Thank you so much for your kind words/for your letter.

非常感謝你的善意美言／你的來信。

This is to let you know that the report you requested will be mailed as soon as it is completed (Dec. 3).

這封信是為了讓你知道，你所要求的報告，在其完成後（十二月三日）便會盡快郵寄給你。

We are pleased to send you the enclosed information about Weycock United Sugar Company.

我們很高興能寄給您附件中關於偉客聯合砂糖公司的資料。

We thank you for your inquiry, and are pleased to enclose a sample snack bar.

謝謝您的詢問，我們很樂意隨信附上燕麥棒樣品。

You have asked me to estimate the fees that would be required for our services.

您請我估算我們服務所需的費用。

03

回
應

段落

Your grant proposal has been read with great interest. We will want to have several other people read and evaluate it before submitting it for discussion at our weekly meeting. I will let you know as soon as we have made a decision.

我們對您的補助金提案很有興趣。在上交至每週討論會前，想讓其他幾個人也讀一讀、評估一下。當我們做出決定，我會盡快讓您知道。

Thank you for your inquiry about Gabbadeo Wines. Enclosed are several brochures describing our vineyards and products and a list of vendors in your area.

謝謝您對於迦巴迪奧酒莊的詢問。隨信附上幾份介紹我們葡萄園與產品的冊子，以及在您當地的銷售點清單。

In response to your fax of June 3, I'm sending the three original contracts along with two copies of each, four pro forma invoices with two copies of each, and a bill of lading. Please let us know at once if everything is in order.

為回應您於六月三日的傳真，我在此寄給您三組原始合約（每組皆有兩份）、四組形式發票（每組皆有兩份）以及一張提單。當一切準備就緒，請立即讓我們知道。

Thank you for your generous and sincere apology. I am entirely willing to put the incident behind me, and I look forward to continuing our old association.

謝謝您寬容而真心的致歉信。我完全願意將這個事件拋諸腦後，並期待我們能繼續往日情誼。

In response to your letter of September 16, we have made a number of inquiries and are pleased to tell you that most of the staff here is agreeable to helping you with your research project. Please telephone the department secretary Arthur Eden to let him know what day or days you would like to spend with us.

為回應您於九月十六日的來信，我們已經多方詢問，並很高興能告訴您，這裡多數的工作人員都願意協助您的研究專題。請打電話至部門祕書亞瑟・艾登，讓他知道您在哪（幾）天會與我們一同度過。

03

回應

Dear Mr. Ruggles,

Thank you for your inquiry about Red Gap. We are enclosing some Chamber of Commerce brochures, a map of the area, and a list of events and activities through the end of the year.

If we can be of any further assistance, please let us know. We hope that you enjoy your stay in Red Gap.

Sincerely,

魯格斯先生您好：

謝謝您對於紅丘的詢問。隨信附上一些商會的手冊、本區地圖以及整年活動盛事一覽表。

若需進一步協助，請讓我們知道。希望您喜歡紅丘。

○○敬上

Dear Ms. Stedman:

Thank you for your interest in our Quick Mail program. Due to an overwhelming demand, requests for our brochure and explanatory CD have far outpaced our supplies. However, a new shipment has been ordered, and we'll send you your materials as soon as we receive them.

Once you receive our kit, you'll learn all about the money-saving ideas that our program has to offer—reducing your mail float time, accelerating your cash flow, escalating your postage discounts, and still other techniques.

We look forward to hearing from you after you have had a chance to examine the materials.

Sincerely,

史蒂曼小姐您好：

謝謝您對我們快信系統的興趣。由於索取人數過多，我們生產手冊與說明光碟的速度已經趕不上索取的速度。不過，我們已經新訂了一批貨，一旦我們收到，就會立即將資料寄給您。

當您收到我們的套組，您會了解我們系統提供的所有省錢訣竅：減少您為確認帳款而耗費於信件往來的時間、加速您的金流、提升您的郵資折扣以及其他技巧。

在您有機會檢視我們的資料後，希望能得到您的回應。

○○敬上

03

回應

Dear Mr. Einhorn:

In response to your inquiry of December 3, I am sorry to tell you that Mr. Belton was with us for only a short time and our records do not indicate a forwarding address. I believe he used to also work for Lorraine Linens. You might try them.

安洪先生您好：

在此回應您在十二月三日的問題：我很抱歉必須告知您，貝爾頓先生只與我們共事很短的一段時間，而我們的紀錄並未顯示轉寄地址。我相信他之前也為勞蘭尼亞麻織品工作過，您也許可以試著聯絡他們。

Dear Barbara and Garnet,

Your love and support these past few weeks have been a great comfort to all of us. I am especially grateful for the way you took over with the children when I couldn't. And, Garnet, thank you for being a pallbearer. I know Edward would have wanted you there. I hope you have not exhausted your reserves of friendship, because I feel I am going to need your kindness and understanding for a while yet.

With love and gratitude,

親愛的芭芭拉與迦內：

在過去幾週，你們的愛與支持，對我們大家是極大的安慰。我特別感謝你們在我無法照顧孩子時幫忙接手。還有，迦內，謝謝你擔任抬棺人。我知道愛德華會希望你在那裡。我希望你們還沒耗盡你們保留的情義，因為我覺得我這一陣子還會需要你們的好意與理解。

愛你們與感謝你們的○○

03

回應

✉ 參見：05 敏感信件、12 致謝函、13 致歉信、14 收件通知、17 後續追蹤信、21 接受、22 拒絕、28 求職信、33 商譽信、35 客訴處理信、47 給親友的信

Chapter 04

遲回的信
Belated Letters

遲到的人通常比等待他們的人更快樂。

——英國劇作家 E·V·盧卡斯（Edward Verrall Lucas）

拖太久的回信是最難寫的。日子一天天過去，我們的罪惡感也一天天加深，我們也越來越不想動筆。最後，一個字也沒寫。

幾世紀前，蒂托·李維（Titus Livius）就曾建議過：「晚做總比不做好。」以寫信這件事來說，「晚做」是不太體貼，但「不做」就是難以原諒的。只要你付出了心力去寫信，即便遲了，對方也仍是感激的。

派蒂·杜夫（Pat Dorff）說道：「可能的話，最好馬上回信。拖延得越久，你的回信就會變得越長。」她說得沒錯。原本在信中你只需要說聲「是」，或確認預約日期或請求資訊就好，如今你還需要道歉，或許還得解釋延遲的理由，並且因為遲誤，你的口氣必須更溫暖一些。

PART 1 說明篇

哪些信件可能會遲回？

敏感議題的信件	給親友的回信	拒絕請求信
參見：05 敏感信件	參見：47 給親友的信	參見：22 拒絕
慰問信	收到禮物的致謝	
參見：45 慰問信	參見：12 致謝函	

該怎麼說？

- 為了避免延遲回覆信件，在一開始先根據重要性排列信件。在處理完最重要的信件前，不要回覆那些沒那麼困難的信件。
- 用簡短幾句話承認自己的遲誤，然後直接進入主題。

什麼不該說？

- 別嘮嘮叨叨說你有多麼抱歉，也別長篇大論解釋延遲的細節。《愛麗絲夢遊仙境》作者路易斯·卡羅（Lewis Carroll）曾說：「別用一頁半以上的篇幅為無法早點回信道歉！」當你自責時，便是把焦點從對方身上移開，聚焦到自己身上。
- 別暗示你的遲誤是對方的錯，如：「每當我寫信給你時，我總是很緊張，因為你的信寫得太好了」或「我不希望你因為我們的拒絕而受傷，所以才比較晚動筆」。

寫作訣竅

- 平時可收集明信片。當你發現快來不及回信時，先寄張簡單的明信片，告知對方你已經收到信，並會盡快回覆。這麼做能讓你不再因為有事情還沒做而焦慮，而當你動筆寫該寫的信時，你也會發現變得簡單許多，畢竟明信片已經寄了，心裡覺得坦蕩。
- 商管書作者唐納德·E·沃克（Donald E. Walker）曾說：「拖延這條路，會引領你走向一事無成。」既然如此，就好好面對吧。在空白信封上先寫下對方地址，接著打開電腦或拿起紙筆。你會感覺到事情已經開始一半，而這股力量會推著你前進，使你更容易完成任務，因為你很希望這個信封趕緊從桌上消失。
- 雖然你延遲了，但不代表你要把信寫到三倍長，或刻意討好對方。這種壓力會讓你更不想動筆。請用你原本寫信的方式來寫這封信。

特殊狀況

- 在**商務書信**中，不管是運貨延誤、信件未回或是訂單未填，拖延是禁止的。不過，這種事還是會發生，而且時常發生。針對這種延誤，可參考本章提供的建議，但你若想獲得對更有力的建議，請參見：35 客訴處理信、13 致歉信。
- 若你拖延的是**致謝函**，請用最多一句話的篇幅道歉，如 My thanks are no less sincere for being so unforgivably late.「這封信的遲到真是無可原諒，但我感激的心意未有絲毫的減少。」；I am sorry not to have told you sooner how much we enjoyed your homemade chutney.

「我很抱歉，我應該早一點告訴你我們有多麼喜歡你的自製酸辣醬。」太晚致謝這種事，其實沒有什麼好藉口，所以不用解釋緣由，反正全都站不住腳。直接說你沒有藉口並感到抱歉，接著便可表達你的謝意。但你可能必須比馬上回信來的更熱情、更仔細措詞。「禮貌小姐」茱蒂絲・馬丁（Judith Martin）曾說：「拖延得越久，你越有義務道謝。你等得越久，你的謝意就得越熱情奔放。」

格式

- 所有遲回信件都依照原本來信的格式回覆。致謝函親手書寫，商業信則以電腦打字在有信頭的信紙上。

PART 2 應用篇

單字

absentminded *(a.)* 健忘的	forgive *(v.)* 原諒	overlook *(v.)* 忽略	remiss *(a.)* 怠慢的
apology *(n.)* 歉意	inadvertently *(adv.)* 不慎地	pardon *(v.)* 寬恕	sheepish *(a.)* 膽怯的
distressed *(a.)* 沮喪的	negligence *(n.)* 疏忽	regret *(v.) & (n.)* 後悔	sorry *(a.)* 抱歉的
embarrassed *(a.)* 慚愧的			

詞組

accept my apology 接受我的道歉	I don't know how it happened that 我不知道這是如何發生的
asleep at the wheel/on the job/at the switch 未能保持警覺／未盡職責	delayed answering your letter because 未能更早回覆你的來信，因為……
intended to write immediately 本想要馬上寫信	much to my regret 我很後悔
embarrassing to discover that 很慚愧發現……	no excuse for 對……沒有藉口
excuse the delay 抱歉延遲了	not from any lack of 不是因為缺乏……
feel sorry/terrible/bad about 對於……覺得很抱歉／糟糕／遺憾	pardon my late response 原諒我遲來的回覆
forgive my tardiness 原諒我的遲誤	reproach myself 覺得自責
I am upset about 對於……我感到不安	slipped my mind 我一不留神忘了

句子

I apologize for not having responded sooner.
我很抱歉沒有早點回覆。

I hope my tardiness in answering your question has not greatly inconvenienced you.
對於太晚回答您的問題，希望沒有造成您太多不便。

I imagine that everyone but me has written by now to congratulate you on your promotion and exciting move to Los Angeles.
我想，除了我以外，每個人應該都已經恭喜你升職與搬家到洛杉磯。

I'm sorry for the delay in getting back to you—I've been out of town the past three weeks.
我很抱歉那麼久才回覆您；過去三週，我不在城裡。

I'm sorry—this letter is badly overdue.
我很抱歉，這封信實在是遲了太久。

I've been writing you in my head for weeks—it's time to get it down on paper.
過去幾週，我一直想著要寫信給你，現在是時候動筆了。

My delay in acknowledging the touching gift of your father's stamp collection is simply inexcusable.
我已經收到令尊的集郵冊，好感人的禮物；拖了那麼久才告訴你，我實在是不可原諒。

My tardiness is due to bouts of extreme busyness and bouts of extreme laziness—I don't know which is worse.
我之所以會延誤，是因為前一陣子又是極度忙碌，又是極度懶惰——我不知道哪種比較糟糕。

Our best wishes for your 75th birthday are no less warm and heartfelt for being so late.
我們在您七十五歲大壽獻上的真心祝福，不會因為晚了這麼久而減少。

Our holiday greetings are late this year, frankly for no good reason.
今年我們的節慶問候遲了，坦白說並沒有什麼特別理由。

Please forgive me for not writing sooner to thank you for the unique and useful fleur-de-lis letter-opener.
謝謝你送來那獨特又有用的鳶尾花拆信刀，請原諒我沒有早一點回信給你。

Please forgive the delay in responding to your letter of June 14.
請原諒我無法更早回覆您於六月十四日的來信。

段落

Well, yes, it's me responding with my usual promptness. I wish that I had any kind of excuse (I've been hospitalized, I've been imprisoned, I've been on a secret mission, I'm a finalist with Publisher's Clearing House), but sadly I do not.

好吧,是的,我又像平常一樣迅速回覆了。我真希望我有任何藉口(我住院了、我入獄了、我去執行祕密任務、我進入出版結算中心的決賽),可惜我並沒有。

I might have to borrow Groucho Marx's explanation for his belated letter: "Excuse me for not answering your letter sooner, but I've been so busy not answering letters that I couldn't get around to not answering yours in time."

我可能必須引用格魯喬‧馬克思在延誤回信時的解釋:「抱歉我無法更早回覆你的來信,但我正忙著不要回信,所以我無法抽出時間及時不回你的信。」

Many and fervent (but, alas, belated) good wishes to you on your birthday. I've got a bad sector in my brain, and can't remember if it was this year or last year that I sent you the birthday card with the warthogs on it. However, I'm betting on last year.

為你的生日獻上滿滿的熱情祝福(但是,哎呀,遲來了)。我的腦袋不靈光了,記不起來我是今年還是去年送給你那張有著疣豬的生日卡片。不過,我賭是去年。

We apologize for the delay in scheduling your tree trimming. The cleanup after the May 30 storm left us shorthanded for everything else. A crew is available at 8 a.m. on the following dates: June 6, 9, 10. Please call with a day that is convenient for you.

我們很抱歉未能及時為您預約修剪樹木的時間。五月三十日風災來襲後,我們全員皆投入了清理工作,因此在其他方面缺乏人手。有一名工作人員在以下日期的早上八點有空:六月六日、九日、十日。請致電告知哪一天對您比較方便。

04

遲回的信

Dear Mr. Cuff,

You will receive the ten (10) hanging pedestals (model #233-1010) for your workstation modulars this week. We apologize for the delay in getting this part of your new workstations to you, especially since you received the other modulars some time ago. Our supplier had an unexpected shortfall of the hanging pedestal.

I hope the delay has not inconvenienced you too much. You are one of our four-star customers and we look forward to doing business with you for many more years to come.

Sincerely,
Rachel Verinder

P.S. Enclosed is a certificate good for $200 off on your next order—our way of saying, "Sorry for the delay."

卡夫先生您好：

這週您會收到您電腦工作站的十個檔案櫃（型號 233-1010）。自您多日前收到工作站的其他零件後，經過這麼久時間才將這個部分寄送給您，我們深感抱歉。我們供應商的檔案櫃意外缺貨。

我希望此次延誤沒有帶給您太多不便。您是我們的四星客戶，期盼在未來能繼續與您合作。

瑞秋・費林德敬上

註：隨信附上 200 元折價券，供您在下次訂購時使用。我們希望藉此告訴您：「真的很抱歉送貨延誤」。

Dear Mrs. Carthew,

Please forgive our tardiness in thanking you for your most generous and valued donation to the Community Affairs Treasure Chest. Because moneys received in our current fund drive are being matched, your contribution is a significant one for us.

Thank you for being one of our most consistent and openhanded supporters.

卡修太太您好：

感謝您對社會事務募捐箱如此慷慨、寶貴的捐獻，請原諒我們過了這麼久才寫信給您。此募捐活動得到的款項，企業會比照捐款，因此您的貢獻對我們來說相當重要。

謝謝您一直以來對我們堅定、大方的支持。

Dear Mala Tarn,

Six weeks ago you requested information about filing deadlines for the current round of state artist-in-residence grants.

I regret my delay in responding. You will know how much I deplore my oversight and how deeply sorry I am when I tell you that the deadline was August 1, two days ago.

I have no way of making my negligence right with you. I can only hope you will accept my apologies.

I have put your name on our mailing list so that from now on you will automatically receive all news of grants, and their deadlines.

Yours truly,

瑪拉‧塔恩您好：

六週前您來信詢問申請本次州政府「居家藝術家」補助金的截止日期。

很抱歉我過了這麼久才回覆。對於我的疏忽，我感到相當自責，在此必須非常遺憾地告訴您，截止日為八月一日，即兩日前。

我無法彌補我的疏忽，只希望您可以接受我的道歉。

我已經將您加入我們的寄件名單，故從今日起，您會自動收到所有關於補助金及其截止日期的消息。

○○謹上

- - -

Dear Mrs. Tuke,

I apologize most sincerely for the delay in getting our estimate to you. You should have had it within days of our estimator's visit to your office. I'm sorry to say that it's entirely my fault (I put the estimator's notes in the wrong file). I hope I have not, by my delay, caused you to lose interest in Trevor Floor Coverings as the best company to install your hardwood flooring.

Attached please find an itemized estimate of all materials and labor plus information on installation services, site cleanup procedures, and our company lifetime guarantee.

Our policy is to match wherever possible any other estimates you might have received. To discuss this, please call Alban Roche, Manager of Trevor Floor Coverings at 555-1234.

Thank you.

塔克太太您好：

很抱歉，我過了這麼久才將估價回覆給您。在估價員拜訪您的辦公室後，您本該在幾日內便獲得估價，這完全是我的錯，我很抱歉（我將估價員給的文件放至錯誤的文件夾）。崔佛地板公司是您鋪設硬木地板的最佳選擇，我希望我的延誤不會讓您對本公司失去興趣。

隨信附上分項條列的估價單，包含材料費與人工費用，鋪設服務、現場清潔程序及本公司終身保固服務的資訊也包括在內。

我們的估價絕不高於其他公司的報價，這是我們的政策。若您想討論，請致電崔佛地板公司經理阿班‧羅奇，555-1234。

謝謝您。

 參見：05 敏感信件、12 致謝函、13 致歉信、14 收件通知

Chapter 05

敏感信件
Sensitive Letters

> 發生意料之外的壞事時，
> 沒有什麼比一封短小又小心翼翼的信更有用了。
>
> ——美國小說家瑪格麗特・德蘭（Margaret Deland）

碰到困難的處境，寫信也許比當面傳達更好。美國溝通專家黛安・布赫曾說：「有些人坐著比站著想得更清楚。」寫信時，你有時間去思考所發生的事，能了解相關或有幫助的實情，也可以好好選擇最能傳達想法的字詞，還能不斷重寫到能準確傳達你的立場。

 PART 1 說明篇

什麼樣的信需要小心處理？

提出不受歡迎的建議	澄清不公的指控	傳達孩子的不良行為
取消邀約	傳達壞消息	報告性騷擾
向朋友家人借錢	結束關係 取消婚約	回信給得重症的人 參見：44 早日康復信

提醒尚未還錢	詢問是否收到禮物 或支票	告訴對方他們錯了
表明自己的功勞	訓斥員工 參見：38 職場相關信	拒絕錄取熟人

該怎麼說？

1. 立刻就寫。拖延只會讓原本已經很難寫的信變得更難寫。

2. 首先，有禮貌地說一件你同意或有共同點的事，無論這件事看起來有多微不足道。

3. 承認你對這個情況感到不自在。

4. 清楚直接講出問題。不要在信中使用艱澀的字或拐彎抹角的句子，只會產生反效果。如果這個部分你寫不出來，可以試著先大聲說出你想表達的信息，好像你在跟朋友說話一樣。接著，將你的「對話」簡化成一、兩個能傳達核心的句子。

5. 列出與事件相關的事實與細節。

6. 傳達你對於對方立場的理解。

7. 如果有的話，承認你在這個事件中錯誤的地方。如果你願意為你的作為負責，那對方也比較可能承認自己的錯誤。

8. 問問自己，看看是否有協商的空間。你是否願意交換條件？你能否接受不如你預期的結果？

9. 寫出你的要求或你希望的解決方式。

10. 結尾時，向對方表達你希望能將此事拋諸腦後、你相信事情能夠解決、你認為一個合適的解決方式會使雙方都受益，或是用一句話表達你的善意。

什麼不該說？

- 不要告訴對方該怎麼做。must（必須）、ought（應當）與 should（應該）這樣的詞很容易激怒別人，可以改用 might like to（或許想要）、could consider（可以考慮）或其他比較開放式的詞語。

- 不要侮辱對方。

- 不要使用會引起對方負面反應的詞語，如 obviously（明顯地）與 clearly（清楚地），這些字暗示對方傻到看不清楚事情；you appear to think（你顯然認為）、according to you（根據你的說法）、you claim（你宣稱）與 if you are to be believed（如果我可以相信你的話），

這些都是貶低對方的用語；you must agree（你必須同意）或 at least you will admit（至少你會承認），這些詞組反而會讓對方不想同意、不想承認。

- 不要使用 problem（問題）、argument（爭執）、battle（衝突）、disagreement（異議）這種負面或敵對的詞。

- 不要誇大。「你嚴重低估了」；「在我的教練生涯中，這是我見過最誇張的事」；「我永遠都不會忘記你的所做所為」；「你對部門毫無貢獻」。當 never（從不）與 always（總是）這樣的詞出現時，你就是在誇大或加油添醋。英國小說家艾薇・坎頓－伯內特（Ivy Compton-Burnett）曾表示：「誇大事實並不能改善情勢。」

- 寫到敏感議題時，不要太「敏感」：「我在寫這封信之前猶豫了很久……」；「我不想寫這封信，因為我知道你很心煩。」；「現在，請別生氣，但是……」；「答應我，你不會誤解我的意思……」。冷靜中立地陳述事件，別把（對方的與你的）情緒摻進來。

- 專注在事實，而非感受。與「我覺得不公平」相比，「根據比賽規定……」更加有力。

- 別假設你已經了解全部事實。檢視你的假設，特別是當很多人牽扯在內時，事件會更加混亂。

- 如果你不想協商，就別讓你的決定聽起來有轉圜空間。明確告訴對方答案是「不」、消息很糟糕、結果不佳等，反倒比較仁慈。

- 別在信中提及其他無關的事情。人們會用無關緊要或漫不經心的話語來隱藏信中難以啟齒的內容，但這對壞消息一點幫助也沒有。

- 如果你有想達成的目的（歸還工具、償付欠款、停止某種行為、修正錯誤），不要教訓對方、說教或為他們的行為貼上標籤。不過，你若只是想發洩，以後再也不需見到對方，那你說什麼就都沒關係。

- 不要攻擊或毀謗對方的個性、特質、智商或外貌，以免對方擺出防禦姿態。如果你讓對方覺得自己愚蠢而渺小，他們越不可能給你想要的。專注在行為、事實，與核心問題上。人身攻擊只是讓你的立場更為薄弱，而前美國國務卿丹尼爾・韋伯斯特（Daniel Webster）也說過：「憤怒並不構成理由。」

- 不要語帶威脅（告上法院、絕交、採取某種行動），這不僅無法解決問題，還會減弱自身立場。專欄作家艾比蓋兒・范布倫（Abigail Van Buren）曾說：「不要給別人最後通牒，除非你已做好輸的準備。」

寫作訣竅

- 給對方不請自來的建議之前，先三思。美國小說家葛楚・史坦（Gertrude Stein）曾說：「知道什麼該管，什麼不該管，是非常重要的。」

- 寫信前，先完成以下句子：「我希望他們……」。你希望他們退錢、換貨還是修理？你想要的是道歉、修正的聲明或功勞？你希望某件事情重來一次嗎？你希望對方相信某個事實、數據或想法是錯的？要了解你的目標。
- 提到一些能連結到這個壞消息的好消息。這個好消息不能是假的或不相關的。積極樂觀的事情能為信中令人不開心的部分帶來一些希望。
- 幫對方保留面子。你要創造一種情境，讓對方能照著你說的做，同時又讓他們覺得自己很大方、高尚、有能力且心甘情願。
- 在敏感的情況下，被動式會比較得體。不要寫 You did this.「你做了這件事。」，而要寫 This was done.「這件事發生了。」
- 你可以告訴對方你很生氣、失望、苦惱、痛苦、害怕或任何其他感受。當你越仔細去選擇形容你的立場的詞語時，你們的溝通便會越順暢。你不該做的是用言語侮辱對方。這之間的差異，通常在於「我」跟「你」的使用：「我因為車門上的凹痕而不高興」是適當的說法；「你真是個白痴，他們應該吊銷你的駕照」則不適當。盡力寫出一封講求事實、冷靜客觀、體貼而公正的信。在盛怒之下寫的信，絕對不要馬上寄出，在接下來幾天多次重讀、重寫。
- 寫到敏感議題時，在寄出信件前請某個你信任的人幫你檢查內容。

特殊狀況

- 當你**收到刻薄、偏頗、充滿敵意的信件時**，要小心處理。若你覺得寫這封信的人可能是危險人物，請向警察或律師諮詢。無論如何，你不需回應惡意信件。如果對方只是在發洩怒氣（而你覺得需要回應），你可以回覆：I am sorry to hear you feel that way.「我很遺憾你有這樣的感受。」
- 寫信**向朋友或親戚借錢時**，要有條有理，告訴對方你需要多少錢、借錢的理由，以及何時還錢。你可以提議簽訂協議。向對方保證，如果他們必須拒絕，你也可以理解。
- **性騷擾**包括不情願、不請自來、單向的性挑逗，如提出性愛要求、故意的肢體接觸或開黃腔。通常是由有權力的一方向弱勢的一方提出。評論、笑話、眼神、談話中的影射、肢體接觸皆包含在內，他們會強調性方面的角色比任何工作能力更重要。這是違法的。
  如果你是承受這種行為的一方，第一步可以寫信告知對方你認為他的行為是性騷擾。過去大家認為，說出某個人的冒犯行為不僅沒有用，還會招來麻煩，但現在並非如此。根據你的情況，有時一封安靜的通知就已足夠。
  要是你是騷擾他人的一方，且收到了抗議信，你可以：
  (1) 了解性騷擾，直到你明白界線該劃在哪裡；
  (2) 寫封簡短的道歉信，感謝對方讓你知道，並告訴對方你會遵照要求去做；
  (3) 絕不再重蹈覆轍。對於不了解事情嚴重性而現在已悔改的初犯，大多數人不會追究。

- 若是**遇到強烈的意見分歧**，先在信中提及之前的聯絡內容，或是寫出讓你想寫這封信的事件。簡述兩種相對立的觀點或行動。清楚列出（或標出序號）你採取此立場的原因，提出統計數據、引用員工守則中的句子、援引相關軼事資料，或列舉目擊者或贊同你的人的姓名（須經他們同意）。如果合適的話，可向對方提議談判：回應你的信件中的特定問題；做進一步調查；雙方進行一場會議，也可以找第三方到場；拜訪律師、會計師或其他適合的專家。如果雙方的糾紛已經到了可以有效處理的階段，請明確指出你想要的結果。結尾時，告訴對方你很期盼能找出雙方都能接受的解決辦法，也期望未來能有良好的關係。
- **向別人請求幫助時**，當你也感到不自在，可以向對方承認這點。如果你能接受答案是「否」，而你也向對方明確表達了這點，那麼做出請求也會變得比較容易。
- **寫信訓誡員工時**，先說正面或稱讚的話，接著描述員工的行為，告知公司無法接受這種行為的原因。提到你如何注意到此事。建議員工改善或改變的方式。列出先前的類似行為紀錄（須標上日期並歸檔）。告知繼續此種行為的後果。明確說出希望員工做的事情（道歉、上課、跟你談談、不要重複問題行為），並告訴對方這封信會放入他們的檔案中。結尾時，告訴對方你相信這個情況會成功獲得改善。你可以要求員工在信上簽名、註明日期，以確認他已閱讀。訓誡信是簡短、尊重、激勵且正面的（不要寫「勿寄任何有錯字的信」，而要寫「請使用拼字檢查功能，並用字典來檢查有問題的字」）。
- **不要做太多假設**。不要假設寄出邀請函後，每個人都可以參加。不要假設離婚是好的或壞的。不要假設死亡是種「祝福」或「解脫」或「上帝的旨意」。不要假設生孩子是全天下人類的共同職責；有些人正因想有孩子卻無法生育而痛苦，有些人則有其他不生小孩的合理理由。簡而言之，要體察他人的現實狀況。當你處理敏感情況時，一定要再三閱讀你的信，不要對別人與別人的感受有任何假設。

格式

- 商業上的敏感議題會打在有信頭的信紙上，以正式中立的態度傳達；這是一種「冷調」的寫法。要是這個商務事件涉及私人層面，則用手寫；這是「暖調」的寫法。
- 私人敏感議題會手寫或打字在私人信紙上。
- 電子郵件與傳真並不適合用來處理敏感議題。

PART 2 應用篇

單字

ambiguous *(a.)* 含糊不清的	distressing *(a.)* 令人痛苦的	negotiate *(v.)* 談判	troublesome *(a.)* 麻煩的
annoyance *(n.)* 煩惱	disturbing *(a.)* 令人不安的	object *(v.)* 反對	troubling *(a.)* 令人煩惱的
arrange *(v.)* 安排	embarrassment *(n.)* 困窘	oppose *(v.)* 反對	unfavorable *(a.)* 不利的
bothersome *(a.)* 惱人的	extent *(n.)* 程度	predicament *(n.)* 困境	unfortunate *(a.)* 不幸的
burdensome *(a.)* 有負擔的	hardship *(n.)* 困難	problem *(n.)* 問題	unhappy *(a.)* 不愉快的
circumstances *(n.)* 情況	impede *(v.)* 妨礙	protest *(n.) & (v.)* 抗議	unpromising *(a.)* 不樂觀的
complex *(a.)* 複雜的	inconvenient *(a.)* 不便的	puzzling *(a.)* 令人費解的	unsuccessful *(a.)* 不成功的
difficult *(a.)* 困難的	inopportune *(a.)* 不合適的	refusal *(n.)* 拒絕	untimely *(a.)* 不合時宜的
dilemma *(n.)* 兩難	intervene *(v.)* 干預	regrettable *(a.)* 令人遺憾的	unwilling *(a.)* 不情願的
discuss *(v.)* 討論	involved *(a.)* 牽扯在內的	reluctant *(a.)* 不情願的	upsetting *(a.)* 令人心煩的
disinclined *(a.)* 不情願的	mediate *(v.)* 調解	thorny *(a.)* 棘手的	worrying *(a.)* 令人擔心的

05

敏感信件

agree to disagree 同意持有不同意見	look forward to 期待
apologize for my part 為我的部分道歉	pleased to be able to discuss 很高興能夠討論
appreciate your willingness to 感謝你願意	rough going 很難辦
come to terms 達成協議	state of affairs 事態
deal with 處理	ticklish situation 棘手的情況
difficult to understand 難以理解	with your help 在你的幫助下
find a middle ground 找出平衡點	work for a happy ending 為了快樂的結局而努力
give and take 互相讓步	work out a solution 找出解決辦法
happy to sit down and discuss 很高興能坐下討論	would like to hear your side 想聽聽你的立場
in the future 在將來	

05

敏感信件

Do you have time to discuss this over a cup of coffee?
你有時間喝杯咖啡討論這個問題嗎？

I feel sure you will make the best decision for all involved.
我相信你會為所有相關人士做出最好的決定。

I hope you will understand that while I am in the early stages of recovery I simply can't be around some of my old friends—wish me well and I will call you when I can.
我希望你能明白，由於我才剛開始康復，所以我真的無法跟你們這些老朋友聚會。祝我好運，當我狀況好轉時會再打電話給你。

I understand you have some thoughts about my work, behavior, and looks, and I would like to discuss these with you directly instead of hearing them second hand.
我知道你對我的工作、行為和外表有一些看法，我想直接與你討論，而不是只從傳聞得知。

The language and tone of your last letter is unacceptable to us. Please forward our file to someone else in your organization who can handle this matter.
你最後一封信的用語和語氣是我們無法接受的。請將我們的檔案轉寄給你們公司中能處理此事的其他人。

You don't have to understand where I'm coming from or agree with me or even like what I'm saying, but would you—as my good, dear friend—do me the great favor of not using crude language around me?
你不必理解我為什麼這麼做，或同意我的意見，或甚至是贊同我說的話；但是，你是我親愛的好朋友，所以，請不要在我身邊講粗話好嗎？

05
敏感信件

段落

I'm sorry to have to write again about the $500 you owe me. I helped you with the clear understanding that the money would be repaid within two months. I've given you at least a month's grace, but I must insist on receiving the money before the end of the week.

我很抱歉，我不得不再次為了你欠我的 500 元寫信給你。我答應幫忙，是因為我清楚知道這筆錢會在兩個月內還清。我已經給了你至少一個月的寬限期，但我必須堅持在本週結束之前收到錢。

I was surprised to learn last week from Miles MacPhadraick that you and he had been discussing your new alarm system. I suspect I misunderstood him because it sounded like the system I've been working on. You might be interested in seeing my record of invention (enclosed). I'd be happy to show you what I'm doing if you stop by the lab sometime.

我上週從邁爾斯‧麥費傑克那裡得知，你和他這陣子在討論你的新警報系統，這令我深感驚訝。我擔心我誤解了他，因為那聽起來很像我正在做的系統。你或許會有興趣看看我的發明紀錄（如附件）。如果你有空經過實驗室，我會很高興告訴你我在做什麼。

Alert! Alert! Jay, I need my kayak. Now! Every time I've called I was sure we understood each other. Maybe a note will do the trick. Just keep saying to yourself: Kayak. Back. To Jack.

注意！注意！傑伊，我需要我的獨木舟。現在就要！每次我打電話給你，我都以為你明白我的意思。或許一張紙條會更有用。請不斷告訴自己：把獨木舟，還給，傑克。

As you know, the Financial Commission has been very pleased with your work. Unfortunately, there is not quite enough of it. Your coffee breaks and lunch hours have been growing increasingly lengthy over the past few months. I realize it's tempting to slip out to run an errand or two or to go to the gym for a workout, but the company has a zero tolerance policy for short workdays. Please let us have a full measure of your fine work.

如你所知，金融委員會很滿意你的工作表現。但是很遺憾的，你的工作量還不夠。過去的幾個月，你的休息時間和午餐時間越來越長。我知道溜出去辦一兩件事，或去健身房運動一下，是很誘人的主意；但是，公司對於工時不足是完全無法容忍的。請讓我們擁有你完整的工作時間。

05
敏感信件

As you can imagine, I wish I had any other response to give you. I would have enjoyed working with you. The decision has been made, however, to hire someone with more experience in livestock production.

我想你也知道，我真希望我能給你其他回應。我會喜歡和你一起工作的。然而，我們已經決定聘請一名在畜牧生產方面有更多經驗的人。

示範信

Dear Mrs. Burdock,

You may not have noticed the wine stains on my linen tablecloth when you returned it. Because they had set, the stains needed special treatment by the dry cleaners.

Knowing you, I thought you would want to take responsibility for the dry cleaning bill, which I'm enclosing.

(This will also make me much more likely to lend it the next time!)

Sincerely,
H. Rimini

伯多克夫人您好：

您也許沒有注意到，當您把我的亞麻桌布還回來時，上面有酒漬。由於汙漬已經凝固，須靠乾洗店的特殊處理才去得掉。

我明白您的為人，所以我想，您會希望負起乾洗費用的責任，帳單如附件。

（這也會讓我下次比較願意出借！）

H・里米尼敬上

Dear Sandra,

We feel so lucky to have you as our Babysitter in Chief—the children are crazy about you. We're looking forward to seeing you again this weekend.

One thing: Our last phone bill had a number of long-distance charges that we didn't recognize. Upon checking the dates and after speaking with several of the recipients of the calls, we realized they were yours.

I'm enclosing a copy of the bill with those calls circled. I noticed that all the calls were made after 10:30 p.m., when the children would have been asleep. This agrees with my sense of you—that you would not be talking on the phone when the children were awake. Because of this good sense of responsibility, I felt you would want to reimburse us for the calls.

And, now, that's the end of that, OK?

親愛的珊卓：

　　我們真是幸運，能有你當我們的「最強保姆」。孩子們都為你著迷，我們期待這週末再次見到你。

　　但有一件事，我們最近的電話帳單有一些我們沒打過的長途電話費用。在查看日期並與幾個電話號碼的主人交談後，我們發現這些電話是你打的。

　　隨信附上電話帳單，圈起來的便是上述那些電話。我注意到這些電話都是在晚上十點三十分後打的，那時孩子們已經熟睡。這跟我的感覺一致，我知道你不會在孩子醒著時講電話。由於你有這樣的責任感，我覺得你會希望補償我們電話費。

　　那麼，這件事就這麼落幕，好嗎？

My dear Bryn,

　　I've been doing a lot of thinking lately. I know you noticed because you've asked me several times what's wrong. What's wrong is that I've realized I don't have the kind of feelings for you that I want to have if we are to spend the rest of our lives together.

　　I think the world of you—and you know that's true—but I'm convinced my love for you is not a marrying kind of love. It's a friendship kind of love.

　　I waited to write this letter until I was very, very sure of my thoughts and feelings. You've done nothing wrong and there is nothing you can do to spark something that isn't there. I don't want to leave you with any doubts or hopes about what I'm saying.

　　I'm probably the last person who can be of support to you, but if there's anything I can do to make this easier, let me know. In the meantime, know that you are and will always be one of the dearest people in my life.

我親愛的布萊恩：

　　最近我思考了很多。我知道你也注意到了，因為你問了我好幾次哪裡錯了。錯的是我發現我對你沒有我想要的那種感情，倘若我們要共度餘生的話。

　　我非常愛你，你也知道這是真的，但我確信我對你的愛不是那種想結婚的愛，而是一種友情。

　　一直到我非常確定自己的想法和感受時，我才開始寫這封信。你沒有做錯什麼，也沒有什麼可以做的，因為不存在的東西不可能激發出來。我不想讓你對我說的話抱有任何懷疑或希望。

　　我想我大概是最不能提供你安慰的人，但要是我能做些什麼讓這一切比較容易，請讓我知道。同時，希望你知道，你永遠會是我一生中最愛的人之一。

TO: Gus Parkington
FROM: Alice Sanderson
DATE: Nov. 13, 2017
RE: Request

I need to tell you that repeatedly touching my arm or putting your arm around my shoulder is inappropriate in a business setting (it would actually also be inappropriate outside the business setting because I don't welcome such gestures from people I don't know well). In the office, this is considered sexual harassment. I would appreciate keeping our exchanges on a professional level. Knowing how intelligent and quick-on-the-uptake you are, I feel sure we need never discuss this again.

收件人：葛斯・帕金頓
寄件人：艾莉絲・山德森
日期：二〇一七年十一月十三日
關於：請求

我必須告訴你，不斷觸摸我的手臂或摟著我的肩膀，在商務場合中是不合適的（事實上，這在商務場合之外也不合適，因為我不歡迎不熟的人對我做這樣的動作）。在職場上，這被視為性騷擾。我希望我們只在專業上交流。我知道你很明智、理解力強，所以我確信我們不會再需要討論這個問題。

✉ 參見：05 遲回的信、22 拒絕、24 反對信、25 抱怨與客訴、35 客訴處理信、45 慰問信

Chapter 06

預約會面
Appointments

> 出現，佔了百分之八十的人生。
>
> ——伍迪・艾倫（Woody Allen）

以電話安排好的會面、面試（interview）與會議，有時會透過信件、傳真或電子郵件的方式加以確認。

預約會面信很單純，目的可以是確認或修改預約，或提醒他人預約時間，或拒絕或取消預約。

不過，如果這封預約會面信的目的是為了推銷公司產品或服務，那這封信就必須相當出色才行，因為你得讓對方相信與你見面對他們有利。

如要確認是否獲得工作面試機會，可以寄給對方一封結合履歷、求職信或申請信的特製信函（參見：27 申請信、28 求職信、29 履歷）。

 PART 1 說明篇

何時要寫預約信？

接受約定	要求預約	取消預約	拒絕預約
改變預約時間 延後或延遲	確認預約	感謝預約	

- **請求會面**：若對方不認識你，先自我介紹；解釋會面的原因；告訴對方會面的好處；所需的時間，如十五分鐘或是 no more than half an hour of your time「佔用不到半小時的時間」；提出可以見面的日期、時間與地點；提及其他出席者；提供你的地址、電話號碼、電子郵件地址及傳真號碼；感謝對方注意到你的請求。有時你也可以告知你會打電話詢問對方意願的時間。

- **同意會面**：告訴對方答應會面；重述見面的目的、日期、時間，地點與會議長度；表達愉悅的心情或致謝（參見：21 接受、14 收件通知）。

- **再次確認約定**：提及上次的討論；重述約定細節，包括日期、時間，地點與目的；在結尾表達愉快的心情，如 look forward to discussing this「期盼與您討論」。

- **更改或延後會面**：提及原訂的時間、日期與地點；列出想更改的時間；為造成的不便道歉；請對方確認新的時間。

- **拒絕會面**：謝謝對方的來信或來電；說「不」時保持禮貌與中立；必要時，提出另一種不需會面也能達成目標的方法；也可以解釋不接受請求的原因，但一句簡單的 I am unable to meet with you.「我無法與您會面。」其實就已足夠。

- **取消會面**：重述時間、日期與地點；簡短解釋原因；為所造成的不便道歉；適合的話，提出替代方案。

- **會面後，寄發後續追蹤信（follow-up）時**：提及見面的日期；告訴對方你對完成的事項感到開心；附上答應傳送的資訊或資料；表達希望未來還能繼續會面／聯絡／生意往來。

- 如果不想和對方見面，或是想取消會面，就不要用 postpone（延後）或 delay（延遲）兩字，直接用 cancel（取消）一字，也避免在信中提及未來計畫。

- 取消或改變預約時，不必表現得太過抱歉，除非情況特殊（你請求開會，該公司邀請高層主管參加，還準備了茶點與攝錄設備）。一般來說，你只需要簡短說一句 I'm sorry to have to cancel/change/postpone...「很抱歉我必須取消／修改／延後……」如果情況比較複雜，請參見：13 致歉信。

寫作訣竅

- 安排會面時要堅定；如果交由對方決定（I'd appreciate hearing from you.「希望能得到您的回覆。」），就很可能得不到回應。
- 當會面的人數超過兩人，向安排這次會面的人道謝。
- 有些人會非常堅持要跟你見面，例如某個很想了解你的祖宗八代或想跟你打橋牌的鄰居，或是無法接受自己被拒絕的推銷員。如果對方是你會繼續遇到的人（如鄰居），你可以寫張字條，用得體而堅定的語氣說：I know you will understand, but I must say no.「我必須說不，我知道您能理解的。」當對方很堅持的時候，絕不要告訴對方你為何拒絕。當你說出無法見面的原因時（「我目前真的很忙」），他們便能做出回應（「這只需要一點時間」）。當你給出另一個理由，他們又會找出其他反駁的方式。他們的招數之一，就是讓你陷入疲憊的辯論之中。為了讓對方閉嘴而選擇妥協的人，你絕不會是第一個。不斷重複簡單的一句 I'm sorry, but no.「抱歉，但我無法。」是最有效的，以文字呈現這句話時，效果更是加倍。

特殊狀況

- 為了銷售或工作面試而請求會面，可以在信中引起對方的好奇心，讓他們想要見你。推銷你的產品或你自己，但別講得太多，否則對方會覺得不須會面，反正也無法知道得更多。
- 如果你忘了去面試、赴約或開會，請立刻寫一封真誠的道歉信，詢問對方你該如何補救。

格式

- 商務往來、工作面試，與工作會議相關的預約會面信，會打字在有信頭的商用信紙或個人對公司用（personal-business letter）(註)的信紙上。
- 公司內部的會議安排，可使用備忘錄用紙或電子郵件。
- 一般私人預約，可用電腦打字，也可以手寫。手寫與否，取決於此次會面的正式或私人程度。

註：指的是以個人身分寫信給公司機關的信件，可以是寫信要求換貨、詢問產品服務；要求公司加薪；或是請求捐款等。這類信件並不會有信頭。

✉ PART 2 應用篇

💬 單字

accept (v.) 接受	contact (v.) & (n.) 聯絡	notify (v.) 通知	session (n.) 開會期間
arrange (v.) 安排	discussion (n.) 討論	pleasure (n.) 愉悅	unable (a.) 無法
confer (v.) 商議	examine (v.) 檢查	postpone (v.) 延後	
consult (v.) 商談	interview (n.) & (v.) 面試	review (v.) & (n.) 仔細審核	

06

預約會面

💬 詞組

already committed/have plans 已經投入／完成計畫	meet with you 與你見面
another engagement 其他約會	move up the date to 把日期提早到……
an unexpected complication 意想不到的困難	of interest to you 你會有興趣的
can't keep our original date 無法維持原來約定的時間	previous commitments 先前的承諾
convenient time 方便的時間	set a time and date 訂下日期與時間
introduce you to 把你介紹給……	unfortunately obliged to 可惜必須
looking forward to seeing/meeting you 期待見到你／與你會面	when you are able 當你可以……的時候

may I suggest	won't be free
我可否建議……	不會有空

would be convenient for me
對我比較方便

句子

Can we change our meeting on July 15 from 2 p.m. to 4:30 p.m.?
我們可否將七月十五日下午兩點的會議改至四點半？

I am unfortunately obliged to change the date we set earlier.
可惜我必須更動我們先前訂下的時間。

I don't believe a meeting would benefit either of us.
我不認為這個會議對我們任何一方有任何益處。

If you're unable to make the meeting on the tenth, please let my assistant know as soon as possible.
如果您無法在十號開會，請盡快讓我的助理知道。

If you would like to discuss this, I could meet with you at a time convenient for you.
若您想要討論此事，我可以在您方便的時間與您見面。

I'll give you a call in a couple of days to see if you can schedule a meeting with me.
幾天後我會打電話給您，確認您是否能安排時間與我開會。

I'm not able to meet with you for several months—please contact me again in late January.
接下來的幾個月我都無法與您會面，請於一月底時再次與我聯繫。

I would be happy to meet with you in my office on Friday, November 8, at two o'clock to discuss your invention.
我很樂意於十一月八日（週五）兩點，在我的辦公室與您討論您的發明。

I would appreciate twenty minutes of your time this week.
本週您若能空出二十分鐘的時間，我會很感激。

I would like to meet with you to discuss Jackie's progress so far on the new medication.
我想要與您見面討論賈姬服用新藥後的復元狀況。

I would like to review with you my current salary, which I believe no longer reflects my responsibilities and contributions.
我想要與您重新討論我目前的薪資，我認為目前薪資不符合我現在的職責與貢獻。

Let me know as soon as possible if this is convenient for you.
請盡快讓我知道這個時間是否方便。

May I stop by your office for a few minutes next week to drop off our latest samples and catalog and to explain how our new service contract works?
我下週可否到您的辦公室拜訪幾分鐘，給您看我們最新的樣品及型錄，並向您解釋我們新的服務條款如何運作？

Mr. Patterne is seriously ill and will be unable to keep his appointment with you on June 23 at 1:30.
派特恩先生病得很重，無法按照約定與您在六月二十三日下午一點半見面。

Thank you for your time yesterday—I enjoyed meeting with you.
謝謝您昨日撥冗，我很高興與您見面。

This will confirm your appointment with Ms. Tucker on Tuesday, December 18, at 3 p.m.
謹以此信向您確認，您與塔克小姐訂於十二月十八日（週二）下午三點會面。

We would like to discuss with you, either in person or over the telephone, our concerns about the academic progress of our daughter, May Bracknel.
我們想跟您討論我們的女兒梅·布雷克諾的學業表現，當面或電話討論皆可。

段落

After you have evaluated my application and résumé, I hope we can arrange an interview at a mutually convenient time. I note several areas where the company's areas of emphasis and my areas of expertise overlap, and I would like to discuss these aspects of the position. You will no doubt have questions for me as well. I look forward to hearing from you.

在您評估過我的申請書與履歷之後,我希望可以在彼此都方便的時間安排一場面試。我發現貴公司著重的幾個領域,與我本身的專業多有符合之處,我希望能與您討論與這些領域相關的職務,相信您也有想詢問我的問題。期盼收到您的回覆。

Charlotte Moulin, managing director of Hardy's Cycle Supply, will be in Alberta the week of August 4, and would like to tour Wheels Unlimited while she is there. Please let me know if something can be arranged.

哈迪汽機車零件供應公司總經理夏綠蒂‧穆琳,於八月四日那一週會待在艾柏塔,她希望能在期間參訪輪胎無限公司。請讓我知道能否安排此次參訪。

I understand you are looking for acreage east of town. May I come in and speak with you sometime this week about the property I have for sale?

我知道您正在找尋位於城東的土地。我可否於本週前往拜訪您,跟您討論我正在出售的土地呢?

Thank you for the copies of the contracts, which we received October 31. As we review them with our lawyer, a few questions occur to us. We would appreciate being able to sit down with you and your lawyer to discuss a few of them. When would this be possible?

謝謝您寄來合約的影本,我們已於十月三十一日收到。在與律師一同檢視合約時,發現一些問題,希望能與您及您的律師一起討論這些問題。請問您們何時方便呢?

Did I have the date wrong? I thought we had a meeting scheduled for 1:30 yesterday. I'm afraid I won't be free again until late next week, but maybe we can arrange something then. Please let me hear from you.

我是否記錯時間了呢?我以為我們約好昨天一點半開會。我恐怕要到下週快結束時才會再有空檔,或許我們可以安排在那時。請讓我知道您的想法。

Dear Mr. Stobbs:

I've received your letter of June 16 requesting an appointment to see me about your Handley Cross computer software.

We have been using the Surtees line of software for all our business needs for the past three years, and we are very satisfied with it. I don't see a meeting benefiting either of us.

Thank you, however, for thinking of us.

Yours truly,

史道博先生您好：

我已收到您於六月十六日的來信，在信中您希望能會面討論您的韓德利克勞斯電腦軟體。

過去三年，我們一直都使用舒緹出的軟體來應付我們所有的工作需求，而且我們對其相當滿意。我不認為安排會面會帶給我們雙方任何益處。

不過，還是謝謝您想到我們。

○○謹上

Dear Lionel,

I have to cancel the meeting we set up for Friday, September 3, at 2:30 p.m., as we've got a little trouble at the Valliscourt plant. I should be back on September 6 and will call you then to set up another appointment.

Thanks for understanding.

Sincerely,

親愛的藍納爾：

我必須取消原訂於九月三日（週五）下午兩點半的會議，因為我們在瓦利斯柯的工廠出了一些狀況。我應該會於九月六日回去，屆時會再打電話給你安排另一個會議。

謝謝你的諒解。

○○敬上

Dear Ms. Vulliamy:

People with disabilities get hired for one very special reason: they're qualified.

I would like to tell you about some of the highly qualified people listed with the Ogilvy Employment Agency who could make a positive and energetic contribution to your organization.

May I meet with you sometime next week?

Sincerely,

芙莉雅美小姐您好：

　　殘障人士得到工作的原因就只有這麼一個：他們有實力。

　　我希望能與您談談奧杰偉職業介紹所中一些實力超群的的人選，他們能為您的公司帶來正面、積極的貢獻。

　　我可否在下週與您會面？

○○敬上

Dear Laura Payton:

　　Our longtime supplier of plastic tubing has recently informed us that they are discontinuing their plastic tubing division. Our vice-president of purchasing will be visiting several plastic tubing manufacturers in your area next week.

　　Would it be possible for you to schedule a meeting and plant tour for him on Tuesday or Wednesday of next week? Enclosed are data on our projected needs for plastic tubing, our production schedules, and delivery requirements that may be helpful to you in preparing for his visit.

　　Thank you.

Sincerely,

勞菈・珮頓您好：

　　我們長期合作的塑料管供應商，最近告知他們即將關閉塑料管部門。我們採購部的副部長，下週會訪視位於您負責區域的幾間塑料管工廠。

　　您可否在下週二或週三為副部長安排會議與工廠參訪？在附件中，您可以看到我們預估的塑料管製作需求、製作時程以及運送要求，這些資料或能協助您安排參訪。

　　謝謝您。

○○敬上

Dear Ms. Green,

　　According to the article about you in last Sunday's paper, you are researching the Arapaho peoples for your new book. My great-grandmother was an Arapaho, and I have a number of papers, mementos, and other belongings that might be of interest to you. I am at home most evenings if you would like to call for an appointment to see if I have anything that interests you.

　　Congratulations on your most recent book, which I read with great pleasure.

With best wishes,

格林小姐您好：

　　根據上週日報紙上關於您的文章，我得知您正在為您的新書研究阿拉帕荷人（註）的資料。我的曾祖母便是阿拉帕荷人，而我手上有一些文件、紀念物及其他屬於曾祖母的物品，您或許會有興趣。如果您想與我約時間，看看我是否擁有一些讓您感興趣的東西，傍晚時我大多都在家。

註：北美印地安人的一支。

恭喜您最近出版了新書，我讀得很開心。

○○敬啟

✉ 參見：12 致謝函、14 收件通知、17 後續追蹤信、18 邀請函、20 請求與詢問、21 接受、22 拒絕、
36 職場相關信

Chapter 07

恭賀信
Congratulations

以「恭喜！」起頭的信往往是最令人開心的一種信函，跟「我愛你」的程度差不多。這種信通常寄信者發自內心而寫，而且內容完全正面，所以這樣的祝賀函相當適合用來為各種私人或商業關係增添亮點。你不必等到大日子才寄祝賀信，小小的里程碑與成就也有其甜美之處，而收到信的人會一直記得你的體貼。

PART 1 說明篇

什麼值得祝賀？

個人成就 畢業、得獎、獲得榮譽	**工作升遷** 新工作、新職位、退休	**職場上的成就** 業績優良、締結合約、新店開張、自立門戶、保住經銷權
各式紀念日 生日、就職服務紀念日	**顧客有好消息** 或發生人生大事	**訂結婚** 參見：43 紀念日、50 婚禮相關信
嬰兒出生 或領養小孩	**宗教上的里程碑** 洗禮、割禮、或成年禮	**消費相關的好消息** 參見：42 銷售信

個人生活的改變	當選幹部	付清貸款
買新車、換新家、換新工作	一般或社會組織、委員會、專業協會	參見：41 信貸相關信

該怎麼說？

1. 讓 congratulations（恭喜）一詞早點出現在信裡。

2. 陳述理由。

3. 向對方表達你的開心、驕傲或印象深刻，並說明開心的理由。英國作家威廉・赫思禮（William Hazlitt）曾說：「取悅他人的祕訣在於取悅自己。」

4. 告訴對方你從何得知消息。如果在報紙上看到，可附上剪報或新聞連結。

5. 將祝賀的事情連結到相關的過往故事、回憶或想法。

6. 結尾時，祝福對方順心；祝福對方工作成功；表達你對他的情感、愛、崇拜、至高的祝福、興趣、快樂、喜悅，或在商業上持續的支持。

什麼不該說？

- 別太諂媚，如「注意啦，美國企業，她來了。」；「我知道我很快就會寫信恭喜你得到諾貝爾獎了。」這會讓對方感到不自在。一句簡單的「恭喜！」，再用幾句話表達個人感受，就足以帶來喜悅。

- 勿加入與好消息無關的問題、資訊、推銷或業務。

- 別拿自己做過的好人好事來跟對方的好消息做比較。讓對方獨自享受這閃耀的時刻。

- 祝賀別人時別提到 luck（運氣），這暗示對方的成功出於機運，而非才華與努力。

- 別讓你的祝賀帶來反效果。不要說「我從來都沒想過你做得到。」或「過了那麼久，你終於辦到了。」請告訴他 I'm so impressed with your energy and determination.「你的活力及決心令我印象深刻。」；Congratulations on your hard work and perseverance.「恭喜你的努力與堅持有了成果。」

寫作訣竅

- 祝賀信不是非寫不可，除非當你收到對方書面的通知信（如畢業）。
- 在聽到消息後立即寄發祝賀信。當消息還熱騰騰時，祝賀的效果最好。如果你延遲了，只要簡單道個歉就好。
- 即便你與收信人很親近，仍然要讓祝賀信保持簡要且有些正式，這樣效果更佳。

特殊狀況

- **在職場上寄出祝賀信**（如祝賀生小孩、結婚、升職、創立新業務），能增加商譽。
- **當商業的成功**屬於整個公司、部門或分部時，可以寄發一封祝賀信給全體同仁，列出所有相關員工的姓名，如 Congratulations on surpassing this year's collection goal/securing the new account/your speedy inventory reduction/a new sales volume record/a smooth departmental reorganization.「恭喜你們超越今年的催款目標／簽約新客戶／快速減少存貨／達成新的銷量紀錄／順利部門重組。」
- **得知他人的訂婚消息時**，回信一定要是愉快、充滿祝福的。如果你對這對準新人的關係有疑慮，請私下處理，別在信裡提及。有警告意味或有所保留的祝賀，比完全不祝賀更糟。傳統而言，congratulations（恭喜）是給訂婚的男方，best wishes（最好的祝福）則是給女方；不過只要使用適當，男女雙方都適用這兩種祝賀方式。
- **收到離婚的消息**，有幾種信可作為回應：收件通知、慰問信（a letter of sympathy），或是祝賀信。祝賀信很少用於這種情況，且只會用在非常熟悉的人。不過，不一定要祝賀對方離婚，你也可以恭喜對方度過最艱難的時期。
- **祝福嬰兒出生**，是最喜悅的一種祝賀信。如果嬰兒早產，請按照一般情況寄送祝賀信、禮物與祝福，不要等到孩子確定平安才寄。

  如果對方生下一個以上的孩子，請別問對方是否使用人工受孕，也別說或暗示「可憐的你！」只要說句「恭喜！」即可。
- 要是**新生兒的健康有問題**或殘障，告訴對方你聽說他們有了小孩，而你正想著他們，請別使用市面販售的卡片，也別以一般的方式祝賀，但是也不要表達慰問。這些新手爸媽可能會聽到這種不祥的話：「你不會把他留下的，對吧？」；「我認為你應該控告醫院」；「你們之中有人有這種病史嗎？」；「也許這孩子活不下來，但這是最好的結果」；「是誰的錯？」；「你懷孕時有喝酒嗎？」；「原本可能更糟的。」；「上帝只會將重擔施予有能力承擔之人。」在知道父母的真實感受（絕望、擔心但樂觀、無論如何都很開心能把孩子生下來）之前，絕不要表現出你的想法，因為你可能錯得離譜。在確定父母的感受後，你的回應才可以訴諸感情。

07

恭賀信

- **祝賀別人領養小孩**，絕不要寫「我打賭你現在就會懷孕」。人們領養小孩的原因與生育力無關，而領養也絕不是解決不孕的方法（領養後懷孕的發生率，差不多等同於夫妻處理不孕問題時懷孕的發生率）。不要詢問孩子的背景或親生父母。絕不要使用「real parents」一詞，因為你現在寫信的對象就是真正的父母。不要說你很「佩服」對方領養小孩，至少不要超過你「佩服」某人親自生小孩的程度。那麼，你該寫什麼呢？請父母跟你聊聊孩子，以及他到來的那一天；告訴他們你等不及要拜訪，並祝福他們幸福快樂。
- 有些祝賀信也是推銷的一種（參見：42 銷售信）。

格式

- 多數的祝賀信是張簡短的便箋，寫在私人信紙、折頁卡片或便條卡上。
- 市面上有適用於各種祝賀場合的卡片；不過，請在內頁或背後親筆寫上祝福話語。
- 在商業、政治、俱樂部與機構組織場合中寄送祝賀信，按照寄件人與收件人之間的熟悉度及消息的重要程度，可以寫在有信頭的商用信紙、個人對公司用的信紙，或公司內部用的備忘錄用紙上。
- 有些祝賀信可以透過電子郵件寄發，特別是辦公室同事之間的祝賀。

PART 2 應用篇

單字

accomplishment *(n.)* 完成	appreciate *(v.)* 感激、讚賞	cheer *(v.) & (n.)* 歡呼	contribution *(n.)* 貢獻
achievement *(n.)* 成就	asset *(n.)* 才能	commend *(v.)* 表揚、推薦	creative *(a.)* 有創意的
admire *(v.)* 崇拜	brilliant *(a.)* 傑出的	compliment *(v.) & (n.)* 讚美	dazzling *(a.)* 耀眼的
applaud *(v.)* 喝采	celebration *(n.)* 慶祝	congratulate *(v.)* 恭賀	début *(n.)* 初登場
dedicated *(a.)* 專注的	happy *(a.)* 開心的	peerless *(a.)* 無雙的	talent *(n.)* 才華
delighted *(a.)* 高興的	hero *(n.)* 英雄	performance *(n.)* 表現	thrilled *(a.)* 興奮的
dependable *(a.)* 可靠的	honor *(n.)* 榮譽	perseverance *(n.)* 堅持不懈	tradition *(n.)* 傳統
distinguished *(a.)* 優異的	imaginative *(a.)* 富於想像的	pleasure *(n.)* 喜悅	tremendous *(a.)* 極好的
effort *(n.)* 努力	impressed *(a.)* 印象深刻的	progress *(n.)* 進展	tribute *(v.)* 尊崇
enterprising *(a.)* 有進取心的	incomparable *(a.)* 無可比擬的	prolific *(a.)* 多產的	triumph *(n.)* 勝利
esteem *(n.)* 尊敬	innovative *(a.)* 創新的	proud *(a.)* 驕傲的	unforgettable *(a.)* 難以忘懷的
excellent *(a.)* 傑出的	inspiring *(a.)* 激勵人心的	recognize *(v.)* 認可	unique *(a.)* 獨特的
exceptional *(a.)* 出色的	invaluable *(a.)* 無價的	resourceful *(a.)* 足智多謀的	unparalleled *(a.)* 空前未有的

exciting *(a.)* 令人興奮的	inventive *(a.)* 發明的	respected *(a.)* 受尊敬的	unrivaled *(a.)* 無敵的
extraordinary *(a.)* 非凡的	kudos *(n.)* 讚揚、名聲	salute *(v.)* 致敬	valuable *(a.)* 無價的
feat *(n.)* 功績	leadership *(n.)* 領導才能	satisfying *(a.)* 令人滿意的	victory *(n.)* 勝利
finest *(a.)* 最優秀的	legendary *(a.)* 傳奇的	sensational *(a.)* 精采的	vision *(n.)* 遠見、眼光
foresight *(n.)* 先見之明	meaningful *(a.)* 意義非凡的	skillful *(a.)* 嫻熟的	vital *(a.)* 不可或缺的
future *(n.)* 未來	memorable *(a.)* 難忘的	special *(a.)* 特別的	well-deserved *(a.)* 值得的
generous *(a.)* 慷慨的	milestone *(n.)* 里程碑	success *(n.)* 成功	winner *(n.)* 贏家
genius *(n.)* 天才	momentous *(a.)* 重大的	superb *(a.)* 極棒的	
gift *(n.)* 禮物	occasion *(n.)* 歡慶場合、盛會	superior *(a.)* 佔優勢的	
gratifying *(a.)* 令人滿意的	outstanding *(a.)* 優異的	superlative *(a.)* 最好的	

詞組

delighted/happy/thrilled to hear/read/receive the news 很高興／開心／興奮能聽到／讀到／收到這個消息	impressed with this latest award/honor/prize/achievement 對最近這個獎／榮譽／獎賞／成就印象深刻
achieved your goals 達成你的目標	in awe of all that you've done 佩服你所做的一切

couldn't let this happy occasion go by without
不能在沒有……之前，就讓這快樂的時刻過去

an impressive record/achievement
了不起的紀錄／成就

another success
另一個成功

good/great/sensational/joyful/thrilling news
好／極好／轟動的／開心的／令人興奮的消息

cheerful/cheering news
令人開心的消息

continued health and happiness/success
持續保持健康與快樂／成功

all possible joy and happiness
喜悅滿滿

accept my heartiest congratulations on
接受我對……衷心的祝賀

high quality of your work
高品質的工作表現

wishing you all the best/much success/continued success
祝福你萬事如意／馬到成功／持續成功

many congratulations and much happiness
祝福與幸福滿滿

take this opportunity to wish you every happiness
利用這個機會祝福你幸福滿滿

I especially liked the way you
我特別喜歡你……的方式

joins me in sending best/good/warm wishes
跟我一起致上最棒的／美好的／溫暖的祝福

know that you're held in high esteem
知道你深受敬重

beyond all expectations
超出期待

offer my warmest/sincerest/heartiest congratulations
致上最溫暖／最誠摯／最真心的祝賀

red-letter day
大日子

rejoice with you
與你一同喜悅

sharing in your happiness
共享你的快樂

significant/valuable contribution
重要／珍貴的貢獻

sincere wishes for continued success
真心祝福持續成功

take great pleasure in sending congratulations to you
很高興能祝賀你

with all good wishes to you in your new venture
為你的新冒險致上美好祝福

wonderful ability to get things done— and done well
能把任務完成，而且好好完成，是很棒的能力

your important contribution
你的重要貢獻

恭賀信

were thrilled to hear about
非常興奮能聽到

you've done a superb job of
你把……做得極棒

spectacular achievement
驚人的成就

句子

Baxter called this evening to tell us that the two of you are engaged to be married, and we wanted to tell you immediately how happy we are for you.
今天傍晚貝斯特打電話跟我們說，你們兩人已經訂婚並準備結婚，我們想立刻告訴你們，我們真的很為你們開心。

Best wishes from all of us.
我們所有人致上至高的祝福。

Congratulations on opening your own chiropractic office!
恭喜你開了你自己的脊骨按摩診所！

Congratulations on the littlest Woodley—may she know health, happiness, and love all her life.
恭喜小小伍德莉出生，祝她一生健康、快樂、擁有許多的愛。

Good news travels fast!
好事傳千里！

Hear, hear!
說得好，說得好！

I am almost as delighted as you are with this recent turn of events.
我跟你一樣相當樂見這件事情最近的轉折。

I couldn't be happier if it had happened to me.
如果這是發生在我身上的話，我一定開心死了。

I hear wonderful things about you.
我聽說了一些關於你的超棒事蹟。

I hope we will enjoy many more years of doing business together.
我希望我們能持續生意上的合作。

I just heard the news—congratulations!
我剛聽到消息，恭喜了！

I'm proud to know you/to be your friend!
我很驕傲能認識你／成為你的朋友！

I'm so impressed!
我印象非常深刻！

It was a splendid performance/great triumph/brilliant speech.
那是很傑出的表現／極大的勝利／出色的演說。

I understand that congratulations are in order.
我知道有很多人在排隊等著祝賀。

I've just heard from Choi Nam-Sun that two of your poems will be included in the next issue—congratulations!
我剛從崔南善那邊聽說，你的兩首詩會被刊登在下期的期刊中，恭喜了！

I very much admire your organization al skills/perseverance/many achievements/ingenuity/calm in the face of difficulties.
我非常佩服你的組織能力／堅持不懈／許多成就／獨創眼光／面對困難時的冷靜自持。

I wanted you to know how proud and happy I was to hear that your short will be shown at the Brooklyn Film Festival.
我想讓你知道，當我聽說你的短片會在布魯克林電影節放映時，我有多麼驕傲又開心。

I wish I could be with you to share in this happy occasion.
我真希望我也能在場，與你一同分享這個快樂的時刻。

My hat's off to you!
我向你致敬！

My heartiest congratulations to you both.
向你們倆獻上最真心的祝賀。

My thoughts are with you today as you celebrate.
在你今天慶祝時，我的精神與你同在。

My warmest congratulations on your graduation from Columbia!
你從哥倫比亞大學畢業了，我獻上最溫暖的祝賀！

This is the best news I've heard in a long time.
我很久沒有聽到這麼棒的消息了。

We are pleased with your work on ethics-in-government legislation.
我們很滿意您在政府工作倫理規範制定上的成果。

Well done!
做得好！

We've all benefited from your expertise and creativity.
我們都受益於您的專業與創意。

What terrific news!
真是個大好消息！

With best wishes for fair weather and smooth sailing in the years ahead.
深深祝福未來都能在美好的天氣中順利出航。

You certainly haven't let the grass grow under your feet.
顯然你完全沒有浪費時間。

Your reputation had preceded you, and I see you intend to live up to it.
你的聲名遠播，而我看得出來你為了無愧於名聲而作的努力。

You've done it again!
你又做到了！

You've topped everyone in the store in sales this past month—congratulations!
過去這個月，你的業績是全店之冠，恭喜你！

段落

I was delighted (although not surprised) to hear that you won the Schubert piano concerto competition this year. Congratulations! I've watched you develop as a fine pianist over the years, and it is a thrill to see you rewarded for your talent—and, above all, for your hard work.

我很高興（但卻不意外）聽到你贏得今年的舒伯特鋼琴協奏曲大賽。恭喜你！這些年來，我看著你成長為一名優秀的鋼琴家，實在很開心見到這個獎肯定了你的才華，以及——最重要的——你的努力。

Please accept the congratulations of everyone here at Avonia-Bunn Title Insurance Company on your Outstanding Service Award. Your industry, your attention to detail, and your creative problem-solving have been an inspiration to all of us.

雅馮布恩產權保險公司全體恭喜您獲得優秀服務獎，請接受我們的祝賀。您的企業、您對細節的重視以及您以創意解決問題的方式，激勵了我們所有人。

You remind me of something I read by Elinor Smith: "It had long since come to my attention that people of accomplishment rarely sat back and let things happen to them. They went out and happened to things."

你讓我想起愛林諾・史密斯寫過的一句話：「我很久以前就發現，有成就的人很少會束手看著事情發生；他們會邁步出去，引導事情的發生。」

示範信

Dear Raoul,

Felicitacións on being named the company's Man of the Year, Panza-Spain Division. Having recently visited one of your division branches, I know that you very much deserve this honor. (As Miguel de Cervantes once said, "By a small sample we may judge of the whole piece.")

I'm looking forward to seeing you at the May banquet when you accept your plaque. Until then, best wishes and hasta la vista!

Sincerely,

07
恭賀信

親愛的勞爾：

　　恭喜你被選為公司西班牙分部的年度員工。我最近才去過你們其中一間分部辦公室，所以我知道你完全值得這個榮譽。（一如《唐吉軻德》作者塞萬提斯曾說的：「由小知大」。）

　　五月時，你會在宴會上受頒匾牌，我很期待屆時見到你。在那之前，我祝福你事事如意。晚點見了！

○○上

Dear Debbie and Jeff,

　　Congratulations on your engagement. Although our record on marriage is not very good as a society, I am optimistic about the two of you. Seldom have I seen such a hardworking, loving, sensible (yet wildly romantic) pair. I like the way you respect and support each other. I like the way you make difficult decisions together. Offhand, I'd say you've struck gold!

　　I'm looking forward to your wedding.

Love,

親愛的戴比與傑夫：

　　恭喜你們訂婚。儘管這個社會中的婚姻並不總是美好，但我對你們倆很有信心。我很少看到如此努力工作、相親相愛又理性（但卻非常浪漫）的情侶。我喜歡你們相互尊重、扶持的模樣，也喜歡你們一同做出困難決定的方式。我可以不假思索地說，你們挖到寶啦！

　　我期待參加你們的婚禮。

愛你的○○

07
恭賀信

Dear Liz,

　　Congratulations on your new job in the animal research lab. I know this is something you've wanted for a long time. I also think they are lucky to have you, with your background and experience with animals. I hope it turns out as well for you as I think it will.

Love,

親愛的麗茲：

　　恭喜你得到動物實驗室的新工作。我知道你很久之前就想要這份工作；我也認為他們很幸運能錄取你，因為你有與動物相處的背景與豐富經驗。我希望你在那邊的發展就像我預想的一樣好。

愛你的○○

✉ 參見：03 回應、11 表揚信、33 商譽信、36 職場相關信、42 銷售信、47 給親友的信、50 婚禮相關信

Chapter 08

佳節問候信
Holiday Letters

因為節日，人們有機會回顧與前瞻，
並透過內在的羅盤重新調整自我。

——美國女性作家梅·薩藤（May Sarton）

市面上有越來越多種問候卡片，以及因應各種節慶的特賣會（紀念日特賣！感恩節特賣！母親節特賣！父親節特賣！），因此，除了過新年或感恩節這種傳統節日，我們也會注意到越來越多的其他節慶。

節日是寫商譽信給顧客、同事與員工的絕佳機會。基本上，家人或朋友一年只會寄一、兩次信問候節日與報告近況，尤其是在年末或新年。人們在過節時也比較願意捐獻，所以募款組織常會在九月底寄送最重要的募捐信。可想而知，十二月期間的郵件數量總是達到高峰。

因此，節日問候信最好能早點寄出，以平衡郵件流量，並降低郵差加班費的成本。自十一月二十三日至十二月三十一日的節慶期間，美國境內約會收到兩百億封信件。

據統計，私人信函當中有 43% 是佳節問候卡片（其他問候卡佔 21%，信件則佔剩下的 36%）。

✉ PART 1 說明篇

佳節問候信包括哪些？

聖誕節	母親節	父親節	新年
情人節、七夕	萬聖節	感恩節	兒童節
教師節	商譽信		

該怎麼說？

1. 以適合的節慶問候開場。
2. 如果是私人的信，可詢問對方的近況，並說說自己的近況。若是商務信件，可向對方表達感謝，並希望未來能繼續服務對方。
3. 祝福對方快樂、成功、健康，或生意興隆。

什麼不該說？

- 別只靠問候卡片幫你說話。如果你沒有什麼話要跟對方說，只想在市售卡片印好的感性語句後簽個名，那你寄卡片的這個舉動可說是毫無意義。打開卡片卻沒看見任何親筆訊息，多數人都會因此失望。
- 寄商譽信給員工時，不要藉此責備員工或傳達辦公室的消息。
- 不要在佳節問候中加入強勢的推銷訊息（佳節問候本就是商譽信），除非節日與商品間有合理的關聯，如花商與母親節，或糖果與情人節。

寫作訣竅

- 不是每個家庭都幸福美滿。有些人失去摯愛，有些人則擔憂生計、罹患疾病或有其他負擔。不要使用商務用節慶制式信；反之，選擇低調、能傳達祝福的問候方式，不要表現得太愉悅，這可能會冒犯到對方。

- 應盡量尊重對方的信仰。除非你跟收件人很熟，否則不要寄與宗教有關的卡片與看法給對方。不要隨便就把跟宗教有關的元素帶進商譽信中，這很可能會被對方認為是虛偽自私的。你可以詢問不同宗教的信徒，確認他們對你的信有何感受。由於絕大多數的佳節問候信都是在十二月寄發，你也可以祝對方新年快樂。在信中指明年份，如 to wish you success and happiness in 2018「祝您二〇一八年成功快樂」，才不會與其他宗教相關紀年法搞混。不然的話，也可以使用 the holidays（這個國定假日）、this season（這個節慶假期）、at this time of year（每年的這個時間）這類的詞。

- 寄佳節問候信給家人與朋友時，你可以順便分享近況，如更改新地址、訂婚、新生兒誕生，或換了新工作。

- 像離婚這樣的消息，加在年終問候信的最後是很方便的，但記得要早點寄，以免朋友已經以你們夫妻為對象寄出聖誕節或新年祝福，這會讓朋友有些尷尬。

- 若由一個人代表全家寫信並替每個人署名，以名或姓署名都是可以的。

特殊狀況

- 以公司管理階層、高級職員或董事會為名**寄發佳節問候信給員工**，能提升商譽、增加員工對公司的認同感。在信中祝福員工於公於私都美滿快樂、恭賀過去一年順利度過並感謝員工的貢獻。

- 最常見的**顧客商譽信**，大概就是年末的佳節問候信。如果你的信或卡片只是為了喚起顧客對公司的印象，那你隨時都可以把信寄出去；但要是十二月是個很重要的銷售或募款時節，你便得在十二月初或甚至是十一月就將信早早寄出，以免人們收到信時已經花光能用來購物或捐獻的錢。

- 有些人認為佳節問候絕不能用同個內容寄給所有人，但也有些人很喜歡這樣的信。使用這種信的爭論持續多年後，安·蘭德斯（Ann Landers）在她的讀者中做了調查，而後她寫道：「結果很明確，一百比一」，**佳節制式信**獲得了勝利。以前的人的朋友圈很小，都在同一個鎮上，不須用書信溝通。然而，對現代的家庭而言，通訊錄有數百個聯絡人稀鬆平常，用同封信寄給所有人是較便利的方式。這種信件也可以寫的很有趣，你可以將信件內容分成兩部分，一是通用的內容，一是根據不同收信者所量身訂製的內容。

通用的內容可以先用打字的方式印出，內容先報告整體狀況，如年度大事、生活中的改變、旅行、或在職場與學校發生的事。安排內容時，可以按照時間或主題排列，或分給每個家庭成員一個段落。如果你能分享你的想法或你參加的活動，例如你對環境的關懷、推薦好書、參加的課程、今日電視內容、對政治的觀點，信件會變得更有趣。你也可以加入軼事、引言、剪報影本或快照。要具體明確，不要只說某件事很「棒」或「美」，而要描述細節。

接著在手寫的部分（這是必要的，就算只寫一、兩句話也行）投對方所好。你可以聊到上一封信的內容、問問他們的生活。

如果你在年末收到好幾封制式信，那你自己也可以用。倘若與你通信的人都沒有使用這種方式，可能是因為你自成一格，而這也是他們喜歡你的原因。

格式

- 卡片是很受歡迎的方式，但請務必親筆寫上內容。若你的姓名已經印或刻在卡片上，那就加一些個人感言。印製姓名在卡片上時，不要寫上稱謂，直接印姓名即可，如 Eddie Swanson、Goldie Rindskopf、Bill and Sarah Ridden 或 Bill and Sarah。小孩的名字通常會列在第二行。如果是單親家庭，或家長的姓氏與小孩不同，那麼小孩的姓氏便也會印出來，如 Annie, Miriam, and Minnie Wells。

- 商務上的佳節問候，通常都是用電腦打字，有些公司也會寄卡片、明信片或是有彩色圖片的特別印製信函。信件比問候卡更顯得親近，也可以囊括更多訊息。如果你有研究卡片與信件的成本，你會發現後者比較便宜，即便你加上特殊效果、裝飾、有顏色的信封亦然。你可以用一個檔案夾存放過去其他公司曾使用的問候妙招。不過，這種吸睛的寫信方式並非適用所有場合；像銀行、法律事務所、保險公司這樣的地方，太過「有創意」的信件便不恰當。

- 人們越來越常用電子郵件互寄佳節問候信，吸引人目光的電子卡片能幫你完成所有該做的事情，只差送不了小禮物。不過，電子郵件比較適用在平常就以電郵聯絡的對象（或是寄給我們電子卡片的人）。

✉ PART 2 應用篇

單字

blessing *(n.)* 福氣	health *(n.)* 健康	prosperity *(n.)* 事業興旺	serenity *(n.)* 寧靜
celebration *(n.)* 慶祝	joy *(n.)* 愉悅	rejoice *(n.)* 欣喜	success *(n.)* 成功
gratitude *(n.)* 謝意	peace *(n.)* 平安	remembrances *(n.)* 回憶	wishes *(n.)* 祝福
happiness *(n.)* 幸福快樂	pleasure *(n.)* 樂趣	season *(n.)* 節慶	

詞組

all the best of the season 為此佳節獻上最深祝福	magic of the holiday season 節慶的魔力
at this time of year 每年的這個時間	much to look forward to 非常期待……
compliments of the season 恭賀佳節	season's blessings/greetings 佳節祝福／問候
during this season and always 佳節期間與永遠	sincere wishes for 誠摯祝福……
great/happy/festive time of year 一年中美好／快樂／節慶的時光	this festive season 歡慶的時節
happy memories 快樂的回憶	warmest regards/wishes to you 為你獻上溫暖的問候／祝福
wonderful holiday season 美好的節慶假期	wishes for a joyous season 祝福有一個愉快的假期

holiday greetings
佳節問候

wishing you love
願你擁有愛

in commemoration/celebration of
為了紀念／慶祝……

with warm personal regards
獻上溫暖的個人問候

have appreciated your patronage over
the past year
謝謝你過去一年來的惠顧

句子

As we at the Bennett Company look back over 2018, we remember with appreciation our friendly, faithful customers.
當班內特公司集體員工回顧二〇一八年，我們滿懷感恩地想起我們友善、忠實的顧客。

Best wishes for a bright and beautiful season/for a New Year of happiness.
祝福你有一個燦爛美好的假期／快樂的新年。

Everyone here at Taunton-Dawbeney sends you best wishes for happiness, health, and prosperity throughout the coming New Year.
湯森－道班尼的全體員工在此向您致上最深的祝福，祝您未來的一年快樂、健康、生意昌盛。

"Here's to your good health, and your family's good health, and may you all live long and prosper." (Washington Irving)
「敬你的健康，以及你的家人的健康，祝你們全都長壽。」（華盛頓·歐文）

Holiday greetings and best wishes for the New Year.
佳節愉快，新的一年一切順心。

I hope that 2018 was a good year for you and that 2019 will be even better.
我希望二〇一八年對你來說是美好的一年，而二〇一九年會是更好的一年。

I hope the New Year brings you health, happiness, and small daily joys!
我希望新的一年會帶給你健康、快樂，每天都有小確幸！

May the beauty and joys of this season stay with you throughout the year.
希望這個假期的美好與快樂會整年都伴隨著你。

May you be inscribed and sealed for a happy, healthy, and prosperous year.
願你有一個快樂、健康而富足的一年。

May your shadow never be less!
祝你青春永駐！

Our best wishes to you for a Merry Christmas and a prosperous New Year.
我們祝福你聖誕快樂、新年興旺。

Skip this part if you are allergic to form letters, if you don't care what we've been doing, or if you can't remember who we are.
如果你對制式信很感冒，或你不在乎我們做了些什麼，或不記得我們是誰，請跳過這個部分。

The best part of this beautiful season is keeping in touch with special friends like you.
在這美好的假期中，最棒的就是能跟像你這樣特別的朋友聯絡。

This is just a note to say we're thinking of you at Thanksgiving/Hanukkah/Christmas/Passover/Easter.
我們只是想透過這張字條告訴你，在感恩節／光明節／聖誕節／逾越節／復活節，我們都想著你。

This time of year inspires us to count our blessings—and good customers like you are chief among them!
每年的這個時候，都讓我們想細數身邊的祝福，而擁有像您這樣的好顧客，就是最大的福氣！

Though we can't be with you at the Thanksgiving table, our hearts are there.
雖然我們無法與你同用感恩節大餐，但我們的心與你同在。

Warm wishes to you and your dear ones this holiday season.
在這個佳節中，祝福你與你愛的人。

We're remembering you at Passover and wishing you happiness always!
現在是逾越節 [註]，我們都惦記著你，並祝你如以往一樣開心！

We send our warmest wishes for health and happiness—and to borrow my Irish grandfather's blessing: "I hope we're all here this day twelvemonth."
我們致上最溫暖祝福，願你健康快樂；套一句我愛爾蘭的祖父常掛在嘴邊的祝福：「希望明年此時我們全都在這裡。」

We wish for you the gifts of love, friendship, and good health.
我們祝福你能獲得愛、友情與健康。

We wish you all the best in the coming year.
我們祝你在新的一年一切順利。

註：逾越節為重要的猶太教宗教節日，落在尼散月（宗教曆的正月，即西曆三月至四月期間）十四日，紀念上帝殺死埃及人，帶領以色列人離開埃及免於奴役。

段落

Anaïs Nin once wrote, "Each friend represents a world in us, a world possibly not born until they arrive, and it is only by this meeting that a new world is born." We're grateful for the worlds in us that you've made possible, and the New Year seems a good time to celebrate this.

阿娜伊絲‧寧曾經寫道:「每個朋友都代表我們心裡的一個世界,在他們進入我們生命之前,那個世界也許都還沒生成。只有藉由彼此的相遇,新世界才會誕生。」我們心中的那個世界,是因為你才出現,我們覺得很感恩。新年的來臨,似乎是為此慶祝的好時機。

Mother's Day is coming soon, and Rowley Floral Shops (with twenty-three metro-area locations) are offering a Mother's Day special you'll want to consider. Choose from one of six stunning floral arrangements (and six surprisingly low prices) to tell that very important person in your life how much she means to you. Included in your one low price is delivery anywhere in the metro area and a special Mother's Day card with Anne Taylor's charming verse:

>Who ran to help me when I fell
>And would some pretty story tell,
>Or kiss the place to make it well?
>My Mother.

Come in today and see which of the six arrangements will bring a smile to YOUR Mother's face!

母親節就要來了,勞利花店(在都會區共有二十三家分店)的母親節特惠活動,一定會讓您駐足考慮。從六種絕美的花藝款式(價格也是令您意外的實惠)中挑選一種,送給你人生中那個最特別的人,讓她知道她對您的重要性。這極低的價格還包括都市區內免費運送服務,以及一張特別的母親節卡片,上面寫著安‧泰勒的迷人字句:

>跌倒時,是誰趕來幫我
>是誰為我講好聽的故事
>或親了親跌傷的地方安撫我?
>是我母親。

歡迎今天就來店裡挑選,看看六種款式中,哪種會為您母親的臉上帶來笑容!

To start the New Year off right and to show our appreciation for your patronage last year, I'm enclosing a certificate good for one free meal with the purchase of another of equal or greater price.

為了讓新年有個好的開始，並感謝您去年的惠顧，在此附上一張優惠券，當您購買一份餐點時，便能免費獲得同等或較低價位的餐點一份。

This Thanksgiving, as you reflect on your blessings, take a minute to consider those who have been overwhelmed by adversity. Help us provide traditional home-cooked Thanksgiving dinners with all the trimmings for the hungry and homeless during this Thanksgiving season. You can feed ten hungry people for $13.90, twenty for $27.80, or one hundred for $139. Won't you help?

這個感恩節，當您回顧一年來獲得的祝福時，也花一分鐘想想那些被困境擊敗的人們。請協助我們，在這個感恩節假期，讓我們為飢餓與無家之人提供有各種佐料的傳統家常感恩節晚餐。只需13.9 元便能使十個人飽足，27.8 元二十人，或 139 元一百人。您願意幫忙嗎？

示範信

Dear Carol and Cecil,

We're remembering you at Passover and wishing you happiness always!

Alison, Jordan, Rebecca, and Jeremy will be home next week and both sides of the family will be coming here for the Seder.

When are you coming to visit? We miss you!

親愛的卡蘿與瑟希爾：

就要逾越節了，我們正在想著你們，祝你們永遠幸福！

艾莉森、喬丹、麗貝卡與傑瑞米下週會回家，兩邊的家族會一起過來這裡享用逾越節晚餐。

你們什麼時候會來拜訪呢？我們很想念你們！

TO: All Norton employees
FROM: Marda Norton, President
RE: Martin Luther King Jr. Day

Beginning this year, Martin Luther King Jr. Day will be a paid holiday for all employees. This day has particular significance for us as I believe Norton represents in many ways the lived-out reality of the dream for which Martin Luther King Jr. lived and died.

We urge employees to devote at least a part of the day to some community service. Bob Gates in Personnel has a list of suggestions if you are interested.

Also, for this, our first holiday, you are invited to a potluck dinner in the upper cafeteria at 6 p.m. on January 16. Please call Bob Gates, ext. 42, with your reservation, and bring a covered dish. Depending on the interest shown in this year's potluck, we may continue the tradition.

收件人：諾頓全體員工
寄件人：總裁瑪姐・諾頓
關於：馬丁・路德・金紀念日

　　從今年起，馬丁・路德・金紀念日將成為帶薪假日，所有員工皆適用。這個節日對我們有特別的重要性，馬丁・路德・金為了他的夢想而活，也為其而死，我相信我們公司在許多方面都代表著他的夢想的實踐。

　　在這一天，我們鼓勵每位員工都至少用部分時間做一些社會服務。如果你有興趣的話，人事部的包柏・蓋茲有一張建議活動列表。

　　另外，為了我們的第一個節日，歡迎你們參加一月十六日傍晚六點在樓上餐廳舉辦的家常菜派對。請向包柏・蓋茲報名，分機42，並請攜帶以罩子覆蓋的一道菜。根據今年派對的參與情況，我們會決定明年是否繼續此傳統。

Dear Homeowner,

It's not too late! If you haven't put in your shrubs and trees and perennials yet, Verrinder Garden Center's big Memorial Day sale will make you glad you didn't get around to it!

Enclosed is a checklist of our complete tree, shrub, perennial, and annual stock (helpfully marked to show sun/shade requirements) so that you can walk around your yard and note what you need. Bring the list with you and you won't forget a thing! Not only that, but when you check out, show your checklist and you will receive a 10 percent discount on your entire order!

Have a safe and happy Memorial Day weekend!

親愛的屋主您好：

　　現在還不遲！如果您尚未把灌木、喬木、多年生植物種下，維林德園藝中心的將士陣亡紀念日大特賣，會讓您很慶幸您還沒花時間在這上面。

　　隨信附上我們完整的喬木、灌木與多年生植物的清單，以及每年存貨量（並貼心標示日照／陰蔽條件），您可以拿著清單在院子裡巡視，同時記下需要的植物。帶著這張清單，您便不會有任何遺漏！不只如此，在結帳時出示這張清單，您該次購買的全部商品就能獲得九折優惠！

　　祝您有一個安全、快樂的紀念日週末！

Dear Mr. and Mrs. Burdock,

Will you be entertaining family and friends over the Fourth of July weekend?

How about inviting just one more to the celebration? Galbraith Catering—a full-service, licensed, insured caterer—can provide you with box lunches, a full multi course buffet, or anything in between. If you want to make the main course, we'll bring salads, breads, and desserts. Or vice versa!
Feel like a guest at your own party! We provide servers, clean up crew, tables, chairs, linens, dishes, and expert advice and assistance.

We are glad to supply references, and as a concerned member of the community, we recycle all papers and plastics, and we donate extra food to the Vane County Food Shelf.

For special events, you may want to make an appointment to come taste some of our specialties and choose the ones you think your guests would like. For simpler events, you are only a phone call away from trouble-free hospitality!

Happy Fourth of July! And, remember, we can help with everything but the fireworks!

柏朵克先生與夫人您們好：

在國慶日週末，想為家人與朋友帶來一些歡樂嗎？

不如為慶祝派對再添加一個成員吧？加布雷斯外燴公司提供完整服務，有執照、有保險，能為您準備餐盒或包含多道菜的自助餐，或是規模在兩者之間的供餐選項。如果您想要親自製作主餐，我們則能帶來沙拉、麵包與甜點；反之亦然！

在您自己的派對上像客人一樣享受吧！我們提供服務生、清潔人員、桌椅、桌巾、餐具以及專家建議與協助。

我們很樂意提供推薦人，而身為關心這個社會的一員，我們回收所有紙類與塑膠，並將多餘的食物捐給范恩郡食物銀行。

若須舉辦特別活動，您可以預約時間來試吃我們的一些特色餐點，並挑選您認為客人會喜歡的品項。而若是比較簡單的活動，你只需一通電話，便能不費周章熱情招待客人！

國慶日快樂！請記得，除了煙火之外，我們什麼都能幫忙！

Dear Mrs. Gorsand,

If you're a kindergartener, Halloween can be scary. If you're a homeowner, it can also be scary—if you've gotten that far into fall without finishing your yard chores!

The MORGAN RENTAL BARN has everything you need to prepare for winter: leaf blowers, power rakes, lawn vacs, aerators, trimmers, chippers, shredders, drop spreaders, tillers—even lawnmowers if yours didn't make it through the season and you don't want to give a new one house room over the winter!

(And if you do finish your chores in time and want to celebrate Halloween with the kids, check out our rental party supplies!)

葛森太太您好：

如果您是個幼稚園小朋友，萬聖節想必很嚇人；而要是您是個一家之主，萬聖節還是可能很嚇人，因為秋天都已經快結束了，您卻還來不及把後院整理好！

摩根穀倉出租公司能提供您所有冬季需要準備的東西：樹葉吹掃機、電動翻地耙、吸草機、土地打孔通氣機、修剪工具、切木機、碎木機、播種機、耕作機；如果您入秋至今尚未割草，而且您想在冬天前就擺脫它的話，您甚至可以租借割草機！

（要是你已經及時整理好了後院，並想要跟孩子一起慶祝萬聖節，您可以看看我們的派對租借商品！）

December 2017

Greetings Dear Family and Friends,

Seasonal salutations to you! We hope this finds you in good health and spirits.

The year 2017 has been especially noteworthy for our family. We saw Kalli play the clarinet at Carnegie Hall, Lauren's soccer team win the World Cup, Leah awarded the Nobel Prize for Literature, and Paul discover the cure for cavities. Not bad for a year's efforts.

Wait a minute! Wait a minute! Just testing to see if you were really reading this. Actually, it has been a fine year, mostly filled with all of the usual family business— school, soccer, piano lessons, soccer, gymnastics, soccer, clarinet, soccer, and softball. Favorite activities included skiing, hiking, swimming, camping, golfing, eating in, and eating out.

As the wonderful holidays approach, we want to take this opportunity to send you our best wishes. Even though in miles you may be far away, in spirit you're close to our hearts.

All the best to you and yours in 2018!

Lots of love,
Paul, Terry
Kalli, Lauren, and Leah

二〇一七年十二月

各位家人、朋友你們好：

致上佳節問候！希望這封信到達時，你們是健康、有精神的。

對我們的家族來說，二〇一七年是特別重要的一年。凱莉在卡內基音樂廳表演豎笛、勞倫的足球隊贏了世界盃、里亞得到諾貝爾文學獎、保羅發現齲齒蛀洞的療法。這一年付出的努力，成果還真不錯。

等一下！等等！我只是在測試你有沒有認真讀信。事實上，這一年確實過得很好，日常家庭活動填滿了大多的日子：學校、足球、鋼琴課、足球、體操、足球、豎笛、足球、壘球。最愛的活動包括滑雪、登山、游泳、露營、打高爾夫、在家吃飯與出外吃飯。

美好假期就要來了，我們想要藉此機會致上最深的祝福。儘管我們之間的距離遙遙，但在精神上，我們卻心心相印。

祝你與你的家人在二〇一八年一切順心！

愛你的
保羅、泰莉
凱莉、勞倫與里亞

參見：07 恭賀信、33 商譽信、39 募款信、42 銷售信、47 給親友的信

Chapter 09

介紹信
Letters of Introduction

為什麼總是那個不需要任何介紹的人花最久時間介紹？
——美國作家瑪瑟琳・考克斯（Marcelene Cox）

現今介紹信已經不常見，因為電話等通訊軟體已經取代了介紹信大部分的功能。而且，多數人都已經擁有太多社會與商業上的人脈，所以人們並不會特別想把人介紹給朋友，除非他們確定雙方能因為認識對方而受益。

儘管如此，還是有人會透過信件介紹兩人互相認識，但現在比較常見的介紹信，通常是用來向顧客介紹新的銷售業務、新產品或新服務。

介紹信與推薦信（recommendation）很相似，都是甲把乙介紹給丙的行為。不過，介紹信比較像是那種在大型派對上膚淺的介紹，而推薦信則像是場嚴肅的談話，談話的主軸是你朋友想雇用的某個人。

 PART 1 說明篇

需要為誰寫介紹信？

轉介業務或員工	求職者	向新鄰居介紹產品
轉介朋友給當地友人 旅遊或搬家到新城市	**加入組織的新成員** 新同事、新合夥人	**新產品** 新服務

新政策	新公司地址	在其他研究領域做
新計畫、新價格	新部門、新商場	研究的研究員
欲加入組織的人	對方主動請求第三方轉介	

該怎麼說？

1. 先說明寫信原因。自我介紹、向收信人介紹某人，或建議收信人會面某個來拜訪的人，或某個初到他們領域的人。

2. 提供該人的全名、職稱、職位，也可以提供一些「標籤」，讓收信人更認識你要介紹的人。

3. 無論你要介紹的是自己或第三方，都要說些關於你要介紹的人的事情，讓收信人想與你介紹的人見面，如 She has collected paperweights for years, and I know this is a great interest of yours.「她收集了多年的紙鎮，我知道你也對此很有興趣。」提及雙方都認識的人、工作或學校上的交集，或共同興趣。

4. 說明你與介紹的人之間的關係或如何認識。

5. 解釋與這個人聯絡的好處。

6. 建議會面方式。由收信人聯絡你介紹的人（提供地址與電話號碼）；或由你介紹的人打電話給收信人；或你邀請雙方一起吃午餐。

7. 結尾表達敬意或友誼，並感謝或讚揚對方，如 I will be grateful for any courtesies you can extend to Chadwick.「如果您能向查德維傳達您的善意，我會非常感激。」

09

介紹信

什麼不該說？

- 不要輕易當介紹人，這件事需要承擔責任、耗時耗力，且會牽涉到很多人。只為特別的人保留介紹的機會。
- 不要堅持讓兩個人見面，或預測他們會喜歡彼此。沒人知道誰會喜歡誰。你只需要強調他們的共通點，收信人會自行評估與對方見面能帶來多大好處。

- 別讓對方覺得必須照你的想法做，勉強會面不會有好結果。讓對方保留思考的空間。由於對方可能會拒絕你，所以你可以替對方保留面子，如 I realize you may not be free just now.「我知道你目前也許沒有時間。」

寫作訣竅

- 給予介紹信的方式有兩種：
  (1) 把信交給你介紹的人，由那個人拿著介紹信去拜訪第三方。信封不必封口，表示信中的內容是得體且圓融的。
  (2) 直接寫信給第三方，詢問他們是否能會見或幫助你介紹的人。
- 明確指出你希望對方做的事。邀請你的朋友吃晚餐；把他介紹給鄰居；向他說明當地的工作機會。

特殊狀況

- 在以前的社交場合上，介紹信是必須的，不像推薦信是經要求才須附上。亞歷山大・L・薛弗與愛德娜・英格斯寫道：「介紹信是為了朋友而寫，不是為自己而寫。」這在今日的社交場合仍舊適用，但在商場上，建立人脈的方式已經不同。你可以告訴某人你想要進入某個領域，或是你正在找工作，等對方將你介紹給朋友或同事；你也可以主動請求他人介紹。
- 當你希望甲照顧乙，你可以直接寫信給甲，並請對方給你回覆，這樣乙就不必親自遞交介紹信，也不會因為沒時間或沒興趣而遭拒，同時甲也不會在毫無準備的狀況下被迫去做不想做的事情。
- **有人幫你寫了介紹信**後，請寫一封致謝信或表揚信給引薦人。你也要寫一封信給對方，為他展現的善意表示感謝。
- 將**新員工介紹給同事時**，可寫封一到兩段長的信給全體同事，內容包含新員工的姓名、職位、上班日期、職責與工作關係、最重要的專業背景，並請大家歡迎他。

- **新業務初次拜訪顧客之前**，公司可以先寫介紹信將新業務轉介給顧客，讓新業務的路好走許多，也是有利商譽的做法，能讓顧客感受到公司對他們的重視。告訴顧客你對新業務的能力很有信心。
- **介紹帳務處理流程上的變更**（新到期日、新的自動轉帳程序、新的結算單格式等）時，要先解釋為何做此變更，可以的話，附上一份流程示範說明。著重在此變更對顧客的價值，而不要強調它對公司的價值。當你感謝顧客的訂購，並告知此變更能改善服務時，你就把介紹信變成了商譽信，甚至成了銷售信。
- **介紹新產品或新服務**跟銷售信很類似。只有加上 we are pleased to introduce...「我們很高興能向您介紹……」這樣的一句話，才能讓它稱得上是一封介紹信。

格式

- 商務場合的介紹信（包含請求介紹、介紹信本身，以及後續的致謝信）都是打在有信頭的商務信紙或個人對公司的信紙上。隨信附上名片，或將名片交給請求介紹的人。你可以在名片上手寫一些訊息來增添人情味。
- 以前在社交場合上需要手寫的介紹信，如今已非必要。
- 當你需要同時向多人介紹，且介紹內容並不是特別私人時，此時可以使用同種文字內容的制式信，例如向遍布各地的會員介紹名單上的新幹事，或向上千、上萬名顧客介紹新系列產品或新的付款時程安排。
- 電子郵件適用於非常不正式的介紹。

單字

acquaint (v.) 使認識	contact (v.) 聯絡	meet (v.) 見面	receive (v.) 收到
announce (v.) 宣布	coworker (n.) 同事、同仁	notify (v.) 通知	sponsor (n.) 贊助人
associate (n.) 同事、夥伴	greet (v.) 問候	pleasure (n.) 愉悦	suggest (v.) 建議
colleague (n.) 同事	hospitality (n.) 殷勤招待	present (v.) 引見	visit (v.) & (n.) 拜訪
connections (n.) 人脈	introduce (v.) 介紹	propose (v.) 提議	welcome (v.) 歡迎

09

介紹信

詞組

acquaint you with
讓你認識

I think you'll like
我想你會喜歡

bring together two such
讓兩個如此……的人互相認識

known to me for many years
與我相識多年

bring to your attention/notice
讓你注意到

longtime friend
多年朋友

get together with
與……聚在一起

please don't feel obliged to
請不必覺得有義務去做

I'd like to introduce to you
我想要向你介紹

present to you
向你引見

if you have time
如果你有時間的話

shares your interest in
在……方面與你有共同興趣

I'm happy to introduce you to
我很高興把你介紹給

similar background
類似的背景

the bearer of this letter
持有此信者

we're pleased to introduce
我們很高興介紹

this letter/note will introduce
這封信／便條會介紹

you've heard me mention/talk about
你曾經聽我提起／講過

we'd like to tell you about
我們告訴你關於……的事

句子

Dr. Roselli plans to be in Rome for the next two years, so if you feel able to offer him any hospitality during that time, I would be most grateful—and I think you'd enjoy meeting him.
洛瑟里博士在接下來兩年會住在羅馬，如果在這段時間，你可以招待他一下的話，我會非常感激，而且我覺得你會喜歡跟他見面的。

I'd appreciate any consideration you can extend to Mr. Chevenix.
如果你可以花點時間照顧崔文尼先生的話，我會很感謝。

I feel sure you would not regret meeting the Oakroyds.
我確定你不會後悔跟奧克羅一家見面的。

I'll appreciate any hospitality you can offer Harriet.
如果你可以稍微招待哈里耶特的話，我會很感謝。

I think you and Nathan would find you have a great deal in common.
我相信你跟內森會發現你們有很多共同點。

I've always wanted to bring you two together, but of course it will depend on whether you are free just now.
我一直都想要介紹你們兩人認識，不過當然這取決於你們是否有時間。

I've asked Adela to give you a call.
我已經請愛德菈打電話給你。

Thank you for whatever you may be able to do for Ms. Ingoldsby.
無論你能為英葛斯比小姐做什麼，都先謝謝你。

There is little that Ms. Trindle does not know about the field; I suspect that you would enjoy talking to her.
崔多小姐對這個領域幾乎無所不知，我想你會喜歡跟她聊聊。

This letter will introduce Nicholas Broune, president of our local professional editors network, who will be spending several weeks in New Orleans.
這封信將為您介紹我們在地專業編輯協會的會長尼可拉斯‧布魯恩，他即將在紐奧良待個幾週。

This will introduce a whole new concept in parent-teacher conferences.
這將會為親師懇談會帶來全新的觀念。

We are pleased to introduce the Reverend Duncan McMillan, who will be serving as weekend presider as of June 1.
我們很高興能向您介紹鄧肯‧麥米蘭教士，自六月一日起，他將擔任週末彌撒的司祭。

段落

Sarah Purfoy of Clark Machinery will be in San Francisco February 3, and I've given her my card to present to you. I wasn't sure if you knew that Clark is working on something that may solve your assembly problem. If you haven't time to see her, Ms. Purfoy will understand.

克拉克機械公司的莎拉・佩芙會於二月三日到達舊金山，而我給了她一張我的名片，讓她向你出示。克拉克正在進行的案子有可能可以解決你的組裝問題，我不太確定你是否知道此事。如果你沒有時間與她見面，佩芙小姐也會理解的。

Dear friends of ours, Ellen and Thomas Sutpen, are moving to Jefferson later this month, and I immediately thought of you. They've bought one hundred acres not far from you, and their two children, Henry and Judith, are almost the same ages as your two. I know you're busy just now, so I'm not asking you to entertain them or to do anything in particular—I just wanted you to know that the Sutpens are delightful people, and I think you'd enjoy them. Remember us to them if you do meet them.

我們親愛的朋友艾倫與湯瑪斯・索朋，這個月會搬到傑佛遜，而我馬上就想到了你。他們在離你不遠處買下了一百英畝的土地，而他們的兩個孩子亨利與茱蒂絲，跟你的兩個孩子年紀幾乎一樣大。我知道你最近很忙，所以我並不是在要求你招待他們，或做任何特別的事情；我只是想讓你知道，索朋一家很可愛，我相信你會喜歡他們。如果你確實見到他們，請代我們向他們致意。

I would like you to meet Rachel Cameron, as I think she would be a wonderful person to run the Good Samaritan program. I'm having a small cocktail party Friday night, and I thought I could introduce you to her then. Will you come?

我希望能讓你見見瑞秋・卡麥隆，因為我認為她是負責樂善好施專案的絕佳人選。週五晚上我會舉辦一場小型雞尾酒派對，我在想我屆時可以把你介紹給她。你會來嗎？

示範信

Dear Edwin,

I'm going to be in New York for three weeks in June, trying to find a publisher for my book. I know that you have extensive publishing contacts there, and I wonder if you might know anyone in particular I ought to see and, if so, if you would be so kind as to

09

介紹信

provide me with a letter of introduction.

I hope this is not an imposition, and I wouldn't want you to do anything you're not comfortable with, so I'll understand perfectly if you don't feel you have any information that would be useful to me.

In grateful appreciation,

Henry

親愛的艾德溫：

我在六月時會去紐約待三週，試著幫我的書找一間出版社。我知道你在那裡認識很多出版界的人士，所以我在想，在你認識的人中，有沒有我應該見見的人；若有的話，不知道你能不能幫我寫一封介紹信？

我希望這不會造成你的負擔，我也不希望你做任何讓你感到不自在的事情，所以若你覺得你沒有任何對我有用的資訊，我完全可以理解。

非常感激。

亨利上

Dear Henry,

Congratulations on finishing the book! I'm so pleased for you. And, as a matter of fact, I do know someone I think you ought to see while you're in New York. Maud Dolomore has her own literary agency and she deals almost exclusively with biographies.

I'm enclosing a brief letter that will introduce you to her. In this case I feel that I am doing both you and Maud a favor by putting you in contact with each other—I suspect your book is something she would be pleased to handle.

Let me know how things turn out.

With best wishes,
Edwin

親愛的亨利：

恭喜你完成那本書！我真為你高興。而且，事實上，我確實認識某個你在紐約應該見見的人。茉德·多洛默擁有她自己的版權代理事務所，而且她幾乎都是處理傳記類的書籍。

我在此附上一封將你介紹給她的信。這麼一來，我覺得我幫了你也幫了茉德，因為我讓你們能互相認識。我認為她會很樂意處理你的書。

讓我知道事情進展得如何。

祝福你。

艾德溫上

Dear Henry,

I'm pleased to hear that you've finished the book! Unfortunately, I've looked through my files but don't see anyone who would be particularly useful to you or to whom I'd feel comfortable writing a letter of introduction.

Most of my contacts are now older and retired, spending their limited time and energy on their own projects. I hope you understand.

Sincerely,
Edwin

親愛的亨利：

　　聽到你已經完成你的書，我真是高興！可惜的是，我翻閱了我的檔案，卻沒有一個人對你特別有幫助或讓我能自在寫介紹信。

　　我認識的人，現在大多年紀比較大且退休了，他們會將有限的時間花在他們自己的事情上。我希望你能理解。

艾德溫上

Dear Edwin,

　　I am grateful for the letter of introduction you wrote to Maud Dolomore on my behalf.
I had lunch with her, and she decided to represent my book. From finding an agent to finding a book contract is a long way, but I am pleased that the manuscript is in good hands.

　　The next time you are in town for a conference, would you let me know ahead of time so I can take you to lunch?

　　I will let you know immediately if Maud manages to find me a book contract. Thanks again.

Yours truly,
Henry

親愛的艾德溫：

　　我很感謝你幫我寫介紹信給茉德・多洛默。

　　我跟她吃了午餐，而她決定要代理我的書。從找尋版權代理人到找尋一份好的出書合約，這是一段很漫長的路，但我很高興現在我的手稿在值得託付的人手中。

　　下次當你來到城裡參加會議時，能不能提前讓我知道，我好請你吃頓午餐？

　　如果茉德幫我找到好的出書合約，我會立即讓你知道。再次感謝你。

亨利上

09
介紹信

✉ 參見：10 歡迎信、12 致謝函、14 公告通知、20 請求與詢問、22 拒絕、27 申請信、30 推薦信

Chapter 10

歡迎信
Letters of Welcome

傍晚來，或早晨來，
在我想你時來，或不說一聲就來。
我隨時在這裡以親吻與歡迎等著你。
你越常來這裡，我便越愛慕你。

——愛爾蘭作家湯瑪斯‧奧斯本‧戴維斯
（Thomas Osborne Davis）

歡迎信並不是一定要寫的信，因此，收到歡迎信總讓人感到快樂。在商務上，歡迎信是很有力的推銷利器，而在人際互動上，它也能鞏固並加深我們與鄰居、同事等的關係。對於天生就熱情好客的人來說，寫歡迎信是一種生活方式、一種快樂。

PART 1 說明篇

可以寫歡迎信給誰？

新的合作對象	社區新來的業者	新同事	新組織成員
新鄰居	新老師或新學生	潛在客戶	未來女婿或媳婦

該怎麼說？

1. 告訴對方你多麼高興他能加入這裡。
2. 提議協助對方認識新環境、職務、同事或鄰居。
3. 讚美對方加入的新環境。如果有特別活動即將到來，可在信中提及，讓對方有可以期待的事。
4. 釋出善意，可提議之後一起開會、吃飯，或邀請對方打電話給你。至少告訴對方你期待早日見到他。向對方保證你很樂意回答問題（可附上電話號碼）。

什麼不該說？

- 不要提及新環境的缺點，例如上個員工留下了堆積如山的業務，或是前房客因為屋頂問題而困擾。
- 不要說 Good luck.「祝你好運。」，這暗示對方需要運氣克服不好的狀況。
- 歡迎新顧客時，要避免過於強烈的推銷手法。

寫作訣竅

- 立刻寄出歡迎信；當新成員還惴惴不安時，他們會更感謝你寄的信。
- 找出你或你的組織與新成員之間的共通點，如 I understand you're a gardener—you'll be interested to know that many of us are!「我知道你喜好園藝，想必你會有興趣知道我們之中很多人也有相同喜好！」
- 歡迎信也很適合向新成員介紹一些組織中的不成文規定，如 Although there's never time to chat during office hours, I'd like to get to know you better over lunch someday.「儘管辦公時間沒有聊天的空檔，我希望能找一天利用午餐時間更認識你。」；We look forward to seeing you once you're settled in—but do give us a call first.「一旦你安頓下來，我們很期待能立即見到你；不過請事先給我們打個電話。」

特殊狀況

- **歡迎新進員工時**，請在信中附上員工守則，避免以後有所誤會，包括工時、職責、薪水、職稱、到職日，與其直屬主管的相關資料。如果公司會發給新進員工一袋資料（包括大樓規定、福利與聯絡電話），可用歡迎信作為資料的第一頁。若主管能寫一封手寫信個別寄發給員工，會是激發忠心與熱忱的好方法。

- **新學年開始前**（約八月底），有些小學老師會寄明信片歡迎學生回到學校，讓他們不那麼抗拒回學校上課。老師可以提到班上同學會喜愛的未來活動或節慶，或說 I think we're going to have a great year.「我認為新的學年會很棒。」如果你的孩子不想回學校上學，你可以在時間或金錢方面協助老師完成歡迎信。
- 如果你的**銷售區域出現新的合作對象或新家庭**，要讓他們對你的名字與產品留下印象。你可以提供免費服務或產品，向對方介紹你們的商品與服務，並鼓勵他們造訪你的辦公室或店面。附上一張優待券，讓對方能得到小禮物或折扣。在給新顧客的禮物中，「資訊」可說是成本相對較低卻很有效的一種，例如列有區域服務中心、醫院、托兒所、學校、專線電話號碼的小卡。在歡迎信中，不明顯且輕鬆的推銷方式是比較有效的。為潛在顧客個別準備歡迎信，並加上主管或總裁的簽名，這種做法會比大量生產發放宣傳單更符合成本效益。
- **顧客消費之後**，可以寄出一封歡迎信給對方。如果你之前不曾這麼做，現在可以提供一些折扣或優惠券，鼓勵顧客再次消費，這樣顧客才有可能漸漸養成習慣。
- 若想**邀請潛在顧客參加**招待會或造訪新店面，可參見：18 邀請函。

10
歡迎信

格式

- 給新鄰居、未來姻親、新學生、新老師的信，會手寫在折頁卡片或私人信紙上。
- 帶有推銷目的的商業歡迎信，以及給新員工、同事、組織成員的信，會打在有信頭的信紙或私人商用信紙上。
- 明信片常用來歡迎新顧客，並隨信附上特別優惠或折扣。

✉ PART 2 應用篇

單字

community *(n.)* 社群	greetings *(n.)* 問候	meet *(v.)* 會見	reception *(n.)* 接待茶會
congregation *(n.)* 集會、人群	hope *(v.) & (n.)* 希望	neighborhood *(n.)* 鄰里社區	together *(adv.)* 一起
delighted *(a.)* 開心的	hospitality *(n.)* 熱情好客	organization *(n.)* 組織	visit *(v.) & (n.)* 拜訪
excited *(a.)* 興奮的	introduce *(v.)* 介紹	pleased *(a.)* 愉悅的	
future *(n.)* 未來	invite *(v.)* 邀請	question *(n.)* 問題	

詞組

bid a cordial welcome 熱烈歡迎	look us up 拜訪我們
delighted to make your acquaintance 很高興認識你	make yourself at home 像在自己家一樣輕鬆
eager to serve you 渴望為您服務	open arms/door/house 張開雙臂歡迎／敞開門歡迎／招待會
to help you get acquainted 幫助你熟悉	pleasure to welcome you 很高興能歡迎你
extend a welcome 表示歡迎	so happy you can join 很開心你可以加入
family circle 大家族	take great pleasure in 非常樂意

help you get established
幫助你得到認可

warm reception waiting
溫暖的接待茶會正等著您

look forward to meeting/seeing you
期待見到你

welcome aboard/back
歡迎加入／回來

expect long and fruitful years of
association
期待長久且富有成果的合作

句子

I look forward to a mutually satisfying business relationship.
我期待這次是能讓雙方都滿意的業務關係。

I'm pleased to welcome you to the Board of Directors of the Margaret Peel Museum.
我很高興能歡迎您加入瑪格麗特皮爾博物館的董事會。

It is with the greatest pleasure that I welcome you to Paragon Photo Processing.
非常高興歡迎您來到典範照片處理公司。

Let us know how we can help you feel quickly at home.
讓我們知道如何能讓您快速感到賓至如歸。

The door is always open to you.
大門永遠為您敞開。

The Packles & Son Theatrical Agency is pleased to welcome you to our select family of talented clients.
帕克斯戲劇社很高興能歡迎您成為我們特選傑出客戶家庭的一員。

To introduce you to the faculty, there will be a welcome reception Thursday, September 8.
我們在九月八日星期四將舉辦歡迎會，把你介紹給所有教職員。

We believe you will enjoy meeting this challenge with us.
我們相信你會喜歡與我們一起迎接這個挑戰。

We hope you'll enjoy this area and the great neighbors as much as we have.
我們希望你會像我們一樣喜歡這個地區與這裡的好鄰居。

Welcome to the team!
歡迎加入團隊！

We welcome you to Daphnis Wool and Textiles and look forward to a long, productive, and satisfying collaboration.
歡迎您來到黛芙妮絲羊毛與紡織品公司，期待能與您有長期、有效且令人滿意的合作。

You've made a wonderful choice (in my opinion)!
你做了一個絕佳的選擇（我是這麼覺得）！

10

歡迎信

段落

Welcome to the Guest & Company family of shoppers! It is always a pleasure to greet a new customer. Customer satisfaction has had the highest priority at Guest & Company since 1860. Although the value, variety, and depend-ability of our products probably inspired your first order, it is only great service that will keep you coming back. If you are not satisfied with your purchase for any reason, just return it for a refund, exchange, or credit—no questions asked! Thank you for shopping with us, and we hope you are pleased with your first order.

歡迎來到賓客公司消費者家族！能問候新的顧客，總是一件樂事。自一八六〇年以來，顧客滿意度就一直是賓客公司最重視的一環。讓您第一次下訂單的原因，或許是我們產品的價值、多樣與可靠，但只有好的服務能讓您不斷回購。如果您對您的採購有任何不滿，請退還商品，我們會退款、換貨或將帳款歸還帳上，不會詢問任何問題！感謝您在我們這裡消費，我們希望您對您的第一次訂購感到滿意。

10

歡迎信

It is my great pleasure to welcome you to the Rivermouth Centipedes. The enclosed preapproved membership card entitles you to all benefits and privileges of club membership.

我很高興能歡迎您加入河口蜈蚣。隨信附上的已預先批准的會員卡，讓您可享有俱樂部會員的所有優惠和特別福利。

We officially welcome Ottila Gottescheim as Director of Education on Friday, August 7 at 6:30 p.m. Please join us for services and an Oneg Shabbat in her honor.

我們將於八月七日星期五下午六點三十分正式歡迎歐蒂拉·葛泰舒出任教育長。請加入我們為她舉辦的禮拜儀式與安息日聯歡晚宴。

Welcome to *SportsStory*, the best sports fiction published today! You will receive your first issue shortly. Don't forget to vote for your favorite story every month on our Internet site.

歡迎來到《運動故事》，時下最棒的體育小說！您很快就會收到您的第一本刊物。別忘了每個月在我們的網站上投票選出你最喜歡的故事。

Dear Rose Lorimer:

Welcome back! We're pleased that you are renewing your membership in the Medieval History Round Table. We know you'll continue to be satisfied with the many benefits that are yours to enjoy in the next year.

You are entitled to tuition discounts at the University, admission discounts at all conferences, workshops, and special lectures, and a subscription to the monthly newsletter. A less tangible benefit is the opportunity to meet people with interests and pursuits like your own.

Your membership dollars help support our programming, and your participation helps make the Round Table more responsive to the people it serves.

Sincerely,

蘿絲・洛里莫您好：

歡迎回來！我們很高興您續訂中世紀歷史圓桌會議的會員資格。我們知道您會繼續對明年可享有的諸多福利感到滿意。

您可享有大學學費折扣；所有研討會、工作坊和特別講座入場折扣；並可訂閱每月會員報。另一個無形的好處是，有機會認識志趣相投、目標相似的人們。

您的會員費能支援我們的活動，而您的參與能讓圓桌會議帶來更符合需求的服務。

○○敬上

Dear Dr. and Mrs. Townshend-Mahony,

Welcome to Buddlecombe! We're having a neighborhood barbecue/potluck dinner on August 3 at our place, and we would love to have you come. Most of the neighbors will be there, and we think you'll enjoy meeting them. If you'd like to bring something, a cold salad would be perfect.

Yours truly,

湯亨德－馬宏尼博士與夫人您們好：

歡迎來到巴德康！在八月三日，我們將在我們家舉行社區烤肉／各家一菜聚餐，我們很希望您們能來。大多數鄰居都會到場，我們認為您們會想要跟他們見見。如果您想帶點東西，涼拌沙拉就很完美了。

○○敬上

✉ 參見：33 商譽信、36 職場相關信、42 銷售信、48 給鄰居的信

Chapter 11

表揚信
Letters of Appreciation

我到現在還不曾對讚美感到厭煩。

——奧圖·范·易許（Otto Van Isch）

表揚信是寫起來最簡單、也是收件人最為開心的一種信。寫表揚信不是出於義務，也不必遵守任何期限，唯一的原則只有發自內心。付出一點點心力，向別人展現慷慨善意，也是人生的小小幸福。

表揚信跟收件通知（acknowledgment）、恭賀信（congratulations）和致謝函（thank-you letter）有點類似，但我們收到後面三種信時並不會感到驚訝，但表揚信則是會讓人出乎意料的。當艾絲崔拉姑姑送你禮物時，你會感謝她；當艾絲崔拉送給你兒子畢業禮物時，你的兒子要感謝她，而你則會寫一封表揚信，告訴她，一直以來她給你兒子的支持對你多麼重要。

當別人迅速繳費、準時交報告、根據表現給予獎金，或將你遺失的皮夾原封不動歸還，你並不需要感謝他們，因為他們只是做了應該做的事情。不過你可以表達你的讚賞，一如美國總統林肯所言：「人人皆喜讚美。」

寫表揚信的時機：員工把「一般」工作做得非常好；你遇到的服務人員給予高效率與高品質的服務；朋友或親戚為你付出額外的心力；有人介紹工作或客戶給你；或你在報紙上讀到有某個人為你所處的群體做出貢獻。

PART 1 說明篇

何時要寫表揚信？

得到獎章或榮譽	員工或團隊表現良好	公眾人物的作為讓你欣賞
受到稱讚 鼓勵或讚揚	感謝客戶的合作 迅速匯款、建立合作關係	參加演講 工作坊或研討會
完成志工服務	得到財務上的援助	對方自願奉獻
收到稱讚公司的信 或稱讚員工、服務或產品	雇主給予福利 加薪或升遷	收到慰問信 參見：12 致謝函、 14 收件通知
有人引薦客戶給你	得到引薦	得到有用的建議

該怎麼說？

1. 描述要表揚的事情（一項才能、一頓商務午餐、新大樓的平面圖）。
2. 讓以下關鍵字早點出現在信中：appreciation（表揚、感激）、congratulations（恭賀）、gratitude（謝意）、admiration（欽佩）、recognition（認可）。
3. 具體描述對方的成果、才華或行動：You're a delight to work with because...「跟你一起工作很令人開心，因為……」；Your work has meant a lot to the company because...「你的工作對公司很重要，因為……」。
4. 也可以提到一則軼事或共同回憶，或抒發讓你想要寫下祝福的原因。
5. 結尾祝福對方持續獲得成功，或表達未來在生意上或私下聯絡的期盼。

什麼不該說？

- 別添加其他資訊，諸如提醒開會日期或推銷都不應提到。這封令人愉悅的信函，只該包含一個主題，才能發揮最大的影響力。
- 別誇大感受。選擇讓你覺得真誠、自在的詞彙；勿過度熱情、誇大或過度諂媚。
- 表達讚賞時，別提到 luck（運氣）。這暗示對方的成就只是偶然，與才能或努力無關。
- 如果寫信的目的是推銷商品，別用表揚信當藉口寄信給客戶。

寫作訣竅

- 保持簡短、溫暖與真誠。保持「簡短」很容易，但要是無法展現溫暖與真誠，那你得重新思考這封信的目的為何。或許你需要寄的並不是表揚信。
- 要有點正式。即便寫信的對象跟你很熟，但當信看起來比較正式時，其影響力也隨之增加。
- 保持正面。不要寫「我以前從不覺得你做得到」；請告訴對方「你讓我們了解到，擁有活力與決心的人潛力無限」。
- 當有人寄給你表揚信，請仔細想想這封信讓你高興的原因。下次當你寫表揚信時，記著這個原因。

11 表揚信

特殊狀況

- **寄給現有或潛在客戶的表揚信**，更像是銷售信。（參見：42 銷售信）。

- 真誠**寫一封簡短的表揚信給員工、客戶或供應商**，會為你的公司帶來許多好評。一旦你開始尋找讚美別人的方法時，你便會發現處處皆值得讚許。你可以每個月都寄出幾封表揚信，讓這個舉動成為一個習慣。

- **拒絕對方的好意**，如禮物、邀請、會員資格，但對方的心意讓你感到榮幸開心，此時你可以寫一封半感激、半拒絕的信（參見：22 拒絕）。

- 可以一次寫表揚信給多名員工，例如表現特別良好或解決問題的小組、部門、分公司或企業。

- 電視名人珍妮佛·威廉斯（Jennifer Williams）曾說：「**粉絲的來信**，是一種經得起考驗的證據，證明我的傑出。它是一種介於情書與榮譽學位證書之間的獨特信件。」寫粉絲信給電影明星或公眾人物時，請長話短說（不要超過一頁）。請求對方打給你或與你見面並沒有意義，只是做白日夢。你可以請對方給你照片，不過不是每個人都會回信。不要寄禮物，因為對方不太有機會看到（通常都會捐贈給非營利組織）。

- 若遇上**公司年度贈禮**，在寄送禮品同時可附上一張表揚信，讓禮品效果加倍。八十五年前，阿格妮絲·雷普利爾（Agnes Repplier）曾寫道：「忙碌的男女花時間寫信，本身就是種慷慨的表現。」在節奏飛快的現代商業文化中，這種慷慨更是應受到尊重。比起口頭的讚美，表揚信可以被一讀再讀。

格式

- 只有一、兩句話的表揚信，可以寫在明信片上。你可以使用印有所在城市風景的明信片，寄給不住在這個城市的人。你也可以使用藝術明信片，或與公司或興趣有關的老電影明信片，甚至是一張突顯你的工廠、辦公室、辦公大樓或其他設施迷人之處的照片。

- 私人表揚信可以手寫在折頁卡片或私人信紙上。

- 撰寫正式的商業表揚信，可用電腦打字在有信頭的信紙上。在較不正式的情況下，可以把表揚信寫在備忘錄用紙上。

- 電子郵件雖然不適合寄發有標準格式的致謝函，卻很適合用來發送表揚信。有些事情太過瑣碎，動用信紙與筆小題大作，但用電子郵件則剛剛好，如 Great presentation!「很棒的簡報！」（若是來自主管，手寫的字條會比較適合）；I noticed your rose garden when I drove by the other day—fabulous!「我前幾天開車路過你的玫瑰花園，真美！」；Heard you got another patent—way to go!「聽說你拿到另一項專利，做得好！」

PART 2 應用篇

單字

admire *(v.)* 欽佩	engaging *(a.)* 迷人的	generous *(a.)* 慷慨的	inspired *(a.)* 受到激勵的
appreciate *(v.)* 感激、讚賞	enjoyable *(a.)* 有趣的	gracious *(a.)* 親切的	kindness *(n.)* 好意
commendable *(a.)* 值得讚美的	fascinating *(a.)* 極好的	honor *(n.)* 榮幸	knowledgeable *(a.)* 知識豐富的
delightful *(a.)* 愉快的	favorite *(a.) & (n.)* 最愛的	impressive *(a.)* 令人印象深刻的	large-hearted *(a.)* 心胸寬大的
memorable *(a.)* 難忘的	remarkable *(a.)* 傑出的	stunned *(a.)* 深深感動的	triumph *(n.)* 勝利
one-of-a-kind *(a.)* 獨一無二的	respect *(v.) & (n.)* 尊敬	superb *(a.)* 一流的	unique *(a.)* 獨特的
overwhelmed *(a.)* 被征服的	satisfying *(a.)* 令人滿意的	thoughtfulness *(a.)* 深思熟慮	valuable *(a.)* 有價值的
pleased *(a.)* 高興的	sensational *(a.)* 轟動的	thrilled *(a.)* 興奮的	welcome *(v.)* 歡迎
recommend *(v.)* 推薦	sincere *(a.)* 真誠的	touched *(a.)* 感動的	
refreshing *(a.)* 耳目一新的	special *(a.)* 特別的	treasure *(v.) & (n.)* 珍惜；珍寶	

11

表揚信

I appreciate the time and effort you expended on
我很感謝你花費在……的時間與心力

I want you to know how much we/ I appreciate
我希望你能知道我（們）有多麼感激

as a token of our gratitude/appreciation
以表達我們的謝意／感激

job well done
做得好

delighted to learn about
很高興知道……

let me tell you how much I liked
我想告訴你我多麼喜歡

grateful to you for
謝謝你，因為……

offer my compliments
獻上我的讚美

heard about your success
聽聞你的成功

realize the worth of
了解……的價值

held in high regard
深受尊敬

set great store by
十分重視

hope I can return the favor someday
希望我有一天可以回報

think highly of
對……評價很高

I am impressed by/with
我對……印象深刻

we can point with pride
我們可以驕傲地指出

appreciate your contributions to
感謝你對……的貢獻

wish you well
祝你一切都好

important contribution
重要貢獻

without your dedication and expertise
若無你的貢獻與專業

it was thoughtful of you to
你對……真是考慮周到

would like to compliment you on
想要在……方面讚美你

句子

As principal of Jerome Elementary School, you might like to know that we think Miss Eurgain is an absolute treasure.
作為傑洛小學的校長，您或許會想知道，我們都認為尤根小姐是個不可多得的人才。

Can you stand one more compliment?
您願意再接受一句讚美嗎？

Customers like you are the reason we stay in business.
像您這樣的客戶，是我們待在業界的理由。

I'd like to express my appreciation for the knowledgeable and sympathetic care you gave me during my hospitalization for bypass surgery.
我想要向您表達感謝，在我因繞道手術住院的期間，給了我專業而體貼的照顧。

I don't know how I would have managed without your help.
要不是有你的幫忙，我真不知道該怎麼辦。

If I can repay your kindness, let me know.
如果有能回報你好意的機會，請讓我知道。

I'm impressed!
我很驚艷！

I sincerely appreciate your time and attention.
我誠摯感謝您投入的時間與心力。

I want to express my appreciation to all of you for the extra hours and hard work you put in last week to secure the Gryseworth contract.
我想要向各位表示感謝。為了確保拿下葛斯渥茲的合約，你們上週都付出了額外的時間與努力。

I want to tell you how much I appreciate what you are doing for the recycling program in our neighborhood.
我想讓您知道，我們有多麼感激您為社區回收計畫所付出的一切。

My hat's off to you!
謹讓我向您致上敬意！

Thanks again for your clever and useful suggestion.
再次謝謝您明智又受用的建議。

The Ridley County School Board would like to add its thanks and appreciation to those of the recipients of the scholarships you made possible.
雷利郡學校委員會想對您表達感謝與讚賞，您讓這些得獎者如願以償獲得獎學金。

This past year has been a banner year for the company, and you have contributed significantly to its success.
過去一年公司大豐收，而你對公司的成功有很重要的貢獻。

We are all happy for you.
我們都為你感到開心。

Well done!
做得好！

Your efforts have made this possible.
你的努力使這一切成真。

Your support is greatly appreciated.
非常感謝您的支持。

You've done it again!
你又做到了！

段落

As Bette Midler once said, "People are not the best because they work hard. They work hard because they are the best." And you are the best! Know that we appreciate you!

就像貝蒂‧蜜勒（Bette Midler）曾說過的：「頂尖人才並非因為努力工作才成為頂尖；他們努力工作是因為他們是頂尖人才。」而你就是最頂尖的！要知道我們都很佩服你！

Thank you for your timely and excellent solution to the problem of tangled hoses. Only those of us who have struggled with this annoying and time-consuming inconvenience can appreciate what a delight the new boom system will be. You will be receiving an Outstanding Contribution award in May, but I didn't want to wait that long before telling you how pleased and impressed we all are.

謝謝您迅速完善解決了管線纏繞的問題。這個惱人又耗時的問題困擾我們已久，也因此我們更能體會這個新的吊架系統的完成有多麼令人欣喜。五月時您將會頒卓越貢獻獎，但我等不及要告訴您我們有多麼高興又佩服。

All of us here at Legson Ltd. enjoyed your enthusiastic letter about the quality of our lace goods. We are proud to offer such a wide selection of fine handiwork from all four corners of the globe. Please accept with our appreciation the enclosed 20 percent discount coupon good on your next order.

雷格森公司的全體員工都很高興收到您的來信，在信中您熱烈讚美了敝公司蕾絲產品的品質。我們提供來自世界各地多樣化的手工藝品，對此我們深感自豪。請接受我們的謝意，隨信附上八折優惠券，您可在下次訂購時使用。

Appreciation and thanks go to Angela Messenger and her Documentation Department for a successful transformation of the tracking system. The new equipment and its faster, more accurate method of record-keeping will help keep us in the forefront of the Stout, Old, Mild, Bitter, Family Ales market. Our success here at Marsden & Company is due to an exceptional group of talented employees.

謹向安琪拉‧梅森傑及其檔案紀錄部門表示讚賞與感激，因其成功改善了貨品追蹤系統。全新設備加上更快、更確實的紀錄保存方式，能使我們在司陶德啤酒、老艾爾、淡艾爾、苦艾爾、家庭艾爾啤酒市場中保持不墜的地位。瑪斯登公司的成功，來自於頂尖優秀的員工。

示範信

Dear Dr. Rowlands,

Your suggestions for next year's technical forum are much appreciated. I've turned them over to the steering committee, although I suspect you'll be invited to join them. I hope you will accept—your ideas seem as workable as they are useful.

Sincerely yours,

羅蘭博士您好：

很感謝您對明年技術論壇提出的建議。我已經將您的建言交給籌劃委員會，不過我想您也會受邀加入他們。希望您會接受邀請，因為您提供的意見切實可行又有效。

○○敬上

Dear Mrs. Sixsmith,

Thank you for accompanying the fifth and sixth graders to Language Camp last weekend. I understand you chaperoned the group on your own time. Since Ronald arrived home, I've heard dozens of stories of your helpfulness, good humor, and ability to make the camp a home-away-from-home for these youngsters.

We felt a lot better knowing you would be with the group, and we appreciate Ronald's opportunity to spend time with a dynamic adult who's a good role model.

With best wishes,

西史密斯太太您好：

謝謝您上週末陪伴五、六年級學生前往語言學習營。我知道您是用私人時間護送他們。自羅納德回家後，我便不斷聽到他描述您的友善協助與幽默言談，讓這些孩子在營隊中有家的感覺。

當我們知道您會陪伴他們一起前往時，我們感到安心許多。我們也很高興羅納德有此機會與您這樣有活力的大人相處，您是他們的楷模。

祝福您。

○○敬上

11
表揚信

✉ 參見：07 恭賀信、12 致謝函、14 收件通知、33 商譽信

Chapter 12

致謝函
Thank-You Letters

他的禮貌可說是有點泛濫了。
當有人寫信謝謝他寄送結婚禮物，他會再回信感謝對方。
倘若對方跟他一樣細心謹慎的話，
那他們的通信往返要到死亡的那一天才能結束。

——英國小說家伊夫林‧沃（Evelyn Waugh）

致謝函能加強商務與一般人際關係，並能為寫致謝函的人帶來豐厚報酬。儘管如此，大多數人還是覺得致謝函很難寫，而這大概是為什麼致謝函經常遲到或甚至根本沒寄出的原因。

不確定寄致謝函是否必要時，最好還是以「必要」作為答案。即便你已經親自向對方表達過感謝，對方仍會期待收到書面的致謝函。

關於結婚禮物的致謝函，參見：50 婚禮相關信。

PART 1 說明篇

何時必須寫致謝函？

得到恭賀 表揚或讚美	**收到貢獻** 募款活動、慈善活動	**收到慰問**
收到錢 禮物、獎金或借款	**得到幫助** 恩惠、建議或特殊協助	**受到熱情招待**

獲得銷售機會 或收到請求的資訊	**獲得轉介** 顧客或病患	**員工表現出色** 或付出努力
收到新訂單	**顧客光顧**	**得到工作面試機會**

該怎麼說？

1. 具體描述你想要感謝的是什麼（而不只是寫「可愛的禮物」或「很好的禮物」）。

2. 用熱情讚賞的口氣表達你的感謝。

3. 繼續描述你的感激之情。告訴對方你收到的東西有多麼實用或合適、你會如何使用它、把它放在哪裡，或是它如何改善你的生活。具體傳達你為什麼喜歡它。

4. 以一、兩句話收尾，但內容與你感激的事物無關，例如你可以答應對方你們很快會見到面、問候其他家庭成員，或說些讚美捐款人的話。

什麼不該說？

- 不要納入其他消息、資訊、問題或評論，這會稀釋你的感謝。

- 如果收到重複的禮物，不要向送禮者提起。

- 不要為了換貨而詢問禮物是在哪裡買的。

- 有些禮儀專家建議，收到禮金時，致謝函中不要提到金額，只要講到送禮者的好意與慷慨，也可以說錢給得太多。不過，只要你與送禮者對於提到金額都感到自在便可隨意。

- 儘管幾位寫信專家不喜歡以 Thanks again.「再次感謝。」結尾，但有非常多致謝信或紙條都是這麼收尾的。如果你喜歡就放心使用。

- 「不要說的比感受到的更多。」對致謝函而言更是如此。我們習慣用冗言贅句來彌補不夠熱情的部分，但一句簡單的 thank you（謝謝你）就足夠。

寫作訣竅

- 立刻就寫。趁感激之情未消退前,比較容易下筆。此外,這樣也比較有禮貌。比起得到感謝,多數送禮者其實是要知道禮物收到了沒(特別是禮物是從店裡直接寄出)以及你是否喜歡。

- 有些人認為,收到禮物後三天內應寄出致謝函,最晚須在兩週內寄出。若是要感謝對方的借住,請在一至三天內寄出,最晚一週內。感謝晚餐或其他招待時,請在一到兩日內寄出。若要回應慰問信,則可以有六週的時間,因為這涉及困難的狀況。收到早日康復的禮物,則等到身體恢復時再回信(可請其他朋友先幫你寄發收件通知)。

- 一張照片抵過千言萬語。你可以附上一張禮物使用情況的照片,如裝著紅酒的玻璃杯,或是穿在狗狗身上的新格子外套。收到雙人按摩禮券的夫妻,則能附上按摩前疲憊易怒,按摩後輕鬆快樂的對比照片。

- 以下情況則沒有義務要寫致謝信(如果你寫了,這會是很高尚又備受讚賞的做法):參加派對,但你不是主要嘉賓;一個隨興休閒的聚餐派對;收到生日、紀念日、祝賀、早日康復卡片的問候;你很親近的人(手足、鄰居)的協助與招待,而且你已經做好報答的安排。在這些狀況下,你可以用電話表達謝意,或下次見到他們時再傳達。

- 受到留宿招待,一定要寫致謝函,通常也會贈送禮物,你可以在留宿當天就把禮物帶去,也可以之後再寄(受歡迎的禮物包括特產、室內植物、花朵、可放在家中的飾品、給孩子的玩具)。當你寫信的對象是一個家庭,請以家長為主軸,並提及孩子的名字(如果你稱讚對方的孩子,對方更會覺得這次邀請你很值得)。若你只寫給邀請你的那個人,或最熱情款待你的那個人,請也在信中問候其他家人。

特殊狀況

- **延遲的致謝函**比其他信件的延遲更不應該,但延誤總比完全不寫好。請用最多一句話的長度為遲寄致謝函道歉:My thanks are no less sincere for being so unforgivably late.「儘管晚得不可原諒,我的感謝仍然一樣真心。」;I am sorry not to have told you sooner how much we enjoyed the petit fours.「我很抱歉沒有更早跟你說我們有多喜歡那些小蛋糕。」

- **收到答謝的禮物後**,請回覆一封感謝函給對方。

- 有人**以你或已故親人的名義捐款給慈善機構**,該機構會寄確認信給你跟捐款人,但你仍然要寫感謝函感謝捐款人。

- **紀念日、慶生會或送禮會(shower)的主辦人**,除了必須收到特別感謝函外,還應該收到一個小禮物。

- **感謝面試官**不僅是求職的重要技巧，也是種禮貌。在面試後立即寫信，且要在對方做出決定前寄達。告訴對方你喜歡這次面試、這間公司，或這個職位。簡要具體強調你適合這份工作的原因。解釋面試時對方對你資歷的擔憂。提及任何你未有機會講到的議題。如果你覺得你在面試時說錯話，或留下了不太好的印象，這封致謝函便是修正的機會，但要簡短而不著痕跡，畢竟你不會想讓面試官回想起你的弱點。

- **儘管商務上的招待**通常被視為理所當然，但對方仍會感謝你寄發致謝函，這也有助於建立良好關係。寫信給同事、客戶、員工或供應商，可以激發忠心、熱忱與生產力。若有業務往來的人寄給你禮物，你可以回覆致謝信，儘管你覺得對方應該送了上百個禮物給上百個跟你一樣的人。當你無法收受商務禮品，避免暗示對方不得體，只須簡單解釋公司不允許收受禮品。

- 在商場上，頻繁寄發致謝函可以帶來商業上的成功，其影響是難以估計的。從得到面試的「謝謝你」，到退休派對的「謝謝你」，你的職業生涯可以因為簡單的感謝信而受益良多。成功的企業家、暢銷作家兼知名演講家哈維·麥凱曾說：「太過忙碌而沒時間說謝謝的人，能說這句話的機會便越來越少。」

- 如果**禮物在活動之前就寄達**，等活動結束後再寫感謝函。如賓客贈禮若於結婚典禮前抵達，新郎或新娘只要於婚禮結束後再寫感謝函就可以了。

- **收到多人合送的禮物**，請寄送感謝函給每個人。但在以下狀況例外：送禮者是一個家庭（即便五個人全都簽了名也一樣）；禮物來自一個團體，如你的橋牌社、你學校裡的老師，或你的同事。你可以直接寫一封信給整個團體，然後輪流傳閱或貼在某個地方，讓有參與的每個人都能看到。

- **辦完喪禮後**，須寄致謝函給送花或捐款的人，以及那些協助準備熱食、主持晚餐、安排外地親戚住宿、借椅子或給予其他支持的人。你也需要回應寄來的慰問信（例外：只有簽名、沒有其他個人留言的市售卡片）。你可以使用殯儀館提供的印製小卡，但必須加上你要說的話。倘若與死者最親近的家屬無法處理這些信件，其他家屬或朋友應代表他們致謝。這種信不必太長，而且一般而言，在葬禮結束後你有六週的時間寄送。為了知道有誰送了花，家屬或殯儀館人員須收集花上的小卡，並在小卡上記錄花的種類。

- **潛在客戶致電或親自拜訪後**，需寄感謝信給他們。你花幾分鐘寫的這封信，能讓潛在客戶留下好印象，增加下次再與你談話的意願。寄出幾封這樣的信之後，你也會驚訝地發現，你開始愛上工作中的這一部分。

- 如果**收到很特別的禮物**，可以考慮寄兩封致謝函，收到禮物時寄第一封，使用後寄第二封，如當你收到支票，你的第二封信可以寫 We used your gift to enroll in a ballroom dancing class, something we've wanted to do for years.「我們用你的禮物報名了國標舞課，這是我們好幾年前就想做的事。」或你收到的是火鍋鍋具時：We invited the cousins over for fondue and told them that they could thank you too!「我們邀請了表兄弟姊妹一起來吃火鍋，並跟他們說要謝謝你！」

格式

- 致謝函幾乎都是親筆寫在折頁卡片、空白小卡或私人信紙上。如果感謝的訊息包含在給家人或朋友的私人長信中，那麼打字也可以。

- 重要場合（如婚禮）的致謝函，請使用正式印製或刻印的信紙。

- 商場上的致謝函會打在有信頭的信紙、私人商用信紙或品質好的書寫紙上。如果想呈現比較溫暖的氛圍，則改用手寫。

- 印有 Thanks 或 Thank you 的市售折頁卡片，是方便且合宜的選項，但應在內頁親筆寫上幾句話。

- 若需要感謝的對象有好幾個人，可以選擇在報紙上刊登致謝通知。特別是幫助重病痊癒的護士、醫師、醫院人員、朋友與家人，更適合這樣的感謝方式。而公眾人物的逝世，其家屬可能會收到上百封慰問信，此時也可利用報紙來傳達謝意。當選的候選人也可透過這個方式，感謝協助競選的團隊與投票給他的人。遣詞用字簡單、溫暖即可：We wish to thank all the generous and loving friends and family who sent cards and gifts on the occasion of our twenty-fifth wedding anniversary.「我們想要感謝所有慷慨、深情的朋友與家人，謝謝你們在我們的結婚二十五週年紀念日寄來的卡片與禮物。」

- 致謝函的重點在於它很私人，儘管電子郵件有許多優點，但卻不夠親切與正式。多數情況下，電子郵件並不適合用來表達謝意。不過，電子郵件可以用於多年老友之間，以及在對方幫了小忙（協助借書、幫忙買午餐等）之後的快速致謝。電子郵件也可以作為寄出「真正」致謝函前的預告，主要是為了告知對方禮物已寄達、致謝信很快會寄出。

- 若要感謝購買產品的顧客，禮貌小姐建議不要使用傳真，因為這樣對方必須負擔傳真的成本（包括傳真用紙、信件佔用傳真機的時間、傳真機的折舊率）。

12

致謝函

單字

appreciate *(v.)* 感激、欣賞	gracious *(a.)* 親切的	overwhelmed *(a.)* 不知所措的	tasteful *(a.)* 有品味的
bountiful *(a.)* 慷慨的	grateful *(a.)* 感激的	perfect *(a.)* 完美的	terrific *(a.)* 了不起的
captivated *(a.)* 著迷的	hospitable *(a.)* 好客的	pleased *(a.)* 高興的	thoughtful *(a.)* 體貼周到的
charming *(a.)* 迷人的	impressed *(a.)* 印象深刻的	priceless *(a.)* 無價的	thrilled *(a.)* 興奮的
cherished *(a.)* 珍惜的	indebted *(a.)* 感激的	remarkable *(a.)* 卓越的	timeless *(a.)* 永恆的
classic *(a.)* 經典的	invaluable *(a.)* 無價的	satisfying *(a.)* 令人滿意的	timely *(a.)* 及時的
delighted *(a.)* 欣喜的	keepsake *(n.)* 紀念品	sensational *(a.)* 絕妙出眾的	touched *(a.)* 感動的
elegant *(a.)* 優雅的	kindness *(n.)* 友善	sophisticated *(a.)* 老練的	treasure *(v.)* 珍惜
enchanted *(a.)* 入迷的	largehearted *(a.)* 度量寬大的	special *(a.)* 特別的	treat *(n.) & (v.)* 對待
enjoyed *(a.)* 享受的	lovely *(a.)* 可愛的	spectacular *(a.)* 壯觀的	unique *(a.)* 獨特的
excited *(a.)* 興奮的	luxurious *(a.)* 豪華的	striking *(a.)* 引人注目的	useful *(a.)* 有用的
fascinated *(a.)* 迷人的	memorable *(a.)* 難忘的	stunned *(a.)* 驚呆的	valuable *(a.)* 貴重的
favorite *(a.) & (n.)* 最愛的	needed *(a.)* 需要的	sumptuous *(a.)* 豪華的	well-made *(a.)* 製作精良的

12

致謝函

flattered
(a.) 受寵若驚的

one-of-a-kind
(a.) 獨一無二的

superb
(a.) 極佳的

wonderful
(a.) 美好的

generosity
(n.) 慷慨

overjoyed
(a.) 喜出望外的

surprised
(a.) 感到驚喜的

詞組

absolutely perfect choice for me
絕對是我完美的選擇

appreciate your confidence/interest/
kind words/referral
感謝你的信心／興趣／好話／轉介

a rare treat
一次難得的享受

cannot tell you how delighted I was
無法告訴你我有多高興

charming of you
迷人的你

enjoyable and informative tour
愉快且知性的旅遊

how kind/dear/thoughtful/sweet of you
to
你這麼做真是好／可愛／體貼／親切

excellent/splendid suggestion
優秀／出色的建議

felt right at home
就像在家裡一樣舒適

from the bottom of my heart
從我的心底

consider me deeply in your debt for
我欠你很多恩惠

please accept my gratitude/our sincere
appreciation
請接受我的感謝／我們的衷心感謝

deeply appreciate
深深感激

derived great pleasure from
從……得到很大樂趣

did us good/our hearts good
對我們的好／使我們開心

perfect gift/present
完美的禮物

convey my personal thanks to everyone
who
向所有人表達我的感謝

pleased as Punch
興高采烈

profoundly touched by
深受……的感動

quite out of the ordinary
頗不尋常

12

致
謝
函

generous gift
慷慨的禮物

great gift for us
對我們來說是非常棒的禮物

heartfelt/hearty thanks
衷心感謝

enjoyed it/ourselves enormously
非常喜歡它／感到非常享受

how much it meant to us
這對我們有多重要

I am indebted/very much obliged to you for
我非常感激你因為

I have seldom seen such
我很少見到這麼

I'll long remember
我會永遠記住

important addition to
重要的新增

I plan to use it for/to
我打算把它用在／用它去做

I really treasure
我真的很珍惜

it was a great pleasure
這是非常快樂的事

it was hospitable/kind of you to
你這麼做很好客／親切

I will never forget
我永遠不會忘記

really appreciate your help
真的感謝你的幫助

seventh heaven
歡天喜地

so characteristically thoughtful
像以往一樣如此體貼

thoroughly enjoyed myself
非常享受

tickled our fancy
勾起興趣

we want you to know how much we value
我們希望你知道我們有多重視

truly grateful
真心感謝

very special occasion
非常特殊的節慶場合

truly a marvel
真是一個奇景

we were especially pleased because
我們特別高興，因為

most sincerely grateful to you for
因為……非常衷心感謝你

what a joy it was to receive
多麼高興能收到

will be used every day/often
將每天／經常使用

with your usual inimitable flair/style
一如你無與倫比的品味／風格

made us feel so welcome
使我們感到賓至如歸

many thanks
非常感謝

meant a great deal to me
對我來說意義重大

more people have remarked on the
越來越多的人讚美

more than kind
不只是親切

we were simply thrilled/delighted/
stunned with
我們因……太興奮／高興／震驚

one of the most memorable days of my
trip
旅程中最難忘的日子之一

much obliged
不勝感激

most thoughtful and generous
最體貼和慷慨

wonderful addition to
美妙的增添

you made me feel so special by
藉由……你讓我覺得如此特別

you may be sure that I appreciate
你可以確定我真的很感激

you must be a mind reader
你一定是個讀心術士

your generous gift
你慷慨的禮物

your gift meant a lot to me at this time
because
此時你的禮物對我的意義重大，因為

your thoughtful/kind expression of
sympathy
你體貼／善意的慰問

one of your usual inspired ideas
一如你往常的靈機一動

句子

All of us were touched by your thoughtfulness.
我們所有人都被你的體貼感動。

As soon as we decide what to do with your wonderful gift/money we will let you
know.
一旦我們決定如何處理你送的美好禮物（錢），我們會讓你知道。

How dear of you—we are delighted!
你真好，我們很高興！

How did you know we needed one?
你怎麼知道我們正需要一個？

I appreciate your advice more than I can say.
非常感謝你的建議。

I can't remember when I've had a better/more pleasant/more relaxing/more enjoyable time.
我不曾有過比這更好／更愉快／更輕鬆／更享受的時間。

I can't thank you enough for chauffeuring me around while my knee was in the immobilizer.
在我的膝蓋穿戴關節固定器期間，謝謝你到處接送我，真的感激不盡。

I'll cherish your gift always.
我會永遠珍惜你的禮物。

I love it!
我好喜歡它！

I'm grateful for your help, and hope that I can reciprocate some day.
我很感謝你的幫助，希望有一天能回報。

In the past several weeks, you have kindly referred Harvey Birch, Frances Wharton, and Judith Hunter to the Cooper Architectural Group—we are grateful!
在過去幾週，你好心將哈維・伯奇、法蘭西絲・沃頓和茱蒂絲・亨特介紹給庫珀建築集團，對此我們非常感謝！

I owe you one!
我欠你一個人情！

I plan to use your gift to buy a wok—we've always wanted one.
我打算用你的禮物買一個炒鍋，我們一直想要一個。

I treasure the paperweight—it will always remind me of you.
我會珍惜這個紙鎮，它會讓我一直想起你。

It was kind of you to let me know about the job opening—I'll keep you posted.
你真好心，讓我知道這個職缺，我會告訴你結果的。

I very much appreciate your concern.
非常感謝你的關心。

Madeleine will be writing you herself, but I wanted to thank you for knowing just what would please a nine-year-old.
瑪德琳會自己寫信給你，但是我想感謝你，你完全知道九歲的孩子喜歡什麼。

More people have remarked on our new Mondrian glassware.
越來越多人讚美我們新的蒙德里安式玻璃器皿。

On behalf of the family of Violet Effingham Chiltern, I thank you for your kind expression of sympathy.
我代表薇歐蕾・艾芬漢・奇登的家屬，感謝您好心的慰問。

Special thanks to the doctors and the nurses at Trewsbury County Hospital.
特別感謝楚伯里郡立醫院的醫生和護士。

Thanks a million.
太感謝了。

Thanks for recommending Bates Craters and Freighters—they've been as good as you said they were.
謝謝你推薦貝茨裝箱承運公司，他們就跟你說的一樣好。

Thanks for the great advice on patio brick—I'm pleased with what we finally bought.
感謝你對露臺磚塊提出好建議，我很滿意我們最後買到的東西。

Thanks for thinking of me.
謝謝你想到我。

Thanks for your order and for the interest in Leeds Sporting Goods that prompted it.
感謝您的訂單以及對利茲體育用品的興趣。

Thank you for including me in this memorable/special event.
感謝您邀請我參加這個令人難忘／特別的活動。

Thank you for opening a charge account with us recently.
感謝您近期在我們這裡開設了信用帳戶。

Thank you for shopping regularly at Farrell Power & Light.
感謝您時常光臨費洛電力與燈光公司。

Thank you for your courtesy and patience in allowing me to pay off the balance of my Irving Products Inc. account in small installments.
感謝您的禮遇和耐心，讓我能分期還清在歐文用品公司積欠的餘額。

Thank you for your generous donation to the Dunstone Foundation in memory of James Calpon Amswell; he would have been pleased and I appreciate your comforting gesture very much.

感謝您慷慨捐助鄧斯頓基金會，以紀念詹姆斯·卡彭·安斯威；他一定會很高興，我非常感謝您這樣表達安慰。

Thank you for your kind hospitality last night; I have never felt less a stranger in a strange city.

謝謝你昨晚的熱情招待；在陌生的城市裡，我從未覺得自己如此不像個異鄉人。

Thank you so much for agreeing to speak to our study club.

非常感謝您同意為我們的讀書會演講。

The letter of reference you so kindly wrote for me must have been terrific—Goodman & Co. called yesterday with a job offer!

您好心為我寫的參考信想必很厲害，因為古德曼公司昨天打電話來錄取我了！

This is just a note to thank you for rushing the steel shelving to us in time for our event.

這是一封簡單的感謝紙條，謝謝您幫我們的鋼架趕工，及時趕上我們的活動。

Visions of Paradise is a stunning book, and we are all enjoying it immensely.

《天堂的遠景》是一本令人驚嘆的書，我們都非常喜歡。

We all thank you for the tickets to the science museum.

我們都很感謝你的科學博物館門票。

We are thrilled with the handsome brass bookends you sent!

你寄來的黃銅書擋很美麗，我們都好喜歡！

We will never forget the autumn glories of the North Shore—thank you so much for inviting us to share your cabin with you last weekend.

我們永遠不會忘記北岸的秋日美景，非常感謝你上週末邀請我們與你一起住在你的小屋。

You can see what a place of honor we've given your gift the next time you stop by.

下一次你路過我們家時，可以來看看我們把你的禮物擺在什麼榮譽位置。

You couldn't have found anything I'd enjoy more.

這是我收到最棒的禮物了。

You shouldn't have, but since you did, may I say that your choice was absolutely inspired!

你不必送的，但既然你送了，我想說，你的選擇真是絕妙！

段落

We are still talking about the wonderful weekend we spent with you—thank you, thank you! You are the busiest people we know, yet you welcomed us into your home as if nothing in the world were more important. We particularly enjoyed the comedy at the Wharton Theater—sharing a laugh with dear friends is surely one of life's greatest pleasures.

我們還在討論我們與你一起度過的美好週末，謝謝你，謝謝！你是個大忙人，但你仍慎重招待我們去你家。我們特別喜歡沃頓劇院的喜劇，與親愛的朋友一同歡笑，絕對是人生最大的樂趣之一。

The extravagantly flowering azalea plant absolutely transformed my hospital room and has given me a great deal of pleasure these past few weeks. I'm looking forward to thanking you in person once I get back on my feet.

盛開的杜鵑花盆栽完全改造了我的病房，並在過去幾週給了我很多快樂。一旦我能起身，我很期待親自感謝你。

Thank you for agreeing to write a letter of recommendation for me, especially since I know how busy you are this time of year. I'm enclosing a stamped envelope addressed to the personnel officer at Strickland Construction. I will, of course, let you know at once if I get the job. In the meantime, thanks again for your kindness.

謝謝您同意幫我寫推薦信，尤其因為我知道您每年此時有多忙。在此附上回郵信封，可以直接寄給史翠克蘭建築公司的人事幹事。當然，要是我獲得了這份工作，我會馬上讓你知道。於此同時，再次感謝您的好意。

I want to thank you for all the time you put into coaching the Crossley-area baseball team this summer. It was a joy to watch you and your enthusiastic players model sporting behavior and team spirit to some of the younger teams. The assistance of our volunteer coaches is crucial to the survival of this program, and the Board of Directors joins me in sending you our admiration and thanks.

我想要感謝今年夏天您投注在訓練克斯利區棒球隊的時間。您與您充滿熱忱的球員，向年輕球隊示範了運動家與團隊精神，看著這樣的您們，我總感到愉悅。志工教練的協助對這個計畫的生存至關重要，董事會在此與我一起向您致上敬意和謝意。

Your dad said you picked out my tie all by yourself. Thank you! Aunt Belinda just took a picture of me wearing the tie and eating a piece of birthday cake. When we get the pictures developed I'll send you one so you can see how nice I look in my new tie.

你爸說這條領帶是你親自挑選的,謝謝你!貝琳達姑媽剛才拍了一張我戴著領帶吃生日蛋糕的照片。照片洗出來之後,我會寄給你一張,你就知道我戴著新領帶的模樣有多麼好看。

On behalf of the directors, staff, and employees of Mallinger Electronics, I want to thank you for your splendid arrangements for the Awards Banquet Night. Decorations, food, program, and hospitality were all first-rate. Please convey our admiration and thanks to your committee chairs. If you can possibly face the thought, we'd like you to chair next year's celebration. The evening was an outstanding success in every way, primarily due to your organizational abilities, creativity, and interpersonal skills.

謹代表馬林傑電子公司的董事、職員和員工,感謝您對頒獎晚宴的出色規畫。裝飾品、食品、節目和招待都是一流的。請代我們向委員會主席致上敬意與感謝。如果您願意接受,我們希望能由您主持明年的慶祝活動。當天晚上的活動在各方面都非常成功,主要歸功於您的組織能力、創造力和人際交流能力。

It is my understanding that you wrote a letter supporting my nomination by the Department of Materials Science and Engineering as a Distinguished Professor. I am happy to inform you that I was indeed honored with this title on June 3, 2018. I am deeply appreciative of your kind support in this regard. Many thanks.

據我所知,您寫了一封信支持材料科學與工程學系建議將我提名為「傑出教授」。我很高興通知您,在二〇一八年六月三日,我獲頒這個頭衛。我真心感激您對我的支持,非常感謝。

12

致謝函

示範信

Dear Major Hugo Cypress,

Thank you so much for agreeing to speak to our study club. We are looking forward to hearing your presentation.

Our district includes ninety-seven veterans, although usually only twenty-five to thirty attend the study club meetings.

The best way to reach the St. George Hotel is to take the Arlen exit off I-35 north. Continue one mile west to 100 Arlen Avenue.

Again, thank you.

Best regards,

雨果・塞普勒斯少校您好：

非常感謝您同意為我們的讀書會演講。我們很期待聽到您的演說。

我們這個地區有九十七名退伍軍人，但通常只有二十五到三十人會出席讀書會。

抵達聖喬治酒店的最佳方式，是從 35 號州際公路往北於艾爾倫的出口下來後，繼續向西開一英里到艾爾倫大道 100 號。

再次感謝您。

〇〇敬上

Dear Elsie and Joe,

You made our day with your funny anniversary card and warm message. In one way or another, you've been a part of many of our "big" days, so it was good to have you with us again, in a manner of speaking, on our twenty-fifth wedding anniversary.

We both send our thanks and love for your faithful friendship (with the promise of a letter to follow).

Fondly,

親愛的艾西與喬：

你們寄來好笑的週年紀念卡片和溫暖的信息，讓我們樂壞了。無論如何，你們參與了我們的許多「大」日子，所以在我們的二十五週年結婚紀念日上，能再次與你們一起度過（就意義上來說是如此），真是太好了。

為了你們忠貞的友誼，我們在此獻上感謝與愛（之後保證會再寄信）。

愛你們的〇〇

Dear Mr. Hollingford,

Thank you for remembering my five-year anniversary with the company. I didn't think anyone would notice except me! I've enjoyed working here and plan to stay as long as you'll have me. Thank you, too, for the gift certificate to Sweeney Inn. I have another anniversary coming up (three years of marriage), and I know where we'll celebrate it.

Sincerely,

霍林福先生您好：

謝謝您記得我的入職五週年紀念日。我以為除了我沒有人會注意到！我很喜歡在這裡工作，也打算繼續待下去，只要您還會雇用我。也謝謝您贈送的史維尼飯店禮券。我的另一個週年紀念日（結婚三年）快到了，現在我知道我們該去哪裡慶祝了。

〇〇敬上

Dear Millicent,

The dinner party was elegant and memorable, and we were delighted to be included.

I don't know anyone who has as much flair and style as you do when it comes to entertaining!

Fondly,

親愛的米利森：

晚餐派對高雅而令人難忘，我們很高興能被邀請。說到招待活動，我找不到比你更有眼光與格調的人！

○○上

✉ 參見：03 回應、04 遲回的信、11 表揚信、14 收件通知、21 接受

Chapter 13

致歉信
Apologies

道歉是生活的強力膠，能修復一切。
——漫畫家琳恩・強斯頓（Lynn Johnston）

比起當面或以電話道歉，寫信道歉通常是更好的方式，因為你可以好好斟酌用字。當你不確定對方是否想跟你說話時，寫信也是較為合適的選項。對方收到致歉信時，不一定會馬上回應，他們會花一些時間消化信中的內容，再決定如何反應。

無論你認為道歉是一種禮節、道德、正義，或是一種交易，它都是生活中必備的工具。人人都會犯錯，當你犯錯時，對方通常不會像你一樣不滿。寫致歉信時，請維持自己的尊嚴。美國心理學家蘇珊・傑弗斯（Susan Jeffers）說過：「如果你最近沒犯什麼錯，那你想必做錯了什麼。」

 PART 1 說明篇

何時需要致歉？

收到東西未能即時回覆 收到禮物、好處、邀請等	**帳務上出現失誤** 或是貸務、財務上	**孩童有不良行為** 或造成損害
員工發生問題 不誠實、服務不周、 工作不符要求	**業務上出現失誤** 訂單出錯、合約出錯、 商品缺陷不良或毀損	**寵物咬人** 毀損物品或造成麻煩

說出傷人言論	對他人財產造成損害	發生性騷擾
發生個人失誤 忘記邀請某人、 未能遵守保密約定	**無法遵守約定** 無法赴約、趕上期限、 準時付款	**做出不得體行為** 酒醉或莽撞行事

該怎麼說？

1. 簡述過失並為此致歉，如 I'm so sorry about the damaged book.「我很抱歉把你的書弄壞了。」若是處理客訴，簡述對方申訴的問題，如 I understand you were twice given incorrect information.「我明白您已經兩次都得到錯誤資訊。」多數情況下，可用 I apologize.「我致上歉意。」或 I am sorry.「我很抱歉。」

2. 感謝對方的來信或來電，或感謝對方讓你知道問題。

3. 適合的話，表示你理解對方立場：I can see how disappointing this must have been.「我能理解這會讓您多麼失望。」；You have every right to be upset.「您確實有理由不滿。」

4. 適合的話，告訴對方你打算採取的改變或補償，如 I will replace the shovel.「我會置換鏟子。」；A refund check is being sent.「會寄給您退款支票。」或是提出修正問題的方法。可提供數種的解決方式，並詢問對方偏好哪種。

5. 向對方保證不會再發生。

6. 如果是商務信件，在結尾表達期待未來繼續往來。

什麼不該說？

• 別為這件事情以外的情況道歉。

• 避免概括性的用詞，例如你多麼的笨手笨腳，或你總是遇到這類的事情。

• 不需以不同方式多次道歉，別太戲劇化。只須簡要地致歉一次即可。避免以下說法：You will probably never want to see me again after what I did.「在我這麼做之後，你大概再也不想看到我了。」；I wish I were dead after the way I behaved last night.「想到我昨晚的表現，我倒不如一頭撞死算了。」；I am very, very, very sorry.「我真的非常、非常、非常抱歉。」；This is the worst thing I've ever done in my whole life.「這是我這輩子做過最糟的事。」

- 別找藉口，別說「我很抱歉，但我還是覺得我是對的」這類的話逃避責任。如果要道歉，必須發自內心。倫理學家傑瑞米・伊格斯（Jeremy Iggers）認為，道歉必須是單方面的，當我們計較他人對我們作了什麼事情時，我們便失去了道歉時的道德立足點。無論別人對我們做了什麼，都不能與我們的錯誤一概而論。
- 別暗示對方也有錯。在商業往來上，如果在信中暗示顧客也有錯，不如什麼都別寫。只要展現出一點點的不真摯，便是在表示遺憾的同時，逃避承擔不完全屬於你的責任。如果對方也需負部分責任，那就只為你犯錯的那一部分道歉，別多說其他無關的事情。
- 別怪罪給電腦。電腦錯誤是人為的。這種不誠實的藉口只會惹惱別人。也別告訴對方這種事不時會發生，儘管你所言不假，但這會讓你看起來疏忽怠慢。
- 勿以白紙黑字寫下所有疏失。若人為疏忽是造成重大過失的原因之一，請先諮詢律師，提供適當的寫信建議。勞夫・斯洛溫科（Ralph Slovenko）表示，醫生在慰悼病患死亡時必須非常小心，因葬禮上的悼詞「在律師有技巧的操作下，可能變成失職的自白」。

寫作訣竅

- 儘快寫道歉信。一旦拖延，這類信件便得花費更多心力撰寫，可能因此需要道歉兩次，一次為你犯的過失道歉，一次為你遲來的道歉道歉。
- 有些狀況是情有可原的，如發生罷工或爆發傳染病。不過在多數情況下，解釋原因只會減弱道歉的力道，例如為做出粗魯的行為找理由，或為了孩子說謊找藉口。

特殊狀況

- **當孩子惹惱他人、傷害別人或損壞物品**，父母須寫致歉函。不過，孩子也應以符合其年齡的方式向對方道歉。大人可在信中這麼寫：Of course, Drusilla will want to apologize to you herself.「杜希拉也想要親自道歉。」
- **員工要為工作失誤或失當行為向老闆道歉時**，可以在信中詳細解釋發生的事情，因為老闆可能必須向更高層的人士報告，需要了解所有相關的資訊。
- **性騷擾**的問題越來越受到重視，不再被當做「只是胡鬧」或「開個玩笑」。任何與性有關的言語騷擾、脅迫、暗示或舉動都是違法的。只要做出會被解釋成性騷擾的行為，就應該真心道歉，騷擾者須完全了解自己錯在哪裡（而不是只把道歉當成權宜之計）。道歉或許阻擋不了公司的懲戒或甚至是法律制裁，但這種可能性也還是存在。無論如何，受到性騷擾的人，必須得到道歉。除了表達懊悔外，騷擾者還須保證不會再犯。因性騷擾而被告上法院的人，通常都是累犯，他們難以理解自己的行為有多法理不容。多數人會原諒當初不了解事情嚴重

性而現已悔改的初犯。

- 在商場中，道歉有其特殊地位。商業書作者瑪莉‧德芙萊（Mary A. De Vries）曾說：「對不起這三個字會帶你度過商業世界中許多艱難時刻。」寫好道歉信，客戶就可能因此心滿意足。有時加上退款、折扣、免費通關券或其他實質的東西來補償顧客。**向顧客寫致歉信時，請以正向的聲明作結**：We look forward to continuing to serve you.「我們期盼繼續為您服務。」或 We value your patronage and your friendship.「謝謝您的惠顧與情誼。」

格式

- 一般社交的致歉信，可使用私人信箋或繪有裝飾的卡片。雖然卡片會印上親切有趣的文句表達「對不起」，還是必須加上手寫文字。
- 寫給顧客或供應商的職場道歉信，需使用商務用信紙。不過，要是涉及個人行為（主管公開藐視某人，或組長無正當理由扣某人的薪水），也可以將道歉信手寫在個人對公司的信紙上。
- 例行性的道歉信（出貨延遲、商品缺貨）可以用制式信處理。
- 以電子郵件寄發的道歉信並不太有說服力，只使用在想立刻向對方道歉，但卻不能使用電話的情況。

13

致歉信

PART 2 應用篇

單字

absentmindedly *(adv.)* 健忘地	ill-advised *(a.)* 輕率的	misleading *(a.)* 誤導的	repay *(v.)* 償還
accidental *(a.)* 意外的	imperfect *(a.)* 不完美的	misprint *(v.)* 印刷錯誤	responsible *(a.)* 有責任的
acknowledge *(v.)* 承認、告知收到	imprudent *(a.)* 不謹慎的	misquote *(v.)* 引用錯誤	restitution *(n.)* 賠償
admit *(v.)* 承認	inaccurate *(a.)* 不準確的	mistaken *(a.)* 弄錯的	restore *(v.)* 修復
awkward *(a.)* 笨拙的、不熟練的	inadequate *(a.)* 不足的	misunderstanding *(n.)* 誤解	sheepish *(a.)* 膽怯的
blunder *(v.) & (n.)* 犯錯；大錯	inadvertent *(a.)* 粗心的	muddle *(v.)* 弄糟	short-sighted *(a.)* 短視的
careless *(a.)* 不小心的	incomplete *(a.)* 不完整的	negligence *(n.)* 疏忽	slip *(n.)* 疏漏
compensate *(v.)* 補償	inconsiderate *(a.)* 不體貼的	omitted *(a.)* 省略的	tactless *(a.)* 不得體的
distressed *(a.)* 沮喪的	inconvenience *(n.)* 不便	overlooked *(a.)* 忽視的	thoughtless *(a.)* 欠缺考慮的
disturbed *(a.)* 心緒不寧的	incorrect *(a.)* 不正確的	pardon *(v.) & (n.)* 原諒	unaware *(a.)* 沒有察覺的
embarrassed *(a.)* 窘迫的	insufficient *(a.)* 不充分的	rectify *(n.)* 改正	unfortunate *(a.)* 不幸的
erroneous *(a.)* 錯誤的	irresponsible *(a.)* 不負責任的	red-faced *(a.)* 羞愧的	unhappy *(a.)* 不快的
error *(n.)* 錯誤	lax *(a.)* 散漫的	redo *(v.)* 重做	unintentional *(a.)* 不是有意的

13

致歉信

excuse *(n.) & (v.)* 寬恕	miscalculation *(n.)* 計算錯誤	regrettable *(a.)* 令人遺憾的	unsatisfactory *(a.)* 不滿意的
explain *(v.)* 解釋	misconception *(n.)* 錯誤認知	reimburse *(v.)* 退還款項	unsound *(a.)* 不穩固的
failure *(n.)* 失敗	misconstrued *(a.)* 錯誤推斷的	remiss *(a.)* 怠慢的	unwarranted *(a.)* 無保證的
fault *(n.)* 過失	misinterpreted *(a.)* 錯誤解讀的	repair *(n.) & (v.)* 修理	unwise *(a.)* 不明智的

詞組

absolutely no excuse for 絕對不是……的藉口	**I am so sorry for** 我為……深感抱歉
accept the blame for 為……接受指責	**I don't know how it happened that** 我不知道這為何會發生
admit that I was wrong 承認我是錯的	**avoid this in the future** 未來會避免此事
angry with myself 對自己生氣	**I'm sorry you were dissatisfied with** 很遺憾你對……不滿意
appreciate your calling our attention to 感謝你讓我們注意到……	**it was embarrassing to discover that** 發現……很令人羞愧
asleep at the wheel/on the job/at the switch 未能保持警覺／未盡職責	**sorry for the inconvenience/confusion/mix-up/misunderstanding** 抱歉造成不便／困擾／混亂／誤會
I have thoroughly investigated/looked into the matter and 我已經徹底調查／檢視這個事件，發現……	**I was distressed to hear/read/discover/learn that** 聽到／讀到／發現／知道……令我沮喪
breach of good manners 違背禮節	**make amends/restitution** 修正／賠償

correct the situation
修正這個情況

make right with you
為你修復

express my regret
表達我的遺憾

much to my regret
我很遺憾

feel sorry/terrible/bad about
為……感到抱歉／糟糕／不快

my apologies for any inconvenience
造成任何不便我很抱歉

how can I apologize for
我該如何為……致上歉意

owe you an apology for
欠你一個道歉

I am not excusing our/my errors, but
我並非在為我（們）的失誤找藉口，但……

it was most understanding of you to
你做……實在非常體貼

sorely regret
極度懊悔

I am most upset about
我對……最為苦惱

please accept my/our apology/apologies for
請接受我（們）對……的道歉

presumed where I shouldn't have presumed
我在不該自作主張時貿然做主

the least I can do is
至少我可以做的是

to compensate for
彌補

prevent a recurrence
預防再次發生

under the mistaken impression that
受到錯誤印象的影響

put to rights
恢復正常

until you are completely satisfied
直到你完全滿意

reproach myself
責備我自己

weighs on my mind
我心頭的重擔

sincerely regret/apologize
真心感到後悔／抱歉

we regret to inform our customers that
我們很遺憾必須通知我們的顧客

you were entirely right about
你對於……的看法完全正確

句子

Although I apologized to you last night for our guests blocking your driveway, I want you to know how sorry we are and to assure you that it won't happen again.
儘管我昨晚已為我們客人擋住您的車道向您道歉，但我想讓您知道我們有多麼抱歉，並向您保證這種事不會再次發生。

As you rightly pointed out, a mistake has been made on your July bill.
您說得沒錯，您的七月帳單出現了錯誤。

I am extremely embarrassed about my behavior last night.
對於我昨晚的行徑，我感到極度羞愧。

I am sincerely/very sorry.
我真心／非常感到抱歉。

I apologize for Jimmy's behavior.
我為吉米的行為道歉。

I can only hope you will forgive this serious lapse of good taste on my part.
我只希望您能原諒我表現得如此不得體。

I don't blame you for being upset.
我不怪您感到不愉快。

I don't like being on the outs with you, particularly since it was my fault.
我不喜歡與你爭辯，尤其當犯錯的人是我的時候。

I hope this situation can be mended to everyone's satisfaction.
我希望這個情況可以改善，讓大家都滿意。

I'm sorry for telling everyone in the office your good news before you could tell them—I don't know what I was thinking.
我很抱歉在你開口之前，就先把你的好消息告訴辦公室的每個人，我真不知我當時在想什麼。

I'm sorry you were treated so disparagingly by the salesclerk.
我很抱歉您受到店員如此屈辱地對待。

I only realized later how insulting my remarks might have appeared.
我後來才察覺我說的話聽起來多麼無禮。

I understand how disappointed you must have been to receive only half your order.
我能理解當您只收到一半的貨時，您會有多麼失望。

I've taken steps to ensure that it doesn't happen again.
我已經採取行動，確保這不會再次發生。

I was totally out of line this morning when I insisted on knowing what your salary is—I can only hope you will forgive my poor taste and insensitivity.
今天早上我堅持要知道你薪水的行為實在欠妥。我只希望你能原諒我如此沒格調又不體貼的行為。

My face gets red every time I remember that night.
每當我想起那一晚，我就感到羞愧。

Please accept my apology for the oversight.
請接受我的道歉，是我疏忽了。

Please excuse my inattention/shortsightedness/thoughtlessness.
請原諒我的粗心／短視／欠缺考慮。

Please forgive me.
請原諒我。

Thank you for advising us of this error/for bringing the matter to my attention.
謝謝您告訴我們這個錯誤／讓我注意到此事。

Thank you for your letter of July 15 telling us about the unfortunate remark made by one of the security guards.
謝謝您於七月十五日來信，告訴我們有名警衛對您出言不遜。

Thank you for your patience and understanding.
謝謝您的耐心與諒解。

This will not, of course, happen again.
當然，這不會再次發生。

We apologize for the delay—it is unfortunately unavoidable.
我們對於延誤感到抱歉；遺憾的是，這是無可避免的。

We are sorry/apologize for any embarrassment this has caused you.
讓您陷入尷尬的處境，我們很抱歉／致上歉意。

We look forward to continuing to serve you.
我們期待繼續為您服務。

We owe you an apology.
我們欠您一個道歉。

We were caught napping on this one.
我們對此措手不及。

You were right, I was wrong, and I'm sorry.
你說得沒錯，我做錯了，而我很抱歉。

段落

We are unable to deliver the spring fabric samples by the date promised. The product supervisor promises me that you will have them by January 5. If this is unsatisfactory, please telephone me. It isn't often we have to renege on a delivery date, and we're not happy about it. Please accept our apologies for the delay.

我們無法在先前約定的日期前運送春季布料樣品,但產品主管答應我會讓您在一月五日前收到樣品。如果您對此有不滿意之處,請致電給我。我們鮮少違背出貨日期的約定,所以我們對此也很是不快。這次的延誤,還請您接受我們的歉意。

Please accept our apologies for what's recently happened at your house. We're all working hard to find other homes for the bunnies. When Hillel assured you that both bunnies were female, he relied on the green-striped ribbons they wore around their necks. None of us knew that a four-year-old neighbor had switched a green-striped ribbon for a yellow polka-dotted ribbon that the male rabbits were wearing. I know this doesn't make up to you for what you've been through, but I thought you should know that our intentions were good. Again, we're sorry and we'll let you know as soon as we've found ten good homes.

對於近日貴府發生的事件,請接受我們的歉意。我們正努力為這些兔子找尋其他收容處。儘管西列爾向您保證兩隻兔子皆為雌性,但這是他憑脖子上的條紋綠緞帶所做的判斷。我們並不知道,有名四歲的鄰居孩童將雄兔戴的黃點緞帶換成了條紋綠緞帶。我知道這並無法撫慰您,但我希望讓您知道我們抱著善意。我們再次致上歉意,並會在找到十個收容處後盡快讓您知道。

It occurred to me in a dream, or maybe it was in the shower, that you had asked for the return of your baby books some time ago. I suppose the friend's child has gone off to college by now. I'm sorry for the tardiness—they're in today's mail.

我在夢中想起——或在洗澡時想到——之前你曾經要我把育嬰書籍還給你。我猜那位朋友的小孩現在都已經上大學了。很抱歉我拖了那麼久,在今天的郵件中我一併附上了這些書。

We erroneously mailed you the same order you placed last month. This month's order has been sent this morning, and we've marked the box plainly with AUGUST written in large red letters. If you will please refuse acceptance of the first box, the carrier will bring it back to us. We apologize for the error.

左側邊欄:

13

致歉信

我們錯將上個月的訂單寄給您。這個月的訂單已於今早補寄給您，並在箱子上寫了一個大大的「八月」字樣。煩請您拒收第一個貨箱，運送人員會將之帶回給我們。我們很抱歉發生這個失誤。

We were sorry to hear that the last neon tetras you bought from us were infected with ich and subsequently infected your entire aquarium. As tropical fish enthusiasts ourselves, we appreciate how devastating this has been. I immediately spoke to our supplier about the problem, and she has assured me this was an isolated slip-up. In the meantime, please restock your aquarium at our expense. Thank you for your understanding. I hope you will continue to be one of our most valued customers.

聽聞您上次向我們購買的霓虹燈魚感染了白點病，而使您的整缸水族箱都受到感染，對此我們深感抱歉。同樣身為熱帶魚的愛好者，我們非常能體會這有多麼令您震驚。我已立刻向我們的供應商反映這個問題，而她已向我保證，這種錯誤只會有這麼一次。同時，煩請您重新購買水族箱裡的魚，支出將由敝店承擔。很感謝您的諒解，您是我們最重視的一位顧客，並希望您能持續光臨敝店。

示範信

Dear Dorothea,

　　I feel dreadful about ruining your lovely luncheon yesterday by arguing with Celia about Will Ladislaw. You certainly did everything you could to save the situation, and I apologize most humbly for ignoring good taste, old friendship, and common sense in pursuing a "discussion" that was completely inappropriate.

　　I spoke with Celia first thing this morning and attempted to mend my fences there, but I feel a great deal worse about what I did to you. The luncheon was delicious, and the first two hours were delightful. I hope you will someday be able to forgive me for blighting the last half-hour.

Your friend,

親愛的桃樂絲：

　　我實在感到不好受，由於我與希莉亞針對威爾·雷蒂斯洛的爭論，而毀了你昨日溫馨的午餐會。你已經盡力控制場面了，我必須非常虛心向你道歉，因為我舉止失當，忘了我們的多年情誼，也忘了常識，我不該「討論」完全不適合討論的事。

　　我今早的第一件事便是找希莉亞談談，並試圖亡羊補牢。但我對你所做的事情，更是令我心神不寧。午餐會的餐點很好吃，前兩個小時也令人十分愉悅。我希望有一天你會原諒我毀了最後半小時。

你的朋友〇〇上

Dear Mr. Ravenal:

As editor of the *Cotton Blossom newsletter*, I want to apologize for omitting your name in the last issue. Captain Hawks asked me how I could have possibly forgotten to include our hottest new actor! In proofreading the copy, my eyes failed to notice that your name wasn't where my brain expected it to be. I'm sorry. A correction will appear in the next issue.

Regretfully,

拉梵納先生您好：

我是《棉花報》的新聞主編，很抱歉在上一期報紙中略去了您的姓名。浩克斯隊長說我怎麼可以忘了我們最火熱的新演員！在校稿時，我的大腦已經預期會看見您的名字，所以我的眼睛沒有注意到您不在上面，我很抱歉。在下一期的報紙中，我們會刊登修正版。

○○謹上

Dear Hsiao-Wei,

I apologize for not showing up at the meeting this afternoon. Although there is no excuse for such a thing, I will say that I was involved in an automobile accident on the way to work and what with filling out forms, notifying my insurance company, and arranging for a rental car, I completely forgot about the meeting.

Can we reschedule for this Thursday, same time? Thanks—and again, I'm sorry.

Regards,

親愛的小葳：

我很抱歉今天下午未出席會議。儘管這種事是沒有藉口的，但我在來公司的路上出了車禍，必須填寫表格、通知保險公司、安排租車。我完全忘了要開會。

我們可否把會議改到這週四相同的時間呢？謝謝。還有，再次致上歉意。

○○敬上

Dear Merton Denscher,

Thank you for your letter of March 19. I am sorry that the background research I submitted was unusable. A careful re reading of your instructions showed me at once where I'd gone wrong. I do apologize.

With your permission, I would like to resubmit the work—this time correctly. I believe I can get it to you by the end of next week since I am already familiar with the relevant sources for your topic.

Please let me know at once if you prefer me not to go ahead.

Sincerely,

莫頓・丹雪您好：

　　謝謝您於三月十九的來信，我很抱歉我繳交的背景研究是不能用的。我仔細重讀了一次您的指示，馬上理解我錯在哪裡。我真的很抱歉。

　　若您許可，我想要重新繳交一份──這一次會是正確的。我相信我能在下週結束前交給您，因為我已經很熟悉與這個主題有關的資料。

　　如果您不希望我這麼做，請立即讓我知道。

○○敬上

✉ 參見：03 回應、04 遲回的信、05 敏感信件、14 收件通知、25 抱怨與客訴、35 客訴處理信

Chapter 14

收件通知
Acknowledgments

人生雖短，總有展現禮節的時間。

——愛默生（Ralph Waldo Emerson）

收件通知與確認信（confirmation）很類似，收件通知會寫 I received your letter (telephone call, gift, materials).「我收到了你的信（或電話、禮物、資料）。」確認信則會寫 I received your letter (message, contract) and we agree about the matter.「我收到了你的信（或訊息、合約）且我們對此事達成共識。」

確認信可以作為非正式的合約。

收件通知可以當作致謝函，或通知對方你已收到訊息，並於稍後回覆或將之交給負責人員。收件通知也可以是商務信函，確認收件（如收到訂單、款項）的同時，傳達額外的商務訊息。

當你收到慰問信時，也須回以收件通知。此外，收到如週年紀念日、生日問候、恭賀、道歉或離婚宣告時，也要以收件通知回覆對方。

 PART 1　說明篇

收件通知和確認信的使用時機

收到恭賀	收到禮物	收到慰問
週年紀念、生日問候	結婚禮物 參見：50 婚禮相關信	或弔唁

收到款項	收到抱怨	代收主管郵件
收到邀約 演講日期、邀約日期	收到訂單或商品 參見：37 訂單處理信	達成協議
收到資訊 信件、文件、資料	收到報告 提案、檔案、文稿	收到問題或請求

該怎麼說？

1. 明確說明收到的內容或要確認的內容。
2. 提及與對方最近一次接觸的日期與場合。
3. 說明正在執行的細節。
4. 告訴對方進一步回覆的時間。
5. 如果對方問起，請解釋你在收到信件、請求或禮品後，無法立即給對方答覆的原因。
6. 表達感激之情，可以是感謝之前的聯絡、對方的善意，或事業上的合作。
7. 最後以有禮的措詞結尾，或表達你期待對方的聯繫。

什麼不該說？

- 別解釋太多。收件通知與確認信通常都很簡短。
- 避免負面的口氣，如 I thought I'd make sure we're both talking about the same thing.「我還以為我們講的是同一件事。」就事論事，複述確認收到的細節即可。

寫作要點

立即回覆。收件通知是在收件後馬上就該寄出的信，弔唁信的收件通知則是例外，由於收件者正處於艱難時期，所以可以至多六週後再回覆。或者，也可以由逝者家屬的近親代寫收件通知：Mother asked me to tell you how much she appreciated the loving letter of sympathy and the memorial you sent for Dad. She will be in touch with you as soon as she is able to.「母親要我轉

告您，她十分感謝您好心寄來的弔唁信，以及您悼念父親的話語。當她狀況較佳時，會盡快與您聯絡。」

特殊狀況

- **來信者詢問的問題較適合其他人處理時**，可以將該人的名字、地址與電話號碼回覆給對方作為收件通知。也可以將信同時轉寄給適合處理問題的人。
- **收到例行商務往來信**（訂單、寄送商品、付款）時，不需寄出收件通知。但發生特殊狀況時，就需寄出收件通知。如之前訂貨並未如期寄達，就須寄出通知，讓對方知道這次的貨送到了。如你之前寄發催款信，也要讓對方知道帳款收到了（並暗示不會再寄催款信）。
- **收到大額帳款、重要訂單或出貨，或第一次與該客戶合作**，亦須寄送收件通知。
- **無法立即回覆寄來的信件**，請寄發收件通知，這樣寄件人便知道你正在處理。
- **當主管或同事不在時代為收件**，應寄送收件通知，提及主管或同事目前不在辦公室，但不須道歉或解釋原因，也不需提到寄件中的內容。
- **代收到訃文或重病的通知**時，需先代主管或同事表達慰問，並告知會盡快寄出弔唁信。
- **接受捐贈的機構**，須寄發收件通知給捐贈人，並通知獲得捐贈的家庭，這樣他們才能私下感謝捐贈人。
- **預約或確認訂房**通常透過電話，不過有些時候，書面確認是必要的，例如有特殊條件或計畫改變。信中應包含你的需求，如日期、天數、房型、價格、額外要求（例如房中有嬰兒床）、無障礙空間、游泳池、HBO 電視臺、娛樂設施等。若是預約國外的飯店或渡假村，請要求對方寄發確認信，並附上你的電子信箱地址或傳真號碼，在有些情況下，你也可以附上國際回信郵票券（International Reply Coupon，IRC，可在郵局購得）方便對方寄回。
- **收到離婚通知**，請不要恭賀或慰問（除非你知道哪個才是對方想要的）。在多數情況下，你只須回應你已知悉這個消息。
- **收到致歉信時**發出的收件通知，是為了讓對方知道你收到了他的歉意（並接受道歉，如果你想這麼做的話）。
- **收到許多求職者履歷時**，可以寄發收件通知告知對方已收到履歷，或感謝他們前來面試，告訴求職者你會盡快讓他們知道結果（如果你已經大致知道結果何時會出來，也請告知），並感謝他們應徵你的公司。

格式

- 例行的商務收件通知與確認信，可用電子郵件寄發。為記錄商業往來，請備份所有交易相關文件。
- 較複雜的商務收件通知或確認信，請使用有信頭的信紙或備忘錄用紙。
- 婚禮禮物或慰問信的數量很多，可以事先印好收件通知小卡，屆時就可以快速寄出收件通知。
- 如果是寄給公眾人物的弔唁，他的家人會收到許多陌生人的弔唁，此時也可使用事先印製的通知小卡，註明不須回覆。
- 私人的收件通知與確認信，可以手寫於非正式信紙；電子郵件可用於較輕鬆的交流。

PART 2 應用篇

單字

accept *(v.)* 接受	approve *(v.)* 允許	ensure *(v.)* 確保	reassure *(v.)* 再次保證
acknowledge *(v.)* 通知收到	assure *(v.)* 保證	indicate *(v.)* 指出	receipt *(n.)* 收取
affirm *(v.)* 證實	confirm *(v.)* 確認	notice *(n.)* 通知	reply *(v.) & (n.)* 回覆
agree-upon *(v.)* 同意	corroborate *(v.)* 確證	notify *(v.)* 通知	respond *(v.)* 回應
appreciate *(v.)* 感謝	endorse *(v.)* 贊同	reaffirm *(v.)* 再次證實	settle *(v.)* 安排

詞組

as I mentioned on the phone
如我在電話中所言

as we agreed yesterday
如我們昨日的協議

I enjoyed our conversation of
我很享受我們關於……的討論

in response to your letter
在此回覆您的來信

I sincerely appreciated
我真心感謝

look forward to continuing our discussion
期待繼續我們的討論

thank you for the package that
謝謝您的包裹

this will acknowledge the receipt of
在此通知你，已收到……

to confirm our recent conversation
作為我們最近談話內容的確認

want to confirm in writing
想要以書面確認

we have received
我們已經收到……

will respond as soon as
會盡快在……回應

句子

I enjoyed speaking with you this afternoon and look forward to our meeting next Thursday at 2:30 at your office.
我很享受與您在今天下午的談話，期待下週四兩點半在您辦公室舉行的會議。

Just a note to let you know that the printer ribbons arrived.
僅以此信告知，印表機碳帶已送達。

Thank you for remembering my ten-year anniversary with Lamb and Company.
謝謝您記得我在蘭牧公司工作的十週年紀念日。

Thank you for the wallpaper samples, which arrived this morning.
謝謝您的壁紙樣品，今早已寄達。

Thank you for writing me with your views on socialized medicine.
謝謝您寄來您對於公費醫療制度的看法。

Thank you for your order, which we received yesterday; it will be shipped to you this week.
謝謝您的訂單，我們昨日收到了，本週就會出貨給您。

The family of Annis Gething gratefully acknowledges your kind and comforting expressions of sympathy.
安妮絲・葛庭的家人感謝您善意體貼的慰問。

The members of the Board of Directors and I appreciated your presentation yesterday and want you to know that we are taking your concerns under serious advisement.
董事會與我感謝您昨日的簡報，並想讓您知道我們正在認真評估您的建議。

This is to acknowledge receipt of the rerouted shipment of Doncastle tennis rackets, catalog number AE-78573.
在此通知您，我們已收到改道運送的唐堡網球拍，貨號 AE-78573。

This is to confirm our recent conversation about the identification and removal of several underground storage tanks on my property.
在此與您確認我們最近一次的談話內容：我們談到在我的所有地上確認並移除數個地下貯存槽。

This will acknowledge receipt of your report on current voter attitudes.
在此通知，您的目前選民態度調查報告已寄達。

This will confirm our revised delivery date of November 6.

在此與您確認，我們修正後的出貨日為十一月六日。

We are proceeding with the work as requested by Jerome Searing in his May 3, 2017, telephone call.

我們正按照傑若‧錫林於二〇一七年五月三日的來電內容處理此事。

We hereby acknowledge that an inspection of the storm drain and street construction installed by the Bagshaw Company in the Rockingham subdivision has been completed.

我們在此確認，由貝格蕭公司負責的洛京安分部雨水下水道與街道工程，現已完成。

14

收件通知

段落

Your letter of July 16 has been referred for review and appropriate action. We value you as a customer and ask your patience while a response is being prepared.

您於七月十六日的來信已進入審查與後續處理階段。我們很重視顧客的看法，煩請耐心等候回應。

Thank you for the update on the preparation of the Price-Stables contract. I appreciate knowing what progress you're making.

謝謝您為我更新「普萊斯－史戴伯」一案的合約準備情況，感謝您讓我得知您的進度。

I've received your kind invitation to join the Friends of the Library committee. I need to review other commitments to be sure that I can devote as much time to the Friends as I'd like. I'll let you know next week. In the meantime, thanks for thinking of me.

我已收到您邀請我加入圖書館之友委員會的邀請函。我必須先評估一下我目前的工作，以確保我能依我所願為圖書館之友投入足夠時間。下週我會讓您知道我的決定；同時，也感謝您邀請我。

I'm glad we were able to reach an agreement on the telephone this morning. I'll have the contracts retyped—inserting the new delivery date of March 16, 2018, and the new metric ton rate of $55—and sent to you by the end of the week.

很高興我們今早在電話中達成協議。我會重新擬定合約，加入二〇一八年三月十六日為新的出貨日，並將每公噸的運費改設為 55 元美金。本週結束前，我會將新合約寄給您。

I wanted you to know that I received your letter this morning, but as I'm leaving for Dallas later today I won't have time to look into the billing problem with the contractor for another week or so. If you need action sooner than that, give Agnes Laiter a call.

我想讓您知道，今早已收到您的來信。不過由於今日稍晚我便要前往達拉斯，所以在未來一週左右，我不會有時間處理與承包商的帳款問題。若您必須在一週內處理問題，請聯繫亞格妮絲‧萊特。

Thank you for telling me about the divorce. It's been too long since I've seen you. Can we get together sometime? How about breakfast Saturday morning? That used to work for us.

謝謝你通知我離婚的消息。從上次見到你之後，已經好久不見。要碰個面嗎？週六早上一起吃個早餐如何？以前我們這個時間都有空。

信件範例

Dear Mr. Borkin:

To confirm our telephone conversation, Barry Studio Supplies will be happy to provide you with all your photographic needs. We make deliveries in the metropolitan area within twenty-four hours of receiving an order.

Enclosed is a copy of our current catalog, a pad of order forms, and my card. As your personal representative, I can answer any of your questions and help you with special orders.

Sincerely yours,

博金先生您好：

在此與您確認我們的電話會談：巴瑞工作室很高興能為您提供所有您需要的攝影用具。在市區，貨品會於收到訂單後的二十四小時內寄達。

附件為我們目前的商品目錄、訂購單及我的名片。我是您的聯絡人，可以回答您任何問題，並協助您處理特殊訂單。

○○謹上

Dear William Beevor,

We have received the blueprints for the Brass Bottle Hotel. As soon as Mr. Ventimore and the staff have had time to look at them, I'll call you to set up a meeting. Until then, Mr. Ventimore sends his regards.

Yours truly,

威廉‧畢佛先生您好：

我們已收到您為銅罐飯店繪製的設計藍圖。在樊丁默先生與職員評估後，我會盡快與您聯繫以安排開會事宜。在此之前，樊丁默先生祝福您一切順心。

○○敬啟

Dear Mrs. Beddows,

This is to acknowledge your kind expression of sympathy and the lovely floral arrangement you sent on the occasion of Mr. Holtby's death. Mrs. Holtby will be writing you a personal note as soon as she can. In the meantime, she appreciates your friendship and concern.

Sincerely,

貝多思太太您好：

　　謝謝您在霍特比先生的葬禮上送來的悼詞與花飾。霍特比太太會盡快親自給您回覆。於此同時，她很感激您的情誼與關心。

○○謹啟

Dear Mrs. Cammysole,

　　Thank you for sending the lease for the apartment on Thackeray Street.

　　We are having our lawyer look at it tomorrow afternoon, and we will be in touch with you as soon as possible after that.

With best wishes,

凱米索太太您好：

　　謝謝您寄來薩克萊街公寓的租約。

　　明日下午我們會請律師詳閱這份租約，之後會盡快與您聯繫。

○○敬上

Dear Member,

　　Thank you for your order.

　　Unfortunately, we're temporarily out of stock on the item below. We've reordered it and expect to have a new supply in a few weeks. We'll ship it as soon as it arrives.

Sincerely,

親愛的會員您好：

　　謝謝您的訂單。

　　遺憾通知您，以下商品暫時缺貨。我們已經重新訂購，並希望能在幾週內收到。一旦商品寄達，我們就會立刻出貨。

○○敬啟

參見：03 回應、06 預約會面、12 致謝函、17 後續追蹤信、21 接受、42 銷售信、49 旅遊相關信、50 婚禮相關信

14
收件通知

Chapter 15

公告通知
Announcements

這是個好消息，值得大家知道！
不過，還是沒好到如美夢成真。

——英國新教徒牧師馬修・亨利（Matthew Henry）

無論是正式或非正式的公告通知，都要用最少的字講出最重要的事實，就像這句話一樣。

 PART 1　說明篇

公告通知的使用時機

新居落成 換地址	**政策變更** 程序變動、津貼福利更動	**舉行會議** 舉辦工作坊或研討會
訂結婚 參見：50 婚禮相關信	**新工作夥伴加入**	**升職**
結婚紀念 參見：43 紀念日	**新辦公室落成** 增設新事業、新部門或子公司	**解雇** 參見：36 職場相關信
嬰兒出生 或領養嬰兒	**新政策頒布** 新經營方針、新管理方針	**辭職或退休** 參見：36 職場相關信

畢業	產品撤回	價格或租金調動
收購公司 公司合併或重組	催繳帳款 參見：38 催款信	學校公開日 公司參觀日
死亡	離婚或分居	開業通知

該怎麼說？

- 除了宣布死訊或離婚，請用愉悅的口氣宣布。
- 列出與這個消息或事件有關的重要細節：誰、什麼、何時、何地、為什麼。
- **布達會議**請包含以下訊息：主辦單位名稱、會議日期、時間、地點及目的。要求收信者不克參加時通知聯絡人。你可以用事先印好的明信片、內部備忘錄用紙或電子郵件。
- **宣布董事會會議**，請根據公司章程或法律規定的格式寄發通知。
- **放棄通知書或授權委託書**通常都會與回郵信封（self-addressed stamped envelope, SASE）一併附在通知信中。
- **宣布新事業或新店面開張時**，用邀請函邀請顧客至招待會或特賣會。
- **宣布公司政策變更時**，納入以下內容：表達對此變更的喜悅，並描述變更內容。若須說明，可提及變更前的政策。解釋此變更對員工或顧客的意義。若適宜的話，可附上指示說明或教學。闡述變更的原因。此變更的執行日期、聯絡人姓名與電話號碼。最後，熱情表達你對於此變更的期待，並感激收件者協助執行此變更。
- **通知新生兒誕生**或領養時，可用打字或親筆寫、或市售或親自設計的信箋。請包含以下內容：嬰兒的全名，要是從名字看不出嬰兒的性別，或是尚未命名，也可以附註是個男孩或女孩；出生日期（也可以列出時間）或年齡（如果小孩是領養的）；父母的全名；手足的名字（可省略）；使用一些表達喜悅的句子，如 pleased to announce「很高興宣布」。
這類通知可能來自**未婚父母**（Julia Norman and Basil Fane announce the birth of their son, Alec Norman-Fane.「茱莉亞．諾曼與貝錫．芬恩宣布他們的兒子艾列克．諾曼芬恩出生了。」）、**單親家庭**（Jean Emerson announces the birth of her son, Howard Thede Emerson.

「珍・艾默森宣布她的兒子霍華・賽德・艾默森出生了。」），或**已婚夫婦**。夫婦二人應使用各自的姓名。

在報紙上刊登孩子出生請包含出生日期、孩子性別及名字（若已取名）、父母姓名及家鄉，與祖父母的姓名。有些報紙也允許刊登體重身高，以及一些感性的句子，如「welcome with love」（用愛歡迎），或列出嬰兒的親戚，如「many aunts, uncles, and cousins」（許多姑姨、叔伯、表堂兄弟姊妹）。請向要刊登的報紙確認這些規定。

- **通知地址變更時**，可以使用政府通報服務（如中華郵政或美國郵政署）、市售的地址變更信或印好的卡片：As of July 1, Sybil Knox (formerly Sybil Coates or Mrs. Adrian Coates) will be living at 15 Morland Drive, Houston, TX 77005, 713-555-1234.「自七月一日起，西碧兒・納克斯（前為西碧兒・寇特斯或亞卓安・寇特斯太太）將搬到郵遞區號 77005，德州休士頓默蘭街十五號，電話是 713-555-1234。」

- **宣布畢業時**，由於各校的畢業典禮時間都很接近，大家通常都只會宣布這個消息，很少會邀請收件人參加典禮。收到此種通知時，收件人沒有義務送禮（但通常會寄一張祝賀卡片），但因為很多人都認為自己必須送禮，所以這種通知信最好只寄給親近的人。

- 向親戚朋友**通知分居或離婚**（可選擇不要宣布），簡單敘述即可：We regret to inform you that our divorce was finalized on December 1.「很遺憾通知，我們的離婚手續已在十二月一日生效。」可透過變更地址的方式委婉通知此消息，告知對方某個日期之後兩人與孩子會分別住在哪裡。不必在信中說明發生了什麼事，如果收信者從字裡行間感受到想保留隱私的暗示，那下次碰面時，便會比較容易應付。通知銀行、公司、賒銷帳戶及債權人這項變動。如果寄發**離婚通知**的女性恢復了原本的姓，請如此稱呼她。

- **死訊**可由以下幾種方式宣布：(1) 在報紙的訃聞區插入訃告（通常需要付費）；(2) 刊登新聞文章，描述死者的成就與貢獻；(3) 將印製的訃告寄給遠方的朋友與熟人；(4) 將手寫信寄給遠方的親朋好友。你可以從死者的通訊簿中找出應該通知的人。在報紙上的訃告應包含：死者姓名，如果死者是女性且沒有使用原來的姓名，請也列出她的原來姓名。地址、死亡日期、逝世時的年齡。死者家屬的名字、與死者的關係及家鄉。隸屬的單位；私人或事業相關資訊；葬禮與埋葬的日期及地點；葬禮是否不公開，或公開給親戚朋友；在葬禮上獻花或致上悼詞的建議；葬禮場地的名稱、地址及電話號碼。由於訃聞馬上就要刊登在報紙上，你可以親自遞送至報社，或在電話上口述。

什麼不該說？

- 別提及不相關的資訊或消息。儘管確實有些例外（例如公司政策變更），但一般來說，布達通知信不該有太多解釋、指示或描述。如果太冗長，通知信的效果會減弱。

寫作訣竅

- 事件發生後，盡快寄出通知信。美國作家黛安‧布赫（Dianna Booher）曾說：「宣布事情的黃金準則是，在收件人從其他管道得知消息前，你的通知就必須寄達。如果你公告的內容已是舊聞，表示它太晚寄達。」
- 請別人幫你檢查拼字與整體內容。宣告內容如果有誤，別人知道的事情便與你希望傳達的事情有很大落差。

特殊狀況

- **例常的公告事項**（帳單新增類別、新地址、開會通知等），可直接寫在商業問候信或銷售訊息中。
- 若**宣布的是大眾會有興趣的消息**（產品撤回；年度或季度財務報告；開業紀念日；資金籌集活動；新計畫政策的實施；新高層主管就任；公司達成新成就、合併或收購），可將**新聞稿**寄給報紙編輯、廣播電臺或電視臺的新聞節目製作人。除了要宣布的消息外，新聞稿中也要包含組織名稱與地址，以及聯絡人的姓名與電話號碼。新聞稿必須寄給特定的人，如果你不知道要寄給誰，請打電話詢問。

  新聞稿需以雙行或三行間距撰寫，設定足夠的頁面邊界空白，並在第一段或前兩段就回答「是誰、是什麼、何時、何地、為什麼、如何」。重複檢查內容是否正確，若有少見的專有名詞，請加以解釋。在新聞稿中，每一頁的最下方通常會註明「接下頁（more）」，最後一頁則會顯示「- 30 -」或「＃＃＃」來表示結尾。

格式

- 商業上的公告通知信常打在有信頭的信紙上。若須寄給許多人，則可以使用制式信。
- 公司內部布達事項（如新的福利津貼、彈性工作程序變更）可使用備忘錄。有時傳送電子郵件也是不錯的選擇。
- 正式的通知信以黑色墨水列印或鋼印在白色或奶油色的卡紙上（配上同色信封）。文具店與影印店通常會提供通知信的樣本，從傳統到現代流行樣式都有，可挑選字型、紙張、墨水與格式。
- 給親朋好友的通知信，通常會手寫在折頁卡片或私人信紙上。
- 明信片適合用於通知地址變更、會議與特賣會。

✉ PART 2 應用篇

單字

announce *(v.)* 宣布	happy *(a.)* 開心的	mention *(v.)* 提到	reveal *(v.)* 揭露
celebrate *(v.)* 慶祝	honor *(n.) & (v.)* 榮幸	notice *(n.) & (v.)* 通知	share *(v.) & (n.)* 分享
delighted *(a.)* 愉快的	inform *(v.)* 通知	pleased *(a.)* 高興的	signal *(v.)* 示意
gratified *(a.)* 滿意的	introduce *(v.)* 介紹	report *(n.) & (v.)* 報告	

15

公告通知

詞組

happily announce the merger of/a new subsidiary
開心宣布……合併／新的子公司

joyfully announce the birth/adoption/arrival of
開心宣布……的誕生／領養／到來

are pleased/proud/happy to announce
很高興／驕傲／開心地宣布

make known/public
讓大家知道

give notice that
給予通知

notice is hereby given that
在此通知

announces the appointment of
宣布委任

public announcement
公開宣告

have the honor of announcing
有這個榮幸宣布

take pleasure in announcing
愉快地宣布

it is with great pleasure that we announce
我們很開心地宣布

wish to announce/inform/advise you
要向你宣布／通知／建議

A meeting of the Broadway-Aldine Community Council will be held October 3 at 7 p.m. in the NewBank boardroom to elect board members and officers for the coming year.
百老匯阿爾汀協會會議將於十月三日晚上七點在新銀行會議室舉行，以選出下一年的理事會成員及理監事。

Ben Bowser announces that by permission of the court of Ramsey County, New Jersey, April 18, 2017, he will now be known as Benjamin Middleton.
班‧保瑟在紐澤西州藍西郡法院的許可下，已於二〇一七年四月十八日改名為班傑明‧米道頓。

Broadbent Civil Engineering, Inc., is proud to announce the opening of offices in Denver and Salt Lake City.
布羅本土木工程公司在此驕傲宣布丹佛及鹽湖城辦公室的開幕。

Dolores Haze (formerly Mrs. Richard F. Schiller) has changed her address to 155 Carol Avenue, Gilberts, IL 60136.
桃樂絲‧海茲（前為理查‧F‧席勒太太）已將住址改為60136伊利諾州吉爾柏市卡羅大道155號。

Important notice of change in terms: Effective January 1, 2017, your credit card agreement will be amended as follows.
條款變更重要通知：您的信用卡約定條款將會有以下變更，自二〇一七年一月一日起生效。

Isabel Wahrfield and Frank Goodwin announce the dissolution of their marriage, effective July 15.
伊莎貝爾‧瓦菲德與法蘭克‧古德溫宣布離婚，自七月十五日起生效。

Mrs. Rachel Dean announces the engagement of her daughter Susan to Richard Tebben.
瑞秋‧狄恩太太宣布她的女兒蘇珊與理查‧泰本訂婚。

Nguyen Van Truy and Tran Huong Lang are proud and happy to announce the birth of their son Nguyen Van Tuân on March 11, 2017.
阮文水與陳香郎驕傲又開心地宣布，他們的兒子阮文段在二〇一七年三月十一日出生了。

Please be advised that your payment due date has been changed to the sixteenth day of each month.
請留意，您的付款期限已改為每個月的第十六日。

Vanderhof Industries, Inc. is pleased to announce the acquisition of the Connelly-Smith-Dulcy Energy Group, a Gordon-area company with ninety-seven employees that specializes in energy development services.
范德霍夫工業公司很高興宣布收購康納利史密斯杜西能源公司，這間位於高登地區的公司，擁有九十七名員工，專精能源發展服務。

With great sadness we announce the death of our husband and father, Leon Gonsalez.
謹以悲痛的心情通知您，外子，同時是孩子父親的里昂・貢薩勒茲去世了。

15

公告通知

段落

Fairford Corporation, Cooper City, announces that it has reached a distributorship agreement with Antoine-Lettice, based in Paris, France, granting them exclusive marketing rights for its Superbe! ultra-high-pressure waterjet equipment in France and Italy, with nonexclusive rights for the rest of Europe.

庫柏市的費佛公司宣布已與法國巴黎之安東樂提斯公司達成經銷協議，於法國及義大利地區給予 Superbe! 超高壓噴水器的獨家經銷權，歐洲其他地區則予非獨家經銷權。

Averill Airlines will now serve Paris's Charles de Gaulle Airport (previously Orly). Airport transfers included in any of our vacation packages will provide convenient motorcoach transportation between Charles de Gaulle Airport and Port Maillot Station in Paris (formerly Montparnasse Station).

艾維爾航空自現在起於巴黎戴高樂機場提供服務（先前於奧利機場）。套裝行程所包含的機場接送，將會改為戴高樂機場與巴黎馬約門站（先前於蒙納帕斯站）之間的巴士接送服務。

Miles and I have decided that we would make better friends than spouses. As of last week, we have canceled our engagement. We are both, I think, quite relieved, although we still think the world of each other. I know how happy you were for me when I wrote about our engagement, so I wanted to let you know right away that you can still be happy for me—but not because I'm engaged.

邁爾斯與我決定，比起夫妻，我們更適合當朋友。我們已經在上週取消了婚約。我想我們兩人都鬆了一口氣，儘管我們依然十分重視彼此。當我宣布訂婚時，我知道你有多為我高興，所以我想立刻讓你知道。你仍然可以為我開心，雖然我沒有訂婚。

Carrie and Frederick Josser, New London, celebrated their twenty-fifth wedding anniversary on March 2. An open house was hosted by Cynthia and Ted Josser of Collins. Eight proud children and many friends and relatives were there.

來自新倫敦的凱莉與費德烈・喬瑟於三月二日慶祝了他們的結婚二十五週年紀念日。來自柯林斯的辛西亞及泰德・喬瑟負責舉行了家庭招待會。八個驕傲的孩子以及許多親朋好友都在場。

15
公告通知

I'm sorry to tell you that Mother died on July 11 of a heart attack. I know how much your friendship and your lively letters meant to her over the years. She spoke of you often.

遺憾告知您，母親於七月十一日因心臟衰竭逝世。我知道您的友誼與充滿活力的來信對她來說有多麼重要。她時常提起您。

Thanks to you, and the orders that have been pouring in for our special line of children's clothing, we are able to make greater bulk purchases of raw materials and thus manufacture at a lower cost. We are proud to announce that we are passing on these savings to you. Enclosed is our current catalog, but please note the new low prices printed in red.

感謝您踴躍下單訂購我們的特製兒童服裝，我們因此能採購更大量的原料，進而以較低的成本製作生產。我們很驕傲向您宣布，我們將把省下來的成本回饋給您。附件請見我們目前的型錄，請注意新價格是以紅字呈現。

示範信

Dear Friend,

　　We have moved! During the past fifteen years we were so crowded in our old location that sometimes customers had to stand shoulder to shoulder or squeeze through the aisles. Nowadays you'll find it much easier to shop at Taylor & Company.

　　Convenient parking facilities in our parking lot and pleasant offices will make it simple for you to meet all your printing needs.

　　Enclosed is a map showing the new location, along with a one-time 10 percent discount coupon. Come in and see us while the paint's still fresh!

Sincerely yours,

親愛的朋友您好，

　　我們搬家了！過去十五年來，我們的店面實在擁擠不堪，有時顧客甚至得摩肩擦踵或在走道上人擠人。現在，您會發現，在泰勒公司購物變得容易多了。

　　有了停車場便利的停車設施與明亮的辦公室，您所有的影印需求都能輕鬆解決。

　　附件中您會看到新店位置圖，以及一張單次購物九折優惠券。趁我們剛粉刷（一切還新）的時候，快來找我們吧！

○○敬上

FOR: Immediate Release

Boorman, Inc. of Menzies announces the recall of its fresh and frozen sandwiches because of the discovery of bacterial contamination during a recent Food and Drug Administration (FDA) test. Some of the sandwiches were found to contain Listeria monocytogenes, a bacterium that can endanger fetuses, infants, pregnant women, the elderly, and people with weakened immune systems.

No illnesses have been reported.

Please destroy all Boorman QuickWich sandwiches from lot 480032 or return them to Boorman for a refund.

致：速報公司

曼茲的布爾曼公司宣布撤回新鮮冷凍三明治，因最近於美國食品藥物管理局（FDA）檢測中發現細菌汙染。部分三明治發現含有李斯特菌，此種細菌可能危及胎兒、孕婦、老年人與免疫系統功能較弱者。

目前未出現致病報告。

請銷毀全部來自貨號 480032 的布爾曼快吃三明治，或將之退回至布爾曼公司辦理退款。

Paul J. Maggio, D.D.S.
and Matthew J. Maggio, D.D.S.
announce the opening
of their new office
at 1099 Kenyon Road
Fort Dodge, Iowa 50501
(515-576-1981)
and an open house
on July 15, 2017

保羅・瑪吉歐牙醫師
與馬修・J・瑪吉歐牙醫師
宣布開設
新辦公室
位於 50501 愛荷華州道奇堡
肯揚路 1099 號
（515-576-1981）
於二〇一七年七月十五日
將舉辦招待會

✉ 參見：28 求職信、33 商譽信、42 銷售信、50 婚禮相關信

Chapter 16

指示說明信
Letters of Instruction

現今的指示說明信已被制式信、說明書、指導手冊、產品手冊、藥房藥品使用說明、其他打字或預先印製的資料所取代。

指示說明信可以是器械設備操作說明、安全指導、組裝步驟、安裝教學、信用卡扣款爭議處理說明、申請出入許可說明、合約或租約簽署指示、退還商品指示、退款或換貨說明，或替換零件指示等。商業上的說明指示可能牽涉到受傷、錢財損失與損害，當然也會與商譽與顧客回購有關，因此，這些說明指示必須非常準確、仔細。主持人維吉尼亞・葛雷漢（Virginia Graham）曾說：「要慎重閱讀廠商給的說明……這是世界上最難寫的一種文章，它必須反映事實、準確無誤且淺顯易懂。」

有些公司偶爾會寫指示說明信，一般是為了回答顧客的問題。公司內部也會寫說明信，通常是以備忘錄的形式呈現。

以下這些時候也需要說明信：將孩子托給他人或托兒所照顧時；讓病人進行某種特別療程；請鄰居小孩幫你的花園澆水；請木工裝修你的房子。

✉ PART 1 說明篇

何時需要寫指示說明信？

簽署協議 合約或租約	**交付孩子給他人照顧** 保姆或托兒所	**遺囑變更** 或其他法律問題
填寫表單說明 申請書或問卷	**托他人照顧房屋** 植物、花園或寵物	**實施新政策**
操作說明 器械、工具或設備	**退還商品說明** 修理或替換商品	**使用商品說明** 註冊或保養商品
裝運指示	**樣品使用說明**	**支付帳款**

該怎麼說？

1. 若是為了回應對方的信件、電話或拜訪，先感謝對方。或先指出這封信的目的， 如 To help you get the most out of your new software, we offer the following suggestions for use.「為讓您從新軟體中獲取最大效益，我們有以下使用建議。」；These instructions will help you care for your instrument so that it will give optimum performance pleasure.「以下說明有助您保養樂器，讓樂器能發揮最令人愉悅的演出。」

2. 為每一步驟標號列出順序，或按照步驟描述。

3. 可以的話，提供聯絡人姓名、電話與地址，或其他可以給予進一步協助的資源。

4. 在結尾處，愉悅表達感謝，表達期盼未來的訂購，或希望對方喜歡新產品。

- 不要用否定句給予說明。使用肯定的語氣。當你在說明中看到 don't（不要）、never（絕不）與 should not（不應該）時，請將句子改寫為肯定句。

- 不要使用 simple（簡單）與 obvious（明顯）這類的詞。通常這種詞的出現，代表接下來的內容既不簡單也不清楚，會讓讀者覺得自己無法理解其他人顯然都能理解的內容。

- 不要使用高傲的語氣。舉例來說，有時候儀器「壞掉」只是因為沒有插電，所以疑難排解的第一條通常會建議查看儀器的插頭。做此建議時，要用中性的語氣，這樣當問題真的出於沒插電時，顧客才不會覺得自己很愚蠢。

寫作訣竅

- 要簡短。寫出來之後須加以刪減，留下重點。羅馬天主教樞機若望・亨利・紐曼（John Henry Cardinal Newman）曾說：「儘管我們想壓縮篇幅，但是在我們處理下，說明卻越來越多。」

- 要具體。如果你說「整晚浸泡隱形眼鏡」，請同時明確指出要泡幾個小時，因為「整晚」對每個人的意義並不一樣。若要建議顧客定期清潔設備，請指出最適合清潔的產品與程序，並說明「定期」是什麼意思。請解釋或以圖示呈現各個零件，以免讀者不清楚專有名詞。

- 要容易閱讀。若你正在撰寫一份會使用上千次的說明信，請找部門外的人幫忙看過。寫得最差的說明書時常是由專家寫的，他們對於自己的領域太過熟悉，無法理解外行人的想法，所以難以清楚解釋任何事情。瑪莉・歐文・克勞瑟在書中建議：「電影沒有文字說明，要是你的話一旦被曲解，那便一定會成真，這是理所當然的」。

- 要保持有禮委婉。有些疑難雜症對你來說可能很愚蠢，而且答案太過明顯，以致你不知道該如何回答。不過，人類大腦的運作方式各有不同，對方也許是用與你完全不同的角度看待事情。所以，儘管那是個「很笨」的問題，為了保持良好關係，你必須像回答其他問題一樣展現禮貌與願意協助的態度。

- 可以的話，用心說明「為什麼」要（或不要）這麼做。舉例來說，「若在雨天或氣溫低於華氏三十二度時，不要使用此複合物。」很多人都會毫不懷疑地接受這項指示，但也有人會想知道雨水與寒冷的天氣到底會造成什麼影響，還有些人會忽略它，覺得這一點也不重要。如果你加上一句「因為此複合物會吸收水分、結凍、膨脹，而可能導致破裂。」使用者便更有可能會遵守指示，你收到的客訴也會減少。美國華裔小說家譚恩美（Amy Tan）說過：「有些事如果我一開始就不懂，之後我也不可能記起來。」

特殊狀況

- **封面信**時常也會包含說明指示。如寄出樣品、合約與產品時,你可以說明解讀或使用方法。
- **必須簽名的文件**(合約、租約、股票轉移書),都會伴隨一封說明信解釋哪裡必須簽上姓名或姓名字首字母、文件上的簽名是否須認證或公證、哪幾張文件交由收件人留存、其他非留底的文件要寄到哪裡。
- **組裝、安裝、操作方法與安全指示**通常都會寫在使用者手冊裡。不過,你也可以在寄手冊時附上一封說明信,強調特別須注意的要項,如 Please particularly note the section on fire hazards.「請特別留意關於火災危險的部分。」

格式

- 公司對外的說明信會打在有信頭的信紙上。
- 公司內部的說明信會打在備忘錄用紙上,簡短隨意的說明可用手寫。
- 常使用的說明信會製作成制式信。

16

指示說明信

單字

advice (n.) 建議	explanation (n.) 解釋	method (n.) 方法	simplify (v.) 簡化
carefully (adv.) 小心地	guideline (n.) 準則	operation (n.) 操作	step (n.) 步驟
caution (n.) 謹慎	how-to (n.) 基本指南	policy (n.) 政策	system (n.) 系統
demonstrate (v.) 展示	illustrate (v.) 闡述	precaution (n.) 預防措施	warning (n.) 警告
description (n.) 描述	indicate (v.) 指出	procedure (n.) 程序	warranty (n.) 保證書
detail (n.) 細節	information (n.) 資訊	regulation (n.) 規定	

詞組

alert you to
提醒你注意

always check to see
務必檢查

as the illustration shows
如圖例所示

before you use your appliance
在使用裝置前

commonly used to
通常用來……

much more effective to
做……效果更佳

note that
注意

once you are familiar with
一旦你已經熟悉……

point out
指出

recommend/suggest that you
推薦／建議你

16
指示說明信

important safety instructions
重要的安全指示

standard operating procedure
標準操作程序

it requires that you
你必須

you will find that
你會發現

句子

Caution: please read the rules for safe operation before plugging in your Villamarti "Thinking Bull" table lamp.
注意：為您的維拉馬帝「沉思牛」桌燈插上電源之前，請仔細閱讀安全規章。

Follow the illustrated instructions to trim hair at home quickly and professionally with your Clavering Clippers.
按照圖示執行，您便能在家用克萊福林理髮刀快速專業修剪頭髮。

I am not sure which model of the Thursley Electric Toothbrush you have, so I'm enclosing instructions for all of them.
我不確定您擁有的瑟司利電動牙刷型號，所以我在附件中將所有型號的說明書都寄給您。

If you have more questions, call our hotline at 800-555-5379.
若您有更多問題，請撥打我們的專線 800-555-5379。

If you plan to deliver your baby at Malmayne's Old St. Paul's Hospital, please note the following instructions for preadmittance.
若您計畫在茂湄的舊聖保羅醫院生產，請詳閱以下入院前須知。

Please note the following guidelines.
請留意以下準則。

We are happy to be able to clarify this matter for you.
我們很高興能為您說明此事。

You don't need special tools to install this fixture, but follow the steps in the order given.
安裝此設備，您並不需要特殊工具，但請按照以下步驟安裝。

Your Aldridge electric knife will provide you with a lifetime of use if you follow these care instructions.
只要按照以下說明照護，您的愛德奇電子刀能使用一輩子。

段落

Enclosed is the final version of the contract, which constitutes the complete and entire agreement between us. Please read it carefully and consult with your attorney before signing all three copies on the bottom of page 5. Please also initial clauses C1 and D3 to indicate your awareness of the changes we have agreed upon. Return all three copies to me along with a check covering the agreed-upon amount. One copy of the contract will be countersigned and returned to you.

附件為合約的最終版本，我們之間完整的協議條列如上。請詳讀，並諮詢您的律師，並請在第五頁最下方簽名，一式三份都須簽名。也請在 C1 與 D3 這兩項條款旁簽上姓名字首字母，表示您已知悉我們先前變更的協議。請將合約一式三份都寄還給我，隨信也請附上支票，支付先前談定的金額。其中一份合約經我們簽名後，會寄回給您。

Thanks for taking care of the hamsters while we're away. If you can stop by once a day, that'd be great. Give everybody one-quarter cup of hamster food. Fill their water bottles. Give Furball an apple slice and Marigold a banana slice from the fruit in the plastic box (they don't care if it's old and brown). The others don't need any special treats. We'll be back before the cages need cleaning, so don't worry about that.

謝謝你願意在我們外出時幫忙照顧倉鼠。如果你能一天來一次是最好的了。給每隻倉鼠四分之一杯的飼料；幫牠們的水瓶裝滿水；給毛球一片蘋果，萬壽菊一片香蕉切片，你可以在塑膠盒裡找到水果（即使水果已經呈現棕色、不新鮮了，牠們也不會介意）。其他隻倉鼠則不需要特別零食。在籠子需要清理之前，我們就會回來了，所以不必擔心這點。

To obtain a credit card for another member of your immediate family, please complete the enclosed form, making sure that both your signature and the new cardholder's signature appear on the indicated lines.

若要為您的其他直系親屬申請信用卡，請填寫附件中的表格，並務必確認您與持卡人都已在指定的地方簽名。

示範信

Dear Mrs. Dollery:

We were sorry to hear that your AutoAnswer communication system is unsatisfactory. All our equipment is carefully checked before leaving our Chicago factory. However, in rare cases, an intermittent problem may have been overlooked or something may have happened to the equipment during shipping.

Please return your system to us, following these steps:

1. Use the original carton and packing materials to ship the system back to us.
2. Address the box to: Customer Service, P.O. Box 1887, Woodlanders, IL 60031. (The California address is only for placing orders.)
3. Enclose a letter describing the problem (a copy of the letter you originally sent us would be fine) and mention whether the trouble occurred immediately or after use. The more information you can give us, the more quickly we can locate the problem.
4. Fasten the enclosed RUSH label to the top right-hand corner of your letter. This will ensure that you receive a fully functioning machine (your present system or a new one) within ten working days.

Thousands of satisfied customers are experiencing the delight and time-saving features of the AutoAnswer communications system every day; I want you to be one of them very soon.

朵樂瑞夫人您好：

　　自動答錄通訊系統不符您預期，我們感到抱歉。我們生產的器材在離開芝加哥的工廠之前，全都受到仔細查驗；然而，在一些罕見的情況下，間歇性的問題可能未得到注意，或在運送途中儀器遭受了某些狀況。

　　請按照以下步驟，將通訊系統退還給我們：

一、使用原箱與包裝材料，將通訊系統寄還給我們。

二、在箱上寫好以下地址：Customer Service, P.O. Box 1887, Woodlanders, IL 60031。（加州廠只負責訂購事宜。）

三、附上一封信說明問題（也可以附上您原先寄給我們的信件副本），並說明此問題是收到貨時便已出現，或是使用後才出現。您提供給越多資訊，我們能越快找出問題所在。

四、將附件中的「急件」標籤貼在信件右上角，這能確保您能在十個工作天內收到功能完好的機器（是您目前的機器型號，或是新型號機器）。

　　目前有數千名滿意的顧客，每天都享受著自動答錄通訊系統帶來的快樂與省時特色；我很快就會讓您成為其中一員。

TO: Estabrook County Residents
FROM: Estabrook County Board of Commissioners
DATE: October 2
RE: Yard Waste

The amount of garbage each of us produces is enormous, and so are the problems and costs of disposing of it. During the summer months, grass clippings make up 24 percent of residential garbage.

Legislation passed earlier this year requires us to separate grass clippings and leaves—yard waste—from regular trash after January 1.

How do we do this?

1. Leave grass clippings on the lawn. This is the most cost-effective and environmentally sound way to deal with grass clippings. They decompose, returning nutrients to the soil, and never enter the waste stream.

2. Bag grass clippings and take them to one of the six County compost sites (list of compost sites is enclosed). Empty your bags of grass clippings and fill them with free compost for your garden.

3. Use grass clippings as mulch around trees and shrubs (if your grass has not been chemically treated).

4. Bag grass clippings and pay a trash hauler to collect them separately. For additional information call 661-555-2117, Estabrook County's Compost Center.

P.S. We've had a number of calls asking if grass clippings will ruin the lawn if left on it. You can leave grass clippings on the lawn and still keep it healthy by (1) not letting the grass get too long before mowing (clippings should be no more than one inch long in order to filter down into the soil); (2) using a sharp mower blade (the sharper the blade the finer the clippings and the faster they decompose); (3) avoiding overfertilization (dense grass doesn't allow clippings to reach the soil to decompose); (4) removing excessive thatch (1/2 inch is ideal); (5) mowing the lawn when it's dry.

收件人：伊斯布魯克郡內居民
寄件人：伊斯布魯克郡立委員會
日期：十月二日
回覆：庭院廢棄物

　　我們每個人製造的垃圾量相當龐大，因垃圾而產生的問題與處理費用也同樣驚人。在夏季期間，修剪下來的草屑便佔了家庭廢棄物總量的百分之二十四。

　　今年稍早時已通過一項法案，自一月一日起，我們必須將草屑及葉子（即庭院廢棄物）與一般廢棄物分開處置。

　　我們可以怎麼做呢？

　　一、將草屑留在草坪上。這是最符合經濟效益也最有利於環境的草屑處理方式。草屑會分解、將養分歸還土地，永遠不必成為廢棄物。

　　二、將草屑裝袋，帶到其中一間郡立堆肥中心（共有六間，清單如附件）。將您袋子中的草屑清空，再裝滿免費的肥料，供您的院子使用。

16
指示說明信

三、將草屑當作喬木或灌木下的護土覆蓋物（如果您的草坪未灑過農藥的話）。

四、將草屑裝袋，付錢給垃圾處理公司，讓他們分開處理草屑。

若需額外資訊，請致電伊斯布魯克郡立堆肥中心 661-555-2117。

附註：我們接到數通電話，詢問將草屑留在草坪上是否會造成破壞。藉由以下做法，您便能將草屑留在草坪的同時，維護草坪的健康：（一）別等到草長得太長才割草（草屑需短於一吋才能滲入土壤）；（二）割草的刀片必須鋒利（刀越鋒利，草屑品質越好，分解速度也越快）；（三）避免過度施肥（草長得太過密集，會導致草屑無法接觸到土壤進行分解）；（四）移除過長的茅草（二分之一吋最為理想）；（五）在草坪乾燥時割草。

TO: All employees

FROM: Buildings and Grounds

DATE: July 6, 2017

RE: Parking lot resurfacing

The north parking lot will be resurfaced beginning July 15. This means the lot will be unavailable for employee parking July 15–17. We ask that, if possible, you share rides to work on those days. For those three days only, parking will be allowed along the east side of the access road and in the visitor parking places in the east lot (visitors will be able to park around the entrance circle). The Lerrick Mall management has also agreed to let us use the row of parking along its east side (that is, next to Morgan Road) July 15–17. We ask that you do not use any other spaces in the mall parking lot. As a last resort, use the Lerrick parking ramp and take city bus #78 (there is a bus every 12 minutes) or plan to walk (about 7 minutes). Thank you.

收件人：全體員工

寄件人：建築土地部

日期：二〇一七年七月六日

關於：停車場路面重鋪工程

自七月十五日起，北停車場將進行路面重鋪工程，故於七月十五至十七日期間，員工將無法使用此停車場。若可能的話，我們希望在這幾天上班時，各位能與其他人共乘。在這段期間，東側通路與供訪客使用的東停車場將開放停車（將開放訪客於大門前圓環停車）。萊瑞克百貨管理部也同意在七月十五至十七日間讓我們使用其東側（即摩根路旁）路邊的停車位。請勿使用百貨停車區的其他空間。萬不得已時，可以使用萊瑞克機械式停車位，再搭乘 78 號市內公車（每十二分鐘一班）或走路（約七分鐘）。謝謝。

✉ 參見：03 回應、23 建議信

Chapter 17

後續追蹤信
Follow-up Letters

我的不屈不撓，連鬥牛犬也認輸。

——美國作家瑪格麗特・荷賽（Margaret Halsey）

根據先前的信件、對話或會議，寄發後續追蹤信，是一種優雅的收尾方法，可提醒對方接著執行承諾過的行動，或以先前的方式為基礎繼續合作。有時你得寫好幾封後續追蹤信，像鬥牛犬一般不屈不撓，配上一些魅力與創意，才能達成目的。

紐約禮儀書作家兼前白宮社交祕書蕾蒂莎・鮑德瑞奇（Letitia Baldrige），建議用後續會議或午餐聚會搭配後續追蹤信。「這種私人會面也許只會花你三分鐘，卻能讓對方印象深刻。在商場上這麼做的人往往很傑出，是能一躍而上的類型。」

 PART 1 說明篇

後續追蹤信可以做什麼？

提供更多資訊	總結討論事項	感謝給予面試機會
加深印象	補寄資料 修改先前內容	回應客戶問題 確認出貨問題

確認資訊	請求回覆	參觀單位後表達謝意
會議日期、口頭協議	問題、資訊、商品	參觀學校或參與會議
提醒下次會議或預約	確認是否收到禮品	

該怎麼說？

1. 說明寫信的理由，如 I haven't heard from you.「尚未收到你的消息。」；I wanted to remind you.「我想要提醒你。」
2. 提到相關內容（上次會議或上封信）。
3. 在信中提及上次與對方聯絡的內容。必要的話，再次自我介紹，如 We met last week at the performance boats trade show.「我們上週在遊艇展銷會曾見過面。」
4. 說明希望對方收信之後的回應。收到商品時給予收件通知、打電話聯絡、支付帳款，或回覆之前的信。
5. 最後，感謝對方的時間與關注，或告訴對方你很期盼未來在生意上的合作或聯繫。

什麼不該說？

- 寫信提醒對方尚未回覆信件，或收到禮物但尚未寄發收件通知時，絕不要暗貶對方粗心大意。儘管信件不太可能會寄丟，但你必須允許這種可能性。即便收件人真的有錯，把對方的錯誤指出來是很沒禮貌又有害事業的做法。
- 後續追蹤信不能只是重述之前的資訊（除非你只是要確認先前的討論內容）。你必須要有一個確切的寫信理由，如寄送新的資料、請求回覆、給予特別優惠，或感謝先前的訂單或會議。

寫作訣竅

- 寫後續追蹤信請求對方回應先前請求時，可以重複寄發先前的訊息（或附上之前訊息的副本），並簡短強調回應的必要性。
- 有些公司會要求對未回覆的信件做後續追蹤。在每次寄出信件之後（如邀請某人演講），在一週或兩週後的月曆上做標記，確認你是否在該時間前收到回應。未回覆的信件可以存放在一起，以寄發後續追蹤信的日期排序。

- 寄出結算單或發貨單後，若對方尚未回覆，你在後續追蹤時，可以用「a brief reminder」（簡短的提醒）的簡短信件提醒對方，寫上必要的資訊（金額、帳戶號碼、到期日期、逾期天數）。很多時候，這麼一張通知便已足夠，因為有些人逾期付款只是因為疏忽。若這封信仍未帶來任何回應，請參見：38 催款信。

特殊狀況

- **在接受工作面試後**，在對方做出決定前立即寄送後續追蹤信。書信專家哈洛・E・梅耶（Harold E. Meyer）曾說：「在工作面試後的後續追蹤信，常是讓你得到工作的臨門一腳。」在信中告訴對方你很享受面試，並再次描述你的能力及對該職位的興趣。要強調一個特別有力的重點。若在面試中有任何誤解，或有未能說清楚的地方，也可以在信中彌補。結尾時，表達你的謝意與禮貌，如 I look forward to hearing from you.「我期盼得到您的消息。」

- **工作面試後若沒有被錄取**，還是要寫後續追蹤信。感謝對方付出的時間，得體地表達你的失望，並請他們保留你的履歷，最後感謝對方與對方的公司。

- **若尚未收到禮物的收件通知**，你可以寫後續追蹤信（大約在寄出禮物後八週再寄）。工作上所送的禮物通常是由員工打開，不一定是由你的收件對象打開，結婚禮物也容易誤收。因此，你的口氣要中立，強調你關心的是對方是否收到禮物，不是對方忘了寄出收件通知。

- **若會議或活動日期早在好幾個月前就安排好**，請寄出後續追蹤信提醒參加者。重述所有相關資訊，並愉悅表示期待見到對方。

- **銷售信的後續追蹤**很重要。當你向客戶報告完商品簡報或是拜訪完客戶，就要立刻寫信。當客戶詢問產品手冊或產品問題、到展銷會上參觀攤位或回應廣告後，馬上寫信。若你寄了銷售信卻未收到回音，也可以寄後續追蹤信。

  先提到之前的聯絡經驗，如 I wrote you several weeks ago to tell you about...「我在幾週前寫信告訴您……」或 Did you receive the certificate we sent you, good for...?「您是否收到我們寄給您的優待券，效期到……？」接著感謝對方的興趣與花費的時間；提供新資訊；根據先前的接觸，強調對方最有興趣的一兩項產品特色；強化銷售信中的重要賣點；鼓勵對方採取行動：下訂單、打電話給你、訂閱試用專案，或使用附件中的優惠折扣。

  如果這是第二封信，可以強調自家產品或服務有什麼好處或特色。

- 成功的企業會**在顧客購買產品或服務後保持聯繫**，寄給顧客後續追蹤信，藉以了解他們的使用情況、通知新產品的上市，或感謝之前的購買並希望能再次提供服務。

- **在會議後**，寫一封後續信給所有參與者。信中列出討論過的議題與決定，為會議中說過的話留下紀錄。在《The 100 Most Difficult Business Letters You'll Ever Have to Write, Fax, or E-mail》（暫譯：一百種最困難的商業書信）一書中，作者伯納德・海勒（Bernard Heller）建議，寄出後續追蹤信或備忘錄，可確保你在會議中貢獻的意見確實會歸功於你。信中可提及你對討論的進一步看法，並將所有意見整理出來，如：This is the gist of the ideas I offered. A detailed explanation of each one is on the pages that follow. 「以下是我提供的一些構想，針對各要點的詳盡解釋則列於後頁。」《Never Work for a Jerk!》（暫譯：別幫混蛋老闆工作）的作者派翠西亞・金（Patricia King），則建議寄給老闆一份會議書面紀錄，自己也保留一份。

格式

- 商務上的後續追蹤信多半使用有信頭的信紙或是備忘錄用紙。一般信件與提醒用的簡短通知則可以手寫。
- 儘管這個方法並不常見，你也可以用「提醒」小卡片來確認電話邀約的後續狀況。將資訊手寫在印刷卡片、折頁或私人信紙上：This is to remind you that Mr. and Mrs. Louis Rony expect you on... 「在此提醒您，路易斯・隆尼先生與夫人期望您在……」。

17
後續追蹤信

PART 2 應用篇

單字

reply *(v.) & (n.)* 回覆	mention *(v.)* 提及	remind *(v.)* 提醒	summarize *(v.)* 總結
acknowledge *(v.)* 給予收件通知	notify *(v.)* 通知	repeat *(v.)* 重複	feedback *(n.)* 回饋意見
confirm *(v.)* 確認	prompt *(v.)* 促使	review *(v.)* 審核	response *(n.)* 回應
inform *(v.)* 通知	remember *(v.)* 記得	suggest *(v.)* 建議	

詞組

about a month ago, we sent you/wrote you
約一個月前，我們寄出／寫信給你關於

about a little/brief reminder
一個簡短提醒

am writing to remind you that
在此寫信提醒你

appreciate your interest in
感謝你對於……的興趣

as I have not heard from you
由於一直沒有收到你的消息

since we haven't heard from you
由於我們尚未得到你的消息

beginning to wonder if you received
開始擔心你有沒有收到

now that you've had time to consider/review/familiarize yourself with
現在你有時間可以考慮／審核／了解

just a note to remind you
只是一個提醒通知

thought you might like to be reminded
認為你或許需要提醒

I am still interested in
我仍對……有興趣

as mentioned in your letter
如你信中所言

if you want further documentation on
若你在……方面想要進一步的文件

as we agreed yesterday
如我們昨日所同意的

make sure you're aware of 確保你知道	prompt you to 促使你去
I know how busy you are, so 我知道你很忙，所以	thank you for your letter telling us about 謝謝你寄信告訴我們
in reference/reply/response to 關於／回覆／回應	jog your memory 喚起你的回憶
as I mentioned on the phone this morning 如我今早於電話中所提及的	

句子

After visiting with you at the textile trade convention last week, I telephoned Yvonne Dorm, our representative in your area, and asked her to call on you.
上週於織品展銷會上與您見面後，我打電話給我們在貴區的銷售代表伊芳‧朵恩，請她去拜訪您。

Did you receive the Blake River catalog and discounted price list that you requested?
您是否有收到布雷克河的型錄，以及您要求的折扣價格列表？

I am writing to follow up on our conversation about the three-party agreement among Clara Hittaway, Amelia Fawn, and Georgiana Fawn.
我們談過在克萊拉‧希塔威、艾美莉亞‧芳恩與喬治安娜‧芳恩之間的三方協議，故在此寫信了解後續情況。

I appreciate the time you gave me last week to demonstrate our unique Lammeter Integrated Phone Service System.
謝謝您上週騰出時間讓我展示我們公司獨特的藍米特電話服務整合系統。

I enjoyed visiting with you last week when you stopped in to pick up some brochures at Spina Travel Consultants.
上週與您的會面相當愉快，當時您來到史賓娜旅遊顧問公司索取指南手冊。

If you did not receive my materials, I would be happy to send you another set.
如果您沒有收到我的資料，我很樂意再寄一套給您。

I'm wondering if you received my telephone message last week.
我想確認您是否收到我上週的電話語音留言。

It's so unlike you not to have responded that I suspect you didn't receive the wedding invitation.
你一直沒有回應，這太不像你的作風，所以我猜你沒有收到喜帖。

I wanted to follow up on our phone conversation of yesterday.
我想要確認我們昨日的電話談話內容。

I wanted to make sure you're aware of the service warranty on your new microwave.
我想確認您已經清楚新微波爐的保固服務。

Just a note to see if you received the message I left for you Friday.
只是張通知，看看你是否已經收到我星期五留給你的訊息。

Now that you have had a chance to tour the proposed site, I'd like to set a date to discuss our options.
既然您已經參觀過所提議的地點，我想找一天來討論我們有哪些選擇。

On February 7, I sent a questionnaire to you on the departmental reorganization.
我在二月七日寄了一份部門重組的問卷給您。

Reminder: staff meeting 3:30 p.m. Thursday in the teachers' lounge.
提醒您：員工會議，週四下午三點半，在教師休息室。

Thank you for letting me help you with the purchase of your new home, which I hope you are enjoying—I'm enclosing my business card in case I can be of further service to you or to anyone you know.
謝謝您給我機會協助您購入新家，希望您喜歡。隨信附上我的名片，希望未來還有機會為您或您認識的人服務。

Thank you for taking the time this morning to describe the media buyer position, to show me around the complex, and to introduce me to other members of your staff.
謝謝您今早花費時間為我解釋媒體採購的職務內容、帶我認識這棟大樓，以及將我介紹給您的其他員工。

段落

I was delighted to meet with you at your home and hear your thoughts about our community. The best part of running for the Bonville City Council is the opportunity to talk with neighbors like you about our future. Please call my office with your concerns, and remember to vote on November 7!

我很高興能拜訪貴府，聽聽您對於我們社區的看法。競選邦維市市議員的最棒之處在於，有機會與您這樣的好鄰居聊聊我們的未來。若您有任何想法，請致電到我的辦公室。還有，別忘了十一月七日要去投票！

On October 26, I submitted to you a letter of application in response to your advertisement for a moldmaker. I hope you have not yet filled the position and that you are considering my application. Could you please let me know where you are in this process? Thank you.

我在十月二十六日寄了申請信給您，回應貴公司應徵鑄模師的職缺。希望您還沒找到此職缺的人選，並正在考慮我的申請。可否請您告訴我目前的處理狀態呢？謝謝您。

I'm looking forward to having dinner with you Friday evening. I'll be waiting in the lobby of the Rosalba Hotel at 7 p.m. See you then!

期待週五傍晚與你共用晚餐。下午七點，我會在蘿薩芭旅館大廳等你。到時見了！

Several weeks ago we sent you a packet of informational materials on Topaz Island Resort. Now that you've had a chance to look over the color photographs of our unique vacation paradise, would you like to reserve vacation time in one of the ultra modern cabins? Our spaces fill up quickly after the first of the year, so make your choice soon!

幾週前我們寄給您黃玉島度假村的資料，現在在看過這間獨特度假天堂的精美照片之後，不知您想不想預約我們的超現代風格小木屋？我們的空房在年初之後預約得很快，所以要趕快決定喔！

As you know, the Norrington Trolley and Lunch Tour will begin its expanded summer schedule on June 2. Please let me know if we are on schedule to have the new seat covers installed by the May 25 date we agreed on. Thank you.

如您所知，自六月二日起，諾林頓電車與午餐之旅便會啟用擴增的夏季行程表。請讓我知道能否在約定的五月二十五日前如期安裝新椅套。謝謝。

17

後續追蹤信

I know you've been especially busy these last few weeks trying to settle into your new home, but I'd like to make sure that you received a package I mailed you a month ago. It was a house warming gift, of course. I did insure it, so if it's lost I can have a tracer put on it. Do let me know, won't you, if it hasn't shown up?

我知道你為了整頓新家,這幾週很忙。但我想確認你是否有收到我一個月前寄給你的包裹。那當然是個喬遷禮物。我有為它保險,所以如果它被寄丟了,我還是能追蹤回來。如果它沒有出現,一定要讓我知道,好嗎?

示範信

Dear Professor Fansler,

As one of the contributors to *The Handbook of English Studies*, you will want to know that there have been two changes: (1) the handbook is scheduled to appear in early December of this year, not in May, as previously planned; (2) it will be published in four volumes rather than two.

Many authors exceeded their space allocations, making a two-volume set unmanageable (it would have run nearly 1,300 pages per volume). Also, a smaller size per volume and thus a lower volume price will result in a larger sales potential (each volume is available individually).

All authors who contributed to the original volume I will still receive complimentary copies of volumes I and II, and those who contributed to original volume II will receive both volumes III and IV as complimentary copies.

Sincerely,

樊斯勒教授您好:

您身為《英文學習指南》的作者之一,想必會想知道本書有兩處變更:(一)此書將於今年十二月上旬出版,而非之前計畫的五月;(二)此書將分成四冊出版,而非兩冊。

本書多數作者寫作篇幅超出預定,所以無法以兩冊出版(否則一冊會將近一千三百頁)。此外,當每冊以較少頁數出版時,單冊價格便可降低,這會帶來更大的商業效益(每冊個別販售)。

所有參與原版第一冊的作者,仍會收到免費贈送的第一、二冊;參與原版第二冊者,則會收到免費贈送的第三、四冊。

○○敬上

TO: Johannes Rohn
FROM: Oren Cornell
DATE: February 10, 2017

We have not yet received your year-end report. I'm enclosing a copy of my original letter and another copy of the report form. Please complete it and turn it in as soon as possible. We now have all the evaluations but yours, and need to process them before the winter recess.

收件人：約翰尼斯・羅恩
寄件人：奧倫・康尼爾
日期：二〇一七年二月十日

我們尚未收到您的年終報告。隨信附上我上封原信的副本，以及另一張報告表格。請完成這張表，並盡快繳交。我們現在已經收到所有評估表，只差您的，而我們必須在冬休前將處理完畢。

Dear Ms. Collen:

We hope you are as pleased with your Safe-Home Security System as we were pleased to install it for you. Let us know if you experience any problems in these first few months. Very few of our customers do, but we're available if anything should come up.

You did not choose to purchase our Monthly Inspection Service at this time. However, if you change your mind, we can easily arrange it for you.

It was a pleasure doing business with you!

Sincerely yours,

科倫小姐您好：

我們很高興能為您安裝安全家庭保全系統，希望您跟我們一樣高興。在一開始的幾個月若有任何問題，請讓我們知道。我們的客戶很少回報問題，但若有任何問題出現，我們都會為您處理。

這次您並未購買我們的每月檢查服務；不過，要是您改變心意，我們可以立刻為您安排。

很高興能與您合作！

〇〇敬上

✉ 參見：03 回應、11 表揚信、12 致謝函、14 收件通知、36 職場相關信、41 信貸相關信、42 銷售信

Chapter 18

邀請函
Invitations

> 邀請是最真摯的奉承。
>
> ——瑪瑟琳・考克斯

身為群居動物的我們，喜歡邀請家人朋友參與人生中許多大大小小的事件，也會因為好玩而慶祝一些較不重要的事情。社交聚會為我們帶來友誼、娛樂與消遣。邀請時，你可以隨意在明信片下寫上 Come visit!「來拜訪我們！」，也能用刻印的邀請帖正式邀請對方參加晚餐舞會。

商場上的宴會、午餐、雞尾酒派對、茶會與招待會，讓我們有機會招攬生意、提升員工士氣，並鞏固跟顧客或供應商的關係。

 PART 1　說明篇

邀請函可以用於什麼情況？

展覽或宴會 如時裝秀、貿易展、書展	**募款活動**	**學校活動**
銷售會 參見：42 銷售信	**週末招待活動**	**演出活動邀請** 表演、演講

會議	款待他人	聚會
工作坊、論壇	午晚餐、茶會、派對	同事、朋友或家人之間
開放參觀	**訂結婚**	**宗教相關儀式**
如工廠、辦公室	或準媽媽派對	洗禮

該怎麼說？

1. 說明參加的場合類型，如招待會、授獎宴會、紀念日慶祝會、晚餐舞會或退休派對）。

2. 說明參加的時間。月、日、星期、上午或下午。在正式邀請函中，時間必須以英文完整寫出，如 seven o'clock in the evening，不使用 a.m. 或 p.m.。

3. 給予地點地址。必要時，附上開車路線指示（附近停車場）或地圖。

4. 合宜的話，提及準備了哪些茶點。

5. 若須收費，請寫出價錢。

6. 正式邀請函會附上一張刻印或印刷的接受回函及信封，在邀請函上註明「RSVP」（敬請回覆）。

    (1) 稍微不正式的邀請函，則會在左下角寫上「RSVP」、「Rsvp」、「Please respond」（請回覆）或「Regrets only」（不能出席請回覆），並提供連絡地址或電話。非正式邀請函可用電話回覆。

    (2) 合適的話，給予回覆的期限。

7. 必要時，在邀請函右下角列出服裝規定（黑色領帶、白色領帶、正式、非正式、休閒、變裝）。

8. 告訴過夜的客人你希望他們幾點到達與離開、需要準備的特殊服裝（網球衣、泳衣、登山裝）、是否會與小孩同房、是否需要睡袋、是否有其他客人。詢問對方是否能容忍動物、香菸的味道或其他可能造成不便的事。

9. 提供額外的資訊，包括停車位、雨備行程、接送服務。

10. 最後，表達你對此次聚會的期待。

- 不要寫 request the honor of your presence（敬請蒞臨），除非是喜帖。
- 正式邀請函不要使用縮寫，除非是 Mr.、Mrs.、Ms.、Dr.、Jr. 或軍階。也避免在提及姓名時使用姓名字首字母。正式邀請函中，在姓名後完整寫出 Second（二世）或 Third（三世），你也可以使用羅馬大寫數字，如 Jason Prescott Allen III（傑森・普斯考特・艾倫三世），姓名與數字之間不需逗號。州名須完整寫出來，要寫 Alabama（阿拉巴馬州），而不能寫 Ala. 或 AL。時間亦然，如 half past eight o'clock（八點半）。

寫作訣竅

- 辦活動的每個人都需在邀請函上署名。可在邀請函上使用任何受邀人想用的名字（如女性婚後使用的姓名、工作使用的姓名、出生的姓名），而受邀人也用邀請函上的姓名回覆。若不確定該如何稱呼該女性，可打電話詢問。

  寄發工作上的邀請，使用公司名字與職稱。

  朋友可以一起署名寄發邀請函。也可以用團體名義寄發，如 The Castorley Foundation invites you「卡斯托利基金會邀請您」或 The Central High School senior class invites you「中央高中高年級邀請您」。

- request(s) the pleasure of your company（敬邀參加）這句話適用於任何邀請函，但不適用在非常隨意的邀請。

- 若你需要知道有誰會出席，請附上一張回覆卡。回覆卡的用紙、風格與格式都與你的邀請函一致，並會伴隨一個小信封（至少 3.5×5 吋的大小，以符合明信片的尺寸），將你的地址印刷或刻印於信封上，並貼上郵票。回覆卡上寫：[Ms., Mrs., Miss, Mr. Name to be filled in] regrets / accepts [one is checked] for Saturday, November 20「受邀人＿＿＿〔填入 Ms.、Mrs.、Miss 或 Mr.，以及姓名〕於十一月二十日星期六不克參加／接受邀請〔擇一勾選〕」。

  在有些情況下，accepts（接受邀請）與 regrets（不克參加）會分開寫，由客人劃掉不適用的或圈選適用的。影印店會有邀請函樣版，他們能建議你適合的格式。

- 若是邀請單身的人，或你對其私生活並不清楚的人，請在邀請函中註明：(1) 是否只邀請對方一人，或 (2) 可以帶朋友，或 (3) 只要事先通知人數皆可。

- 寄發邀請函給家中有幼兒的家庭時，信封上需在家長姓名下方寫出每個小孩的名字，不要只寫「and family」（及其家人）。若有其他成人跟那個家庭住在一起，不要在邀請函中納入他的姓名，而要另外寄發一封專屬的邀請函。十三歲以上的孩子也應收到專屬邀請函。

18
邀請函

- 在邀請函中暗示對方送禮物是不恰當的（如給願望清單，或表明想要金錢作為禮物）。不過，有些人會聲明不必送禮物（例如某人慶祝八十大壽，而他並不需要禮物，也沒空間可以擺）。如果希望對方不用送禮物，可參考安·蘭德斯的專欄讀者所提出的兩種寫法：

  (1) Your friendship is a cherished gift. We respectfully request no other.

  「你的友誼就是珍貴的禮物，敬請您不必再送其他禮物。」

  (2) We request your help in compiling a book recalling memories from our parents' first fifty years of marriage. On the enclosed sheet, we ask that you write one memory or event that you have shared with them and return it to us by April 26. We believe that the loving memories they have shared with you, their friends, would be the most treasured gift they could receive; therefore, we request that no other gift be sent.

  「我們希望您能協助我們編撰一本集結回憶的書，是關於我們父母的前五十年婚姻生活。在隨信附上的單子中，請您寫下一項您與他們共享的回憶或事件，並於四月二十六日前寄還給我們。我們相信他們與您們共享的這些深情回憶，就是他們能收到最珍貴的禮物；因此，我們敬請您不必寄送其他禮物。」

- 在家中舉行的晚餐活動，通常會明確指出客人應到達的時間與上菜時間。會寄這樣寫邀請函的人，通常都曾因為有人遲到而毀了他們之前主辦的晚餐派對。

- 需規定服裝規定時，須遵循以下規則：

  (1) 白領帶是最正式的服裝，男性須穿戴白領帶、翼領及燕尾服，女性則須穿著正式長禮服。

  (2) 黑領帶或所謂的正式服裝，對於男性來說，是指無尾禮服與襯衫及領結（深色西裝並不符規定），而對於女性來說，則是講究的洋裝、及膝洋裝或長禮服。

  (3) 半正式服裝意指男性穿著獵裝外套或西裝，女性穿著洋裝（而非長禮服）或較講究的上衣與褲子。牛仔褲與 T 恤並不適合半正式的場合。

- 寄發重要場合的邀請函給外地的客人，應提早半年郵寄。郵寄邀請函的時間建議：

  (1) 正式晚餐、宴會、舞會、慈善活動、接待會、茶會的邀請函在四至六個月前就須寄發；

  (2) 接待會或雞尾酒派對，則在兩至四週前寄送；

  (3) 猶太成年禮，於三週前寄發；

  (4) 一般晚餐或聚會於兩週前郵寄。

特殊狀況

- **為一般商業招待活動寄發邀請函時，**可以使用備忘錄或電子郵件，內容包括：活動類型（退休、離職、入職紀念日、客座演講）；時間、日期、地點；是否備有茶點；是否需要捐款；可供確認或詢問的分機號碼。

- **宗教儀式的邀請函內容包括**：日期、時間、地點、儀式類別、儀式後茶會或聚會的相關資訊。猶太成年禮的邀請函，可用刻印或印刷，或用手寫，內容包含：年輕人的全名；時間、日期、地點；會後茶會或慶祝會的資訊。

- **女兒首次出席社交場合的邀請函**會由父母寄發，無論女兒是否結婚、寡居、離婚或分居，如：Sir Arthur and Lady Dorcas Clare request the pleasure of your company at a dinner-dance in honor of their daughter Millicent on Saturday...「亞瑟爵士與朵卡斯‧克萊兒夫人邀請您於週六參加晚餐舞會，以祝賀他們的女兒米莉森……」。若是在家中接待客人，邀請函可以這麼寫：Mrs. Sybil Fairford and Miss Elizabeth Fairford will be at home Sunday the second of June from five until half past seven o'clock, One Cooper Row.「喜碧兒‧費爾芙夫人與伊莉莎白‧費爾芙小姐於六月二日星期日五點至七點半會在家中，庫柏路一號。」

- **募款活動的邀請函**必須明確寫出接受邀請者需要做的事情，如 $100 donation suggested「建議 100 元捐款」或 Tax-deductible contribution of $500 per couple suggested.「建議每對夫妻捐款 500 元，可抵稅。」你的用詞會受限於 tax deductible（可抵稅）與 donation（捐款）所指涉的意涵。附上一回郵信封，讓對方方便回覆；若你不這麼做，則告知對方要把支票寄到哪裡，以及如何取得門票。有些主辦人無法成功舉辦募款活動，是因為捐款人都很忙碌，他們沒有時間仔細閱讀邀請函上的小字體，也沒功夫猜測該如何回覆邀請。為了他們，請把一切簡化。義賣活動、公開慈善宴會及其他募款活動都不需要寄發回函，因為購買門票就表示接受邀請。

- **邀請演講者時**，邀請函內容須包含：活動名稱與贊助機構；日期、時間與地點；觀眾類型（人數、興趣、過去對演講主題的認識）；演講類型；分配的演講時間長度，及演講開始的大約時間；可使用的器材；住宿與交通資訊，或是演講地點的路線指示；是否有問答時間；節目表；是否提供餐點；聯絡人姓名；關於酬勞的細節；向演講者表示願意進一步協助的意願；告訴演講者你很高興他能為你的組員演講。此時你也要向演講人要求提供自傳，才能放入節目表。

- **銷售信**有時會以邀請函的形式出現，邀請顧客前往展示會、特賣會、招待會或操作示範會，或邀請顧客成為會員、開戶或訂閱。

- 根據一般公司規章，**年會的舉辦**皆須寄發正式通知，不過你仍然可以寄送邀請函，特別是年會後還有宴會或晚餐時。對方不須回覆是否參加年會，但通常必須回答是否加入晚餐。

- 當你**邀請的人尚未回覆**，但你必須提早計算參加人數，請直接打電話詢問。有名新婚女性投稿至「親愛的艾比」（艾比蓋兒‧范布倫 Abigail Van Buren）專欄，提到她與未婚夫寄出的一百張喜帖中，只收到三封回郵回函，但幾乎所有邀請的人都出席了婚禮。「親愛的艾比」提出的預防方法，是將 RSVP（敬請回覆）替換成白話的英文：Please let us know if you are able to attend—and also if you are not.「請讓我們知道您是否能夠出席，或是不能出席。」除了正式或大型的活動外，最好是用電話（或是利用語音信箱）或通訊軟體邀請客人，而後

再寄發邀請函作為提醒。

- **若要取消或延後邀請**，使用與原邀請函相同的格式、風格與紙質。倘若還有時間，則可以像原邀請函一樣用刻印或印刷回覆；也可以用手寫通知，並採用與原邀請函一樣的行文風格：Mr. and Mrs. Hans Oosthuizen regret that it is necessary/that they are obliged to postpone/cancel/recall their invitation to dinner on...「漢斯・烏斯紹森先生與太太很遺憾必須／不得不延後／取消／撤銷他們於……的晚餐邀請」或 We must unfortunately cancel the dinner party we had planned for...「可惜的是，我們必須取消為……安排的晚餐派對」。若是緊急狀況，請打電話。

- 如果**在接受邀請後取消**，須立即打電話給活動主辦人，接著再寄出一封短信向對方道歉。在短信中強調你的遺憾，並給予充分的理由。若你到最後一刻才取消，或是你的取消造成對方許多不便，你也可以隨道歉信一同寄出一束花。

格式

- 正式的邀請函是刻印或印刷於品質好的信紙上，分行書寫，並採用第三人稱，如 Terence Mulvaney requests the pleasure of your company at a dinner-dance in honor of his daughter...「泰倫斯・莫凡尼敬邀您參加為他女兒舉辦之晚餐舞會……」影印店、文具店與百貨公司都有提供多種邀請函風格、紙張、墨水與設計。邀請函也可以用手寫的，格式與措詞與印製之請帖相同。像 requests the pleasure of your company（敬邀您參加）這樣的句子適用於所有的請帖，但喜帖除外。在信封或邀請函寫上每位受邀者的全名及敬稱（Ms., Mrs., Miss, Dr., Mr.）。所有的字、州名與小於一百的數字都須完整拼出，絕不使用縮寫。電話號碼與郵遞區號則從來不會出現在正式邀請函上；郵遞區號通常只會出現在回信地址或回郵信封。商業上的正式邀請函（如授獎宴會），會採用標準的正式邀請函格式。

- 非正式的社交邀請函會手寫在非正式的信紙或折頁卡片上，採用一般的寫信風格（第一人稱、不分行連續書寫）。內容通常會寫在折頁卡片的第一頁，而要是這一頁已經寫有你的名字，你可以將細節內容寫在你名字的下方。市面上有賣那種只須在空白處寫入內容的邀請函，這使用在非正式的聚會是沒有關係的；事實上，這種邀請函有時還很幽默巧妙。

- 非正式的商務邀請函可以寫在有信頭的信紙上；公司內部的邀請函則可以採用備忘錄用紙，有時甚至可以使用電子郵件寄發。

- 實際內容為銷售信的邀請函，通常會使用制式信。

- 如果你時常招待客人，可訂購已刻印或印刷且設有空白處的邀請函，這樣你就能在需要時填入內容，如 Mr. and Mrs. Desmond Mulligan request the pleasure of [name's] company at [event] on [date] at [time] o'clock, 1843 Thackeray Street.「戴斯蒙・莫利根先生與太太敬邀〔姓名〕參加〔活動〕，於〔日期與時間〕，地點在薩克萊街 1843 號。」

💬 **單字**

attend *(v.)* 出席	début *(n.) & (v.)*（女性）初次 出席社交場合	occasion *(n.)* 場合	salute *(v.)* 致敬、祝賀
cancel *(v.)* 取消	fête *(n.)* 喜慶日	pleasure *(n.)* 愉悦	solemnize *(v.)* 隆重慶祝
celebration *(n.)* 慶祝	honor *(n.) & (v.)* 榮幸	postpone *(v.)* 延後	welcome *(v.)* 歡迎
commemorate *(v.)* 紀念	installation *(n.)* 就任	rejoice *(v.)* 深感欣喜	

💬 **詞組**

accept with pleasure 樂意接受	looking forward to seeing you 很期待見到你
be our guest 做我們的客人	obliged to recall/cancel/postpone 不得不撤銷／取消／延後
bring a guest 帶客人來	owing to the illness/death of 由於⋯⋯生病／去世
cordially invites you to 真心邀請你們	request the pleasure of your company 敬邀你參加
have the honor of inviting 有這個榮幸邀請	we are celebrating 我們即將慶祝
in commemoration/celebration of 為了紀念／慶祝	we would like to invite you to 我們想邀請你來
in honor of 為了祝賀	you are cordially invited 誠摯邀請你
invite you to 邀請你前往	kindly respond on or before 在⋯⋯當日或之前回覆

句子

A revolutionary new service is now available to valued customers—and you're among the first invited to enroll.
一項革命性的新服務已可供尊榮客戶使用，而您就是我們第一批邀請註冊的貴客。

Are you free after work on Friday to join a few of us for dinner?
週五下班後，有空跟我們幾個去吃晚餐嗎？

Business attire is suggested.
建議穿著適宜之商務正裝。

Come hear noted Reformation scholar and professor of history Dr. Margaret Heath speak on September 12 at the 8:30 and 11:00 services at Gloria Dei Lutheran Church, 1924 Forster Avenue.
請來聽宗教改革學者兼歷史教授瑪格麗特‧璽思博士的演講，於九月十二日的八點半及十一點兩場禮拜舉行，地點在福斯特大道 1924 號的光榮路德教會。

I'm pleased to invite you to acquire the Golden American Bank Card.
我很高興邀請您申請美國銀行金卡。

It will be so good to see you again.
到時能再次見到你，真是太好了。

I urge you to look over the enclosed materials and consider this special invitation now.
我建議您仔細檢視附件中的資料，並且立即考慮這個特別的邀約。

Mr. and Mrs. Alex Polk-Faraday regret that it is necessary to cancel their invitation to brunch on Sunday, the sixteenth of August, because of the illness of their daughter.
艾力克斯‧波克－法拉岱先生與夫人在此遺憾宣布，因為女兒生病，他們必須取消本週日（八月十六日）的早午餐邀約。

Please confirm by June 6 that you can attend.
若您能參加，請於六月六日之前回覆確認。

Please join us for a farewell party in honor of Veronica Roderick, who is leaving Wain International to pursue other business interests.
請加入我們為薇若妮卡‧羅德里克舉辦的歡送派對，她即將離開韋恩國際另覓其他事業。

You are invited to a special evening showing of our new line of furniture from European designers.
敬邀您參加一場特別展示晚會，我們將展出一系列由歐洲設計師設計的新式傢俱。

段落

Please plan to attend the Hargate Open House this Thursday, September 26, at 7 p.m. You will have the opportunity to meet the school staff, sit in on each of your student's classes during a simulated (but greatly shortened) school day, and talk to other parents during the social hour that follows. (A contribution for the refreshment table will be greatly appreciated.)

請考慮出席哈門招待會，於九月二十六日本週四傍晚七點舉行。您將有機會見到學校職員、在模擬（但大幅縮短）的學校日活動時間至各班入座聽課，並在其後的交流時間與其他家長分享討論。（若願意贊助茶點，我們將感激不盡。）

The Jervis family invites you to help Laura and Frank celebrate their Golden Wedding Anniversary. An Open House will be held at the Russell Eagles Hall, from 1 to 4 p.m. on Sunday, March 10, 2017.

傑維斯家族邀請您一同慶祝勞菈與法蘭克的金婚紀念日。招待會將於二〇一七年三月十日（週日）下午一至四時在羅素老鷹會堂舉行。

You are invited to attend the Fall Family Festival this Tuesday evening from 6 to 9 p.m. at Temple Beth Shalom, 14 Burnsville Parkway. There will be puppet shows, activity booths, games, and refreshments!

敬邀您參加秋季家庭慶典，本週四傍晚六至九時於貝斯索隆猶太會堂（伯恩維爾大道十四號）舉行。屆時會有布偶秀、活動攤位、遊戲與茶點！

Kindly respond on or before
September 18, 2017
M _____
accepts/declines
Number of persons _____

敬請於以下日期當日或之前回覆
二〇一七年九月十八日
受邀人_____
接受邀請／不克參加
人數_____

18
邀請函

You are invited to hear the National Liturgical Choir under the direction of Maugrabin Hayraddin at 4 p.m. Sunday, September 28, at Quentin Methodist Church, 1823 Scott Avenue. The sixty-voice chorus will sing Russian liturgical music by Gretchaninof and Kalinikof and selections by Bach, Shaw, and Schutz. The cost is $5 ($3 for seniors and students).

敬邀您前來欣賞由毛格賓・黑拉汀指揮的國家詩歌合唱團表演，於九月二十八日週日下午四時舉行，地點在昆汀循道教會，史考特大道 1823 號。六部合聲合唱團將演唱格列恰尼諾夫與卡林科夫創作之俄羅斯聖樂，以及巴哈、蕭伯納與舒茲的音樂選集。門票價格為 5 元（敬老價與學生價為 3 元）。

You are invited to join the Henderson Film Club for one month—at absolutely no cost to you. Tell us which four selections you want, and they will be sent the same day we receive your order.

敬邀您加入韓德森電影俱樂部，第一個月完全免會員費。告訴我們您想要哪四種選集，我們便會於收到您訂單的當日將選集寄出。

The tenth annual Public Works Open House will be held on Tuesday, October 3, from 4 to 7 p.m. at the Evans Street yards, a block south of Owen Avenue. The whole family will enjoy it. Get your picture taken on a Public Works "cherry picker." Car buffs can tour the biggest maintenance and repair shop in the city. There will be drawings for prizes, music, food, and entertainment. Some lucky winner will take home an actual traffic signal used for fifty years on the corner of Blodwen and Marquand Streets.

第十屆年度公共事務招待會將於十月三日（週二）下午四至七時舉行，地點在伊凡斯街庭院，位於歐文大道南方一街區處。這是全家人都能享受的活動。您可以在公共事務「吊車」上照相；汽車迷可以參觀市內最大的維修廠。屆時還會有抽獎、音樂、食物與娛樂活動。一名幸運得主將能帶回一面有五十年歷史的交通號誌，曾實際使用於布洛溫街與馬昆街交口。

示範信

Mr. and Mrs. Seymour Glass
joyfully invite you
to worship with them
at the Bat Mitzvah of their daughter
Muriel
Saturday, the tenth of July
Two thousand seventeen

at ten o'clock in the morning
Mount Zion Temple
1300 Summit Avenue
Colorado Springs, Colorado

西莫·葛拉斯先生與太太
開心邀請您
與他們一同
慶祝他們女兒莫瑞兒的
成年禮
二〇一七年
七月十日星期六
上午十時
於錫安山會堂
科羅拉多州科羅拉多泉市
頂峰大道 1300 號

Owing to the illness of a family member
Blanche Hipper and Loftus Wilcher
are obliged to recall their invitation
for Saturday, the seventeenth of April
two thousand seventeen

由於家人生病
布蘭琪·希波與洛弗特斯·威爾契
必須取消他們於
二〇一七年
四月十七日星期六的邀約

Dear James Ayrton,

You are invited to become a member of the Brodie Community Anti-Crack Coalition. Formed eight months ago, this coalition of three community councils and six community organizations was formed to oppose the activity and effects of illegal drug use and trafficking in Easdaile and especially in the Brodie neighborhood.

The Brodie Community Council already has two delegates to the coalition, but we believe it would be helpful to have one more. Your name has been mentioned several times as someone with the necessary experience and enthusiasm.

I'll call later this week to discuss the possibility of your participation.

詹姆士・艾頓您好：

　　敬邀您成為布洛迪社區反毒聯盟的一員。本聯盟於八個月前創立，是由三個社區委員會及六個社區組織組成，在伊斯達利地區，尤其是布洛迪這一帶，我們反對非法毒品的使用與交易，及其相關活動與影響。

　　布洛迪社區委員會已派兩位代表加入聯盟，但我們相信多增加一位將大有助益。而因為您擁有我們需要的經驗與熱情，您的姓名曾多次被提起。

　　本週內我會再打電話給您，與您討論參加的可能性。

Dear Mrs. Lucas,

　　We are having a reception on Sunday, May 5, from 1 p.m. to 4 p.m. to celebrate our joy in the adoption of our new son, Philip. It would mean a great deal to us to have you join us.

Sincerely,

盧卡斯太太您好：

　　我們將在五月五日（週日）下午一至四時舉辦一場茶會，歡慶我們領養了新的兒子菲利浦。您的參與對我們意義重大。

○○敬上

Special Savings Invitation!

Dear Martin Lynch Gibbon:

　　As one of our Preferred Customers, you are invited to save 10 percent on every purchase you make at Murdoch Jewelers on July 14 and 15. This discount applies to both sale-priced and regular-priced merchandise, and includes our line of dazzling Iris diamonds, the ever-popular Headliner watches for men and women, and our complete selection of wedding gifts.

　　You deserve the best, and for two days this month, "the best" comes with a discount just for you!

Note: The discount does not include labor or service charges.

特別優惠邀請！

馬汀・林區・吉本您好：

　　您是我們禮遇的貴賓，我們敬邀您一同參與：七月十四、十五日當天，在茉朵克珠寶購買的每項商品皆可獲得九折優惠。此優惠適用於特價及原價商品，也包括我們的閃亮艾莉絲鑽石系列、一直廣受歡迎的頭條男女錶系列以及所有結婚禮物商品。

　　您值得最好的，而在本月的這兩天，您可以用專屬優惠得到「最好的」！

附註：本折扣不包括人力或服務費用。

✉ 參見：03 回應、12 致謝函、14 收件通知、19 社團組織相關、21 接受、22 拒絕、42 銷售信、43 紀念日、50 婚禮相關信

Chapter 19

社團組織相關
Organizations and Clubs

請接受我的退出，我不想參加任何願意讓我加入的社團。
——美國喜劇演員格魯喬·馬克思（Groucho Marx）

湯姆森·蓋爾（Thomson Gale）撰寫的《Encyclopedia of Associations》（暫譯：美國組織百科全書）中，列有三萬五千個非營利、會員制組織，以及許多較沒那麼正式的俱樂部、協會、團體，供人們分享興趣、目標、專業資訊與娛樂活動。

多數社團或組織的通信通常都很簡短、有規律、措詞淺白。但是，組織每次寄發的宣告、邀請或信件，對於會員與大眾而言，就是代表著組織本身。也因此，這些文件必須正確無誤且有吸引力。

 PART 1 說明篇

何時要寫組織／社團相關信件？

布達消息	**邀請參加活動**	**引薦新會員**
開會、提醒或變更 參見：15 公告通知	或邀請講者 參見：18 邀請函	參見：30 推薦信
退出組織	**請求** 加入會員、贊助、 志工服務、提供資訊	**歡迎新成員** 參見：10 歡迎信

該怎麼說？

- **若要通知開會**，內容須包含：組織名稱；會議日期、時間與地點；聯絡用的電話號碼；至少提供一個吸引對方出席會議的理由（名人講座、特別選舉、座談會、簽書會）。

- **邀請演講者時**，內容須包含：組織完整名稱；預估聽眾人數；組織的主要目標與會員興趣所在，演講者才能為聽眾量身打造演講內容；可使用的器材（懸掛式投影機、麥克風）；路線指示圖；聯絡人姓名與電話號碼。

- **招募新會員時**，設計一本介紹組織的小冊子，內容包含最能將組織「推銷」給別人的組織目標與活動。將小冊子與一張封面信一起寄送，在封面信中可強調組織的重要目標，並向對方解釋他為何適合你的組織。

什麼不該說？

- 避免將負面的事情寫進信裡，如個性衝突、對於政策的意見分歧與爭論、效忠對象的改變，這些雖為組織帶來活力與獨特色彩，但最好面對面再談。當這些棘手的情況被寫進信裡，最後便會成為公開的文件，這可不明智。

- 避免在信中顯露專制、上對下的語氣。今日，多數組織都更崇尚同儕關係而非階級關係。雖然仍有負責人或領導者，但每個成員都認為自己對組織有部分的所有權。

寫作訣竅

- 有人也許會請你協助社團或你不太認識的會員，或幫他寫推薦信。同為協會或社團成員，你會感受到微妙的壓力，讓你覺得必須接受。但是這種情況就跟任何其他情況一樣，你並沒有義務幫忙（參見：22 拒絕）。

- chairman（主席、議長）一詞現在基本上已為 chair 所取代。其他選擇包括 moderator（會議主席）、committee/department head（委員會／部門主任）、presiding officer（主席）、presider（主持人）、president（會長、主席）、convener（會議召集人）、coordinator（協調人）、group coordinator（小組負責人）、discussion/group/committee leader（討論會／小組／委員會負責人）、head（主任）、organizer（籌備人）、facilitator（推動人）、officiator（主持人）、director（主導人）、administrator（管理人）。有些人會使用 chairwoman 與 chairman，但 chairwoman 感覺起來較不有力，很少被視為能與 chairman 完全對應的詞彙。人們會有意識地使用 chairperson 來稱呼女性。簡短的 chair 是原始的用法

（一六四七年出現），chairman 到一六五四年才出現，chairwoman 則是一六八五年。chair 可以作為名詞與動詞，就像 head 能當名詞與動詞一樣。人們雖然討厭別人用傢俱來形容他們，但顯然並不排斥被稱為主導部門、分公司或團體的「頭」。同理，也不會有人錯以為 chair 是用椅子來主持會議。

格式

- 所有社團或組織信件都必須用打字的，除非該社團為社交型社團，成員都互相認識，並喜歡寄給彼此手寫信。
- 電子郵件與明信片可用在寄發會議通知、宣布事項、邀請函與簡短訊息。
- 無論組織大小，通訊錄都應該輸入電腦；將這種通訊錄結合多數文字處理系統，能大大簡化通信過程。

19

社團組織相關

單字

action *(n.)* 行動	coalition *(n.)* 聯盟	heritage *(n.)* 遺產、傳統	practical *(a.)* 實際的
affiliation *(n.)* 隸屬單位	committee *(n.)* 委員會	ideal *(n.) & (a.)* 典範；典型的	principle *(n.)* 原則
agenda *(n.)* 議程	constitution *(n.)* 章程	improve *(v.)* 改善	procedure *(n.)* 程序
allegiance *(n.)* 忠誠	contribution *(n.)* 貢獻	league *(n.)* 社團、聯盟	program *(n.)* 計畫
alliance *(n.)* 聯盟	establish *(v.)* 建立	legacy *(n.)* 留給後人的東西	progress *(n.)* 進度
association *(n.)* 協會	generous *(a.)* 慷慨的	nominate *(v.)* 提名	project *(n.)* 專案
benefit *(n.)* 義賣、義演	guild *(n.)* 互助會、協會	policy *(n.)* 政策	qualification *(n.)* 資格
bylaw *(n.)* 內部章程	headquarter *(n.)* 總部	positive *(a.)* 正面的	regulation *(n.)* 規定
rule *(n.)* 規則	support *(v.) & (n.)* 支持	valuable *(a.)* 珍貴的	worthwhile *(a.)* 值得的
society *(n.)* 協會、社會	unwavering *(a.)* 堅定的	welcome *(v.)* 歡迎	

19

社團組織相關

詞組

a credit to the organization
為組織爭光

join forces
同心協力

affiliated/associated with
隸屬於／與……有關

minutes of the meeting
會議記錄

all-out effort
全力以赴

service to the community
為社區效力

board of directors
董事會

slate of officers
幹事候選人名單

committee chair
委員會主席

take pride in nominating
自豪地提名

cooperative spirit
合作精神

unfortunately must resign
很遺憾必須退出

credit to us all
歸功於我們全部

worthwhile cause
值得的目標

have been elected a member of
已被選為……的一員

would like to nominate you for
想要提名你為

common goal
共同目標

19

社團組織相關

句子

Enclosed please find names of hosts, meeting dates, and topics for the next six months.
在附件中您能看到未來半年的主持人姓名、會議日期與開會主題。

I am sorry to inform you that family illness obliges me to step down from the club vice-presidency, effective immediately.
很遺憾地通知大家，由於家人生病，我必須卸下俱樂部副主席的職位，即刻生效。

It is with great pleasure/regret that I accept/decline your nomination to the Board of Directors of Montmorency House.
我很樂意接受／遺憾拒絕您提名擔任蒙莫倫希之家的董事會成員。

I would be happy to discuss any questions you have about the Club over lunch some day next week.
我很樂意於下週某天的午餐時間與你討論對俱樂部的任何問題。

I would like to recommend/wish to propose Brander Cheng for membership in the Burke Orchestra Society.
我想推薦／希望布蘭德‧程能成為柏克管絃樂協會的一員。

Join now and take advantage of this limited offer to new members.
現在就加入，享受新會員的獨享優惠。

Our annual fundraising meeting to plan events for the next year will be held August 3 at 7 p.m.—all are invited.
我們的年度募款會議將於八月三日傍晚七時舉行，會中將計劃未來一年的活動，誠邀所有成員參加。

Please accept my resignation from the Rembrandt Society.
請接受我的林布蘭學會退會申請。

To join the Frobisher Society today, simply indicate your membership category on the enclosed form and return it with your check.
想在今日加入佛比西協會，您只須在附件中的申請表上勾選您的會員類型，並與您的支票一起寄回。

Would you be willing to staff the Club's concession stand at the High-Lake Street Fair?
您是否願意擔任高湖街展銷會上社團攤位的工作人員呢？

Would you please place the following three items on the agenda for the November meeting?
您可否將以下三項議題加入十一月會議的議程？

段落

The Belford Area Women in Trades Organization invites you to attend its next monthly meeting, Thursday, June 14, at 7:30 p.m. in the old Belford Union Hall. Get to know us. See what we're trying to do for women in trades in this area. And then, if you like what you see, join up! Introductory one-year membership is $45, and we think we can do as much for you as you can do for the Organization!

貝爾福地區女性貿易協會邀請您出席下一月度會議，於六月十四日星期四傍晚七點半在舊貝爾福聯合會堂。來認識我們，看看我們想為本地貿易界女性做的事情。而後，如果您喜歡您所見到的，加入我們！新會員一年會費為 45 元。我們相信，我們能為您做的，就跟您能為協會做的一樣多！

I understand you and some other employees have formed several noon-hour foreign language clubs. I would be interested in joining your Italian-speaking group. Can you put me in touch with whoever is in charge of it? Thanks.

我知道你與其他員工組成幾個午間外語小組。我希望能加入義大利語小組；你能不能把我引薦給負責的人呢？謝謝。

Thanks so much for helping to clean up after the dance last Saturday. It's certainly not a popular job, which makes me appreciate all the more the good-hearted folks who did pitch in. The next time you're on the cleanup committee, you can put my name down!

謝謝你在上週六的舞會後協助清理環境。這絕不是人人搶著做的工作，所以像你這樣願意貢獻的好心人讓我更是感激。下次當你參加清潔委員會時，你可以加上我的名字！

示範信

TO: Admissions Committee
FROM: Paul Dombey
DATE: April 16, 2017
RE: Recommendation for membership

　　It is my pleasure to propose Louisa and John Chick for membership in the Granger Social Club. I know Louisa and John both personally and professionally; he is a fellow merchant, owner of Chick Book & Stationery, and she is Louisa Dombey, my sister. I recommend them to you highly.

They are both graduates of Walter Gay University, members of Trinity Lutheran Church, and hosts of a weekly book club. In addition, Ms. Chick is currently president and part owner of the Women's Collective and Mr. Chick has served as vice president of the local merchants' group.

They are charming people, committed and accomplished tennis players, and assets to the community. I think the Club would benefit from welcoming them as members.

Sincerely,

收件人：審查委員會
寄件人：保羅・東比
日期：二〇一七年四月十六日
關於：會員推薦信

　　我很樂意推薦露易莎與約翰・奇可夫婦加入格蘭傑社交俱樂部。我與露易莎及約翰於公於私都有交情。約翰經商，是奇可書籍與文具公司的所有人，而露易莎・東比是我的姊姊。我強烈推薦他們。

　　他們都是華特蓋伊大學的畢業生、三一路德教會的一員、每週讀書會的主持人。此外，奇可太太目前還是婦女會的主席與共同所有人，奇可先生則為本地商業團體的副主席。

　　他們都很有魅力、是認真的網球高手、是社會的資產。讓他們加入會員，我相信會為俱樂部帶來助益。

〇〇敬上

To: Board of Directors

It is with much regret that I resign my position as Secretary of the Macduff Drama Club. Family complications oblige me to withdraw from any evening activities at least for the foreseeable future. If I can be of any help to my successor, I am available by telephone.

I have thoroughly enjoyed my association with the Macduff Club. Best wishes to all of you. I look forward to joining you again as soon as possible.

致：董事會

　　我很遺憾必須辭去麥道夫戲劇社的祕書一職。由於家庭狀況，我必須空下傍晚的時間，至少在可見的未來皆須如此。若我能在任何方面協助我的繼任者，請隨時以電話與我聯絡。

　　我非常享受在麥道夫戲劇社度過的時光。深深祝福您們，並期待能盡快再次加入您們。

✉ 參見：03 回應、10 歡迎信、15 公告通知、18 邀請函、20 請求與詢問、22 拒絕、30 推薦信、39 募款信

Chapter 20

請求與詢問
Requests and Inquiries

> 要知道怎麼問問題。
> 對一些人來說，這實在太困難了；
> 對其他人來說，則是再簡單也不過。
>
> ——十七世紀西班牙思想家巴爾塔沙·葛拉西安
> (Baltasar Gracián)

要維持個人或組織之間的想法及資源交流，請求信（請求某件事情）與詢問信（想知道某件事情）是很重要的。這兩種信是雙方首次接觸的契機，無論是在企業與潛在客戶之間，或是求才者與應徵者、出版社與賣家之間。正因如此，這些信必須扮演優秀的外交大使才行。

只有在有問題出現時，才需要寫請求信與詢問信。

最常見的請求（更改保險受益人、申請保險理賠、購屋）通常會先從打電話開始，再填寫適當的表單。

 PART 1 說明篇

何時需要寫請求／詢問信？

提出客訴 參見：25 抱怨與客訴	**提出建議** 參見：34 報告與提案	**請求會面或開會議** 參見：06 預約會面	**請求面試** 參見：27 申請信、 28 求職信
請求介紹 參見：09 介紹信	**請求捐贈** 參見：39 募款信	**請求協助**	**請求延後**

請求原諒	請求借錢貸款	請求付款	申請信用資訊
參見：13 致歉信	參見：41 信貸相關信	參見：38 催款信、 41 信貸相關信	參見：41 信貸相關信
邀請講者	詢問商品	申請文件資料	投標與估價
詢問訂位	請求加薪	詢問是否收到禮物	
參見：49 旅遊相關信	參見：36 職場相關信	參見：17 後續追蹤信	

該怎麼說？

1. 清晰、簡短陳述你的請求，以有禮貌的詞組起頭，如 Please send me...「請寄給我……」或 May I please have...「請給我……」。

2. 提供細節資訊，這樣對方才能把你需要的東西正確寄給你（參考號碼、日期、描述、標題）。

3. 如果適合，以及如果這能讓對方更準確提供你所需要的，簡要解釋如何使用這些資料。（寫信給病理學家詢問一起謀殺案牽涉到的程序時，若你能告訴對方你是個推理小說作家在收集背景資料，而不是準備立案的檢察官或需要醫療紀錄的醫生，對方才會知道要給你什麼。）

4. 指出希望對方採取的具體行動或給予的回應。

5. 提供能讓收件人想要回信的理由。法國哲學家拉布魯耶（La Bruyère）曾說：「要在世上出人頭地的最好方法，是讓人們相信，幫助你對他們有好處。」

6. 適合的話，主動提議由你支付影印、郵資或手續費等費用。

7. 明確指出須獲得回應的期限。

8. 如果信很長，最後把請求再講一次。

9. 感謝對方付出的時間與關注。結尾時，表示有信心對方會給予正面回覆。

10. 適合的話，隨信附上回郵信封。或請對方把資料寄送某地址，或打電話、傳真或寄電子郵件給某人。

- 不要只說索取「information」（資料）。有些公司有上百種手冊說明其產品與服務，當你的請求不明確時，就得不到需要的資訊。如果你不知道有哪些資料可供索取，可以加一句：I would appreciate any other information you think might be helpful.「如果有任何其他資料您認為有幫助，我也會很感謝。」

- 不要表現出抱歉的態度（除非你的請求真的很耗費時間或很難解決）。避免這類的句子：I hope this is not too much trouble.「我希望這不會太麻煩您。」；I'm sorry to inconvenience you.「我很抱歉帶給您不便。」只須順道提起你對於對方時間、才能與資源的敬重，如 I know how busy you are.「我知道您有多忙碌。」但不要老往負面想。每個人都有請求，當你越實事求是且有禮貌，你便越有機會能獲得正面的回覆。

- 避免顯得太過霸道，不要暗示你有權利獲得資訊、服務或幫助。你要做的是請求，而非要求。

20 請求與詢問

寫作訣竅

- 要簡短，避免不必要的解釋，也不需用不同的方式問相同的問題。再三重讀你的信，確認你的問題很容易就能回答。櫃檯人員有太多信要回覆，但他們沒有足夠的時間細看。

- 利用主旨列，使收件人能迅速掌握情況：Re: piano tuning rates「關於：鋼琴調音價格」；Subject: airbag safety information「主旨：安全氣囊使用安全須知」；Re: mountaineering and ice climbing expeditions in North America「關於：北美登山與攀冰探險」；Subject: recipes using cranberries「主旨：蔓越莓食譜」。若是簡單、講求效率的請求，不須寫出信首稱謂，而主旨列可獨立存在。

- 當請求有一個以上時，請分行書寫，並在前面加上數字（從最重要到最不重要），收件人便能在回應每個請求後標上記號。

- 具體描述需要的資訊：退還硬碟的郵寄教學、如何向地方法院申請變更法定名稱、旺季的空房與價格、一月一日至六月三十日期間的缺勤人數等。你提供越多資訊，你得到的資料便會越有幫助。

- 有些寫信專家會建議不要用「thank you」（謝謝您）或「thanking you in advance」（提前謝謝您）結束請求信（因為這些句子暗示交流已進入尾聲），但現在這種用法已經很常見且

得到認可。有些人喜歡這種用法，認為能讓信結束得乾淨俐落，所以不自覺就會使用。你也可以用 I appreciate your time and attention.「謝謝您的時間與關注。」或 I look forward to hearing from you.「我期待您的回覆。」來結尾。

- 要讓對方很容易就能回覆你：附上調查表或問卷；提供貼有回郵的明信片，上面印有訊息及可填入資訊的空格；在每個問題下空出一些空間，對方就能快速寫下回應，再放入隨附的回郵信封中寄回。當對方願意協助你，而你們兩人之中必須有人負擔郵資、材料費或其他協助費用，那當然你要提議由你來支付這些費用。當你請求某人幫你做事情時，務必附上回郵信封；但如果你詢問資訊的對象是想跟你做生意的公司，便不必這麼做。

特殊狀況

- **寫信詢問對方是否已經收到禮物時**，描述禮物、寄送的時間，並幫對方找一個保留面子的藉口，如 I know you are especially busy just now.「我知道你最近特別忙。」你也可以告訴對方，你之所以寫信詢問，是因為你有幫這個包裹保險，所以如果它沒寄達，你想要追蹤它的去向，或考慮停止支票的支付。你並不一定要解釋詢問的理由，但這麼做是很得體的。

- 為研討會、銷售簡報及其他商業活動**預約設備**時，首先必須打電話去了解價格、可預約日期與設備類型。寫信確認預約時，須包含：時間、日期、預計出席人數、所需器材與用品、茶點安排、帳單資訊、公司中的聯絡人姓名（如果不是你的話），以及其他達成共識的事項。

- 以寫信的方式（而不是面談）**要求加薪時**，首先說明你在公司裡的職位，以及希望提高的金額。列出你認為應當加薪的理由：工時過長、職責過多、工作上取得的成就、重要的業績、習得新技能。盡可能使用數據說明，如「increase of 10 percent」（增加百分之十）。強調自上次加薪以來你完成的工作。抱怨部門中的其他人做得比你少、拿得比你多，是不會有結果的。在結束前重複你最有力的論點，再以祝福與感謝收尾。

- **申請醫療紀錄**給其他醫師、醫院或保險公司時，可寫：
Dear Dr. [name], I hereby authorize you to release my medical file to [name of recipient]. I will appreciate this being done as soon as possible. Thank you.
〔姓名〕醫師您好：我在此授權給您，請將我的醫療紀錄寄發給〔收件方名稱〕。我希望此手續能盡快完成，謝謝您。

- **請求使用版權物時**，要讓對方很容易點頭答應。寄送兩份表單或你的信，讓對方可以簽名、填上日期，並將其中一份寄還給你。附上回郵信封。確切描述你希望使用的內容（書或文章標題、頁數、行數或段落數、節錄內容的影本）。告訴對方你打算如何使用此材料（你的書或文章的標題、預計出版日期、出版社、價格、預計印刷份數、其他與預期讀者群及發行有關的資料）。告知對方你會如何在作品中聲明版權，並請求對方同意。感謝對方考慮你的請求，如果你希望的話，也可以讚美對方的作品。

- **邀請某人演講時**，提供下列資訊：你的組織名稱；日期、時間、活動地點、路線指示或地圖；希望的演講長度與主題；舉辦活動的理由或活動焦點；描述組織的興趣與背景，讓演講者對於聽眾有基本了解；預估聽眾人數；預計演講者須到達及可離開的時間；是否會支付報酬、補償演講者的交通費與住宿費；可用的器材（麥克風、投影機）；聯絡人的姓名與電話號碼（如果不是你的話）。
- **請求估價或投標時**，要具體：數量、時限（招標、完工）；特殊條件；類型、型號、顏色；你希望包含在總價中的項目列表。為確保不會遺漏任何重要事項，可使用之後會給對方簽署的合約內容作為寫信的範本。
- **若須比較不同公司的服務**（辦公室維修、草坪維護、駕訓班、地毯清理），可將同一封詢問資訊的信，寄給當地所有提供該服務的公司。

格式

- 公司外部的商務請求信必須用打字的，通常會打在有信頭的信紙上。備忘錄用紙則是用於公司內部請求。
- 私人請求可以打字或手寫在商務或私人信紙上。越私人的請求，越適合手寫在折頁卡片或私人信紙上。
- 明信片很適合用於只有一行的請求。
- 如果你必須重複請求同一件事，可使用制式信，或在備忘錄用紙上留下空格，讓你填入想請求的商品名稱。
- 當你請求的對象是一間有官方網站的公司時，時常會使用電子郵件。電子郵件也可以用於較不正式或例行的請求。

PART 2 應用篇

單字

appeal (n.) & (v.) 請求	grant (v.) & (n.) 給予；補助金	product (n.) 產品	refer (v.) 參考、提及
assistance (n.) 協助	grateful (a.) 感謝的	prompt (a.) 迅速的	require (v.) 需要
brochure (n.) 小冊子	immediately (adv.) 立即地	query (n.) & (v.) 疑問；提問	rush (n.) & (v.) 匆忙
expedite (v.) 加速執行	information (n.) 資訊	question (n.) 問題	seek (v.) 尋找
favor (n.) 幫助	inquiry (n.) 詢問、調查	questionnaire (n.) 問卷	solicit (v.) 請求
furnish (v.) 提供	instruction (n.) 指示	quickly (adv.) 快速地	urgent (a.) 緊急的
generous (a.) 慷慨的	problem (n.) 問題	reconsider (v.) 重新考慮	

詞組

additional information/time 額外資訊／時間	direct me to the appropriate agency 將我介紹給合適的機構
answer the following questions 回答下列問題	have the goodness to 有……的好意
anticipate a favorable response 期待正面回應	hope you are able to 希望你能夠
please provide us with/send details about 請提供我們／寄關於……的詳情	I'd appreciate having/receiving/obtaining 我希望能有／收到／獲取

appreciate any information/your cooperation/your help
感激任何資料／你的合作／你的幫助

as soon as possible
盡快

count on/upon
依賴

I'm writing to ask you
我寫信是為了問你

institute inquiries
展開調查

offer some assistance
給予一些幫助

it would be most helpful
這會很有幫助

I would appreciate your assessment of
我會很感激你對……的評估

I would be grateful/most grateful if/for
如果／為了……我會很感激

look forward to hearing from you
期待得到你的回音

interested in receiving information/learning more about
想收到資料／知道更多關於……的事

of great help to us
幫我們很大的忙

on account of/behalf of
由於／代表

please call me to discuss
請打電話給我討論

if you can find time in your busy schedule to
如果你能在百忙中抽空去做……

if you think it might be possible
如果你覺得這是可能的

by return mail
儘快回信

please let me have your estimate by
請在……之前讓我知道你的估價

apply/ask for
申請／請求

reply by return mail
以信件儘快回覆

respectfully request
恭敬地請求

take into consideration
納入考慮

thank you for your efforts in/to
謝謝你在……的努力

trouble you to/for
麻煩你

we would appreciate your taking a few minutes to
若你能花幾分鐘去……我們會很感謝

would you be willing to/good enough to
你是否願意／勞煩你

your considered opinion
你在深思熟慮後的意見

please reply by
請以……方式回覆

句子

Can you tell me which government agency might be able to give me background information on Minamata disease in Japan?

你可否告訴我，哪個政府單位能提供日本水俣症的背景資料？

Do you remember that you once offered to lend me Grandma's pearl ring for a special occasion?

你曾提議借出祖母的珍珠戒指讓我參加特殊場合，還記得嗎？

Enclosed is a self-addressed stamped envelope/an International Reply Coupon for your reply.

隨信附上回郵信封／國際回信郵票券，供你回覆。

How can a private citizen be named to the task force on the Resolution Trust Corporation?

普通公民如何才能加入清債信託公司的特別工作小組呢？

I am preparing a report for which I need annualized total returns for one, three, and five years through December 31—can you provide these by March 15?

我正在準備一份報告，因此需要一年、三年、五年內截至十二月三十一日的年度總收益，你可以在三月十五日前給我這些資料嗎？

I'd like to know how one goes about getting on your talk show.

我想知道如何才能參加你的脫口秀。

I have a favor to ask you, but I take "no" very well!

我想要請你幫個忙，你說「不」我也可以接受！

I'm wondering if you have the time to give us a little guidance.

我想知道您是否能抽空指導我們。

Is it true that it's possible to have stars named for people and, if so, how does one go about it?

可以用人名為星星命名，這件事是真的嗎？如果是真的，該怎麼做呢？

I would be interested in seeing some of the material that went into the preparation of your most recent occupational titles handbook.

我想看看你在準備最近一本職稱手冊時所使用的一些資料。

May I use your name as a reference when applying for a cashier position with Mawson's Country Inn?

我能不能將你列為我申請茂森鄉村飯店出納員的推薦人呢？

Please forward this letter to the appropriate person.
請將這封信轉寄給負責人。

Please send me any literature you have on antioxidant vitamins.
請寄給我你手邊關於抗氧化維生素的文獻。

This is a formal request to you to make some other arrangements for your cats; your lease clearly states that animals are not allowed in the building.
這是一個正式的請求，請你為你的貓另做安排；租約清楚寫明在此建築中不允許飼養動物。

We are contacting several industrial window cleaning firms to invite estimates.
我們正在聯絡數間工業廠房窗戶清潔公司提供估價。

We do not understand footnote (b) of Exhibit H—could you please explain it?
我們不能理解陳列品 H 的註腳 (b)，可以請你解釋嗎？

Will you please send me a copy of your current foam and sponge rubber products catalog along with information on bulk order discounts?
可否請你寄給我一份目前泡沫海綿橡膠的產品型錄，以及大量訂購的優惠資訊？

Will you please send me a list of those trash haulers in Willard County that contract by volume rather than by flat fee?
可否請您寄給我一份清單，上面列有威勒郡中以量計費（而非固定費用）的垃圾處理公司？

Your order forms, prices, and ordering instructions are oriented toward institutions—can you tell me how an individual can obtain your materials?
貴公司的訂購表格、價格與訂購指示都是針對機構的，可否告訴我，個人客戶要如何訂購你們的材料？

段落

My Maundrell watch, which is still under warranty, has stopped running for no apparent reason. I'm told there is nothing wrong with the battery. Please tell me where to bring or send it for repair under the warranty.

我的蒙瑞爾手錶仍在保修期，但它無緣無故停止運作。據我所知，電池沒有問題。請讓我知道我該把它帶或寄到哪裡，以使用保修服務。

Please send a copy of your guide to the best American colleges. Enclosed is my check for $21.95.

請寄給我一份最佳美國大學指南。隨信附上 21.95 元支票。

We are interested in replacing the decorative stone brick on our home and would like you to give us an estimate on your lightweight "cultured stone." Please call either of us at work during the day or at home during the evening (see enclosed business cards) to set up an appointment. Thank you.

我們想要替換我們家的裝飾石磚，所以希望你可以針對你們的輕量「人造石」為我們估個價。請打電話給我們其中一人預約時間，日間請打到公司，傍晚打到家裡（請見附上的名片）。謝謝。

Several bowling teams in the tri-county area are establishing a league that will sponsor a series of competitions. We will be needing trophies, plaques, and ribbons. We are also interested in seeing your line of name tags, medals, incentives, T-shirts, caps, and jackets. Please send your catalog and price lists. Thank you.

三郡區域的幾支保齡球隊正在建立一個聯盟，以後會主辦一系列的比賽。我們會需要獎盃、匾牌、緞帶。我們也有興趣看看你們名牌、獎牌、獎品、T 恤、帽子與夾克等產品線。請寄給我們型錄與價目表，謝謝。

20

請求與詢問

Dear Werfel Credit Advisers Inc.,

I believe I need a credit counselor to help with my current financial goals: to reestablish a good credit rating, to set up a workable debt repayment plan, to analyze and prioritize my present spending patterns, to learn how to budget, and, in general, to get my finances under control.

Would you please send me complete information on your services, including fees? I would also like the names of several people with whom you have worked who would be willing to recommend you. What I absolutely do not need at this time is more delay and confusion in my money life.

Thank you.

威佛信用顧問公司你好：

我需要一名信用顧問來協助達成目前的財務目標：重新建立良好的信用等級、制定可行的債務償付計畫、分析我目前的消費模式並排出優先順序、學習如何規劃預算。整體而言，我希望我的財務狀況可以穩定下來。

你可否寄給我完整的服務資訊，包括價格？我也希望你提供幾個你曾經協助過、願意推薦你的人的姓名。我目前最不需要的，就是在我的金錢世界中出現更多的遲滯不前與混亂困惑。

謝謝。

Dear Mr. Eldrige:

Would you be willing to speak to the *Challis University English Department* about your recent book, Grammar and the Grammarian, sometime this next spring? Several department members have heard you speak; all of us have read your book. We meet the third Wednesday of every month and hope that one of those Wednesdays will fit into your schedule.

If you think this is possible, please call me to discuss the honorarium.

Hoping for a favorable reply, I am

Sincerely yours,

艾德里吉先生您好：

接下來的春季，您是否願意在查利斯大學英文系上講講您最近的新書《文法與文法家》？系上有幾名成員都聽過您的演講，而我們大家都讀過您的書。我們固定每個月的第三個週三聚會，並希望其中一個週三可以排進你的行程中。

若您覺得這是可能的安排，請打電話給我討論酬金。

希望能得到您的正面回覆。

○○敬上

20

請求與詢問

Dear Mr. Imhof,

Would it be possible for me to move my desk?

A number of factors about my desk's present location make concentration difficult at times. The shipping clerk traffic just outside the door adjacent to my desk is unrelenting and distracting, the lighting over my desk is poor, and I have a direct view of an office in which the person spends some time every day tending to matters of personal hygiene.

The spot to the left of the lightboard would be perfect for my desk. I'd need an extension cord to reach an outlet for my computer and desk light, but that should be no problem. If Mr. Wahnschaffe could spare ten minutes to help me move my desk and computer, I'd be all set.

I would really appreciate being able to move. Thank you!

印賀夫先生您好：

我有沒有可能換位置呢？

很多因素影響之下，我目前的位置使我很難專心。在門外靠近我桌子的地方，總是持續有運貨員來來往往令我分心；我桌上的燈光很暗；我目光直接對到的房間，裡頭是一位每天多花費相當多時間處理個人衛生的人。

在透明光板左方的位置，會是擺放我的桌子的絕佳地點。我會需要一組延長線，不然我的電腦與桌燈無法插上插座，不過這應該不是個問題。如果萬薛佛先生可以挪出十分鐘幫我移動桌子與電腦的話，那我一切就準備就緒了。

如果能夠移動，我真的會非常感激。謝謝您！

Dear Morris,

I'm thinking of leaving Langdon Glass Works (I'll tell you why next time I see you) and am currently on the lookout for a good sales management position.

You seem to know everyone in the industry (and everybody knows you)—would you mind letting me know if you hear of any openings?

I appreciate being able to ask you this. Let's get together soon.

Sincerely,

親愛的莫里斯：

我在思考離開蘭登玻璃工藝（下次見到你再告訴你原因），所以現在正在找尋不錯的銷售管理職位。

你似乎認識這個產業的每一個人（而每個人也都認識你）；如果你有聽說任何職缺，你是否願意讓我知道呢？

能向你詢問這件事，我覺得很感激。我們趕緊聚會吧。

〇〇上

✉ 參見：03 回應、06 預約會面、09 介紹信、12 致謝函、18 邀請函、33 募款信、36 職場相關信、37 訂單處理信、38 催款信、41 信貸相關信、42 銷售信、49 旅遊相關信

Chapter 21

接受
Acceptances

理智給我們千百種說不的方式，
但說「是」的方法只有一種，也就是發自內心。

——美國電視主持人蘇西・歐曼（Suze Orman）

一旦你決定接受邀請或請求，不妨直接說出口；這是最簡單的一種信。

如果你的「是」並非發自內心，你的接受函也會看起來冷淡疏離，不久後你甚至可能反悔。下定決心說「是」，比寫接受函本身更難。

PART 1 說明篇

接受函的使用時機

同意加入 學校、俱樂部、組織協會	**接受邀請** 聚餐、會議、派對	**給予會員身分** 董事會、委員會、組織協會
同意加盟	**接受提案**	**提供工作**
接受演講邀請 研討會、工作坊、宴會	**同意請求** 答應參與、給予協助	**接受婚禮邀請** 參見：50 婚禮相關信

該怎麼說？

1. 表達接受邀請、提議、出價或請求的喜悅。
2. 複述對方提到而你也接受的細節，如會面時間、出價金額或你貢獻的程度、提供協助的具體方式、或你答應承擔的責任。
3. 提出特定需求：符合免稅標準之捐贈收據、邀請人聯絡資訊、演講所需器材、或其他相關單位名單。
4. 在結語表達喜悅之情，或提及未來的行動，如預計完成的事項、預計採取的行動、或回報的方式。

什麼不該說？

勿給太多但書，避免寫出以下句子：「我很忙，但我應該處理得來」；「我已有兩個行程，但會試著過去打聲招呼」；「我不會是個好講者，但我會試試看」。給一個直截了當的「是」；如果你猶豫，拒絕是比較好的選擇。

寫作要點

- 盡快寄出接受函。如果遲寄可以道歉，但不需詳述理由。
- 接受函多半簡短，而且只跟「接受」有關。
- 知名修辭專家魯道夫‧傅萊區（Rudolf Flesch）曾說：「如果你對一個請求的回應為『是』，那麼以『是』作為一封信的開頭，是很不錯的選擇。」
- 展現熱情。直接告訴對方你樂意接受，並複述與邀約相關的細節。如果你能再說一些私人、有趣或輕鬆的話題，那你與邀請人、雇主或朋友的關係會更好。
- 收到的邀請函上有一個以上的署名時，請在回覆中提及所有名字。可將接受函寄給信中的聯絡人，或第一個署名的人。
- 如果你收到的邀請函寫著「請回覆」（RSVP 或 Please reply.），請立即回覆，這是義務的、必要的且重要的。

特殊狀況

- **收到錄取工作通知時**，請寫一封接受函表達你的熱忱與喜悅，並確認工作相關細節。
- **寫接受函通知申請人錄取工作時**，納入以下內容：恭喜申請人獲得錄用的賀詞，並讚賞對方資歷、經驗或面試表現；工作相關資訊—職責、薪資、主管姓名與到職日；公司聯絡人姓名

與電話；公司在員工待遇方面的優勢。請強調為你們公司工作的一些好處，吸引錄取者接受這份工作。

- **參加婚禮時**，夫妻可以一人接受邀請、一人拒絕。請與邀請人確認這是否可行。
- **兒童收到邀約時**，也可以寫簡短的接受函：Thank you for inviting me to your Halloween party. Wait till you see my costume!「謝謝你邀請我參加你的萬聖節派對，期待我的服裝吧！」

格式

- 以收到的邀請函格式作為回覆的範本。如果邀請函是用手寫的，回覆也請用手寫；如果對方用有正式信頭的信箋，你也使用有信頭的信紙回覆；邀請函是以電子郵件寄達，也請以電子郵件回覆；要是邀請函採用非正式的用語，你的回覆也保持非正式；當你回覆正式邀請函時，請用與邀請函幾乎完全相同的文字、編排與文體。

21

接受

單字

accept (v.) 接受	gratifying (a.) 滿意的	satisfying (a.) 滿足的	touched (a.) 感動的
approve (v.) 同意	pleased (a.) 樂意的	thoughtful (a.) 體貼周到的	willing (a.) 願意的
welcome (v.) 歡迎	delighted (a.) 高興的	thrilled (a.) 興奮的	pleasure (n.) 喜悅
certainly (adv.) 一定			

詞組

able to say yes
同意

accept with pleasure
欣然接受

agree to
同意做……

glad to be able to vote yes
很高興能投贊成票

happy to let you know
很高興告訴你

I am pleased/happy/honored to accept
我很高興／開心／榮幸接受……

it is with great pleasure that
樂於……

it was so thoughtful of you to
您做……真體貼周到

it will be a pleasure to
很樂意能……

pleased to have been invited
很高興能被邀請

thank you for asking me to
謝謝您邀請我……

thank you for nominating me for
謝謝您提名我……

we are delighted to accept
我們很樂意接受……

we are sincerely happy to join you
真的很高興能加入您們

we have accepted your bid of
我們接受您對於……的出價

we look forward with pleasure
我們滿心喜悅期待

句子

After reviewing your application, we are pleased to be able to offer you the funding requested.
在審查您的申請後，我們很高興提供您所申請的補助金。

I accept with pleasure the position of senior research chemist.
我很榮幸接受這個資深化學研究員的職位。

I am happy to be able to do this.
我很高興能夠這麼做。

I appreciate very much (and accept) your generous apology.
我感謝（並接受）你誠摯的道歉。

I'll be happy to meet with you in your office March 11 at 10:30 to plan this year's All-City Science Fair.
我很樂意於三月十一日上午十點三十分在您辦公室與您會面，一起計畫今年度的全市科學博覽會。

In a word, absolutely!
簡而言之，當然願意！

In response to your letter asking for support for the Foscari Children's Home, I'm enclosing a check for $500.
回應您來信詢問資助法斯卡利兒童之家的意願，我在此附上 500 元美金支票。

Thank you for inviting me to speak at the Chang-Ch'un Meditation Center next month.
謝謝您邀請我下個月至長春禪修中心演講。

We accept your kind invitation with great pleasure.
我們欣然接受您的盛情邀約。

We are happy to accept your estimate for refinishing our Queen Anne dining room suite.
我們願意接受您修整安妮女王式餐廳傢俱組的報價。

We are pleased to grant you the six-week extension you requested to complete your work.
我們願意按您的要求給您六週延展期完成工作。

We are pleased to tell you that your application for admission to the Emmet School has been approved.
我們很高興通知您，您提出的艾默特學校入學申請已獲准。

We look forward to working with you.
我們期待與您共事。

21
接受

段落

I will be delighted to have dinner with you on Friday, the sixteenth of March, at seven o'clock. Thanks so much for asking me. I can hardly wait to see you and Anders again.

很高興能與你在三月十六日週五七點共用晚餐。非常謝謝你的邀請，我等不及再次見到你與安德斯了。

Thanks for telling me how much the children at St. Joseph's Home liked my storytelling the other night. I'm happy to accept your invitation to become a regular volunteer and tell stories every other Thursday evening. Do you have a CD player so that I could use music with some of the stories?

謝謝您告訴我聖喬瑟夫兒童之家的孩子很喜歡我那晚的說故事活動。我很高興能接受您的邀請成為固定志工，於每隔週週四傍晚為孩子說故事。您是否能提供唱片播放機，方便我幫一些故事搭配音樂呢？

I'm looking forward to your graduation and the reception afterward. Thanks for including me.

我很期待參加你的畢業典禮與接下來的茶會，謝謝你邀請我。

Your bid of $6,780 to wallpaper our reception rooms has been accepted. Please read the enclosed contract and call with any questions. We were impressed with the attention to detail in your proposal and bid, and we are looking forward to our new walls.

您提案以 6,780 元美金為我們的接待室貼壁紙，此報價已獲接受。請詳閱附件的契約書，有任何問題，歡迎打電話詢問。您的提案與報價很注重細節，令我們印象深刻，我們很期待我們的新牆面。

21

接受

示範信

Dear Selina,

Vickers and I accept with pleasure your kind invitation to a celebration of your parents' fiftieth wedding anniversary on Saturday, July 16, at 7:30 p.m.

Sincerely,

親愛的莎琳娜：

於七月十六日下午七點半，維克與我很高興能參加您父母的結婚五十週年慶祝會。

〇〇敬上

Dear Ms. Thirkell,

I am pleased to accept your offer of the position of assistant director of the Gilbert Tebben Working Family Center.

I enjoyed the discussions with you, and I look forward to being part of this dynamic and important community resource.

The salary, hours, responsibilities, and starting date that we discussed during our last meeting are all agreeable to me. I understand that I will receive the standard benefits package, with the addition of two weeks' vacation during my first year.

Sincerely yours,
Laurence Dean

瑟克爾小姐您好：

我很高興能接受這個職位，成為吉爾 · 泰本勞工家庭中心的副總監。

我很享受那天與您的討論，也期待成為這個活躍而重要的社會資源的一部分。

在我們最後一次會面中所討論的薪資、工時、職責與到職日，我都同意接受。我也明白我會獲得標準員工福利，並於第一年享有額外兩週的休假。

勞倫斯 · 狄恩謹上

Dear Mr. Van Druten,

In response to your letter of February 10, we are pleased to grant you a two-month extension of the loan of the slides showing scenes of our amusement park. We appreciate being able to help you add, as you said, "a bit of amusement" to your corporate meetings.

We offer this extension with our compliments.

Cordially,
Laura Simmons

范杜騰先生您好：

在此答覆您於二月十日的來信。我們很樂意讓您的租期展延兩個月，此期間您可繼續租用展示我們樂園的投影片。

我們很高興能夠協助您；如您所言，望貴公司會議能因此增添「些許樂趣」。

我們以此展延信向您問候。

勞菈‧西蒙斯敬啟

Dear Dr. Cheesewright:

Thank you for inviting me to speak at your county dental society's dinner banquet on October 26 at 7:00. I am happy to accept and will, as you suggested, discuss new patient education strategies.

I'm not sure how much time you have allotted me—will you let me know?

With best wishes,

契斯萊特醫師您好：

謝謝您邀請我於十月二十六日七點在您們州內的牙醫協會晚會進行演講。我很高興能接受您的邀請，並會如您所建議的，在演講中討論新的衛教策略。

我不太確定您安排給我多長時間做這場演講，可以麻煩您告訴我嗎？

○○謹復

Mr. Clarence Rochester
accepts with pleasure
William Portlaw and Alida Ascott's
kind invitation to dinner
on the sixteenth of June at 7:30 p.m.
but regrets that
Dr. Maggie Campion
will be absent at that time.

克勞倫斯‧羅徹斯特先生
欣然接受
威廉‧波洛與愛莉姐‧艾絲考特
盛情的晚餐邀約
於六月十六日下午七點半
但遺憾告知
瑪姬‧坎朋博士
此次無法到場。

✉ 參見：03 回應、22 拒絕

Chapter 22

拒絕
Refusals

多數的人都討厭說不，
但遠不及他們討厭聽到不的程度。

——溝通專家兼作家黛安・布赫（Dianne Booher）

當我們對邀約的活動毫無興趣，並有合理的理由拒絕時（例如不在國內或是沒錢），寫拒絕信相當容易。但在其他情況下說不，便是個挑戰。

寫拒絕信（letter of refusal，也稱做 regret 或 rejection）之前，你必須先確認你確實想說不，因為模稜兩可的態度只會削弱你的口氣。適合用來說不的方式之一，是一句簡單的「我不想」。如果你有具體理由，可以寫出來，不過你其實沒有義務要為你的拒絕辯護。對方若因為你說不而感到憤怒、試圖控制你，或想讓你有罪惡感，那他想必是把請求誤以為要求了。

 PART 1 說明篇

用拒絕信向什麼說不？

客訴或索賠	申請	禮物	邀約
提案	請求	銷售	婚禮邀請

該怎麼說？

1. 具體描述對方的提議、請求或邀請，並表達感謝。
2. 客氣地同意對方：目標值得追求、提案考慮周全、履歷令人印象深刻、邀請很吸引人。
3. 說不。表達你的遺憾，因為你必須這麼做。
4. 若你希望的話，可以解釋你的立場。
5. 若適合的話，可提議替代的行動或其他資源。
6. 在結尾處，以愉悅的口氣表示你希望下次能幫得上忙、能再次見到對方，或祝福對方成功。

什麼不該說？

- 你的回應不該讓對方感到疑惑。用堅定語氣說「不」。
- 不要說謊。如果你拒絕的理由是根據某部分的事實，你面對自己與對方都會感到比較自在。
- 不要長篇大論，或用複雜難懂的藉口或辯解。這並沒有說服力，儘管你說的都是事實。英國小說家阿道斯・赫胥黎（Aldous Huxley）曾說過：「一個藉口總是比多個藉口更令人信服。」
- 不要針對個人做任何主觀性評論（關於外表、個性、行為、語言能力）。儘管你認為這對他有幫助，但這種評語還是留給他們生命中的其他人來說吧。

22
拒絕

寫作訣竅

- 立即回覆。古羅馬文學家普布里烏斯・西魯斯（Publilius Syrus）說過：「拒絕得越迅速，造成的失望便越小。」有事相求或邀請你去某個活動的人，通常必須趕快得到回應。你早點拒絕，他們才有時間找其他解決方案或邀請別人。
- 要得體。不要用對方的邀請內容作為拒絕的理由；反之，以自己的不足作為拒絕理由，如 need someone who is bonded「需要有第三方保證」；another meeting that day「當天已有會議」；will be out of town「會去遠門」；或直接說 will be unable to help「無法協助」。
- 拒絕之前先說出理由，如此收信人便有了心理準備，也不會因為被拒絕太過失望而「聽」不進去你的理由。不要說「我無法參加你的畢業典禮，因為我那一週要去加州」，而要說 I am going to be in California the week of June 2, which means I won't, unfortunately, be able to attend your graduation.「我在六月二日那一週要去加州，這也表示我很可惜無法參加你的畢業典禮。」
- 在有些情況下，你可以用 policy（政策）這個字，這表示你的決定沒有商量的餘地，如 The family has a policy that leaves donations to the Board's discretion.「家族政策是交由董事會處理捐款。」policy 表示你已經考慮過你受到的限制，而這些限制難以反駁。

- 你也可以打出「個人」牌：I'm dealing with several difficult issues right now and I don't feel I can handle anything else. But thanks for asking. 「我目前正在處理數件困難的問題，無法再應付別的事情，但還是謝謝你問我。」這是你對於自己的評估，文明人是不會跟你爭執這點的。

- 降低失望。提供其他協助；建議其他可能提供協助的人選；贊同他們提到的某一點；為無法同意請求致上歉意；指出你的回絕能帶來的好處；感謝他們的興趣、請求或關心。

- 不過，禮貌小姐茱蒂絲‧馬丁不建議把失望降到最低。她認為，當你拒絕別人，對方一定會覺得遭到否定；要是他們不覺得遭到否定，他們就不會放棄。無痛的拒絕便不是拒絕，所以，請不要給予錯誤的希望。她建議拒絕信要寫得溫和、平淡、不必講求創意。

- 有時候，你拒絕申請人、提案、投標案或其他業務的方式，可能會讓你惹上官司。如果你擔心，在寫信前請先諮詢律師。

特殊狀況

- **無法出席邀約時**，而邀請卡上標有 RSVP「敬請賜覆」、Please reply「請回覆」或 Regrets only「不能出席請回覆」，請務必回信。這是義務的、強制的、必要的、強迫的、有責任的且重要的。

- 若**邀請函上有一個以上的署名**，在拒絕信中需寫出所有的姓名，並寄給 RSVP 下方列出的姓名，或寄給署名列於第一的姓名。

- **拒絕邀請時**，使用的格式應與邀請函完全相同。如果邀請函是用手寫的，你的回覆也用手寫；如果對方寄來有信頭的商用信紙，你也使用有信頭的信紙；要是邀請函採用非正式的用語，你的回覆也保持非正式；當你回覆正式邀請函時，請用與邀請函幾乎完全相同的文字、編排與文體。

- **拒絕應徵職位的申請人時**，包含以下內容：感謝對方的申請；簡單告知你無法錄取對方；需要時可以解釋原因；讚美申請人的資歷、能力、面試表現或履歷；適合的話，可以邀請對方下次再來應徵；祝福對方找到一個合適的職位。有些公司不會通知沒有錄取的申請人；不過，寫一封簡短、得體的信，能提升公司形象。若是收到不請自來的工作申請，你可以在回覆中感謝對方想到你們公司，並告訴對方目前沒有職缺，或提議保留對方的履歷並邀請他下次再聯絡。

- **拒絕一份工作時**，先感謝並讚美對方公司、面試官或人力資源部門。表達你的遺憾。合適的話，可以告訴對方你為何做此決定，但要著重在你的需求，而非對方的不足。以正面的話結尾，為未來的可能性開一扇門。

- **拒絕員工要求晉升、加薪或申請內部職位時：**
  (1) 感謝員工的貢獻，並列出對方具體的才能與長處；
  (2) 誠實且具體解釋為拒絕的理由；
  (3) 給予可能獲得晉升、加薪或其他職位的建議，而要是你的決定是基於跟對方無關的考量（主管太多、預算不足），則可告知什麼樣的改變才能使下次的請求成功。你的目標是讓員工覺得獲得尊重、動力與鼓勵。

- **拒絕客戶申訴或索賠申請時**，仍要盡可能留住顧客。語氣要得體、貼心。可以的話，提出替代或折衷方案。向顧客表達你理解他們的立場、你們已仔細評估他們的申訴、你也很希望能答應他們。接著，為你的「不」給一個合理的解釋。利用事實或文件來證明你們並不保證能處理客訴。一封簡短、明確的書面拒絕信，便能讓多數的顧客滿意。有些顧客會回信逐條反駁；當這種情況發生時，須展現堅決的「不」，不必多做解釋。

- 許多公司與政府機關會明文規定處理招標的程序。當你有選擇時，請盡快通知投標廠商你們的條件。**拒絕投標案時**，要有禮貌、表現支持的態度，如果可能的話，簡短解釋投標遭拒的理由（尤其當對方未能遵照指示或符合某些原則時），或是中標者獲勝的原因。對你的承包商來說，這種資訊很有用。結尾時，表達感謝，並傳達未來可以合作的可能性。你並不需要說出得標者。

- **拒絕借貸的請求時**，要圓滑，畢竟對方仍然是你的顧客、潛在顧客或是朋友。感謝對方的詢問，謝謝他們關注你的公司或相信你們的友誼。
  如果對方申請的是**商業信貸**，須告訴對方你是如何做出決定（根據申請書、雇主推薦、背景調查、商業徵信所的檔案）。建議申請人改善信用等級，或尋找其他信貸來源，或在一段時間或解決某些財務問題後重新申請。
  若對方申請的是**個人信貸**，則可省略給予建議的步驟，直接告訴對方你這次幫不上忙。

- **拒絕稿件時**，大多都是以制式明信片或制式信通知。很少人能如字典之父詹森（Samuel Johnson）一樣風趣：「你的稿子不僅寫得好，也很有原創性；只是寫得好的部分沒有原創性，而有原創性的部分寫得不好。」寫信給作者時，要強調這個決定是出於你們出版社的需求與興趣，其他出版社可能會有所不同。向對方保證你已經仔細考慮過這個作品、謝謝他想到你，並祝福他將來能成功。

- **多數募款信**都是以大宗郵件寄出，如果你沒興趣，就不需回覆。不過，若你收到一封以限時郵件寄出的私人信函，且上面署名的是你認識的人，就會需要回覆。首先，讚美對方組織進行的工作，再給一個合理的藉口解釋不捐款的原因，最後致上祝福。你不必提供其他你不想揭露的細節；籠統告訴對方你目前已有其他負擔，也是可以的。如果你拒絕的原因在於不同意該組織的目標或政策，直言無妨。

- **終止商業合作或一段關係時**，要盡量達成「無過失」分開，不要怪罪另一方或翻舊帳。自己擔起分離的責任，替對方保留面子。要誠實，同時也要得體而友善。最重要的是，要簡短、明確；當你是真心想要結束一段關係時，解釋太多或太少都是很致命的。最後以鼓勵與讚美結尾。

- **拒絕異常堅持的人的請求時**，必須堅決、簡單、明確。不須解釋拒絕的原因，一句 I am sorry but I will not be able to.「我很遺憾但我無法。」便已足夠。當你說出拒絕的原因（「我目前真的很忙。」），他們就能立即做出回應（「這只需要一點時間。」）；而當你給出另一個理由，他們又會找出其他反駁的方式。他們的招數之一，就是讓你陷入疲憊的辯論之中。不斷重複「抱歉，但不行」是最有效的。

- **必須拒絕對方的禮物時**，先感謝對方的體貼、選了很好的禮物；解釋你必須退還的原因，如 Employees are prohibited from accepting gifts from suppliers.「員工禁止接受供應商的禮物。」 或 I hope you will understand, but I would feel uncomfortable accepting such an expensive gift from a client.「我希望您能理解，但從客戶手上收到這麼貴重的禮物，讓我心裡過意不去。」在拒絕信中要小心措詞，不能讓對方覺得送禮是個錯誤判斷。

22

拒絕

格式

- 商務上的拒絕信會打在有信頭的信紙上。
- 私人拒絕信通常是用手寫的。
- 例行的拒絕信可用制式信處理。
- 當別人以電子郵件寄出，也可以用電子郵件回覆拒絕。

單字

awkward *(a.)* 尷尬的、棘手的	impractical *(a.)* 不實際的	refuse *(v.)* 拒絕	unavailable *(a.)* 沒空的；缺貨的
contraindicated *(a.)* 禁忌的	obstacle *(n.)* 障礙	regretfully *(adv.)* 遺憾地	unfavorable *(a.)* 不利的
decline *(v.)* 婉拒	opposition *(n.)* 反對	reject *(v.)* 拒絕	unfeasible *(a.)* 不可行的
difficult *(a.)* 困難的	overextended *(a.)* 過分擴張的	reluctantly *(adv.)* 不情願地	unfortunately *(adv.)* 不幸地
dilemma *(n.)* 兩難	overstocked *(a.)* 庫存過剩的	respond *(v.)* 回應	unlikely *(a.)* 不可能的
doubtful *(a.)* 疑惑的	policy *(n.)* 政策	sorry *(a.)* 抱歉的	
impossible *(a.)* 不可能的	problem *(n.)* 問題	unable *(a.)* 沒有辦法的	

詞組

after much discussion/careful evaluation 多次討論／仔細評估之後	beyond the scope of the present study 超出本研究的範疇
although I am sympathetic to your problem/plight/situation 雖然我理解你的問題／困境／狀況	I know how understanding you are, so I'm sure 我知道你很通情達理，所以我確信
although the idea is appealing 雖然這個主意很吸引人	current conditions do not warrant 目前的狀況我無法保證
appreciate your asking me/us, but 謝謝你問我／我們，但是	disinclined at this time 這次需婉拒

company policy prohibits us from
公司政策禁止我們做

because of prior commitments
由於先前的承諾

previous commitments
先前的承諾

due to present budget problems
由於目前的預算問題

hope this will be of some help even though
儘管……希望這會幫上一點忙

I appreciate your asking me, but
謝謝你問我，但是

if it were possible
倘若可能的話

I'm sorry to tell you
我很遺憾告訴你

I must say no to
我必須向……說不

I regret that I cannot accept
我很遺憾我無法接受

it is, unfortunately, out of the question that
可惜這是毫無疑問的

it's a wonderful program, but
這是個很好的計畫，但是

it's currently impossible
目前這是不可能的

runs counter to
與……衝突；強碰到……

difficult decision
困難的決定

doesn't qualify/warrant
不合格／保證

don't have enough information
沒有足夠的資訊

not an option at the moment
不是目前可行的選項

not currently seeking
目前沒有在尋找

no, thank you
不用了，謝謝

not interested at this time
目前不感興趣

puts me in something of a dilemma
置我於兩難之中

regret to inform you
遺憾通知你

remain unconvinced of the value of
仍然無法確信……的價值

must decline/demur/pass up/ withdraw from/say no to
必須婉拒／反對／放棄／撤回／拒絕

sincerely regret
非常遺憾

sorry about this, but
對此很抱歉，但是

your idea has merit, but
你的想法有其價值，但是

I would like to help, but
我想要幫忙，但是

we appreciate your interest, but
我們感謝你的關注，但是

I wish I could say yes, but
我真希望我能答應，但是

we find that we cannot
我們發現我們無法

normally I would be delighted, but
通常我會很高興，但是

we have concluded with regret
我們遺憾地做出結論

not a choice I can make right now
不是我目前能做的選擇

we have now had a chance to review
我們現在有機會審核

unable to help/comply/grant/send/
contribute/offer/provide
無法幫忙／遵從／給予／寄送／捐贈／提出／
提供

句子

Although we appreciate your interest in Dempsey Toys, we do not feel that your product is one we could successfully market.
雖然我們很感謝您對丹普西玩具的興趣，但我們不認為我們能夠成功行銷您的產品。

Although your entry did not win, we wish you good luck and many future successes.
雖然您的參賽作品未能獲勝，我們仍祝福您一切順利、有成功的未來。

At this time there does not appear to be a position with us that is suited to your admittedly fine qualifications.
目前我們沒有職缺適合您的優秀資歷。

Fundraising is not one of my talents—is there anything else I could do for the committee?
募款並非我的強項，我能否在其他方面協助委員會？

I appreciate your offer but I want to try a few things before I go outside the firm for a solution.
我很感激你的提議，但我想在尋求公司外部協助之前，先嘗試一些方法。

I don't have the energy just now to do the project justice.
我目前分身乏術，難以公正處理此專案。

I don't think this will work for us.
我不認為這行得通。

If you reread your contract, specifically clause C1, you will see that we have no legal obligations in this regard.
若您重看一次合約，尤其是 C1 條款，您會發現我們在此方面並無法律義務。

I have taken on more projects than I can comfortably handle.
我負責的專案量已經超出我能妥善處理的範圍。

I hope this will help you understand why we are unable to furnish the additional funding you are requesting.
我希望這有助您了解為何我們無法提供您所要求的額外資金。

I know we'll be missing a wonderful time.
我知道我們會錯過許多美好時光。

I'm completely overwhelmed just now, and can't take on anything new.
我現在已經完全忙不過來了，無法再處理新的業務。

I'm sorry not to be able to give you the reference you requested in your letter of November 3.
你在十一月三日的來信請我提供參考信，但恕我無法提供。

I sympathize with your request and wish I could help.
我理解您的請求，但願我幫得上忙。

It's possible we would be interested sometime after the first of the year.
也許在一月一日後我們會有興趣。

I've made it a policy never to make personal loans.
我已經正式決定再也不會私下借款。

I will be out of town that evening—I regret that I'm unable to accept your kind invitation.
那天傍晚我要出遠門，很遺憾我無法接受你好意的邀請。

I wish I could be more helpful, but it's not possible now.
但願我能幫得上忙，但目前實在不可能。

I wish I didn't have to refuse you, Jerry, but I'm not in a position to make you the loan.
但願我不必拒絕你，傑瑞，但我現在的立場並不適合借錢給你。

May I take a rain check?
我可以推遲一會嗎？

Our present schedule is, unfortunately, inflexible.
可惜我們目前的時程無法更動。

Regarding your request to use my name in your fundraising literature, I must say no.
你請求在你的募款資料中使用我的姓名，但我必須拒絕。

Thank you, but we have had a regular purchasing arrangement with Burnside Office Supplies for many years.
謝謝，但多年以來我們一直都是向伯塞辦公用品公司進行採購。

The Board has, unfortunately, turned down your request.
很遺憾，董事會已經駁回你的請求。

The position at Locksley International for which you applied has been filled.
您向洛克斯利國際公司應徵的職缺目前已找到人選。

Unfortunately, this is not a priority for Pettifer Grains at this time.
可惜這並不是派特菲穀物目前優先考慮的事項。

We appreciate your asking us, and hope that we will have the opportunity of saying yes some other time.
我們很感激您詢問我們，並希望下次我們會有機會答應。

We are unable to approve your loan application at this time.
我們這次無法通過您的貸款申請。

We have decided to accept another proposal.
我們已經決定接受另一項提案。

We have reviewed your credit application and regret to inform you that we are unable to offer you a bank card at this time.
我們已經審查過你的信用申請，很遺憾通知您，我們此次無法將銀行卡提供給您。

We regret that your work was not selected for inclusion in the symposium.
我們很遺憾，你的文章並未獲研討會的青睞。

We regret to inform you that Spenlow Paint & Tile is no longer considering applications for its sales positions.
我們很遺憾通知您，史本洛油漆與磚瓦公司已不再考慮任何應徵業務職位的申請。

We regret to say that a careful examination of your résumé does not indicate a particular match for our present needs.

很遺憾，在仔細審核您的履歷後，我們認為您並不符合我們目前的需求。

Your request comes at a particularly difficult time for me—I'm over-scheduled for the next two months.

你的請求恰好在我最忙的時候出現；我接下來兩個月的日程大爆滿了。

22

拒絕

段落

Thank you for your résumé. We considered your application carefully but have decided to offer the position to someone else. We will keep your application on file, however, and will contact you if we have a similar opening later. Please accept our best wishes as you seek a challenging and rewarding position.

謝謝您的履歷。我們仔細考慮了您的申請，但已決定將此職缺給予另一個人。不過，我們會保留您的申請文件，若我們之後有類似的職缺，會再聯絡您。在您尋找有挑戰性又有意義的職位的同時，請接受我們最深的祝福。

I am sorry to report that we are unable to extend credit to you at the present time. Our decision is based primarily on your lack of a credit record and on the brevity of your employment history. Please contact us again in six months, when we would be happy to discuss your request again.

我很遺憾告知您，我們目前無法讓您賒帳。我們做此決定，首先是因為您缺乏信用紀錄，而您的工作經驗也較短。請在六個月後再次聯絡我們，屆時我們很樂意再次與您討論您的請求。

Thank you for your invitation to join Glowry Health Services as a pharmacy technician. The beautiful new facilities, the friendly staff members, and the good interview I had with you were all very persuasive. However, I have also been offered a position forty-five minutes closer to home. To have more time with my family, I plan to accept it. I thank you for your time, attention, and good humor. I hope our paths cross again someday.

謝謝您邀請我加入葛羅瑞健康服務擔任藥房技術員。美麗的新設施、友善的公司成員以及與您的面試，都令我非常心動。然而，我也錄取了另一份工作，離我家近了四十五分鐘。為了有更多時間與我的家人相處，我打算接受那份工作。謝謝您的時間、關注與幽默。希望有一天我們有機會再次合作。

I've checked our production schedule and see no way of moving up your deliveries by two weeks. We are dependent on materials shipped to us by suppliers in other states who are unable to alter their timetables.

在查看我們的生產時間表之後，恕我無法將您的出貨日期提前兩週。我們需要來自不同州的供應商寄來的材料才能生產，而他們的時程表已無法更動。

22

拒絕

Dear Ms. Partlit,

Your request for a transfer to the Manufacturing Operations Department has been carefully considered. We are sympathetic to your reasons for asking for the transfer and we hope to find a way of accommodating you in the future.

For the moment, however, you are irreplaceable where you are. In addition, the MO Department is in the process of downsizing so there is little likelihood that they would take on anyone else at this point.

I wish the answer could have been yes...

帕里特小姐你好：

你請求調任至製造運作部門，而我們已仔細考慮你的請求。我們理解你申請調任的理由，也希望未來能找到方法顧及你的請求。

然而，就目前而言，你在你的部門是無可取代的。此外，製造運作部門正在縮減人力，所以目前他們實在不太可能接受任何人。

但願我的答案是「沒問題」……

Dear Ms. Murchison,

We were sorry to hear about the problem with your Wimsey Electronic Digital Computerized Hairdryer.

Although your appliance is still under warranty, we are unable to repair it for you free of charge. The terms of the warranty appear to have been violated, which renders the warranty null and void. The machine was plugged into a European 220-volt outlet when it was intended for use only with 110-volt outlets or for 220-volt outlets with a converter. (This is explained in the owner's manual, and a small tag is affixed near the plug warning to use only 110-volt current.)

If you wish us to repair the machine at an approximate cost to you of $120, please let us know. Otherwise, we will return it to you.

We wish we could be more helpful, but the terms of the warranty are carefully spelled out. We cannot make exceptions, no matter how sympathetic we might feel.

Sincerely,

莫奇森小姐您好：

我們很遺憾聽聞您在使用溫希電子數位吹風機遇到了問題。

儘管您的吹風機仍在保修期間，但恕我們無法免費為您修理。您顯然已經違反了保修條款，故保修書是無效的。吹風機被插入了歐洲 220 伏特的插座，但它僅能使用於 110 伏特的插座，或須透過轉換器才能插入 220 伏特的插座。（使用說明書有解釋此點，在插頭旁也貼有小標籤警告只適用 110 伏特的電壓。）

若您希望我們修理這臺機器，並同意由您支付約 120 元的費用，請讓我們知道；不然的話，我們會將吹風機寄還給您。

我們希望能幫上忙，但保修條款已明文規定，無論我們如何同情您的遭遇，我們都無法破例。

○○敬上

Dear Dean Arabin:

I regret that I am unable to represent Barchester College at the inauguration of Dr. Eleanor Bold as new president of Century College on September 16. I wasn't able to reschedule a previous commitment for that day.

My wife is a graduate of Century, so I would have particularly enjoyed being part of the ceremony. Thank you for thinking of me. I was honored to be asked to represent the College and would be glad to be of service some other time.

I hope you are able to make other arrangements.

Sincerely,

狄恩‧阿拉賓您好：

在九月十六日愛倫諾‧柏德博士成為世紀學院新院長的就職典禮上，我很遺憾無法代表巴切斯特學院出席。當天另一個先前已經安排好的行程，我無法挪開。

我的妻子是世紀學院的畢業生，所以能成為這個典禮的一分子，尤其令我開心。感謝您想到了我。您邀請我代表學院出席，使我深感榮幸，下次會很樂意效勞。

我希望您能做出其他安排。

○○敬上

Dear Margaret Ivory,

We have appreciated having you as a patient these last two years. At this time, however, we feel that your best interests are not served by continuing treatment in this office.

We would like to recommend that you make an appointment with Dr. Royde-Smith, Dr. Owen, or a dentist of your choice. We will be happy to send along your dental records, including X-rays.

Let us know how we can facilitate this change in dental care providers.

瑪格麗特‧艾佛里您好：

過去兩年以來您一直是我們的患者，對此我們感到非常感謝。然而，現在我們認為，繼續在此診所接受治療對您並不是最好的選擇。

我們建議您與羅伊德－史密斯醫師、歐文醫師或你選擇的其他牙醫預約時間。我們很樂意協助寄送您的牙醫紀錄，包括 X 光片。

請讓我們知道我們如何能協助您轉診其他牙科醫師。

✉ 參見：03 回應、05 敏感信件、06 預約會面、24 反對信、41 信貸相關信

Chapter 23

建議信
Advice

給予建議是會上癮的。今天你給了一個朋友一點忠告，
下週你便會發現自己又給了兩、三個朋友忠告；
再下一週，則是一打朋友；
接下來的一週，獲得你忠告的人已經成群！

——美國作家卡洛琳・威爾斯（Carolyn Wells）

只有當你願意接受建議時，才向他人尋求建議。若你已經知道自己想要什麼樣的「建議」，就不該尋求建議，那對花費時間回覆你的人來說並不公平，而你自己也會感到不滿又驚訝。

如果你是給予建議的一方，請只回應對方提出的議題，別冒險越線。

如果別人還沒問你意見，逕自開口是很危險的。英國作家瑪麗瑪莉・藍（Mary Lamb）曾說：「當你跟朋友說話時，偶爾插入一兩句建議無傷大雅。但在信中給人建議則容易犯下大忌，因為對方只想讀到好話，或是回憶過去的美好。」

總括來說，只在有人誠摯向你尋求意見時才給予建議。

 PART 1 說明篇

與建議有關的信

尋求建議	給予提議	回覆請求徵詢信
給予建言	拒絕建議	感謝給予忠告

該怎麼說？

- **尋求建議時**：簡要列出欲詢問的問題。也可以說明這次選擇寄信給他們的原因。如果你必須在某個期限前得到建議，請告知。向對方保證他們不回應也沒有關係，並感謝他們願意與你聯繫。

- **給予建議時**：先以換句話說的方式重述對方的請求（You asked my advice about your college plans.「關於你大學期間的規劃，你向我詢問建議。」）或說明寫信的理由（無意中看到某個資料，認為對方有興趣，或你有個可能有用的想法）。闡述你的看法、建言或提議；必要的話，解釋你的論理依據；提出你認為對方可以採取的行動；納入一句免責聲明：this is only my opinion「這只是我的看法」、I know you will use your own good judgment「我知道你會自己做出明智的判斷」、just an idea「只是個想法」。最後，告訴對方你相信他們會做出好的決定、解決難題、成功客服挑戰。

- **對建言表達感謝時**：如同像收到禮物般表達謝意，並告訴對方他們的建議很有幫助。如果你不接受對方的建議，可以感謝對方付出了時間、心力與關心。如果你收到的建議並不適宜，或者是你不想要的，禮貌起見，請假設他們是出自好意，並感謝他們的關心。

什麼不該說？

- 別解釋得太多，只須用幾個句子來簡述你的建議或做法。古羅馬詩人賀拉斯（Horace）說過：「無論你給什麼建議，請長話短說。」寫信給予建議時，保持簡潔很難，因為我們總是很想展現這輩子累積的智慧。請忍住，寫完之後，刪去一半的內容。如果對方想知道更多，他們會主動問你。

- 避免使用 should（應該）這類命令式字眼。沒有人可以告訴別人「應該」或「理當（ought to）」怎麼做，請用更有彈性的措詞來表達你的意見。

- 別在字裡行間暗示你找到了唯一的正解。反之，請提供選項、可能性、或是新穎的方法。

寫作訣竅

- 給予建議時，措詞須委婉、委婉、再委婉。重讀你寫的信，好似這封信是寫給你的。這封信讓你有什麼感覺？找別人幫你看一次，確保這封信不會傷人或顯得太過自負。英國詩人塞謬爾‧泰勒‧柯勒律治（Samuel Taylor Coleridge）曾說：「建言如雪；它落得越輕巧，就能維持得越久，並在心中留下越深的痕跡。」

- 以讚美或愉快的句子起頭，讓建議看起來較為正面。

- 可能的話，將建議歸功給另一個人。尤其是當你主動給予建議時，可以透過另一人提出你想給的建言。父母給孩子的建議一般都不受歡迎，但若此建議出自第三方，孩子通常會接受；高層給的建議，或許比同事給的建議更容易接受（或反之）。

- 具體明確。「冷靜！」或「好好做！」或「再努力一點！」並不算是建議。美國作家米格恩‧麥克勞林（Mignon McLaughlin）曾寫道：「『振作吧』這句話，通常都不是講給做得到的人聽的。」必要的話，附上相關資源的聯絡人姓名與電話、所建議的行動所需之花費，與達成目標的確切步驟。

- 當你主動給予建議時，請保持尊重並保持低調，溫和告訴對方這可能是他們想要參考的建議。在這種狀況下，被動語句或委婉的措詞很有用，例如以 If the loans could be consolidated「如果可以將貸款整合」取代 If you would consolidate your loans「如果你整合貸款」。你也可以寫 I noticed that...「我注意到……」或 Do you need nay help?「你需要幫忙嗎？」先不要直接給予建議，先告訴對方你很樂意協助。

特殊狀況

- **給予專業建議時**（如律師、醫生，或是老師給予專業上的建議），要比一般建議信更小心謹慎。所提供的建議必須在專業上站得住腳，同時附上參考資料或建言出處。保存信件影本（有時也可以寄給第三方）。有些時候，你或許需要另一人的意見來加強論點，並保護你自己。我們的社會是很愛爭論的；熱心的善行並不受到法律保護。

- **尋求金錢投資建議，或是會帶來重大後果的狀況時**，請向對方強調他們不必為結果負責。有了書面免責聲明，他們會在給予建議時較為自在。不過，最好還是向專業人士諮詢（財務顧問、心理學家、律師、房地產經紀人），畢竟一分錢一分貨。

- 如果你**寄出的第一封建議信石沈大海或是被拒絕**，停止再向對方寄出任何一封建議信。美國作家漢娜‧惠塔‧史密斯（Hannah Whitall Smith）曾說：「在你誠心誠意給予建議後，無論對方接受與否，你都無需動搖，也不用堅持糾正對方，這便是給予建言的真正祕訣。」

23
建議信

- 不要提供不利於他人、公司或產品的建議與警告，否則會惹上法律問題。基本上，向別人推薦一個人或一間公司是沒什麼關係的；但要是你是公眾人物，或許會有人要求你解釋不推薦其他人的原因。

格式

- 寫給公司外部的商業夥伴時，使用有信頭的信紙。寫給公司內部人員時，可用備忘錄用紙或有信頭的信紙。寫給有交情的人時，可採用非正式的信紙。
- 手寫與電腦打的建議信，會讓你的信有不同的調性。給員工的手寫信，會傾向私人並帶有歉意；由電腦打出來的內容則顯得客觀、就事論事。另一方面，在一些敏感的商務場合中，若你寫了一封私人信箋，表示你不僅是以朋友的身分寫信，也是以顧客、客戶或主管的身分寫信。

23

建議信

💬 單字

advantageous *(a.)* 有優勢的	debate *(n.) & (v.)* 辯論	instruction *(n.)* 指示	resource *(n.)* 資源
advisable *(a.)* 可建議的	desirable *(a.)* 令人滿意的	open-minded *(a.)* 心胸寬廣的	sensible *(a.)* 明智的
advocate *(v.)* 提倡	direction *(n.)* 方向	opinion *(n.)* 意見	study *(n.) & (v.)* 研究
appropriate *(a.)* 合適的	encourage *(v.)* 鼓勵	persuade *(v.)* 說服	suitable *(a.)* 適合的
apt *(a.)* 傾向於	examine *(v.)* 檢驗	practical *(a.)* 實際的	urge *(v.)* 促使
beneficial *(a.)* 有益的	expedient *(a.)* 有利的	precaution *(n.)* 預防措施	useful *(a.)* 有用的
careful *(a.)* 仔細的	fitting *(a.)* 適當的	principle *(n.)* 原則	valuable *(a.)* 有價值的
caution *(n.)* 警覺	forethought *(n.)* 事先考慮	prudent *(a.)* 謹慎的	warn *(v.)* 警告
consider *(v.)* 考慮	guidance *(n.)* 指導	rational *(a.)* 理性的	weigh *(v.)* 權衡利弊
consult *(v.)* 諮詢	guideline *(n.)* 指導準則	reasonable *(a.)* 合理的	wisdom *(n.)* 智慧
counsel *(v.)* 商議	insight *(n.)* 真知灼見	recommend *(v.)* 推薦	worthwhile *(a.)* 值得的

23

建議信

詞組

alert you to the possibility
提醒你這個可能性

as I understand it
就我所理解的

backseat driver
愛管閒事的人

compare notes
交換意見

consider carefully
仔細考慮

I am convinced that
我相信

I don't like to interfere, but
我無意干涉，但是

I feel/assume/presume/think
我感覺／假定／推測／認為

if you don't mind
如果你不介意的話

look into
深入研究

might want to
也許會想要

piece of advice
一點建議

so far as I know
就我所知

speak for
代表……說話

I have the impression that
我對……有印象

take it amiss/the wrong way
錯以為／想錯了

I noticed that
我注意到……

I take it that
就我的理解

it seems to me
就我看來

just wanted to suggest/recommend
只是想提議／推薦……

keep a lookout for/an eye on
在……保持警覺

kick around this idea
聊聊這個想法

think through
全盤考量

to my way of thinking
就我來看

to the best of my knowledge
據我的了解

take to heart
認真關注

think about
想一想

weigh both courses of action
衡量兩種行動

take care of 處理	what you could do 你可以做的是
take into account 納入考量	whether you take my advice or not 無論你是否接受我的建議
in my estimation/judgment/opinion/ view 就我的估計／判斷／看法／觀點	you've probably already thought of this, but 也許你已經想到這點了，但是……

句子

Although I liked what you wrote about switching your major from Physics to Astronomy, I have a suggestion you might want to consider.
我認同你想從物理主修轉為天文的想法，但我有些建議你也許會想參考一下。

Do you have any advice about how I can raise morale in the Accounting Department?
關於提升會計部士氣的方法，您有什麼建議？

Ever since you asked my opinion about the Middlemarch line, I've been mulling over the situation, weighing the benefits against the rather considerable cost.
在您詢問我對於米德鎮鐵路的看法後，我就一直在思考這個問題並衡量獲益，因為成本將會相當高。

I don't usually give unsolicited advice, but this seems to me to be a special case.
我通常不會擅自提出建議，但這件事對我來説比較特殊。

I hope this is the sort of advice you wanted.
我希望這個建議是你想要的。

I'm considering a switch from the technical to the management ladder—do you have any wise, helpful words for me?
我正在考慮要從科技轉為管理，對此您是否有任何明智、有用的建議能提供給我呢？

I'm writing to you for advice.
我寫信給您，是希望能得到您的建議。

I thought I should mention this.
我想我應該告訴你這件事。

I took your excellent advice and I'm grateful.
我採用了您絕妙的建議，非常感謝。

I will appreciate any comments or advice you'd care to give.
如果您願意提供任何評論或建議，我將會非常感激。

I would be grateful for your frank opinion about our registering Jermyn for kindergarten this year (he won't be five yet) instead of waiting another year.
我們不想再等上一年，打算在今年讓傑瑞米上幼兒園（他還不到五歲），若您能大方分享您的看法，我會很感激。

I wouldn't ordinarily presume to tell you your business, but I'm concerned.
我通常不會冒昧干涉你的事業，但我很擔心。

Thank you for your unerring advice about our hot rolling equipment—we're back on schedule.
謝謝您在熱軋設備問題上提供可靠建議，一切終於恢復正常運作。

There is one thing you might want to consider.
有件事你也許想要納入考量。

We are unable to take your advice just now, but we're grateful to you for thinking of us.
我們目前無法採納您的建議，但我們很感謝您為我們著想。

Would you be willing to tell me quite frankly and confidentially what you think about my interpersonal skills?
關於我的社交技巧，您是否願意私下坦白告訴我您的看法呢？

You asked for my opinion about switching service providers—here it is.
您詢問我對於改行作服務供應商的看法，請見下文。

You must, of course, use your own judgment, but I would suggest this.
當然，你必須自己做出判斷，但我會這麼建議。

Your counsel and advice have meant a great deal to me.
您的忠告與建議對我來説非常重要。

Your idea is excellent and I may regret not going that route, but I'm going to try something else first.
您的主意非常好，也許我會後悔沒有選擇那條路，但我決定要先試試別的。

You were kind enough to ask my advice about the Hexam-Riderhood merger—this is what I think.
謝謝您詢問我對於海森與萊德瑚合併案的建議，以下是我的看法。

段落

You asked what I thought of the new store hours. They are certainly more convenient for customers and will bring us the early evening business that can make a difference in our year-end numbers. However, I wonder if it is profitable to stay open so late on Saturday evenings. Could we keep a record of Saturday evening sales for a month?

你曾問我對新營業時間的看法。新的時間確實對客人來說比較方便,也會帶給我們下午近傍晚時段的生意,這可能會提升我們年底的業績。不過,在週六晚上營業到這麼晚是否真能帶來收益,對此我仍有疑慮。我們可否記錄一個月的週六晚上銷售額呢?

You might want to hire an investment banking firm to help with your financial restructuring. Such a firm can assist you in exploring strategic alternatives to rebuild your liquidity and improve value for shareholders.

您也許可以雇請一間投資銀行公司,來幫助您進行財務重組。這種公司會協助您找出策略來恢復流動性,提升股票的價值。

I would like to suggest that you examine the issue of cooperation versus competition in the school environment. In the three years our children have been students here, I've noticed the school is strongly oriented toward competition, with little value assigned to cooperative learning, cooperative sports, and cooperative activities. I'm enclosing several reports and studies on this issue. May I stop in and speak with you about this next week?

我想建議您了解一下校園的合作與競爭情形。我們的孩子已在這間學校當了三年學生,我注意到學校非常鼓勵競爭,卻極少重視合作學習、團隊運動與團體活動。隨信附上幾份關於這個議題的報告與研究。下週可否造訪並與您談談此事呢?

I'm flattered that you want my advice on choosing a college. However, you seem interested in the eastern colleges, and I know little about them. I wonder if you wouldn't want to talk to Ling Ch'ung, who in fact is quite knowledgeable about many of them.

我很高興你向我詢問選擇大學的建議;不過,你似乎對東部的大學較有興趣,而我對此所知甚少。我在想你是否願意找鍾玲聊聊,其實她很了解東部的大學。

Thanks so much for your advice on the hip roof and preparing for the building inspector. I doubt if she would have given me the building permit the way I was going about things!

真是非常感激你對於四坡屋頂以及應對建築視察員的建議，否則她恐怕不會就這樣給予我們建築許可！

I'm grateful to you for the time you took to outline a solution to our current problem. We are interested in your ideas. However, we just started working on another approach last Thursday and I'm going to wait and see how that develops. I'll let you know if we are later able to consider your plan. In the meantime, thanks for your helpful suggestions.

感謝你花費時間為我們眼下的問題提供解決之道。我們對你的想法很感興趣，不過上週四我們才剛嘗試另一個方法，所以我會先等等看成果。若我們之後能將你的計畫納入考慮，我會讓你知道。與此同時，很感謝你的提議。

書信範例

Dear Mr. Brimblecombe:

　　I was present at the Music Educators' Conference when your elementary school jazz band performed. I was impressed to hear that out of a school population of 640, you have 580 students in your instrumental music program. This is unusual, as I'm sure you know.

　　Do you have any advice for other elementary music directors trying to increase the number of student musicians? If you do not have the time to respond by letter, perhaps you could indicate on the enclosed postcard a time and date when I could call you long-distance. I'd appreciate any tips you might have.

Gratefully,

賓柏克比先生您好：

　　您的國小爵士樂團於音樂教育研討會上表演時，我也在場。貴校學生共有六百四十人，其中便有五百八十人參加您的樂器課程，這令我留下深刻印象，我想您也明白，這是相當難得的事。

　　如果他校的音樂組長想增加學生音樂家的人數，您是否有什麼建議呢？如果您沒有時間回信，您也可以在隨信附上的明信片寫下您方便的日期與時間，我會打長途電話過去。若您能分享您的祕訣，我會非常感激。

○○謹上

Dear Tony,

As one of our most aggressive sales representatives, you have an enviable record and I expect you will be up for an award at the end of the year. The flip side of this aggressiveness is, unfortunately, a certain abrasive attitude that has been reported by several customers.

I'd like to suggest two things. One, come in and talk this over with me. I can give you some idea of how people are responding to you and why it's a problem over the long term if not the short term. Two, spend a day or two with Tom Jerningham. He has a manner that is effective without being too insistent.

Let me hear from you.

Sincerely,

親愛的東尼：

你是我們公司最積極的銷售代表之一，有著令人稱羨的業績，我想年底的獲獎人非你莫屬。不過，這種積極的另一面卻可能是惱人的，好幾個客戶都曾申訴你的態度問題。

我想要建議兩件事。第一，來我的辦公室與我談談。我可以告訴他人對你的看法，還有長期而言這為何會是個問題，儘管短期來說問題也許不大。第二，花一、兩天跟著湯姆·傑寧漢，他的態度既有效又不會太過強硬。

讓我聽聽你的想法。

〇〇上

Dear Shreve,

We are both proud of how well you're doing in college—your grades, your job, your friends. I think we've told you often how much we love you and admire the way you handle things. BUT... (did you know there was a "but" coming?) we are extremely concerned about one new thing in your life: cigarettes. Will you please think about what it will mean if you let this habit take hold?

I'm enclosing some literature on the subject.

We won't nag you about this, but we had to speak up strongly at least once and say that, based on our experience, knowledge, and love for you, this is not a good choice.

Love,

親愛的薛弗：

你在大學的表現，包括你的成績、工作、和交友狀況，都讓我們很驕傲。我想我們已經常常告訴你我們有多愛你、多佩服你處理事情的方式。但是……（你有猜到會有個「但是」出現嗎？）我們非常擔心你生活中的一項新事物：香菸。要是你養成了習慣，會有什麼影響，可以請你好好想想嗎？

隨信附上相關文獻。

我們不會因此對你嘮叨，但我們至少要有這麼一次嚴正提出我們的看法，因為我們的經驗、知識與對你的愛，我們必須告訴你這不是個好的選擇。

愛你的〇〇

Dear Marion and Leopold,

Thanks so much for driving all the way into the city just to look over the situation with the house. The decision whether to repaint or put on all new siding was really getting us down. Your advice was excellent, and we feel good about our decision. It was also wonderful to see you again!

Love,

親愛的瑪莉詠與李奧帕德：

謝謝你們開了這麼遠的路進城，只為了檢查房子。究竟要重新粉刷還是要全部鋪上新的牆板，這問題真的讓我們很煩惱。你們的建議實在太棒了，我們對這個決定很滿意。而且真的很高興再次見到你們！

愛你們的○○

Dear Uncle Thorkell,

Thank you for your letter. I appreciated your advice about my earrings. I know it doesn't seem "manly" to you, but my friends and I like earrings. I'm coming home at the end of the month for a visit, and I don't want you to be disappointed when you see that I still have them. Although I am grateful for your concern, I am going to keep wearing earrings. I hope this won't hurt our good relationship.

Love,

親愛的索克爾叔叔：

謝謝您的來信，我很感激您對我戴耳環的建議。我知道您認為帶耳環不夠「男子氣概」，但我與我的朋友都很喜歡耳環。這個月底我會回家一趟，而我不希望您因為我仍戴著耳環而失望。雖然我很感謝您的建議，但我會繼續戴耳環。希望這不會影響我們之間的良好關係。

愛您的○○

23
建議信

✉ 參見：05 敏感信件、12 致謝函、16 指示說明信、20 請求與詢問、22 拒絕、41 信貸相關信

Chapter 24

反對信
Letters of Disagreement

不認為凡事都有一體兩面的人，
自己大概也是個問題。

——蒼耳（The Cockle Bur）

有些人喜歡製造衝突，有些人則為了避免衝突而耗盡心力。如果這兩種人活在現實世界的話，他們遲早得寫一封反對信給對方。表達異議不算好事也不算壞事，但你表示異議的方式，會影響接下來的事件、感受與人際關係。

PART 1 說明篇

反對信牽涉到哪些事情？

合約	口頭協議	款項支付
人事問題	政策、計畫、程序或規定	地產分界

該怎麼說？

1. 提及相關的談話內容或事件。

2. 列出兩種對立的觀點或行動。

3. 為你的立場清楚解釋理由（可列點）並引證支持，如統計數據、引用員工守則、相關軼事資料，或列舉目擊者或贊同你的人的姓名（須經同意）。

4. 如果合適的話，邀請對方進行協商或調解；請對方回應信件中的特定問題；做進一步調查；進行協商，也可以找第三方到場；諮詢律師、會計師或專家。

5. 如果雙方的糾紛已經進展到可以有效處理的階段，請明確說出你想要的結果。

6. 結尾時，表達你期盼能找出雙方都能接受的解決辦法，也期望未來能有良好的關係。

什麼不該說？

• 不要引發對方的戒心。多用「我」（I）而少用「你」（you），因為包含「你」的句子聽起來容易有控訴的意味。請確保你的信不會讓對方覺得心情不好、受到羞辱、笨拙無能或虛弱無力。被你輕視的人，不會讓你得到你想要的東西。

• 避免負面用詞，如 ridiculous（荒謬的）、egregious（爛透的）、brainless（無腦的）。這些詞不只會帶來反效果，還毫無說服力，甚至還會暴露你的脆弱。雨果（Victor Hugo）曾說：「強硬尖銳的言詞，反映的是軟弱無力。」

• 避免情緒化用詞。訴諸事實，而非感受。告訴對方「我相信這是不公平的，因為在七名祕書中，只有一個人總是被要求加班，卻沒有加班費」，比起只說「我覺得這不公平」更有力。

寫作訣竅

• 信件呈現出的調性，決定你的意見能不能獲得傾聽。盡力寫出實事求是、不情緒化、體貼而公平的信函。

• 把需求講清楚。下筆之前，先想一想：「我希望他們做什麼？」你想要的是折扣、換貨或修理？想要對方道歉、改正結算單或給予信貸？想讓對方承認錯誤嗎？還是你想要事情能重來一遍？

• 顧全對方的面子。你要設定出一種情境，讓對方能照著你說的做，同時又讓他們覺得自己很大方、高尚、有能力且心甘情願。

• 儘管主動語態大部分比被動語態更好，但處理反對意見時，可以使用比較圓滑的被動語態。不要說 You did this.「你做了這件事。」，而要說 This was done.「這件事發生了。」

• 檢視自己的立場，看看有沒有談判的空間。你可不可以與對方交換條件？你能不能接受不如預期的結果？

- 若要寫信反對某法案的通過，先留意此法案屬於何種層級，再寫信給適合的立法委員或政府官員。

特殊狀況

- 如果遇到下列情況會需要**諮詢律師**：收到分居的另一半寫信要你認錯、要求或威脅；需要將非正式的口頭協議轉化為書面協議；家人間為了不動產的爭執益加嚴重；有人因為某件事情控告你；爭紛越演越烈，對方威脅要告上法院。
- 有些團體會透過**集體寫信來抗議有爭議的議題**。響應者會收到示範信，便照著寫，並以自己的名義簽名寄出。如果是議員想知道支持與反對該議題的人數時，這種集體寫信的活動是很有意義的。不過，一封文筆流暢、有原創性的信函，比上百封制式信更能吸引目光。要先去了解集體活動在哪些狀況下有效、哪些狀況下無效。律師佛羅倫斯・甘迺迪（Florynce B. Kennedy）曾說過：「若你是國家，你寧願在門口看到什麼？一隻獅子，或是五百隻老鼠？」
- **寫信給立法委員講述對某議題的看法時**，你並不想收到對方寄來一封長達三頁的回信解釋他們的立場，因為你早已從新聞中了解他們的立場。既然如此，請用這句話為你的信函收尾：Please do not respond to this letter. I know your views; I wanted you to know mine. 「您不必回覆這封信，因為我已經知道您的立場；我希望的是讓您知道我的看法。」

格式

- 與商務有關的糾紛，請打在有信頭的信紙上。
- 私下寫信表達反對意見時，手寫信會顯得較友善，也比較有調解的空間。若你想要看起來堅定、不容談判，那麼打字是最好的選擇。

單字

argument *(n.)* 爭論	dispute *(n.)* 爭執	standstill *(n.)* 停滯	displeased *(a.)* 不悅的
conflict *(n.)* 衝突	estrangement *(n.)* 失和	feud *(v.) & (n.)* 長期不和；宿怨	disturbing *(a.)* 令人不安的
contention *(n.)* 主張、爭吵	faction *(n.)* 內訌	quarrel *(v.) & (n.)* 爭吵、不合	incompatible *(a.)* 處不來的；不相容的
contradiction *(n.)* 矛盾	friction *(n.)* 摩擦	protest *(v.) & (n.)* 抗議	infuriated *(a.)* 觸怒的
controversy *(n.)* 爭議	impasse *(n.)* 僵局	break *(v.)* 違反；決裂	irritating *(a.)* 惱人的
dead-end *(n.)* 困境	misunderstanding *(n.)* 誤解	differ *(v.)* 分岐	regrettable *(a.)* 後悔的
deadlock *(n.)* 僵局	offense *(n.)* 冒犯	disapprove *(v.)* 不同意、反對	unfortunate *(a.)* 不幸的
dilemma *(n.)* 兩難	stalemate *(n.)* 僵持狀態	reconcile *(v.)* 調和、和解	unhappy *(a.)* 不開心的
dissatisfaction *(n.)* 不滿意	rift *(n.)* 嫌隙	object *(v.)* 反對	

24

反對信

詞組

agree to differ/disagree
同意各自保留不同意見

believe you should know that
相信你應該知道

as I understand it
就我的了解

in the best interests of
對……最有益

at cross-purposes
目的相反；相互誤解

be at odds with
與……不一致

in my estimation/judgment/opinion/
view
就我的估計／判斷／看法／觀點

bone of contention
爭議點

bury the hatchet
握手言和

come to terms
勉強接受

complicated situation
複雜的情況

conduct an inquiry
展開調查

difference of opinion
意見不同

direct your attention to
將你的注意力轉到

disputed point
爭議點

do a disservice to
對……造成損害

fail to agree
無法同意

I am convinced that
我相信

I assume/presume/think/have no doubt
that
我假定／推測／認為／深信不疑

I take it that
我認為

it seems to me
就我看來

matter/point in dispute/at issue/
under discussion/in question
爭執／議論／討論／質問的項目／事件

my information is
我得到的資訊是

part company with
與……分道揚鑣

point of view
觀點

question at issue
造成議論的問題

register my opinion
提出意見

strongly oppose
強烈反對

take into consideration
納入考慮

think differently
想得不同

to my way of thinking
以我的思考模式

to the best of my knowledge
就我所知

wonder if you are aware that
想知道你是否察覺

I have the impression that
我的印象中

句子

Are we ready to put this to a vote?
還是我們來投票表決好了？

Do you think it would help to call in an arbitrator?
你覺得我們找一位仲裁員幫助如何？

Enclosed please find several abstracts that may be helpful.
隨信附上摘要，可能會有所幫助。

I agree with the necessity of fundraising for the purchase and maintenance of band instruments, but I disagree with the fundraising program adopted for next year.
為了購買與維修團樂器，我們需要募款，這點我贊同，但是我並不贊同明年即將採用的募款計畫。

I am convinced that the passage of this bill would do more harm than good/is not in the best interests of the state/would be a grave error.
這項法案若通過，我相信它帶來的傷害會超過益處／並不符合本州的最大利益／會是個嚴重的錯誤。

I disagree with the store policy of filling prescriptions with generic drugs without notifying the customer.
依貴店政策，處方箋上的藥品會以學名藥取代，不會另行通知顧客，這點我並不贊同。

I found the language and tone of your last letter completely unacceptable; please put us in touch with someone else in your organization who can handle this matter.
我認為你最近一封信中的用詞與口氣令人完全無法接受；請將我們轉介給貴公司內能處理此事的其他人。

If you would like some background reading on this issue, I would be happy to furnish you with some.
若你想參考與此議題有關的讀物，我很樂意提供你一些。

I received your letter this morning and am sorry to hear that you cannot accept our terms.
我今早收到您的信，很遺憾您無法接受我們的條件。

Several of the points you mention are negotiable; some are not.
在你提到的幾點當中，有一些是可以協商的，有一些則無法。

We are submitting this matter to an independent referee.
我們正要將此事件交予獨立仲裁員。

We still have one major area of disagreement.
我們在一項主要議題上仍未取得共識。

What would make the situation more agreeable to you?
如何能讓您比較願意接受這個情況？

段落

I realize that there is technically no more to be said about the Dillon-Reed merger, but I would like to state for the record that I strongly oppose the move. I refer you to the enclosed independent report that we commissioned from Elkus Inc. This is the classic situation where one owns a dog but persists in barking oneself. The Elkus people, acknowledged experts in the field, advised us against the merger. Do we have strong enough grounds for rejecting their conclusions? I think not.

我明白迪倫與理德合併一案基本上已成定局，但我還是希望留下發言紀錄，在此聲明我強烈反對此舉。請見附件中我們委託艾可思公司撰寫的獨立報告。這正是花錢雇人代勞卻仍親自操勞的典型狀況，艾可思公司的知名專家都建議我們不要合併。我們是否有足夠的理由反對他們的結論？我想沒有。

I know we've talked about this until we're both blue in the face, but I feel strongly that Great-Aunt Elsie is not yet ready for a nursing home. It would make her unhappy and shorten her life to be placed in one prematurely. What changes would you need to see before you could feel comfortable about her remaining in her apartment?

我知道我們討論此事到最後，雙方都很生氣，但我真的覺得，愛希曾祖母還沒有準備好去住療養院。貿然把她放到療養院，會讓她過得不開心，縮短她的壽命。你想要看到什麼樣的改變，才能接受她繼續住在她的公寓裡呢？

My lawyer requested the addition of the following clause to the contract: "Clause S. This agreement will expire ten years from the date of execution." The clause does not appear in the final contract. I know this issue was in dispute at one time, but I understood that you had finally agreed to it. I am returning the unsigned contracts to you for correction.

我的律師曾要求在合約中加入以下條款：「第 S 條　本協議將於生效日起十年後失效。」這項條款並未出現在最終版的合約中。我明白我們曾經爭論過這件事，但我知道您最後已經同意加入這項條款。我會將未簽名的合約寄還給您修改。

We seem to be at an impasse on determining the boundary line between our properties. Would you be interested in sharing the costs of hiring a surveyor?

在劃定地產邊界一事上，我們似乎陷入了僵局。您是否有興趣與我們共同分擔雇用勘測員的費用？

24

反對信

示範信

Dear Senator Burrows,

I urge you to oppose the Television Soundtrack Copyright Reform Bill.

As you know, music performance rights for syndicated television programs are licensed in one of four ways: (1) a blanket license with a performing rights society; (2) a per program license; (3) a source license; or (4) a direct license. This bill would mandate that music performance rights for syndicated television programs be licensed in only one way, at the source in conjunction with all other broadcast rights for the program.

The current system has been used since the beginning of television and has been upheld in court challenges. It assures a fair return based on performance to composers and songwriters who create television music. The proponents of the bill have a heavy burden to demonstrate the need for Congress to interfere in the current system and mandate a single way of doing business.

They have not met their burden, and I oppose the legislation.

Sincerely,

布羅斯參議員您好：

我在此要求您反對電視原聲帶版權改革法案。

如您所知，聯賣電視節目的音樂表演權許可來自以下四種：(1) 由一表演專利協會給予全面版權許可；(2) 按節目給予版權許可；(3) 由來源給予版權許可；(4) 直接版權許可。此法案會使得聯賣電視節目只剩下一種音樂表演版權許可，即從來源處與節目的所有其他播放專利一起取得授權。

目前的制度是從有電視節目開始就一直使用的，且在法院多次質疑後依然屹立不搖。透過此制度，創作出電視音樂的作曲家與詞曲創作人能從表演中獲得公平的回饋。此法案的支持者要求國會介入目前的制度，改為單一授權方式，卻難以解釋為何有這樣的需求。

他們無法提供合理解釋，所以我反對這項法案。

○○敬上

Dear Ms. Burling-Ward:

I enjoy working for Stegner Publishing, and you in particular have been most helpful in introducing me to people and showing me around.

When I was interviewed for the job, Mr. Oliver consistently used the term "production editor," and the job duties he listed were those generally associated with the position of production editor.

During my three weeks on the job, I have done nothing but copyediting. After speaking with you yesterday and discovering that this was not just a training stage but my permanent position, I suspect there has been a misunderstanding.

I would like to meet with you and Mr. Oliver sometime soon to clarify this situation.

Sincerely,

24
反對信

博林－瓦德小姐您好：

　　我很享受在史德納出版社的工作，並特別感謝您協助我認識同事與環境。

　　當我面試此職缺時，奧利佛先生不斷使用「製作編輯」一詞，而他列出的工作職責基本上也都屬於製作編輯的範疇。

　　在我入職的三週以來，我除了文字的編輯外，其餘都未曾接觸。在昨日與您談話後，我發現這並不只是訓練階段的狀況，而是我的正式職務，因此我認為這其中應該有所誤會。

　　我希望能盡快與您及奧利佛先生一起開會，釐清目前的狀況。

○○敬上

Dear Nandie and Victor,

　　Our jazz trio has been so compatible and has had such a good time these last three years that I'm uncomfortable with our present disagreement. I think we're used to getting along and thus don't know how to handle it when we don't agree.

　　Here's my suggestion. Next Thursday night, instead of rehearsing, let's meet at Saduko's Restaurant for dinner. Each of us will bring three 3×5 cards with our reasons for changing the trio's name.

　　After a good meal and some nonwork conversation, we will exchange cards so that each of us is holding the three viewpoints. I hope we can then come to a good decision.

　　What do you think?

Angelo

親愛的南蒂與維克多：

　　我們的爵士三人組一直都是那麼合拍，過去三年一起度過了美好的時光，所以我們最近的爭執實在令我難受。我想這是因為我們一直都很合得來，所以不知道該如何處理不同的意見。

　　我的建議是這樣的：下週四晚上，我們不要彩排，而是到沙杜可餐廳吃晚餐。我們每個人都帶三張 3×5 的卡片，上面寫著我們想改團名的理由。

　　在享用美食、聊聊與工作無關的話題後，我們就可以交換卡片，這樣每個人手上便都握有三種觀點。我希望這能使我們做出一個好的決定。

　　你們覺得呢？

安傑羅

24

反對信

✉ 參見：05 敏感信件、22 拒絕、25 抱怨與客訴、48 給鄰居的信

Chapter 25

抱怨與客訴
Complaints

> 如果你不寫客訴信,就永遠拿不到商品。
> 等你寫了信,那在這封憤怒的信件寄達之前,你就會收到商品。
>
> ——美國作家亞瑟·布洛可(Arthur Bloch)

你並不是唯一一個寫抱怨信的人,這世上有成千上百萬人每年都在寫這種信。有間食品公司每年都會收到三十萬通客訴電話與信件。

有些抱怨可以透過電話傳達,不過,寫客訴信(claim letter,或稱 consumer action letter「顧客行動信」)效果更好。第一,某人的桌上因此會擺上一封實體的信,所以他非得處理這封信不可。第二,信件措詞會更得體。第三,能更清楚傳達細節資訊(你可以在信中仔細打上日期、姓名、發貨單號碼,但透過電話卻很難如此謹慎)。第四,如此一來,你手上便握有抱怨信的紀錄。

如果你的抱怨對象是一般大眾,請參見:26 致編輯函。

若你需要回應別人的抱怨,參見:35 客訴處理信,或是 13 致歉信。

 PART 1 說明篇

何時需要寫抱怨信?

訂單出錯	發生延誤 出貨、退款、 付款或供貨遲誤	商品缺損 價格過高、廣告不實、 缺少零件

孩童行為失當 或造成損害	**員工服務不周** 無禮、粗魯或效率低落	**個人失誤** 發生誤會
出現擾民或擾鄰問題 成人書店、環境髒亂、 派對吵雜	**立法不周** 稅金過高、法律不公、 議案未決	**鄰居糾紛** 參見：48 給鄰居的信
寵物造成損害 有攻擊行為	**政策出現問題** 不夠理想、限制過多、 歧視	**學校出現問題** 懲戒不當、課程不良

該怎麼說？

1. 描述問題，包含問題內容、發生時間，以及所造成的困擾。

2. 提供確實的細節資訊。

- **跟商品有關**：購買日期與地點、銷貨發票號碼、商品描述、序號或型號、支付金額、銷售員姓名、你的帳戶號碼或信用卡號。

- **跟服務人員有關**（無禮或效率低落）：事件發生日期與時間、服務人員姓名（若知道的話）、發生地點、目擊者姓名、行為描述。

- **與印刷錯誤、陳述錯誤或內容缺失有關**：日期、章節、頁數、欄位、應修正的內容；正確的內容；你的電話號碼。

- **與航空公司有關**：班機號碼、航行日期、出發地點與目的地、問題或事件的描述、發生地點與時間。

3. 附上相關文件：銷貨單、收據、保固單與保證書、過去通訊紀錄、缺損商品照片、修理或服務訂單、取消的支票、合約書、已付款之發貨單。（請寄影本。）

4. 告訴對方必須解決這個問題的理由。

5. 清楚陳述希望對方做的事：退款、替換新品、換貨還是修理。若你想要的是錢，可明說金額。請提出合理的解決方式。

6. 提議一個解決問題的期限。

7. 提供聯絡細節：姓名、地址、家中及辦公室電話號碼、電子郵件地址。

8. 結尾時，告訴對方你相信他們會做出正確判斷，並有能力解決問題，例如 I am sure you will find a solution for this problem. 「我確信您會有辦法解決這個問題。」；I am confident that you will want to replace this defective scanner.「我相信您會替換這臺損壞的掃描機。」

- 別用主觀的句子，如 I want（我要）、I feel（我覺得）及 I need（我需要）。提供數字、日期、事實、照片及文件，才更有說服力。
- 別放任自己發洩情緒。若你希望對方處理問題、道歉或正面給予回應，請別把能幫助你的人當成敵人。負面的信函不僅沒效果，還會讓你看起來很蠢（當你回想時，你也會覺得自己很蠢）。
- 別負面思考，如「我不認為您對這有什麼辦法。」請假設對方很想要幫忙（至少在你發現並非如此之前）。

- 別威脅要控告對方。這種話通常都只會被當成吹噓。真正會提出告訴的人，會讓律師出擊。若你決定訴諸法律，再告知對方，這也是種快速的解決方式。（請注意，有些法律行動是有時限的。）
- 別控訴他人說謊、不專業、欺騙、偷竊或扭曲事實，這會惹上法律麻煩。
- 別暗示要得到免費產品或超出應得的補償。

寫作訣竅

- 立即寫信。這樣你對細節記得比較清楚，也較容易得到正面回應。
- 保持簡短。一頁以內的信是最容易讓人讀下去的。
- 保持禮貌。收信對象可能跟你遇到的失誤一點關係也沒有，當你的態度冷靜且得體時，對方也會更願意提供協助。你可以適當加入幾句正面的評價，如你為什麼選擇該產品或該公司服務、產品你已經使用了多久、你相信此次事件必定是個例外。
- 一封信只聚焦在一項抱怨或議題。若你在同一封信提到推銷員無禮、停車位不足、商品價格標示錯誤、開罐器什麼都打不開，那你很可能只會得到一封含括所有問題的道歉信，個別問題卻無法得到具體的處理。
- 把重點擺在解決問題上。不需在細節、自身感受以及問題帶來的災難著墨太多。著重於解決問題，並在解決方法上取得共識。
- 顧及對方的面子。要是你透過脅迫或操控解決問題，表示你並不相信對方也是有禮、慷慨的人。
- 如果抱怨的事件不只一件（遺漏的訂購項目、一連串的事件），將這些項目以條列方式（可編號或加項目符號）呈現。
- 所有的電話、信件、行動都要留下紀錄，並記錄日期、聯絡人姓名及職稱與大致的結果。

- 所有通訊紀錄、購物明細、支票、銷貨單與相關文件，都要留正本。

- 若你是第一次寄抱怨信給一家公司，先不要將副本寄給第三方。給這家公司一個解決問題的機會。如果你沒有得到滿意的回應，之後你便可以把副本寄至監督單位、同業公會或消費者保護機構。利用電子郵件的「cc:」（副本）欄位加入你寄副本的對象。

- 「找能幫你的人抱怨。」（南斯拉夫諺語）好好寫了一封信，卻寄給錯誤的對象，再也沒有比這更沒效率的事了。最好將抱怨信寄給特定的人。一封未明確寫出收件者的信，最後便沒有任何人需要負責。

- 寫信給立法委員或政府官員，可寄信至各縣市政府的市民信箱；在網路上搜尋立法委員的專頁或寄信至其辦事處。

- 寫信給一般公司時，可以先打電話到對方公司詢問姓名及職稱，或是在網路上查找。把信寄到該公司的公關部門也是不錯的選擇，因為此部門專門處理客戶遇到的問題。如果該公司無法給你滿意的答覆，你可以透過以下單位處理：行政院消費者保護會、消費者文化基金會，相關消費者團體或同業公會。當你尋求這些團體的支持時，請描述問題、條列出已採取的行動，並附上你已聯絡過的人名與職稱。

- 如果與你有爭執的是專業人員，你可以寫信給批准其執照的政府單位。

- 如果你常寫抱怨信，可以參考以下書籍：
  《Shocked, Appalled, and Dismayed! How to Write Letters of Complaint That Get Results》，作者：Ellen Phillips

特殊狀況

- **信用卡購物若出現糾紛**，先聯絡信用卡公司，請他們在處理問題期間暫緩付款。

- **若要抗議租金上漲，或汽車、醫療、房屋等保險費增加**，信中須包含：姓名、地址、電話號碼、公寓或保險單號、向該公司租屋或保險的年數、歷史費率，以及你提出異議的原因。要求對方派人打電話給你討論此事。

- **若孩子在學校發生問題**，請先假設你對事情細節不知情，以問句釐清狀況：Can you tell me...?「是能否告訴我……？」；Is it true that...?「……是真的嗎？」學校與家長之間很容易發生誤會，所以在要求對方改變或道歉前，請先釐清問題。

- **學校向家長傳達怨言時**，電話是雙方溝通的第一選擇。不過，當校方須寫信給家長時，校方的用詞需得體圓滑、實事求是。簡要客觀陳述發生的事情。提議一個日期與時間會面，或請家長打電話給你。附上校規影本，點出孩子違反的規範，或請家長參閱學生手冊。告知家長校方正如何處理此事，或將採取什麼行動。

- 如果你是**跟著大型團體一起抗議**某個行動、產品、服務或某企業採取的措施，請以個人名義寄信，不要寄制式信件或團體聲明信。比起上百封內容一模一樣的明信片，機構組織更願意回應一封細心書寫的原創信函。有些情況下，大量的抱怨信確實很有說服力，但一般來說，量產的抱怨信只是浪費時間與郵資而已。

- **寫信給當選的官員提出建議**時，請在第一句或主旨提及你有異議的議題或法規，如「Re: property taxes」（關於：財產稅）或「Subject: HR4116」（主旨：HR4116）。清楚陳述你的看法與立場，如 I strongly disapprove of...「我強烈反對……」或 I urge you to...「我強烈要求……」。告訴對方你採取此立場的理由。若原因很多，分別條列，在每一點前加上序號、星號或項目符號。指出你希望對方採取的行動，或你希望得到的回應。如果你對此議題特別了解，可以向對方表示你願意提供協助。信件結尾感謝對方的關切與時間。

- 有時候，陷入糾紛的雙方都需要道歉。儘管你的抱怨合情合理，但也許你犯了一些小錯導致情況惡化。為自己的行為道歉不僅是一種誠實（如有需要的話），也有助於獲得想要的回應。

💬 格式

- 有信頭的商務信紙、個人對公司用信紙，或有信頭的私人信紙，都很適合用來寫抱怨信。
- 最好以電腦打字。如果你只能用手寫，請確保你的字體整齊且好閱讀。

PART 2 應用篇

單字

action *(n.)* 行動	impolite *(a.)* 無禮的	misleading *(a.)* 誤導的	replace *(v.)* 替代
adjustment *(n.)* 客訴處理	inaccurate *(a.)* 不準確的	misprint *(v.)* 印刷錯誤	resolve *(v.)* 解決
agreed-upon *(a.)* 已同意的	inadequate *(a.)* 不適合的	misquote *(v.)* 引用錯誤	restore *(v.)* 恢復
breakdown *(n.)* 故障	inappropriate *(a.)* 不適宜的	misrepresented *(a.)* 扭曲事實的	short-sighted *(a.)* 短視的
compensation *(n.)* 補償	incident *(n.)* 事件	missing *(a.)* 缺少的	slipshod *(a.)* 懶散的
concerned *(a.)* 有關的	incomplete *(a.)* 不完整的	misstatement *(n.)* 錯誤陳述	thoughtless *(a.)* 輕率的
damaged *(a.)* 損壞的	inconsistent *(a.)* 不一致的	mistake *(n.)* 過錯	uncooperative *(a.)* 不合作的
defective *(a.)* 缺損的	inconvenient *(a.)* 不方便的	misunderstanding *(n.)* 誤解	unfortunate *(a.)* 不幸的
disagreement *(n.)* 爭論	incorrect *(a.)* 不正確的	nonfunctioning *(a.)* 沒有作用的	unfounded *(a.)* 沒有事實根據的
disappointed *(a.)* 失望的	inexperienced *(a.)* 沒有經驗的	off-putting *(a.)* 令人厭惡的	unjustifiable *(a.)* 沒有正當理由的
displeased *(a.)* 不悅的	inferior *(a.)* 品質較差的	omission *(n.)* 遺漏	unpleasant *(a.)* 不高興的
dispute *(n.)* 爭執	insufficient *(a.)* 不足的	overcharged *(a.)* 收費過高的	unprofessional *(a.)* 不專業的
dissatisfaction *(n.)* 不滿意	lax *(a.)* 散漫的	overestimated *(a.)* 估價過高的	unqualified *(a.)* 資格不足的

25

抱怨與客訴

embarrassing *(a.)* 窘迫的	misapprehension *(n.)* 錯誤理解	overlooked *(a.)* 疏忽的	unreasonable *(a.)* 不合理的
exasperating *(a.)* 令人惱怒的	miscalculation *(n.)* 錯誤計算	oversight *(n.)* 疏忽	unreliable *(a.)* 不可靠的
experience *(n.)* 經驗	misconception *(n.)* 錯誤觀念	regrettable *(a.)* 遺憾的	unsatisfactory *(a.)* 不令人滿意的
fault *(n.)* 錯誤	misconstrued *(a.)* 推斷錯誤的	reimburse *(v.)* 償付	unsound *(a.)* 不安全的
flaw *(n.)* 瑕疵	mishandled *(a.)* 處理錯誤的	remake *(v.)* 重做	untidy *(a.)* 不整潔的
grievance *(n.)* 不滿	misinformed *(a.)* 誤傳的	repair *(v.)* 修理	untrue *(a.)* 不真實的
ill-advised *(a.)* 不明智的	misinterpreted *(a.)* 解讀錯誤的	repay *(v.)* 償還	unwarranted *(a.)* 沒有保固的

25
抱怨與客訴

💬 詞組

does not meet our performance
standards
不符合我們的性能標準

appealing to you for help
向你請求協助

are you aware that
你是否察覺……

as a longtime customer
作為長期的客戶

call to your immediate attention
請求你立即關注

correct your records
修改你的紀錄

I was displeased/distressed/disturbed/
offended/disappointed by
我因……感到不悅／苦惱／心亂／冒犯／失望

I wish to be reimbursed for
我希望因……而獲得賠償

I would like to alert you to
我想要讓你注意到……

may not be aware that
也許未察覺……

not up to your usual high standards
不符合貴公司一貫的高標準

register a complaint about
提出關於……的申訴

deceptive advertising
廣告不實

defective upon arrival
到貨時有缺損

a mix-up in my order
我的訂單有錯誤

expect to hear from you soon
期盼盡快得到你的回應

expensive maintenance
昂貴的保養費

has not met my expectations
不符合我的期望

high prices
高昂價格

hope to resolve this problem
希望能解決這個問題

I am concerned about
我擔心……

I feel certain you would want to know that
我確信你會希望知道……

inefficient design
缺乏效率的設計

it has come to my attention that
我注意到

we were unhappy with
我們對……感到不悅

you have generally given us excellent service, but
你通常都提供很棒的服務，但是……

serious omission/problem
嚴重的遺漏／問題

shoddy workmanship
粗劣的品質

slow delivery
貨運緩慢

under the conditions of the warranty
在保固的條件下

unpleasant incident
令人不悅的事件

unresponsive personnel
反應遲鈍的工作人員

unsafe product
不安全的產品

unsatisfactory performance
令人不滿意的表現

warranty inaccuracies
保修單不確實

it is with reluctance that I must inform you
我不得不通知你

with all possible speed
以最快的速度

would like credit for
希望……得到認可

it was disconcerting to find that
很不安地發現……

句子

Anything you can do to speed matters up/resolve this problem will be greatly appreciated.
希望您能盡快處理／盡力解決這個問題，我會非常感激。

Here are the facts.
事實如下。

I am confident that you can resolve this.
我確信您能解決它。

I am expecting the courtesy of a prompt reply.
我期盼您的迅速回覆。

I am writing regarding my last bill, invoice #G4889, dated August 15, 2017.
我寄信是為了最近一次的帳單，發貨單號 #G4889，日期為二〇一七年八月十五日。

I believe that an apology is due us.
我相信我們應該得到一聲道歉。

I expect an adjustment to be made as soon as possible.
我希望能盡速做出處置。

I hope you will take this complaint in the helpful spirit in which it is meant.
我希望您能把這封抱怨信視為一種幫助，因為我的意圖僅是如此。

I know you will want to see that such an incident does not occur again.
我知道您也希望這種事件不會再次發生。

I like your product but I object strongly to your advertising.
我喜歡您們的產品，但強烈不認同您們的廣告方式。

I'm concerned about Coach Ingelsant's angry, abusive manner with the junior soccer players.
我對英格桑教練對待青少年足球隊員的憤怒粗魯態度感到憂心。

I'm confident that we can resolve this matter to our mutual satisfaction.
我確信我們能找出讓雙方都滿意的解決方式。

I regret/am sorry to inform you of the following unpleasant situation.
很遺憾通知您以下令人不悦的狀況。

I strongly oppose your position on this weapons system.
我強烈反對您對此套武器系統的立場。

It is my understanding that it will be repaired/replaced at your expense.
就我的理解，修理／替換費會由您支出。

I will send a check for the balance as soon as I receive a corrected statement.
待收到修正的月結單後，我會馬上寄出支票償清餘款。

I wish to receive credit on my account for this item.
我希望能將此品項退費至我的帳戶。

I would appreciate a telephone call from you about this situation.
我希望您能打電話給我說明此情況。

I would like a refund in the amount of $49.99.
我希望收到金額 49.99 元的退費。

I would like to clear up this misunderstanding as soon as possible.
我希望能盡快釐清此誤會。

Let me know what is being done.
讓我知道目前的處理進度。

Please call the principal's office to arrange a meeting with the principal, the school counselor, and myself regarding Christie's suspension.
請致電校長辦公室，安排我與校長及學校輔導員開一場會議，討論克莉絲蒂的停學。

Please contact me within three business days to make arrangements for rectifying the situation.
請於三個工作日內聯絡我，以安排後續事宜改正此情況。

Please let me hear from you at your earliest convenience.
請盡快回應。

Please let me know what options are available to me.
請讓我知道我有哪些選擇。

Thank you for your prompt assistance with this situation/problem.
謝謝您如此迅速協助我處理此情況／問題。

The following situation has come to my attention.
我注意到以下狀況。

The most satisfactory solution for us would be for you to send us a replacement lamp and reimburse us for the cost of mailing the defective lamp back to you.
最能讓我們滿意的解決方法，是寄給我們全新的燈具，並補償我們寄回缺損燈具的運費。

There was too little feedback to us during the design of the #2 unit.
在設計二號組件的過程中，我們收到的回饋太少。

This product has been unsatisfactory in several respects.
這個產品在許多方面都讓人不滿意。

We experienced the following problem in your store/restaurant/hotel last week.
上週我們在貴商店／餐廳／旅館遇到以下問題。

Will you please check on this?
可以煩請您檢查此事嗎？

25

抱怨與客訴

段落

I received the leather patchwork travel bag today (copies of catalog page and invoice enclosed), but the matching billfold was not included. Please send me one as soon as possible, in burgundy to match the bag. Thank you.

我在今天收到了真皮拼貼旅行包（隨信附上型錄的產品介紹影本與發貨單），但成套的皮夾卻未包含在內。請盡速將皮夾寄給我，請寄與旅行包配成套的酒紅色款式。謝謝。

Five weeks ago I mailed you my check for our stay at the Vörös Csillig in Budapest, and I have not yet received confirmation of our reservations. As the rest of my itinerary depends on whether we are able to stay in Budapest, I would appreciate an immediate phone call from you.

五週前我寄出支票，預訂我們在布達佩斯紅星飯店的住房，但我尚未收到訂房確認。由於我們的行程會因是否能住在布達佩斯而改變，我希望您能立即打電話給我。

Channel 12's insistence on running inappropriate programming between 5 p.m. and 7 p.m., when many young people are watching, means that this family at least will no longer turn to Channel 12 for any of its news, entertainment, or programs.

第十二頻道堅持在下午五點至七點間播放不宜觀賞的節目，這個時段有許多小孩在看電視，所以我們全家決定，不再轉到第十二頻道收看任何新聞娛樂等節目。

Please find enclosed a bracelet, a necklace, and a pair of earrings. We would appreciate either repair or replacement of these items. The bracelet has a broken clasp, the gold on the earrings appears to be chipped, and the silver finish is overlaying the gemstone on the necklace. In each case, dissatisfied customers of our store returned the items to us. Your immediate attention to this matter will be greatly appreciated.

請見附上的手鍊、項鍊與一對耳環。我們希望您能修理或替換這些商品。手鍊的鉤環壞了，耳環上的金色部分顯然已剝落，而項鍊上的銀漆則將寶石遮住了。這些瑕疵使我們的顧客不滿，並將商品退還給我們。希望您能立即關注這個問題。

Dear Harter & Benjamin Jewelers:

We, the undersigned members of the Eustace College staff, object to the recent ads for Harter & Benjamin Jewelers that have appeared in the college newspaper. All of them advertise your jewelry with the word Intoxicating and show a young man and young woman obviously drinking alcohol. The artwork features champagne glasses and wine and liquor bottles.

Why are you using alcohol to sell jewelry? There must be many other symbols, appeals, campaigns, graphics that would better sell your product. By associating alcohol with "the good life," you are selling college students on the "joys" of booze. We believe this is undesirable and indefensible.

We've spoken to the newspaper staff and adviser about the wisdom of accepting any more of these ads and have also suggested they write an article explaining why such ads are refused.

We sincerely hope you will consider dropping this particular angle in your advertising, especially in periodicals aimed at young audiences.

Sincerely,

哈特與班傑明珠寶您好：

我們身為尤思塔斯學院的員工（如以下簽名者），反對最近出現在學院報紙上的哈特與班傑明珠寶廣告。這些廣告都用了「令人沉醉」一詞，並以一對年輕男女正在飲酒的形象呈現。廣告中有香檳酒杯與紅酒及烈酒酒瓶。

為何要用酒來銷售珠寶？一定有其他更適合用來販售貴公司產品的象徵、形象、活動或圖案。當您們將酒精與「美好人生」建立起關聯時，貴公司便是以酗酒的「樂趣」來銷售商品。我們相信這並不是大家所希望看到且能接受的。

我們已經與報刊員工及指導教授商談是否要繼續刊登這類廣告，並建議他們寫篇文章解釋這種廣告遭到拒絕的原因。

我們誠心希望貴公司能考慮不再於廣告中呈現這個概念，尤其是不要刊登在以年輕讀者為對象的刊物上。

○○敬上

Dear Dean Higgs:

Last week the College hosted one of the most important international conferences on philosophy in many years—and virtually nobody knew about it.

The Public Affairs Office was briefed about the conference over a period of months: at a two-hour breakfast meeting in March, at three meetings in April, via ten pages of updated notes, details, and list of interview possibilities in May, and at a final one-hour meeting in June.

Despite this, no news releases were sent by the College's publicity department, no photographers were present at major events, the Nobel Prize-winning speakers were not interviewed, and neither of the metro-area newspapers carried articles or features on what was surely an event of local and international significance.

I ask that this situation be investigated, an apology be tendered, and some guarantees for future College publicity be spelled out.

Yours truly,

希格斯院長您好：

上週學院舉辦了多年來最重要的一場國際哲學研討會，卻幾乎沒有人知道這件事。

過去幾個月，我們數次向公共事務處簡報這場研討會：三月的兩小時早餐會議；四月的三場會議；五月提交十頁的最新資訊、細節與訪問人選清單；六月的一小時最後一次會議。

然而，學院的公關部門未曾寄發新聞稿、主要活動時無攝影師到場、曾獲諾貝爾獎的講者未受訪問，而在都會區可取得的報紙，亦沒有一家報導或提及這件在本地與國際上皆很重要的大事。

我要求院方調查此情況、給予道歉，並為未來學院的公關活動提出保證。

○○謹上

Dear Mr. Blowberry,

I would like to register a complaint about one of your employees, Albert Grope. When I was in your bookstore last week, Mr. Grope persisted in answering my questions in a very loud voice, using one-syllable words and enunciating in an exaggerated fashion. Although I have an accent, my English is correct enough to allow me to teach classics at the university level, and I feel his behavior was inappropriate. Between sentences he would archly eye the other clerk, obviously aware of how hilariously "funny" he was. Even if I had as little command of the English language as Mr. Grope assumed, and were dim-witted besides, I believe he owes every customer a certain respect.

I have spoken to you on several occasions and I felt you were the sort of person who would want to know this.

Sincerely,

布婁貝里先生您好：

我要投訴您的一名員工，亞伯特·葛洛普。上週我去貴書店時，葛洛普先生堅持用非常大的音量、單音節字詞與過度清晰的發音來回答我的問題。儘管我有口音，但我的英語程度足以讓我在大學教導古典文學，我認為他的行為很不合宜。說話時，他甚至狡黠地看向其他店員，顯然他知道自己有多「搞笑」。即便我真的像葛洛普先生認為的那樣不擅長英語，甚至很愚笨，我相信他仍應該要尊重每位顧客。

我曾在數個場合與您講過話，我認為您會想要知道此事。

○○敬上

Re: BankCard #2378-54-8970

My statement dated August 28, 2017, shows an entry for $59 payable to NewFit Shoes, Murray Road and Converse Boulevard, Chicago, dated June 30, 2017.

This charge does not belong on my account. I was in California at the time and, in any case, have never been in that particular store.

Please remove this charge from my account. Enclosed is my check for the balance of my account, $148.53. This amount does not include the $59 for the shoes.

Thank you for taking care of this matter.

主旨：銀行卡帳號 2378-54-8970

在二〇一七年八月二十八日的月結單上，顯示二〇一七年七月三十日有一筆 59 元的應付帳款繳給新規格鞋店（芝加哥墨瑞路與康為大道交口）。

此筆金額並不屬於我的帳單。當時我人在加州，而且，我不曾造訪這家店。

請從我的帳單中移除這筆帳款。隨信附上 148.53 元支票支付本期帳單，此金額不含支付鞋子的 59 元。

謝謝您處理此事。

Dear Mr. Tallant:

As you know, a great deal of our work is coordinated with Harvey Crane Construction.

They must complete their paving and other operations before the median work on Pearl Street can begin. I have seen no progress on their part for about a month. Their delays mean that we incur such damages as loss of production, lower profits, winter protection costs, remobilization, accelerated schedules (overtime), and barricade rental—to name just a few items.

As these costs and damages will necessarily be passed on to you, you may want to check into the situation.

Sincerely,

塔倫先生您好：

如您所知，我們有很多工程都與哈維克倫建設合作。他們必須先完成路面鋪設及其他工程，才能開始進行珍珠街上的安全島工程。

他們已經長達一個月的時間沒有進展。他們的延誤會為我們帶來多種損失，包含生產損失、獲利短少、冬季工程保護費用、重新動員費用、趕工費用（加班費）及租借路障的費用，而這些僅是其中一部分的損失而已。

這些費用與損失勢必會成為您的責任，所以您也許會希望了解這個情況。

〇〇敬上

Dear Dr. Blenkinsop,

As you know, we have been satisfied patients of yours for the past six years. However, I wonder if you are aware that the condition of your waiting room is off-putting. The carpet rarely appears vacuumed, the plastic plants are thick with dust, and the magazines and children's playthings are strewn about, apparently untouched from one of our visits to the next. Hygiene seems particularly important in a health care environment, and, although I know what an excellent physician you are, I can't help worrying about how clean everything else is.

I hope you find this letter helpful rather than unpleasant—it was written with the best intentions.

Sincerely,

布倫金索醫師您好：

如您所知，在過去六年來，您一直是我們很滿意的醫生。然而，我不知道您有沒有發現，您的等待室很令人不適。地毯看起來未經清理；假盆栽上滿是灰塵；雜誌與兒童玩具四散各處，顯然，從我們上次造訪以來就沒有人整理過。在醫療照護機構中，衛生是特別重要的一環；儘管我知道您是一位非常優秀的醫師，但我還是忍不住擔心其他設備是否衛生。

我希望您會覺得這封信是有幫助的，而不是令您不悅的，因為我想要表達的只有善意。

○○敬上

✉ 參見：03 回應、13 致歉信、14 收件通知、35 客訴處理信、37 訂單處理信、48 給鄰居的信

25

抱怨與客訴

Chapter 26

致編輯函
Letters to the Editor

> 人人看法相同並不是件好事；
> 有不同的意見，我們才能像賽馬一樣彼此競爭。
>
> ——馬克・吐溫

致編輯函（letter to the editor）是人們最喜愛的一種讀物。也因此，幾乎每份報紙或期刊都會刊出一定數量的致編輯函。每日發行的報紙，會從收到的信件中選出百分之三十至四十刊登；全國性的新聞週刊則只會刊出百分之二至五的來信。不過，幸好我們有辦法可以增加你的信被選上的機會。

PART 1 說明篇

何時可以寫信給編輯？

贊同或反對某篇新聞
　　文章、故事、社論
　　或其他讀者來信

修正刊登的資料

對熱門議題提出看法　　想傳達資訊給更多人知道

該怎麼說？

1. 第一句就提及寫信的原因，如 the Nov. 1 editorial opposing a new hockey arena「十一月一日反對新曲棍球場的社論」，讓讀者馬上知道這封致編輯函的目的。

2. 明確表達立場，是 I agree with（我同意）、I oppose（我反對），還是 I question（我質疑）。

3. 為你的立場提出證據與支持的理由。多數刊物都會為這種信函設定字數限制；若超出字數，編輯可能會把內容修成你不喜歡的樣子。請控制在一百至三百字英文字以內。

4. 提出客觀事實（統計數據、研究資料、文章、紀錄、引言），不要訴諸主觀感受或印象。若你對該議題有特別研究或專業背景，請寫出來，這會增加刊登機率，並讓你的意見看起來更有用。

5. 必要的話，指出希望讀者閱讀之後所採取的行動（建立鄰里守衛隊、打電話給立法委員、抵制一項產品、簽署請願書、停止亂丟垃圾）。

6. 盡可能以強而有力、令人難忘的一句話收尾，這會讓讀者想要回頭重看你的信函。

7. 提供你的全名，或至少名字的首字母加上姓氏、地址與白天的聯絡電話。還有，要簽名——幾乎所有的刊物都會堅持要你這麼做。若給編輯的信上有許多人的簽名，通常只有一、兩個名字會被刊登（後面註記「與其他十六人」），多數刊物寧願把這些空間拿來刊登意見，而非一連串的姓名。

什麼不該說？

- 別用 You won't dare print this letter.「你不敢刊登這封信的。」當做信件開頭，這類句子通常會被刪掉，編輯的確敢把各種意見刊登出來，即使是那些批評他們的信函。

- 不要抱怨，這種信讀起來一點也不有趣。

- 若你在信中大剌剌地為你的公司或團體打廣告，請別期待報紙或雜誌會刊登。如果你希望人們知道一個非營利、與社會公益相關的活動，編輯通常願意在活動專欄中放入這個消息。

- 勿提供半真半假或不正確的言論。編輯會核對信函長度、內容真實性、得體與否、是否符合報紙風格等。

- 勿提供帶有惡意的言論（即便你說的是事實），也別寫任何你無法證明的事（即便你沒有傷人的意圖）；出版社不會刊登任何有毀謗疑慮的文章。

- 別在言詞中顯露威嚇、脅迫、輕蔑或刻板印象。有些讀者確實會同意你，但多數讀者都知道這種言詞反映的是薄弱的論點。英國前首相柴契爾夫人（Margaret Thatcher）曾說：「遭受某種特別傷人的攻擊時，我總是非常高興，因為我心想，如果他們只能做人身攻擊，表示他們沒有任何政治上的論點。」

- 別以 Think about it!「好好想想吧！」收尾。一名編輯曾表示，這句話時常出現在信中，而每次都會被刪除。當你的信出現在社論對頁版（op-ed），就表示人們已經知道這種信函是需要思考的。

- 別在信中寫詩、尋人啟示或私人訊息。

寫作訣竅

- 查看投稿規定或是作者指引（Instructions to Authors）。多數刊物都有其遵守規則。
- 致編輯函的對象是編輯，而不是要為你信件內容負責的人。
- 你也許會想評論先前出版過的致編輯函。儘管區域報紙可能會接受這類信件，但多數全國性報章雜誌都有相關政策，避免刊登回應其他致編輯函的信函。
- 撰寫的議題須符合時事，編輯不太會選擇已經過時的議題。
- 集中講一個主題或一個主要看法。如果你的信沒有重點或重點太多，信件便很可能會被修改，以突顯它的重點。
- 確保有超過一個人（你自己）認為你提出的議題是重要的。讀者並不在乎你的鄰居有多糟糕，除非你能將鄰居的行為連結到一個更重要的議題（如：鄰居不清除人行道的雪）。
- 若你希望寄出的致編輯函能被選上，請以簡潔幽默的筆觸，表達不尋常的資訊或反轉傳統觀念。編輯偏好以下的內容：引發讀者興趣；表達對某爭議的看法；針對廣泛的主題傳達獨特觀點；清楚、有趣而發人深省。
- 若你對某項議題有很強烈的意見，你也可以號召其他人寫信。這些寄至專欄的信件，顯示許多人與你有相同感受。
- 寄出前，先讓別人讀一讀你的信；有時你太專注在議題上，反而看不見這封信會如何影響他人。
- 多數報紙不會頻繁刊登同一作者的信件，頂多一、兩個月刊登一篇。所以，如果你的信才剛被刊登，不必急著寫另一封信。
- 同一封信不可同時寄給很多家出版社，多數出版社不會喜歡看到自己刊登的致編輯函也能在其他刊物上讀到。請確認所投稿的刊物的其他規定。

特殊狀況

- 出版社很少會刊登**匿名信**，因為他們認為讀者有權知道發表意見的人是誰。不過，有些情況是容許匿名的（可能使作者受到傷害或丟掉工作）。編輯會以「Name Withheld」（姓名保留）的名義刊登這種信件。請先打電話詢問，確保這是可行的。在你寫信時，明確指出只有在匿名狀態下你才同意發表此信。
- 讀者專欄在**選舉前**總是特別受歡迎。有些出版社會刊登支持某一候選人或批評另一候選人的信函。在選前幾天或當天，有些出版社會禁止任何與選舉有關的信件，避免有心人士利用此專欄進行最後攻擊。明目張膽的政治活動通常上不了這個版面，這類有宣傳意味，或企圖製造一窩蜂熱潮的內容，編輯都能找得出來。

- **要求修正或撤回不正確的內容時**，先指出該文章的刊登日期、章節、頁碼與欄位。要有禮貌、講求事實、堅定。提供正確數據，與能證實你的主張的資料，並留下電話號碼，供對方核對內容。
- 你也可以寫信給編輯，**推薦對社會有貢獻卻鮮為人知的人物或市民團體**。這樣的信件，不僅能為讀者專欄增添少見的輕鬆氣息，還能建立正向的社會氣氛，促使更多的正向活動發生。然而，請記得這種「和善」的信函並不常被選上，你需要為它添加些幽默、機智或色彩。

格式

- 編輯偏好以電腦打字的致編輯信函。若你用手寫，請確保別人讀得懂你的字。
- 多數出版社接受以電子郵件或傳真寄發的信函。

單字

advice *(n.)* 建議	perspective *(n.)* 觀點	contradict *(v.)* 與……矛盾	prejudiced *(a.)* 有偏見的
aspect *(n.)* 面向	position *(n.)* 立場	disagree *(v.)* 不同意	provocative *(a.)* 挑撥的
attitude *(n.)* 態度	posture *(n.)* 姿態	disapprove *(v.)* 不贊同	doctrinaire *(a.)* 不切實際的
bias *(n.)* 偏見	premise *(n.)* 前提	examine *(v.)* 檢視	dogmatic *(a.)* 固執武斷的
commentary *(n.)* 評論	slant *(n.)* 看法、傾向	express *(v.)* 表達	embarrassing *(a.)* 尷尬的
consensus *(n.)* 共識	stand *(n.)* 立場	infer *(v.)* 推論	inflammatory *(a.)* 有煽動性的
controversy *(n.)* 爭議	view *(n.)* 看法	persuade *(v.)* 說服	insulting *(a.)* 侮辱的
impression *(n.)* 印象	assume *(v.)* 假設	suppose *(v.)* 認為	judgmental *(a.)* 妄下判斷的
misunderstanding *(n.)* 誤會	conclude *(v.)* 總結	surmise *(v.)* 推測	offensive *(a.)* 有攻擊性的
notion *(n.)* 概念	conjecture *(n.) & (v.)* 推測	dissatisfied *(a.)* 不滿意的	one-sided *(a.)* 單方面的
omission *(n.)* 省略	consider *(v.)* 考慮	disturbing *(a.)* 煩人的	unfortunate *(a.)* 不幸的
partisan *(n.)* 支持者			

26

致編輯函

詞組

after reading your Sept. 29 article on
在讀了你於九月二十九日關於……的來信後

I must take issue with
我必須針對……提出異議

a May 3 *New York Post Dispatch* article spoke of
五月三日於《紐約郵報》刊登的文章說到

I was disturbed/incensed/pleased/angry/disappointed to read that
讀到……使我心煩／憤怒／愉悅／生氣／失望

I strongly object
我強烈反對

I really enjoyed
我真的很喜歡

presented a false picture
呈現錯誤的情況

an affront to those of us who
對我們的公開侮辱

did a slow burn when I read
讓我在閱讀時越來越生氣

it seems to me
就我看來

difference of opinion
不同的意見

neglected to mention
刻意未提及

fail to agree
無法同意

made me see red
令我怒火中燒

how can anyone state, as did Laetitia Snap (June 3), that
怎麼有人能像萊蒂莎‧史奈普（六月三日）說出

letter writer Muriel McComber's suggestion (Aug. 9) was intriguing, but
信件作者莫瑞爾‧麥康柏的建議（八月九日）很有趣，但是

I agree wholeheartedly with
我完全同意

one side of the story
單方說法

I am horrified by the Aug. 11 report
八月十一日的報告讓我嚇壞了

on the one hand/on the other hand
一方面／另一方面

I am one of the many "misguided" people who was outraged by
我就是受到「誤導」的其中一人，並因……感到憤怒

I disagree with the Reverend Septimus Crisparkle's premise (Feb. 7)
我不同意賽提默斯‧克里帕可牧師提出的假設（二月七日）。

I am puzzled by the reference to the long-term effects of
關於……的長期影響的資料令我困惑

cartoonist Humphry Clinker should be aware that
諷刺畫家杭弗利‧柯林克應該要知道

I am writing on behalf of
我代表……寫這封信

read with great/considerable interest
饒富興味地閱讀

point in dispute
爭論點

recipe for disaster
災難的肇因

I found the short story in your September issue to be
我認為在你九月期刊中刊登的內容是……

regarding Senator Sam Blundel's new bill for the hearing-impaired
關於山姆·布朗德參議員為聽障者提出的新法案

I take exception to the opinions expressed by
由……表達的意見，我會視為例外

several letter writers have commented upon
多封讀者來信都針對……給予評論

in response to a July 3 letter writer who said
在此回應七月三日的信函作者，該作者提到

the article on women in trades did much to
這篇談論商界女性的文章對……大有助益

infuriating to see that
很憤怒看到

your editorial position on
你在社論中關於……的立場

your Sept. 17 editorial on
你在九月十七日有關……的社論

句子

A Dec. 9 writer is incorrect in saying that the Regional Transit Board was abolished several years ago; we are, in fact, alive and well.
十二月九日的一名作者指出，地區運輸委員會在多年前已廢止，但這個消息是不正確的；事實上，我們仍然存在，且運作良好。

I am writing to express my appreciation for your excellent coverage of City Council meetings on the local groundwater issue.
您在新聞中報導市議會針對城市地下水問題的開會內容，該報導十分優秀，我想表達我的欽佩。

I commend you for your Aug. 11 editorial on magnet schools.
我很讚賞八月十一日時您那篇關於名校的社論。

I disagree with Elizabeth Saunders' Apr. 5 column on city-supported recycling.
我不贊同伊莉莎白·桑德於四月五日之專欄文章，主題為市府支援之資源回收。

I look forward to seeing a published retraction of the incorrect information given in this article.
我期望看見一篇聲明撤回那篇錯誤文章的報導。

In Hennie Feinschreiber's Dec. 9 column on the living will, she uses statistics that have long since been discredited.

荷妮‧范許萊柏在十二月九日的專欄文章中討論生前遺囑，但她使用的統計數據在很久之前便已不受到採信。

In his December 1 Counterpoint, "Tax Breaks for the Rich," Gerald Tetley suggests that out of fear of giving the rich a break, we are actually cutting off our noses to spite our face.

十二月一日，傑拉德‧泰利在〈為富人減稅〉一文中提出反駁，他指出，當我們害怕讓富人減稅時，我們其實是在跟自己過不去。

I was disappointed that not one of the dozens who wrote to complain about the hike in municipal sewer rates noticed that the rates are actually lower than they were ten years ago.

許多人寫信抱怨市內汙水處理費飆升，但卻沒有人注意到，現在的收費其實比十年前還低，對此我實在感到失望。

Many thanks for your unpopular but eminently sane editorial stand on gun control (July 2).

非常感謝您那篇關於槍枝控管的社論（七月二日），雖不受歡迎，卻相當明智。

Please consider the cumulative effect of such legislation on our children.

請考慮這樣的法案對孩子日積月累的影響。

Please do not drop Flora Lewis/Cal Thomas/Ellen Goodman/George Will from your editorial pages.

請不要將芙蘿拉‧李維斯／卡爾‧湯瑪斯／艾倫‧古德曼／喬治‧威爾從貴社論版面移除。

Several important factors were omitted from your Apr. 6 article on wide-area telephone service.

在您四月六日提到廣域電話服務的文章中，有幾項要點被忽略了。

The writer of the Mar. 16 letter against triple trailers seemed to have little factual understanding of semi-truck traffic and professional truck drivers.

三月十六日的作者在信中反對三節貨車，但他似乎對於半掛式卡車的交通運輸及專業卡車司機並無實際了解。

Your Aug. 3 editorial on workers' compensation overlooked a crucial factor.

您在八月三日之社論中討論工傷賠償，但您忽略了一項關鍵要點。

Your June 29 editorial on child care failed to mention one of the largest and most effective groups working on this issue.

您在六月二十九日的社論中談到孩童的照護，卻沒有提及在此議題上最大、最有力量的一個團體。

段落

Has anyone noticed that the city has become overrun with dogs in the last several years? Most of these dogs have no collars and run in packs of five to eight dogs. If I had small children, I'd worry when they played outdoors. Where have these dogs come from? Whose problem is it? The city council's? The health department's? The police department's?

有沒有人注意到，在過去幾年，市內出現越來越多犬隻？這些狗大多沒有頸圈，以五至八隻為單位成群而行。若我有年紀小的孩子，當他們在室外玩的時候，我一定會很擔心。這些狗是從哪裡來的？這是誰該負責的問題？是市議會嗎？還是健康部門？或是警察部門？

Your story on the newest technology in today's emergency rooms featured the views of hospital administrators, medical care givers, and manufacturers' representatives. Nowhere was a patient mentioned. Is overlooking the patient also a feature of today's emergency rooms? (If it is, it's not new.)

您的文章以醫院管理階層、醫療服務人員與廠商代表的觀點，討論到目前急診室的最新科技，但是卻完全沒有提到患者。難道忽略患者也是今日急診室的一大特徵嗎？（若是如此，那也不是新聞了。）

To those of you who have been expressing yourself in these pages about the presence of wild geese in the city parks: Hello! A park is supposed to be natural. It is not meant to be as clean as your kitchen floor. It has messy leaves and gravel and bugs and, yes, goose grease. If you can't handle nature in the raw, there's always your backyard.

致曾在這個版面上針對市內公園的野鵝發表看法的你們：哈囉！公園就應該符合自然，而不該像你的廚房地板一樣乾淨。公園就該有亂亂的樹葉、沙礫、蟲子以及，沒錯，鵝糞便。如果你沒有辦法接受大自然，你還有你家後院可以去。

There was an error in your otherwise excellent article about the Lamprey Brothers Moving and Storage. In addition to brothers Henry, Colin, and Stephen (whom you mentioned), there is also brother Michael, a full partner.

您那篇關於藍普利兄弟運輸倉儲公司的文章近乎完美，但有一處錯誤。除了（您在文中提到的）亨利、柯林與史蒂芬，還有一名兄弟麥可，也是合夥人。

26
致編輯函

I commend Meg Bishop for the use of "people first" language in her Jan. 2 column. By using expressions such as "people with severe disabilities" rather than "the severely disabled" and "people with quadriplegia" rather than "quadriplegics," Bishop helps change the way society views people with disabilities.

梅格‧畢許在一月二日專欄中「以人為先」的表達方式，令我很讚賞。畢許以「有嚴重殘障的人」取代「嚴重殘障者」、以「患有四肢麻痺的人」取代「四肢麻痺者」，像這樣的表達方式，有助改變這個社會看待患有殘疾的人的方式。

示範信

To the Editor:

So the tax collectors and money changers in rural Wayne County are persecuting Amish woodworker Sam Swartzendruber because he will not get a permit for his outdoor privy. They have fined him and charged him with over 100 offenses, one for each day he uses the privy without a permit. Now he will probably go to jail for his refusal to bend his beliefs to those of the bureaucrats who cannot come up with a reasonable way to regulate outdoor privies.

On my farm in a residential zone in Story County, I could build an unlined earthen sewage cesspool with more than 2 million gallons of liquid manure, taking in waste from up to 4,166 factory hogs, with no state or county permits. I could pollute the air for miles around, contaminate groundwater, and pile up my dead hogs daily out by the road with no permits. Not only would I not go to jail, but our governor, Legislature, and the Iowa Supreme Court would all congratulate me and tell me I was helping to build a better Iowa.

Be a good neighbor, go to jail. But build a hog factory, and you're a hero. Iowans ought to give Sam a medal for reminding us all what it means to stand up for our beliefs. We're jailing the wrong people. Let's pen up the mega-hog factory profiteers and turn Sam loose.

致編輯：

在以農業為主的韋恩郡，當地的稅務員與貨幣兌換商正在為難阿米希族的木工山姆‧史瓦森卓柏，因為他無法獲得許可使用他的戶外廁所。他們罰他錢，並控訴他犯下超過一百項違法行為，每當他未經許可使用廁所，他犯的罪條便又添了一項。現在，他大概要去坐牢了，只因他不願折損他的信仰去迎合那些官僚，而這些官僚根本找不到合理的方式來規範戶外廁所。

我在史杜里郡的住宅區擁有一個農場，我可以在農場中建一個未防滲的土製汙水池，內含兩百萬加侖的液態肥料，肥料來源是工廠裡 4,166 頭肉豬的排泄物，而我並沒有任何州或郡的許可。我可以汙染周遭的空氣、弄髒地下水、每天都把死豬屍體堆在路邊，而我還是不需要許可。我不只不會去坐牢，我們的州長、議會與愛荷華最高法院還會恭喜我，說我是在幫忙建設一個更好的愛荷華州。

認真做個好鄰居的人去坐了牢；建立肉豬工廠的人則成了英雄。愛荷華人真應該給山姆一面獎牌，因為他提醒了我們，為自己的信仰挺身而出是有意義的。我們關錯了人。該進監牢的是那些因肉豬工廠而致富的人，讓我們放了山姆吧。

Dear Mr. Scott,

What happened to the ecclesiastical crossword puzzle you used to have every month in *The Abbot*?

史考特先生您好：

您以前每個月都會在《修道院刊》放上基督教會填字遊戲；最近發生什麼事了呢？

To the Editor:

Several months ago, you announced a "bold new look" for the paper. Could we perhaps have the timid old look back?

Sometimes I find the financial pages behind the sports pages, sometimes in a section of their own, and occasionally with the classified ads. Usually the advice columnists and funnies are run together in their own section, but more often they are separated and positioned variously with the sports pages, the community news, the feature section, or the food pages.

I have tried to discern a method to your madness—perhaps on Mondays the sports have their own section, on Tuesdays they appear with the financial papers. No such luck. Somebody down there must just roll dice and say, "Ha! Let them try to find the foreign exchange rates today!"

Is there any hope for a more organized future?

致編輯：

數個月前，貴報宣布要為報紙換上「大膽的新面貌」；但是，我們能不能換回那膽怯的舊面貌呢？

我發現，有時財經版在運動版後面，有時又獨立一頁，偶爾則是跟分類廣告放在一起。而有時提供建議的專欄會與滑稽漫畫放在一起，有時又有獨立頁面，但更多時候它們時常散落各處，與運動版、地方新聞、特別報導或美食版放在一起。

我曾試著要為貴報的雜亂無章理出一個頭緒：或許週一的運動版會有獨立頁面，週二則會與財經版放在一起。可惜我沒那麼幸運。我想，您們那裡一定有個人在丟擲骰子，並說著：「哈！讓他們找找看今天的外幣匯率吧！」

我們可以有一個更有章法的未來嗎？

Dear Mr. Burlap:

The excerpt from *Point Counter Point* in your June issue was excellent. I hope you will continue to offer us selections from lesser-known but high-quality literature.

貝賴先生您好：

您刊登於六月號《針鋒相對》的文摘真的很棒。希望您會繼續節選刊登少為人知卻優異的文學作品。

Dear Editor:

I read with interest the proposal to add four stories to the downtown public library building at a cost of $5.3 million.

I am concerned, however, that no provision has been made for user access. As it now stands, hundreds of thousands of books are all but useless since no one can get to them. There are a handful of metered street parking spaces, but you must be lucky to find one. And then you must not forget to run out every hour and insert four more quarters (the meter readers are particularly active in this area).

How many of you have driven around and around and around hoping for a parking place? How many of you have walked five or six blocks carrying a back breaking load of books? How many of you have gotten $10 tickets because you forgot to feed the meter on time? It is utterly pointless to spend $5.3 million on a facility that no one can use.

編輯您好：

看了以 5,300,000 元為市區公立圖書館擴建四層樓的提案，我很感興趣。

然而，本提案沒有以借閱者使用為出發點作考量。目前有成千上萬本書處於無用狀態，只因為民眾沒有辦法借閱這些書。街上有少數按時計費的停車格可供使用，但你要夠幸運才能找到一個車位。接著你還不能忘了，每小時要趕著出來投四枚 25 分硬幣（這個區域的停車計費器特別有效率）才能繼續使用。

在您們之中，有多少人曾經開著車在附近不斷轉呀轉，只希望找到一個車位？您們有多少人曾經扛著沉甸甸的書本步行五、六個街區？您們又有多少人被開過 10 元的罰單，只因為忘了及時投入硬幣？在一棟沒人可使用的建築上花費 5,300,000 萬，根本毫無意義。

✉ 參見：11 表揚信、24 反對信、25 抱怨與客訴

Chapter 27

申請信
Letters of Application

撰寫求職文件，是多數人最接近完美的時刻。
——肯·卡夫特（Ken Kraft）

想爭取面試機會，有三種方法：

1. 填寫並繳交該公司的職務申請表，隨表可附上一封求職信（cover letter）。信中簡要說明自己適合這份工作的一到兩項理由，並提及文件內包含申請表。

2. 寄出履歷表（résumé）。履歷表上需清楚條列工作經歷、教育背景、技能及職涯目標，並附上求職信。

3. 撰寫一封結合求職信與履歷表的申請信——此信比求職信長，但比履歷表短，且較不拘謹。此信也稱 broadcast letter（自介信）或 letter of interest（意向書）。

哪一種方法最適合？這取決於潛在雇主給的暗示；「填寫申請書」、「把履歷郵寄或傳真」、還是「向以下部門申請」。

除了主動開缺的職位，你也可以申請無開缺的職位（即使沒有職缺，但你還是想去那家公司工作）。若是屬於後者，你便無法得知雇主的偏好。在這種情況下，第三種方法，申請信——詳述履歷內容且具說服力的單頁信——會比傳統的履歷表或求職信更有效。

有些公司相當重視申請信，藉此評斷求職者自我表現能力與書寫能力。

申請信的目的在於吸引雇主的注意力，使之留下印象，從而能將你放進短短的面試名單中。也就是說，申請信是一種自我宣傳，你不僅是推銷員，也是產品本身。

✉ PART 1 說明篇

申請信可以寄到

營隊	社團與團體組織	大學院校	連鎖企業
實習職缺	私立中小學	公司	義工組織

該怎麼說？

1. 針對特定對象撰寫申請信。先確認對方職銜與姓名拼寫否正確，即使名字聽起來很簡單，仍然要檢查拼字：Gene 或許是 Jeanne，而 John 也許應寫成 Jon。

2. 開頭句或開頭段落必須吸引人。

3. 陳述申請該職位與該公司的理由，並說明自己是適當人選的原因。

4. 條列出與該職缺最相關的技能、教育背景及經歷；其他的等到面試時再提出。

5. 請求面試：I will be in Burbank next week and would like to arrange an interview.「下週我會在柏本克，希望能與您安排面試。」

6. 提供地址、日間可聯繫的電話號碼、傳真號碼及電子郵件地址。

7. 以愉悅或期待的語句收尾：I appreciate your time and consideration.「感謝您抽出時間考慮。」；I look forward to discussing this position with you.「我期待能與您討論這個職缺。」

什麼不該說？

• 勿過度使用概括性或模稜兩可的敘述，如 etc.（等等）。精準陳述你的能力與經歷。

• 別耍花招、別用你平常不會用的華麗詞彙、別裝「幽默」，也不要用任何會產生反效果的炫麗設計。保守（不等於無聊）為佳。

• 別自稱 the writer（筆者），如 The writer has had six years' experience as a heavy equipment operator.「筆者有六年的重型機器操作經驗。」

- 勿強調公司能幫你達成何種個人職涯目標，反之，請強調你的能力如何幫公司獲益。不要說 Here is what I can do.「我會做這些。」請修改這句話，告訴對方 Here is what I can do for you.「我可以為您做這些。」
- 別提及現在或過去工作中任何負面的事件。
- 別看輕你取得的資格。
- 別把求職目的建立在你對該職務的需求上，也勿訴諸同情心（如我是我們家庭的唯一支柱）。請專注在你能提供的東西。
- 別在信裡提及薪水話題（儘管職缺要你列出薪資條件）。這類的討論請留到面試。

寫作訣竅

- 別用有前公司信頭的信紙寫申請信。
- 在寄出前重讀一遍，看看你的信是否展現出自信、專業與說服力。試想，如果你是雇主，你會想要面試寫這封信的人嗎？
- 保持簡短有力。申請信的篇幅不該超過一頁。
- 用動作動詞描述你的能力及成就（參見：29 履歷一章中所列出的動詞清單）。
- 為申請職缺的公司量身打造申請信。如果你用同一封信到處投履歷，或按照制式的申請書撰寫，雇主一眼就看得出來。他們會發現你只是想找一份工作，任何工作都好，並不一定非要他們的。
- 加入個人特色。當未來的雇主收到一封特別為他們而寫的信時，這封信便可能得到更多的關注，不像多數的信都只得到六十秒的時間。
- 能否獲得面試機會的關鍵要素，在於你是否為該雇主所需要的人。儘管你很明白自己能付出什麼，但你還必須知道這家公司想從你身上得到什麼。你可以打去公司詢問問題、去圖書館研究這家公司，或跟該公司職員或了解這家公司的人談談。當你以公司的需求為措詞基準，盡全力將自己的形象清晰展現出來時，雇主便能輕易判斷你是否是符合他們需要的人選。
- 你不必告訴對方 References available upon request.「如有需要可提供推薦人。」因為推薦人是必須附上並會加以審核的。
- 避免拼字文法錯誤。不要使用品質不好的信紙，並避免糊掉或不清晰的印刷以及不適宜的行距。傳真時，請選擇「高解析度」設定，寄送的影本越清晰越好。

特殊狀況

- **申請特許經銷權**時,請詳閱相關政府單位規定。你可以請律師在書信往來上給予協助。
- **大學院校就學申請**多半定期舉行且有相關規定。如果你畢業時在班上的排名很高或很低,或你有特殊需求(例如經濟上的援助),你可以求助於高中輔導室、私人諮商師或尋求大量相關文獻。對有些學生來說,申請大學的過程可能會花上數月,而且需要專業意見。
- 如果**你是雇主**,請先了解《就業服務法》與《性別工作平等法》相關法令。雇主不得因種族、階級、語言、思想、宗教、黨派、籍貫、出生地、性別、性傾向、年齡、婚姻、容貌、五官、身心障礙或以往工會會員身分歧視求職者。雇主亦不得要求求職者提供非就業所需的隱私資料,包括醫療檢測、HIV 檢測等「生理資訊」、心理測驗等「心理資訊」,以及信用記錄、犯罪紀錄、懷孕計畫或背景調查等「個人生活資訊」。在**設計求職申請單**時,先請律師檢查,確保內容符合法律規範。

格式

- 申請信要用打字,最好是打在有信頭的信紙上。
- 有些雇主會請求職者以傳真方式遞交資料。除非該公司有特別要求附上履歷,不然你可以傳真申請信即可。傳真前請加上一張空白紙張,或在申請信最上方留出空間提供傳真資訊(參見:02 傳真信)。

PART 2 應用篇

單字

ability *(n.)* 能力	education *(n.)* 教育	opportunity *(n.)* 機會	skill *(n.)* 技能
apply *(n.) & (v.)* 申請	experience *(n.)* 經驗	professional *(a.)* 專業的	suitable *(a.)* 適合的
background *(n.)* 背景	goal *(n.)* 目標	qualified *(a.)* 符合資格的	
credential *(n.)* 證書、資格	objective *(n.)* 目的	responsible *(a.)* 有責任感的	

詞組

applying for the position of 申請⋯⋯職位	interested in pursuing a career with 有興趣與⋯⋯追求事業
arrange a meeting at your convenience 依您方便的時間安排面試	meet and exceed your criteria 不僅符合且超越您的標準
experience that qualifies me for 該經驗使我有資格⋯⋯	serious interest in 對⋯⋯非常感興趣
extensive experience with 在⋯⋯方面經驗豐富	similar to my most recent position 與我最近一份工作的性質相似
good candidate/match for the job 這份工作的適宜人選	skills that would be useful to 對⋯⋯有用的技能
in response to your advertisement 回應您的徵才廣告	ten years' experience with 十年的⋯⋯經驗
may I have fifteen minutes of your time to discuss 能否借用您十五分鐘的時間討論⋯⋯	well suited for 相當適合⋯⋯

According to this morning's paper, you are seeking a storm restoration contractor.
貴公司在今天的早報徵求風災後重建承包商。

After eight years as a senior analog engineer at Blayds-Conway, I am seeking a position in this area because of a family move.
我在貝雷迪康威公司做了八年的資深類比工程師。由於搬家之故，我現在正在找一份同領域的工作。

At the suggestion of Wilhelmina Douglas-Stewart, I am writing to request an interview for the project leader position in your long haul fiber optic communications department.
在葳漢米娜‧道格拉斯史都華的引介下，我寫這封信給您，希望能得到長距離光纖傳輸部門專案組長一職的面試機會。

Because I believe you would find me to be an efficient, experienced, and dedicated legal administrative assistant, I am applying for the position at Wilson & Bean.
我是一個高效率、經驗豐富且充滿熱忱的法務行政助理，因此來應徵威爾森與賓恩事務所這個職務。

Dr. Breuer has informed me that you are currently looking for a part-time veterinary technician.
布爾醫師告訴我，您正在尋找兼職的獸醫技術員。

I am applying for the position of credit research analyst that you advertised in today's paper.
我要應徵您在今日報紙上刊登的信貸研究分析師一職。

I look forward to hearing from you.
期待能收到您的回覆。

I understand from Dr. Demetrius Doboobie that you have an opening for a medical records supervisor.
我從迪米崔‧杜布比醫師那裡得知，您有一個病歷室主任的職缺。

I understand that there is currently no opening in your office, but I would like you to keep my résumé on file and to consider me for any openings that occur.
我明白目前貴公司並無職缺，但我希望您能保留我的履歷，當有職缺釋出時能考慮我。

I was happy to learn that there is an opening for an insurance underwriting coordinator at the Daffyd Evans Marine Insurance Agency.
我很高興知道達菲‧伊凡斯海上保險公司有保險承銷協調人的職缺。

I was pleased to see your advertisement in this morning's paper for a floral designer because I have just moved here and am looking for a position after having worked as a floral designer in Chicago for the past six years.

我很高興在今早報紙上看見您徵求一名花藝設計師。我才剛搬到這裡，並正在找尋工作；在此之前，我在芝加哥擔任了六年的花藝設計師。

I will call you Thursday to discuss setting up an interview.

我會於週四致電給您安排面試。

My eight years as a food microbiologist at Samuel Braceweight, Inc., make me eminently suitable for the responsibilities of the position you are currently advertising.

過去八年我在山謬·布司維公司擔任食物微生物學家，這個經驗讓我非常適合您目前所刊登的職缺。

Please consider me as an applicant for your advertised part-time position as clerical assistant in your business office.

您在廣告中應徵辦公室兼職文書助理一職，請考慮讓我應徵這個職位。

Roger Brevard told me that you are looking for a real-time software engineer.

羅傑·貝瑞福告訴我，您正在徵求一名即時控制軟體工程師。

Thank you for considering my application.

謝謝您考慮我的申請。

The skills and duties outlined in your advertisement in today's paper are almost a perfect match for the position I held until recently at Geoffrey Bentley Publishers, Inc.

您在今日報紙所列出的技能與職責，幾乎跟我之前在喬佛里·班特利出版社的職務是一樣的。

段落

As you know, I have been managing the Albany branch of your Woodstock Bookstore for three years. I understand that you plan to franchise several of your bookstores, and I would like to apply for the franchise for this store, if it is available.

如您所知，您的伍士塔書店阿爾巴尼分店已經由我管理三年了。我知道您打算要出售數個書店的經銷權，若這間分店的特許經銷權尚未售出，我想申請。

Your neighbor, Gina Gregers, who is a friend of mine from high school, told me yesterday that you are seeking a lunch-hour delivery driver for your catering company. I have a valid driver's license, have never had a moving violation, and, as a twenty-year resident of Werle Heights, know my way around the city and suburbs.

您的鄰居吉娜・葛雷格是我高中以來的朋友。她昨日告訴我，您正為您的外燴公司尋找午餐時間運貨司機。我有駕駛執照，從未有交通違規紀錄，而且我在威勒高地住了二十年，城內與近郊的交通都再熟悉不過。

I would like to be considered for your customer service representative position. You requested experience in the transportation industry: I was employed from 2007–2017 as customer service representative for Coldstream Transport and from 2004–2007 as dispatcher for Steenson Intermountain Express.

我希望您能考慮錄用我為客戶服務代表。您要求申請人須有運輸業工作經驗：我於二〇〇七至二〇一七年間擔任冷流運輸公司的客戶服務代表，於二〇〇四至二〇〇七年間擔任史汀森山間快遞的調度員。

示範信

Dear Mr. Hartright,

I heard about your internship through the film scoring department at Berklee College of Music, where I'm currently in my eleventh semester.

Although I will graduate next semester with requirements fulfilled for the four-year program with three majors (film scoring, songwriting, and jazz composition), I intend to specialize in film. I view this internship as one of a number of significant steps in bettering my skills and adding to my experience.

If selected, I can guarantee that you will be pleased with me as an employee. I've been a paid and unpaid composer, music director, and performer, and all my previous employers have been highly satisfied. I tend to work harder than anyone else in the vicinity, turn out twice what ever the goal or assignment is, and am perfectionistic, creative, responsible, and knowledgeable.

My experience with studio work is limited, but I thoroughly understand the function and use of the equipment involved.

Enclosed please find an unofficial transcript, work samples, and letters of recommendation.

I look forward to speaking with you about the internship.

Sincerely,

哈特萊先生您好：

我從柏克萊音樂學院電影配樂系聽聞您提供的實習機會，我目前在該系就讀第十一個學期。

下個學期我便會取得四年學程、三項主修（電影配樂、詞曲創作、爵士作曲）的畢業資格，但我決定要專攻電影。對我來說，這個實習機會是讓我提升能力、增加經驗的重要一步。

如果我被選上，我可以向您保證您會非常滿意我作為雇員的表現。我有作曲（收費或免費）、擔任音樂總監與表演的經驗，並讓所有前雇主都相當滿意。我比周遭的人都更努力工作，無論目標或任務是什麼，我都企圖達成雙倍的成果；我追求完美、充滿創意、盡心負責且專業知識豐富。

雖然我在電影製片廠工作的經驗有限，但我對於相關器材的功能與使用有透徹的了解。

附件中您可以看到非正式成績單、作品集與推薦信。

我期待能與您進一步討論這份實習工作。

○○敬上

Dear Mr. Kringelein,

Please consider me as an applicant for your advertised part-time position as clerical assistant in your business office.

My word-processing and business computer skills, which you require, are excellent: I am completely conversant with the current versions of Windows, Office, and Microsoft Word.

Before my move here last month, I was employed for six years as assistant to the manager of Baum Office Products in Philadelphia on a part-time basis. My duties there included all office word processing, mailing list management, transcription, and such general office functions as telephone answering, faxing, and photocopying.

I look forward to hearing from you.

Sincerely,

克林吉蘭先生您好：

關於您在廣告中刊登的辦公室兼職文書助理一職，我希望您能考慮我的申請。

我的文書處理與商務電腦技能相當優秀，符合您的徵才條件：我非常熟悉目前版本的 Windows 作業系統，以及 Office 與 Microsoft Word 文書作業系統。

在上個月搬來這裡之前，我在費城的邦恩辦公室用品公司工作了六年，擔任經理的兼職助理。我的職責包括所有的辦公室文書處理、郵件名單管理、抄寫，以及其他辦公室雜項事務，如接聽電話、傳真與影印。

期盼能收到您的回覆。

〇〇敬上

Dear Ms. Chuffnell,

We have just moved to Seabury and have heard good things about the Seabury Fitness Center. My husband, three children, and I are interested in applying for membership.

I am enclosing an application and the one-time nonrefundable processing fee of $50. If you need any further information, please call me during the day at 555-2498 or in the evening at 555-9980.

We are looking forward to enjoying the Seabury Fitness Center for years to come.

With best wishes,

巧芙娜小姐您好：

我們剛搬至汐柏里，聽到很多人推薦汐柏里健身中心。我、我的丈夫與三名子女希望能申請會員。

隨信附上申請表與一次性不退款之手續費 50 元。如果您需要任何其他資訊，請致電給我，白天請打 555-2498，傍晚請打 555-9980。

我們很期待往後能享受汐柏里健身中心的服務。

〇〇敬上

27

申請信

參見：17 後續追蹤信、28 求職信、29 履歷、36 職場相關信

Chapter 28

求職信／封面信
Cover Letters

> 據估計，每封商務信只能得到收件人不到三十秒的注意力。
> 即使是非常優異的求職信，得到的注意力也不會多上多少。
>
> ——英國指揮家馬汀·耶特（Martin Yate）

封面信（cover letter，與履歷一起寄出的 cover letter 可稱「求職信」），亦稱送件函（transmittal letter），會伴隨履歷、申請表、稿件、文件、產品資料、帳款、慈善捐款、合約、報告、樣品、數據及其他資料一起出現，是用來說明附件的信。

封面信可以只有短短兩句，簡短說明寄信原因並且有哪些附件。封面信也可以長至兩頁，摘述附件的重點資訊，或解釋無法一眼看出的重點。封面信也能用來推銷商品，與相關報告、樣品、文件、資訊或包裹一齊寄出。

封面信的主要目的在於，快速說服收件人去查看附件中的資料。

封面信與封面（cover sheet）不同，封面隨著傳真發出，上面寫的是寄發傳真的人、收取傳真的人、傳真號碼以及傳真總頁數（參見：02 傳真信）。

 PART 1 說明篇

封面信會伴隨哪些資料？

申請表	月結單或發貨單	合約或協議	慈善捐獻

文件	稿件	提案	問卷
履歷	調查	商品型錄、樣品 參見：42 銷售信	

該怎麼說？

1. 寫上收件人地址。
2. 說明隨信附上的資料，或會在另一封信中寄送哪些資料。若有多份文件，請一一條列。告知對方各種資料的數量與類型、帳款金額或其他描述性的資訊。
3. 告知寄送這些資料的原因。
4. 必要的話，解釋資料內容或使用方式。
5. 總結附件中的重點資訊，如強調你的履歷符合資格，或把對方的注意力吸引到資料中最重要的議題上。
6. 告訴對方你希望他採取的回應，或是你即將採取的行動。
7. 寫下你的姓名、地址、電話號碼、電子郵件地址與傳真號碼。
8. 在結尾處表達感激或未來合作機會。

什麼不該說？

- 勿重複附件內容。可以總結資料內容或提示重點，但要是完全與附件內容重複，收件人之後可能就會跳過這封信。
- 別在結尾時顯得虛弱無力。「如果您希望的話，我可以在您方便的時間前往面試」、「若您有興趣，請打電話給我」這類的話暗示你缺乏信心，避免使用像 hope（希望）、wish（希冀）、if（如果）、should（應該）、could（可以）、might（可能）這樣的字詞。
- 不要用「可愛」的信紙、多重問號或驚嘆號、表情符號或其他花招吸引注意力。在展現熱情自信的同時，不該讓讀者蹙眉。可以先找別人幫你重讀信件。

寫作訣竅

- 例行性的訂單、出貨、或建議信，不需要封面信。若是應對方要求寄送附件，或對方正在等你寄回附件，這類狀況也不需要封面信。
- 不過，以下狀況則須加入封面信：當對方不知道你會寄資料；資料本身無法清楚呈現重點；資料配上說服對方的信件能帶來更大效益。

- 再三檢查姓名、職稱與地址。尤其是寄出履歷或寄送稿件給編輯時，這點十分重要。

- 保持簡短。莎士比亞建議用字要「短而有效」。除非你寫的封面信其實是一封附上樣品、產品文獻或型錄的銷售信，不然封面信都只是甜點，而非主餐。一封優異的封面信不會超過一頁篇幅（五至六段），它會讓收件人期待閱讀附件，而迫不及待把封面信擱到一旁。

- 非裔美國詩人傑西・弗塞特（Jessie Fauset）曾說：「古人說得沒錯，第一印象確實影響深遠。」封面信應該是乾淨、迷人而優雅的，頁面邊緣留下的空白通常頗寬，並且不會有任何拼字、文法或用法錯誤。

- 在《Cover Letters That Will Get You the Job You Want》（暫譯：讓你錄取理想工作的求職信）一書中，史坦利・韋內特（Stanley Wynnett）說道：「我寫過的每一封求職信都是以『謝謝』結尾。」有些專家認為，預先說謝謝唐突又老套，表示雙方的互動已結束。不過，沒有人會拒絕別人的謝意，你可以自行判斷是否要道謝。

- 若想獲得更多幫助，可以參考以下兩本好書：
  (1)《Cover Letters That Knock 'Em Dead》，第七版，作者：Martin Yate
  (2)《Cover Letters》，第二版，作者：Taunee Besson
  若需要隨履歷附上的求職信，可參考：
  《The Perfect Cover Letter》，第三版，作者：Richard H. Beatty
  繳交稿件隨附的投稿信則可參考：
  《How to Write Attention-Grabbing Query & Cover Letters》，作者：John Wood

28

求職信／封面信

特殊狀況

- **為履歷寫張優異的求職信**，絕對是推銷自己的良策。神經科學家瑪格麗特・麥卡錫（Margaret McCarthy）說：「很少有其他信件比隨履歷附上的求職信更重要。」先描述你從何得知此職缺，或稱讚應徵的公司（越具體效果越好）。接著，明確寫出所應徵的職位或工作類型。強調你在哪些方面符合公司的徵才要求（不要重複履歷中已提到的詞彙、日期或資訊）。不要聚焦在你想要的東西上，而要強調你能為公司帶來的貢獻，使對方對你產生興趣。結尾處，請求對方給予面試機會，因為這就是你寄送求職信及履歷的目的：I will call you next week to arrange an interview appointment after you have had a chance to review my résumé.「在您有機會審閱我的履歷後，我會於下週打電話給您安排面試時間。」；I look forward to meeting with you to discuss the match between your requirements and my qualifications.「我期待能與您見面，讓您了解我在哪些方面符合您的徵才條件。」參見：27 申請信，了解更多寫求職信的訣竅。

- **求職信勿超出一頁篇幅**。對於忙碌的工作者來說，過長的求職信很倒胃口，對方可能根本不會看你的履歷。此外，為每間公司量身打造求職信，收件人通常會查看信中與他們公司有關的內容。

- **用電子郵件寄發求職信**，可以將履歷或其他資料接續在求職信下方，不以附件的方式夾帶。有些人不太信任附件，擔心會有病毒。因此，請避免附加照片、寫作作品或其他資料，可先告訴對方這些文件會在要求後寄發。電子郵件的主旨必須簡短、直指重點，像是 Application for Human Resources Opening「申請人力資源職缺」或 Response to Ad for Mosquito Inspectors「回應蚊子稽查員徵才廣告」。在求職信中加上聯絡資訊，並於簽名下方重複打上這些資訊，忙碌的人沒有耐心在信中找尋你的電話或傳真號碼。電子郵件比一般信件更容易出錯，所以在按下「傳送」前，先把郵件列印出檢查。

- **隨稿件寄給編輯的封面信**（又稱 query letter「投稿信」），一般都很簡短，目的是介紹附上的稿件（書或文章的類型、標題、字數）以及你自己（過去的出版紀錄，或是你寫這份稿件的資格）。一封好的投稿信，會有簡潔有力的文字，讀起來就像型錄上的商品介紹。你必須用最棒的寫作技巧來描述你的書或文章，或為其增添風味。請**一定**要附上回郵信封，並禮貌地結束信件。

- **隨報告寄出的封面信**，會以報告的標題來指稱該報告，並提及準備這份報告的動機、授權給你寫這份報告的人以及寫報告的人。在信中，請寫下這份報告的概要（以此報告的序、摘要或總結為基礎）。如果這是一份正式的報告，則封面信會放在標題頁的後面、目錄的前面。

- **隨禮物一起送達的信函**，跟封面信類似。請在信中指出禮物的用處，如 a little something for your birthday「為你生日準備的小禮物」，並加上你的問候與祝福。
  若這封信須附在公司送的禮品寄出，你可以告知這份禮物為何而送，如入職服務紀念日，或完成某個重要專案。請具體寫出對方的工作、才能、紀念日或獎項：I'm particularly grateful because...「我覺得特別感謝，因為……」；You've been a delight to work with because...「我很高興能與你共事，因為……」；Your work has meant a lot to the company because...「你的工作對公司來說相當重要，因為……」。可以用一則故事、一段共同回憶或一些想法來映襯你的祝福。在結尾處，愉快地祝福對方持續獲得成功，或表達你對於未來合作的期盼。若要送禮給託運公司或網路公司工作人員，也可附上差不多的信函，你可以告訴對方你寄了「a little something」（小禮物）或「something I thought you'd like」（您可能喜歡的東西）或「something for your desk」（能擺在您辦公桌上的東西）；如果可能的話，也告知預計寄達的時間。倘若公司送的禮物與手寫的表揚信一起送達，送禮的效果更是會增強百倍。當員工從忙碌的上司手上收到這麼一封信時，他會感到親近、難忘，覺得自己受到了重視。

- **隨樣品或產品資料寄出的封面信**，比較適合視為銷售信（參見：42 銷售信）。

格式

- 除了隨禮物寄出的封面信，或是非常不正式的通信之外，封面信一般都是打在有信頭的商務信紙或備忘錄用紙上（後者適用於公司內部，或是經常聯絡的外部人士或公司）。
- 求職時，使用有信頭或高品質的全白、灰色或米白色信紙。避免花俏的信紙、字型、顏色與圖片。
- 當對方要求你以傳真或電子郵件寄送履歷時，也要一同寄出求職信。傳真時，請按照一般信件的格式，使用有信頭的信紙，並設定以「高解析度」傳送，確保信件寄達時是好看易讀的。
- 若是回應他人要求給予資訊時，可使用制式的封面信。為了讓對方感到重視，請用高品質的紙張，並以姓名稱呼對方（而不是只通稱「親愛的朋友」或「親愛的訂閱人」），最後為每封信親筆簽上名字。若對方在未來可能是重要客戶，請寫一封量身打造的信。

28

求職信／封面信

✉ PART 2 應用篇

💬 單字

announce *(v.)* 宣布	outline *(n.) & (v.)* 大綱；略述	proposal *(n.)* 提案	terms *(n.)* 條款
deliver *(v.)* 遞送	document *(n.)* 文件	prospectus *(n.)* 簡介、簡章	enclosed *(a.)* 附件的
illustrate *(v.)* 闡述	draft *(n.)* 草稿	provision *(n.)* 條款	
summarize *(v.)* 總結	policy *(n.)* 政策	report *(n.) & (v.)* 報告	
notice *(v.) & (n.)* 通知	project *(n.)* 專案	attached *(a.)* 附加的	

💬 詞組

acquaint you with 讓你知悉	for further information 供你未來參考
as promised 一如約定	here are/is 這就是
at your request 如你所要求	I am sending you 我會寄給你……
enclosed is/are 附件是	if you need/want additional information 若需要／想要其他資訊
call with questions 致電詢問問題	I'm also enclosing 我也附上了
complimentary copy 贈送的印刷品	in response to your advertisement 為回應你的徵才廣告

direct your attention to 使你注意到	please note that 請注意
brochure that presents/details/ describes/outlines/explains 展示／詳述／描述／概述／解釋……的冊子	rough draft 初步草稿

句子

After you have reviewed the enclosed proposal, please call me (or Bess Beynon if I'm out of town) to discuss it.
在您審閱完附件中的提案後，請打電話與我討論（若我不在城內，請打給貝絲‧貝儂）。

As a June graduate of Cleveland College with a BA in business, I am looking for employment and wanted to check first with you because I so enjoyed working for The Clement Group as an intern in your marketing department.
我即將於六月拿到克里夫蘭學院的商學學士學位，所以我正在找工作，並希望能先向您詢問，因為我曾在貴公司行銷部門擔任實習生，而我非常喜歡為客萊門集團工作。

As you will see from my résumé, I have a great deal of experience in program development, administration, contract development, and budget planning.
您可以從我的履歷看到，我在程式開發、經營管理、合約建立與預算計畫方面有豐富的經驗。

At your request, I am enclosing three copies of the Empire State Film Festival program.
根據您的要求，在此附上三份帝國電影節的節目手冊。

Complete medical records from the office of Dr. Anna Lakington for Mr. Barnabas Holly are enclosed.
在此附上安娜‧賴金頓醫師診所為巴納博‧霍利先生開立的完整醫療紀錄。

Enclosed are copies of the recorded deeds and easements for the above-referenced properties.
附件為上述財產之契據及地役權狀影本。

Enclosed is a completed application form—please note my four years' experience as an installation technician.
附件為完整的申請表；您可以注意到，我有四年作為安裝技術人員的工作經驗。

28

求職信／封面信

Enclosed is a copy of the survey on equipment rental in the six-county metro area.
附件為六郡地鐵區域器材租賃調查影本。

Enclosed is a quitclaim deed conveying the new Fort Road from Faulkland County to the City of Sheridan.
附件是權利轉讓契據，將新堡路從佛克蘭郡轉讓至薛立登市。

Enclosed is the requested report on the Heat Treatment Seminar, held July 14-17.
應您的要求，附件是七月十四至十七日舉辦之熱能治療研討會相關報告。

Here are the molding samples we'd like you to evaluate.
這些便是我們希望您能評估的模具樣品。

I am enclosing the damaged belt from my twenty-year-old Bannister vacuum in the hopes that you can locate a replacement for it.
隨信附上從使用二十年的班尼特吸塵器拆下的受損皮帶，希望您能協助替換它。

I am interested in your part-time position for a truck unloader.
我對您提供的兼職貨車卸貨員一職有興趣。

I am responding to your advertisement in Sunday's paper for a senior analyst programmer.
我想應徵您刊登於週日報紙上的資深分析程式設計師一職。

I am writing to introduce myself and inquire about openings for a Tae Kwon Do instructor.
我想藉此信向您自我介紹，並詢問跆拳道教練此一職缺。

I believe I am well qualified to apply for your opening for a water quality extension agent.
我相信我符合申請水質推廣員一職的資格。

I'm sending you a copy of the article on the Minnesota Twins that we discussed last week.
如我們上週所討論的，我在此寄給您關於明尼蘇達雙城隊的文章影本。

In response to your ad for a website producer/editor, I'm enclosing my résumé, which details my considerable experience in this area.
為了應徵您在廣告中徵求的網站創建員／編輯員一職，在此附上我的履歷，其中詳列了我在這個領域的豐富經驗。

I understand you are looking for a form tool grinder.
我知道您正在尋找一名成形工具磨床技術員。

I will telephone your assistant Monday morning to see if you can schedule an interview next week to discuss the position.

我會在週一早上打電話給您的助理，詢問您能否於下週安排面試討論這個職缺。

I would like to bring my commercial interior design skills to work for Engelred Offices Inc.

我期望能將我在商業內部設計的才能，帶到英格雷辦公室設計公司。

Ms. DeGroot suggested I contact you about the development grant writer and board liaison position.

德古特小姐建議我向您詢問，關於發展資助金申請寫手暨委員會聯絡人一職。

Please sign both copies of the enclosed letter of agreement and return them to us.

請在附件中的兩份協議書上簽名，再交還給我們。

Prentice Page suggested I write you about the wallpapering specialist position.

普倫提斯·佩吉建議我寫信向您詢問壁紙安裝專員一職。

Thank you for your patience—enclosed please find the replacement part for your Noyes Intercommunication System.

謝謝您的耐心等候，隨信附上諾耶通訊系統零件，供您替換。

Under separate cover I'm sending you samples of our new line of Natural Solution products for the hair.

在另一封信中，我會寄給您我們針對秀髮設計的「自然對策」新系列樣品。

We are pleased to send you the set of deck plans you requested.

我們很高興能回應您的要求，將這套甲板平面圖寄給您。

Will you please look over the enclosed rough draft of your will and let me know if it needs any changes or corrections?

您可否檢閱附件中您的遺囑初步草稿，並告訴我是否需要改動或修正？

段落

I note that you are seeking a ware house manager with five years of supervisory or managing experience and five years of experience in shipping, receiving, and inventory control. This almost precisely describes my qualifications.

我注意到貴公司正在應徵一名倉庫經理，須具備五年以上的監督或管理經驗，以及五年以上的收發貨及存貨控管經驗，而我的資歷幾乎完全符合這些條件。

Enclosed is a sample (ref. #4467-AB) of the film that Alwyn Tower and I discussed with you last Thursday. Please keep in mind that the sample was produced under laboratory conditions. If you have any questions about this material or variations of it, please call Alwyn or me.

隨信附上艾文‧塔爾、我跟您於上週四提到的薄膜樣品（品號 4467-AB），請留意，這些樣品是在實驗室環境中製造的，若您對此材料或其中差異有任何問題，請致電艾文或我。

I am currently employed in an engineering environment by a large independent transportation firm, but I am interested in making a career change into the investment/financial services field. I have recently obtained my CFP designation and hope to find a position as a broker trainee. I am enclosing my résumé for your review and consideration for such a position.

我目前在一間大型運輸公司做工程方面的工作，但我想要改變職涯規劃，轉向投資／財務服務的領域。我最近剛取得理財規劃師證書，並希望能找到一個證券經紀人儲備專員的職位。隨信附上我的履歷供您審閱，望您能考慮給予我這類的職位。

Thank you for your interest in Griffiths Collar and Shirt Company. I'm enclosing a packet of materials that will describe our range of products and services. I will call you next week to see if you have any questions and to discuss how we might be of help to you. You are, of course, always welcome to visit our offices and factory here in Lycurgus.

謝謝您對葛林芬斯製衣公司的興趣。隨信附上一組資料，供您了解我們的產品與服務種類。下週我會打電話給您，詢問您是否有任何問題，並與您討論我們能協助您的方式。當然，歡迎您隨時前來我們位於呂庫古斯的辦公室與工廠。

The attached set of project plans covers work through the end of 2019. The plans have been generated in consultation with each of the key people involved. We expect to review progress the first of each month and to adjust the work accordingly. You will note that we are dependent on the work of others in the office and that they are in turn dependent on us. Please review the scheduled work and give me your comments.

附件的專案計畫書，包含直至二〇一九年年底的工作計畫。在諮詢與此專案相關的每一位重要人員後，本計畫書才制定而成。我們期盼能在每月首日檢視進度，並據此調整工作計畫。請注意，我們都仰賴辦公室其他人的工作成果，而其他人也仰賴我們的工作成果。請仔細閱讀工作期程，並讓我知道您的意見。

示範信

Dear Ms. Lownie:

As an editor with eighteen years' experience, I think I may be well qualified for the position of Editor advertised in *Engineering Today*. You will see from the enclosed résumé that I have edited both technical and trade publications. In each case, I was able to raise the standards of the editorial content, increase ad sales (in one case by 120 percent), and attract new subscribers in significant numbers.

Having met and exceeded my goals in my present position and knowing that the assistant editor here is more than capable of taking over, I want to challenge myself with a more demanding position. *Engineering Today* appeals to me very much as this type of challenge.

Thank you for considering my application.

Sincerely,

勞尼小姐您好：

我有擔任編輯長達十八年的經驗，因此，我認為我符合《今日工程》所刊登的編輯職缺應徵資格。您可根據附件中的履歷，得知我有技術類與貿易類刊物的編輯經驗。我提升了這兩種刊物的內容品質、增加其廣告收入（其中之一的增幅為 120%），並吸引了大量新訂閱戶。

我已經在我目前的職位上達成目標，甚至超越了自己的期許，同時，我也知道目前公司的助理編輯很有能力，可接手我的職務，因此我希望能自我鞭策，尋找一個更有挑戰性的職位。《今日工程》正是這種有挑戰性的工作，深深吸引了我。

謝謝您考慮我的申請。

〇〇敬上

Dear Customer,

Thank you for writing for your free sample of the "world's toughest disposable rubber gloves!" Please read through the enclosed flyer for the many ways you can use these gloves to save your hands from damaging liquids and abrasives. Then go ahead and try the last word in convenience, comfort... and toughness! You will never want to use any other glove again.

We would appreciate hearing your comments on the gloves after trying them. Enclosed is a postage-paid reply postcard.

親愛的顧客您好：

謝謝您來信索取「世界最耐用拋棄式橡膠手套」的免費樣品！請詳閱附件中的傳單，了解使用此手套的多種方法，它能保護您的手不受有害液體及磨蝕性物件的傷害。接著，請直接試用這雙完美手套，你會發現它的方便、舒適……與強韌！從此以後，你再也不想使用其他手套。

試用後，我們希望能了解您的想法，因此，隨信附上回郵的回覆卡。

Dear G. E. Challenger,

I was intrigued with the ad in Sunday's paper seeking someone experienced with high pressure liquid chromatography—first, because there aren't that many openings in this field and, second, because my experience and background match almost precisely what you appear to need.

I was further intrigued when I called the number given in the ad and discovered that this is your company. I have never forgotten several of your research papers that were required reading when I was in college.

After you have a chance to read my résumé, I hope you will agree that an interview might be interesting for us both.

G・E・查仁傑您好：

我對您於週日報紙刊登的徵才廣告非常有興趣，該則廣告徵求一名對高壓液相層析法有經驗的人員。首先，因為此領域的職缺並不多；第二則是因為我的經驗與背景幾乎完全符合您的需求。

當我打電話至廣告中提供的號碼，並發現徵才單位的是貴公司時，我更是深受吸引。我永遠忘不了您的數篇研究論文，那都是我在大學期間的必讀文獻。

在您有機會審閱我的履歷後，希望您會同意為我安排一場面試，這應是我們雙方都樂見的。

參見：20 請求與詢問、27 申請信、29 履歷、42 銷售信

28
求職信／封面信

Chapter 29

履歷
Résumés

我們用自己認為能做到的事情來評斷自己；
別人則用我們已經做過的事情來評斷我們。

——美國詩人亨利・沃茲沃思・朗費羅
（Henry Wadsworth Longfellow）

履歷是對個人資歷與工作經驗所做出的書面總結，讓未來的雇主快速認識你的一張紙。它要能讓雇主相信你是適合此職缺的候選人，並邀請你來做進一步的面試。

雖然履歷上不會有誇大的訴求與華麗的文字，但當你在寫履歷時，你同時是推銷員，也是商品。

應徵工作時，你會用到下列一至二種文件：

(1) 履歷：條列出學經歷與職涯目標的文件；
(2) 求職信：伴隨履歷的簡短介紹信；
(3) 申請信：結合求職信與簡短、非正式履歷的文書。

撰寫後兩者時，可參見：27 申請信、28 求職信。

 ## PART 1 說明篇

何時需要寄發履歷？

申請特許經銷權	申請會員資格	應徵工作 或實習缺
回應徵才廣告	詢問公司職缺	申請大學 或學位學程

1. 在履歷最上方右側或最上方中央（左上方可能會裝訂或打洞）寫上姓名、地址、日間電話號碼、電子郵件地址或傳真號碼。

2. 具體寫出應徵的職位名稱或工作類型。

3. 詳盡列出相關工作經歷與技能。方法有兩種，後者在今日較常見。

   (1) 以傳統倒敘格式列出工作經歷。從最近的職位開始，接著根據時間一條條往回寫。這種格式簡單，強調如雇用日期、雇主名稱與完整地址、工作職稱與工作職責等具體資訊。必要的話，也可寫出離職原因。但要是你剛入職場、工作經歷之間有空白期、或是先前工作與應徵職缺關係不大，這種格式就有缺點。

   (2) 非時序式的履歷（也稱為職能取向履歷，或功能型履歷）強調資歷與能力，根據技能類別區分工作經驗。舉例來說，在「領導能力」下面會寫「在霍普公司管理夜班員工兩年」；在「人際溝通能力」下寫「身為市長的糾紛調解專家，我時常被召去解決爭紛、談判合約，或在艱難的狀況下處理選民、政治人物與市府人員的問題」；「組織能力」則可能包含「我受雇於阿諾－布朗公司，任務是重組會計部門，當時因員工流失、士氣低落、缺乏部門指導方針與辦公空間配置不當，該部門幾乎停擺。兩年後，我因『絕佳組織能力』而受到公司總裁表揚。」

   也可以結合兩種履歷格式，例如在每個倒序排列的工作下方，以該職位用到的技能類型來進一步歸類。或者，直接以正在應徵的工作作為寫履歷的依據，只列出基本資歷，以及與應徵職位相關的具體工作經歷。

4. 提供學歷重點資訊：學校名稱、所在之城市與國家、就讀期間、獲取的學位或證書、修習的課程名稱、特殊訓練、重要榮譽或會員資格。

5. 如果合適的話，可列出出版作品。

什麼不該說？

- 不要加上私人資訊（年齡或出生年、體重、身高、兵役或財務狀態、小孩、種族、身心障礙、宗教或政治立場），除非與應徵的工作有關。若你應徵的是體重控制班的老師，就須提供體重紀錄。一般來說，雇主詢問年齡、性別、種族與宗教是違法的。

- 不要提及希望公司為你做的事情（「這個職位是讓我學習銷售汽車的絕佳機會」），改強調你能為公司帶來的貢獻。

- 談到你的成就時，不要只說「這是我做過的事情」，而要注意用詞遣字，讓這些經歷透露出「這是我能為你做的事情」的訊息。比如說：This position is a wonderful opportunity to

29
履歷

learn about the marketing side of the automotive industry. 「此職缺是我能夠學習汽車產業行銷面的一個絕佳機會。」

- 不必將做過的每件事一一寫出。把會減弱履歷的項目過濾掉。有些人認為，把額外資訊都列出來「並不會有壞處」，但這種說法有待商榷。不見得要包含童年、早期教育、嗜好或興趣等資訊（除非與應徵的職位有直接關聯）。過去做過但不願再做的工作，也可省略不談，除非這會讓你的履歷出現無法解釋的漏洞。

- 不要美化誇大、講半真半假的話，也不要說謊。很多公司都有負責調查履歷真偽的專員，要是被發現作假，你會遭到免職，還可能面對訴訟。當你試著想讓自己看起來優秀一點時，這可能就是個警訊：也許你並不符合這個職位的資格，或是你在這個職位上不會做得開心。

- 不要太過謙虛，也不用貶低自己的成就。可以請某個認識你的人幫你評估履歷完稿。

- 不要使用「etc.」（等等）。這無法提供任何訊息，還會讓你的履歷看起來過度隨興。

- 不要使用虛弱的形容詞與副詞。移除每個 very（非常），以及每個像 good（好）、wonderful（很棒）、exciting（令人激動的）一樣溫和無力的詞語。反之，要使用強勢（甚至是特別的）名詞與動詞。請見本章的形容詞、名詞與動詞清單。

- 不要使用術語、複雜長句，以及平常不會使用的單字或縮寫（除非你的領域中這個縮寫非常普遍，若完整寫出來反而像是在羞辱對方）。

- 不要在履歷中提到薪水，這種事最好在面試時討論（屆時要試著讓面試官比你先說出金額）。

寫作訣竅

- 寫履歷之前，先收集兩種資訊：關於你自己的事，以及關於雇主與職缺的資訊。你可以打電話到對方公司詢問問題；上網研究；找該公司員工或了解這家公司的人聊聊。主動告訴雇主能為他的公司貢獻什麼時，這暗示對方，你有深入研究這家公司，所以你知道哪裡適合你發揮，而這點是很吸引人的。儘管你無法改變工作經歷，但要是你知道雇主要的是什麼，你便能強調他們看重的技能與資歷。比如說，雇主想要的是創意，但你之前的工作都不怎麼相關時，你可以從其他面向思考，找出曾經展現創意的時刻，如美術課、攝影嗜好，或指導陶藝。當雇主發現這份履歷是專為他們準備時，他們便願意給你更多時間，而不像其他履歷只能得到六十秒的關注。若你能按照雇主的需求展現自己時，你便是在幫他們快速做出決定。琳達·史鄧建議：「如果你有工作，每週花十五小時在履歷上；若你沒工作，每週則要花三十五小時以上。在你認識的人中，若有人與你的目標有關聯，務必要打電話給他們每一個人，並請求他們提供資訊。詢問工作機會，每六週就打電話確認一次⋯⋯要找到一份好工作，請有心理準備要花六個月或以上的時間。」上述不一定適用於每個人的情況，但要找到好工作確實不容易。

- 履歷可能會經過人資部、電腦掃描，及招聘人員三方看過，所以它必須讓這三方都喜歡才行：簡短的段落、足夠的留白，以及清楚的標題抓住人資部的目光；大量、貼切且適合的關鍵字方便電腦處理；有邏輯、有說服力的內容組織吸引招聘人員。

- 大公司會使用光學字符識別器（optical character readers）掃描寄來的履歷。軟體會辨識關鍵字，然後將履歷存在大型資料庫中。當公司需要新員工時，便能以關鍵字搜尋資料庫，找出具有所需技能的應徵者。職業諮商顧問建議，在履歷中添加特別關鍵字的項目，列出能讓你被找到的字詞；有些則認為，電腦可以辨別這些字詞是否處於同一段落或分散四處，無需額外增加條目列出。無論如何，你的履歷必須包含關鍵字詞，這些字詞與你想要的職位最為相關，也能讓你的履歷更快速被挑出來。若履歷會經過掃描，寫作訣竅如下：第一行只放姓名，因為這是軟體所預設的；使用你的領域中常用的術語、縮寫及其他字詞，以及同義詞；具體寫出你會的技能，例如寫出你熟悉的電腦軟體名稱（別只是寫「文書處理能力」）；使用同種字的不同詞類，如 administrator（管理者）與 administered（管理），這樣軟體只須搜尋其中一個就能找到你；越具體越好，例如要寫「廣告經理」而不只是「經理」，那麼公司不管怎麼搜尋，都能找到你；寫學歷時，只需寫一個日期（獲取學位的日期），不然軟體會解讀成你只是在那裡度過一段日子；把縮寫與全名（如 R.N. 和 Registered Nurse（護理師））都放入履歷，以免對方只搜尋其中一種稱呼；和徵才廣告作對照，確認廣告中使用的字詞都已出現在履歷中。

- 多數專家建議履歷維持在一到二頁之內。在《The Smart Job Search》（暫譯：聰明找工作）一書中，馬克・馬可斯（Mark L. Makos）寫道：「除非你不在乎找不找得到工作，否則一頁的履歷是你的唯一選擇。」

  不過，若是學術或專業職缺，會需要兩頁以上，最多十二頁的履歷，因為需列出長串的出版作品、專利、個案或研討會簡報等逐條紀錄的列表。

  無論是一頁或十二頁，履歷都必須簡潔、易讀：使用簡單短句與簡短段落、留下大量空白與邊緣空間。寫作專家拉瑟・布魯門賽（Lassor A. Blumenthal）表示：「把履歷想成六十秒的電視廣告，因為收件人大概只會花這麼多時間在上面。」

- 以下是履歷中常見的標題（使用的數量不會超過六個），能幫助你架構履歷：

Activities 活動	Extracurricular Activities 課外活動
Additional Accomplishments 其他成就	Highlighted Qualifications 重點資歷
Additional Experience 其他經歷	Interpersonal Skills 人際溝通能力
Awards, Honors, Offices 獎項、榮譽、要職	Job Objective 工作目標
Background Summary 背景概要	Key Qualifications 重點資歷

Career Highlights 職涯亮點

Career Objective 職涯目標

Career Summary 職涯概要

Communication Skills 溝通能力

Copywriting Experience 文案經驗

Editorial Experience 編輯經驗

Education 學歷

Employment Objective 工作目標

Executive Profile 執行管理概要

Experience 經歷

Overview of Qualifications 資歷總覽

Professional Achievements 專業成就

Professional Affiliations 專業組織成員

Professional Background 專業背景

Professional Experience 專業經驗

Professional History 專業經歷

Professional Profile 專業概要

Professional Qualifications 專業資格

Promotional Skills 推銷能力

Related Experience 相關經驗

Relevant Accomplishments 相關成就

Relevant Experience 相關經驗

Leadership Skills 領導能力

Management Profile 管理概要

Managerial Experience 管理經驗

Memberships 會員資格

Negotiating Skills 談判能力

New Product Development Skills 產品開發能力

Office Management Skills 辦公管理能力

Office Skills 辦公能力

Organizational and Managerial Skills 組織管理能力

Résumé 履歷

Skills 技能

Skills Summary 技能概要

Special Skills 特殊技能

Summary of Qualifications 資歷概要

Summary of Work History 工作經驗概要

Supervisory Skills 監督能力

Systems Skills 電腦系統技能

Technical Experience 技術工作經驗

Training 訓練

Volunteer Work 志工活動

Work Experience 工作經驗

Retail Sales Experience 零售銷售經驗

- 著墨在你的優勢上。在撰寫每個你認為雇主會想要的特質時（領導能力、負責任、問題解決能力、自動自發），要從工作經驗中找尋例子。
- 履歷中有三種提到自己的方式：

  (1) 第一人稱，如 I managed the Midway Pro Bowl for three years, and saw it double in profits during that time.「我管理米德威美式足球職業盃三年，期間收益成長了兩倍。」

  (2) 第三人稱，如 She has worked in a number of areas of radio broadcasting, including...「她曾在許多廣播領域工作，包括……」；Dr. Patikar organized a new patient outcare service.「帕提卡醫生成立了新的病患門診照護服務。」

  (3) 不使用代名詞，如 developed a new method of twinning steel「發展初始鋼產生雙晶變形的新方法」。

  每種方式都有其優缺點。第一種不斷出現的「我」易令人倦怠（盡量省略）；第二種看起來較有距離且做作；第三種顯得有些唐突。使用讓你覺得最自在的方法，無論你是否覺得有利或不利。不管怎麼樣，都別稱呼自己為「the writer」（筆者）。

- 使用有力的動作動詞。不要使用虛軟無力的動詞，如 I did this.「我做過這個。」或 I was responsible for that.「我負責那個。」，改寫成 I managed（我管理）、I developed（我開發）、I directed（我指揮）。請見本章所列之動作動詞清單。

- 所有項目用平行句型撰寫：要寫「I directed... I supervised... I increased...」（我指揮……我監督……我增加……）；而不要寫「I directed... I was a supervisor... I have increased...」（我指揮……我擔任過監督……我曾經增加了……）。

- 履歷中會使用到兩種時態：

  (1) 現在式會用於職涯目標與技能等類別，如「Desire position with...「渴望……的職位」，或是 I am fluent in French, Italian, Spanish, and German.「我能流利使用法語、義大利語、西班牙語及德語。」

  (2) 過去式則會用於工作經驗與專業成就等類別，如 Headed all major advertising campaigns「領導所有主要廣告活動」，或是 I won a six-state cabinetmaking competition.「我贏得六州聯合櫥櫃製作大賽。」

- 使用數字呈現工作成果。銷售額成長、開支減少，或十年來第一次未超出預算等等，儘管你跟這些成就只有部分關聯，還是要寫出數據。列出你管理的人數、你的書賣出的數量、你監督的專案數、你為公司省下了多少時間或金錢、你負責的預算金額、你的部門的缺勤率降低了多少、你的工作站的生產率提升了多少。數字最有說服力。

- 在這個資訊與科技快速發展的世界，韌性是一項重要特質。透過讓過去的工作經歷看起來各有不同，能突顯你的可塑性，以及學習新事物、適應新環境的能力。舉例來說，如果你曾經做過很多執行助理的工作，你可以在一個職位列你曾經重組檔案系統，在另一個職位列出你曾訓練新員工使用新的電話系統，接著，在另一個職位列出你曾在主管請假時管理辦公室

29

履歷

三個月。

- 標示工作經歷的日期時，只使用年份，勿使用月份。

- 不必解釋辭職的原因；如果雇主想知道，面試中自然會問到。可接受的理由包括：搬家、回歸校園深造、尋找更好的職位、前一份工作出現意外的改變。

- 舊式履歷常會出現「如有需要可提供推薦人」，但這是不必要的，因為大家早已有此共識：等到之後的階段，雇主會要求推薦人，而你必須提供。只在你想填滿履歷最後的空白處時，才加上這一句話。一定要提前詢問別人願不願意當你的推薦人。

- 每份履歷皆是為特定公司量身訂做，都是才剛打好或列印出來的。

- 在檢查完完稿後，至少請兩個人幫你讀一讀。三人之中，有兩個人都忽略的錯誤，還是可能馬上就被未來雇主注意到。

- 不要使用訂書針、黏膠，或將履歷放進封口的活頁夾或文件夾（除非對方要求）。文件不須裝訂，只須用迴紋針夾起，對方會比較容易處理。將履歷與封面信裝入寬 9 吋、長 12 吋的信封郵寄，這樣它們到達對方手上時，才會是沒有折痕、乾淨整潔的模樣。

- 有些情況下，可附上作品集、出版品或其他補充資料。

- 查找履歷撰寫的專書，這裡推薦兩位作者：
  (1) 作者 David F. Noble 的《Gallery of Best Résumés: A Collection of Quality Résumés by Professional Résumé Writers》
  (2) 作者 Wendy S. Enelow 的相關書籍

特殊狀況

- 若你**不希望讓目前雇主知道你在找工作**，使用家中地址，並請對方等到你與未來雇主都感到比較確定時，再向目前的雇主尋求推薦信。

- 若**對方給你一張申請表**來應徵職缺，你可以將履歷附在後面。

- **第一次進入職場的人**，會遇到一種典型的挫折：他們不雇用我，因為我毫無經驗，而我沒有經驗是因為他們不雇用我。然而，儘管沒有華麗的工作經驗，還是可能寫出一張誘人的履歷。暑期打工反映出你的可靠、自動自發、負責任；課外活動顯示你的領導潛力、完成專案的能力與特別的興趣；獎項、榮譽、成績、幹部與獎學金，則展現你的成就，以及長期以來比同儕更優異的表現；志工、體育活動與組織成員資格，顯露了你的特質，給予你清晰的形象。像這樣的履歷，很適合用職能取向的格式；展現出你是一個負責任、可靠、努力、學習快速或忠誠的人，並提供實例。

- 若對方要求你為節目單、新聞稿或公司刊物**提供一篇簡短的自傳**（biographical sketch 或 bio），那你的履歷會很有幫助。自傳是敘述性的文章，比履歷更簡短，但不必那麼具體，目的是展現專業生涯中的精髓，而非細節。

格式

- 所有的履歷都應打字在品質好的白色或米色紙上，只印單面。以清晰黑色墨水印製，字體為 elite[註1] 或 pica[註2]（不要使用書寫體或奇特的字型），這能讓履歷看起來專業、保守而直接。在某些領域，設計非常有創意的履歷，例如加入圖片、彩色墨水、非主流的排版，反而能讓你獲得工作。不過，要使用這個方法前，你必須了解你的市場，例如你知道公司中的某個人也是藉此得到職缺。

- 如果你的履歷會經過掃描時，只用白色紙張；不要使用任何圖片、小型字體或特殊字型（Times Roman 或 Arial 是較佳的選擇）；不要使用斜體字、底線或粗體字；使用星號（*），而不要使用項目符號，因為項目符號會被軟體認成句點。光學字符識別器喜歡無聊、同質性高的履歷，所以請只給它這樣的風格。

- 只有在對方要求或對方必須立即收到時，才使用傳真。傳真後的履歷，模樣就不像印在履歷紙上那麼好看。

- 有些情況下可以用電子郵件寄發履歷：分類廣告提供電子郵件地址，並要求應徵者寄至該信箱；你從公司網站看到職缺，而他們鼓勵以電子郵件寄送履歷。先向對方確認寄電子郵件是否有任何特殊規定。

註 1：活版印刷單位，一吋含十二個符號，約為今日之十號字體。

註 2：活版印刷單位，一吋含十個符號，約為今日之十二號字體。

單字（動作動詞，皆為過去式）

accelerated 加速	appointed 任命	calculated 計算	communicated 溝通
accentuated 突出	appraised 評估	captured 獲得	compared 比較
accepted 接受	approached 接近、聯繫	carried out 執行	compiled 匯編
accommodated 適應、調和、顧及	appropriated 撥款	carved 開創	completed 完成
accomplished 完成	approved 批准	catalogued 編錄	composed 構成、調停
accounted for 負責	arbitrated 裁定	categorized 分類	computed 計算
achieved 實現	arranged 安排	caused 引起	conceived 構思
acquired 取得	articulated 闡述	celebrated 慶祝、舉行	conducted 實施
acted 行動	assembled 召集	centralized 集中	confirmed 確認
adapted 適應	assessed 評估	chaired 主持	connected 連接
added 添加	assigned 指派	challenged 挑戰	conserved 保存
addressed 處理	assisted 協助	championed 倡導	considered 考慮
adjusted 調整	attained 獲得	charged 收費、使承擔責任	consolidated 合併、鞏固

29
履歷

administered 管理	attended 出席	charted 繪製	constructed 建構
adopted 採用	augmented 增強	checked 檢查	consulted 諮詢
advanced 促進	authored 編寫	chose 選擇	contacted 聯繫
advised 建議	authorized 授權	clarified 闡明	continued 繼續
advocated 主張	awarded 頒發	classified 分類	contracted 簽約
aided 輔助	balanced 使平衡	cleared 清除	contributed 貢獻
allayed 平息	began 開始	closed 關閉	controlled 控制
alleviated 緩解	bettered 改良	coached 執教	converted 轉換
allocated 分配	bid 投標	collaborated 合作	cooperated 合作
altered 改變	blended 協調	collated 核對	coordinated 協調
amassed 積累	boosted 提升	collected 收集	corrected 修正
amended 修正	bought 購買	combined 結合	corresponded 通信
analyzed 分析	brought 帶來	commanded 指揮	counseled 商議
anticipated 預期	budgeted 編入預算	commissioned 委託	crafted 精心製作
applied 應用	built 建立	committed 致力於	created 創建

cultivated 培養	elaborated 闡述	financed 資助	incorporated 合併
cut 削減	eliminated 消除	finished 完成	increased 增加
dealt 處理	emphasized 強調	fixed 固定	indexed 編索引、指示
decided 決定	enabled 使能夠	focused 聚焦	influenced 影響
decreased 降低	enacted 頒布、制定	followed 跟隨	informed 通知
defined 定義	encouraged 鼓勵	forecast 預測	infused 灌注
defrayed 撥款支付	enforced 實施	forged 鍛鍊	initiated 開始
delegated 委派	engineered 策劃、建造	formed 形成、成立	innovated 革新
delivered 發表、運送	enhanced 加強	formulated 制定	in-serviced 在職服務
demonstrated 展示	enlarged 擴大	forwarded 轉發、促進	inspected 檢查
deployed 部署	enlisted 招募	fostered 培養、促進	inspired 啟發
designated 指定	enriched 充實	fought 爭取	installed 安裝
designed 設計	enrolled 招收	found 發現	instilled 灌輸、教導
detailed 詳盡呈現	ensured 確保	founded 成立	instituted 制定
detected 發現	entered 進入	framed 構思、建造	instructed 指示

determined 決定	enticed 促使	fulfilled 實現	integrated 整合
developed 開發	equipped 使有能力	functioned as 作為	interacted 互動
devised 設計、制定	established 建立	funded 資助	interpreted 解讀
diagnosed 診斷	estimated 估計	furnished 提供	intervened 介入
directed 指揮	evaluated 評估	furthered 推動	interviewed 採訪
disbursed 支付	examined 檢查	gained 獲得	introduced 介紹
discovered 發現	exceeded 超過	gathered 聚集	invented 發明
dispatched 發送、迅速處理	exchanged 交換	generated 產生	inventoried 編製目錄、清點
dispensed 分配、執行	executed 執行	governed 治理	invested 投資
displayed 顯示	exercised 行使	grew 成長	investigated 調查
disseminated 傳播	exhibited 顯示	grouped 編組	invited 邀請
dissolved 解散	expanded 擴張	guided 指導	involved 參與
distributed 分發	expedited 加速	handled 處理	isolated 隔離
diversified 分散投資；增加產品	experienced 體驗	headed 主導	issued 發行
divided 劃分	experimented 試驗	heightened 提高	itemized 逐項列出

documented 記錄	exported 出口	held 舉行	joined 加入
doubled 使翻倍	extended 延伸	helped 幫助	judge 判斷
downsized 縮減	extracted 提取	hired 雇用	justified 證明
drafted 草擬	fabricated 製造	hosted 主辦	launched 開辦
drew up 制定	facilitated 促進	hurried 敦促	learned 學到
drove 駕駛	factored 代理經營	identified 識別	lectured 講授
earned 獲得	familiarized 使熟悉	illustrated 說明	led 主導
economized 節省	fashioned 塑造	implemented 實施	lessened 減少
edited 編輯	fielded 回答、處理（問題）	imported 進口	leveraged 發揮重要功效
educated 教導	filed 歸檔	improved 改善	licensed 准許
effected 實現	finalized 完成、定案	improvised 即興發揮	liquidated 清理債務、消除
litigated 提出訴訟	notified 通知	processed 處理	reduced costs 降低成本
located 查明	obtained 獲得	procured 努力取得	reengineered 重新設計
logged 記錄	offered 提供	produced 產生	referred 提及
lowered 降低	officiated 主持	profiled 呈現概況	regained 重獲

maintained 維持	opened 打開	programmed 制定計畫	registered 登記；提出
managed 管理	operated 操作	progressed 取得進展	regulated 規範
mandated 授權	optimized 優化、充分利用	projected 預計	rehabilitated 修復
maneuvered 巧妙處理	orchestrated 精心安排、協調	promoted 促進	reimbursed 償還
manufactured 製造	ordered 訂購；下指令	proofread 校對	reinforced 強化
mapped 詳細計劃	organized 組織	proposed 提議	rejuvenated 恢復活力
marked 標記	originated 發起	protected 保護	related 涉及；認同
marketed 行銷	outdistanced 遠遠超過	proved 證實	remained 保持
mastered 精通	outlined 概述	provided 提供	remedied 補救
masterminded 精心策劃	outsourced 外包	publicized 宣傳	remodeled 改建
maximized 最大化	overcame 克服	published 發表	rendered 提供、提出
measured 測量	overhauled 全面檢修；追上	purchased 購買	renegotiated 重新談判
mediated 調解	oversaw 監督	quadrupled 翻四倍	renewed 更新
mended 改良	paced 調整步調	qualified 使有資格	reorganized 重組
mentored 指導	packaged 包裝	quantified 量化	repaired 修復

merged 合併	packed 包裝	quoted 報價	replaced 替換
met 會見；達成	parlayed 談判	raised 提高	replicated 複製
met deadlines 在時限內完成	participated 參加	ran 經營	reported 報告
minimized 最小化	partnered 合作	ranked 排名	repositioned 重新定位
mobilized 動員	perfected 完善	rated 評分	represented 代表
modeled 展示	performed 執行	reached 達到	reproduced 複製
moderated 主持	persuaded 說服	read 讀懂	researched 研究
modernized 使現代化	piloted 帶領	realigned 重新調整	reshaped 重新塑造
modified 修正、微調	pinpointed 查明	realized 實現	resolved 解決
molded 塑造	pioneered 開創	rearranged 重新安排	responded 回應
monitored 監控	placed 放置；投資；下訂單	rebuilt 重建	restored 恢復
motivated 激勵	planned 計劃	received 收到	restructured 重組
mounted 上升	positioned 就位	recognized 認可	retained 保留
moved 移動	predicted 預測	recommended 推薦	retooled 改組
multiplied 倍增	prepared 準備	reconciled 調和	retrieved 取回

29

履歷

named 命名	prescribed 規定	reconstructed 重建	returned 歸還；恢復
narrated 敍述	presented 呈現	recorded 記錄	revamped 改造、翻新
narrowed 縮小	preserved 保存	recovered 恢復	reversed 扭轉、徹底改變
navigated 引導	presided 主持	recruited 徵募	reviewed 審查
negotiated 協商	prevented 預防	rectified 矯正	revised 修訂
netted 獲取	printed 印製	redesigned 重新設計	revitalized 重振
nominated 提名、任命	prioritized 優先考慮	redirected 重新定向	revived 復興
revolutionized 徹底改變	sold 賣出	supported 支持	trimmed 修整
rotated 輪流	solicited 徵集	surpassed 超越	tripled 翻三倍
routed 安排程序	solidified 鞏固	surveyed 調查	troubleshot 分析解決問題
safeguarded 防衛	solved 解決	synchronized 使協調	turned around 周轉
salvaged 挽救	sorted 整理	synthesized 合成	tutored 教導
satisfied 滿足	sourced 獲得	systematized 系統化	typed 打字
saved 節省	spearheaded 帶領	tabulated 製表	uncovered 揭露
scanned 掃描	specified 具體指明	tackled 對付、處理	underlined 強調

scheduled 安排	speeded 加快	tallied 符合、計算	undertook 進行、保證
screened 篩選	spent 花費	tapped 開發	underwrote 同意
searched 搜尋	spoke 陳述意見	targeted 作為指標、瞄準	unified 統一
secured 保證	sponsored 贊助	taught 教導	united 聯合
selected 選擇	stabilized 使穩定	tended 傾向	unraveled 弄清、解決
sent 發送	standardized 標準化	terminated 終止	updated 更新
sequenced 排序	started 開始	tested 測試	upgraded 升級
served 擔任	steered 導引	topped 突破	upheld 維護、贊同
serviced 服務	stimulated 激發	totaled 總計	urged 敦促
set strategy 設定策略	streamlined 簡化程序	traced 追踪	used 使用
set up 設置	strengthened 加強	tracked 追踪	validated 確認
settled 安頓	structured 建構	trained 訓練	verified 核實
shaped 塑造、計劃	studied 研究	transacted 交易	viewed 查看
shepherded 看管	submitted 提交	transcribed 轉錄	volunteered 自願
shipped 出貨	succeeded 達成成功	transferred 調動、轉變	widened 拓寬

shortened 縮短	suggested 建議	transformed 改造	withstood 承受、抵抗
showed 顯示	summarized 總結	transitioned 轉變	won 贏得
signed 簽約	supervised 監督	translated 翻譯	worked 工作
simplified 簡化	supplied 供應	traveled 旅行、出差	wrote 撰寫

單字（名詞）

ability 能力	education 教育	initiative 積極進取	references 參考人
background 背景	experience 經驗	objective 目標	skill 技能
credential 資格	goals 目標	opportunity 機會	

單字（形容詞）

adaptable 適應力強的	creative 有創意的	dynamic 有活力的	enthusiastic 熱情的
ambitious 有雄心壯志的	decisive 果斷的	eager 渴望的	flexible 靈活的
assertive 堅定自信的	dedicated 專注的	effective 有效的	friendly 友善的
capable 有能力的	dependable 可靠的	efficient 有效率的	honest 誠實的

competent 能幹的	determined 有決心的	energetic 有活力的	imaginative 有想像力的
conscientious 勤勉盡責的	discreet 慎重的	enterprising 有事業心的	independent 獨立的
industrious 勤勞的	open-minded 思想開明的	professional 專業的	tactful 處事得體的
innovative 創新的	optimistic 樂觀的	progressive 進步的	tenacious 堅韌的
intelligent 聰明的	persuasive 有說服力的	qualified 合格的	trustworthy 值得信賴的
intuitive 直覺的	persistent 堅持不懈的	reliable 可靠的	versatile 多才多藝的
loyal 忠誠的	pioneering 開創的	resourceful 足智多謀的	well-organized 井井有條的
mature 成熟的	practical 實際的	responsible 負責任的	
methodical 有條理的	problem-solver 能解決問題的	self-confident 有自信的	
motivated 積極的	productive 富有成效的	steady 穩定的	

詞組

believe I could contribute/have a strong aptitude for 相信我能貢獻／有優秀的資質去	may I have fifteen minutes of your time to discuss 能否借用您十五分鐘的時間討論
analytical and critical thinking skills 分析和批判性思考能力	my five years as 我在五年間作為

able to present facts clearly and succinctly
能清晰簡潔地呈現事實

would enjoy attending/working/belonging
會想要出席／工作／歸屬於

considered an enthusiastic worker
被認為是具有熱忱的員工

responsible for
負責

experience that qualifies me for
經驗使我有資格去

serious interest in
對……深感興趣

extensive experience with
在……方面的豐富經驗

sound understanding of
對……很了解

good candidate/match for the job
適合的候選人／符合這個職位的條件

specialized in
精通、專攻

good sense of/working knowledge of
對……有良好判斷力／工作知識

supervisory abilities
監督管理能力

in response to your advertisement
回應你的徵才廣告

take pride in my work
以我的工作為榮

in this capacity
在這個職位上

technical skills
技術能力

interested in pursuing a career with
有興趣與……一同工作

well suited for
非常適合

qualities that would be useful in
在……方面有用的特質

willing to travel
願意出差

句子

I achieved a 19 percent capture rate on grants proposals submitted to local funders.
在提交給當地資助者的補助金提案中，我拿到補助金的機率達到百分之十九。

I am able to travel.
我接受出差。

I am a skilled operator of the Bridgeport mill and radial drill.
我能熟練操作橋港牌銑床與懸臂鑽床。

I have experience with light clerical duties.
我有處理辦公事務的經驗。

I have three years' experience in product development.
我有三年的產品開發經驗。

I met every deadline while working at Brooker Associates, some of them under fairly difficult circumstances.
我在布魯克公司工作期間，都在時限內完成業務，其中有些情況是相當艱難的。

In my last position I performed complex CNC turning operations on diversified parts with minimum supervision, and also had Mazatrol experience.
在我上一份工作，我需要操作複雜的電腦數值控制車床，其中牽涉各式各樣的零件，但我僅須最少量的監督。我也有操作 Mazatrol 系統的經驗。

In my two years at Arrow Appliance, I helped increase productivity by approximately 25 percent and decrease absenteeism by almost 20 percent.
在飛箭器材設備公司的兩年時間裡，我幫助提高了大約百分之二十五的生產力，並將曠工率降低了近百分之二十。

I successfully reduced stock levels while maintaining shipping and order schedules, resulting in lower overhead costs.
我成功降低存貨量，同時維持了出貨與訂單進度，從而降低了間接成本。

I was responsible for all aspects of store management, including sales, personnel, inventory, profit and loss control, and overseeing the annual budget.
我負責管理店面的各個面向，包括銷售、人事、存貨、損益控制，並監督年度預算。

My work skills include data entry, alphabetical and numerical filing, photocopying, typing skills, good organizational skills, an affinity for detail, and previous experience in a legal office.
我的工作技能包括數據輸入、按字母和數字歸檔、影印、打字技巧、良好的組織能力、對細節的重視以及在法律事務所的經驗。

Previous employers have found me responsible and innovative.
以前的雇主認為我負責、有創意。

段落

Part of my duties as music director and liturgist involved instrument acquisition and maintenance, including revoicing seven ranks of the organ, constructing small percussion instruments, enlarging the handbell set from sixteen to thirty-seven, and acquiring a new studio piano for the choir. I also obtained estimates and made plans for a major overhaul of the forty-rank 1926 Casavant organ.

我作為音樂總監和禮拜儀式專家，有一部分的職責是樂器的取得與維護，包括調校管風琴七個音管的聲音、打造小型打擊樂器、將手搖鈴從十六組擴增到三十七組，以及為合唱團購買新的直立鋼琴。我也負責詢問估價，並為一九二六年卡薩翁管風琴制定全面檢修計畫。

Because my previous jobs have all involved public contact, I am comfortable dealing with people on many levels. As an academic adviser in the MBA program at McKeown College, I provided academic guidance and course selection assistance to adult graduate students and program applicants, recruited students, and promoted the program in talks and seminars.

我先前的工作都跟接觸大眾有關，所以很習慣跟各行各業的人打交道。擔任麥康學院 MBA 學程的導師期間，我負責指導研究生和學程申請人，並協助他們選課。我也協助招募學生，並在講座和研討會上推廣學程。

I am highly skilled in the use and interpretation of specifications drawings and measuring instruments, generally knowledgeable about mechanical and electrical principles, and have experience in the construction, maintenance, and machine repair industries.

我擅長使用和解讀說明書圖紙與測量儀器，對機械和電氣原理有基本的了解，並有在建造，維修和機器修理業工作的經驗。

My responsibilities at Edwards International included invoicing, logging deposits, resolving billing problems related to data entry, managing four other accounts receivable employees, and filing a monthly report on the department.

我在愛德華國際的職責包括開發票、記錄存款、解決與數據輸入有關的帳單問題、管理其他四名應收帳款人員，以及編寫月度部門報告。

JOAN PENROSE

Present Address	**Permanent Address**
14 Grace Lane	#4 Route 9N
Chance, UT 84623	Fairfield, UT 84620
801-555-2241	801-555-2789
penrose@email.com	penrose@email.com

OBJECTIVE

An entry-level management position in transportation and logistics with the opportunity to contribute to the efficient operation of a firm and to earn advancement through on-the-job performance.

EDUCATION

Bachelor of Business Administration, May 2009, from Merriam University, with a major in Transportation and Logistics and a minor in Psychology. Major GPA: 4.0; cumulative GPA: 3.4.

Coursework: Logistics Law, International Transportation and Logistics, Strategic Logistics Management, Transportation and Public Policy, Transportation Carrier Management, Transportation Economics; Accounting I and II, Business Communications, Business Law, Community and Regional Planning, Computer Science, Economics, Operations Management.

Financed 100% of college expenses through work, work-study programs, and grants.

EXPERIENCE

Merriam University Computer Lab, 2006–2009; supervised three other students; oversaw hardware repairs and updating of software library; assisted users with various software (15 hours/week, September to May only).

Swinney's Book Store, summers, 2005–2007: assembled and packed book, magazine, and giftware shipments; trained twelve employees (20 hours/week).

Creston Food Stores Inc.: Deli Manager and Clerk, summers, 2005–2007; controlled all facets of delicatessen, including catering large and small events; worked at five different stores (20 hours/week).

Lorimer Industries, Salt Lake City, June and July 2008, Transportation/Distribution Intern: facilitated the relationship between Transportation and Customer Support Inventory Planning and Purchasing; assisted in the routing and controlling of inbound raw materials; gained experience in outbound logistics management, including warehousing and distribution.

Blaydon Logistics Case Study, August 2008: one of seven students selected to participate in logistics project at Blaydon Corporate Headquarters, San Diego;

29

履歷

evaluated performance measures used in the areas of transportation, customs, and export administration; presented initial findings and suggested alternative measures.

STRENGTHS

Communication: communicate well when speaking and writing; able to act as liaison between different personality types; comfortable and effective communicating with both superiors and staff.

Leadership: able to motivate a project team; background in psychology provides wide range of interpersonal skills to encourage and instruct others.

Responsibility: accustomed to being in positions of responsibility; self-motivated and willing to set goals and work to achieve them; never assume "the other person" is responsible.

Organization: use time and resources effectively; consider efficiency, planning, and accountability very important.

Computer expertise: experienced in Lilypad 1-2-3, Savvy Pagemaker, WordAlmostPerfect 9.0, ELEMENTAL programming, Venus-Calc spreadsheets, Cambridge Graphics, MacroTough Advance, and Bytewise.

Other: willing to relocate anywhere; have traveled to Europe (three times) and to the Orient (once) and thus have a global awareness of business and politics; quick learner and trained in analytical problem-solving skills; solid work ethic that finds satisfaction and pleasure in achieving work goals; daily reader of *Wall Street Journal, The Journal of Commerce, Christian Science Monitor*, and *The Utah Times*.

ACTIVITIES

Treasurer, Transportation/Logistics Club

Member, University Finance Club

Campus Chest (student-operated community service organization), business manager, 2008, public relations, 2009

Member, Professional Women in Transportation, Utah Chapter

Coordinator of the Business Council Peer Advisory to Transportation and Logistic Undergraduate Students

AWARDS

Creston's Employee-to-Employee Courtesy Award

Dean's List, eight semesters

Golden Key National Honor Society

National Collegiate Business Merit Award

29 履歷

瓊 · 潘洛斯

現居地址

84623 猶他州錢斯市葛雷思巷 14 號

801-555-2241

penrose@email.com

永久地址

84620 猶他州費菲爾德市 9N 號公路 4 號

801-555-2789

penrose@email.com

目標

在運輸和物流方面的初級管理職位，有機會為公司的運作效率做出貢獻，並通過在職表現獲得晉升。

學歷

企業管理學士，梅里亞姆大學，二〇〇九年五月，主修運輸和物流，副修心理學。專業科目 GPA：4.0；總平均 GPA：3.4。

課程：物流法、國際運輸與物流、策略物流管理、運輸與公共政策、運輸公司管理、運輸經濟學；會計一與二、商業溝通、商事法、社區和區域規畫、電腦科學、經濟學、經營管理。百分之百通過工作、工讀計畫和獎學金來支付大學學費。

經驗

梅里亞姆大學電腦實驗室，二〇〇六至二〇〇九；指導另外三名學生；監督硬體維修和軟體更新；協助使用者執行各種軟體（每週十五小時，僅九月至五月）。

史維尼書店，二〇〇五至二〇〇七年夏季：書籍、雜誌與禮品之裝配與包裝；培訓十二名員工（每週二十小時）。

克雷斯頓食品公司：熟食店經理和記帳員，二〇〇五至二〇〇七年夏季；掌管熟食店的各個面向，包括為大小活動提供餐飲；在五個不同分店工作（每週二十小時）。

鹽湖城羅里默工業，二〇〇八年六至七月，運輸／分銷實習生：促進運輸部與顧客支持及存貨計劃與採購部門之間的關係；協助路線安排並控制原料的進入；獲得外向物流管理經驗，包括倉儲和分銷。

布雷頓物流案例研究，二〇〇八年八月：七名入選學生之一，在聖地亞哥的布雷頓公司總部參與物流專案；在運輸、海關和出口管理方面評估績效指標；提出初步結果和建議替代措施。

優勢

溝通：口語與寫作溝通良好；能夠成為不同性格的人之間的橋樑；自在且有效地與上級和員工溝通。

領導：能夠激勵專案團隊；心理學背景提供各種人際互動能力，能鼓勵和指導他人。

負責：習慣承擔責任；自我激勵，願意設定目標並努力實現；永遠不會假設是「另一個人」要負責。

組織：有效利用時間和資源；認為效率、計畫與責任制非常重要。

電腦專業：有使用 Lilypad 1-2-3、Savvy Pagemaker、WordAlmostPerfect 9.0、ELEMENTAL 程式設計、Venus-Calc 電子表格、Cambridge Graphics、MacroTough Advance 及 Bytewise 的經驗。

其他：願意分發到任何地方；曾旅行歐洲（三次）與東方（一次），因而對於商業與政治有全球性的認知；學習快速，並曾接受分析解決問題的訓練；具強烈的職業道德感，從達成工作目標之中獲得滿足與快樂；《華爾街日報》、《商業雜誌》、《基督科學箴言報》與《猶他時報》的忠實讀者。

活動

運輸／物流俱樂部，會計

29

履歷

大學金融俱樂部，成員

校園資金（由學生營運的社區服務組織），業務經理，二〇〇八年，公關，二〇〇九年

運輸專業女性協會，猶他分會，成員

商務委員會，運輸物流系大學生同儕顧問統籌人

獎項

克雷斯頓食品公司內部員工禮貌獎

院長獎，八個學期

金鑰匙全國榮譽協會

全國大學生商務人才獎

FROM: Pip Thompson
TO: Raindance Film Festival
DATE: 4-9-2017
RE: bio for film festival program

Pip Thompson graduated magna cum laude from Yale University with a BA in Anthropology and Theater Studies. Two years in the film industry as script supervisor, production coordinator, and short-film director were followed by graduate school; she will receive her MFA in film (directing) from Columbia University in 2017.

Although Thompson admits her areas of specialization may seem unrelated to each other and a strange base on which to build a film career, she feels that anthropology, literally "the study of people," uncovers truths about human behavior while both theater and film convey those truths viscerally. Her viewfinder might not look like a microscope and her notebook contains storyboards, not observations on Inuit rituals, but she strives to direct films that give viewers insight into different cultures as a means of better understanding their own ways and the broader human experience.

A native of Minnesota, Thompson brought her interest in anthropology home with "The Windigo." Set in the preserved wilderness of northern Minnesota, the story derives its title and subject from a local Ojibwe Indian myth and dramatizes the misunderstandings that can arise between cultures. Gerard strives to emulate native ways, but he embodies a recent trend that appropriates Indian legends and beliefs without truly understanding them. Sandy, on the other hand, learns the hard way that he is biased in favor of laboratory wisdom. "The Windigo" examines ancient myths through the eyes of contemporary culture in order to shed light on the past and the present.

寄件人：琵普・湯普森
收件人：雨舞影展
日期：二〇一七年四月九日
關於：影展節目手冊自傳

琵普・湯普森以極優等的成績畢業於耶魯大學，獲得人類學和戲劇研究學士學位。研究所畢業後，在電影界工作兩年，期間擔任劇本監製、製作協管與短片導演；她將於二〇一七年從哥倫比亞大學獲得電影（導演）的藝術創作碩士。

湯普森也承認她的專業領域看起來彼此並不相關，在此基礎上建立電影事業也頗為奇特；然而就她看來，人類學在字面上即是「對人的研究」，它揭露的是人類行為的真相，而戲劇和電影則是從內在來傳達這些真理。也許她的取景器看起來並不像顯微鏡，也許她的筆記型電腦裝著的是分鏡腳本，而不是對因紐特人儀式的觀察報告；但她努力想拍出的電影，便是能讓觀眾在其中洞察不同的文化，藉此讓人們不僅更理解自己的行為，也對廣泛的人類經驗有更多了解。

　　身為土生土長的明尼蘇達人，湯普森透過「溫迪戈怪物」把她對人類學的興趣帶回了家鄉。場景設於明尼蘇達州北部的原始森林，故事的標題與主題源自當地奧傑布瓦印第安人的神話，並將文化之間可能產生的誤解加進了戲劇張力。杰拉德力求本土化，但是他體現的是近年的一種趨勢：盜用印地安的傳說與信仰，卻不曾真正理解其內涵。另一方面，桑迪則在歷經種種困難後，才發現自己贊同的是科學的智慧。「溫迪戈怪物」透過當代文化審視古代神話，讓人們能進一步了解過去和現在。

JAMES PAWKIE

1822 Galt Road

Woodland, AL 36280

205-555-1234

pawkie@gmail.com

OBJECTIVE

An entry-level position offering future management opportunity and present learning challenges.

EDUCATION

Bachelor of Business Administration, Alabama University, 2008

Private security office license, Alabama Department of Public Safety, 2006

Certificate: Certified Security Officer, 2007

WORK EXPERIENCE

P. Picklan International, 2008–present. Duties include monitoring inventory of supplies, accounting, purchasing, stocking, clerking, scheduling, supervising five coworkers, and training fifteen new employees.

W.S. Caption Security Inc., 2007–2008. Duties included enforcing safety and pilferage rules, processing invoices, and data entry.

Alexander Clues Manufacturing, 2004–2007. Duties included assisting manager with inventory control operations, ticketing and distributing orders, receiving and shipping freight, evaluating daily reports, working with computer system, answering customer inquiries concerning inventories.

ACTIVITIES

Scoutmaster, 2006–present

Member, Rotary International

Commissioned Second Lieutenant, U.S. Army, 2004

Dean's List all four years of college

傑米‧鮑奇

36280 阿拉巴馬州伍德蘭市蓋特路 1822 號

205-555-1234

pawkie@gmail.com

目標

初級職務，未來能提供管理機會，且目前能帶來學習上的挑戰。

學歷

企業管理學士，阿拉巴馬大學，二〇〇八年

私人保安執照，阿拉巴馬州公共安全部，二〇〇六年

證書：合格保安人員，二〇〇七年

工作經驗

皮克蘭國際，二〇〇八年至今。職責包括監督存貨供應、會計、採購、庫存、記帳、安排時程、管理五個同事和培訓十五名新員工。

開普迅安全公司，二〇〇七至二〇〇八。職責包括執行安全防盜守則、處理發票和輸入數據。

亞歷山大製造公司，二〇〇四至二〇〇七。職責包括協助經理進行存貨控制、處理票務與分配訂單、接收與運輸貨物、評估每日報告、使用電腦系統、回答顧客關於存貨的詢問。

活動

童子軍團長，二〇〇六年至今

國際扶輪社成員

美國陸軍少尉，二〇〇四年

大學四年皆獲院長獎

29

履歷

✉ 參見：06 預約會面、12 致謝函、17 後續追蹤信、27 申請信、28 求職信、30 推薦信、36 職場相關信

Chapter 30

參考信與推薦信
References and Recommendations

參考信是用來擔保一個人的個性與人格，讓第三方知道這個人在社會中是負責有用的一員。參考信是種證明：「是的，我已經認識這個人一段時間了。」推薦信則著重於具體呈現一個人的專業態度，通常是由認識申請人且了解雇主方的人來寫。推薦信是一種背書：「是的，這個人是個出色的候選人，適合你們的計畫。」推薦信與參考信有著緊密的相關性，所以寫作的原則也差不多。

稱讚信（letter of commendation）則是用來恭賀某人的成就，結合了表揚信與恭賀信的功能，請參見相關章節。

 PART 1 說明篇

參考信與推薦信的使用時機

申請加入組織或公司	請求別人代表你寫信	信用參考
參見：19 社團組織相關		參見：41 信貸相關信
拒絕寫信	請求前雇主提供資訊	感謝對方幫忙寫信
參見：22 拒絕	從求職者提供之參考信獲得資訊	參見：12 致謝函

＊參考信可用來保證：前員工／學生／朋友／家庭成員／顧客／鄰居／褓姆

推薦信可用來推薦：個人／想法／公司／專案／產品／服務／計畫／工作坊／新程序／管理決策／行動計畫／官方辦事處

該怎麼說？

1. 在參考信或推薦信開頭提到求職者全名，而後在每一段第一次提到他時，以 Ms.、Mr. 或 Dr. 加上姓氏來稱呼，在此之後則以 she 或 he 稱之。絕不要只寫名字。

2. 描述你與求職者的關係（前雇主、老師、主管、指導教授、同事、鄰居、導師）以及認識的時長，如 for five years（長達五年）。

3. 一般的參考信，著重在求職者的特質（值得信賴、有責任感、極富熱忱、機智圓通）。若是推薦信，著重在工作經驗與技能（與你共事的時長、特殊能力與成就、你對於考慮雇用他為員工的看法）。以事實或範例來支持你的論點。

4. 結尾時，以一句話作為總結，你可以重申你對這個人的推薦，或你對他的信心。

5. 如果適當的話，可表示願意提供進一步的資訊。若你沒有使用有信頭的信紙的話，請附上全名、地址與電話號碼。

6. 將參考信或推薦信交給求職者，信封不必封口，對方想看的話可以打開看。如果你被要求將信直接寄給人事部門、獎學金委員會或其他調查機構，則須將信封封口。有的時候，你或許會被要求在封口處簽名，以確保機密性。一般來說，封口的信比未封口的信更具說服力。

什麼不該說？

- 不要使用過多讚美之詞，也不要使用太多最高級形容詞，這會降低可信度。專注描述兩、三個特質，並給予實例。

- 避免說出你無法證明的事情。儘管比起給予過多正面評價，這還算不上是全然的不誠實，但卻可能對求職者不利。

- 不要指示潛在雇主該怎麼做，如「如果她是在我們這裡求職的話，我一定會馬上雇用她」；「如果我是你，我會趕快把這個人搶下來」；「我想不出比他更值得這項獎學金的人了」。多數人都討厭別人對他們下指導棋。你要做的是提供資訊，他們才是做決定的人。

寫作訣竅

- 要簡短。一頁就好，至多兩頁，這便足以傳達整體概況，並能避免內容重複、使用不必要的詞彙、過度讚美或令對方感到無聊。

- 要具體。不要只是說說，而要展示給收件者看。不要只說這個人很誠實，而要舉例說明他能打開收銀機，但即便在財務上有困難時，他交上來的收據都是正確無誤的。不要只說這個人很有同情心，而要描述他如何為了幫助遇到麻煩的同事而錯過了晚餐派對。

- 申請工作職位時，推薦信不必隨著履歷與申請信或封面信一起寄送。等到對方要求時再寄。

30

參考信與推薦信

特殊狀況

- 當你**想把某個人列為推薦人時**，先打電話或寫信給對方取得許可。

- **請別人幫你寫參考信或推薦信時**，須提供對方足夠的資訊，他們才能在信中突顯對你最有幫助的要點，如 I am applying for a position as a claims examiner.「我要申請的是理賠審查員。」幫寫信的人才能根據你轉述的公司需求與條件，寫出相應的內容。隨信附上一個回郵信封，或附上一貼有郵票的信封，並寫下推薦信收信人的地址。表達感謝。給對方二至三週的時間寫信。

- 感謝為你寫推薦信或參考信的人後，可以向對方分享你找工作、申請會員、或申請入學的新消息或進度。即便你沒有得到職位，或決定不選這個職位，你都還是要**向代表你寫信的人致上謝意**。

- 如果你無法幫某個前員工寫正面參考信或推薦信，**可以拒絕幫忙**。多數員工都能取得員工紀錄，所以要是他們不喜歡你寫的內容，他們或許會想對你採取法律行動。此外，根據調查，許多雇主很擔心惹上官司，所以在取得員工書面同意書與免責聲明前，他們不會提供任何關於前員工的資訊。有些公司甚至無論如何都不提供推薦信，因為打一場誹謗的官司會花費成千上萬元，即便公司贏了亦然。很多公司與人事部門訂有政策，規定只以電話提供訊息（如此便不會留下書面證據），或只寄發制式確認這個人曾在此工作並核實受雇日期。這種信可能還會加一句 It is against our policy to discuss the performance of former employees.「我們的政策規定不可討論前員工之工作表現。」

- **推薦一項服務或產品時**，要納入自己的經驗，但避免整篇都是讚美。可以給予幾項聲明：This is only my opinion, of course.「當然，這只是我的看法。」；You may want to see what others think.「你也許會想知道別人的看法。」；It may not work for everyone, but we liked it.「也許不是每個人都適用，但我們很喜歡。」

- **當你想正式建議某種行動、政策變更或決策**，內容須包含：在主旨欄或第一個句子中點出這封信的主題；總結建議；提出事實支持；表達你願意接受進一步的談判、加入進一步的研究或繳交額外資料。如果你的建議具批判性或是負面的，要小心措詞。在提及不力條件時，也要點出優勢所在，但要明確表示你認為前者比後者的影響更大。

格式

- 參考信與推薦信都是打在有信頭的信紙上。
- 寄致謝函給幫忙寫信的參考人或推薦人時，可打字或手寫在素雅的私人信紙或折頁卡片上。
- 與公司政策有關的內部建議信，會打在備忘錄用紙上。

單字

admirable *(a.)* 可敬的	effective *(a.)* 有效的	integrity *(n.)* 正直	resourceful *(a.)* 足智多謀的
approve *(v.)* 贊同	efficient *(a.)* 有效率的	intelligent *(a.)* 聰明的	respect *(v.) & (n.)* 尊重
capable *(a.)* 有能力的	endorse *(v.)* 贊同	invaluable *(a.)* 無價的	responsible *(a.)* 負責任的
commendable *(a.)* 值得讚美的	energetic *(a.)* 精力充沛的	inventive *(a.)* 善於創造的	self-motivated *(a.)* 自動自發的
competent *(a.)* 能幹的	ethical *(a.)* 道德的	loyal *(a.)* 忠誠的	sensible *(a.)* 明智的
congenial *(a.)* 令人愉快的	excellent *(a.)* 優異的	meticulous *(a.)* 一絲不苟的	successful *(a.)* 成功的
conscientious *(a.)* 勤勉認真的	experienced *(a.)* 有經驗的	outstanding *(a.)* 出色的	suitable *(a.)* 適合的
considerate *(a.)* 體貼的	first-rate *(a.)* 一流的	personable *(a.)* 優雅的	tactful *(a.)* 機智圓通的
cooperative *(a.)* 合作的	hardworking *(a.)* 努力的	praiseworthy *(a.)* 值得稱讚的	thoughtful *(a.)* 考慮周到的
creative *(a.)* 有創意的	honest *(a.)* 誠實的	productive *(a.)* 富有成效的	trustworthy *(a.)* 值得信賴的
dependable *(a.)* 可靠的	imaginative *(a.)* 想像力豐富的	professional *(a.)* 專業的	valuable *(a.)* 珍貴的
diligent *(a.)* 勤勞的	indispensable *(a.)* 不可或缺的	recommend *(v.)* 推薦	
discreet *(a.)* 謹慎的	ingenious *(a.)* 心靈手巧的	reliable *(a.)* 可靠的	
dynamic *(a.)* 有活力的	initiative *(a.)* 積極進取	remarkable *(a.)* 卓越的	

30

參考信與推薦信

able to energize a group of people
能夠激發團隊的活力

great respect for
對……充滿敬意

acquits herself/himself well
表現良好

happy to write on behalf
很樂意代表……寫信

asset to any organization
是任何組織的資產

has three years' experience
有三年的經驗

attentive to detail
注意細節

have been impressed with
因……而印象深刻

broad experience/range of skills
經驗豐富／能力多元

held in high regard here
在此受到高度器重

can attest to
可以證實

held positions of responsibility
足以擔負需承擔責任的職務

creative problem-solver
有創意的問題解決者

highly developed technical skills
非常熟練的技術

skilled in all phases of light clerical
duties
各方面的辦公事務都很熟練

I heartily/ wholeheartedly/highly
recommend
我真心／全心／極度推薦

did much to improve/increase/better/
upgrade
為了改善／增加／改進／升級……做了很多努力

in response to your request for
information about
在此回應將……的資訊提供給你的請求

discharged his/her duties satisfactorily
滿意地卸下職責

many fine contributions
許多傑出的貢獻

distinguished herself/himself by
在……表現出色

matchless record
無與倫比的紀錄

do not hesitate to recommend
毫不猶豫地推薦

nothing but praise for
只能為……讚美

energetic and enthusiastic worker
有活動、充滿熱忱的員工

one in a thousand
萬中選一

every confidence in
對……非常有信心

first-rate employee
一流的員工

for the past five years
在過去五年

gives me real satisfaction to
做……讓我非常滿足

responsible for all aspects of security
負責安全作業的各個面向

satisfactory in every way
在每個方面都令人滿意

set great store by
相信……很重要

dependable/eager/hard worker
可靠／熱切／努力的員工

sterling qualities
優秀的特質

outstanding leadership abilities
出色的領導能力

rare find
稀有的人才

recommend with complete confidence
非常有信心地推薦

take-charge person
負責人

take genuine pleasure in recommending
非常樂意推薦

takes pride in his/her work
為他／她的工作感到驕傲

vouch for
為……擔保

well thought of
受敬重的

句子

Although company policy prohibits my writing you the recommendation you requested, I certainly wish you every success with your career.
因為公司政策，我不能答應你的請求為你寫推薦信，但我真心祝福你在職場上獲得成功。

Ann Shankland has highly developed sales and marketing skills and has also proven herself invaluable in the recruiting, training, and supervising of an effective sales team.
安・雪克蘭擁有純熟的銷售與行銷技巧，並已證明她在招募、訓練與督導一支業績良好的銷售團隊方面，有著不可估量的價值。

Elizabeth Endorfield is one of our most knowledgeable people when it comes to custodial chemicals, equipment, and techniques.

在化學物質管理、器材與技術方面，伊莉莎白‧恩多菲是我們之中最學識淵博的人之一。

Hiram G. Travers was in my employ for ten years.

西藍‧G‧崔佛斯受雇於我長達十年。

I've known Richard Musgrove as a neighbor and employee for six years.

理查‧穆斯果夫是我的鄰居與員工，我們已認識六年。

I am proud to recommend Ellen Huntly to you—I always found her work, character, and office manner most satisfactory.

我很驕傲地向您推薦艾倫‧杭特莉，她的工作表現、人格特質與辦公態度一直都讓我非常滿意。

In response to your inquiry about Chester Nimmo, it is only fair to say that he seemed to need constant supervision and our association with him was not an altogether happy one.

在此回應您對於切斯特‧尼莫的詢問。平心而論，他似乎需要不斷的監督，而我們與他的往來整體來說並不是特別愉快。

In response to your inquiry about Michael Condron, we were obliged to let him go because of our own financial difficulties—he was a superior scaler and riveter.

在此回應您對於麥可‧康卓的詢問。由於我們本身的財務困難，我們不得不讓他離開；他是一名優異的測量繪圖員與鉚工。

I would prefer not to comment on Jean Emerson's employment with us.

我不願針對珍‧愛默森的在職表現做任何評論。

Mary Treadwell worked as an X-ray technician at Porter General Hospital from 2009 to 2016.

瑪莉‧崔德威在二〇〇九至二〇一六年期間於波特綜合醫院擔任 X 光技術員。

Mr. Tamson's record with our company was excellent.

湯森先生在我們公司的紀錄非常優異。

Thank you for the wonderful and apparently persuasive recommendation you wrote for me—I've been accepted at the Maxwell School of Political Science!

謝謝您為我寫這封推薦信，文采優美，而且顯然非常有說服力。我已經錄取麥斯威爾政治學院！

Working with you has meant a great deal to me and I'm wondering if I may give your name as a reference when I apply for my first "real" job.

與您共事對我的意義重大，而我想知道，在我應徵第一份「真正的」工作時，我是否能將您列為參考人。

段落

In order to fully evaluate your suitability for the sales position you applied for, we need to speak to at least four former employers or supervisors. Please provide us with names, addresses, and daytime phone numbers of people we may contact. You will hear from us as soon as we have made a decision.

為全面評估您是否適合您所應徵的業務職位,我們必須與至少四名前雇主或主管會談。請提供我們可聯絡的姓名、地址與日間電話號碼。我們做出決定後,會立即與您聯繫。

The position turned out to be different from what I'd expected and I ended up declining it. I'm grateful to you for the positive recommendation you wrote (one of the reasons they wanted to hire me, I know!), and I'd like to use it again sometime. I'll let you know what happens.

我後來發現該職位與我期待的不同,所以我最後婉拒了。很感謝您為我寫的正面推薦信(我知道這是他們想雇用我的原因之一!),我之後想要再次使用,屆時我會讓你知道結果。

It is a pleasure to confirm Kenneth Eliot's employment with Meynell Associates from 2007 through 2017. Mr. Eliot carried out his responsibilities with diligence and punctuality, and was a definite employee asset. We have no reservations about recommending him highly.

我很樂意向您確認,肯尼斯‧艾略特於二○○七年至二○一七年受雇於梅諾公司。艾略特先生在履行其職責時總是勤勉、準確,絕對是公司的資產。我們毫無保留,極力推薦。

You asked what I thought of the Vanever-Hartletop contract. After looking into the matter, my best recommendation would be to return the contract unsigned with a request for renegotiation of the default clause.

你問我對於范諾維－哈特塔合約的看法。在了解情況後,我能給的最好建議是不要簽名、直接將合約歸還,並要求針對違約條款重新協商。

Dear Ms. Tartan,

You once offered to write me a letter of reference if ever I needed one. I would like to take you up on your kind offer now.

I am applying for a part-time teaching position in the Glendinning-Melville School District and have been asked to supply several letters of reference. In the hopes that you have the time and are still willing to write a letter, I'm enclosing an instruction sheet from the school district outlining what they need in a letter of reference as well as a stamped envelope addressed to the district personnel offices.

If for any reason you cannot do this, I will understand. Know that I am, in any case, grateful for past kindnesses.

Sincerely,

塔坦小姐您好：

您曾經提過，在我需要時您可以幫我寫推薦信，現在我想要接受您的提議。

我正在申請葛倫汀寧－梅維爾學區的兼任教職，對方要求我提供數封參考信。抱著您有時間且仍願意寫參考信的希望，我在此附上學區提供的說明書，上面列有他們必須在信中看見的事項，同時也附上能寄至學區人事辦公室的回郵信封。

若您因為任何原因無法協助，我都能理解。無論如何，我都很感謝您過去給我的善意，希望您了解這點。

○○敬上

TO: Office of Admissions
FROM: Dr. Charles Kennedy
RE: Steve Monk
DATE: November 15, 2017

I have known Steve Monk for four years, first as a student in my earth sciences and biology classes and later as his adviser for an independent study in biology. I am currently helping him with an extracurricular research project.

Mr. Monk is one of the brightest, most research-oriented students I have encountered in eighteen years of teaching. His SAT and achievement test scores only begin to tell the story. He has a wonderful understanding of the principles of scientific inquiry, a passion for exactitude, and a bottomless curiosity.

I will be happy to provide any further information.

收件人：入學審查辦公室
寄件人：查爾斯‧甘迺迪博士
關於：史帝夫‧蒙克
日期：二〇一七年十一月十五日

我認識史帝夫・蒙克已有四年時間，一開始他是我地球科學與生物學課堂上的學生，而後我成為他在生物學獨立研究的指導教授。目前我正在協助他進行一項課外研究專題。

　　在我十八年的教學生涯中，蒙克先生是我見過最聰明、對研究最有興趣的學生之一。他的SAT與能力考試成績只是故事的一部分而已；此外，他對於科學調查的原則有著深刻的理解，態度嚴謹、好奇心無限。

　　我很樂意提供任何進一步的資訊。

Dear Ms. Burnell,

　　You requested employment information about Dan Burke.

　　Mr. Burke was employed with us from 2011 through 2018 as a structural engineer. His work was satisfactory, and I believe he left us to pursue a more challenging job opportunity.

　　If we can be of additional assistance, please call.

Sincerely,

博納小姐您好：

　　您詢問關於丹・柏克的資訊。

　　柏克先生在二〇一一年至二〇一八年間受雇於我們，擔任結構工程師。他的工作表現令人滿意，而我相信他離開我們，是為了追求一份更有挑戰性的工作。

　　若有我能提供額外協助的地方，請打電話給我。

○○敬上

✉ 參見：09 介紹信、11 表揚信、12 致謝函、19 社團組織相關、20 請求與詢問、29 履歷、36 職場相關信

Chapter 31

投稿信或提案信
Query Letters

投稿信（query letter，有些狀況中可稱提案信）是一種雖簡短但講究的信件，為的是讓編輯有興趣出版你的文章或書籍，最理想的結果是讓編輯主動向你邀稿。投稿信結合了請求與推銷，可以用來說服作家經紀人代理你的作品，或吸引別人對你的提案產生興趣。

編輯很喜歡收到投稿信，因為這能幫助他們迅速決定你的提案是否適合他們、是否值得出版。他們自己也會利用措詞講究的投稿信，在編輯會議上把想法推銷給其他同事。

如果作家沒有經紀人，而編輯也不收毛遂自薦的文稿，投稿信便是唯一能接近編輯的方法。如果編輯接受文稿，先寄出投稿信也是接洽的好方法。一旦編輯回應你的投稿信，並邀請你寄給他文稿時，請在稿件包裹上標示「Requested Material」（應邀寄發資料），這樣你的文稿才不會被扔進廢稿堆。透過事先寄發投稿信，你也能事先知道對方是否需要這樣的作品。

 PART 1 說明篇

為了什麼寫投稿信？

劇本	書籍	雜誌文章
期刊或文獻	作家經紀人	提議商業機會

該怎麼說？

1. 要寄給正確的對象。先了解該出版社或投稿期刊的性質，確認你的內容投其所好。找出符合你的文稿類型的專職編輯，取得該編輯的姓名與職稱。打電話確認該編輯仍在那裡工作、正確的姓名拼寫方式，以及目前的職稱。（不需要求與該編輯說話，編輯很容易被這種電話惹惱；前臺接待人員與編輯助理就足以回答你的問題。）

2. 讓收信人立刻就能抓到重點，如 Would you be interested in seeing a 10,000-word article on...?「您是否有興趣閱讀一篇關於……的文章，約一萬字？」

3. 要勾起編輯的興趣，讓他繼續讀下去。有些投稿信會以文章或書的第一段為開頭。

4. 告訴對方你的書或文章是什麼類型（工具書、傳記、童書）、字數、目標讀者與標題。接著用幾句話描述作品內容，讓編輯迫不及待想讀一讀；這一段你必須寫得最好才行。

5. 告訴對方你的文章或書與其他類似主題的作品不同之處、為何你是寫這個主題的最佳人選（提及你的相關專業或知識），以及選擇這間出版社的原因。

6. 列出過去著作。

7. 感謝對方付出時間與關心。

8. 附上回郵信封，務必每次都要附上。

什麼不該說？

• 不要在投稿信中討論稿費、版稅、權利或其他交易上的問題。這個階段這麼做並不適當。

• 勿納入與作品無關的個人資訊（如年齡、婚姻狀態、嗜好、教育背景）。除非這些資訊與你的作品高度相關。當然，你必須提供基本聯絡方式，即全名、居住地址、電話號碼、電子信箱與傳真號碼。

• 別用花招吸引編輯的注意力。編輯知道如何找出作品核心，不會因彩色的字體、開場的笑話或謎語（當然，除非那是本笑話集或謎語書）或炫目的招式而分心。他們通常認為，只有業餘人士才會耍這些花招。

寫作訣竅

• 按照出版社提供的投稿指示寫投稿信。如果出版社能接受電子信件，他們會在指示中明說；若他們提及回郵信封，表示他們偏好書面郵件。多數出版社會提供作者須知（writer's guidelines）；當你想把作品推銷給某間出版社時，請先向對方索取一份須知（可從網站下載，或寫信索取並附回郵信封）。

- 一般而言，投稿信會寄給協同編輯與助理編輯。比起執行編輯或總編輯，他們更有機會讀你的信。
- 長度最好保持一頁，至多兩頁。編輯主管珍·范梅倫（Jane von Mehren）表示：「投稿信就像是釣魚；別在魚鉤上放太多餌，否則釣不到魚。要簡潔、吊人胃口！」
- 傳達你對作品的熱情。
- 機智、難忘或有趣的作品標題（但要適合作品）能幫助你達成目的。不必是定稿標題，挑選一個暫定標題，或專門為投稿信寫一個標題。
- 再三檢查投稿信，越多次越好，確保沒有任何拼字、標點、文法或用字錯誤；這種錯誤是致命的。
- 重複投稿（multiple submission）指的是把同一份文稿同時寄給多名編輯。作者與編輯對重複投稿是否合宜各持不同意見。一般來說，你可以同時寄同一份投稿信給多名編輯，等到有數名編輯都回覆並要求你寄發文稿時，才需要思考重複投稿的問題。
- 若需要更多撰寫投稿信上的協助，可參考以下書籍：
  《How to Write Attention-Grabbing Query & Cover Letters》，作者：John Wood
  《How to Write Irresistible Query Letters》，作者：Lisa Collier Cool
  《How to Get Happily Published》，第五版，作者：Judith Appelbaum

特殊狀況

- 傳統上，投稿信在只用在紀實類的文稿，但在今日，出版社也會要求**虛構小說**的作者寄送投稿信。在這種情況下，投稿信其實就像是求職信的角色，隨信附上內容大綱與試閱章節。
  投稿文件即使是虛構小說，還是可以按照本章原則撰寫投稿信，但在簡述故事的段落須描述情節、角色、衝突與決心。
- **尚未出版作品的作家**，常擔心出版社的人會在讀完投稿信後，會偷走他們的點子，但這其實極度罕見。事實上，新點子一直不是重點，只有包裝與呈現想法的方式才是真正發揮創意的地方。即便兩個人都想到了相同的點子（據說戲劇的情境總共只有三十六種），作品也會迥然不同。而且，要是不寄投稿信，你如何才能出版作品？
- 當你**將投資的提案或想法推銷給收信人時**，要附上能展現成功紀錄的圖表或報告，你的履歷、信用與推薦書，或任何與你的提案有關的資料。你的目標是說服對方與你見面討論此提案。這種信跟文學作品投稿信不一樣，你可以參見其他章節：27 申請信、28 履歷、34 報告與提案、42 銷售信。

格式

- 投稿信務必用打字的，最好使用私人信頭信紙。不要試圖縮小字體，或減少邊緣留白處，來打進更多的字。
- 有些編輯可以接受以電子郵件寄發的投稿信。請事先確認是否有任何關於電子郵件的特殊規定。
- 只有當對方請你以傳真寄發詢問函，才能用傳真的方式寄出。

單字

appeal *(n.) & (v.)* 吸引力；訴求	feature *(n.) & (v.)* 特色；主打……特色	nonfiction *(n.)* 非虛構小説	round-up *(n.)* 綜述、概要
audience *(n.)* 讀者群	fiction *(n.)* 虛構小説	outline *(n.) & (v.)* 大綱；概述	summary *(n.)* 總結
consider *(v.)* 考慮	interested *(a.)* 感興趣的	overview *(n.)* 總覽	synopsis *(n.)* 概要
contemporary *(a.)* 當代的	manuscript *(n.)* 文稿	publication *(n.)* 出版作品	viewpoint *(n.)* 觀點
expertise *(n.)* 專業	material *(n.)* 材料	review *(n.)* 評論文章	

詞組

about 2,500 words 大約兩千五百字	previous works include 過去的作品包括
aimed at long-distance runners 針對長跑運動員	professional background supports 專業背景支持
first-person narrative 第一人稱敘事	publication credits include 出版紀錄包括
most recent publications include 最近的出版作品包括	sample chapters and outline 試閱章節與大綱
mystery series 推理小説系列	trade journal appeal 以貿易期刊為訴求
personal experience with 個人在……的經驗	

句子

As you do not currently accept unagented submissions, I'm writing to ask if you'd like to see a picture book manuscript.
由於您目前不接受不是由經紀人經手的投稿，我在此想詢問您是否有意願看看一份繪本手稿。

Can the market stand one more book on weight control? If it's this one—written by a physician with thirty years' success in helping patients lose weight—it can!
市場還能接受更多關於體重控制的書嗎？撰寫這本書的醫師在過去三十年間成功幫助病人減肥，如果是這本書的話，市場能接受！

Enclosed are three sample chapters and an outline.
隨信附上三章試閱章節以及一份大綱。

Enclosed is a SASE for your response.
隨信附上回郵信封，供您回覆。

I can submit the article by e-mail or as hard copy.
我可以透過電子郵件寄出文章，或繳交書面稿件。

I could deliver a 5,000-word article by September 1.
我可以在九月一日前寄出一篇五千字的文章。

I look forward to hearing from you.
我期待得到您的回覆。

It was a dark and stormy night—or was it?
那是個漆黑、風雨交加的夜晚，不是嗎？

Thank you for your time and consideration.
謝謝您的時間與關心。

Would you be interested in seeing a 40,000-word mystery for children set in the 1920s in one of Upper Michigan's Finnish settlements?
您是否有意願看看這本四萬字的兒童推理小說？場景設於一九二○年代，在上密西根的一個芬蘭移民家庭。

31
投稿信或提案信

段落

If education is not a preparation for life but life itself (John Dewey), why does today's education so little resemble the real world? What would happen if it did? Would you be interested in considering for publication the 75,000-word story of a real-life experiment in education?

如果教育本身就是人生，而非適應人生的準備階段（由杜威提出），那為何今日的教育卻與真實世界如此迥異呢？若教育與真實世界相像，會發生什麼事？這個七萬五千字的故事，便是關於一項針對教育的真實實驗，您是否有興趣出版呢？

What happens to romance after a couple has a baby? What can you do before the baby arrives to "baby-proof" your relationship? What skills and strategies will actually deepen your love after the baby arrives? As a family counselor with a new baby herself, I have been collecting anecdotes, quotations, studies, and firsthand stories to help your readers answer these questions.

夫妻有了孩子後，愛情會有什麼變化？在孩子出生前，您能做什麼來「寶護」夫妻關係呢？什麼樣的技巧與策略，能在孩子出生後加深愛情？我是一個有孩子的家庭諮商師，一直以來我都在收集相關的軼事、語錄、研究與第一手資料，為的就是幫助您的讀者回答這些問題。

A man with amnesia tries to negotiate the tricky steps of the life he is told is his. A familiar plot? Not in this novel.

一名患有失憶症的男子試圖度過人生中的棘手事情，但他的人生卻只能透過別人告訴他。很耳熟的劇情嗎？在這個小說中可不一樣。

Thank you for sending the submission guidelines for *Stucco City*. Having studied the guidelines and having also been a subscriber to your magazine for more than five years, I believe the article I want to submit to you is as new as it is highly appropriate to your readership.

謝謝您寄給我《灰泥城市》的投稿須知。我已經仔細研讀須知，本身也訂閱您們的雜誌長達五年以上，所以我相信，我投稿的文章內容不僅新穎，也非常適合您們的讀者閱讀。

---

31 投稿信或提案信

I've been a season ticket-holder for the past three years and have thoroughly enjoyed your theater company's vitality, intelligence, and creativity. I am also a playwright with a script that I think is particularly appropriate for your ensemble.

過去三年我持續買了貴劇場的季票,也相當享受貴劇場公司具有活力、才智與創意的戲劇。本身也是劇作家的我,手上有份劇本,我認為特別適合您的劇團。

示範信

Dear Ms. Dakers,

As the curator and principal scientist at the Leys Marmot Living Museum, I am in a unique position to write about the little-known but fascinating marmot (some species of which are more familiarly known as woodchucks). Studying them has given me a sense of the uncharted boundaries between so-called human and animal behavior.

I think the readers of *Animal Life* would be interested in the daily routine of a yellow-bellied marmot family, from the moment they wake up in their single-family dwelling to the moment they signal whichever family member has been guarding the door that it's time to come in and go to bed.

I am thinking in terms of a 10,000-word article with several sidebars on the folklore of the marmot. I can supply high-quality color slides.

I'm enclosing a SASE for your reply and I look forward to hearing from you.

達克斯小姐您好:

我是里斯旱獺生活館的館長與主要研究員,我的特殊職位讓我得以將少有人了解卻迷人的旱獺寫成文章(其中有些品種以土撥鼠之名較廣為人知)。研究牠們的同時,我發覺在所謂的人類與動物行為之間,有著未知的分界。

我想,《動物生活》的讀者會對黃肚皮旱獺家族的作息感到興趣,從牠們在只住了同一家族的居處起床,到牠們發出信號叫守門的家族成員回家睡覺。

我正在考慮寫篇一萬字的文章,並會加入數個與旱獺有關的民俗小故事作為補充。我可以提供高畫質彩色簡報。

隨信附上回郵信封供您回覆,期待得到您的回應。

Dear Ms. Ryder,

I am a regular customer of Ryder Exercise Equipment Inc. I am also the owner of three juice bars in the metropolitan area.

It occurred to me that a small line of take-home health foods and juices might be welcomed by your customers.

Enclosed are some articles on the growing popularity of juice bars and a summary of my own stores' financial health.

At this point, I am interested simply in exploring the possibilities of such an arrangement.

Would you like to discuss this sometime? Perhaps we could meet at my Mulcaster Avenue store, which is not far from you. I'd especially like to see what you think of our Apple-a-Day juice.

Sincerely,

瑞德小姐您好：

　　我是瑞德運動器材的常客，本身經營三間都會區果汁吧。

　　我有個想法，或許您的顧客會對可帶回家的健康食品與果汁有興趣。

　　隨信附上一些關於果汁吧越來越受歡迎的文章，以及我的店舖的財務總結報告。

　　在這個階段，我只是單純想知道這種安排的可行性。

　　您是否想要找時間討論一下呢？我們可以在我的穆卡斯特大道分店見面，這間離您不遠。我也很想知道，您對我們的「一天一蘋果」果汁吧有什麼看法。

○○敬上

From: jhall@email.com
To: query@email.com
Date: 06/26/2017 01:41 PM MST
Subject: Query: Renting a villa in Sicily

Hello. For my third stay in Sicily this fall, I'm renting a villa. Would you be interested in a 1,200-word piece comparing the benefits of villa life with hotel life, using as examples three of my favorite Sicilian hotels (one on the north coast, one on the south coast, and one in Taormina)? Travel information layered into the article includes getting to Sicily; the best times to visit; auto rental peculiarities there; the three best areas in which to rent villas and the day trips that are possible from each; the sites that no visitor to Sicily should miss.

I've written eighteen books published by mainstream publishers as well as a number of magazine and other articles. I'll be in Sicily Oct. 13–Nov. 13 and could get the piece to you several weeks after that. Because Sicily is best traveled in spring or fall, the article might appear in the spring for fall travel.

Thanks for your time and attention.

寄件人：jhall@email.com
收件人：query@email.com
日期：06/26/2017 01:41 PM MST
主旨：詢問：租用西西里島別墅

　　哈囉，這個秋天我將會第三次前往西西里島，我打算在那裡租一間別墅。我在一篇一千兩百字的文章中，比較了別墅生活與飯店生活帶來的好處，並以我在西西里島最喜歡的三間飯店為範例（一間位於北岸、一間於南岸、一間在陶美那），您是否有興趣一讀呢？文章會有一個部分提供旅遊資訊，包括如何到達西西里島；最佳旅遊時間；當地租車特色；三個最適合租別墅的地點，以及在各個地點適合的一日遊行程；西西里島遊客絕不能錯過的景點。

我寫過十八本書，皆由主流出版社出版，此外還有多篇雜誌文章與其他文章。於十月十三日至十一月十三日期間，我會在西西里島，結束行程的數週後，我可以把稿件給您。由於西西里島最適合在春季或秋季遊覽，這篇文章或許可以在春季出版，人們在秋季旅遊時便能使用。

謝謝您付出的時間與關注。

Dear Randy Shepperton,

Would you be interested in seeing an 85,000-word novel, *The Boarding House*?

Wealthy, intelligent, and isolated, Marshall is a house divided against himself. Denying important and life-giving facets of his self from an early age, he surrounds himself with shadows formed by his projected unacceptable imaginings. In this literary exploration of the divided self, Marshall struggles to resolve the four basic human conflicts—between freedom and security, right and wrong, masculinity and femininity, and between love and hate in the parent-child relationship. In daring to love with maturity and without reserve he is finally able to deal with the boarders living in his house and to trade his mask for a real face.

I can send the complete manuscript or, if you prefer, sample chapters and a detailed synopsis.

I am also the author of a number of short stories, one of which won the Abinger Prize last year, and I was recently awarded a grant by our state arts board based on a sample from this novel.

Enclosed is a SASE for your reply.

藍迪・薛普頓您好：

你是否有興趣看一本八萬五千字的小說《寄宿公寓》？

馬修富有、聰明而孤僻，他就像一間把自己分隔成兩半的房子。從很小的時候起，他便否認自己擁有那些重要、生活必需的特質；他讓自己被陰影包圍，而陰影來自他腦中那些無可容忍的幻象。在這個探索分裂自我的文學作品中，馬修為了解決四種人類基本衝突而掙扎：自由與安全；正確與錯誤；男子氣概與女性氣質；親子關係中的愛與恨。當他勇敢、無保留地展現成熟的愛，他終於能夠與寄宿在他房子中的房客相處，並將面具卸下，換上真實的面孔。

我可以將完整的手稿寄給您；若您希望的話，我也可以只寄試閱章節與詳細的劇情梗概。

我本身亦是許多短篇故事的作者，其中一篇在去年獲得了亞賓杰獎。最近，州立藝術委員會也根據這本小說的一份試閱文稿，頒發給我一項獎金。

隨信附上回郵信封供您回寄時使用。

✉ 參見：20 請求與詢問、28 求職信、34 報告與提案、42 銷售信

Chapter 32

備忘錄
Memos

> 只談生意，然後迅速處理那筆生意。
> ——義大利印刷之父阿爾杜斯・馬努提烏斯（Aldus Manutius）

備忘錄快絕跡了。

備忘錄（memo，是 memorandum 的簡稱；複數為 memos、memoranda 或 memorandums）的出現，是為了提升公司內部員工之間的通訊效率，達成迅速、直接、扼要的溝通。也因此，當通訊對象是你經常需要溝通的同仁、主管與經理，且他們都了解自己的公司時，便沒有必要使用有信頭的信紙、「Dear」、「Sincerely」以及其他禮貌性的開頭與結尾用語。

不過，電子郵件也符合備忘錄的特色，具有迅速、簡單的優勢。

儘管如此，備忘錄還是很有用的。當辦公室很小，且不是每個人都有電腦收發電子郵件；當你要傳達的資訊具機密性質；隨備忘錄一起寄送的報告頁數太多或有太多圖表，難以透過電郵傳送；當你希望這項資訊能按順序傳遞，並讓各經手人簽名、簽署姓名字首字母或評論；當你必須與公司外部的顧客或供應商進行溝通（訂單、資料傳送、收件通知、確認、詢問）。

在《How to Survive From Nine to Five》（暫譯：如何戰勝朝九晚五的工作人生）一書中，作者吉莉・庫柏（Jilly Cooper）寫道：「備忘錄最主要的功能，是作為追蹤紀錄，這樣你才能在六個月後向某人發怒：『嗯，你應該要知道這件事的，因為我有寄給你一張備忘錄』」。

PART 1 說明篇

什麼可寫在備忘錄中?

布達事項 政策變更	**公司內部活動**	**指示**
會議	**提醒**	**報告**

該怎麼說?

1. 備忘錄的標題欄須包含四項要素。最常見的呈現方式是將四行靠左條列:

    TO: Blanche Challoner

    FROM: Francis Levison

    DATE: Nov. 20, 2017

    SUBJECT: employee stock purchase

也可以只將字首字母大寫:

    To: Blanche Challoner

    From: Francis Levison.

    Date: Nov. 20, 2017

    Subject: employee stock purchase

你也可以像這樣編排:

    TO: Blanche Challoner

FROM: Francis Levison

 DATE: Nov. 20, 2017

    RE: employee stock purchase

或是以兩欄的格式呈現:

    TO: Blanche Challoner   DATE: Nov. 20, 2017

    FROM: Francis Levison   RE: employee stock purchase

2. 仔細選擇主旨用詞，使讀者一眼就明白備忘錄的重點，如 new flexible tubing「新型彈性管線」；personal telephone calls「私人來電」；medical benefits enrollment「醫療福利登記」；change in library hours「圖書館開放時間變更」。

3. 在主旨下方二至四行處開始寫備忘錄內容，從左邊往右寫。內文的所有段落都從最左側開始書寫，段落間相隔一行空行（段落內的文字不必空行）。

4. 在結尾處寫上希望對方採取的行動。需要的話，也給予一個採取行動的截止日期：Please call me before Tuesday.「請於週二前打電話給我。」；Please inform others in your department.「請通知你部門內其他人。」；Send me a copy of your report by Oct. 13.「於十月十三日前寄一份你的報告給我。」

5. 在備忘錄最下方簽名，或是在標題欄你的姓名旁簽名或簽上姓名字首字母。

6. 寄人姓名字首字母（reference initials）與附件（enclosure notation，若有的話）會打在備忘錄下方靠左處。

什麼不該說？

- 不必包含開頭與結尾問候語，或任何標準商務信件常用的敦促或安撫用句。你很有禮貌，但直接進入重點。

- 正式信件不使用備忘錄（如升職與退休），要打在有信頭的信紙上。

寫作訣竅

- 第一句就寫出備忘錄的目的。

- 簡短扼要。使用簡單短句、現在式及主動動詞。一般來說，備忘錄長度不限，但一般都維持在一至二頁，除非是報告或議題備忘錄。備忘錄越短，收件人越有可能立刻閱讀。

- 備忘錄的特色在於它不正式，比信件更短更單純。備忘錄的文字也較為直白，且可以使用公司內部熟悉的術語與縮寫。內文會使用「我們」，而非「藍普利－伍德塢電信公司」。

- 當你要寄備忘錄給一人以上時：

  (1) 只有幾名收件人，則在「To:」後面列出所有收件人姓名。

  (2) 寄給大量的人，在「To:」後面列出主要收件人姓名，其餘姓名則列於備忘錄最下方「cc:」之後。

  (3) 將所有收件人姓名列於備忘錄最後一頁的分發名單中，並在「To:」後面打上「See distribution list on page 2」（見第二頁分發名單）。姓名前方不須加上敬稱（如 Ms.、Mr.），不過有時可以加上專業頭銜（如 Dr.）。若名單包含主管，他們的姓名通常會按照職等排序。在有些公司，則會按照字母順序排序。

特殊狀況

- **議題備忘錄**是一種陳述事實的報告,用以總結重要資訊,決策才得以制定。組織資料的有效方法,通常包含下列部分或全部項目:

  (1) 講述議題內容,須提供脈絡或背景資訊;

  (2) 列出可行或建議選項,或解決方法,以及各項的優缺點;

  (3) 詳述各選項的成本、財務影響及對其他計畫的影響;

  (4) 若情況適宜且公司歡迎的話,可列出執行各選項時所需步驟;

  (5) 提出你自己的建議;

  (6) 建議下一步可採取的行動(繼續研究、開會、投票、主管決策)。

- 可利用備忘錄**邀請員工參加公司內部活動**,這比電子郵件更「有誠意」。(寫作方法參見:18 邀請函)

格式

- 不須使用有公司信頭的信紙。有些組織會提供印有公司名字、或最上方簡單寫著「Memo」,或印好標題的備忘錄用紙。不過,電腦與電子郵件的普及,備忘錄用紙在今日已越來越不常見。

PART 2 應用篇

單字

announcement *(n.)* 宣告	information *(n.)* 資訊	policy *(n.)* 政策	report *(n.)* 報告
attachment *(n.)* 附件	instruction *(n.)* 指示	procedure *(n.)* 程序	request *(n.) & (v.)* 請求
deadline *(n.)* 截止日期	listing *(n.)* 列表	progress *(n.) & (v.)* 進度；進行	status *(n.)* 狀態
feedback *(n.)* 反饋意見	notice *(n.)* 通知	proposed *(a.)* 提議的	summary *(n.)* 總結
guideline *(n.)* 指導原則	outline *(n.) & (v.)* 概要；概述	reminder *(n.)* 提醒	

詞組

appreciate your comments on
謝謝你對……的評語

route this message to
將此訊息傳遞給

background information
背景資訊

see below for
見下文了解

clarify recent changes in procedure
說明最近的程序變更

summarize yesterday's discussion
總結昨日的討論

effective immediately
立即生效

would like to announce the following
想宣布以下事項

pleased to report
很高興報告

request a response by
請在……之前回覆

句子

Attached is a "get well" card for Ethel Ormiston—sign it if you like and pass it on to the next name on the list.
附件是給艾瑟‧歐密斯頓的「早日康復」卡，若願意的話請簽名，再傳遞給名單中的下一個人。

I've had phone calls from the following people about the new hook lifting devices—will you please return their calls and let me know what the problem is?
我接到以下幾個人來電詢問吊鉤起重裝置，你可否打電話回覆他們，並讓我知道是出了什麼問題？

Please initial this memo to indicate that you've read it.
請在這張備忘錄上簽上姓名字首字母，表示你已經看過。

Please read the attached proposal before tomorrow's meeting.
請於明日會議前讀完附件的提案。

Please sign up below for staff lounge cleanup duty and route this memo as indicated.
請在下方登記員工休息區清潔職責，並按照指示傳遞這張備忘錄。

The attached outline covers projected work through the end of the year.
附件中的大綱是關於現在到年底的預期工作。

There's been some confusion about the new procedures for travel reimbursements—please note and file the following guidelines.
大家對於新的旅費報帳程序仍有一些疑惑，請注意以下準則並存檔。

This memo will serve to authorize the preparation and filing of a patent application in the United States Patent and Trademark Office for a Quick-Drying Colorless Gesso Substitute.
關於快乾無色石膏替代品之專利申請，謹以此備忘錄核准向美國專利及商標局申請專利之準備及申請作業。

We are pleased to announce that last week's sales figures as reported by the branch offices (see below) constitute a record for us.
我們很高興宣布，上週各分公司回報之銷售額（見下文）達成我們的新紀錄。

We suggest you keep these fire drill instructions posted near your desk.
我們建議你將這些消防演習指示貼在你的辦公桌附近。

段落

The attached outline covers projected work through the end of the year. The outline was generated in consultation with department heads. We will review progress on the first of each month and adjust the work and timelines accordingly. We are highly interdependent in this company and we need the interlocking pieces to fit comfortably. Please review the scheduled work and let me know your opinion, particularly of the feasibility of project goals and deadlines.

附件中的大綱是關於現在到年底的預期工作。此大綱是根據諮詢各部門主管的結果所制定。我們會在每月第一日檢視進度，並對工作與時程做出相應之調整。在這個公司，我們都非常依賴彼此，我們必須緊密聯繫才能相互自在配合。請查看時程表中的工作，並讓我知道你的想法，並請特別針對此計畫目標與時程的可行性發表看法。

As of January 1, all customer 612 area code numbers given on the attached sheet will be changed to 651. Please correct your files. Note that 612 area codes not on this list remain 612. Also attached is a list of the three-number prefixes that take 612 and those that take 651 so that you can verify the correct area code for any new numbers.

自一月一日起，所有在附件表單上列出的顧客 612 區域代碼都會改成 651。請修正你的文件。請注意，沒有列於這張表單上的 612 區域代碼仍然維持 612。另外一份附件條列使用 612 三碼代碼者以及使用 651 代碼者，如此你便能確認任何新號碼的正確區域代碼。

Devizes Inc. will be selling company cars that are more than two years old. Employees will be given priority. Please see the attached list of vehicles with descriptions and prices.

狄維齊公司將出售兩年以上之公司用車。員工將有購買之優先權。請見附件車輛清單以及相關敘述與價格。

The Pudney Summer Soccer Camp has approached Potter Commercial Development Corp. to ask if some of our employees would be interested in volunteering at the Soccer Camp this summer. Attached is a brochure describing the camp and an application form for volunteers. Thank you for considering their request.

帕尼足球夏令營聯繫波特商業發展公司，詢問我們是否有員工有興趣在這個夏天至足球夏令營擔任志工。附件為該夏令營之介紹手冊及志工申請表。感謝你考慮他們的邀請。

示範信

TO: All employees
FROM: Raymond Berenger, Building Services
DATE: November 15
SUBJECT: Building maintenance
Please be reminded that the building custodian was terminated a week ago, on the day of the merger announcement. I ask that all employees cooperate by keeping your areas clean. Thanks.

收件人：全體員工
寄件人：雷蒙‧貝倫格，大樓服務
日期：十一月十五日
主旨：大樓環境維持
請記得，大樓管理員已於一週前宣布合併的當天解雇，我希望全體員工皆能配合維持環境清潔，謝謝。

....

TO: Delina Delaney Deli counter clerks
From: M. De Maine, Manager
Date: June 15
Re: Soliciting from the homeless/vendor safety

The presence of homeless people in this area of Manhattan is a fact. Occasionally, as you know, a homeless individual will venture into our shop and ask for handouts of food. Sometimes he or she will simply take a loaf of bread or a muffin without asking.

Now that summer is here we see more of this activity and all staff must adhere to our policy: Never say no to a homeless person's request for food. Some of these visitors are mentally unstable, some may carry weapons. Give them the food they want and politely escort them to the door. The cost of the food involved is not worth the risk to your safety.

There is always the possibility that we will thus get a reputation on the avenue for having free food. If interference with regular business escalates, we will reevaluate our policy.

收件人：蒂琳娜‧蒂蘭妮熟食店收銀員
寄件人：M‧狄曼，經理
日期：六月十五日
主旨：奉勸注意街友／攤位安全
　　曼哈頓的這個區域確實有許多街友。如你們所知，有時會有街友闖入我們店鋪請求給予食物，也有時他或她會未經詢問直接拿走一條麵包或一個鬆餅。
　　現在，由於夏季來臨，我們見到更多這樣的事件，而所有工作人員都必須遵照我們的政策行事：絕不拒絕街友對於食物的請求。有些街友精神狀態不穩定，有些則可能攜帶武器。請給他們

想要的食物，並有禮貌地送他們至門口。食物的費用並不值得拿你們的安全冒險。

我們當然有可能因此得到免費給予食物的名聲。倘若這類干擾例常業務的事件增加，我們會重新評估此政策。

TO: All employees
FROM: Staffing
DATE: February 5
SUBJECT: Half-time employees
Following is the full list of half-time employees (continuing with, however, full benefits) during the merger transition with Half Moon Press for a period of half a year effective February 8. HALF a good day!

Anne Frith, editorial
Eden Herring, editorial
Maria Lousada, production
Luke Marks, production
Hope Ollerton, order fulfillment

收件人：全體員工
寄件人：人事
日期：二月五日
主旨：兼職員工
在與半月媒體合併之半年過渡時期，兼職員工的完整名單如下（但繼續擁有全職員工之福利），自二月八日生效。祝你有美好的「半」天！

安・費里茲，編輯
艾登・海林，編輯
瑪麗亞・羅莎達，製作
路克・馬克斯，製作
霍普・歐勒頓，訂單履行

TO: Olive Chancellor
FROM: Varena Tarrant
SUBJECT: Patent authorization for: "Three-Dimensional Blueprint Acrylic Viewer"
DATE: June 16, 2017
This memo will serve to authorize the preparation and filing of a patent application in the United States Patent and Trademark Office.
The invention provides a method for viewing blueprints that allows ready discrimination of varied elevations.
The inventors and I will provide additional information and any experimentation necessary to file the application. We suggest that this application be filed by outside attorney.

Basil Ransome (Ransome & Birdseye) who is familiar with the inventors and technology.

Varena Tarrant

Senior Patent Liaison Specialist

收件人：奧利佛・錢斯勒
寄件人：瓦雷娜・塔朗特
主旨：授權專利申請：「三維藍圖壓克力看版」
日期：二○一七年六月十六日

謹以此備忘錄核可向美國專利及商標局申請專利之準備及申請作業。

這項發明提供一種觀看藍圖的方法，可輕易辨別各種立面圖。

發明者與我將提供申請專利所需之額外資訊並配合任何實驗測試。我們建議此申請交由外部律師巴齊爾・蘭桑（蘭桑與博瑟事務所）處理，他很熟悉發明與科技相關業務。

瓦雷娜・塔朗特
資深專利事務聯絡專員

TO: Dick Phenyl

FROM: A. W. Pinero

DATE: March 3, 2018

SUBJECT: Internet training session on March 10

So far the following people have signed up for the class. Will you please arrange with their supervisors for their absence that day? It also looks as though we're going to need a larger room and a few more computers. Can you arrange it? Thanks.

收件人：迪克・芬尼爾
寄件人：A・W・皮內洛
日期：二○一八年三月三日
主旨：三月十日的網路訓練課程

目前有以下幾個人報名了這堂課。他們那天無法工作，能不能麻煩你協助向他們的主管協調？此外，我們也需要一間大一點的教室，以及多幾臺電腦，你可以幫忙安排嗎？謝謝。

✉ 參見：01 電子郵件、03 回應、14 收件通知、15 公告通知、16 指示說明信、20 請求與詢問、34 報告與提案

Chapter 33

商譽信
Goodwill Letters

只謀求今天的收益是不夠的，
因為你的競爭者已經在爭取明天的商譽了。

——系統公司（The System Company），
《How to Write Letters That Win》

商譽信是一種銷售信，不過賣的不是商品或服務，而是公司的價值、名聲、友善、誠信與競爭力。你希望讀者對你的公司有良好觀感，並期盼他們未來購買商品或服務時會想到你。

推銷多半強調商品價格、顏色、尺寸或服務特色等顧客能直接感受的東西，但有時，我們也能訴諸感受與態度，商譽信針對的，便是會影響顧客做決定的非物質因素。

 PART 1 說明篇

商譽信有哪些種類？

恭賀	**布達事項** 價格、人事、政策異動 參見：15 公告通知	**表揚** 優良付款記錄、業績
產品服務問卷	**節慶問候** 參見：08 佳節問候信	**特殊活動或優惠** 樣品、禮券、招待會
紀念日或人生大事 入職紀念日、婚禮	**致謝** 參見：12 致謝函	**歡迎歸隊或蒞臨** 參見：10 歡迎信

該怎麼說？

1. 以一句友善或讚美的話開場。
2. 寫出此信的主要目的（恭賀、致謝、保持聯絡、佳節愉快、「只是看看你過得如何」），並展現你對顧客或員工的重視。
3. 以主要目的為基礎拓展內容，如 I'm particularly grateful because...「我想特別感謝您，因為……」；You've been a delight to work with because...「與您共事很愉快，因為……」；I hope the New Year is a happy and healthy one for you and your family.「我希望對您與您的家人來說，新的一年會是開心又健康的。」
4. 聚焦在對方身上，因為這是一封關於對方的信函。
5. 結尾時，用愉快口氣祝福對方成功，並提及未來會再次聯絡或繼續維持聯繫。

什麼不該說？

- 別在商譽信中進行強烈推銷。只需稍微帶過你的產品或服務，或完全不要提。
- 不要在信中尋求業務合作、請求協助、要求更多工作成果，或納入商業新聞或評論，這會稀釋商譽信的影響力。這些主題先留起來，等下次寫別種信時再列入。
- 不要太過熱情奔放。使用自然隨性的語氣，展現真誠與友善。

寫作訣竅

- 在公司內部寄發商譽信。儘管你沒有義務要恭喜員工的入職紀念日，但這麼做能提昇員工士氣，加強忠誠度。若要代表公司主管、高級職員或董事會寄商譽信給員工，節日會是完美的時機。
- 利用平時寄發公告或通知（寄出新帳單、通知新地址或會議通知）的機會寫商譽信（感謝顧客消費，或感謝員工一年來的辛勞）。
- 年末的節慶假期是寄發商譽信的絕佳時機，但要提早郵寄，才不會與其他十二月的信混雜在一起，顧客也才不會在其他地方花光買禮物的預算。

特殊狀況

- **顧客產品服務問卷**也能作為一種商譽信。多數人喜歡被徵詢意見,也喜歡因提供協助而被感謝。為了確保顧客會覺得愉快而沒有負擔,問卷務必簡短、容易填寫,並容易寄回(如附上回郵信封)。
- **商譽禮物**,如樣品、試用包、搶先體驗包等顧客不必消費也能得到的禮物,通常會伴隨一張封面信。你不必在信中用力推銷,因為免費的產品本身就已經是種推銷。不過,你必須在幾週後追蹤這封信的成效,屆時便可以加強推銷的力道。(參見:17 後續追蹤信、28 求職信、42 銷售信)

格式

- 所有的商譽信都是打在有信頭的信紙上,除非是給員工與同事的祝賀短箋,這種可以打在備忘錄用紙上,手寫也是可以的。
- 寄發佳節問候或其他內容較廣泛的信件給員工或顧客時,通常會使用仔細撰寫過的制式信,這是大眾可接受的做法。

33

商譽信

單字

appreciate *(v.)* 感謝、欣賞	kindness *(n.)* 好意	sensational *(a.)* 轟動的	unique *(a.)* 獨特的
delighted *(a.)* 開心的	memorable *(a.)* 難忘的	special *(a.)* 特別的	valuable *(a.)* 珍貴的
enjoy *(v.)* 享受、喜歡	pleased *(a.)* 愉悅的	superb *(a.)* 極好的	
grateful *(a.)* 感謝的	remarkable *(a.)* 卓越的	terrific *(a.)* 了不起的	
inspired *(a.)* 受到激發的	satisfying *(a.)* 令人滿意的	thoughtful *(a.)* 考慮周到的	

詞組

happy/pleased to hear 很高興聽說	look forward to your next 期待你下一個
how are you getting along with 你在……的進展如何	pleased to be able to 很高興能夠
just thinking about you 剛好想到了你	show our gratitude for 為……表達我們的感謝
just to let you know 只是想讓你知道	wanted you to know 想要你知道
keep us in mind 把我們放在心上	wishing you all the best 為你獻上最深的祝福
let us know if 讓我們知道是否	like to keep in touch with 喜歡與……保持聯繫

33

商譽信

would be glad to have you stop in again when
當……時，希望您能再次造訪

句子

All of us here at Larolle International send you warmest holiday greetings and our best wishes for a happy, healthy new year!
萊羅樂國際公司全體在此致上我們最溫暖的佳節問候，祝福您新的一年快樂、健康！

As one of our longtime customers, you may be interested in our new, faster ordering procedures.
您作為我們的長期顧客，或許會想了解我們更新、更快的訂購程序。

Because we appreciate the responsible handling of your account, we are raising your credit limit to $15,000.
我們很感謝您對帳款的用心管理，所以我們在此將您的信用額度提升至 15,000 元。

Congratulations on your ten years with us—you're a key player on our (thanks to you!) successful team.
你在我們的團隊已經第十年了，恭喜！在這個成功的團隊裡（多虧了你！），你是我們的核心隊員。

Enclosed is an article on retirement savings that we thought you'd like to see.
附件是關於退休儲蓄的文章，我們認為您應該會想看看。

I heard something pretty special is going on over there!
我聽說那裡有很特別的事情正在發生！

Sawbridge Training Services Inc. now has a special customer hotline—at no charge to the calling party—for all your questions and concerns.
見橋訓練服務公司現在推出特別顧客專線（撥打方免付費），解答您所有的問題與擔憂。

The Pig and Whistle invites you to a customer appreciation sale, but bring this card with you as the sale is "invitation only."
豬與哨邀請您前來感謝顧客特賣會，但由於此特賣會僅限邀請者參加，故請務必攜帶此卡。

段落

You used to order regularly from us, but we haven't heard from you for some time now. To help you remember how easy it was to order and how much you enjoyed our high-quality camping merchandise, we're enclosing a "welcome back" certificate good for 15 percent off your next order. We hope you use it—we've missed you!

過去您時常向我們訂購商品，但目前我們已經有一陣子未聽見您的消息。為了提醒您訂購有多麼容易，以及您以前有多麼喜歡我們的露營商品，我們在此附上一張「歡迎回來」的八五折優惠券，可用於下次訂購。希望您會使用。我們想您了！

I noticed the handsome photograph of you and your husband in Sunday's paper—congratulations on twenty-five years of marriage! Do stop by the office the next time you're in the store so I can congratulate you personally.

我注意到週日報紙上有一張好看的照片，上面是你與你的丈夫。恭喜你們結婚二十五週年！下次當你來到店裡，請進來坐坐，讓我親自恭賀你。

Thank you so much for referring Stanley Purves to us. It is because of generous and appreciative customers like you that Dorset Homes has been growing by leaps and bounds. We will give Mr. Purves our best service—and we are always ready to help you in any way we can. Thanks again for passing on the word!

非常感謝您將史丹利‧普夫斯介紹給我們。多虧有您這樣慷慨又有眼光的顧客，多賽家居公司才能飛躍成長。我們會提供普夫斯先生最好的服務，也隨時準備好盡我們所能協助您。再次感謝您幫忙傳話！

You are cordially invited to an Open House on January 29 from 5 to 8 p.m. to celebrate our fiftieth anniversary. We are taking this opportunity to show our appreciation to our many fine customers. Do come—we will have a small gift waiting for you!

誠心邀請您參加一月二十九日下午五至八時的招待會，與我們一同歡慶五十週年紀念日。我們希望藉此機會，向許多優良顧客表達感謝。請務必前來，有小禮物等著您！

33
商譽信

Dear Chung Hi,

We thank you—as always—for choosing Levi-Ponsonby Office Products for all your business office needs. You regularly receive our big catalog, the one that puts 20,000 office products at your fingertips.

We're proud of being able to supply every office product made. But we began to wonder if we weren't offering almost too many products!

Today I'm sending you a smaller catalog containing only our bestselling items. A select group of customers is receiving this special catalog. If it seems to be helpful to our customers, we may begin publishing smaller catalogs every few months while reserving the big catalog for once a year.

I hope you enjoy seeing what other businesses consider the most essential office products.

Sincerely,
Peter Levi
Levi-Ponsonby Office Products

鍾熙您好：

感謝您一如往常選擇了賴維龐森比辦公用品公司，滿足您所有商務辦公需求。您定期會收到我們的大本型錄，兩萬種辦公用品就近在手邊。

我們一直很自豪能提供每種辦公用品；不過，我們開始擔心我們是否產品種類過多！

今天，我在此寄給您較小本的型錄，僅包含我們的暢銷商品。只有一部分精心挑選出的顧客會收到這本特製型錄。若這種做法能幫助我們的顧客，我們會每幾個月就印刷一次小本型錄，大本型錄則是一年出刊一次。

在這本型錄中，您會看到各公司行號公認最重要的辦公用品，我希望您會喜歡。

彼得・賴維敬上
賴維龐森比辦公用品公司

Dear Mr. Purdie,

We are pleased to have you enrolled at Okinawan Karate ("The Ultimate in Self-Protection and Self-Perfection") for the fall season. Welcome back!

For your convenience, we're enclosing a bookmark with our hours and telephone numbers. You might note on the back our standing invitation to take any other class on a trial basis, free of charge!

Stop in at the office any time and say hello!

普狄先生您好：

很高興您報名沖繩空手道（「終極自我防衛與自我完善」）秋季班課程。歡迎回來！

為了您的便利，我們在此附上一張書籤，上有我們的營業時間與電話號碼。如您在書籤背面可見，我們邀請您試用任何其他課程，沒有期限、不必付費！

隨時歡迎您過來說聲哈囉！

Dear Jules,

I see that the bank is celebrating an important birthday—congratulations! You must be proud to see what a success Mignaud et Fils has become one hundred years after its founding by your great-grandfather.

All of us here at Philips Deluxe Checks wish you continued success and prosperity.

Sincerely,

親愛的朱爾：

我知道銀行正在慶祝一個很重要的生日，恭喜！在你曾祖父創建銀行的一百年後，米諾與菲爾變得如此成功，想必你一定深感驕傲。

飛利浦高級支票的全體人員，祝福你繼續成功、昌盛。

〇〇敬上

Dear Mr. and Mrs. Charles:

It has been three months since your new floor tiles were installed. I hope you've been enjoying them. We have customers who still rave about floor tile they bought from us thirty years ago.

If we can be of service to you in the future, keep us in mind. We're planning a store-wide three-day sale on all floor coverings in late January in case you're interested in doing any other rooms.

Thanks again for choosing a fine floor product from Geiger Tiles.

Yours truly,

查爾斯賢伉儷您們好：

從貴府安裝新的地板磁磚以來已經三個月了，希望您們都很滿意。我們有客戶至今仍極力讚揚三十年前向我們購買的地磚。

未來若有我們可服務的地方，請務必聯絡我們。如果您們想要安裝其他房間的地板，我們正在規劃為期三日的全店特賣會，會於一月底舉行，屆時所有的地板材料都會有折扣。

再次感謝您選擇蓋格磁磚的優良地板產品。

〇〇敬上

✉ 參見：07 恭賀信、08 佳節問候信、10 歡迎信、11 表揚信、12 致謝函、43 紀念日、44 早日康復信、
　　45 慰問信、48 給鄰居的信

Chapter 34

報告與提案
Reports and Proposals

哈潑兄弟出版公司（Harper & Brothers）
或許說過我拒絕了他們的提案，
但若有後續我也歡迎他們來找我。

——抒情詩人埃德娜・聖文森特・米萊（Edna St. Vincent Millay）

標準的提案與報告並不是以信件形式呈現，但當提案內容較短，便可以寫成信件或備忘錄寄送。此時用字會比較簡白，也沒有標題、小標題與條款，比較不正式，也較不複雜。

提案可以是經要求而寫（對方請求估價、投標或為某個行動做計畫），或是出於自發而寫（主動推銷計畫、服務或方案）。無論是哪種情況，提案都是一種推銷工具，讓對方確信你們公司就是做此項業務的最佳選擇，或讓對方相信確實需要你提議的服務。

 ## PART 1 說明篇

報告與提案信包括哪些？

各式提案	出版提案	各式報告	信用報告
產品提案、銷售提案	參見：31 投稿信	進度報告、銷售報告	參見：41 信貸相關信
			回應提案或報告
投標與估價	推薦或建議	確認收到提案或報告	參見：21 接受、22 拒絕

該怎麼說？

1. 開頭先以一句話點出主題。
2. 指出寄這份報告或提案的原因，如 as requested「按照要求」；for your information「供您參考」；Charles O'Malley asked me to send you a copy.「查爾斯‧歐馬利請我寄給您一份。」；in response to your request for a quotation「為回應您的估價請求」。
3. 以一至兩句話描述報告內容。
4. 報告或提案的正文必須明確清晰、按照邏輯組織。詳細解釋想法、提供預估花費、規格、期限，與應用示範。
5. 以一至兩句話總結報告內容。
6. 列出為此報告或提案付出努力的參與者。
7. 表達可以進一步給予資訊，或提供聯絡人的姓名及聯絡方式。
8. 告訴對方應採取的下一步，或你的期望，如 call me「打電話給我」；sign the enclosed contract「在附件的合約上簽名」；Please respond with a written evaluation of the proposal.「請以書面回覆對此提案的評估結果。」
9. 感謝對方付出時間閱讀提案或報告。

什麼不該說？

- 不要納入其他主題或業務。報告與提案內容須明確專一。
- 不要使用術語，除非你很確定收件人也熟悉這些用語。

寫作訣竅

- 在寫報告或提案前，先確認你能回答以下問題：誰會讀這份文件？目的是什麼？它包含哪些資料？這些資料應如何呈現？
- 提案或報告信的正文，可以是一個段落，也可以一段以上，並以傳統報告的元素來分段：標題頁；總結、大綱或摘要；前言、序、導言、沿革或背景；致謝詞；目錄；說明數據、選項、結論與建議；附錄、參考文獻、文末註解、引用文獻、附加輔助文件的提醒。
- 在寄發提案或報告前，找一名了解此議題的人（有時可以找律師）讀一讀，評估內文是否清晰準確。再三檢查提案，確保對方要求的所有事項都已經包含在內。
- 如果時間是會影響報告或提案的重要因素，可以在寄送時請求回條，這樣你便能確認對方收到的日期。

特殊狀況

- **寫補助金計畫書時**，有三項原則能增加你獲選的機會：
  (1) 嚴格遵照指示，不可與規定的格式有任何偏差；
  (2) 準確無誤的呈現資料，整齊地打在高品質的紙上，一絲不苟、行距適當；
  (3) 以絕佳的文筆撰寫內文，立場要偏向資助單位。因此，同一份資料通常不會寄給兩個不同的團體。有時你的資料也會被同領域的人評估。
- **進度報告**通常各公司有各自格式規定，不過也可以用信件敘述。內容須包含：在報告期間完成哪些業務；目前正在做什麼；有哪項出色的專案正等著公司關注；報告期間的好消息與壞消息；其他需要讓公司、部門或上司知道的其他事情。
- 如果對方已表態會接受提案，你可以在提案信的結尾加上一句 Read and approved on [date] by [signature and title].「〔簽名與職稱〕於〔日期〕已詳讀並同意。」使提案信具有法律約束力。如果此提案隸屬於一份範圍更大的合約，請加上 pursuant to the Master Contract dated March 2, 2017, between Raikes Engineering and Phillips Contractors「根據雷克斯工程與菲利浦承包公司於二〇一七年三月二日訂立的主合約。」（參見：40 具合約效力信）

格式

- 報告與提案信會打在有信頭的信紙或備忘錄用紙上。
- 如果時間上較為緊急，可用電子郵件或傳真寄發，但同時也要將紙本郵寄過去。
- 制式表單很適合用在信用報告、進度報告、例行生產報告以及其他多為數字或敘述較短的報告。

單字

abstract *(n.)* 摘要	**display** *(v.)* 顯示	**judge** *(v.)* 判斷	**recommendation** *(n.)* 推薦、建議
advise *(v.)* 建議	**draft** *(n.)* 草稿	**layout** *(n.)* 版面編排	**representation** *(n.)* 代表
agenda *(n.)* 議程	**establish** *(v.)* 建立	**method** *(n.)* 方法	**research** *(n.) & (v.)* 研究
analysis *(n.)* 分析	**estimate** *(v.) & (n.)* 估計；估價	**monograph** *(n.)* 專題論文	**result** *(n.)* 結果
application *(n.)* 應用	**evaluate** *(v.)* 評估	**notification** *(n.)* 通知	**review** *(v.) & (n.)* 審查；評估報告
appraise *(v.)* 評價	**exhibit** *(v.)* 展示	**offer** *(v.) & (n.)* 提議；報價	**statement** *(n.)* 聲明、結算單
approach *(n.)* 方法	**explanation** *(n.)* 解釋	**opinion** *(n.)* 意見	**strategy** *(n.)* 策略
assess *(v.)* 評估	**exploration** *(n.)* 探索	**outcome** *(n.)* 結果	**study** *(n.) & (v.)* 研究
calculate *(v.)* 計算	**exposition** *(n.)* 說明	**outline** *(n.) & (v.)* 大綱；概述	**subject** *(n.)* 主題
compute *(v.)* 計算	**finding** *(n.)* 調查結果	**performance** *(n.)* 表現	**suggest** *(v.)* 建議
conclude *(v.)* 得到結論	**forecast** *(v.)* 預測	**policy** *(n.)* 政策	**summary** *(n.)* 總結
condition *(n.)* 條件	**gauge** *(v.)* 估計、判斷	**preface** *(n.)* 序言	**system** *(n.)* 系統
consider *(v.)* 考慮	**guesstimate** *(v.)* 猜測	**preliminary** *(a.)* 初步的	**technical** *(a.)* 技術的

34

報告與提案

critique	inquiry	presentation	terms
(v.) 批判	*(n.)* 詢問、調查	*(n.)* 簡報	*(n.)* 條款
decision	inspect	procedure	text
(n.) 決定	*(v.)* 視察	*(n.)* 程序	*(n.)* 本文
design	instruction	program	undertaking
(v.) & (n.) 設計	*(n.)* 指示	*(n.)* 計畫	*(n.)* 任務、承諾
diagram	introduce	project	venture
(n.) 圖表	*(v.)* 介紹	*(n.)* 專案	*(v.)* 大膽行事
disclose	investigation	projection	
(v.) 揭露	*(n.)* 調查	*(n.)* 規劃	
discussion	issue	prospectus	
(n.) 討論	*(n.) & (v.)* 議題；發行	*(n.)* 簡章	

💬 詞組

a considerable/significant/important advantage
大量／顯著／重要的優點

address the problem of
針對……的問題

supplies/offers/provides some distinct advantages
提供一些明確的優勢

as you can see from the data
一如你在數據上所見

ballpark figure
大概的數字

close/exhaustive inquiry
密切／徹底的調查

rough computation/calculation/draft/guess
粗略的計算／估算／草稿／猜測

map out
詳細籌劃

matter at hand/in dispute/under discussion/at issue
當前／爭執中／討論中／待裁決的事情

planning stages
計劃階段

plan of action
行動計畫

position paper
意見書

copy of the proceedings 會議紀錄副本	make inquiry/known/public 詢價／揭曉／公開
detailed statement 詳盡的結算單	subject of inquiry 調查主題
educated guess 有根據的猜測	summarizes the progress of 概述……的進度
estimated value 估計的價值	along these lines 與之類似的
give our position on 表達我們對於……的立場	take into consideration 納入考量
gives me to understand 讓我能理解	take measures/steps 採取措施／步驟
in-depth account of/look at 詳盡記述／檢查	under consideration/discussion 考慮中／討論中
institute inquiries 展開調查	

句子

Data on in-line skating injuries in the United States during the past two years are charted below.
美國於過去兩年間的直排輪受傷數據，如下圖所示。

East Side Neighborhood Service Inc. has developed a proposal to make our streets safer and cleaner.
東側鄰里服務公司發展出一個提案，能使我們的街道更安全、更乾淨。

I propose that we set up a subcommittee to study flex hours for all salaried employees.
我提議組成一個小組委員會，研究如何讓所有支薪員工獲得彈性工時。

Our annual report on homelessness in the six-county metro area reveals both good news and bad news.
我們針對六郡都會區街友的情況做了年度報告，其中包含好消息與壞消息。

Re: Acquisition of the Cypress Spa Products Corp.
關於：收購柏木溫泉產品公司

Sperrit-Midmore Landscape Supply Center has had one of its most successful quarters ever—see below for details.
史畢禮－米德莫景觀供應中心剛度過數一數二成功的一季，詳情請見下文。

Subject: Proposed staffing changes in conference catering.
主旨：研討會飲食服務人員變更提議

The following report was prepared by Robert Famish and Narcissa Topehall.
以下報告由羅柏‧菲明許與娜西卡‧托普霍準備。

34

報告與提案

段落

Your book proposal has been read with great interest. We will want to have several other people read and evaluate it before submitting it for discussion at our weekly acquisition meeting. I will let you know as soon as we have made a decision.

我們對您的書籍提案很有興趣,在上交至每週採購會議前,想讓其他幾個人也看過並評估。當我們做出決定,我會盡快讓您知道。

This report is a summary of your benefits and any optional coverage you have chosen as of January 1. Your benefits booklet provides further details. If you have any questions, please see your supervisor or the Benefit Information Coordinator. Although this report has been prepared for you as accurately as possible, the Company reserves the right to correct any errors.

這份報告總結了你自一月一日起的福利津貼與你選擇的加保項目。你的福利手冊有更詳盡的內容。若你有任何問題,請與你的主管討論,或聯絡福利資訊負責人。儘管我們在準備這份報告時力求準確,但公司仍保留修正錯誤的權利。

Since our letter of September 3, in which we compared electroplating and sputtering for production of thin alloy films for recording, we have done some additional research on this subject. We have found that as long as the proper microstructure is achieved, both electroplating and sputtering are effective. It appears too early to exclude either of the processes. It may be helpful, however, to do a rough cost analysis either as more data from research in these two areas become available or by making a number of assumptions.

在九月三日寄出的信件中,我們比較了能製造錄製用合金鍍膜的電鍍法與濺鍍法;而後,我們針對此主題又做了一些額外的研究。我們發現,只要達成適當的微結構,電鍍與濺鍍皆有效果,所以目前排除任何一種工法都言之過早。不過,做一個粗略的成本分析或許會有幫助,一方面這兩種工法的研究數據現在皆可供使用,而另一方面也可以做一些假設來進行估算。

Dear Etta,

    Re: Proposed Budget for Design of Streets DRS—821.01

    We have estimated the design cost to produce final plans for the relocation of Concannon Street from the bypass to the railroad tracks, and for Concannon Bypass from Blake Avenue to Nicholas. The design of Concannon Street is for a length of approximately 2,000 feet and consists of five traffic lanes, curb and gutter, and a raised median over 25 percent of its length. The Concannon Bypass design covers approximately 2,500 feet and includes curb and gutter along the outside lanes and median, pavement widening, intersection improvements, acceleration and deceleration lanes, and signals at three locations. The cost works out to $255,000, and we therefore propose that a budget for this amount be approved.

    Please call me if you have any questions concerning our estimate. Thanks.

                         Sincerely,

親愛的艾塔：

    關於：街道設計預算提議 DRS—821.01

    為將康坎能街從外環道路改到火車鐵路，並將康坎能外環道路從布雷克大道改至尼可拉斯大道，我們已經估算了設計費用，以供最終版計畫書的撰寫。康坎能街的設計長度大約 2,000 呎，包含五條車道、路緣與排水溝，以及長度超過街道總長百分之二十五的中央分隔島。康坎能外環道路的設計則大約為 2,500 呎，包含沿著外車道的路緣與排水溝，以及中央分隔島、路面加寬、道路交叉口改良、加速車道與減速車道、在三處添加號誌。所需成本為 255,000 元，因此提議通過此金額的預算。

    若你對我們的估算有任何問題，請打電話讓我知道。謝謝。

                         ○○敬上

34

報告與提案

Proposal

Marryat Insulation Systems Inc.

54 Easthupp Boulevard Frederick, IA 50501

Proposed work:

• Install fiber glass under boards in 900 sq. ft. attic area of two-story house.

• Remove and replace necessary boards.

• Install wind tunnels.

• Install 2 R-61 roof vents.

• Install fiberglass in sidewalls, approx. 2,000 sq. ft.

• Drill siding and redwood plug, chisel and putty, owner to sand and paint.

• Remove and replace siding, drill above second floor windows only.

• Install 4 8" x 16" soffit vents, 2 front, 2 rear.

We propose hereby to furnish material and labor—complete in accordance with above specifications—for the sum of cash on completion, $5,307.

All material is guaranteed to be as specified. All work to be completed according to standard practices. Any alteration or deviation from the above specifications involving extra costs will be executed only upon written orders, and will become an extra charge over and above the estimate. All agreements are contingent upon strikes, accidents, or delays beyond our control. Owner to carry fire, tornado, and other necessary insurance. Our work is fully covered by Worker's Compensation Insurance.

Note: This proposal may be withdrawn by us if not accepted within 10 days.

Date: May 3, 2018

Authorized signature: F. Marryat

Acceptance of proposal: The above prices, specifications, and conditions are satisfactory and are hereby accepted. You are authorized to do the work as specified. Payment will be made upon completion.

Date of acceptance: May 6, 2018

Signature: Jack Easy

施工提案

馬力亞隔熱系統公司

50501 愛荷華州費德里克郡東霍普大道 54 號

工程提議：

- 在兩層樓房的閣樓區域（900 平方呎）木板下安裝玻璃纖維。
- 有必要的話，移除、置換木板。
- 安裝風洞
- 安裝兩個 R-61 屋頂通風口
- 在邊牆安裝玻璃纖維，約 2,000 呎長。
- 在邊牆鑽孔、放入紅木塞、鑿刻、塗油灰，由屋主打磨與油漆。
- 移除、置換邊牆，只在二樓窗戶上方鑽孔。
- 安裝四個 8×16 吋下楣通風口，兩個在前、兩個在後。

我們在此提議由我們提供材料與人力，並根據上述規格完成工程，完成後須支付之現金總價為 5,307 元。

所有材料皆保證與上述完全相同。所有的工程皆按照標準程序完成。所有變更或偏離上述規格之處，若涉及額外費用，則僅在有書面訂單的情況下才得以實施，且額外費用不包含在上述估價金額中。所有的協議可能因不可抗力之罷工、意外或延誤而異。屋主須握有火災、風災及其他必要保險。我們的工程具勞工災害補償保險的全額保障。

注意：若未能於十日內接受，此提案可由我們撤回。

日期：二〇一八年五月三日

授權簽名：F・馬力亞

接受提案：上述金額、規格與條件符合要求，故在此接受提案。你已獲授權，可按照上述規格進行工程。報酬將於工程完成時支付。

接受日期：二〇一八年五月六日

簽名：傑克・伊齊

✉ 參見：03 回應、14 收件通知、16 指示說明信、21 接受、22 拒絕、28 求職信、30 推薦信、32 備忘錄、41 信貸相關信、42 銷售信

Chapter 35

客訴處理信
Letters of Adjustment

對任何公司來說，能快速且完善處理客訴的美名，
絕對是強而有力的公關工具。

——商業書作者蘇・保芙、瑪莉德・富萊爾、大衛・湯瑪斯
（L. Sue Baugh, Maridell Fryar, David Thomas）

收到客戶的抱怨信（letter of complaint，亦稱 claim letter「投訴信」）時，可以寫封客訴處理
信作為回應。帳單錯誤、商品缺損、帳款拖欠等的業務缺失並不少見，因此處理客訴信是例行
公事的一部分。美國作家梅格兄妹曾說：「保住舊客戶，就跟獲得新客戶一樣重要。」

客訴處理信的功能有三：

(1) 改正錯誤，並為公司不足之處給予補償；

(2) 合理提供全面或部分補償，以維持關係；

(3) 技巧性拒絕不合理的要求，重獲顧客的信任。

在經典的《Handbook of Business Letters》（暫譯：商業書信手冊）一書中，作者弗雷利（L.
E. Frailey）建議，用看待訂單的敬意來看待客訴信件，讓客戶知道你渴望服務他們，一如你
渴望把商品賣給他們。

美國實業家莉莉安・維儂（Lillian Vernon）曾說：「每個不滿意的顧客都會把糟糕的經歷告訴
十個人，但開心的客戶也許只會告訴三個人。」

比起抱怨的顧客，更可怕的是不抱怨卻跑去別家消費的顧客。客訴信提供重新贏得顧客心意的
機會。當顧客回心轉意，你就會知道，你寫了一封成功的客訴處理信。

若想提出客訴，請參考：25 抱怨與客訴。

✉ PART 1 說明篇

客訴信的使用時機

帳單、發貨單有誤	解釋疏忽或錯誤	修理缺損
退還款項	修正新聞報導	延長時間
商品缺損 退款、給予折扣、換貨	拒絕受理 參見：22 拒絕	

該怎麼說？

1. 用誠摯的直述句起頭，感謝對方讓你注意到這件事：Thank you for your letter of June 3.「謝謝您於六月三日的來信。」或帶著感情告訴對方 We were sorry to hear that...「我們很抱歉……」。

2. 說明失誤之處，並註明日期、金額，與發貨單號碼。

3. 如果客戶所說屬實，請誠實以對。

4. 對客戶造成造成的疑惑、混亂或失誤表達遺憾。

5. 如果許可，說明公司客訴處理政策。

6. 說明解決問題的方式，或已經採取的行動。也可以提供選項，如換貨、退款或將款項歸還至帳戶等，供顧客選擇。

7. 說明問題大約多久能得到解決，即便只說 immediately（立刻）、at once（馬上）或 as soon as possible（盡快）也好。

8. 再次向客戶保證，該失誤極少出現，未來不會再次發生，公司會盡全力滿足客戶的需求。

9. 最後，感謝客戶的耐心，請求對方繼續造訪，提出進一步合作的機會，並再次申明公司的善意以及商品的價值，或傳達你期待客戶繼續支持公司的服務與商品。

35

客訴處理信

- 別用 claim（投訴）、complaint（抱怨）。這些字眼有指控批判的意味，多數客戶都認為自己的投訴應當得到處理。改用 report（報告）這類中性的字眼。

- 別對客戶的抱怨表現出驚訝，如「我真不敢相信這會發生。」或「過去二十年，我們從不曾遇到這個問題。」除非真的是例外中的例外。客戶認為這種失誤既然發生在他們身上，也可能發生在別人身上，當你這麼說時，便失去了信用。

- 不必重述或過度強調問題細節，快速聚焦在解決問題上，而非問題本身，因為你希望顧客趕快淡忘這個失誤。

- 避免冗長解釋。顧客不在乎你遇到了什麼困難，他們只希望問題能得到處理。如果你真的想解釋，請將篇幅限縮在幾個字之內，如 due to a delayed shipment「由於發貨延遲」或 because of power outages last week「因為上週停電」。

- 勿過度道歉。簡單的一句 We regret the error.「我們很抱歉出現失誤。」已足夠。

- 別怪罪給電腦。電腦是由人操作，這種藉口很容易惹惱對方。

- 別暗示這種問題時常發生，儘管是事實，但會讓你的公司留下草率隨便的印象。

- 別用不情願、憤怒、沒耐心或屈就的口氣來處理客訴，別在文句中暗示對方你是好心幫他大忙。處理客訴時保持親切，就事論事，即便顧客很生氣或粗魯也一樣。展現友好、善解人意的態度，才能獲得好的商譽與顧客滿意度。

- 信件結尾勿再次提及顧客投訴的問題。這麼一來，顧客只會記得問題，而不會記得你的善意與處理。

- 勿誇大公司過失，或以白紙黑字寫明公司疏失。如果問題確實是公司疏失導致，最好請教公司律師這封信該怎麼寫。

寫作訣竅

- 迅速回覆，展現善意。

- 明確描述問題、採取的行動步驟以及顧客在未來可期盼的結果。模糊不清的回應，會讓顧客期待過高，當他們得不到預期的結果，便會心生不滿。

- 如果情況允許，用主動的語氣 We sent the wrong monitor.「我們寄出了錯誤的螢幕。」取代被動句 The wrong monitor was sent to you.「錯誤的螢幕被寄送給您。」負起責任。

- 如果顧客遭受不便，請不吝展現同理心。有些公司深怕這種開放的態度會反遭顧客「利用」，而不願給予顧客應有的權益，因此造成顧客滿意度下降，得不償失。

- 有時可釋出善意，如贈送折價券或禮券，或在下次訂單給予折扣。

- 如果公司有既定的客訴處理規定，遵循公司規定即可，並公平處理所有類似的事件，不必費心思考每封信該怎麼寫。
- 《The Book of Letters》（暫譯：書信大全）作者瑪莉·歐文·克勞瑟（Mary Owens Crowther）曾說出以下歷久不衰的名言：「把法規當成藉口，在處理客訴時是行不通的。顧客的不滿也許合理也許不合理，但滿意的顧客才可能帶來生意。也因此，問題不在於證明誰對誰錯，而在於如何讓顧客滿意。這個原則雖然非盡善盡美，但倘若真的出了差錯，做得過多總比做得太少安全。」
- 對需要經常處理客訴信的人來說，以下是很棒的參考書：
《Customer Service Letters Ready to Go!》，作者：Cheryl McLean

特殊狀況

- **如果不是公司的錯**，也勿怪罪顧客，這會讓你建立的信任毀於一旦。如果公司與顧客都不是完全做錯的那一方，你可以提出折衷的方案，或給予數個選項（換貨、給予折扣等）。德國經濟學家路德維希·艾哈德（Ludwig Erhard）曾說：「所謂折衷，是一種分蛋糕的藝術，你必須讓每個人都相信自己分到最大的一塊蛋糕。」
- **拒絕顧客要求**（例如全額退費），請解釋原因，如事件的調查結果不支持此項要求（隨信附上相關文件或詳細列舉調查結果）；公司的標準程序不允許此類做法（而且在此案例中，違反程序是不可能的）；該商品已不在保固期間；或顧客使用該商品的方式是明文禁止的。你必須親切以對，同時保持堅定立場。告訴顧客你能理解他們的看法、說明你們已仔細評估來信、訴諸他們對於公平公正的要求，並以正向的說法作為信件結尾（如：感謝對方過去在商業上的合作；提供折價券；告訴對方這封信雖難寫，卻是表達你重視公平、願意負責的唯一方法）。
- **寄出產品撤回通知**（recall notice）之前，先諮詢律師。因為措詞非常重要。多數的撤回通知是以印刷函件的形式發布，其中描述了須撤回的產品以及產品的問題，並解釋顧客如何能得到補償、換貨或退款。

格式

- 若你處理的是少見的客訴問題，使用有正式公司信頭的信紙。至於常見的客訴問題，則使用半張紙大小的備忘錄用紙或印刷函件，這種信紙上有空白欄位，供你填寫細節資訊。
- 小公司也許會寄回客訴信的影本，上面附加一張手寫的紙條：We apologize for the error. Enclosed is a check for the difference.「我們很抱歉出現失誤，隨信附上彌補差額的支票。」
- 如果你是透過電子郵件或傳真收到顧客投訴，使用相同方式回覆。

💬 **單字**

accommodate *(v.)* 顧及、調整	correct *(v.)* 改正	refund *(v.)* 退款	replace *(v.)* 替換
amend *(v.)* 修改	credit *(v.) & (n.)* 歸還帳款；信用	regulate *(v.)* 制定規章	return *(v.)* 回寄
apologize *(v.)* 致歉	rebate *(v.)* 退還部分款項	reimburse *(v.)* 歸還款項	satisfaction *(n.)* 滿意度
arrange *(v.)* 安排	rectify *(v.)* 修復	remedy *(v.)* 補救	settle *(v.)* 解決
compensate *(v.)* 補償	redress *(v.)* 賠償	repair *(v.)* 修理	solution *(n.)* 解決方法

💬 **詞組**

appreciate your pointing out 謝謝您指出來……	reduce the price 降低價格
corrected invoice/statement/bill 修正的發貨單／報告書／帳單	sincerely sorry to hear that 得知……真心感到抱歉
greatly regret your dissatisfaction 對您的不愉快感到十分遺憾	prevent a recurrence 預防再次發生
I'm sorry to learn that 我很遺憾得知	sorry to learn that 很遺憾得知……
make amends for 為……彌補過失	until you are completely satisfied 直到您完全滿意
our apologies 我們致歉	will receive immediate credit 會立即收到退款

please disregard
請忽略……

you are correct in stating that
您所說的……是對的

sorry for the inconvenience/
misunderstanding
很抱歉造成不便／誤解

句子

I'm sorry about the error in filling your order—the correct posters are being shipped today.
我很抱歉在填寫訂單時出現錯誤——正確的海報在今天會出貨給您。

Thank you for bringing to our attention the missing steel pole in the tetherball set you ordered from us.
謝謝您讓我們知道您向我們訂購的梨球套組中少了鐵桿。

Thank you for giving us the opportunity to correct the erroneous information published in the last issue of *Tallboys' Direct Mail Marketer*.
謝謝您讓我們有機會修正最新一期《高個子直郵營銷商》的錯誤資訊。

Thank you for your telephone call about the defective laser labels—you will receive replacement labels within two to three business days.
謝謝您致電告知雷射標籤受到毀損；在二至三個工作天內，您便會收到替換的標籤。

We appreciate the difficulties you have had with your Deemster Steam Iron, but all our appliances carry large-print, bright-colored tags alerting consumers to the safety feature of the polarized plug (one blade is wider than the other and the plug fits into a polarized outlet only one way).
我們很遺憾您在使用大法官蒸汽熨斗時遇到困難，但我們的所有電器都貼有大型亮色警示，要求顧客留意定極插頭的安全設計（插頭的其中一腳比另一腳寬，且插頭只能以單一方向插入定極插座）。

We are pleased to offer you an additional two weeks, interest-free, to complete payment on your formal-wear rental.
我們很樂意給您額外兩週時間（免利息）來付清您租借正式服裝的費用。

We hope to continue to serve your banking needs.
我們希望能繼續在銀行業務上為您服務。

We regret the difficulties you had with your last toner cartridge.
我們很遺憾您在使用最後一個墨水匣時遭遇困難。

We're sorry you had to write; this should have been taken care of some time ago.
我們很抱歉，勞煩您寄信了；這個問題之前就應該得到處理。

We were sorry to learn that you are dissatisfied with the performance of your Salten personal paper shredder.
我們很遺憾得知您不滿意薩頓個人碎紙機的性能。

Your business and goodwill are important to us.
您的訂購及信任對我們很重要。

You're right, the self-repairing zippers on your Carradine Brent Luggage should not have seized up after only two months' use.
您說得對，您的卡拉汀‧布蘭特行李箱上的自我修復拉鍊，不應在使用短短兩個月後就卡住。

You will receive immediate credit for the faulty masonry work, and we will send someone to discuss replacing it.
由於石造工程的錯誤，您會立即收到退款，我們也會派人與您討論替換事宜。

段落

Thank you for responding to our recall notices and returning the Small World farm set to us for a refund. Small World has been making quality toys for children since 1976, and we regret the design error that made this set potentially dangerous to young children.

謝謝您回應我們的撤回通知,並將小世界農耕套組寄回給我們換取退費。自一九七六年,小世界便一直為兒童製造高品質玩具,我們很遺憾此次設計有誤,導致本套組可能對幼兒有潛在危險。

Thank you for calling to our attention the pricing error on our Bluewater automatic pool cleaners. Enclosed is a check for the difference. We look forward to serving you again.

謝謝您讓我們注意到碧水泳池自動清潔機的標價有誤。隨信附上補償差額的支票,我們期待再次為您服務。

After carefully reading your letter of August 4, I consulted our shipping department. It appears that we did comply with the terms of the contract (documents enclosed).

在詳讀您於八月四日的來信後,我已諮詢我們的運輸部門,我們確實有遵守合約中的條款(隨信附上相關文件)。

I am sorry that your order was filled incorrectly. Enclosed are the back issues that you ordered. Please keep the others with our apologies.

我很抱歉錯填您的訂單。附件為您訂購的過期雜誌。為表示我們的歉意,您可以保留其他的雜誌。

示範信

Dear Ms. Jordan,

This will confirm the arrangements made by telephone this morning. We apologize for your conference tables arriving with a center inlay color of Vanilla Illusion rather than the Blackstar Aggregate that you ordered.

The correct order will be delivered on June 7, and the other conference tables will be picked up at that time. As I understand it, only one table of the first shipment was unboxed. If you can have that one reboxed or protected enough to be returned to us, we will appreciate it.

There will, of course, be no charge and in recognition of the inconvenience to you, we are enclosing a coupon good for $100 off your next order. We have always appreciated your business and look forward to serving you again.

Sincerely,

喬丹小姐您好：

謹以此信確認今日早晨的通話內容。很抱歉寄給您錯誤的會議桌，其中央鑲嵌色為「香草幻影」，而非您訂購的「黑星群集」。

正確的商品將於六月七日寄送給您，屆時也會取走錯誤的會議桌。據我所知，在第一次貨運中，您只拆開了其中一張桌子的包裝。若您能將該會議桌重新裝箱，或協助使它在退還時有足夠的保護，我們將感激不盡。

當然，我們不會收任何費用。由於造成您的不便，我們也附上一張 100 元的禮券，供您下次使用。一直以來，我們很感謝您的訂購，並期盼能再次為您服務。

○○敬上

Dear Lucy Snowe,

Thank you for your letter requesting a correction of several statements that appeared about you and your company in the most recent issue of *Small Business Today*. The information we were given was not double-checked; we apologize.

The correction appears on page 4 of this month's issue.

Sincerely,

露西・史諾您好：

謝謝您來信要求修正最近一期《今日小企業》對您與貴公司的描述。我們要為沒有再三確認刊登資訊一事向您致歉。

修正的資料會刊登於敝雜誌本月號的第四頁。

○○敬上

Dear Mrs. Painter,

Thank you for telling us about the infestation in our Wheatley cereal. We are sorry you had this experience and want you to know we share your concern.

Consumer satisfaction is most important to us, and we sincerely regret your recent experience with our product. Our company has strict standards of quality control. We carefully examine each lot of raw materials when it arrives. Sanitarians inspect our manufacturing plant continually and, in addition, make periodic checks of our suppliers' facilities. Food samples are collected all through the manufacturing process and are analyzed in our laboratories. We enforce these stringent procedures to ensure the production of high-quality, insect-free products.

The information you gave us about our product is being brought to the attention of the appropriate company officials.

Again, thank you for writing.

Yours truly,

佩特太太您好：

謝謝您告知在我們的惠特里玉米片裡發現蟲子，我們很抱歉讓您有這樣的遭遇，並希望讓您知道我們跟您一樣關切此事。

對我們來說，顧客的滿意度是最重要的，所以我們非常遺憾我們的產品在最近帶給您的不快。我們公司在品質管理上有非常嚴格的標準。每一批原料抵達時，我們都會仔細檢驗；公共衛生官員亦持續監督我們的製造工廠，並定期檢查供應商的設備。在製造過程的各個階段，我們都會收集食物樣本，送到我們的實驗室進行分析。我們採用這些嚴格的程序，確保我們生產出高品質、無蟲害的產品。

您提供給我們的產品資訊，已交由相關公司高層處理。

再次感謝您的來信。

○○謹上

Dear Mr. Magnus,

We were unhappy to hear that you felt the installation of your fiber-optical cable was "sloppily done" and the electricians "unprofessional."

We now have the report of two inspectors, one from our company and one from an independent oversight bureau, who visited your offices on November 11 and 12. Their evaluations indicate that the installation was meticulously done, that code standards were met or exceeded, that site cleanup was faultless, and that, in fact, there was no findable cause for objection.

Interviews with your staff members who had contact with the electricians turned up no negative information about their behavior.

In the light of these reports, we are unable to offer you the requested deep discount on our services.

馬格尼斯先生您好：

聽聞您覺得您的光纖電纜「安裝草率」，且電工技師「很不專業」，我們同感到不悅。

我們已收到兩名稽查員的報告，一名來自我們公司內部，一名來自獨立監督機構，他們於十一月十一、十二日曾造訪您的辦公室。根據他們的評估，電纜安裝一絲不苟，符合安裝規範，甚至超出期待；安裝場地的清理工作亦無可挑剔；事實上，他們未發現任何可能導致異議的原因。

在與負責貴辦公室安裝工程的技師接觸過的員工訪談中，亦不曾提及任何負面行為。

有鑑於這些評估報告，我們無法按照您的要求在服務時給您額外折扣。

✉ 參見：03 回應、13 致歉信、14 收件通知、04 遲回的信、22 拒絕、25 抱怨與客訴、41 信貸相關信

Chapter 36

職場相關信
Employment

當你要求加薪時，工作彷彿一文不值；
而當你想要請假時，工作又變得極其重要。
這真是有夠奇怪。

——霍伊・萊瑟特（Howie Lasseter）

魔術師羅伯・奧本（Robert Orben）曾說：「每天早上起床，我都會查看富比世的美國富豪榜。如果沒看到我的名字，我就去工作。」我們，如同大多數人，都會像他一樣去工作。

工作時，雇主與員工之間的信件，會影響工作士氣、效率與和諧。

員工會受到各種信件的影響，例如請求加薪的信，或要求解釋退休金的信，其影響可能是直接或間接的。而雇主必須要把信寫好，才能維持良好的勞雇關係，並解決會妨礙公司目標的人事問題。

 PART 1 說明篇

哪些信與員工有關？

收件通知	建議或抱怨	公告通知	同意、核准
參見：14 收件通知	參見：23 建議、25 抱怨與客訴	參見：15 公告通知	參見：21 接受
恭賀或稱讚	**應徵工作**	**經營商譽**	**拒絕**
參見：07 恭賀信	參見：37 申請信、28 求職信、29 履歷、30 推薦信	參見：10 歡迎信、11 表揚信、12 致謝函	參見：22 拒絕

邀請	面試	會議相關	請求
參見：18 邀請函	參見：06 預約會面、 17 後續追蹤信、 29 履歷	參見：03 預約會面	參見：20 請求與詢問
建立人脈	引薦與推薦	退休	辭職或解雇
參見：09 介紹信	參見：30 推薦信	參見：07 恭賀信、 14 收件通知、 15 公告通知、18 邀請函	

該怎麼說？

- 每封信或備忘錄都要註明日期。

- **回應應徵申請時**，若你無法馬上在應徵者中做出選擇，先寄出收件通知，或感謝他們前來面試。可以的話，告知你何時會通知結果。感謝他們有意願應徵你的公司。

  拒絕對方時，先感謝對方的時間與意願，再直接告知你無法錄取對方。適合的話，也可以簡述理由。最後可以針對應徵者的資料給予讚美、邀請對方下次再來應徵（如果你確實這麼想的話），並告訴對方，你深信他能找到一個合適的職位。

  錄取某人時，在開頭恭賀、讚美對方，接著與對方確認工作內容，並提供能進一步回答問題的聯絡人姓名與電話。重述一到兩項公司的特色，增加對方來就職的機會。最後，讓錄取者知道你對他在公司的未來深具信心。

- **宣布公司政策、程序或規定上的變更時**，請包含以下內容：描述新政策；可比較舊政策並提出解釋；簡述變更理由；變更後預期產生的效益；執行變更的日期；加入進一步解釋變更的指示或附件；能回答問題或協助解決問題的聯絡人姓名與電話；表達對於變更的熱烈期盼。

- **安排公司內部會議時**：解釋會議目的、提供可能的日期與時間、感謝對方留意你的請求。若要改變會議時間，一定要提及原來的日期與時間，並請對方確認新的時間。若要取消會議，須重述日期與時間、告知你必須取消會議（簡單解釋理由）並為造成的不便致歉。要是你錯過參加會議，要馬上寫一封誠摯的道歉信。

- **寫信請求加薪時**，要保持簡要並實事求是，附上的證明資料越多越好（表揚信、銷售紀錄、專利證書、研究論文、審核結果、獎項列表）。沒有人有必須獲得加薪的「權利」，所以絕不要用這種態度寫信。不要威脅辭職，除非你真的打算這麼做。別比較你與他人的薪水，這不僅不得體，也沒有意義，反而會讓收信人心生防禦。你要做的，是讓對方知道你現在的工作對公司有更多的貢獻，或是以「調薪」為切入點，希望薪資能反映你額外付出的時間、責任或生產力。

- **寫信訓誡員工時**，先說正面或稱讚的話。接著按照事實描述員工的行為，必要時也可以告訴對方這是公司無法接受的。若合適的話，說明你如何注意到此事。建議員工做出改變的方式。告知繼續此種行為的後果。結尾時，告訴對方你相信這個情況會獲得改善。訓誡信應是簡短、尊重、激勵且正面的（不要寫「當病患在等候室時，不要打私人電話」，而要寫「請只在等候室沒有病患時撥打私人電話」）。你寫訓誡信的目標，並不是要復仇或發洩，而是要改變員工的行為。避免譴責、貶抑、喋喋不休、說教、責備或擺架子。
- **通知員工暫時停工或解雇的程序**，現在都有明文規定，因為會有法律後果，處理這種事時遵守規則是最妥當。寫信時，要很簡短，並包含下列內容：暫時停工或解雇的聲明；對必須採取這樣的措施表示遺憾；暫時停工或解雇的生效日期；關於遣散費、分紅、退休金與醫療保險的細節；若是暫時停工，提供可能的時間長度；詳述公司對暫時停工或解雇的政策、職涯諮商服務、推薦信的提供、可取得之公共援助方案，及其他能幫助員工度過暫時停工或解雇時期的資訊；能回答問題的聯絡人姓名及電話。

  若員工是因為糟糕的工作表現或行為而遭解雇，必須仔細遵守公司與法律規定。告訴對方為什麼會遭到開除，並將先前的警告留底保存。

- **辭職時**，口頭通知就已足夠。不過對雇主與員工雙方來說，一紙書面的辭職紀錄是很有幫助的。一般的做法是，先當面告知辭職的計畫，再交上辭職信。在信的開頭，首先讚美你要辭去的職務、公司或組織。接著告知辭職的生效日。在多數情況下，也會給一個辭職的理由，例如健康狀況不佳、年齡、搬家、與工作相關的健康問題、有其他更好的發展機會、另一間公司提供更高的薪水或更好的工作地點、想轉換跑道、最近發生影響職務的變化。如果你離開是因為管理問題、同事關係、公司政策限制或其他負面原因，要模糊帶過，如 For personal reasons, I am resigning effective March 1.「由於私人原因，我會於三月一日辭職。」別用你的信來發洩情緒，離開時也要有禮貌、有尊嚴，儘管你還有未說出的真相。一方面是因為你可能需要推薦信，另一方面，雖然雇主應保密，但在你的專業領域中，這種怒氣沖沖的信會一直跟著你。而且，你不知道未來還有沒有與這間公司交涉的可能。

  如果**你是因公司違法或違反誠信的行為而辭職**，請將握有的資料（相關紀錄越多越好）帶到外部的政府或專業機構。

  若你是被要求辭職，別在信中提到這點，只說你要辭職，否則會在正式檔案留下記錄。合適的話，可以告訴雇主你願意幫忙尋找或訓練接任者。最後以愉悅的口氣結尾，表達你的感謝，因為你在公司學到很多、因為你的同事、因為你能在這麼有活力的公司工作、因為你參與了公司的新發展。在某些情況下，你也可以只寫一句話告知你要辭職，不提供任何解釋。

- **回覆辭職信時**，先以一句聲明表示「遺憾」（with regret）接受辭職要求，再稱讚對方在公司中的表現，最後祝福對方的未來。

什麼不該說？

- 別在信中對員工或可能成為員工的人說出可能會被告的話。你可以依常識判斷。如果你不確定，可先向律師諮詢敏感信件（如訓誡信或解雇信）的遣詞用字。
- 別表現出負面情緒。你可以簡單陳述負面事件，但信中的口氣必須是客觀的，而不是憤怒、心存報復、煩躁、偏頗、傷人或輕蔑的。如果你陷入過度情緒化的狀態，可請別人幫你寫信。

寫作祕訣

- 保持簡短。簡單扼要的備忘錄與信件，更受到歡迎（別人也會更快回覆）。檢查信中的字詞、句子與段落，把影響理解的部分刪除。
- 要展露專業與禮貌。即便你寫信的對象與你很熟悉，還是要保持專業的口吻。寫在紙上的一切，都可以保存重讀。從嘴巴不慎說出的話可以被忘記，在紙上不慎寫下的句子卻會永久留存。
- 使用相符的姓名形式。如果你在信的開頭稱呼對方為 Dear Hazel Marston，那你最後的署名便是 John Reddin；若你稱對方為 Hazel，你便自稱 John。在工作面試後，如果你覺得比較適合以名字稱呼對方（Dear Henry），那你在簽名時也只簽上名字（Ferris），簽名下方則打上你的全名（在地址欄也是打上收件人的全名）。

特殊狀況

- 寄恭賀信或表揚信的時機：員工完成專案、獲得新客戶或對公司有其他貢獻；同事或員工升職或獲獎；公司人員的入職紀念日；員工、同事或主管慶祝人生大事（孩子出生、結婚）。你沒有義務要寫這種信，但這卻是最有影響力的一種工作信件。即便是像「謝謝你，湯姆，你太棒了」這種非常簡短的信，也能激發對方交出更亮眼的成績。

格式

- 多數公司內部的通信都是採用備忘錄的形式。較為正式的通知或信件（如升職或辭職），因為會列為個人紀錄，所以會打在有信頭的信紙上。
- 電子郵件很適合用在簡短的一般聯絡上；不過，具機密性或重要性的事項，則不能用這種方式寄送。

單字

accomplishment *(n.)* 成果	objective *(n.)* 目標	regulation *(n.)* 規定	supervise *(v.)* 監督
achievement *(n.)* 成就	operation *(n.)* 經營	success *(n.)* 成功	conduct *(v.)* 實施、進行
behavior *(n.)* 行為	policy *(n.)* 政策	training *(n.)* 訓練	recognize *(v.)* 認可
cutback *(n.)* 裁員	position *(n.)* 職位	capable *(a.)* 有能力的	regret *(v.)* 遺憾
goal *(n.)* 目標	procedure *(n.)* 程序	competent *(a.)* 有能力的	
morale *(n.)* 士氣	process *(n.)* 過程	outstanding *(a.)* 出色的	

詞組

accepted another position 接受了另一個職位	ask you to accept my resignation 請接受我的辭職
after much deliberation 在深思熟慮後	have no other option but to 不得不
an opportunity has recently arisen 最近出現了一個新的機會	highly motivated 非常積極
appreciate having had the opportunity to work 感謝有這個機會共事	cannot presently offer you any encouragement 目前無法給你任何激勵
must advise/inform you 必須勸告／通知你	proposed termination date of 預計的解雇日為

36
職場相關信

financial problems/difficulties have forced/obliged us
財務問題／困難迫使我們

not adding to/expanding our staff at the moment
目前沒有要增加／擴增員工

company cutbacks/merger
公司裁員／合併

submit/tender my resignation
繳交／提出我的辭職信

considered for the position of
考量到……的職位

under consideration
考慮中

due to economic conditions
由於經濟狀況

value your contributions
重視你的貢獻

eliminate certain positions
取消某些職位

expect to fill the vacancy
期望錄取該職缺

with great personal regret/great reluctance/mixed feelings
個人非常遺憾／不情願／心情複雜

句子

According to the terms of my contract, I hereby give four weeks' notice that as of April 18 I am terminating my employment as freight transportation manager with Sweedlepipe Inc.
根據合約內容，我在此於四週前給予通知，自四月十八日起，我將辭去在史威德派公司的貨運經理一職。

Although your credentials are impressive, we are offering the position to someone who also has the grain futures experience we are looking for.
雖然您的資歷令我們印象深刻，但我們要找的是有穀物期貨經驗的申請人，因此我們將此職位給予符合此條件的人。

Because Don Rebura Associates was not awarded the Marryat contract, we are obliged to consider employee layoffs.
由於唐里布拉公司未能與馬雅簽約，我們不得不考慮暫時停工。

I accept with pleasure the offer to join Potticary Dairy Products as institutional services manager.
我很高興接受此職位，加入波堤凱利乳製品公司擔任機構服務經理。

I am proud to be part of such a creative and enthusiastic team—I hope you are too.
我很驕傲能加入這麼獨具創意、極富熱忱的團隊，我希望你們也一樣。

I'll be happy to recommend you highly to potential employers.
我很樂意將你鄭重推薦給可能的未來雇主。

I'm concerned about the infractions of our safety regulations.
我很擔心違反我們的安全規章。

I'm looking forward to a long and challenging association with Willard Electronics.
我很期待能與威來電子公司建立長期而充滿挑戰的關係。

I've seen your wonderfully creative and appealing display windows and want to congratulate you on your excellent work.
我看到你設計的展示窗，既創新又吸引人，恭喜你做出這麼棒的成果。

I would like to meet with you to review the circumstances leading to my termination notice.
我希望與您見面討論，了解我收到解雇通知的相關理由。

On behalf of the management of Steenson Engineering, I am happy to inform you that you have been promoted to Senior Research Engineer, effective March 1.
謹代表史汀森工程公司的管理階層，很高興通知你，你已晉升為資深研究工程師，自三月一日生效。

Our decision in no way reflects on your excellent qualifications.
我們的決定並不會影響您優異的資歷。

Thank you for applying for the position of commercial plant specialist with Calvert Tropical Plants.
謝謝您向卡維特熱帶植物公司應徵商用植物專員一職。

The award properly belongs to the entire department.
這個獎項是屬於整個部門的。

The position for which you applied has already been filled.
您應徵的職缺已有錄取人選。

This is to advise you that you are being laid off in compliance with Article XXXI, Section 6, of our current labor agreement.
在此通知您，依照我們目前勞雇協議第三十一條第六項之規定，您已被解雇。

This letter will give formal notice of my resignation from Toddhunter Associates as Media Specialist effective April 1.
此信作為辭職的正式通知，自四月一日起，我將辭去淘杭特公司媒體專員一職。

Unfortunately we are not able to offer you a position with Roehampton Ltd. at this time.
可惜我們這次無法提供您羅漢頓公司的職位。

We accept your resignation with regret, and wish you well in future endeavors.
我們遺憾地接受你的辭職,並希望您未來一切順利。

We are pleased to offer you the position as warehouse attendant for Landor Textiles.
我們很高興錄取您為藍朵織品的倉務員。

We are sorry to see you leave.
你的離去,我們深感遺憾。

We have received a number of responses to our advertisement, and we ask your patience while we evaluate them.
我們收到很多回應徵才廣告的申請,在我們的評估期間,煩請您耐心等候。

We hope to be able to consider you for another position soon.
我們希望很快能在另一個職務上考慮您的申請。

We hope you will be available for recall.
我們希望您屆時能夠歸隊。

We will let you know/contact you/notify you/be in touch with you/write or call you about the status of your application sometime before June 1.
在六月一日前,我們會讓您知道／聯絡您／通知您／與您保持聯絡／寄信或打電話給您告知申請狀態。

段落

A one-hour presentation on workplace e-mail usage, covering such issues as privacy, monitoring activities, retention and documentation, and definitions and consequences of personal use will be offered Tuesday, June 6, every hour on the hour from 9 to 5 in the conference room. Please reply to this e-mail with your name and the hour you will attend in the subject line.

於六月六日（星期二）九點至五點間，每個整點都會給予一小時的簡報，主題為職場電郵使用，內容包含隱私、監督活動、保存與歸檔、私人使用之規範與後果，地點在會議室。請回覆這封電子郵件，在主旨中寫明你的姓名與參加時間。

We are seeing more travel expenses turned in after the fact, whereas company policy states that all travel expenses must be preapproved. If you have questions about how to handle travel expenses, call Michael Lambourne in Human Resources, extension 310.

我們發現，多數差旅費用都是事後才申報，但根據公司政策，所有的差旅費用都應預先申請並核准。若對於差旅費用的處理有所疑問，可打電話至人力資源部的麥可‧藍本，分機 310。

Last month, we lost $3,780 worth of clothing to shoplifters. There is an informational seminar on shoplifting scheduled for June 16 at 3 p.m. In the meantime, we ask all employees to be especially vigilant.

上個月我們共被偷走價值 3,780 元的衣物。六月十六日下午三時，我們將舉辦防盜講座。同時，我們也希望所有員工保持警戒。

I am obliged to resign my position with the Van Eyck Company because of ill health. I appreciate the good employer-employee relationship we have enjoyed over the years and will be watching the company's growth with much interest. If I can be of any assistance to my successor, I will be glad to help out.

由於本人健康狀況不佳，我必須辭去在范艾可公司的職位。我很感謝過去這些年與公司保持良好的勞雇關係，並會真心祝福公司持續成長。若我能在任何方面協助我的接任者，我很樂意幫忙。

We are sorry to announce that Jeanne Beroldy has resigned from the firm effective July 1. She has accepted the position of Managing Director with Christie Packaging Corp. Although we will miss her, we wish her every success in her exciting new position.

我們很遺憾宣布金妮‧貝洛迪已於七月一日從本公司辭職。她已接受克莉絲蒂包裝公司董事總經理一職。雖然我們會很想念她，但仍希望她在這令人興奮的新職位上，一切順利成功。

36

職場相關信

Dear Frank,

Welcome to Pierpont Industries! I hope you have a good first day on the job, and that it only gets better after that. We're very pleased to have you on our team, and hope that you're equally glad to be here. If any of us can make these first weeks smoother for you, don't hesitate to let us know.

親愛的法蘭克：

歡迎來到派龐工業！我希望你在新職位上的第一天一切順利，而後的每一天則是越來越順利。我們很高興你來到我們的團隊，希望你也一樣高興加入我們。如果我們之中有誰能在前幾週助你一臂之力，請別猶豫，一定要讓我們知道。

Dear Marcus,

As you are no doubt aware, I recently received a raise, and I am of course grateful not only to have a job that I enjoy so much but to be appreciated in this very practical way.

However, I am not sure how the raise was determined. As I look back over my five years here, I see a fairly quick rise from the position I originally accepted (word processor) to my current position as department manager. All performance reviews have been particularly favorable, including the last one. Despite these outstanding reviews, and three successive promotions within the last two years, my recent raise was just 1.5% above the company average.

As my immediate supervisor, you are perhaps in the best position to tell me (1) if this is consistent with policy throughout the company; (2) if there is something I should be doing to let others know my achievements, qualifications, and general worth.

If you have time to discuss this in the next couple of days, I'd be grateful for your time.

Sincerely,

親愛的馬可斯：

想必您已經知道，我最近獲得了加薪。我當然非常感謝，因為我不只能做我喜歡的工作，還能以這麼實際的方式得到嘉獎。

然而，我不太確定此次加薪是如何決定的。我回顧在這裡工作的五年，我發現我很快就從一開始的職位（文字編輯）升至目前的部門經理。我所有的業績審核結果都非常正面，包括最近這一次的結果。儘管我的評核結果優異，並於過去兩年連三次獲得晉升，但我最近加薪後的薪水，只高於公司平均值 1.5%。

您是我的直屬上司，也許您最適合為我解釋以下問題：(1) 這是否符合公司政策規定？(2) 我是否該做些什麼，讓別人知曉我的成果、資歷與整體價值？

若您在接下來幾天有時間討論此事，我會非常感謝。

〇〇敬上

Dear Mr. Karkeek:

Thank you for your letter seeking employment with our firm.

You have an interesting background. However, we feel your qualifications and experience do not match the needs of the account executive/trainee position presently available in our Chicago office.

We thank you for your interest in Lessways International and wish you success in the attainment of your career objectives.

Sincerely yours,

卡奇克先生您好：

謝謝您來信向我們公司應徵工作。

您的背景相當有趣；然而，我們的芝加哥辦公室目前徵求的是業務企劃／儲備幹部一職，而我們認為您的資歷與經驗並不符合需求。

謝謝您對於雷思威國際的興趣，祝福您能順利達成職涯目標。

○○敬上

Dear Marguerite Lambert,

Thank you for your application for the position of litho stripper, your résumé, and your work samples. They are being carefully considered by our Human Resources Department.

We received a number of other applications, so it may be three or four weeks before we can make a decision. You will be notified either way as soon as we do.
Thank you for your interest in Greatheart Printing Company.

Sincerely yours,

瑪葛瑞特‧藍博您好：

謝謝您針對印刷剝離員一職寄來的申請書、履歷與工作樣品集。我們的人力資源部門正在仔細考慮您的申請。

我們收到許多其他人的申請，所以可能需要三至四週時間才能做出決定，屆時您會立即收到通知。

謝謝您有意願應徵大心印刷公司。

○○敬上

Dear Ms. Moncada:

As you know, I just celebrated five years with Tresham Paper Products. In that time, I've been stimulated by my work, supported by coworkers, and encouraged by management. I've enjoyed being part of the Tresham team.

The recent reorganization has changed things for me, however, and I question whether the next five years will be as fruitful for me as the last five and whether I'll be as useful to the company in my new situation. Because of this, I am accepting a position with Walter & Co. Inc. where I am assured of opportunities for advancement as well as exceptional laboratory support.

Please accept my resignation, effective November 1, along with my appreciation for a satisfying and rewarding five years.

Sincerely,

蒙卡達小姐您好：

　　如您所知，我才剛慶祝在崔漢紙張產品公司工作五週年的紀念日。過去我一直受到工作的激發，同事的支持與主管的鼓勵。我很喜歡作為崔漢團隊的一分子。

　　然而，最近的重組讓一切都改變了，我開始懷疑我在這裡的下一個五年是否能像前一個五年一樣成功，而我在新的職位上又是否能繼續為公司帶來助益。也因此，我將接受華特公司的職位，在那裡我確信能擁有發展的機會與優異的實驗室支援團隊。

　　請接受我的辭職，自十一月一日起生效。我很感謝有那麼令人滿意而成果豐碩的五年。

○○敬上

TO: Dr. Betti Lancoch
FROM: Caradoc Evans
DATE: February 3, 2018
RE: Biodegradable plastics technology

We continue to be very interested in your biodegradable plastics technology, which appears to be the cornerstone for several new products. I understand you're pursuing patents for this technology. We'd like to see your patent applications filed by May 1, 2018, so that we could begin customer contact to clarify performance criteria for several of the products.

I want to emphasize our need for your technology along with appropriate patent protection. If you require additional support, please call. Thanks.

收件人：貝蒂・藍克
寄件人：卡拉達克・伊凡斯
日期：二〇一八年二月三日
主旨：生物可分解塑膠技術

我們依舊對您的生物可分解塑膠技術深感興趣，這項技術顯然是多項新產品的基礎。我明白您正在為此項技術申請專利；我們希望您能於二〇一八年五月一日前取得專利，如此我們便能開始聯絡客戶，向他們解釋多項新產品的性能標準。

我想在此強調，我們需要您的技術以及適當的專利保護。若您需要其他的協助，請致電。謝謝。

✉ 參見：03 回應、06 預約會面、07 恭賀信、10 歡迎信、11 表揚信、12 致謝函、15 公告通知、17 後續追蹤信、22 拒絕、28 求職信、29 履歷、30 推薦信

36

職場相關信

Chapter 37

訂單處理信
Letters Dealing with Orders

> 每次好不容易出了有我很想買且很棒的產品，
> 偏偏就會停產。

——伊莉莎白・C・芬恩根（Elizabeth C. Finegan）

標準化的訂單、採購單與請購單，以及二十四小時免付費訂購專線，再加上便利的網路購物，使訂單處理信形同消失。不過，只要人們繼續訂購商品、填寫訂單，那麼錯誤、例外、問題或是特殊要求就一定會出現，你就會需要寫信處理。

 PART 1 說明篇

何時需要寫訂單處理信？

下訂單	詢問額外資訊 參見：20 請求與詢問	取消訂單 變更訂單	提出抱怨 參見：25 抱怨與客訴
下單後續處理 確認收到訂單、 回覆出貨日期	詢問訂單問題 出貨日、退貨方式	說明訂單流程 參見：16 指示說明信	客訴處理 參見：35 客訴處理信、 13 致歉信
說明變更	逾期支付訂單 參見：38 催繳信、 41 信貸相關信	退換貨	

該怎麼說？

- **要下單卻沒有制式訂購單時**，提供以下資料：商品描述、數量、尺寸、顏色、客製化設計／字母組合、價格。姓名、地址、郵遞區號、日間電話號碼、電子郵件地址、付款方式。若你是用信用卡支付，提供卡號、有效日期與簽名。訂購商品時，先確定運費計算方式，並明確給予包裝或送貨的特殊須知。

- **寫出必須出貨的日期**。如此一來，當未能如期收到商品時，你才有依據取消訂單而不必支付罰金。信件也是一種非正式合約。

- 製作通用的表單，作為收到**訂單後若無法立即處理的回信**。一開始先打上 Thank you for your order. We are unable to ship your merchandise at once because... 「謝謝您的訂單。我們目前無法馬上運送您的商品，因為⋯⋯」，接著羅列出數項收到訂單可能會遇到的問題，以便直接圈選、畫底線或打勾，如 Payment has not been received. 「帳款未收到。」；We no longer fill C.O.D. orders. Please send a check or money order. 「我們不再提供貨到付款服務，請寄支票或匯票。」；We cannot ship to a post office box. Please supply a street address. 「我們無法寄送到郵政信箱，請提供地址。」；We are currently out of stock—may we ship later? 「目前存貨不足，能否晚點出貨？」；We no longer carry that item. May we send a substitution of equal value and similar style? 「此商品已停止供貨，能否改寄給您同等價格、款式類似的替代商品？」；Please indicate size (quantity, style, color). 「請提供尺寸／數量／款式／顏色。」；We must receive shipping and handling charges before processing your order. 「在處理您的訂單之前，我們必須先收到運費與手續費。」

什麼不該說？

- 訂購時，別提到跟訂單無關的事（如索取新型錄、抱怨前次訂購、申請成為優惠客戶），否則會導致出貨延遲。

寫作訣竅

- 寫訂購信時，請適當排版，讓對方一眼就能讀懂內容。不要用句子描述訂單，如「我想要訂購六雙尺寸 11 號的男性白色運動襪，以及四雙尺寸 11 號的男性黑色彈性長襪，一雙各為 7.95 元」，改以分欄或分項的方式呈現資訊，並分行書寫。使用阿拉伯數字，如 12 Menaphon harmonicas「12 個梅納風口琴」，不使用拼寫，因為阿拉伯數字最容易閱讀。

37

訂單處理信

- 不要忘記禮貌。訂購過程須遵循各種規定，容易使我們忘記另一端的人也是活生生的人。因此，請說 Thank you for your prompt attention.「謝謝您迅速處理。」或 Thank you for your order.「謝謝您的訂單。」並聲明隨時都能服務客戶，也感謝顧客的光顧。有禮貌的回應，便是一種商譽信。

特殊狀況

- **初次寄訂單沒有收到回應**，再次訂購相同的商品時，請註明這是重複的訂單，以免對方收到第一張訂單時，又要重新處理一次。
- 當你必須**取消已預付款項的訂單**，或要求退款，請在信中包含：訂單或發貨單號；訂購日期；商品描述。明確指出商品的費用是退還帳戶還是信用卡，或以支票的形式退還。
- **退貨時**，在封面信中包含：你的姓名與地址；商品描述；銷貨單、發貨單或運貨標籤；退貨原因、要求退錢或退款至帳戶或替換商品；並表達感謝。如果商品太大或太脆弱，可先寫信詢問該如何退貨。要求對方補償你所支付的運費（儘管你可能得不到）。

格式

- 訂單很適合以制式化表單呈現。將例行性的訂單、問題處理單、退款退貨單或其他例行文件製作成制式化的表單，簡化訂單處理程序。在表單中加入：顧客姓名、公司名稱或職稱、地址、郵遞區號、包含區碼的電話號碼、電子郵件地址、傳真號碼；顧客帳號；商品描述、商品貨號或連結、數量、尺寸、顏色、款式；客製化設計或字母組合；單件價格；各商品總價格；運送與處理程序圖表；銷售稅資訊；隨信附上的金額；運貨資訊（可能選項與運送時間）；填寫銀行卡號、有效日期與簽名的空間；供採購部門或其他單位簽名的空間。
- 客製化的訂單處理信件，應打在有信頭的信紙或備忘錄用紙。

✉ PART 2 應用篇

單字

billed *(a.)* 已付清帳款的	expedite *(v.)* 迅速執行	item *(n.)* 品項	stock *(n.)* 存貨
cancel *(v.)* 取消	freight *(n.)* 貨物	merchandise *(n.)* 商品、貨物	underpayment *(n.)* 支付金額不足
change *(v.)* 變更	goods *(n.)* 商品、貨物	overnight *(n.)* 隔夜抵達郵件	overpayment *(n.)* 超額支付
charge *(v.)* 收費	handle *(v.)* 處理	urgent *(a.)* 緊急的	warehouse *(n.)* 倉庫
confirm *(v.)* 確認	immediately *(adv.)* 立刻地	receipt *(n.)* 收據	
deposit *(n.)* 訂金	invoice *(n.)* 發貨單	rush *(v.)* & *(n.)* 匆促行動	

詞組

as soon as possible/at once 盡快／立刻	next-day delivery 隔日運送
being shipped to you 已出貨	please advise us/let us know 請給我們意見／讓我們知道
confirm your order 確認訂單	please bill to 請寄帳單給……
delivery date of 運送日期為	prompt attention 迅速關注
enclosed is my check for 隨信附上我支付……的支票	retail/ wholesale price 零售／批發價格

hereby confirm	return receipt requested
在此確認	請寄回收執回條
I would like to order	ship C.O.D.
我想要訂購	以貨到付款方式運送
must cancel my order of	shipping and handling charges
必須取消我的……訂單	運費與手續費

句子

Along with your order I'm enclosing our spring catalog as I think you'll want to know about our new lower prices (many are lower than last year's!) and our completely new line of Strato work clothes.
隨信附上您的訂單以及我們的春季型錄,我想您可能會想知道我們最新的較低定價(很多都比去年更低!)以及全新的史特拉多工作服裝系列。

If you cannot have the storage cabinets here by October 3, please cancel the order and advise us at once.
若您無法在十月三日前送到儲藏櫃,請取消訂單並立即通知我們。

Please bill this order to my account #JO4889 at the usual terms.
請將此訂單以普通條款記在我的帳上(#JO4889)。

Please cancel my order for the Heatherstone china (copy of order enclosed)—the three-month delay is unacceptable.
請取消我的風藥石瓷器訂單(訂單見附件),我們無法接受三個月的延遲。

Please charge this order to my Carlyle First Bank Credit Card #333-08-4891, expiration date 11/10 (signature below).
這筆訂單請從我的卡利爾第一銀行信用卡扣款,卡號 333-08-4891,有效日期至 11/10(簽名如下)。

Please check on the status of my order #90-4657 dated March 1.
請查看我於三月一日下單的 #90-4657 訂單狀態。

Please confirm receipt of this order by fax or telephone.
收到這張訂單後,請透過傳真或電話回覆。

Please include your account number/invoice number/order number on all correspondence.
每封通信往來中，皆請附上您的帳號／發貨單編號／訂單號碼。

We acknowledge with thanks your order of August 19 for one Pumblechook self-closing, self-latching chain-link gate.
謝謝您，我們已收到您於八月十九日訂購潘波趣自關自閂鏈結門的訂單。

We are pleased to inform you that both your orders were shipped this morning.
我們很高興通知您，您的兩筆訂單都已於今日早上出貨。

We are sorry to advise you that we will be out of that particular piano tuning kit (#P11507) indefinitely.
很遺憾通知您，該組鋼琴調音工具（#P11507）將無限期缺貨。

We are unable to fill your order dated June 3 because your account is currently in arrears.
我們無法處理您於六月三日下的訂單，因為您的帳戶目前仍有欠款。

We hope you enjoy your personalized stationery, and will think of us for your other stationery needs.
我們希望您喜歡您的客製化信紙，也希望日後您有其他文具需求時能想到我們。

Your order #KR45G is being processed and should be shipped by August 1.
您的訂單 #KR45G 已在處理中，預計於八月一日前出貨。

段落

This is to confirm receipt of your order #104-1297 dated June 17, 2018. It will be shipped on or about June 26. Please allow two to three weeks for arrival. If you need to contact us again about this order, use our reference number, 442-48895.

在此向您確認，我們已收到您於二〇一八年六月十七日的訂單，編號 104-1297。我們會於六月二十六日前後出貨，須二至三週才會送達。若您要再次聯絡關於這筆訂單的相關事宜，請致電到 442-48895。

We appreciate your order #GR3315 for the exposed aggregate. However, we no longer ship C.O.D. Please send a check or money order for $782.11 so that we can expedite your order.

謝謝您訂購露石混凝土的訂單，編號 GR3315。然而，我們已不再提供貨到付款的服務，煩請將 782.11 元的支票或匯票寄給我們，我們才能加速處理您的訂單。

Please note that you received a special price on the sheet protectors. Your refund check for the overpayment is enclosed.

請留意，您是以特別優惠價購買文件保護套，隨信附上您超額支付金額之退款支票。

With one exception, your order is being shipped to you from our Gregsbury warehouse this week. The six desktop calculators are coming from our Chicago warehouse, and we've been experiencing some delays from that warehouse recently. You may not receive the calculators until approximately March 8. Please let us know if this is acceptable.

您的訂單將於本週自葛斯伯里倉庫出貨，但有一項商品除外；六臺桌上型計算機將從芝加哥倉庫出貨。而最近由此倉庫出貨的商品都有些延遲，所以您要等到三月八日左右才能收到計算機。請讓我知道您能否接受此項安排。

It was my impression that we agreed upon a delivery date of May 15. The confirmation I have just received gives June 15. This will unfortunately be too late for us. Please let me know at once if this was a clerical error or if we have a serious problem on our hands.

印象中，我們雙方同意運送日期為五月十五日，但我剛收到的確認信中，運送日期為六月十五日。遺憾的是，這個日期對我們來說太晚了。請馬上讓我知道這只是辦事人員的失誤，還是我們遇到了嚴重的問題。

示範信

TO: Conford Confections
FROM: Alexander Trott
DATE: June 3, 2018

I have been buying your Conford Confections for family, friends, and business acquaintances twice a year (Easter and Christmas) for many years. I will be traveling in Europe this summer and would like to take along Confections to offer friends and business acquaintances there.

My questions:

1. Do Confections need to be refrigerated, either to maintain good quality and appearance or to ensure that there is no product spoilage?

2. Do you have outlets for your product in Europe? (I would not like to cart them along as a "special treat" and then find them being sold everywhere over there.)

3. Is there any other reason that would prevent me from taking Confections with me? (Do they melt easily, for example?)

If you can reassure me on the above points, please place my order for:

6 boxes	8 oz. Gift Box	$7.95@
10 boxes	14 oz. Supremes	$12.95@

My check for $197.83 (including sales tax and shipping and handling) is enclosed. Please ship to the letterhead address.

If you think the Confections won't travel well, I'll appreciate your saying so and returning my check.

37
訂單處理信

收件人：康福西點
寄件人：亞歷山大‧圖洛特
日期：二〇一八年六月三日

多年來，我每年都會購買兩次（復活節與聖誕節）康福西點給家人、朋友與工作上認識的人。這個夏天我會去歐洲，想帶些西點給那邊的朋友與業界熟人。

我的問題是：

一、西點是否需要冷藏才能維持口感與外觀，或確保不會變質？

二、您們的商品是否能在歐洲買到？（我不希望把他們當成「特別禮物」搬運過去，結果卻發現到處都買得到。）

三、有沒有其他不該把西點帶去的理由？（比如說，會不會很容易融化？）

如果您能向我保證不必擔心以上幾點的話，請處理我的訂單：

六盒	八盎司禮盒	各 7.95 元
十盒	十四盎司特級組合	各 12.95 元

隨信附上 197.83 元支票（含銷售稅、運費與手續費）。請運送至信頭所列之地址。

如果這些西點禁不起旅途運送，請告訴我，並將支票退還給我，非常感謝。

✉ 參見：03 回應、13 致歉信、14 收件通知、16 指示說明信、22 拒絕、25 抱怨與客訴、35 客訴處理信、
38 催款信、41 信貸相關信

Chapter 38

催款信
Collection Letters

催款信的目的是拿到錢，同時又不失去客戶。
——商業寫作書作者梅格兄妹

寫催款信時，需達成兩個相互矛盾的目的——讓客戶付清帳款，並維持與客戶的關係以保住生意。一封絕佳的催款信可以帶來很好的結果，不光是把錢收回，更能將賒帳的客戶變成可靠的客戶。

催款的第一步通常是由公司帳務中心、會計部門或信用部門寄發逾期提醒（past-due reminder）。當帳單逾期三十、六十或九十天，便開始寄發一系列的催款信。只有當這些越來越嚴厲的催款信都被忽略時，公司才會找代客催收欠款業者介入。許多大公司會利用統計方法，預測哪些客戶須更早以較強勢的手段管理。不過請記得，在某些情況下，最有效的催帳方法或許是一通親切提醒繳款的電話。

 PART 1 說明篇

催款信有哪些？

找第三方處理催款的信	私人催帳信	提醒信
如律師或欠款催收公司	給朋友或親戚	
宣告已轉交第三方處理的催款信	一系列愈加強勢的催繳信	感謝付款的致謝信

該怎麼說？

- 信件的語氣須有禮，假設客戶有意願付錢，只是忘了，並假設這是最後一封催款信，所以口氣是樂觀、感激與自信的。

- 內容須包含：客戶姓名、訂單號碼；訂購日期與價格；訂購品項；原付款截止日；希望對方付款的截止日；先前的良好付款紀錄；建議的付款計畫；其他說明。給客戶足夠時間付款（各催帳信之間相隔二至三週）。結尾處加上一句明確的付款要求，並以一句聲明告知對方若已付款可忽略此信。附上回郵信封，鼓勵對方盡快回應。

- 以下是一套包含六封催款信的催款計畫。你也可以寄四或十封信，或更改信件內容以符合需求。

  (1) 寄出多封逾期通知之後（通知上可蓋上 Past Due（逾期）或 Second Notice（第二次通知）的印章或貼紙）未果，便可寄出第一封有禮的催帳信，向對方表明帳款已逾期。保持簡短，只告知該金額之帳款已逾期數週或數月，並以愉悅的口氣要求付款。

  (2) 口氣更堅持一些，提醒客戶帳款仍未收到。請對方給予解釋，或提供幾個為對方保留面子的理由，替對方解釋尚未付款的原因（帳單被忽略了、在郵寄中遺失、客戶不在辦公室）。在結尾表示你相信帳款會立刻付清。

  (3) 語氣變得更為急迫、信變得更長，給客戶一個或數個付清帳款的好理由，如這能保住他們的信用評等與名譽；這跟公平／正義／良心有關；這才是負責任的做法；這對他們來說最為有益。在這封信或下封信中，提出兩種你能接受的付款時程，給客戶選擇的機會。可將逾期的帳款以每週、每半個月、每月分期付款，或分為兩次付款。

  (4) 措詞愈加嚴厲，提醒對方必須付款的理由：你已經提供服務或運送貨品，客戶也須履行義務；欠款的金額很小，不值得為此損及信用評等；客戶不會希望出現在你們的拖欠名單；他們不會希望被告；他們未來無法再向你們提出訂單。這封信中可提到帳單會轉交代收欠款公司處理。

  (5) 事到如今，你會假定客戶已經察覺問題，卻故意不付款。在這封強勢的信中，請宣布你將實行其他必要措施，如交由代收欠款公司催款，或委託律師採取法律行動。（若你決定採取法律行動，信中的措詞請按照律師建議。）不過，在真正採取行動前，此階段仍可以給客戶十天時間安排付款事宜。在信中明確表示這些行動是可以避免的，只要對方立刻回應。

  (6) 在最後一封信中，你相信客戶只有在強迫之下才會付錢。告訴對方從某月某日起，帳款已轉交某代收欠款公司或某律師事務所處理。這封信只是告知你將採取的行動，你不會再試圖說服客戶付款。

- 當你寫信給代收欠款公司時，請提供完整資訊：姓名、地址、電話號碼、帳戶號碼、所有通訊聯絡紀錄、結算單、數據文件。

- 別用代收欠款公司或法律行動威脅客戶，除非你確實準備採取這些手段。如果你說你會在十天內將帳款轉交代收欠款公司處理，請務必實行。

- 勿使用以下的字：failure（失敗、沒有履行），如 your failure to respond「您沒有回應」、failure to pay「沒有付款」；ignore（忽視）如 you have ignored our letters「你忽視了我們的信」；insist（堅持）或 demand（要求），如 we insist that you send payment at once.「我們堅持您必須立刻付款。」這些字會讓對方感到渺小，他們也不會因此喜歡你。

- 別用負面的話術（辱罵、中傷、霸凌、諷刺、傲慢、口頭警告）；這些做法只會帶來負面的結果、毀壞公司名譽。

- 避免自以為幽默、假裝困惑、一點也沒有效果的語氣：「我們只是無法理解為何信用等級這麼高的人……」；「我們很困惑，不知為何我們一直沒有得到你的回應。」；「我們想不透……」。

- 不要說任何會被認為是誹謗的話。

寫作訣竅

- 措詞保持得體。即便是信用紀錄不良的人，也可能覺得自己已經表現得不錯。寫得不好的催款信，會讓對方感到憤怒、自卑或無助，而這些感受並不會激勵他們付錢。

- 催款信之間要有間隔。一開始，每個月寄發一次，從對方未遵守付款日的那天立刻寄送。要給對方足夠的時間回應，或讓他們有因病痛、忙碌、假期而延遲付款的時間。而後，每十天至兩週寄一次信。對方越頑固，你寄信的間隔也越短。如果該客戶的信用紀錄良好，便不須如此頻繁寄信。

- 理論上，與信貸及財務有關的事情都應該保密。請盡全力保護你提供與接收的信用資訊。

- 別把催款信寄到對方辦公的地方，其他人可能會把信拆開。同理，為了隱私，不要用明信片寄發催款信。你不會希望讓客戶難堪，或讓自己被客訴或惹上法律麻煩。

特殊狀況

- 催款時，**若客戶回報他們遇上很糟糕的狀況**（生病、解雇、財務困難），可提供對方可行的付款時程，即使慷慨一點也無妨。透過背景調查，便知道是否應該特別留意這名客戶遭遇的困難。減少債務（無論金額多小）對借貸雙方都有益處，值得你付出最大的努力。

- 若要**提醒朋友或家人借款已到期**，可以幫對方想個藉口，給對方面子，如 I know how busy you are...「我知道你有多忙……」；I wonder if you forgot about...「我在想你是不是忘了……」；Am I mistaken, or did we agree that you'd repay the loan September 1?「不知道是不是我搞錯了，但我們是否說好你會在九月一日前還錢呢？」。如果之前有留下借據或曾在信中列出條件，那會派上用場。第二次寄信時，可以附上此借據的影本。

格式

- 催款信一定是打字於有信頭的信紙上。
- 剛開始的幾封催款信可以使用制式信。第一封信可以是簡單的提醒，只須將金額與付款截止日填入空格。

單字

action (n.) 行動	debt (n.) 債務	notice (v.) & (n.) 通知；注意到	request (v.) & (n.) 請求
advise (v.) 建議	disappointed (a.) 失望的	outstanding (a.) 未支付的	require (v.) 需要
arrangement (n.) 安排	embarrass (v.) 使難堪	overdue (a.) 逾期的	satisfy (v.) 使滿意
balance (n.) 餘額	explanation (n.) 解釋	overlooked (a.) 遭忽視的	settle (v.) 決定、結算
circumstances (n.) 境況	extend (v.) 延長	oversight (v.) 疏忽	statement (n.) 結算單
collect (v.) 催收	liability (n.) 負債、義務	past-due (a.) 逾期的	terms (n.) 條款
concerned (a.) 有關的	misunderstanding (n.) 誤解	propose (v.) 提議	unpaid (a.) 未付的
cooperation (n.) 合作	necessitate (v.) 使成為必需	reminder (n.) 提醒	urge (v.) 極力主張
creditworthiness (n.) 優良信譽	nonpayment (n.) 未付款	repayment (n.) 償清	

38

催款信

詞組

account past due 帳款已逾期	final opportunity 最後的機會
accounts receivable 應收帳款	friendly reminder 友善的提醒

act upon
按照⋯⋯行事

amount/balance due/owed
逾期／欠繳的金額／餘額

appreciate hearing from you
希望得到你的回應

at least a partial payment
至少支付部分帳款

be good enough to/so good as to
煩請

behind with your payments
超過付款期限

call/direct your attention to
讓你注意到⋯⋯

overdue account
逾期的帳款

credit rating/standing/record
信用等級／狀況／紀錄

damaging to your credit record/
standing/rating
損害您的信用記錄／狀況／紀錄

delinquent status of your account
你的帳款到期未付

despite our notice of a month ago
儘管我們在一個月前寄發了通知

did not respond
沒有回應

discuss this with you
與你討論此事

have heard nothing from you
沒有收到你的回應

how can we work together to
我們一起想辦法

immediately payable
立即應支付

important to resolve this matter
解決這個問題是很重要的

in arrears
拖欠的

it is our policy
這是我們的政策

let us hear from you right away
立即回應我們

just a reminder/to remind you
只是要提醒你

legal action/advice/steps
法律行動／建議／措施

I understand and appreciate your
position, but
我能理解並體諒你的情況，但是

mail today
今日寄出

must hear from you
必須得到你的回應

mutually satisfactory solution
讓彼此都滿意的解決方式

no activity on your account
你的帳戶沒有任何活動

easy payment plan
簡單的付款計畫

escaped your attention
使你沒有留意到

outstanding balance
未付的餘額

clear your account before the next
statement period
在下一個結算期前付清帳款

to avoid additional expenses, delays and
unpleasantness
以避免額外費用、延遲與不愉快

perhaps you didn't realize
也許你沒有發現

please let us hear from you by
請在⋯⋯之前回應我們

please mail/send us
請寄給我們

pressing need for action
迫切需要採取行動

prompt payment/remittance
立即付款／轉帳

reasonable payment arrangement
合理的付款安排

recourse to legal action
訴諸法律行動

reduce your balance
減少餘款

resolve this matter
解決這個事件

not made a payment since
自從⋯⋯便沒有付款

now due on your account
現在帳款已逾期

official notice
正式通知

since you haven't replied to our last
letter
由於你尚未回覆我們的上一封信

so that you can maintain your credit
standing
如此一來，你可以維持你的信用狀況

special appeal
特別請求

strongly suggest
強烈建議

suggested payment plan solution
建議作為解決方法的付款計畫

we would appreciate your sending us
如果您寄出⋯⋯，我們會很感激

unacceptable delay
令人無法接受的延遲

valued customer
珍貴的客戶

seriously delinquent
嚴重逾期

several statements and letters
數封結算單與信件

we haven't heard from you
我們尚未得到你的回覆

review of our files/your account shows
在審查我們的檔案／你的帳戶紀錄發現

past-due amount
到期未付的帳款

without further delay
不得再拖欠

句子

After 120 days, we normally/routinely/automatically turn an account over to our attorneys for collection.
一百二十天後，我們通常／按規定／自動會將帳單轉交由律師催收。

A postage-paid envelope is enclosed for your convenience.
為了您付款方便，隨信附上回郵信封。

Despite our last three reminders, your account remains unpaid.
我們已寄出三封提醒信，但您的帳款仍待付清。

Enclosed is a copy of your last statement, showing a balance of $457.89 that is ninety days overdue.
附件是您最近一次的結算單影本，您可以看到 457.89 元的餘款已逾期九十天。

I am sorry, but we are unable to extend you any more time for the payment of your outstanding balance of $896.78.
我很抱歉，但您未付清的 896.78 元餘款，我們無法再延長付款期限。

If we do not hear from you at once/within the next ten days, we will be obliged to pursue other collection procedures/we will have no choice but to engage the services of a collection agency.
若我們沒有立即／在接下來十天內收到您的回覆，我們便必須採取其他催款措施／我們便不得不使用代收欠款公司的服務。

If you have already sent your check/paid your balance of $324.56, please ignore this notice.
若您已寄出支票／付清餘款 324.56 元，請忽略此封信。

If you haven't already mailed in your payment, won't you take a moment to mail it today?
若您尚未郵寄您的帳款，可否於今日撥空寄送呢？

If your financial circumstances make it impossible to pay the full amount at this time, please let us know as I am sure that we can work out an acceptable schedule of installment payments.

若您因財務狀況無法付清全額，請讓我知道，我確信我們可以訂出一個合理的分期付款時程。

If your payment is not received by June 1, we will be obliged to turn your account over to the Costello Collection Agency.

若在六月一日前仍未收到您的帳款，我們就必須將您的帳單轉交卡斯特洛代收欠款公司處理。

It is important that you take some action before this unpaid balance affects your credit rating.

在此項未付餘款影響您的信用評等之前，您必須採取行動。

Just a reminder: your account balance of $106.87 is thirty days past due.

提醒您：您的 106.87 元餘款已逾期三十日。

May we have your check for $89.43 by return mail?

您能否將 89.43 元支票以回信寄給我們呢？

Our records show your account to be seriously in arrears.

我們的紀錄顯示，您的帳款已嚴重逾期。

Please call or write to make arrangements.

請致電或來信做進一步安排。

Please forward payment in the amount of $269.89 promptly.

請立即付款，金額為 269.89 元。

Please mail your check by May 5 so that no future action will be necessary.

請在五月五日前郵寄您的支票，我們便毋須採取進一步的措施。

Thank you for your cooperation/attention to this matter/for taking care of this at once.

謝謝您的合作／對此事的關切／立刻處理此事。

Thank you for your recent remittance, which has allowed us to reactivate your account.

謝謝您日前匯寄的帳款，我們立即重啟您的帳戶。

There may be a good explanation for your lack of response to our requests for payment of your overdue account—won't you tell us about it?

我們請求您支付逾期的款項，但未能得到您的回應，我們相信您或許有適宜的解釋，可否請您告訴我們呢？

This matter must be resolved without further delay.
此項問題必須立即解決，勿繼續拖延。

Unfortunately your payment has not been received.
可惜我們仍未收到您的帳款。

We are disappointed not to have heard from you about your overdue balance of $1,785.97.
未能得到您對於逾期餘款 1,785.97 元的回應，我們感到相當失望。

We ask for your cooperation in paying the balance due.
謝謝您的合作，支付了到期的餘款。

We expect to hear from you by July 15 without fail.
我們期望您務必在七月十五日前回應我們。

We have sent a number of friendly requests for payment but have had no response from you.
我們已寄發數封友善的信函請求您付款，卻未能得到您的回音。

We hope that you will take advantage of this last invitation to settle your account and to avoid further damage to your credit rating as well as the costs of any possible legal action.
我們希望您能接受這最後一次的請求，結清帳款，以免損及您的信用評等，也避免後續法律行動產生的費用。

We look forward to hearing from you.
我們期盼得到您的回應。

We must know your intentions immediately.
我們必須立即了解您的想法。

We provide prompt service, and we expect prompt payment.
我們提供即時的服務，亦期望客戶即時付款。

We resort to legal action with the greatest reluctance.
我們別無選擇，只能訴諸法律行動。

We would be happy to work with you to arrange an easy payment plan suited to your circumstances.
我們很樂意與您一起安排適合您目前處境的簡易付款計畫。

Why not take care of this matter right now?
不如現在就解決這個問題？

You are a much-appreciated customer, and we hope there is no problem.
您是我們相當重視的客戶，我們希望不會出現問題。

You may not realize that your account is ninety days past due.
您或許尚未發現，您的帳款已逾期九十天。

Your account has been turned over to Darley and Havison, our attorneys, for collection and, if necessary, legal action.
您的帳單已轉交給我們的律師達萊與哈維森，他們會負責催款事宜，必要時亦會採取法律行動。

Your payment of $876.23 will be appreciated.
若您能付清餘額 876.23 元，我們會非常感激。

Your prompt payment will protect your good credit rating.
若您立即付款，將有助您維持優良的信用等級。

You will want to mail your check today so that you can continue using your credit privileges.
建議您於今日寄出支票，未來才能繼續享受您的信用卡優惠。

38

催款信

段落

Enclosed are copies of your statements, year to date. Please check them against your records, and let us know if they do not agree with ours. We show an outstanding balance of $1,236.90.

隨信附上您今年至今日為止的結算單影本,請與您保存的紀錄比對,若有不符之處,請讓我們知道。我們的紀錄顯示您有 1,236.90 元的餘款未付。

The nonpayment of your balance is expensive for both of us: it is costing you your excellent credit record as well as monthly service charges and it is costing us lost revenues and extra accounting expenses. We strongly urge you to make out a check right now for the balance due on your account (a self-addressed stamped envelope is enclosed for your convenience). If you wish to discuss some financial difficulty or arrange for a special payment schedule, please call 800-555-1331 today so that we can avoid reclassifying your account as delinquent.

您未付的帳款對我們雙方而言都代價高昂:您因此必須賠上優良的信用紀錄,並須於每月支付手續費;我們的收益則會減少,會計成本亦會增加。我們強烈建議您現在立即開出支票,付清您逾期的帳款(為了您的方便,隨信附上回郵信封)。若您想討論您的財務困難,或安排專屬付款計畫,請於今日致電 800-555-1331,以避免我們將您的帳款列為逾期。

The Locksley-Jones Collection Agency has been authorized by Elliot Lumber to collect the $980.54 past due amount on your account. According to information turned over to us by Elliot, you have not responded to requests for payment made over a period of eight months. This letter serves as your official notice that collection proceedings will begin ten days from the date of this letter unless you contact us to make some satisfactory arrangement for payment.

洛克斯里－瓊斯代收欠款公司已獲艾略特‧朗博授權,得以向您催收您已逾期之帳款980.54元。根據艾略特轉交給我們的資料,您在過去八個月一直未回應其付款之請求。在此正式通知您,催款程序在這封信寄出十天後會啟動,除非您聯絡我們,與我們安排合理的付款計畫。

Thank you for your payment of $763.21, received today. We are happy to be able to remove you from our collection system and to reestablish your line of credit. We do this with the understanding that you will keep your account current in the future. We hope to continue to serve you with all your plumbing and electrical needs.

謝謝您支付 763.21 元，今日已收到。我們很高興能將您移出我們的催款系統，並恢復您信用貸款之最高限額。我們這麼做，是因為我們知道您未來會準時付款。我們希望能繼續在水電管線方面為您服務。

示範信

Dear Sarah Scally:

On September 15, your account (#3178-S) will be transferred to the Bowyer Collection Agency for collection of the past-due amount of $481.69. If we should hear from you before then, we would be glad to make other arrangements. Otherwise, however, you will be hearing from someone at Bowyer.

Sincerely,

莎拉・史卡利您好：

您的帳單（#3178-S）於九月十五日將轉交波爾代收欠款公司處理，由該公司催收您逾期的帳款 481.69 元。若我們在此之前能得到您的回應，我們很樂意為您做別的安排；不然的話，則會由波爾公司的人員與您聯繫。

○○敬上

TO: Gombold Collection Agency
FROM: Van Allen Department Stores
DATE: February 3, 2018

We would like to engage your services to collect a past-due account in the name of:

Hermione Roddice
1921 Lawrence Parkway
Sunnybrook, OH 45043

Enclosed are copies of statements sent, the data sheet on this account, and all correspondence between us and Ms. Roddice to date.

收件者：甘柏代收欠款公司
寄件者：范艾倫百貨公司
日期：二〇一八年二月三日

我們想要使用您的服務，催收下列逾期帳單：

妙麗・羅迪斯
45043 俄亥俄州日溪市勞倫斯公園路 1921 號

隨信附上曾寄過的結算單、本帳單相關數據以及我們與羅迪斯小姐之間的所有通訊紀錄。

Dear Avery,

I'm enclosing a self-addressed stamped envelope along with the form below. I hope to hear from you by return mail.

- -

Please mark one of the responses below and enclose this form in the self-addressed stamped envelope along with your check, money order, or cash.

☐ Whoops! I was just about to send you the $300. Here it is.

☐ The kids need shoes and we don't have any food in the house, but, what the heck, I owe you!

☐ Are you SURE it was $300? Let me check. Yup, I guess it was.

☐ WHAT $300??!! Heh heh, just joking.

☐ I don't know why you should get paid before the dentist, Sears, and the kid who cuts the grass, but, here, take it!

親愛的艾佛瑞：

在此寄給你回郵信封跟下面的回條，希望你能回信。

- -

請勾選下列其中一個選項，並將此回條與支票、匯票或現金一齊放入回郵信封。

☐ 噢！我正準備寄給你 300 元。錢都在這了。

☐ 孩子們需要買鞋，而且我們家斷糧；不過，管他的，這是我欠你的！

☐ 你確定是 300 元？讓我確認一下。是啊，我想是的。

☐ 什麼 300 元？？！！嘿嘿，我只是開個玩笑。

☐ 我不懂為什麼你可以比希爾斯牙醫及修剪草皮的孩子更快拿到報酬，不過，錢在這兒，拿去吧！

Dear Ms. Seebach:

We are concerned about your past-due account of $473.23 and your lack of response to our inquiries about it. We would like to hear from you within the next ten days so that we are not obliged to seek other, more serious means of satisfying this debt.

Please consider protecting your credit rating by sending us a check promptly. You will be glad you did.

Sincerely,

希芭小姐您好：

您的帳款 473.23 元已逾期，而您一直未回覆我們對於此帳款的詢問，令我們十分關切。我們希望能在接下來十天內得到您的回應，以免我們必須尋求其他更嚴厲的措施使此債務得以償付。

為保護您的信用等級，立即將支票郵寄給我們。若您能這麼做，對您也是好事。

○○敬上

 參見：17 後續追蹤信、20 請求與詢問、41 信貸相關信

Chapter 39

募款信
Fundraising Letters

到頭來，募款還是得靠自己親自登門詢問。
這件事是沒有捷徑的。

——美國實業家喬琪・莫斯貝奇（Georgette Mosbacher）

慈善募捐在今日變得益加競爭激烈，這表示你的募款信必須用最少的字展現最強的說服力與吸引力。募款信大概是一般家庭收到數量最多的一種信，僅次於銷售信。你該如何說服讀者保留你的信、把錢捐給你？

如果募款組織本身歷史悠久且信譽良好，那募款就容易許多。但在多數時候，最好的方式還是從寫作下手，在寫作中灌注活力，如扣人心弦的故事、容易理解且有說服力的數據、激發思考的比喻、知名人士的現身說法、使用動作動詞、寫出能讓心與錢包都打開的動人訴求等。想寫出強而有力的募款信，其中一種方法是研究有效果的銷售信。

 PART 1 說明篇

募款信包含哪些？

請求捐獻	捐獻後續追蹤 參見：17 後續追蹤信	回應是否捐獻 參見：03 回應、 21 接受、22 拒絕	感謝捐獻 參見：12 致謝函
徵求募款志工	募款活動邀請函	政治競選活動募款	

1. 用吸引目光的開場白引起讀者興趣。

2. 清楚指出募款的組織單位。

3. 簡短而生動地描述募款單位，使讀者有興趣繼續讀下去：此單位在做什麼、設立目的、獨特之處、最令人印象深刻的成就。

4. 給讀者一個有說服力而急迫的募款需求，請他們協助。

5. 用故事、引言、證詞、案例、描述來打動人心。

6. 用事實、數據、資訊來說服理智。

7. 清楚說明會如何使用捐獻，如 With your help, we want to offer college scholarships to an additional twenty students this year.「有了您的幫助，今年我們會提供大學獎學金給額外的二十名學生。」

8. 提及捐獻的好處（個人獲得滿足、撫平痛苦、改善社會、改變某個人的未來、可抵稅、進入某個由捐款人組成的特別團體、獲得大眾認可、有機會分享一些盈餘、實踐信仰）。

9. 讓讀者相信募款單位的信譽，並向他們保證其捐獻會被有效使用。

10. 感謝讀者的興趣、關注、時間與關心。

11. 附上回郵信封，或可透過信用卡捐款的免付費電話，讓讀者很容易就能捐款。

12. 請最高位階的成員在信上簽名，或由知名公眾人物簽名。

13. 在信末署名之後的附註（P.S.）中，可強調新特色或重點。

什麼不該說？

- 別問問題，或建議讀者思考某件事。你要傳達一個又一個強而有力的訊息，不要打斷這個節奏，不要給讀者思考、「反駁」或理性思考的機會。

- 不要在信中出現任何攻擊或說教的語氣。有強烈信念的人，時常認為別人「應該」要有所貢獻，而信中便容易流露這樣的態度。你不能羞辱或操弄那些潛在的捐款人，因為捐款人相信捐獻是出於自由意志，是出自他們自己的高尚動機，而非你給的壓力。

- 忍住使用以下陳腔濫調的衝動：We need your help.「我們需要你的幫助。」；Why read this letter?「為什麼要讀這封信？」；You don't know me, but...「你不認識我，但是……」；Send your check today!「今天就寄出支票！」；Please take a few minutes to read this letter.「請花幾分鐘閱讀這封信」。想知道哪些話是陳腔濫調，必須讀過上百封募款信才行，但這麼做很值得，因為你能了解哪些信是有效的、哪些是無效的。

39

募款信

- 不要使用華麗的花招，如花俏的字體、過多的底線或大寫字母、彩色墨水或怪異的頁面設計。強而有力的訴求才是關鍵，這些花招幫不了疲軟無力的訴求，還會削弱有效訴求的力道。今日的募款信會用其他的策略，如在信封上使用手寫字體、較小的信紙、隨信附上誘因或提出誘因。

寫作訣竅

- 保持正向。不要告訴讀者若不捐款情況會變得多糟，而要讓讀者知道他們的捐獻能讓情況改善多少。
- 提出的支持要具體明確，不要說「在這個國家，孩子每晚都餓著肚子上床睡覺」，而要說「在這個世界上最富有的國家，四個孩子中就有一個必須每晚餓著肚子上床睡覺」。請求也要具體明確，如 Visit our website today.「今天就上我們的網站。」或是給予一個具體的金額，如 Your $100 will plant four new trees.「您的 100 元能種下四顆新樹。」
- 盡量簡短，你只有幾秒鐘的時間發揮影響力。
- 傳達急迫性。讀者不只是要捐款，還要現在就捐。被放到一旁等等再處理的信件，最後都會被遺忘。你要請求的是立即回應，並至少給一個必須這麼做的好理由。
- 與讀者之間建立一道連結，如 As a parent/teacher/physician, you understand what it means to...「您是一名家長／老師／醫生，想必您了解……的意義。」
- 《How to Write Powerful Fund Raising Letters》（暫譯：如何寫出有影響力的募款信）的作者賀歇爾‧高登‧路易斯（Herschell Gordon Lewis）曾說：「募款時最有效的詞是『你』。」檢查信件，看看哪個字最常出現：「你」或「我們」（或「我」）。
- 將訊息分成兩部分。先給讀者一個鮮明生動的景象，讓他們知道未來可能會是什麼樣子：健康的身心；營養良好的孩童；積極活躍的社區中心；杜絕疾病的蔓延；新的圖書館。接著確切告訴讀者你如何落實這個景象。對於未來的展望是訴諸感情、主觀的，而計畫則是講求事實、客觀的。
- 在募款信也可以呼籲讀者採取行動（簽署請願書、打電話給立法委員、為某項議題投票、參與寫信運動），之後再向讀者募款。
- 嚴謹的捐款人大多會關心募款單位如何運用捐款。附上一份年度報表或是款項使用說明，讓讀者了解有多少比例的捐款用於行政支出、多少用於該單位的主要活動。對捐款人而言，募款單位的信用與責任感是很嚴肅的問題。
- 附註（P.S.）是一封信中讀者最有可能讀的部分，有附註的信也比沒有附註的信有更高的回覆率。吸引目光的附註通常很短（少於五行），能用來鼓勵讀者立刻採取行動、感謝讀者的協助與興趣，或是加入有說服力的資訊。附註多不代表更好；兩個附註反而比一個更沒效果。

- 寄發一系列各有不同重點的募款信，通常很有效，儘管某個訴求無法打動讀者，但另一個訴求也許就正中紅心。

特殊狀況

- **邀請別人參與募款活動**時，要用適當的邀請函格式（參見：18 邀請函），但信中必須清楚講明你希望出席者做些什麼，如 $100 donation suggested「建議捐獻 100 元」或 Tax-deductible contribution of $500 per couple suggested.「每對夫妻建議捐款 500 元，可抵稅。」提到 tax-deductible（抵稅）與 donation（捐獻）這兩個詞時，用詞需精確。
- **邀請加入募款籌備委員會**時，明確說出你希望對方達成的事，成為委員後需要做的事，以及此活動的整體目標（財務與宣傳目標）。

格式

- 絕大多數的募款信都是制式信。你也許以為人們不會回應這種制式信，但事實上，這種信為募款單位募得了很多錢。通用的募款信寫得好，不僅讓人容易接受，而且還很有效。不過，這封信的成效取決於你所鎖定的目標族群。你可以直接將募款信郵寄給所有你所知的地址，也可以只寄給某特定團體的成員或某個人，但相比之下，前者的效果比較不好。
- 用有信頭的公司信紙寫私人募款信會有效果，但也可能引起質疑。只有在雇主同意的情況下，才能這麼做。
- 募款信不會以電子郵件或傳真寄送。

39
募款信

💬 **單字**

advocate *(v.) & (n.)* 提倡;提倡者	**cooperation** *(n.)* 合作	**help** *(n.) & (v.)* 幫助	**request** *(v.) & (n.)* 請求
aid *(v.) & (n.)* 援助	**donation** *(n.)* 捐獻	**humane** *(a.)* 人道的	**rescue** *(v.) & (n.)* 救援
appeal *(v.) & (n.)* 呼籲、籲求	**donor** *(n.)* 捐贈人	**necessity** *(n.)* 必需品	**share** *(v.) & (n.)* 分享
ask *(v.)* 詢問	**encourage** *(v.)* 鼓勵	**need** *(v.) & (n.)* 需要;需求	**solicit** *(v.)* 徵求
assistance *(n.)* 協助	**endow** *(v.)* 資助	**offer** *(v.)* 提供、奉獻	**sponsorship** *(n.)* 贊助
auspices *(n.)* 在……幫助之下	**essential** *(a.)* 必要的	**open-handed** *(a.)* 大方的	**subsidy** *(n.)* 補助、津貼
backing *(n.)* 資助、援助	**favor** *(n.)* 恩惠	**participate** *(v.)* 參與	**supply** *(v.) & (n.)* 供給
befriend *(v.)* 扶助	**foster** *(v.)* 促進	**partnership** *(n.)* 合夥關係	**support** *(v.) & (n.)* 支持
benefactor *(n.)* 捐助人	**furnish** *(v.)* 提供	**patronage** *(v.)* 資助	**tribute** *(n.)* 讚揚
benefit *(n.)* 利益;義演、義賣	**generous** *(a.)* 慷慨的	**petition** *(n.)* 請願	**unsparing** *(a.)* 不吝嗇的
bequest *(n.)* 遺贈、遺產	**gift** *(n.)* 禮物	**philanthropic** *(a.)* 慈善的	**urgent** *(a.)* 急迫的
charity *(n.)* 慈善機構(事業)	**give** *(v.)* 捐贈	**promote** *(v.)* 提倡	
compassionate *(a.)* 有同情心的	**grant** *(v.) & (n.)* 給予;補助金	**public-spirited** *(a.)* 有公益精神的	
contribution *(n.)* 貢獻	**grateful** *(a.)* 感謝的	**relief** *(n.)* 救濟	

39

募款信

a campaign to stop/protect/encourage/support
停止／保護／鼓勵／支持……的活動

acquaint you with
讓你熟悉

adopt the cause of
接受……的目標

all you have to do is
你需要做的只有

as generous as possible
盡可能慷慨相助

as soon as you can
盡快

be good enough to
勞煩去做

broad program of services
廣泛的服務項目

call upon you for
呼籲你為了……

can bring comfort to those in need of
能為那些需要……的人帶來安慰

continue our efforts
延續我們的努力

champion of
……的擁護者

come to the aid of
伸出援手

please join your friends and neighbors in supporting
請加入你的朋友與鄰居，一起支持

financial backing
財務上的支持

for the sake of
為了

give assistance
給予協助

good/guardian angel
守護天使

have the goodness to
勞煩去做

helping hand
援手

humanitarian interests
人道關懷

I am confident that we can
我有信心我們可以

in order to provide the necessary funds
為了提供必要的資金

it can make all the difference
可以為……帶來截然不同的變化

for join forces
聯合協力

make room in your heart for
讓……在心裡佔有一席之地

consider carefully
仔細考慮

make this possible
讓這變得可能

counting on your contribution
仰賴你的捐獻

on account/behalf of
由於／代表……

deserves your thoughtful consideration
值得你仔細考慮

direct your attention to
讓你注意到

pressing need
急迫的需求

our immediate needs are
我們急迫需要的是

rising costs
逐步增加的成本

urgently need you to
迫切需要你去做……

shaping the future
打造未來

welfare of others
他人的福址

special cause/program/need
特別的目標／計畫／需求

with open hands
慷慨地張開雙手

for your contribution will enable
你的捐獻能夠

without your contribution
若沒有你的捐獻

the time has never been better to/for
現在就是……的最佳時機

working together, we can
一起努力，我們可以

your tax-deductible gift
你的可抵稅贈與物

struggling with a worldwide shortage of
為了全球性的……短缺而奮鬥

this program really works because
這個計畫真的有效，因為……

your donation will make it possible
你的捐贈能讓……變得可能

those less fortunate than you
那些比你不幸的人

your past/unselfish generosity
你過去／無私的慷慨

there are no funds presently available for
目前沒有資金供以……

39
募款信

Almost all the money we need to help preserve the Bradgate River Valley comes from people like you.
為了保育布萊門河谷，我們需要您這樣的人的資金協助。

Any amount/contribution is most welcome/appreciated.
我們歡迎／感謝任何金額／捐贈。

Before we can begin raising funds for the new annex, we need volunteers to help with the mailing—will you consider giving several hours of your time to help out?
在我們開始為新附屬建築募款前，我們需要志工幫忙寄信。您是否願意付出幾個小時的時間來幫忙呢？

But without your help, it cannot be done.
但倘若沒有您的幫助，一切不可能成真。

Do it now, please!
現在就做，拜託！

Help us work for a solution to this most tragic disease.
幫助我們為這個不幸的疾病找出解決方法。

Here's how you can help.
您可以協助的方式如下。

I am troubled by the growing incidence of violence in our society, and I know you are too.
社會上層出不窮的暴力事件令我憂慮，我知道您也是如此。

If each family gave only $7.50 we could meet our goal of $5,000.
每個家庭只要捐助 7.5 元，我們便能募得目標金額 5,000 元。

I'll call you next week to see if you can help.
下週我會打電話給您，看看您是否能夠協助。

I'm writing to ask you to join our campaign.
在此寫信邀請您加入我們的活動。

I need your immediate help to make sure our legislation continues to progress despite a fierce lobbying campaign against it.
我需要您立即的協助，以確保我們能繼續推動這項法案的制定，不受到激烈反遊說活動的影響。

In order to take advantage of bulk prices, we need to raise $10,000 before May 1.
為了能使用量販價，我們必須在五月一日前募得 10,000 元。

It can be done!
這能成真！

I thank you from the bottom of my heart.
我發自內心深處感謝您。

It is people like you who make the world a better place.
就是像您這樣的人，才能讓這個世界變得更好。

I want to share a story with you that illustrates for me what heroism is all about.
我想要跟您分享一個故事，在這個故事中我了解到英雄的真義。

I want to tell you about the progress you have made possible.
我想要告訴您現在的進展，這些都因為您而成真。

I will truly appreciate what ever you can give, and I know these young scholars will too.
無論您捐贈什麼，我都會真心感謝，我知道這些年輕的學生也會如此。

Join us today.
今天就加入我們。

Last year, your contribution helped more than 3,000 students come closer to their dream of a liberal arts education.
您去年的捐獻幫助了超過三千名學生，讓他們在人文教育上更接近他們的夢想。

Not a dime of your contribution will be wasted.
您捐獻的一分一毫都不會被浪費。

Now, more than ever, your continued support is needed to help keep the doors open.
現在，我們比任何時候都更需要您的繼續支持，才能持續下去。

Only by working together can we make a difference.
只有齊力合作，我們才能帶來改變。

Our deadline for raising $50,000 is April 1—could you please send your gift by then?
我們募集 50,000 元的截止日期為四月一日，您可以在這之前寄出您的捐贈嗎？

Please be as generous as you can.
請盡可能慷慨相助。

Please encourage your friends and neighbors to call legislators, sign a petition, contribute funds.
請鼓勵您的朋友鄰居打電話給立法委員、簽署請願書並捐獻資金。

Please mail your tax-deductible check in the enclosed postage-paid envelope.
請將您的可抵稅支票放入附件中的回郵信封並郵寄。

Please respond quickly and generously.
請立刻大方回應。

Please take some time to read the enclosed brochure.
請花一些時間閱讀附件中的手冊。

P.S. Write your check and make your phone call today.
附註：今天就開支票、打電話。

Thanks for what ever you can do.
無論您能做什麼，我們都很感謝。

The Cypros Food Shelf presently faces a crisis.
希普蘿絲食物銀行目前正面臨危機。

The people of Port Breedy are counting on you.
布雷迪港的人們正盼望著您的協助。

The Raybrook Foundation is at a financial crossroads this year and we critically need your generous giving to sustain the important work we've begun.
雷布魯克基金會今年遭遇財務困難，我們真的迫切需要您的慷慨捐助，以維持我們開創的重要工作。

We are looking to people like you to help us provide the dollars we need to continue our hospice program.
我們仰賴像您這樣的人提供延續收容所計畫所需的資金。

We invite you to become part of the Annual Giving Campaign.
我們邀請您成為年度捐贈活動的一分子。

We've accomplished a great deal, but much more must be done.
我們已經達成許多成就，但仍有更多尚待完成。

What ever you decide to send, please send it today—the situation is urgent.
無論你決定寄來什麼，請今天就寄，因為情況相當急迫。

When you contribute to the Belknap Foundation, you invest in the future.
當您資助貝克納基金會時，您便是在投資未來。

You don't have to give until it hurts—just give until it feels good.

您不需捐出會讓您心痛的大筆金額——捐出讓您感到滿足的金額就已足夠。

Your contribution will help us expand our resources and do a far more extensive job of protecting our vulnerable waters.

您的捐獻能幫助我們擴增資源，讓我們在保護水源上能做得更多。

Your donation is tax deductible.

您的捐贈可抵稅。

Your generosity to the Boyle County Library Fund will ensure not only that we can preserve existing books, manuscripts, and archives, but also that we can continue to supplement the rising acquisitions budget for new books and periodicals.

您對波爾郡立圖書館基金會的慷慨捐助，不僅讓我們能保住現有的圖書、手稿與檔案庫，還能貼補不斷增加的購書預算，使我們得以添購新的書籍與期刊。

Your generosity will be recognized in *The Anchor*, the monthly organization newsletter.

您的慷慨相助將會刊登於《支柱報》，這是我們機構每月發行的報紙。

Your telephone calls, letters, and checks have made all the difference.

您的電話、信件與支票，讓一切有了不同。

段落

All quality nonprofit organizations need financial resources to help achieve their goals. The Argante Human Services Agency has three basic means of financial support: foundations and corporations; fee services (based on ability to pay); and individuals. Your contribution is, and always has been, critical to our success.

所有優良的非營利組織都需要財務資源，才能達成他們的目標。雅根公共事業機構基本上有三種資金來源：基金會與企業；收費服務（根據經濟狀況付費）；個人。您的捐獻對我們的成功至關重要，現在是如此、一直以來都是如此。

You are cordially invited to the Holiday Open House, to be held Saturday evening December 12, from 7 p.m. to midnight, at the Bildad Mansion on Melville Avenue. This annual fundraiser for Pequod Elementary School is open to the public and will feature Victorian carols and refreshments, old-time vaudeville entertainment at 10:30 p.m., and "Nutcracker" characters circulating all evening long. Join us for a delightful and unforgettable evening of holiday magic. The suggested donation of $20/person is tax deductible.

真心邀請您前來假日招待會，十二月十二日（週日）傍晚七點於梅維爾路上的比達公館舉行。這場為佩果小學募款的年度招待會，開放給大眾參加，會中包含維多莉亞式聖誕頌歌與茶點，以及復古歌舞雜耍演出（晚上十點半），整個晚上還會有胡桃鉗人物在場上巡迴表演。與我們一同享受這個愉快而難忘的魔幻假日傍晚。建議每人捐贈 20 元，可抵稅。

As you know, district school budgets are limited and cannot cover many items we want our students to have. A group of your friends and neighbors wants to raise $3,000 to provide the items on the attached list. Can you contribute to this fund to provide additional learning opportunities for our children? Every cent we receive will go directly to school supplies and services.

如您所知，區域學校預算有限，無法納入許多我們希望學生能擁有的項目。您的朋友與鄰居中，有一群人希望能募集 3,000 元，幫助學生擁有附件清單中的項目。您是否願意為此捐款，讓我們的孩子有其他的學習機會？我們收到的每一分錢，都會直接用於學校用品與服務上。

39

募款信

Will you be breathing cleaner air next year, or not? It's up to you. A bill currently before the state legislature (SF1011) will set new, lower levels of tolerable pollution for rural and urban areas. To convince lawmakers of the importance of this bill, I need you to sign the enclosed petition and return it to me at once. Time is running out—the bill comes out of committee later this month. A successful petition drive requires your signed petition... and your dollars. Along with your signed petition, I'm asking you to return a contribution of $25 or $50 to support lobbying efforts for this important measure. But please hurry!

明年您是否能呼吸到更乾淨的空氣？這取決於您。一項目前尚未經過州議會決議的法案（SF1011）將提出新的修改，以降低農業與都市區的汙染標準值。為了讓立法者了解此法案的重要性，我需要您簽署附件中的請願書，並立即寄還給我。成功的請願活動不只需要您的簽名……也需要您的資助。在您寄還已簽名之請願書時，希望您也能附上 25 元或 50 元的捐款，援助我們對此重要法案的遊說活動。但請立刻行動！

Because the School Enrichment Council is organized for the purpose of lobbying and influencing legislation, your gift or donation is not deductible under current IRS guidelines as a charitable contribution. It may, however, be deductible as a business expense. If you have questions, please contact the SEC or your tax accountant.

由於「改善校園協調會」是為了遊說、影響立法而組成，按照目前國家稅務局的規定，您的贈與物與捐款作為慈善奉獻時無法抵稅。不過，若作為業務支出，則可以抵稅。若您有任何問題，請聯絡證券交易委員會或您的稅務會計師。

示範信

Dear Mrs. Ogmore-Pritchard,
> One can do much. And one and one and one can move mountains.
> —Joan Ward-Harris

Will you be one of the ones who will help us move mountains? We have one particular mountain in mind—the mountain of unconcern, neglect, abuse, and wrongful use of many of our wilderness areas.
The enclosed copies of recent newspaper articles will give you an idea of the problems facing us today. Also enclosed is an invitation to become a member and support our efforts to move this mountain!

奧格默－普里察夫人您好：

一個人能做的有很多，而三個人甚至能移動一座山。

——瓊·沃德－哈里斯

您願意幫忙我們移山嗎？我們心中有著一座山，這座山充滿著對野生區域的不關心、漠視、傷害與濫用。

隨信附上最近的報紙文章，讓您了解我們今日所面臨的問題。同時也附上一張邀請卡，敬邀您成為我們的會員，支持我們移動這座山脈的努力！

Dear Fred and Aline,

I deeply appreciate your contribution. Thanks to the outstanding people who have worked on the campaign, we have accomplished a great deal. My commitment to public education is stronger than ever. I am pleased to have your confidence and support.

The campaign has grown in scope and intensity. In the remaining days, we are reaching out to large numbers of voters in a variety of ways. There is still much to be done. Please remember to tell your friends and neighbors to vote on November 7.

After the election, I will have eight weeks before the important School Board work begins. I will continue to prepare myself for the issues and problems facing our schools. I look forward to your continued input now and in the future.

Thank you again, Fred and Aline, for your help.

Sincerely yours,

親愛的弗雷與艾琳：

真心感謝你們的捐助。多虧了為此競選活動努力的優秀人才，我們才能達成這麼多成果。我對於公立學校的投入更勝以往，我很高興你們對我的信心與支持。

這次的競選活動在規模與強度上都成長許多。在剩下的幾天，我們會用各種方法去吸引大量的選民，所以還有很多要做的事情。請告訴你們的朋友與鄰居，十一月七日務必去投票。

在選舉結束後，重要的學校董事會還有八週才會開始。我會繼續做好準備，了解我們學校面臨的問題與困難。我期盼你們持續的支持，無論是現在或是未來。

弗雷與艾琳，再次謝謝你們的協助。

○○敬上

✉ 參見：03 回應、12 致謝函、14 收件通知、17 後續追蹤信、18 邀請函、20 請求與詢問、21 接受、22 拒絕、28 求職信、33 商譽信

Chapter 40

具合約效力信
Letters that Serve as Contracts

在達成共識的過程中，
溝通不良的程度與花費的金額成正比。

——美國勵志作家羅伯特・林格（Robert J. Ringer）

信件可以作為簡短的非正式合約。這種信是否需要律師檢查，取決於合約內容的複雜度，以及寫不好時可能帶來的負面後果。

 PART 1 說明篇

合約信能做什麼？

達成協議	變更條款	決定租金
取消協議或合約	給予工作指令	制定租約

該怎麼說？

1. 在主旨中寫明合約性質，如Re: Tuckpointing at 1711 Grismer Avenue「關於：葛林斯默大道 1711 號牆面磚縫嵌填」。
2. 以類似的句子起頭：This letter will serve as a contract between...「此封信將作為……之間的合約。」
3. 在協議或合約上，加入立約雙方的姓名與地址。
4. 闡明雙方提供的義務及獲益的事項。
5. 明確指出工作完成及付清款項的日期。
6. 說明合約是否能取消，或在什麼條件之下可取消。
7. 明確指出希望對方在什麼日期之前簽名並寄回此信。
8. 在信件最下方留數行空白，讓雙方能簽名並寫下簽名日期。

什麼不該說？

- 別納入任何與合約無關的內容，這份文件的焦點必須清晰。
- 不要為了讓合約看起來比較專業而使用法律專有名詞（除非你是律師）。請用簡單的標準英文，避免之後另一方聲稱他們「看不懂」部分的合約條款。

寫作祕訣

- 在下筆之前，列出所有能保護這份協約的要素（如：期限、價格上限、獨立督察員）。找了解狀況的人幫你再次檢查。
- 不必擔心你寫出來的語句太過口語化。你可以使用人稱代名詞及正常的句子結構，如 I promise to... in exchange for...「我同意……以交換……」。另一方面，請保持有條不紊的口氣，讓對方信任這封信，增強以此信作為合約的效力。
- 信件的本文可以短至僅有一個段落的篇幅，亦可以長至包含許多段落。若包含數段，務必以清晰、有邏輯的方式組織你的資訊。

特殊狀況

- **制定或取消合約時**，如果時間是很重要的一環，請要求對方回寄回條或收件通知，這樣便能知道對方收到信件的日期。如果租約規定你必須在三十天前給予通知，那這紙回覆就能證明你是在期限內寄達。
- **繳交提案並認為對方會接受時**，可以在最後面加上 Approved by [signature] on [date] by [printed name and title].「由〔印刷體姓名及職稱〕於〔日期〕經〔簽名〕許可。」，將這份提案轉化為具法律約束力的合約或協議。
- **借錢給家人或朋友時**，一封寫明金額、日期與責任的合約信，能讓各方都受益良多。

格式

- 所有合約或具合約效力的信件，都應打在有信頭的商用信紙、或是有信頭的私用信紙，或品質好的證券紙上。
- 如果你的公司時常為同類型的業務制定合約，就可以使用制式信。

單字

agreement *(n.)* 協議	condition *(n.)* 條件	negotiation *(n.)* 談判	transaction *(n.)* 交易
arrangement *(n.)* 安排	confirm *(v.)* 確認	obligation *(n.)* 義務	understanding *(n.)* 理解
assure *(v.)* 使放心	conform *(v.)* 符合	provision *(n.)* 條款、規定	underwrite *(v.)* 簽名同意
bind *(v.)* 使具法律效力	consent *(v.)* 許可、同意	settlement *(n.)* 決議	verify *(v.)* 證實、核對
certify *(v.)* 證明	endorse *(v.)* 贊同	stipulation *(n.)* 條款、規定	warrant *(v.)* 授權
clause *(n.)* 條款	guarantee *(v.)* & *(n.)* 保證	terms *(n.)* 條款、條件	

詞組

agreed-to terms 達成共識的條款	mutual satisfaction 雙方皆滿意
articles of the agreement 協議中的條款	on condition that 在……的條件下
as of the agreed-upon date 自雙方同意之日起生效	please sign and date 請簽名並註明日期
comply with 同意履行	reach an understanding 達成理解
considered complete when 當……視為完成	return this letter by 在……前回寄此信

effective as of/until
自⋯⋯生效／生效至⋯⋯為止

in return, you agree to
作為交換，你同意

terms listed below
下列條款

句子

Enclosed is a check for $500, which will serve as earnest money for the purchase of apartment #37 in the 131 Park Drive building.
隨信附上 500 元支票，作為購買帕克街 131 號大樓 37 號公寓的訂金。

In the event of disagreement about the quality of the work, the dispute will be submitted to independent arbitration with costs being shared equally by both parties.
若對工作品質有異議，將交由獨立的仲裁員裁決，費用由雙方平均分攤。

Note: This contract may be withdrawn by us if not accepted within 10 days.
注意：若未於十日內接受，我們將撤回此合約。

Paragraph N of the contract is irrelevant to the matter at hand; please delete it and initial and return this letter.
合約第 N 項與目前事務無關，請刪除並簽上姓名首字母，然後回寄此信。

The enclosed forward currency contract constitutes an agreement to deliver or receive a present stated amount of currency at a future specified date.
隨信附上之遠期外匯合約，同意於未來指定日期支付或收取合約指定之外幣金額。

This letter serves as a contract between Madge Allen and Cain & Sons for sheetrock and plaster repair to the property at 35 James Court, with the following conditions and specifications.
此信作為梅吉・艾倫與肯恩公司之間合約，規範詹姆斯法院路 35 號建築之石膏板與灰泥整修事宜，包括下列條件與規格要求。

This letter will serve as an informal agreement between us covering the period from January 1, 2018, to December 31, 2019, for the following services.
這封信將作為我們之間的非正式合約，範圍包括二〇一八年一月一日至二〇一九年十二月三十一日期間之下列服務。

段落

We will pay the mortgage payments on your town house from now until Simon graduates next June. Based on Hatty's job, the two of you will pay the Homeowners Association monthly fee, your utilities, and other housingrelated expenses. When Simon becomes employed and your incomes stabilize, we'll discuss selling the town house to you on a contract for deed basis. When you eventually sell it, we expect to receive the $45,000 we have put into it plus a percentage of the appreciation of the town house's value (if it has appreciated 25 percent we will receive $45,000 + 25 percent of that amount).

從現在起至賽門明年六月畢業期間,我們會為你的聯棟別墅支付抵押貸款費用。你們兩人須以哈蒂的工作薪水繳交每月管理委員會費、水電瓦斯費以及其他居住相關費用。等賽門找到工作,你們的收入穩定下來時,我們可討論簽訂房契交付合約,將這間聯棟別墅出售給你們。如果你們最後要把房子賣出,我們希望能拿回我們投入的 45,000 元,外加符合該住宅增值率之漲價金額(若增值率為百分之二十五,我們則應收到 45,000 元加上漲價金額之百分之二十五)。

I am happy to lend you the money to buy the truck. As we discussed, you will repay the $9,000 loan over a period of 36 months in the amount of $250 per month. There will be no interest. Please sign and date the second copy of this letter and return it to me.

我很樂意借錢給你買貨車。如我們所討論的,你會償還 9,000 元借款,分成三十六個月期間支付,每個月支付 250 元,沒有利息。請在這封信的第二份副本上簽名並註明日期,再歸還給我。

I agree to translate your Moroccan contracts, letters, faxes, and other messages for the fee of $35 per hour. I further agree to complete the outstanding translations by February 10. You will pay messenger service fees between your office and mine, parking fees for consultations at your offices, and postage for mail or overnighting services.

我同意為您翻譯來自摩洛哥的合約、信件、傳真與其他訊息,收費為一小時 35 元。我亦同意在二月十日前完成未繳交的譯文。您將支付雙方辦公室間的快遞服務費用、於您辦公室商談時之停車費用,以及信件郵資與隔夜抵達郵遞費用。

Acceptance of contract: The above prices, specifications, and conditions are satisfactory and are hereby accepted. You are authorized to do the work as specified. Payment will be made upon completion. Date of acceptance: May 6, 2018. Authorized signature: Bernard Boweri

同意接受合約:我滿意並接受上述之價格、內容及條件,您已得到授權,可依所述內容進行作業,報酬將於完成時付清。接受合約日期:二〇一八年五月六日。授權簽名:伯納德‧包威禮

Dear Mr. Bowling,

As required by our lease, we hereby give you thirty days' notice of our intention to move from Apartment 2 at 619 Fourth Street.

Please call any evening after 6 p.m. to let us know when you need to show the apartment.

Our rent deposit of $450 will need to be refunded to us as we have not damaged the apartment in any way during our tenancy.

We have enjoyed our two years here very much, and will be sorry to move.

Sincerely yours,

波林先生您好：

根據租約規定，我們特於三十天前通知您，我們希望搬離第四街 619 號第二公寓。

請於任一天傍晚六點後致電給我們，告知您何時會帶客人來看房。

租房期間我們並未對公寓造成任何損害，因此租屋訂金 450 元應退還給我們。

我們很享受住在這裡的兩年時間，很可惜我們必須搬離。

○○敬上

40

具合約效力信

Dear Ms. Hart:

Pryke Financial Services Inc. will be happy to act as Investment Adviser to the Collins Foundation and, as such, will assist with cash management and investment of foundation funds with the exception of the initial investment of the bond issue proceeds from certain bond issues.

We agree to provide the following services:

1. A complete review and analysis of the Collins Foundation's financial structure and conditions.

2. The preparation of written investment objectives outlining preferable investments, portfolio goals, risk limits, and diversification possibilities.

3. The establishment of preferred depository or certificate arrangements with banks or savings and loans.

4. Soliciting bids for guaranteed investment agreements.

5. Monitoring fund transfers, verifying receipt of collateral, completing documentation.

6. Working with a governmental securities dealer to execute governmental security transactions.

7. Meeting with your treasurer and financial adviser periodically and with your board of directors as requested.

8. Providing monthly portfolio status reports with sufficient detail for accounting and recording purposes.

Pryke Financial Services Inc. will submit quarterly statements for services. Our fees will be billed in advance and calculated by multiplying .000375 times the Collins Foundation's invested portfolio at the beginning of each calendar quarter (.0015 annually).

Fees will be adjusted at the end of each quarter to reflect the rate times the average invested balance for the previous quarter. Adjustments will be included in the next billing.

Fees can be reviewed and adjusted annually on the anniversary date of this contract.

This agreement will run from June 1, 2018, through June 1, 2019, but may be canceled by either party without cause with thirty days' written notice.

Sincerely,

Grace Bloom

President

The above agreement is accepted by the Collins Foundation (blanks for date, signatures, titles).

哈特小姐您好：

普萊克金融服務公司很樂意作為柯林斯基金會的投資顧問，將協助管理現金及基金會資金的投資，但某些債券發行之初始投資不包含在管理範圍內。

我們同意提供以下服務：

一、針對柯林斯基金會的財務結構與狀況提供完整的審查與分析。

二、準備書面投資計畫，簡述適宜的投資對象、投資目標、風險限額及分散投資的可能性。

三、安排適合的存儲機構，或銀行證券，或儲蓄信貸。

四、為約定好的投資協議招標。

五、監督資金移轉、確認抵押品的收取、完成文件編整。

六、與政府證券交易商合作執行政府證券交易。

七、與您的財務主管及財務顧問定期開會，並於您要求時與董事會會面。

八、提供每月投資報告，內含可供會計與記帳使用之充分細節。

普萊克金融服務公司每季會提供服務報表。我們會提前寄發帳單，費用之計算方式為柯林斯基金會於每季首日已投資金額乘以 .000375（即每年乘以 .0015）。每季終時將調整收費，以符合前一季平均投資金額乘上費率後之金額。調整後的費用將反映在下一期帳單。

於每年合約週年日時，可審查並調整收費。

本協議自二〇一八年六月一日起生效，效力至二〇一九年六月一日，但任一方皆可於三十日前寄發書面通知後終止協議，毋須特定事由。

總裁葛蕾絲・布倫敬上

上述協議已獲柯林斯基金會接受（留空格供對方寫日期、簽名及職稱）。

參見：14 收件通知、21 接受、35 客訴處理信、37 訂單處理信

40

具合約效力信

Chapter 41

信貸相關信
Letters about Credit

現在這個世界真古怪，
每家銀行都寄信用卡給我們……
想像一下，有家銀行竟然把信用卡寄給兩位超過一百歲的老太太！
這些人究竟在想些什麼？

——美國民權先鋒莎拉與伊莉莎白・迪藍尼（Sarah and A. Elizabeth Delany）

與申請或提供信貸相關的書面文件，大多都已經按照政府或機構的規定與指示，製成標準化的表格。然而，對於非例行的事件，仍須小心撰寫。

 PART 1 說明篇

哪些信件與信貸有關？

申請信用卡 現金卡	**催繳帳款** 參見：38 催款信	**拒絕信貸申請** 參見：22 拒絕
申請貸款	**拖欠帳款**	**與金融聯合徵信中心往來**
銀行帳戶相關 開戶、取消或重啟帳戶	**信用記錄有關** 取得信用記錄、記錄有誤	**解釋信貸申請遭拒理由** 或說明條件
延長繳費期限	**恭喜客戶信用紀錄良好** 參見：42 銷售信	**親朋好友借錢**

該怎麼說？

- **向金融聯合徵信中心申請信用報告時**，須提供雙證件（第一證件身分證，第二證件如健保卡、護照、駕照、新式戶口名簿）姓名，可事先於網站上填寫申請書。

- **寫信給某人或某公司詢問職缺申請人的信用紀錄時**，請提供那個人的姓名及地址、請求相關之信用資訊、簡要解釋你想要這些資訊的原因（如：正在討論合夥）、聲明你會將資訊保密、表達你的感謝，並附上一回郵信封供對方回信。在有些情況下，你也可以說明你是如何找到他們的（如：經由考慮的人選介紹）。詢問問題時則要具體：您認識那個人多長時間？當時您是什麼身分？您提供了哪種信貸？目前的餘額有多少？那個人的付款模式？他在那裡工作了多久？他收入為何？

- **要求修正錯誤的信用紀錄時**，須提供全名與地址、指出紀錄中錯誤的部分，並解釋錯誤的理由。附上相關單據（結算單、貸款文件、納稅申報單、薪資明細表）來證實你的說法。要求對方提供修正後的報告。最後記得感謝對方，畢竟他們極有可能不是犯錯的人，而是能幫助你的人。

- **拒絕提供信貸時**：感謝對方的申請意願；為你無法提供貸款表示遺憾；向對方保證你已仔細評估他們的申請；建議其他做法（分期預付購貨、付現金、小額貸款）以維持合作關係；鼓勵他們之後再次申請。若對方有進一步的問題，可列出你們的信貸條件、指出對方信用紀錄中的問題，並告知你是從哪裡取得信用資料。若是較小額、例行的信貸申請，可以用制式信簡單告知 Your request for a loan has been denied.「您的貸款申請未通過。」下方則以可勾選的清單列出未通過的可能原因：受雇時長、資料不足、債務過多、為該區新住戶故尚未有信用紀錄、付款紀錄不良、債權遭扣押。信中設置空格，填寫你取得資訊的出處。

- **核准信貸申請時**，須聲明你已核准了申請、指明核准的金額與生效日期，並說明還款程序。隨信附上須給對方簽名的文件，以及如何填寫這些文件的說明書。接著你可以歡迎新客戶加入你的信貸機構或公司、感謝他們選擇與你合作，並建議他們將所有信貸需求交給你們公司處理。

什麼不該說？

- 不要寫任何無法以文件證明的事情。像「未付款」或「習慣性逾期付款」這類的詞語，都必須有單據支持，才能證明這些付款習慣。

寫作訣竅

- 信貸相關事務必須保密。要做好一切措施保護你提供或收到的信用資訊。

- 提供他人的信用紀錄資訊時，務必要正確。再三檢查資料、姓名拼寫及帳戶號碼。
- 保持得體。即便是信用紀錄不佳的人，也希望聽到自己的好話。瑪莉・歐文・克勞瑟（Mary Owens Crowther）在其一九二三年出版的書中寫道：「以不得體的方式處理信貸事務，是目前所知最快摧毀商譽的方法。」

特殊狀況

- **親朋好友之間的借貸**，時常會造成財務與交情上的損失。**若想讓對方借錢給你**，必須實事求是、有條有理：告知金額及用錢原因，並提出償付計畫與利息。一定要先給對方臺階下，如 You may have financial problems of your own, for all I know.「就我所知，你可能在經濟上也有困難。」；This may not be a good time for you.「也許這對你來說並不是個好時機。」；You may disapprove, on principle, of loans between friends.「也許你在原則上是不贊成朋友之間借錢的。」向他們保證，即使他們拒絕，也不必有罪惡感。不要哀求他們或博取同情；對一個不願借錢給你的人施加壓力，並不會讓你得到錢，反而會讓你失去一個朋友。
  拒絕借錢給親朋好友時，請簡短回應：I wish I could help you, but it's not possible just now.「我希望我能幫上忙，但目前實在不可能。」不要解釋太多或道歉，或拐彎抹角。如果需要，可以在結尾詢問能否幫其他的忙。
  同意借錢給朋友或家人時，應明確寫下出借的金額、借錢條件與償還日期、利息及其他資訊。寄兩份信函給對方，請他簽名、註明簽名日期，再把一份寄還給你。
  若你**要提醒朋友或家人借款已逾期**，一開始的口氣先保持委婉：I know how busy you've been...「我知道你最近很忙……」；Did you forget about...「你是否忘了……」；Didn't we agree you'd repay the loan December 1?「我們不是說好，你會在十二月一日償付借款？」如果你已經是第二次寄信，可附上協議書的影本，並用比較強硬的措詞表達拿回借款的需求。
- **若你無法按時支付貸款**，應馬上寫信通知對方。先為你的逾期道歉，再告訴對方你會盡快付清，並附上你能負擔的一部分餘款，什麼金額都行。若你能為逾期付款提出合理的理由（疾病、臨時解雇），請讓對方知道；若不然，則不必解釋太多，你的債權人更想知道的是，你會為此帳款負起責任。

格式

- 基本上，信貸相關的事務絕不會使用手寫信。例行的聯繫可以使用制式信，其餘則會打在有信頭的商用信紙上。

PART 2 應用篇

單字

application *(n.)* 申請	installment *(n.)* 分期付款	receipt *(n.)* 收據	reimburse *(v.)* 償還
approval *(n.)* 核准	IOU *(n.)* 借條	requirement *(n.)* 必要條件	repay *(v.)* 償還
arrangement *(n.)* 安排	lender *(n.)* 借出人	guarantee *(v.) & (n.)* 保證	verify *(v.)* 核對、證實
balance *(n.)* 餘額	lessor *(n.)* 出租人	default *(v.) & (n.)* 違約、拖欠	creditworthy *(a.)* 信用可靠的
collateral *(n.)* 抵押品	lien *(n.)* 先得權、留置權	finance *(v.) & (n.)* 提供資金；財務	regretfully *(adv.)* 遺憾地
debt *(n.)* 債務	mortgage *(n.)* 抵押契據	loan *(v.) & (n.)* 貸款	
funds *(n.)* 資金、現款	nonpayment *(n.)* 未付款		

詞組

after careful consideration 在審慎考慮後	due to cash flow difficulties 由於金流上的困難
apply for credit privileges 申請信用優惠	current/up-to-date financial statement 目前／最新的財務報表
although you have only occasional payment problems 雖然你只是偶爾有付款問題	due to a rise in the number of uncollectable past-due accounts 由於無法收回之逾期帳款數目增加

as much as we would like to extend
credit to you
儘管我們真的很想提供信貸給你

cannot justify approval
無法合理通過

cash basis only
只用現金制

consistently on-time credit payments
持續按時償付貸款

in checking your credit background
檢查你的信用紀錄

it is our policy
這是我們的政策

I understand and appreciate your
position, but
我理解且能體會你的立場，但是

late payments
逾期付款

must delay payment
必須延遲付款

one of our credit requirements is
我們其中一項信貸條件為

pattern of late payments
逾期付款的習慣

pay in advance/in full
提前／全額付款

pleased to be able to accommodate you
我們很樂意通融

poor payment history
不良的付款紀錄

credit application/history/record/
standing/rating/limit
信用申請／歷史／紀錄／狀況／等級／限度

excellent credit rating
優異的信用評等

financial difficulties/needs/services
財務困難／需求／服務

preferred customer
貴賓客戶

regret that we are unable to
遺憾我們無法

responsible use of credit
為信貸負責

subject only to normal credit
requirements
只適用一般信用條件

steady credit payments
穩定信用償還記錄

review of our files
審閱我們的檔案

unable to accommodate you at this time
這次無法通融

unpaid balance
未付餘額

we are happy/pleased to approve
我們很高興／樂意能通過

will you please run a credit check on...
你能否檢查……的信用紀錄

Because our inquiries disclosed a number of past-due and unpaid accounts, we are unable to extend the line of credit you requested.
經調查發現，您有數項逾期未付的帳款，所以無法提供您所要求的信貸額度給您。

Could you see your way clear to lending me $200 for approximately three weeks, until I receive my income tax refund (enclosed is a copy of my return, showing the amount I will be receiving)?
你可以借我 200 元嗎？等三週後我收到所得稅退稅款項，便會將錢還你（附件為我的退稅申請，上面有我即將收到的金額）。

Cressida Mary MacPhail, 1968 Taylor Avenue, Bretton, IN 47834, has applied to the Maxwell Credit Union for a loan, and gave us your name as a reference.
葵希妲‧瑪麗‧麥費爾（47834 印第安納州布雷頓市泰勒大道 1968 號）向麥斯威爾信用合作社申請貸款，並將您的名字提供給我們作為信用紀錄查詢對象。

Eileen Schwartz has had an excellent credit history with this company, and we recommend her highly as a credit customer.
愛琳‧史威茲在本公司的信用紀錄良好，我們強烈推薦她成為信用客戶。

I appreciate your courtesy in allowing me to pay off the balance of my account in small installments.
謝謝您的好意，讓我能分期償付帳戶餘款。

I'm writing to notify you of an error in our credit history and to request an immediate correction.
在此告知您，我們的信用紀錄中有一項錯誤，我們請求立即修正。

I would appreciate your raising my credit limit from $10,000 to $20,000.
謝謝您將我的信用額度自 10,000 元提升至 20,000 元。

Please close my Fortis-Pryde account, effective immediately.
請關閉我在福帝普萊的帳戶，立即生效。

Please keep us in mind for your other credit needs.
若您有其他信貸需求，請考慮我們。

The credit bureau cites repeated credit delinquencies.
商業徵信所指出多次信貸拖欠紀錄。

We are pleased to report that our credit dealings with Angela Crossby have been excellent.

我們很高興通知您，安琪拉‧克勞斯比在我們公司的信用紀錄相當優異。

We are puzzled that our application for a home equity line of credit has been refused—please send us a copy of our credit report, if that was the problem, or your explanation for this refusal.

我們想知道為何我們的房屋淨值信用貸款申請遭到退回。若我們的信用報告是問題所在，請寄一份給我們，或請解釋您們退回申請的原因。

We are unable to furnish you with any current credit information on Emerson-Toller—they have not been a credit customer of ours for over ten years.

我們無法提供您任何關於艾默森托勒公司的最新信用狀況，因為他們已經超過十年不是我們的信用客戶。

We expect to be making large purchases of office furniture from your firm as well as routine purchases of office supplies and would like to open a credit account with you.

我們計劃要向您的公司大量採購辦公室傢俱，並會例行向您們購買辦公室用品，故希望能與您們開設一信用帳戶。

We have run into some difficulties checking the references you supplied.

我們在檢查您提供的信用紀錄時遭遇了困難。

We note a persistent pattern of nonpayment in your credit history.

我們注意到在您的信用歷史中有持續的未付款紀錄。

We suggest you reapply for the loan once you have resolved some of these problems.

我們建議在您解決其中一些問題後，重新申請貸款。

We will appreciate any credit information you can give us about Walter Tillotson.

若您能提供任何關於華特‧提洛森的信用資料，我們會非常感謝。

段落

Enclosed please find a check for $457.32, which will bring my account up to date. I am sorry that I let the account become past due. I expect to keep it current in the future.

隨信附上 457.32 元支票以付清餘款。很抱歉帳款逾期了，未來我會按時繳費。

I would like to see the credit record you currently have on me. I am applying for a second mortgage on my home next month, and would not want to be unpleasantly surprised by anything that may be on file. Thank you.

我希望能查看目前您手上關於我的信用紀錄。下個月我將用我的房子申請抵押貸款，所以我不希望在我的檔案上有任何令人不快的意外紀錄。謝謝您。

I am pleased to report that we were able to approve your loan request for the amount of $5,000. A check is enclosed, along with a payment booklet and a packet of payment envelopes. Please read your repayment schedule carefully.

我們很高興通知您，我們已核准您的貸款申請，金額為 5,000 元。隨信附上支票、償付規定手冊與一疊付款信封袋。請仔細閱讀您的還款流程。

We are sorry to report that your loan application has not been approved. Our decision was based primarily on information received from the Carnaby Reporting Services credit bureau. You may want to look at their record on you to verify that it is correct. If it is, we suggest working with a financial counselor, something that has been helpful to several of our customers. We will be happy to review your loan application at a later date if your circumstances change.

我們很遺憾通知您，您的貸款申請未通過。我們的決定主要基於卡納比商業徵信所提供的資料。您或許希望查看他們提供的紀錄，並確認是否正確。若為正確，我們建議您向金融顧問諮詢，我們的許多顧客都因此得到幫助。之後若您的情況有所改變，我們很樂意再次審查您的貸款申請。

41

信貸相關信

In order to set up a credit account for you with Copper Beeches, we need the following information: company name and tax identification number; a copy of your annual report; the names of banks with which you currently have accounts and those account numbers; names and phone numbers of at least three companies from which you have purchased materials in the past six months. We appreciate your business and look forward to serving you.

為了幫您在庫柏畢許開立信用帳戶，我們需要以下資訊：公司名稱與統一編號；一份年度報表；目前已開戶之銀行名稱及帳戶號碼；您在過去半年曾購買材料的公司名稱與電話，至少三家。感謝您與我們合作，期盼能盡快為您服務。

示範信

TO: Dudley Credit Data
FROM: Eustace Landor, Landor First Banks
DATE: September 3, 2018
RE: Edith Millbank
    Will you please run a credit check for us on:
        Edith Millbank
        1844 Coningsby
        Oswald, OH 45042
        Social Security #000-00-0000
    Ms. Millbank is taking out a loan application with us, and we wish to verify the information she has given us with regard to her credit history.
    Thank you.

收信人：達利信用數據
寄件人：尤堤思・藍多，藍多第一銀行
日期：二〇一八年九月三日
回覆：伊蒂絲・米爾班
    可否請您為我們檢查以下客戶之信用紀錄：
        伊蒂絲・米爾班
        45042 俄亥俄州奧斯沃市柯寧斯比 1844 號
        社會安全號碼 000-00-0000
    米爾班小姐正在向我們申請貸款，而我們想確認她提供給我們的信用紀錄資料是正確的。
    謝謝您。

Dear Ms. Panzoust,

Thank you for your letter of March 16 requesting our opinion of the creditworthiness of Valmouth Fiber Arts.

We have had only the most limited business transactions with them and, since they have always been on a cash basis with us, we have no idea of their financial standing. I would not feel comfortable expressing an opinion on so little information.

I'm sorry I couldn't have been more helpful.

彭佐斯小姐您好：

謝謝您於三月六日的來信，信中您詢問我們對於佛茂司纖維藝術中心的信用狀況的看法。

我們與他們之間的交易經驗有限，而且他們一直都是以現金交易，所以我們並不了解他們的財務狀況。由於資訊的不足，我想我並不方便表示意見。

很抱歉我無法幫上忙。

Re: Loan #211925

Dear Ms. Parry-Lewis,

We have reviewed your request for a renewal of your home equity loan, as required by Raine National Bank every five years. In addition to a pattern of late payments and frequent disagreements about interest payments, we find that your current financial obligations seem excessive for your stated income. As a result, we are unable to grant you a renewal.

We would be happy to serve your banking needs in the future. If you meet our criteria for a home equity loan renewal in six months, please reapply and we will waive the newloan fees.

Sincerely,

關於：貸款 #211925

派瑞－李維小姐您好：

我們已經審查您對於房產淨值貸款的展期申請。按瑞恩國家銀行規定，此貸款每五年便須展期一次。您有逾期付款的習慣，且經常不同意利息的支付；除此之外，我們也發現以您填寫的收入而言，您目前的債務似乎已超出負擔範圍。因此，我們無法讓您續約展期。

我們很樂意未來繼續為您提供銀行服務。若您在六個月內達成房產淨值貸款的展期條件，請重新申請，我們會免除您的開辦手續費。

○○敬上

✉ 參見：03 回應、12 致謝函、13 致歉信、14 收件通知、15 公告通知、20 請求與詢問、22 拒絕、
25 抱怨與客訴、35 客訴處理信、37 訂單處理信、38 催款信

Chapter 42

銷售信
Sales Letters

> 廣告是現代文學類型中最有趣也最困難的一種。
>
> ——英國小說家阿道斯·赫胥黎

從公司、企業或組織寄出的信，都算是銷售信，即便是那些與交易無關的信，如慰問信、恭賀信、感謝函與致歉信，都帶有第二層的訊息：希望收信人能想起公司。成功的公司所寄的信，都是有禮貌、清晰、準確而有說服力。

並非每樣產品與服務都適合使用銷售信，不過，透過銷售信，收信人打電話或造訪店面的機會會大大增高，也會帶動實際的銷售。跟印製廣告單或拍廣告相比，銷售信有效又省錢，在多數公司的行銷策略中，銷售信都是核心的一環。

銷售信目前運作已經相當成熟，因此，許多企業不需再親自撰寫這種信，而交給能提供全套服務的事務所來處理所有廣告，包括銷售信。

PART 1 說明篇

銷售信包含哪些？

布達產品消息 推出新品、產品變更	**請求會面拜訪** 參見預約	**郵購廣告** 或網路廣告
後續追蹤 如詢問、銷售	**制式信**	**商譽** 參見：33 商譽信

提供試用	問卷調查	回應問題
特別宣傳 優惠、免費服務、禮物	致謝信 感謝購買或付款	邀請 參與優惠活動、成為新會員

該怎麼說？

1. 用開場的句子、問題，故事或統計數據，引起收件人的注意力。

2. 用一個強烈的關鍵訊息，使對方產生興趣。

3. 使用具體、生動的詞語，以及強而有力的動作動詞，引起收件人對產品的欲望。有一個字永不落伍：new（新的）。

4. 指出你的服務或產品與其他商品有何不同，強調其品質與可靠性。

5. 讓你的讀者相信，回應你的信是聰明之舉，並附上證據（樣品、證詞、統計數據）。

6. 提供獲得產品或服務的管道。

7. 給予一個立即行動的理由：限量、優惠期間即將結束、未來價格上漲、早鳥折扣。

8. 清楚表達希望對方採取何種行動：Telephone now for an appointment.「現在就打電話預約。」；Order one for every family member.「為每位家人都訂一個。」；Call today to arrange a demonstration.「今天就打電話安排產品展示。」；Return the postage-paid reply card now.「現在就回寄已付郵資的卡片。」；Send for your free copy of the planning guide.「寄回即可領取免費計畫指南。」

9. 讓收件人方便回覆：提供訂貨單與回郵信封；附上貼有郵資的明信片，可提供選項，讓收件人勾選是否需要業務去電詢問或索取額外資訊；提供當地經銷商的電話，或直接下訂的免費服務專線；提供現在訂購、稍後付款的服務；列出分店營業時間與地點清單。（比起由買方支付郵資的商務信件，由賣方支付郵資的商務信回覆率高了百分之十到二十。）

10. 最後，用不同方式重複一次開場白。如果你在一開始引用名人說過的話，那最後你可以收尾如下：And that's why So-and-So won't drive anything but a...「這也是為什麼某某人不開其他的車，只開……」

11. 加上一段附註（P.S.），重述重點、強調特色，或提出一個有力的新論點，如保證退款、限時優惠、現在購買的額外折扣：P.S. To offer you these sale prices, we must receive your order by June 30.「附註：為了保證您能用這個優惠價購買，我們必須在六月三十日前收到

您的訂單。」；P.S. Don't forget—your fee includes a gift!「附註：別忘了，您付的費用包含禮物！」；P.S. If you are not completely satisfied, return your Roebel Pager and we will cheerfully issue you a full refund.「附註：如果您對商品不甚滿意，請退還您的魯貝攜帶型傳呼器，我們很樂意全額退款。」林語堂曾寫道：「寫信是一種自言自語，但當信有了附註，便成了對話。」

什麼不該說？

- 一封信不要有太多重點，專注在最強而有力的一、兩點上即可。必要的話，可以把第三點加在附註中，其餘的則等到後續追蹤信時再提。

- 一般來說，不要使用太多驚嘆號或誇大的形容詞，如 astonishing（驚人的）、revolutionary（革命性的）、incredible（不可思議的）、sensational（轟動的）、extraordinary（不凡的）、spectacular（壯觀的）。你要描述的，應該是具體的特色、好處，細節與產品訴求。

- 不要用疑問句，如：「您能禁得住丟掉這封信的後果嗎？」或「現代人少了這個還能過活嗎？」這是很糟糕的心理策略，你把收件人放進了對話之中，但他卻不一定會「正確」回答你的問題。收件人原本是在一列直達訂單的單向火車上，這種問題卻會讓它脫軌，收件人因而意識到他還有拒絕的選項。

- 不要說「我們不打折！我們的原價就已經很低了，所以我們不需要打折」。人就是喜歡打折。即便顧客經常使用你們的產品或服務，也認為你們的價格合理，但他們仍會被特價商品吸引。偶爾提供折扣、優惠、清倉特價和特別商品活動，會為新舊顧客都帶來興奮的心情與購買的意願。

- 避免術語，除非你很確定你的目標客戶很熟悉這些用語。

- 不要威脅對方（「要是不現在就訂購，你一定會後悔」）。這會引發反感，對方會覺得你在虛張聲勢。不過，告訴顧客若不馬上訂購，他們的名字便會從名單中移除，這招有時候倒是有效，因為人都會擔心錯過某些事情。

- 不要說教、責備、糾正或貶低顧客（「您或許不知道這點，但是……」）。請別人幫你檢查你的信，確保信中沒有藏著高高在上的語氣。

- 避免直呼其名，或假裝對方是朋友。商業專欄作家路易斯・魯凱瑟（Louis Rukeyser）曾在刊登一篇銷售信的專欄後，收到一封令他印象深刻的讀者來信。根據他的說法：「假裝的親近特別讓人厭煩」。

- 不要做任何假設。不要假設讀者知道你在說些什麼；不要假設他們熟悉你們產業的用語；不要假設他能在腦海裡描繪出你的產品；不要假設他會同意你的條件。人際溝通大師卡內基（Dale Carnegie）曾寫道：「我只管顯而易見的事。我只呈現、強調、讚揚顯而易見的事，因為顯而易見的事才是人們需要知道的」。

寫作訣竅

- 不管你推銷的是產品、服務、想法、空間、信用或商譽，在撰寫銷售信前須做的準備，比實際寫信更花工夫。你必須全盤了解你的產品、服務，以及你的顧客群，收集越多資料越好。美國實業家哈維·麥凱（Harvey Mackay）曾說：「獲取顧客訊息，就跟了解產品一樣重要。」確切找出一個強而有力的核心賣點，並據此發展銷售信。將其他的因素考量進來（時機、設計、長度、製作優惠券或樣品）。只有充足準備，才能寫出一封成功的銷售信。

- 銷售信的開場，有種公認最好的方式：一炮打響！不過，要用什麼形式來「打響」，並沒有一定，可以是令人吃驚的事實或數據；感人或戲劇性的故事；個人的故事；能省下一大筆錢；提供禮物、優惠券或特惠手冊；一個引發思考的問題或引言；一則笑話或謎語；名人背書、語錄或相關的搭配產品；一段回答是誰、是什麼、何時、何地、為何的段落；最強勁的賣點；描述共通點，或是之前的購買經驗；讓讀者相信他們很特別；請顧客幫忙，或幫助顧客；有時一句負面或意想不到的陳述也會有用。

- 在你決定用創新的方式冒險前，先請他人評估。有時候很難判斷這是巧妙的噱頭、引人注意的手法，或只是自以為可愛。如果確實絕妙，成果必定豐碩；但要是弄巧成拙，後果便是致命的。

- 務必寫出產品或服務的價格。沒寫價錢的銷售信，會被顧客置之不理，因為他們會預設自己無法負荷。多數情況下，價格決定購買意願；要是顧客還得打電話才能知道價錢，那麼在競爭對手已把售價寫進銷售信的狀況下，這種額外的麻煩便顯得不值得。

- 儘管情感與理智兩種訴求都是必要的，但前者通常吸引力更強。將你要傳達的信息訴諸各種情感，如給予愛（「您的孩子能擁有好幾小時的樂趣！」）；對愛的需求（「當你穿上這個，大家都會轉頭看你」）；獲得名聲（「有了……你的家便是最出眾的那個」）；滿足野心（「一夜之間學會新的管理技巧」）；提供安全感（「內建電池檢驗器的煙霧偵測警鈴」）。告訴顧客你的服務或產品如何能讓他們變得健康、受到歡迎、因擁有它而驕傲或有成就感、獲得成功、賺取更多錢、改善外表、過得更舒適而悠閒、在社交與商務上獲得進展、帶來忠誠。

- 從頭到尾，銷售信聚焦的都是潛在的顧客。要頻繁使用第二人稱「you」或「your」。描述產品時，著重在產品對顧客的好處：產品如何連結到顧客需求、問題和興趣；如何改善顧客生活、幫顧客省錢，或使他們感到更有自信。顧客想問的問題只有一個：「它能為我做什麼？」說服潛在顧客時，你要讓他們知道，他們之所以需要你的產品，並不完全是因為它很棒，而是因為對他們來說，這項商品是絕佳選擇。

- 選擇一種能突顯產品或服務的「語氣」，並在整封信上保持一致：友善、如鄰居一般；嚴肅而知性；幽默、生動、緊湊；俐落務實；急迫而激動；成熟老練；撫慰人心、令人安心；神祕；專業，或富含資訊；情感充沛。

- 使用生動鮮活的描述性用詞、有力的動詞，以及吸引人的形象。有些人在寫銷售信時，太專注想著教導潛在顧客，或滿腦子都是統計數據、背景資訊與報告，而忘了這樣的信有多麼無趣、忘了以客戶為主。

- 以重複的方式來強調重點，並說明較複雜的內容，並賦予你的信一種迷人的節奏。

- 銷售信可以模仿其他類似的信：祝賀信、致謝函、產品布達信、邀請函、歡迎信、節日問候。

- 透過實際經驗分享、研究報告、統計數據、公司名聲、產品使用檢測結果、比較類似商品、免費樣品或試用期、保固／保修、名人背書、實際使用照片、使用者調查等，建立並增強顧客對產品或服務的信任。只要有機會，就利用某種方式向顧客保證他們一定會滿意。

- 銷售信篇幅應該多長？關鍵在於，每個字都要有功能、每個字都是推銷工具。一封銷售信要是寫得差，即便縮短也於事無補；而優異的銷售信，即使很長，回覆率依然很高。不過整體而言，短一點比較好。專注在必須提到的要點上，無論這會花上一頁、兩頁、四頁或十頁。但無論是什麼情況，信中的每一個段落都一定要保持簡短。

- 為了增加顧客回信的意願，可提供折扣、優惠價格、特別專案、無息延後付款、禮物、店內禮券、附件資料、優惠券、產品手冊，樣品或試用期。

- 有些吸引目光的招式，能讓你的信更令人難忘。在信封上寫上訊息，刺激收信人打開信封（研究顯示，寄件人有十五秒的機會讓顧客打開信封，超過之後他們便失去了這些客源）；部分內容可用手寫（例如附註的部分）；將關鍵字句畫上底線或以黃色色筆標出，好像你親自在現場強調這些重點一樣；使用彩色墨水或信紙；使用圖片；用問卷或調查；框出重要資訊；斜體字、大寫字母、引號，與不常見的字型；注意排版，如標題、次標題、空白空間、短段落、縮排、有項目符號的清單。不過，這些吸引目光的招式並不適合所有情況。若是推銷銀行卡、壽險、醫護服務，或其他較嚴肅莊重的產品與服務時，則必須使用較傳統的格式。

特殊狀況

- **回應顧客詢問的封面信**，就是一種銷售信，而且是最有效果的一種，因為對方給了你一個可以專心推銷產品或服務的機會。儘管你的附件（或是這些附件所描述的產品）本身就有推銷效果，但封面信能帶來更強烈的訊息、給予額外的動機。

- 如果有**顧客對你的產品接受度很高（因為先前買過）**，那你可以多次聯絡他們，但每一次的重點都要不一樣：新的保險費、產品或服務的額外好處、優惠期間即將結束、買一送一或打折。或者，你可以針對購買一項產品的顧客，在銷售信中宣傳其他產品或服務，這些產品或服務往往是顧客可能忽略的，因為他們已習慣固定的消費模式。舉例來說，時常去美髮廳的顧客，可能已經忘記他們也能在那裡購買各種美髮產品或預約美甲服務。

- 當你**宣傳的是多種產品或服務**（或是同一系列中有不同的產品），你便能將觸手伸及不同目標族群，用的是專為不同族群需求打造的銷售信。製造溫室的廠商，可以寫不同的銷售信給農夫、郊區房屋主人、企業、公寓居民，甚至是大學生（桌上型迷你溫室）。

- **以先前消費過的顧客為對象的銷售信**，可以從以下方面著手：感謝過去的光顧；渴望能再次服務他們；推出新產品或服務；你相信你能滿足他們需求。你也可以詢問他們不再與你做生意的原因，這個資訊可能會很有幫助。

- **電子銷售信**的數量多得爆炸，絕大多數都被視為垃圾郵件，意即人們討厭收到這些信，而且還用擋信軟體把它們阻擋在外。不過，懂得尊重客戶的公司，仍能成功利用電子郵件來推銷產品與服務：

  (1) 他們只會寄電子郵件給主動透過賣方網站聯絡的顧客；

  (2) 他們總是提供收件人取消訂閱的選項，並尊重顧客的選擇；

  (3) 他們很小心不讓電子信箱充斥著他們的信；

  (4) 他們的電子郵件值得一讀，因為會提供特別優惠、折扣或有用的資訊。

格式

- 多數的銷售信都是電腦產出的，有些是制式信，有些則能利用大量郵件的合併功能加入個人化的姓名、地址與稱呼，使信件看起來像量身打造（但如果你把對方的姓名在信中到處穿插，反而會帶來不好的印象）。

- 若收信人是 VIP，請使用高品質的信紙、限時郵件、親筆簽名以及個別輸入的地址。

PART 2 應用篇

單字

absolute (a.) 絕對的	**demonstrate** (v.) 展示	**high-quality** (n.) 高品質	**pledge** (v.) 保證
acquaint (v.) 使認識	**dependable** (a.) 可靠的	**immediate** (a.) 立即的	**portable** (a.) 便攜的
adaptable (a.) 適應力強的	**detail** (n.) 細節	**indulge** (v.) 享受、沉迷	**powerful** (a.) 強大的
advanced (a.) 先進的	**discovery** (n.) 發現	**inexpensive** (a.) 便宜的	**practical** (a.) 實際的
advantage (n.) 優點	**durable** (a.) 耐用的	**informative** (a.) 詳實的	**precision** (n.) 精確
affordable (a.) 可負擔的	**economical** (a.) 實惠的	**ingenious** (a.) 巧妙的	**premium** (a.) 頂級的、優質的
all-new (a.) 全新的	**effective** (a.) 有效的	**innovative** (a.) 創新的	**productive** (a.) 富有成效的
attractive (a.) 有吸引力的	**exceptional** (a.) 出色的	**instant** (a.) 立即的	**professional** (a.) 專業的
authentic (a.) 真實的、可靠的	**exciting** (a.) 令人興奮的	**invaluable** (a.) 無價的	**profitable** (a.) 有利可圖的
benefit (n.) 好處	**exclusive** (a.) 獨家的	**investment** (n.) 投資	**proven** (a.) 已證實的
brand-new (a.) 全新的	**expert** (n.) 專家	**lasting** (a.) 持久的	**quality** (n.) 品質
breakthrough (n.) 突破	**exquisite** (a.) 精美的	**low-cost** (n.) 低成本	**rapid-action** (n.) 快速行動
choice (n.) 選擇	**extensive** (a.) 大規模的	**low-priced** (a.) 低價的	**reasonable** (a.) 合理的
classic (a.) 經典的	**fact** (n.) 事實	**luxurious** (a.) 豪華的	**rebate** (n.)（政府單位的）退款

clever *(a.)* 聰明的	feature *(n.) & (v.)* 特色；主打	moneymaking *(n.)* 賺錢	refund *(n.) & (v.)* （因不滿意而）退款
comfortable *(a.)* 舒適的	flair *(n.)* 天賦、眼光	natural *(a.)* 自然的	reliable *(a.)* 可靠的
compact *(a.)* 小巧的	flexible *(a.)* 靈活的	new *(a.)* 新的	result *(n.) & (v.)* 結果
confident *(a.)* 有自信的	genuine *(a.)* 真正的、非偽造的	nostalgic *(a.)* 懷舊的	revolutionary *(a.)* 革命性的
contemporary *(a.)* 現代的	guarantee *(n.) & (v.)* 保證、保修	offer *(v.) & (n.)* 提議、給予	reward *(n.)* 獎勵
convenient *(a.)* 方便的	half-price *(n.) & (a.) & (adv.)* 半價	opportunity *(n.)* 機會	safe *(a.)*（人）安全的；（物品）不會造成危險的
dazzling *(a.)* 耀眼的	handy *(a.)* 便利的；好上手的	optional *(a.)* 非必須的	satisfaction *(n.)* 滿意
delightful *(a.)* 愉快的	helpful *(a.)* 有幫助的	personalization *(n.)* 個人化	secure *(a.) & (v.)* （物品）牢固的；保衛
solution *(n.)* 解決辦法	successful *(a.)* 成功的	unconditional *(a.)* 無條件的	versatile *(a.)* 多功能的
sophisticated *(a.)* 成熟老練的	super *(a.)* 超級的	up-to-date *(a.)* 最新的	warranted *(a.)* 受到保修的
spectacular *(a.)* 壯觀的	thrifty *(a.)* 節儉的	urgent *(a.)* 緊急的	waterproof *(a.)* 防水的
state-of-the-art *(a.)* 最先進的	tremendous *(a.)* 極大的	useful *(a.)* 有用的	wholesale *(n.) & (a.) & (adv.)* 批發價；批發
stunning *(a.)* 令人驚嘆的	trial *(n.) & (v.)* 試用	user-friendly *(a.)* 方便使用的	
substantial *(a.)* 大量的	unbreakable *(a.)* 牢不可破的	valuable *(a.)* 有價值的	

add a new dimension to
添加一個新特點

direct-to-you low prices
專屬優惠

advanced design
先進的設計

direct your attention to
讓你注意到

all for one low price
用便宜的價格得到全部

discover for yourself
為自己發現

all-in-one convenience
多合一的便利

dramatic difference
極大的差異

as an added bonus
作為額外優惠

easier and more enjoyable/comfortable
更容易且更愉快／自在

at a discount/a fraction of the cost/great savings/no expense to you
折扣價／一點成本／大省一筆／你不須付任何費用

we're making this generous offer because what better way to
我們大方提供這個優惠，是因為還有什麼更好的辦法

more advanced features
更高級的功能

easy/carefree maintenance
維修輕鬆／無憂

be more efficient
更有效率

easy-to-follow instructions
簡單易懂的指示

be the first to
成為第一個

elegant styling
優雅的造型

both practical and beautiful/decorative
既實用又美觀／適合裝飾

engineered for dependability
專為可靠性而設計

budget-pleasing prices
節省預算的價格

exciting details/offer
令人興奮的細節／優惠

built-in features
內建功能

exclusive features
獨家特色

business advancement
業務上的進展

experience the pleasure of
體驗……的樂趣

buy with confidence
有信心地購買

can pay for itself in
在……年內可以回收成本

carefree upkeep
不需費心保養

easier to use than ever before
比以前更容易使用

come in and try
進來試試

compact design
小巧的設計

complimentary copy
免費贈送的一份

provides the finest home hair care at the least cost
以最低價格提供最好的家庭頭髮護理

customer support
顧客支持

cutting edge
最尖端的、處領先地位的

contemporary/gracious design
現代／華美的設計

revolutionary approach
革命性的方法

impressive collection
令人印象深刻的產品系列

improved appearance
改良的外觀

express your personality
傳達你的性格

fast, safe, easy-to-use
快速、安全、容易使用

finely crafted
精心製作的

fit-any-budget price
適合任何預算的價格

fully automated/warranted
全自動／全面保固

get full details
得到完整的細節

gives you your choice of
給你你所選擇的

greater safety/convenience/pleasure/popularity
更安全／方便／愉快／受歡迎

great gift idea
送禮首選

have the satisfaction of knowing
知道……覺得滿意

if not completely satisfied
若不完全滿意

no strings attached
沒有附加條件

now for the first time
現在是第一次

of particular importance to you
對你特別重要

increased enjoyment
升級的享受

incredibly low introductory rate/price of
初期優惠利率／價格非常的低

indulge yourself
寵愛自己一下

influence others
影響別人

intelligent way to
聰明的方式去做

in these fast-moving times
在這個快速變遷的時代

invite you to
邀請你去

join millions of others who
加入數百萬計的其他人

just pennies each
每個只要幾分錢

key to your peace of mind
讓你安心的關鍵

lasting beauty
持久的美麗

lets you enjoy more of your favorite
讓你享受更多你喜愛的

look forward to sending you
期待寄給你

low, low prices
極低的價格

loyal customers like you
像你這樣忠實的客戶

one easy operation
一個簡單的操作步驟

one of the largest and most respected
其中規模最大、最有聲望的

one reason among many to order
只是訂購的很多原因之一

one size fits all
一個尺寸，全都適合

order today
今天就訂購

our top-seller
我們的暢銷商品

outstanding features
突出的特點

over 50,000 satisfied customers
超過五萬名滿意的客戶

perfect gift for yourself or a loved one
適合自用或給摯愛的人的完美禮物

pleased to be able to offer you
很高興能為你提供

preferred customer/rates
貴賓／優惠費率

previously sold for
以前賣的價格是

price you'll appreciate
你會喜歡的價格

pride of accomplishment
達成目標的自豪

privileges include
優待服務包括

make it easy for yourself
給自己方便

professional quality
專業素質

makes any day special
讓每一天都特別

prompt, courteous service
及時、有禮的服務

many advantages of
很多優點

proven reliability/technology
經證明的可靠性／技術

money's worth
錢沒白花

state of the art
最先進的

avoid worry/embarrassment/
discomfort/risk
毋須擔心／尷尬／不自在／冒險

ready to spoil you with its powerful
features
準備用它強大的功能來寵愛你

more money/comfort/leisure
更多的錢／舒適／休閒

reasonably priced
合理定價的

more than fifty years of service
超過五十年的服務

reduced price
降低的價格

most versatile, powerful, and exciting
study aid available
市面上最多功能、強大、令人興奮的學習幫手

if you accept this invitation/respond
right away/send payment now
如果你接受這個邀請／立即回應／現在就付款

no matter which set you choose
不管你選擇哪一套

reward yourself with
用……獎勵自己

no more mess/lost sales/errors/fuss/
worry
不再混亂／流失訂單／出錯／大驚小怪／擔心

you will appreciate the outstanding
quality of these
你會喜歡它們優異的品質

no-risk examination
無風險檢驗

rugged and dependable
堅固可靠

save money/time
節省金錢／時間

under no obligation to
沒有義務去做

satisfaction guaranteed
滿意保證

under our simple plan
在我們簡單的計畫下

security in your later years
你老年的安全

unequaled savings and convenience
無比省錢而方便

see for yourself
親自看看

unique limited edition creations
獨特的限量版

simple steps
簡單的步驟

unique opportunity
獨特的機會

so unusual and striking that
如此不尋常而驚人的

urge you to
促使你去做

special benefits/introductory offer/value
特別優惠／入門優惠／價格

use it anywhere, anytime
隨時隨地使用它

take a moment right now to look over this
現在就花一點時間來看看這個

choose from over 20 styles/cards/ models /varieties
從二十多種款式／卡片／型號／種類中選擇

stop those costly losses with
以⋯⋯終止那些昂貴的損失

risk nothing
沒有風險

supply is limited
限量供應

whole family can enjoy
全家人都可以享受

surprise your special someone with
用⋯⋯給你特別的人一個驚喜

with no obligation on your part
你沒有義務

take advantage of this opportunity
利用這個機會

with our compliments
我們的敬意

take a giant step forward toward
向⋯⋯邁進一大步

won't cost you a thing to
不會花費你的任何成本去做

step in the right direction
邁向正確的方向

won't find better quality anywhere
在任何地方都找不到更好的品質

takes the gamble out of choosing
冒險選擇

world of enjoyment waiting for you
充滿享受的世界等著你

time is growing short
時間越來越少

you can be proud of
你可以為⋯⋯自豪

timeless elegance
永恆的優雅

you don't risk a penny
你不需花費一毛錢

42

銷
售
信

time-tested
經得起時間考驗的

top of the line
最高級的

treat yourself to
款待自己

unconditional money-back guarantee
無條件退款保證

you'll be amazed to discover
你會驚訝地發現

you might expect these to cost as much as
你可能以為這些會花費

your money back
退款給你

句子

At this low price, every home should have one.
如使實惠的價格,每個家庭都應該擁有一個。

Be the first in your community to have one!
成為您社區中第一個擁有的人!

But act now—we expect a sizable response and we want to be certain that your order can be filled.
現在就採取行動吧;我們預期反應會相當熱烈,所以我們要確保您能成功下單。

Call today to arrange a demonstration.
今天就打電話安排專人展示。

Discover savings of up to 50 percent.
發現能讓你最多省上百分之五十的方法。

Discover the elegance of a genuine leather briefcase with discreet gold initials.
發現真皮公文包的優雅,上面印有細膩的金色姓名首字母。

Don't miss out!
不要錯過!

Do your holiday shopping the easy way.
簡單完成假日採購。

Enjoy it for a 15-day home trial.
享受十五天的在家試用期。

Every item is offered at a discount.
全品項皆打折。

If you are not completely satisfied, simply return it for a full credit.
如果您對商品不甚滿意，只須退還，我們將全額退款。

In order to make this offer, we must have your check by September 1.
為了能享有這個優惠，您必須在九月一日前寄出支票。

It's a first!
這是業界首見！

It's a no-strings offer.
這是一個無附加條件的優惠。

Join us today.
今天就加入我們。

Just bring this letter with you when you come in to sign up.
當你進來登記時，只需帶上這封信。

Just what makes the Blount Filing System so great?
布朗特歸檔系統如此優異的理由是什麼？

May I make an appointment with you next week to explain/show/demonstrate our latest line of products?
可否與您預約下週見面，向您解釋／展現／展示我們的最新系列產品？

Now there's a new magazine just for you.
這是本為你量身打造的新雜誌。

Order one for every family member.
為每個家庭成員都訂購一個。

Please don't delay your decision—we expect a heavy demand for the Ellesmere filet knife.
請不要再猶豫；埃斯米爾片魚刀的需求預計將會供不應求。

P.S. To lock in these great rates, we must receive your deposit by October 15.
附註：為了能享有優惠利率，請務必在十月十五日前完成匯款。

Send for your free copy of the Bemerton planning guide.
回信可獲得免費的貝默頓計劃指南。

Send today for free, no-obligation information on rates and available discounts, special services, and easy claims filing.
今天寄送，就可獲得免費、免責的資料，內容關於利率與可獲得的折扣、特別服務及簡單的索賠申報。

Take a look at the enclosed brochure for a sneak preview.
看一看附件的手冊，先睹為快。

Telephone Sarah Lash, your personal representative, for an appointment.
打電話給您的個人業務莎拉‧拉許預約時間。

The Art Deco look fits almost any decorating scheme.
「裝飾藝術」風格適合幾乎所有裝潢。

There is absolutely no risk on your part.
無須承擔任何風險。

There's no cost or obligation, of course.
當然，您不需承擔任何成本或義務。

These low prices are effective only until June 1.
低價優惠僅在六月一日之前有效。

This is just one more reason why our products have won such overwhelming acceptance.
這是我們的產品廣受歡迎的其中一個原因。

Use the order form and postpaid reply envelope enclosed to receive your first Holiday Bell absolutely free.
使用附件的訂貨單和回郵信封，您便能免費收到第一個聖誕鐘。

We cannot extend this unusual offer beyond May 25, 2017.
在二〇一七年五月二十五日後，我們便無法繼續這個特別優惠。

We invite you to complete the enclosed reservation request form and return it now to confirm your choice of dates.
我們邀請您填寫附件中的預約申請表，並立即寄回，以確認您所選擇的日期。

We're making this unprecedented offer to a select group of business executives.
這個前所未有的優惠，只給我們特選的業務主管。

We take all the risks.
我們承擔所有的風險。

We've missed you!
我們想念您了！

You can choose from over 150 different programs.
您可以在一百五十多個頻道中自由挑選。

You'll appreciate these fine features.
你會喜歡這些優異性能。

You'll like our convenient evening and weekend hours; you'll love our brand-new equipment and experienced teachers!
你會喜歡我們便利的傍晚與週末時間；你會愛上我們的全新設備及經驗豐富的老師！

You'll see that Rockminster China isn't like other china.
您會發現羅克明斯特瓷器不同於其他瓷器之處。

You may not have ever used a hibachi, which is why we are making you this no-risk trial offer.
您也許從來沒有使用過木炭火盆，因此我們提供給您這個無風險的試用優惠。

You must see the complete series for yourself to appreciate how it can enrich your life.
您必須親自鑑賞這一個系列，才能體會它能如何豐富您的生活。

段落

Are you still paying premiums for the same homeowner's policy you signed up for ten years ago? Things have changed. You may want to compare what's available today with what you bought ten years ago.

您是否仍在為十年前簽訂的房屋保險支付保費？但時代變了，或許您會想比較今日可保的保險和十年前買的保單。

The enclosed Special Introductory Invitation can be guaranteed for a limited time only. We urge you to reply within the next 10 days.

隨信附上的入會優惠邀請函只在有限的期間內有效，請您在接下來的十天內回覆。

Congratulations on your election to membership in the Society for Historic Preservation! If you accept this membership offer—and I certainly hope you will—you will become part of a unique and influential group. As a member you will enjoy such important benefits as voting privileges on matters of national importance, a subscription to the monthly magazine *Preservation*, and many more. Please mail the enclosed Confirmation of Election by May 31.

恭喜您獲選為歷史保護協會會員！如果您接受此會員邀請（而我當然希望您會接受），您便會成為這個獨特而有影響力的團體的一員。成為會員後，您可以享受許多重要的福利，例如國家重要議題投票特權、《保存》月刊的訂閱等等。請於五月三十一日之前回寄附件中的獲選確認函。

If for any reason, at any time, you are not satisfied with your Haverley Air Cleaner, you can return it to us for a complete and prompt refund. No questions asked.

無論原因、無論何時，只要您對哈佛利空氣淨化器不滿意，您都可以退回給我們，我們會迅速全額退款，不問任何問題。

42

銷售信

Dear MasterGold Cardmember,

A revolutionary new service is now available to valued MasterGold card members—and you're among the first invited to enroll.

CreditReport service is a valuable new credit tool that allows you to guard your privileged credit status. Membership in CreditReport entitles you to:

- Unlimited access to copies of your CreditReport record.
- Automatic notification when anyone receives a copy of your CreditReport files.
- One convenient document that organizes all your personal finances.
- Convenient application for loans or financing at participating credit grantors.
- Credit card protection: At no extra charge we'll register all your credit, charge, and ATM cards in case of loss or theft.

Best of all, your membership includes an unconditional money-back guarantee, so you can enjoy all the privileges of membership without risk.

This is a valuable service for MasterGold card members. I urge you to look over the enclosed materials and consider this special offer now.

Sincerely,

親愛的爵金信用卡會員：

爵金信用卡的貴賓會員現在可享有一項革命性的新服務，而您是第一批受邀加入的人。

信用回報服務是相當有用的新工具，幫助您保護信用狀態。信用回報的會員資格使您能夠：

- 無限制取得您的信用回報紀錄。
- 任何人收到您的信用回報文件時自動通知。
- 只要一份便利的文件，就能統整您所有的個人財務狀況。
- 向特定授信方申請貸款或融資，手續便利。
- 信用卡保護：不需額外費用，我們將登記您所有的信用卡、簽帳卡與提款卡，以防丟失或被盜。

最棒的是，您的會員資格包括無條件的退款保證，所以您可以享受所有的會員福利，而無須承擔風險。

這對爵金信用卡會員而言，是很值得的服務。我建議您詳讀附件資料，並現在就考慮這項禮遇服務。

○○敬上

Dear Executive:

According to several management studies, the single most important characteristic of an effective executive is the ability to manage time.

Are you meeting your deadlines? Can you list your current projects in order of importance? Do you know where you're headed over the next week, month, year? Can you find things when you need them? Do you assign work in the most time-effective ways?

42
銷售信

If you answered no to any of these questions, you're sure to benefit from our popular, effective Time Management Workshop.

In just two days you learn how to set priorities, how to use special tools to help you organize your time, and how to develop interpersonal skills to help you deal with unnecessary interruptions, inefficient staff, and group projects.

In fact, we don't want to be one of those interruptions, so we'll make this short. We simply suggest that you save time by making time for the next Time Management Workshop in your area. You can do this in under a minute by checking off a convenient date and signing the enclosed postage-paid reply card or by calling 800-555-1707 to register.

This is one workshop that won't be a waste of time!

Sincerely,

親愛的經理您好：

根據幾項管理方面的研究，一名善於管理的經理，最重要的特質便是擁有時間管理能力。

您是否都在時限內完成工作？您可以按照重要性排列您目前的專案嗎？您知道下星期、下個月、下一年您會前往哪裡嗎？您可以在需要時找到您要的東西嗎？您是否用最有效的方法分配工作？

如果您對上述的任何一個問題回答了「否」，那這個受歡迎、有效果的時間管理研討會，一定能讓您從中受益。

在短短的兩天時間裡，您將學會如何設定優先順序、如何使用特殊工具來協助您管理時間，以及如何建立人際溝通技巧，讓您能處理不必要的干擾、低效率的員工與小組專案。

事實上，我們不希望成為您的干擾，所以會長話短說。我們只想建議您參加您們地區下一次的時間管理研討會，花一點時間便能幫您節省時間。您只須花不到一分鐘的時間，在貼有回郵的回覆卡上勾選方便的時間並簽名，或撥打 800-555-1707 登記註冊。

這個研討會絕不會浪費您的時間！

○○敬上

42

銷售信

參見：07 恭賀信、08 佳節問候信、11 表揚信、12 致謝函、15 公告通知、17 後續追蹤信、18 邀請函、20 請求與詢問、28 求職信、33 商譽信、37 訂單處理信、41 信貸相關信

Chapter 43

紀念日
Anniversaries

> 我知道很多人都不看好我們，
> 不過我們剛慶祝在一起滿兩個月的紀念日。
>
> ——瑞典女演員布莉特·埃克蘭（Britt Ekland）

現在市面上充斥各種漂亮的祝賀卡，所以很少人會親自寫便條或信函來祝賀紀念日或生日。不過，每個曾經收到只有簽名的市售祝賀卡片的人，都會了解一兩句手寫的問候能帶來多少快樂。對多數人來說，看見手寫信跟收到禮物是一樣棒的事情。

紀念日（anniversary）這個字，以前只代表結婚紀念日，但今日人們也慶祝開業、就職、或個人相關等紀念日，而如果別人記得這些特別的日子，我們也會感到高興。有些公司也會寄生日及紀念日卡片給客戶，表現誠意。

 PART 1 說明篇

使用時機

生日	商業往來	公司紀念日
結婚週年或忌日	參見：33 商譽信	商會、組織
個人成就	**生日或紀念日邀請**	**客戶生日或紀念日**
就職服務紀念日	參見：18 邀請函	參見：42 銷售信

該怎麼說？

1. 說明寄信的原因，如果不知道是幾週年，只須寫出 your service anniversary（你的就職服務紀念日）、your birthday（你的生日）或 the anniversary of Beryl's death（貝瑞爾的忌日）。

2. 在適合的段落寫下一段小故事、一個共同的回憶、沒有惡意的幽默笑話，或用一句話告訴對方他對你的重要性。

3. 最後，為對方的下一個週年或下一年獻上祝福，並堅定傳達你的感情、愛、崇拜、溫情、興趣、快樂、愉悅、在業務上給予支持，或其他合適的情感。

什麼不該說？

- 別離題，勿加入其他不相關的資訊或消息，專注在紀念日或生日上就好，除非你寫信是為了向家人或好友報家常。

- 別在信中以「玩笑」方式提到以下敏感話題，如對方增長的年紀、能力不足、浪費時間、婚姻問題或長年不變的職位。這類關於年齡、婚姻或工作年資的俏皮話，只能讓對方勉強一笑，難以帶來太多溫暖。

- 別挑選有負面語句的卡片，例如有些卡片總假設所有人到了二十一歲都會迫不及待跑去酒吧，或「不惑之年」很令人沮喪，或五十歲的人已開始走下坡。

寫作訣竅

- 要讓你的生日或紀念日祝福變得有個性，可引用語錄：

The great thing about getting older is that you don't lose all the other ages you've been.

變老有個好處：你不會失去你所經歷的任何歲月。

——美國作家麥德蓮・蘭歌（Madeleine L'Engle）

The fact was I didn't want to look my age, but I didn't want to act the age I wanted to look either. I also wanted to grow old enough to understand that sentence.

事實上，我不想理會我的年齡，但我也不想舉手投足像我希望看起來的年紀一樣。我也希望年紀夠大，才能看懂這個句子。

——美國作家爾瑪・邦貝克（Erma Bombeck）

The marriages we regard as the happiest are those in which each of the partners believes that he or she got the best of it.

我們眼中最快樂的婚姻，是婚姻中的兩人都相信自己得到了最好的人。

——美國記者席尼・J・哈里斯（Sydney J. Harris）

- 留些問候卡片在身邊備用。年初時，把該記得的紀念日期標示在行事曆上（只有在第一次整理日期時會比較耗費時間）。在每個月的第一天，為該月生日或紀念日的人挑選卡片，並把地址寫好。在信封的右上角（之後會被郵票蓋住的地方）以鉛筆寫上生日或紀念日的日期，然後在那個日期的幾天前把卡片寄出。

- 收集能放入卡片中的小巧而實用的禮物，如手帕、書籤、郵票、樂透彩券、藝術明信片、鈔票。你也可以在生日或紀念日卡片中放入照片、剪報與收據，信封鼓起來亦無妨。
- 有些網站能讓你自行選擇或親手設計卡片，以電子郵件的方式寄出。

特殊狀況

- 留意公司人員的**入職服務紀念日**。寄封信給對方祝賀其就職服務日，能提升員工忠誠度，如果能加上一句話稱讚對方的工作表現更好。若是寄信給同事，你可以提起一段共同的回憶，增添個人色彩。記得重要供應商與客戶的紀念日，公司商譽也會因此提昇。
- 有時也可**寄生日與紀念日卡片給個人客戶**。在一些可以取得客戶生日或紀念日日期的產業（如保險業），寄卡片是一種與客戶保持聯繫的方法，同時也能讓他們想起你與你的產品或服務。
- 送禮或用字需**考量是否有需注意避免的禁忌**。作家奧莉維亞‧戈斯密（Olivia Goldsmith）曾在其在《The Bestseller》（暫譯：暢銷作品）一書中玩笑表示，在作家生日時祝福他們 many happy returns（快樂常返）是很不妙的，因為對作家來說，returns（返回）指的是沒賣完的書被退還給出版社。
- 在對方**達成個人重要成就**（如戒菸或戒酒）的週年紀念時表示恭喜，對方會很高興，不過這只適用在熟識的人。
- 若親朋好友失去了某個重要的人，你可以在那個人的**忌日寫信**給他們。別擔心這麼做會重提傷心的回憶。安‧蘭德斯曾在專欄中寫道：「過去我也曾以為，聽到別人提起死去的親人會很痛苦，但很多讀者並不這麼認為，現在我也明白。」失去親人的人，其實一直牢記著那個日子，如果別人也記得，他們會覺得感激。如果你的熟人在結婚多年後失去了配偶，可以在他們的結婚紀念日時寄封短信致意。

格式

- 寄給商務銷售相關或官方單位的信件，可以打字或手寫的方式寫在有信頭或個人對公司用的信紙上。
- 市售賀卡也可以用在與工作無關的場合，只要加上幾句手寫的句子。
- 以電子郵件發送生日與紀念日祝福，也同樣受到歡迎。
- 許多報紙提供欄位供刊登生日或紀念日祝福（通常會收取費用）。一般來說，這種形式的祝福會搭配慶祝紀念日的家庭招待會或宴會。

✉ PART 2 應用篇

單字

celebration *(n.)* 慶祝	heartfelt *(a.)* 真心的	milestone *(n.)* 里程碑	remember *(v.)* 記得
congratulations *(n.)* 恭賀	honored *(a.)* 榮幸的	progress *(n.)* 進度	special *(a.)* 特別的
delighted *(a.)* 雀躍的	landmark *(n.)* 轉折點	prosperity *(n.)* 亨通	successful *(a.)* 成功的
future *(n.)* 未來	memorable *(a.)* 難忘的	red-letter day *(n.)* 大日子	unique *(a.)* 獨特的
happy *(a.)* 高興	memories *(n.)* 回憶	remarkable *(a.)* 了不起的	

詞組

all good wishes 美好的祝福	important day 重要的日子
anticipate another period of success 期待下一次成功	look forward to the next ten years 期待下一個十年
celebrate with you 與你一同慶祝	on the occasion of 在……的時候
convey our warmest good wishes 傳達我們真心的祝福	send our love 獻上我們的愛
great pleasure to wish you 開心地祝福你	

Congratulations on forty years of outstanding contributions to Heaslop-Moore Plastics.
恭喜你在喜樂摩爾整形診所服務貢獻滿四十年。

Congratulations on the tenth anniversary of Stanley Graff Real Estate—it has been a pleasure serving all your stationery needs!
恭喜史坦利葛拉夫不動產開業十週年,很高興能持續為您提供文具用品!

Every good wish to both of you for much health, happiness, prosperity, and many more years of togetherness.
祝福兩位賢伉儷健康、快樂且富足,享受彼此更長久的陪伴。

Here's a question for you from Ruth Gordon: "How old would you be if you didn't know how old you were?"
我想問你一個魯斯‧高登曾提出的問題:「如果你不知道自己的年齡,你覺得自己會是幾歲?」

May you enjoy many more anniversaries—each happier than the last.
祝您年年快樂,且一年比一年更快樂。

May you live as long as you want, and never want as long as you live!
祝您長壽、生活富足!

May you live long and prosper!
祝您長壽、發財!

On the occasion of your 25th wedding anniversary, we send you our best wishes for continued love and happiness together.
在您們結婚二十五週年的這一天,我們獻上最好的祝福,祝您們永浴愛河、永遠幸福。

Today marks the fifth anniversary of Archie's death, and I wanted you to know that we still miss him and that you are in our thoughts today.
今天是亞齊的第五個忌日,我想讓你知道我們依然思念他,且我們今天都惦記著你。

段落

Best wishes for a happy anniversary to a couple we have long admired and loved. May your relationship continue to be a blessing to both of you as well as to all those who know you.

致我們多年來崇敬又深愛的夫婦，祝你們有一個快樂的紀念日，希望對你們兩人及認識你們的人來說，你們的婚姻一直都充滿著祝福。

This marks the tenth anniversary of our productive and happy business association. In that time, we have come to appreciate Fausto Babel Inc.'s prompt service, reliable products, and knowledgeable staff. I'm sure the next ten years will be equally happy and successful. Congratulations to all of you.

我們高效率、充滿樂趣的商會，邁入第十年了。在這段日子裡，我們必須感謝法斯科・巴貝爾公司裡每位提供立即服務、可靠產品與專業的工作人員。我確信，下一個十年同樣會是快樂而成功的。恭喜各位。

Happy 1st Anniversary! I have such lovely memories of your wedding day. I hope you have been gathering more happy memories of your first year of married life.

一週年快樂！你的婚禮讓我留下美好的回憶。希望你婚後的第一年能創造更多快樂回憶。

Barbara and Dick Siddal celebrate their 50th wedding anniversary on February 14. They have four children, nine grandchildren, and many wonderful friends. Love and congratulations from the whole family.

芭芭拉與迪克・西道於二月十四日慶祝結婚五十週年紀念日。他們擁有四個孩子、九個孫子女與許多好朋友。我們全家在此致上愛與祝賀。

Sunday is the first anniversary of Vivie's death, and I couldn't let the day go by without writing to see how you are getting along and to tell you that all Vivie's friends here in Cambridge miss her very much.

這個週日是薇薇的第一個忌日。我不能就這麼讓這一天過去，我必須寫這封信看看您是否無恙。我要告訴您，在劍橋這裡，薇薇的朋友都非常思念她。

43

紀念日

Dear Muriel Joy,

Happy birthday! I'm sending you 6 quarters, 6 colored bows for your hair, 6 teddy-bear stickers, and 6 tiny horses for your collection.

How old did you say you are today?

Love,
Aunt Dinah

親愛的莫瑞兒喬伊：

生日快樂！我這次寄了六枚硬幣、六個頭髮綁帶、六張泰迪熊貼紙及六匹讓你收集的小小馬給你。

你覺得你今天幾歲了呢？

愛你的狄娜阿姨

Dear Dr. Arnold,

On behalf of the governing board, I would like to congratulate you on ten years of outstanding service as headmaster. Under your leadership the school has established itself among the premier ranks of such institutions.

Be assured of our continued admiration and support.

Very sincerely yours,

阿諾博士您好：

謹代表理事會向您恭賀擔任本校校長已屆十年。在您的領導下，本校得以在各校中名列前茅。

請讓我們繼續崇敬、支持您。

○○敬啟

Dear Auntie Em,

I send you love and hugs on your 80th birthday. If only I were there to celebrate with you!

I read this once: "Years in themselves mean nothing. How we live them means everything." (Elisabeth Marbury) I hope I live my years as well as you've lived yours!

Speaking of which, how is the bridge group? the golf foursome? the church cleaning crew? your birthday luncheon friends? your bowling game? your Monday night dinners with the family? And are you still going to Las Vegas in February?

(Watch the mail for a small package from me!)

Love,
D.

親愛的艾咪阿姨：

在此為您的八十大壽獻上我的愛與擁抱，真希望我也在場為您慶祝！

我曾經讀到這句話：「歲月是沒有意義的，我們如何度過這些歲月才是意義所在。」（伊莉莎白・馬布里）我希望我能像您一樣度過人生歲月！

話說回來，您的橋牌社如何呢？高爾夫四人組還好嗎？教會清潔順利嗎？參加你生日午餐會的朋友如何呢？保齡球比賽還好嗎？週一仍與家人共進晚餐嗎？二月時您仍有去拉斯維加斯嗎？

（請留意我寄去的包裹！）

愛您的 D

Dear Martin,

All of us here at Eden Land Corporation congratulate you at Chuzzlewit Ltd. on your twenty years of solid contributions in the field of architecture.

We know that when we do business with you we can count on superior designs, reasonable costs, and dependable delivery dates.

May the success of these first twenty years lead to an even more successful second twenty.

With best wishes,

親愛的馬汀：

伊甸園公司的全體員工在此向各位楚澤維公司的同仁致上祝賀，貴公司在建築界貢獻服務已屆滿二十年。

我們總是對貴公司卓越的設計、合理的價格與可靠的出貨日期給予全心信賴。

希望這第一個二十年的成功，能為貴公司帶來更成功的第二個二十年。

○○敬賀

Dear Penrod,

Congratulations on your twelfth birthday. I hope you have a wonderful time and get everything you want (although, from what your father tells me, I hope you don't want another slingshot).

Your uncle and I are sorry we can't be there to celebrate with you, but I'm sending you a little something in a separate package. Have a good time and give everyone a hug for us.

Happy birthday!

親愛的朋羅：

十二歲生日快樂。希望你度過美好的一天，得到所有你想要的禮物（不過，根據你爸告訴我的，我希望你想要的不是另一把彈弓）。

很抱歉我與你叔叔無法到場為你慶生，但我用另一個包裹寄給你一個小禮物。好好享受，並幫我們抱抱每個人。

生日快樂！

 參見：04 遲回的信、07 恭賀信、12 致謝函、14 公告通知、18 邀請函、33 商譽信、47 給親友的信

Chapter 44

早日康復信
"Get Well" Letters

為自己工作是充滿樂趣的。
不過只有在請病假的時候除外，
因為我知道我在說謊。

——喜劇演員麗塔‧拉德納（Rita Rudner）

多數人生病時都會期待收到早日康復卡，但要是你曾經收到什麼都沒寫、或是只簽了名的卡片，你就會知道這有多麼令人失望。你很感謝對方的好意，但你更喜歡親筆寫下的訊息。

如果對方生小病，或你跟對方不算熟稔，那麼早日康復信很容易就能寄出。不過在其他較嚴重的狀況下，我們會感到無力、焦慮，甚至是同情，所以我們不是乾脆不寫，就是寫出一封連自己也覺得尷尬的信。

早日康復信的主要目的，是讓對方知道他們並不是孤單一人，並給予他們毋須質疑的愛與友情作為治癒的力量。你的鼓勵不必冗長、文謅謅或讓人難忘；幾句暖心的話便已足夠。

PART 1　說明篇

早日康復信可以寄給誰？

生病或出意外的同事	生病或復原中的家人	接受戒癮治療的親友
或客戶	朋友、鄰居或同事	或接受飲食控制、心理治療

該怎麼說？

1. 告訴對方你很遺憾他生病、發生意外、接受手術或住院。

2. 關心對方的健康，如 I want you to be comfortable and on the mend.「我希望你狀況良好、逐漸康復。」

3. 語氣要親切、正面而且樂觀。

4. 具體提出能協助對方的方式，如幫忙撥打重要的銷售電話、協助完成專案、參加會議、去圖書館借書給對方看、週末幫忙照顧小孩或平日接送上下學、幫忙打電話取消活動、為對方家人提供食物、把郵件帶到醫院並協助回信、為對方大聲唸信、幫忙跑腿等。模稜兩可的「請讓我知道有沒有幫得上忙的地方」並沒什麼用，因為病人沒力氣思考你能幫什麼忙或打電話給你。可以向對方家人或鄰居詢問有什麼需要做的。

5. 如果對方已臥床多時，或你認為他們喜歡有人陪伴，可以提議去拜訪他們。但一般來說，最好不要去拜訪住院或生重病在家休養的人。「早日康復」信的用處，便是在對方狀況不佳無法見你時，代替你與對方接觸。提議見面時，措詞要讓對方在不想見你時也不會不好意思拒絕。

6. 堅定向對方展現你的感情、關心、溫暖、祝福、愛或祈禱。

7. 最後，表達你的盼望，如不適能緩解、很快康復、病情迅速改善、健康狀態變好。

什麼不該說？

- 不要過度強調對方的疾病或事故，沒必要且不得體。說「你的車禍」，而不要說「那場奪走兩條人命的可怕意外」；說「你的手術」，而不要說「你的迴腸造口手術」。

- 避免用 victim（受害者）、handicapped（殘障的）或 bedridden（久病的）這類的詞，它們暗示著悲劇、絕望與自憐。也要避開戲劇化的負面用詞，如 affliction（苦難）、torture（折磨）、nightmare（夢魘）或 agony（痛苦），除非對方遭遇真的符合這些字詞。

- 考慮對方的身心狀態，不要擅自建議對方該如何看待自己的遭遇。要有同情心，但不要誇大事實或做出誇張的反應。

- 別說空泛、陳腐或假裝樂觀的話，如「這也許是最好的情況了」（病人並不覺得是「最好」）；「我知道你的感受」（你並不知道）；「黑暗中總有一線光明」（被黑暗籠罩的如果是你的話，就不是這麼回事了）；「至少你不必去上班」（比起病床，對方也許更喜歡辦公室）。重讀信件，要是你在相同處境，對這封信會有什麼感覺？

- 不要批評或質疑病人在醫療護理上的選擇，除非你有合理理由這麼做。很多病人會擔心自己未受到最妥善的治療照護，要是朋友又提及這件事，只會助長不安。

- 勿將對方的遭遇與他人比較。也許你們有過相似的經歷，但請等到對方完全康復後再提，這樣你也不必擔心提起此事會有風險。每個人的經歷都是獨特的，都各有自己的憂傷。

寫作訣竅

- 聽到消息後馬上就動筆。
- 聚焦在對方的情況，而不是你自己的無力感。如果你覺得無助又苦惱，可以說出來，但不要執著在此上面。病人的感受比你的感受更重要。
- 用跟生病前一樣的口氣與對方說話。若家人、朋友對待病人的方式是把他當成與從前不太一樣的人，這是很讓患者傷心的。你的收信人依舊是人，他有著一般人都有的希望、興趣、人際關係與情緒。
- 如果對方重病，請長話短說。等之後再寄長一點的便箋或信函。你的信讀起來不能太困難；剛做完手術的人不太適合閱讀潦草的字體。不過，在家養病的人則喜歡有許多新消息的長信。你可以附上一些好笑或有趣的剪報、照片、壓花、漫畫、香包、引文、孩子塗鴉或色彩繽紛的明信片。當你有些話說不出口時（例如對方已病入膏肓），在信中附上小東西也不失為一種好方法。

特殊狀況

- **向住院或生病的員工**保證工作不會受影響，業務會有人代理。適合的話，可向他們保證公司有病假與醫療補助。人們在生病之前通常不會細讀這些規定。直屬上司與人力資源部門可以寄發關於保險、病假與公司政策的資料。如果你跟對方很熟，簡單說一句「不必擔心」就已足夠。來自決策管理階層的「早日康復」信，能強化員工忠誠度，對私人與工作上的關係都有助益。
- **寫信給生病的孩子時**，告訴對方你很遺憾聽說他生病了，並附上色彩繽紛、有娛樂性且適合其年齡的東西，如字謎遊戲、謎語、漫畫、剪報或貼紙書，也可以編有趣的故事，或提到雜誌中看到的故事跟他們分享。或者，也可以寫張「優待券」，上面列出他會開心的事情，如讓他能看從圖書館借來的書，或吃到他最喜歡的速食店外帶餐點（如果對方父母同意）、為他講三十分鐘的故事，或開車帶他的朋友來看他。

  如果這名孩子會回信，可以問對方問題讓他好過一些：醫院病房看起來如何？醫生是誰？生病最大的好處是什麼？最糟之處？你如何度過醫院的一天？康復之後，第一件事情想做什麼？

- **如果對方已經無法康復**，別寄「早日康復」信，也不要寫信告訴他你有多傷心。反之，用一封樂觀的信傳遞你的愛，如 I'm glad you're resting comfortably now.「我很高興你現在正舒服地休養。」；It sounds as if you're getting excellent care.「聽起來你正接受很好的照護。」；I see your grandson's math team is going to the finals.「我知道你的孫子的數學隊進入決賽了。」

  在對方提起前，不要講到死亡。有些人不喜歡討論死亡，有些人則願意，所以請按照對方的意願去做。重看一次信件，確保你沒有下意識寫了封「弔唁」慰問對方即將到來的死期。一封合宜的信，是表達你正想著對方，且正為對方祈禱。加入一段共同的回憶故事，但不要說得像墓誌銘一樣（如「我永遠不會忘記……」；「我會一直記得你是個……的人」）。反之，你可以說：I'm still thinking about your giant pumpkin. I'll bet it would have won first prize at the State Fair.「我還在想著你的大南瓜，我打賭全州農業展示會的第一名本來應該是它。」專注在那些絕症病患仍能感到開心的事情，如寫信或拜訪家人與朋友、閱讀、老電影、卡牌遊戲、口述回憶錄。

- **若認識的人得到愛滋病**，請記得，他們首先是你的朋友、鄰居或親戚，其次才是一個得了絕症的人。寫信的語氣，就與你寫給重病病患一樣，別假設對方的來日不多。醫學上的進步，讓有些愛滋病患者能多享受幾年高品質的生活。寄信展現支持，比說話內容正確與否更重要。著重在對方身上，而不是疾病本身。你也可以提議去拜訪他。在對愛滋病的認知錯誤之下，有些人會躲避罹患愛滋病的朋友，這也是生這個病另一辛苦之處。

- **寫信給接受戒癮、飲食失調等治療的朋友時**，你可以選寫著 Thinking of you（想著你）而非 get well（早日康復）的卡片。加上幾句親筆寫的訊息，用你的話告訴對方 I care about you.「我關心你。」或 You are important to me.「你對我很重要。」

- **當親友受傷或生重病，需要長期照護**，那你不只是要寫信給病人，還要寫信給負責照顧他們的人，如配偶、父母、兒女、親戚。在信中給予情感上的支持，並提議實際的幫助（跑腿、載人、送餐、幫忙陪伴病人讓看護人員休息）。

格式

- 市售卡片適合用在各種「早日康復」場合。有人會跳過印刷的字句，直接閱讀手寫訊息，但也有人會細讀每一個印刷字，好像你是特別為他們寫的。因此，請用心挑選卡片，並且務必在卡片上親筆寫下訊息。你可以在卡片內頁右側底下簡短地寫幾句話，或是在卡片內頁左側（通常是完全空白）寫下長一點的內容。

- 當對方跟你有私交，可手寫在私人信紙、便條紙或卡片上。

- 跟對方是職場關係時，可在商務信紙、個人對公司用信紙或備忘錄用紙上打上訊息。

PART 2 應用篇

單字

accident *(n.)* 事故	disheartening *(a.)* 令人沮喪的	painful *(a.)* 疼痛的	treatment *(n.)* 治療
affection *(n.)* 情感	disorder *(n.)* 失調	recovery *(n.)* 康復	uncomfortable *(a.)* 不舒服的
cheer *(v.)* 鼓舞、加油	distressed *(a.)* 痛苦憂傷的	relapse *(v.)* 舊疾復發	undergo *(v.)* 經歷
comfort *(n.) & (v.)* 安慰；撫慰	heal *(v.)* 癒合	saddened *(a.)* 悲痛的	unfortunate *(a.)* 不幸的
concerned *(a.)* 擔心的	health *(n.)* 健康	sickness *(n.)* 病痛	unwelcome *(a.)* 不受歡迎的
convalescence *(n.)* 恢復期	hope *(v.) & (n.)* 希望	sorry *(a.)* 抱歉遺憾的	
diagnosis *(n.)* 診斷	illness *(n.)* 疾病	support *(v.) & (n.)* 支持	
discomfort *(n.)* 不適	optimistic *(a.)* 樂觀的	sympathy *(n.)* 同情、慰問	

詞組

be up and about 能下床走動	have every/great confidence that 很有信心會
bright prospects 前景光明	quick return to health 快速恢復健康
clean bill of health 身體健康	rapid/speedy recovery 快速康復

devoutly hope
衷心希望

regain your health
重新得到健康

early recovery
及早康復

restore/return to health
恢復健康

encouraging news
令人振奮的消息

sorry/very sorry/mighty sorry to hear
遺憾／很遺憾／非常遺憾聽説

felt so bad to hear
很難過聽説

thinking of you
想到你

fervent/fond hope
熱烈／殷切（但不太可能）的希望

unhappy to hear about
聽説……而心情低落

good prospects
前景樂觀

greatly affected by the news that
深受此消息的影響，以至於

wishing you happier, healthier days ahead
祝你未來更快樂、更健康

句子

Although we'll miss you, don't worry about your work—we're parceling it out among us for the time being.
雖然我們會想念你，但別擔心你的工作，我們已經先幫你分攤了。

Best wishes for a speedy recovery.
真心祝福你儘快康復。

Don't worry about the office—we'll manage somehow.
別擔心辦公室的事，我們會想辦法解決。

Fawnia says you're doctoring that troublesome shoulder again.
芳妮雅説你又在治療那麻煩的肩膀了。

From what I understand, this treatment will make all the difference/will give you a new lease on life.
就我所了解，這個治療會帶給你截然不同的未來／會讓你重獲新生。

Hearing about your diagnosis was a shock, but we're hoping for better news down the road.

聽到你的診斷，我大吃一驚，但我們希望很快能聽到更好的消息。

Here's hoping you feel a little better every day.

希望你每天都一點一點變得更好。

I am concerned about you.

我很擔心你。

I hope you'll soon be well/back to your old self/up and around/up and about/back in the swing of things/back on your feet.

希望你很快就會康復／恢復到原先的你／下床走動／下床走動／回歸日常生活／痊癒。

I hope you're not feeling too dejected by this latest setback.

希望最近這次的復發沒有讓你太沮喪。

I'm glad to hear you're getting some relief from the pain.

我很高興知道你的疼痛能得到些許緩解。

I'm sorry you've had such a scare, but relieved to know you caught it in time.

很遺憾你受到如此驚嚇，但你能及時發現也使我鬆了一口氣。

It's no fun being laid up.

臥病在床一點也不好玩。

I was so sorry to hear about your illness/that you were in the hospital.

很遺憾聽說你生病／住院了。

Knowing your unusual determination and energy, we are anticipating a speedy recovery.

我們知道你比別人都有決心與活力，我們相信你很快就會康復。

The news of your emergency surgery came as quite a shock.

你緊急動手術的消息，真是把我們嚇了一跳。

The office/this place is not the same without you!

辦公室／這個地方少了你，完全變了個樣！

We expect to see you as good as new in a few weeks.

我們期盼幾週後看到你時，你就像全新的人一樣狀態良好。

We're all rooting for you to get better quickly.

我們都在為你加油，希望你快快康復。

We're hoping for the best of everything for you.
我們希望你一切順利。

We're thinking of you and hoping you'll feel better soon.
我們正想著你，並希望你能很快好轉。

What a bitter pill to come through the heart surgery with flying colors and then to break your hip!
先是接受心臟手術成功，接著臀部骨折，你真是經歷了難以忍受之苦！

You're very much on my mind and in my heart these days.
這些日子，你時常出現在我的腦海、我的心裡。

段落

We're relieved you came out of the accident so lightly—although from your point of view, it may not feel all that good at the moment. I hope you're not too uncomfortable.

知道你在這場事故中只受到輕微的影響,我們真是大鬆一口氣,儘管就你的立場來說,目前的狀態也許並不太好。希望你沒有很不舒服。

I was sorry to hear about your arthritis. I hope you don't mind, but I made a contribution in your name to the Arthritis Foundation and asked them to send you informational brochures.

我很遺憾聽說你的關節炎狀況。我以你的名義捐款至關節炎基金會,並請他們將資訊手冊寄給你,希望你不會介意我這麼做。

Can I help with anything while you're out of commission? Because of my work schedule and the family's activities, I'm not as free as I'd like to be. However, some things I would be delighted to do are: pick up groceries for you on my way home from work (about 5:30), run the children to evening school events, have them over on Saturday or Sunday afternoons, make phone calls for you, run errands on Saturday mornings, bring over a hot dish once a week. I'd really like to help. You'd do the same for me if our positions were reversed. I'll be waiting for your call.

在你不能工作的期間,有沒有我能幫上忙的地方呢?由於我有工作與家庭,無法像我希望的那樣有自由時間。不過,有些事情我很樂意幫忙,包括在我下班回家時(大約五點半)幫你提回食物雜貨;帶孩子去傍晚的學校活動;在週六或週日下午照顧孩子;幫你打電話;週六早上幫忙跑腿;一週帶給你一道熱食。我真的很想幫忙。如果我們的立場交換,你一定也會為我做一樣的事。我會等你打電話來。

I'm sending you some old *Highlights for Children* magazines and one new scrapbook. I thought you could cut out your favorite pictures and stories and paste them in the scrapbook. It might help pass the time while you have to stay in bed.

我寄給你幾本《兒童文粹》雜誌,跟一本新的剪貼簿。我在想,你可以把喜歡的照片或故事剪下來貼到剪貼簿上。在你臥床期間,這也許能幫你打發時間。

Dear Damon,

What a shock to get to work this morning and have Harry the Horse explain that the only reason I punched in earlier than you for once was that you'd been in an accident. It was pretty gloomy around here until Little Isadore got some information from the hospital. Your doctor evidently thinks the general picture looks good and you shouldn't be laid up too long.

Last Card Louie has divided up your work between Society Max and Good Time Charlie Bernstein, so don't worry about anything at this end.

Best wishes,

親愛的戴蒙：

今早到辦公室時，馬臉哈利告訴我，我這輩子第一次比你早到的原因，是因為你出了意外，這讓我大吃一驚。這裡的氣氛很沉重，直到小伊薩多帶來醫院的消息。你的醫生表示你的狀況大致良好，應該不會臥床太久。

最終手段路易已經將你的工作分攤給社會馬克思與好日子查理·伯恩斯坦，不用擔心這邊的事。

祝福你，

〇〇上

Dear Uncle Mordecai,

We all felt bad to hear that your tricky hip has landed you in the hospital. Here's hoping that surgery is effective in clearing up the problem and that you aren't uncomfortable for too long.

I went over yesterday and cleared the leaves out of your gutters. I was afraid you'd be worrying about that.

We'd like to stop by the hospital some evening to see you, but I'm wondering if it isn't more important for you to get all the rest you can. If you feel up to company some evening, give us a call. Otherwise, we'll see you when you get home. Take care of yourself. You're pretty important to a few people around here.

With love,

親愛的莫德凱叔叔：

您那難治的髖關節又讓您住進了醫院，我們聽到這個消息都很難過。希望手術能有效解決問題，也希望您不會不舒服太久。

我昨天過去您家裡清理了排水溝的樹葉，因為我怕您會擔心這件事。

我們希望能找個傍晚去醫院探望您，但又擔心是否該讓您好好休息。如果您某個傍晚想要有人陪伴，儘管打電話給我們；不然的話，我們會等您回家後再去拜訪。要好好保重。對這裡的很多人來說，您可是很重要的。

愛您的〇〇

44

早日康復信

Dear Horace,

We were all distressed to hear of your heart attack. Leo says you're doing well and all of us here at Giddens are looking forward to your full and speedy recovery.

You'll be happy to know that even in your absence, it's business as usual; your nephew Ted has been a quick study, and things are going smoothly. We loaded the last shipment of the big Hellman order yesterday, and so far all schedules have been maintained.

It must be difficult to be away from a business you raised from a baby, but you need have no fears about it. I hope you can instead spend your energy regaining your health and strength.

Very best wishes to you and Regina.

Sincerely,

親愛的霍瑞斯：

聽到你心臟病發的消息，我們都很傷心。李奧說你的狀況不錯，我們在吉登斯的所有人都期盼你很快就能完全康復。

你應該會很高興知道，你不在的時候，業務仍如常進行；你的姪子泰德學得很快，事情都進行得很順利。昨天我們將海爾曼那張大訂單的最後一批貨裝運，目前一切都照計畫順利進行。

暫離你一手養大的公司，想必讓你很煎熬，但是你不必害怕，希望你能把精力放在恢復健康與氣力上。

為你與雷吉娜獻上最深的祝福。

〇〇上

Dear Mrs. Gummidge,

We were sorry to learn that you have been hospitalized. I took the liberty of stopping your newspaper and mail delivery for the time being (the mail is being held at the post office). Since I had a copy of your house key, I went in to make sure the faucets were off and the windows shut (except for leaving one upstairs and one downstairs open an inch for air). I've been going in at night and turning on a few lights so it doesn't look empty.

I wasn't sure you were up to a phone call, but I thought you'd want to know that the house is being looked after.

We're praying for your speedy recovery.

With best wishes,

古彌紀太太你好：

很遺憾聽說你住院了。我擅自幫你暫時停掉報紙與信件的寄送（信件會暫存在郵局）。由於我有您家的備用鑰匙，所以我進去確認水龍頭與窗戶有沒有關上（只在樓上與樓下各留一扇窗，開了一吋的寬度讓空氣流通）。晚上我都會進去開幾盞燈，才不會看起來沒有人住。

我不太確定你有沒有辦法講電話，但又覺得你會想知道有人在照顧你的房子。

我們都為你祈禱，望你早日康復。

致上最深祝福，
〇〇上

Dear Ms. Melbury,

The staff and management at The Woodlanders join me in wishing you a speedy recovery from your emergency surgery. We are relieved to hear that the surgery went well and that you'll be back among us before long. For one thing, you are the only one who can ever find the Damson files.

Don't even think about work. Giles Winterborne is taking over the outstanding projects on your desk, and Felice Charmond is answering your phone and handling things as they come up. Marty South will send you a copy of company policy on sick leave and hospitalization costs (both are generous, I think).

Sincerely yours,

梅柏瑞小姐你好：

伍蘭德的主管、同仁與我，一齊在此獻上祝福，望你早日在緊急手術後能康復。聽說你手術成功、不久後就能歸隊時，我們都鬆了一口氣。別的不說，你可是唯一能找出譚森檔案的人。

完全不需要擔心工作。吉爾斯·文特勃恩會負責你桌上那項出色的專案；費莉絲·查蒙則為你接聽電話，並處理接下來的事情；馬蒂·紹斯將公司關於病假與住院費用的規定寄給你（我認為公司在這兩方面都很大方）。

○○上

Dear Jay,

I hear you've been under the weather lately. As soon as you feel up to it, let me know and I'll call Daisy and Tom and Nick—there's nothing like a party for lifting the old spirits.

Best,

親愛的傑伊：

我聽說你最近身體不舒服。當你覺得合適時，馬上讓我知道，我會打給黛西、湯姆與尼克。沒有什麼比一場派對更能振奮衰弱的精神了。

○○上

✉ 參見：04 遲回的信、05 敏感信件、12 致謝函、14 收件通知、45 慰問信、47 給親友的信

Chapter 45

慰問信
Letters of Sympathy

一封好的慰問信就像握手，
溫暖而友善。

——作家莉莉安・艾奇勒・華森（Lillian Eichler Watson）

慰問信與弔唁信（letter of condolence）可說是最難寫的信之一，感到震驚、傷心、無能為力、說不出話的人，必須寫信給深陷於悲傷、脆弱、覺得人生沒有意義的人。

無論有多痛苦，只要你與死者的家人或朋友有私人或商務上的關係，便必須寫慰問信。所愛之人去世是件大事，要是你忽視了這麼重要的事情，對方是很難忘記的。

弔唁信只在有人亡故時才需要寫。慰問信除了可用於遭受死亡，也可以用於遭受天災、人禍（如被搶劫、偷竊、或承受暴力對待）或其他不幸事件（失業、破產、個人挫折）。

PART 1 說明篇

何時需要寄慰問信？

寵物死亡	離婚	家中出事的上司
流產或死產	認識的人的親人過世 朋友、鄰居、親戚、顧客、員工、同事	因病或意外住院 參見：44 早日康復信
忌日 參見：43 紀念日	天災 水旱災、風災、地震	不幸事件 失業、破產、盜竊、暴力行為

該怎麼說？

1. 向對方失去的人或遇到的麻煩，簡單直接表達哀傷。
2. 以名字來稱呼死者或遇到不幸事件的人。
3. 合適的話，告訴對方你如何得知消息。
4. 表達哀痛、驚愕、失落的感受。
5. 給予安慰、關心，為對方祈禱、祝福。
6. 若是有人過世，可提及你喜愛死者的原因。講講開心的回憶、故事、口頭禪，或是他們曾給你的建議；提到他們被人記住的美德、功績或成就；回顧他們曾讓你感動的話語或行為。可以回想死者曾說過的話來讚美、描述死者家屬，這樣的內容特別受人喜愛。你的回憶越具體，你的信便越令人難忘、越撫慰人心。

7. 最後用關心、感性或鼓勵未來的方式收尾：You are in my thoughts and prayers. 「我會想著你，為你祈禱。」；My thoughts are with all of you in this time of sorrow. 「在這個悲傷的時刻，我會一直惦記著你們。」；In the days ahead, may you find some small comfort in your many happy memories. 「在未來，希望你能在許多美好的回憶中找到些許安慰。」

什麼不該說？

- 別說得太少（勿用市售卡片，上面只簽名），也別說得太多（勿說陳腔濫調、給予建議或不合宜的評論）。
- 不要過於戲劇化（「我第一次聽到這麼慘的悲劇」）。如果你確實很震驚、受到了衝擊，直言無妨，但要避免太過傷感、聳動或消極。一句簡單的 I'm sorry.「我很遺憾。」就足以撫慰對方。
- 不要討論哲理，或以宗教的角度評論，除非你確定你們有共通的哲學或宗教思想，且這種思想適合用來安慰對方。避免講出跟宗教有關的陳腔濫調、過於簡化悲劇發生的原因，或毫無根據地解釋神的作為、意圖或介入。
- 不要提供建議，或鼓勵對方做出大改變（離開城市、搬到公寓、賣掉配偶的模型船收藏品）。家屬通常要過好幾個月之後才能清楚思考該做的決定。
- 提議給予協助時，不要太過廣泛，如「讓我知道有沒有能幫忙的地方」或「隨時可以打電話給我們」。對方已經有很多事情要處理了，通常不會理會這麼模糊的提議。反之，請直接做點事情：帶食物、幫對方將要穿去葬禮的洋裝或西裝送去乾洗、幫忙外地來的親戚安排住宿、幫忙照顧孩子、為慰問信的回信寫上地址、接手幾天工作、修剪草坪或鏟雪或為花園澆

水、幫忙整理房子。如果你與對方熟悉，你便知道該如何提供幫助，或知道要向誰（朋友、鄰居）詢問。

- 不要聚焦在自己的感受：「我感到心力交瘁，無法專心做任何事」；「每當我想起他，就會哭出來」；「你為何不打電話給我？」。在琳恩‧肯恩（Lynn Caine）的暢銷書《Widow》（暫譯：寡婦）其中一章〈附註：別跟我說你的心情有多糟！〉提到，這位寡婦收到的慰問信，裡頭講的多半是寫信的人自己的尷尬、苦澀與無能為力，而無關她的憂傷與他們共同失去的人。她說，許多信「內容全都在講寫信的人有多不自在、感到多悲慘，好像他們想要我去安慰他們似的」。表達憂傷與過度誇張，兩者還是有明顯不同的。

- 不要表現出不適宜的愉悅，或說些看似樂觀的陳腐說詞。克莉絲塔‧葛洛默（Crystal Gromer）在《讀者文摘》中〈悲傷的禮儀〉一文寫道：「在一個悲傷的場景中，講陳腔濫調就是不禮貌……『至少他沒有痛苦』、『至少他沒成為植物人。』每當你發現自己即將脫口說出『至少』時，請立即停下。在想像中製造一個更慘的情景，並不會讓當下的現實變好，反而使現實顯得無足輕重。」C‧C‧柯頓（C. C. Colton）曾說：「我們的不幸，通常比朋友的評論更容易忍受。」避免說出以下句子：

Chin up. 振奮起來。	Keep busy, you'll forget. 保持忙碌，你會忘記的。
Be brave. 勇敢起來。	I know just how you feel. 我知道你的感受。
Don't cry. 不要哭。	God never makes a mistake. 上帝永遠不會犯錯。
You'll get over it. 你會克服的。	Be happy for what you had. 滿足於你所擁有的。
It's better this way. 這樣更好。	He's in a better place now. 他現在是在一個更好的地方。
She is better off now. 她現在這樣更好。	It's a blessing in disguise. 這其實是一種祝福。
Time heals all wounds. 時間能癒合所有傷口。	At least she isn't suffering. 至少她不再痛苦。
He was too young to die. 他英年早逝。	You must get on with your life. 你必須繼續你的生活。
Life is for the living. 活著的人生活還是要過下去。	He was old and had a good life. 他年紀大了，而且有美好的一生。

Every cloud has a silver lining.
黑暗中總有一線光明。

I heard you're not taking it well.
我聽說你還沒接受這件事。

You're young yet; you can always marry again.
你還年輕，你可以再婚。

It's just as well you never got to know the baby.
你還沒有機會見到這個孩子，這樣也好。

I have a friend who's going through the same thing.
我有一個朋友正在經歷同樣的事情。

You're not the first person this has happened to.
你不是第一個經歷這種事的人。

Don't worry. It was probably for the best.
別擔心，這或許是最好的。

Be thankful you have another child.
你還有另一個孩子，要覺得感恩。

At least you had him for eighteen years.
至少你與他度過了十八年。

She is out of her misery at least.
至少她已經脫離苦海。

God only sends burdens to those who can handle them.
上帝只會將重擔交給能承擔的人。

Life must go on—you'll feel better before you know it.
生活必須繼續過下去；在你意識到之前，你就會感覺好些了。

I feel almost worse than you do about this.
我對此的感受幾乎比你還要糟。

God had a purpose in sending you this burden.
上帝給你這個擔子，一定有目的。

寫作訣竅

- 即使太晚動筆寫慰問信，還是要把信寄出去。對方可以諒解你的遲到，卻不會原諒你在這種時候忽視他。

- 多數情況下，請保持簡要。在悲傷的時候，太長的信會讓對方難以承受。但要是信件內容長，因為你講到很多關於死者的美好回憶，那對方會很歡迎這封信，並會帶給他安慰。但如果信件內容都是沈溺在負面情緒，或是提到其他消息，就不太妥當。

- 要得體，但不必擔心實話實說，例如你可以使用 death（死亡）或 suicide（自殺）。較迂迴的用詞如 passed on（去世）、passed away（過世）、departed（走了）、left this life（離世）、gone to their reward（駕鶴西去）、gone to a better life（去過更好的生活）。the deceased（亡者）與 the dear departed（摯愛的故人）兩個詞現在已經不太常用。

- 接受這個事實：不管你寫了什麼，都無法讓對方的悲傷消失。悲傷是痊癒的必經階段。太多人為了找到適合的詞彙而苦惱不已，希望能用這些字讓一切重返軌道，但這樣的字並不存在。

- 要注意慰問與同情之間的差異。慰問時，你尊重對方有度過不幸事件的能力；同情時，你則懷疑這個事件已經擊倒了對方。
- 讓對方知道他們沒有義務要回覆信件。寫完致謝函給送花、弔唁、說悼詞、抬棺、給予特別協助的人之後，家屬通常都已經沒有精力再回覆慰問信。
- 寫信給家庭成員之一時，在結尾時必須提到其他家人的名字。
- 為了確保你沒有表露尷尬、同情或不得體的內容，請假裝你是收信人，仔細檢視內容。

特殊狀況

- **流產與死產**是令人非常絕望的，你必須像哀悼任何一個孩子的死亡一樣致上慰問。避免說出像以下評論：「你已經有兩個可愛的孩子了，要為了你擁有的而感恩。」；「這也許是最好的；這個孩子可能有什麼不對勁，這是大自然照顧他的方式。」；「你還年輕，可以再試一次。」最糟糕的評論是：「別那麼難過，畢竟這並不像真正失去孩子那樣。」對方是確實失去了孩子。
- **若死者是自殺**，你要像對待任何死者家屬那樣致上慰問。許多家屬會有罪惡感、深感困惑，或覺得不光彩，因此他們更需要知道你惦記著他們。一般狀況，你可以告訴對方你感到「震驚」，但在這種情況下請避免這種描述。不要問問題，不要猜測如何能預防這個悲劇，也不要沉溺於自殺這個事實。重要的是，對方已經離世，而家屬正陷在悲痛之中。你要說的，是死者影響了你、與你共有的美好回憶，或安慰死者家屬的傷痛。
- **慰問患有愛滋病的人時**，要記住，他們先是你的朋友、鄰居與親戚，接著才是罹患愛滋病的人。你要像對待任何得了重病的人那樣寫信給對方。不要假設對方時間已剩不多；有些愛滋病患可以活得很長。向對方表現支持，比說出完全正確的話更為重要。專注在這個人對你的重要性，而非聚焦在疾病、預後情況與感傷上。詢問他們是否需要陪伴，因為有些人並不願意拜訪愛滋病患者，因此他們會很感激你的拜訪。
- **回應離婚或分居**確實很困難，除非你跟對方很熟悉。在多數情況下，慰問或恭喜都不適當。不過，無論這是否會讓對方過得「比較好」，這種人生轉折總是少不了令人難過、遺憾的一面，所以對方通常能接受你給予慰問與支持。
- 如果**有人經歷了讓他感到丟臉的不幸事件**（例如家中有人犯罪），請別猶豫，儘管寫信給他。如果家人朋友正為此感到心痛，那他們一定會歡迎你溫暖的支持。
- 當**工作上的伙伴或顧客失去親人**，請像寫信給朋友或親戚一樣寫慰問信慰問，不過你的信可以短一些、正式一點。避免做私人評論，告訴對方你正惦記著他們便已足夠。代表公司向家屬表示慰問與哀悼。寫信給已故員工家屬時，你可以提議協助整理個人物品、討論撫恤金或幫他們介紹公司裡能回答問題的人。

- 因為**寵物過世**而悲傷的人，也會很感激你寄來的慰問信。無論你是否認同，但失去寵物會令對方非常沮喪，所以表示慰問是細心有禮的表現。

- 你可以在**死者**的忌日或結婚紀念日寫信給其親屬紀念他們。不必擔心會重提傷心往事，因為對方在那一天本來就無法想別的事，他反而會很感謝你寄信鼓勵他，這讓他知道有人還記得死者。計劃開同學會的人，可以寄卡片或花束給已故同學的父母，使他們知道有人仍記著他們的孩子。

- 寫信給得了**不治之症或重病的人**，其實比較像是在寫慰問信，而不是「早日康復」信，但要小心不要提到對方可能的死亡。除非對方自己提起，並顯露出想談談這個話題的意願，否則絕不要提到。反之，告訴對方你聽說他生病後感到非常遺憾，而你現在正惦記著他。不要選擇「早日康復」卡片，最好選寫著「Thinking of You」（想著你）或沒有任何主題的卡片。

- **寄花束到殯儀館時**，須在花束的小卡上寫下如 The family of Emily Webb Gibbs「艾蜜莉・韋伯・吉伯斯的家屬」的字眼。你可以使用從花店附的白色小卡，或你自己的名片，並在上面寫些簡短的內容，如 Please accept my sincerest sympathy.「請接受我最真摯的悼念。」或 My thoughts and prayers are with you and the children.「我為你與孩子致上關心與祈禱。」**若你用死者的名義捐款至某個慈善機構**，請附上你自己與一名死者家屬的姓名與地址。慈善機構會把捐款通知寄給死者家屬，並告知你捐款已經收到。

格式

- 私人慰問信一定是用手寫，除非有無法手寫的狀況（如有殘疾）。使用素雅的私人信紙或折頁卡片（不要使用亮色系或花稍的設計）。

- 可以使用市售問候卡，記得寫上一、兩句（或更多）自己的話。

- 如果是寫給你不太熟但曾在工作上有交流的顧客、客戶、員工或同事，慰問信可以用打字的。使用私人商用信紙，不要使用標準尺寸的信頭信紙。

💬 單字

affection *(n.)* 情感	distressed *(a.)* 痛苦的	mourn *(v.)* 哀悼	sorry *(a.)* 遺憾的
bereavement *(n.)* 喪親	faith *(n.)* 信念	ordeal *(n.)* 考驗	suffering *(n.)* 痛苦
bitter *(a.)* 苦澀的	grief *(n.)* 哀痛	overcome *(v.)* 克服	sympathy *(n.)* 慰問
blow *(v.)* 打擊	hardship *(n.)* 困難	regret *(v.)* 後悔	touched *(a.)* 感動的
comfort *(v.)* 安慰	healing *(a.)* 癒合的	remember *(v.)* 記得	tragic *(a.)* 悲慘的
commiserate *(v.)* 慰問	heartache *(a.)* 心痛	saddened *(a.)* 難過的	trouble *(v.)* 使憂慮苦惱
compassion *(n.)* 憐憫	heartbroken *(a.)* 心碎的	severe *(a.)* 嚴重的	trying *(a.)* 難受的
concerned *(a.)* 關心的	heartsick *(a.)* 悲痛的	shaken *(a.)* 震驚的	unfortunate *(a.)* 不幸的
consolation *(n.)* 安慰	heavyhearted *(a.)* 心情沉重的	share *(v.)* 分享	unhappy *(a.)* 不愉快的
devastating *(a.)* 心力交瘁的	hope *(v.)* 希望	shocked *(a.)* 驚愕的	upset *(a.)* 不安的
difficult *(a.)* 困難的	misfortune *(n.)* 不幸	sorrow *(n.)* 悲傷	unwelcome *(a.)* 心煩的

45

慰問信

詞組

although I never met
儘管我從未見過

I remember so well
我記得很清楚

at a loss for words
說不出話

deepest sympathy
最真心的慰問

beautiful/blessed/cherished memories
美麗／充滿祝福／令人珍惜的回憶

in your time of great sorrow
在你最悲傷的時候

I was saddened to learn/so sorry to hear that
很難過聽到／很遺憾聽說

legacy of wisdom, humor, and love of family
留下了智慧、幽默與對家庭的愛

deeply saddened
深感悲傷

long be remembered for
長久因……被人們記住

during this difficult time
在這個困難時期

made a difference in many lives
為許多人的人生帶來改變

extremely/terribly/so sorry to hear of
極度／非常／很遺憾聽到

many friends share your grief
許多朋友一同分攤你的悲傷

with sincere feeling/personal sorrow/
love and sympathy/sorrow and concern
帶著真誠的感受／個人的哀傷／愛和慰問／
悲傷和關心

no words to express my great/
overwhelming/sincere/deep sorrow
無法用語言來表達我巨大／令人打擊／真心／
深切的悲傷

sharing in your grief/sorrow during this difficult time
在這艱難的時刻分享你的悲痛／哀傷

offer most sincere/heartfelt/deepest sympathy
致上最誠摯／最衷心／最深切的慰問

feel the loss of
感到失去了……

one of a kind
獨一無二的

grand person
偉大的人

profound sorrow
深沉的悲傷

greatly saddened
非常難過

rich memories
豐富的回憶

greatly/sadly/sorely missed
非常／悲傷地／心酸地想念

grieved to hear/learn of your loss
聽到／知道你的損失，覺得悲痛

grieve/mourn with you
和你一起悲傷／哀悼

heart goes out to
心中惦記著

send my condolences/our deepest sympathy
表示我的哀悼／我們最深切的慰問

terrible blow
可怕的打擊

sick at heart
傷感的

sincere condolences
真誠的哀悼

so special to me
對我來說很特別

sorry to learn/hear about
很遺憾知道／聽說

stunned by the news
因這個消息震驚

sad change in your circumstances
你遭逢劇變

sad event/news/bereavement
悲傷的事件／消息／喪親之痛

feel fortunate to have known
有幸認識

family sorrow
家庭的悲痛

shocked and profoundly grieved/ saddened
震驚而深感悲痛／悲傷

touched to the quick
觸及傷痛

tragic news
悲慘的消息

trying time
難受的時刻

upsetting news
令人沮喪的消息

warmest sympathy
最溫暖的慰問

wish to extend our condolences/sympathy
希望傳達我們的哀悼／慰問

句子

All of us are the poorer for Patrick's death.
我們所有人都為派翠克的離世而難過。

How sad I was to hear of Hsuang Tsang's sudden death.
我聽說宣奘突然死亡的消息時非常難過。

Dora was a wonderful person, talented and loving, and I know that you and your family have suffered a great loss.
朵拉是一個很棒的人，有才華、有愛心，我知道你和你的家人承受了很大的損失。

I am thinking of you in this time of sorrow.
在這悲傷的時刻，我正惦記著你。

I can still see the love in his face when he watched you tell a story.
我仍然記得那時他看著你講故事時他臉上的愛意。

I feel privileged to have counted Fanny as a friend.
我有幸能與芬妮當朋友。

I hope you don't mind, but Marion Halcombe told us about your recent bad luck and I wanted to tell you how sorry we were to hear it.
我希望你不會介意，但瑪莉詠‧哈爾科告訴我們你最近遇上不幸的事，我想告訴你，我們聽到消息時感到很遺憾。

I know how hard it is to lose a beloved father—I hope the memories of the happy times you shared will be some solace.
我知道失去摯愛的父親有多麼難受，我希望你與他共度的快樂時光能帶給你些許安慰。

I know Phillip had many admiring friends, and I am proud to have been one of them.
我知道菲利普有許多令人欽佩的朋友，我很自豪是他們其中的一員。

I remember the way your mother made all your friends feel so welcome with her questions, her fudge, and her big smiles.
我記得你媽媽總是用她的方式來歡迎你的所有朋友，包括她問的問題、做的軟糖與燦爛的笑容。

It seems impossible to speak of any consolation in the face of such a bitter loss.
面對如此慘痛的損失，我似乎找不到任何能安慰到你的話。

It was with great sadness/sense of loss/profound sorrow that I learned of Ramona's death.
當我聽說拉蒙娜過世，我感到非常難過／極度失落／深切的悲傷。

I was so sorry to hear that Mr. Golovin's long and courageous battle with cancer has ended.
我很遺憾聽說戈洛文先生與癌症的長期勇敢抗戰已經結束。

I wish I weren't so far away.
我真希望我不是在離你如此遙遠的地方。

45

慰
問
信

I write this with a heavy heart.
我用沉重的心情寫這封信。

Like so many others who were drawn to Yancy by his charm, courage, and warmth, I am deeply grieved and bewildered by his unexpected death.
就像許多喜歡楊西的魅力、勇氣和溫暖的人一樣，我對他的意外死亡深感悲痛和困惑。

Please extend our condolences to the members of your family.
請向你的家人表示哀悼。

Professor Bhaer will always remain alive in the memories of those who loved, respected, and treasured him.
巴爾教授將永遠活在那些熱愛、尊重、珍惜他的人的記憶中。

The loss of your warm and charming home saddened us all.
你失去了溫暖迷人的家園，我們都很為你難過。

The members of the Crestwell Women's Club send you their deepest sympathy.
克雷斯威女子俱樂部的成員向您致以最深切的慰問。

The world has lost someone very special.
世界失去了一個非常特別的人。

We always enjoyed Dr. Stanton's company and respected him so much as a competent, caring physician and surgeon.
我們一直很喜歡斯坦頓醫師的公司，並且非常尊重他，他是一位有能力又有愛心的內外科醫師。

We were grieved to hear that your baby was stillborn.
聽說你失去了腹中的孩子，我們深感悲痛。

We were stunned to hear that you lost your job, but are hopeful that someone with your experience and qualifications will find something suitable—maybe even better.
聽說你失去了工作，我們感到很震驚，但相信你的經驗和資歷會讓你找到合適的職位，甚至是更好的職位。

We who knew and loved Varena have some idea of how great your loss truly is.
我們這些認識維若娜並愛著她的人，知道你承受的是多麼大的損失。

You and the family are much in our thoughts these days.
這些日子，我們時常惦記著你與你的家人。

Your grief is shared by many.
你的悲傷，許多人都感同身受。

段落

How sad I was to hear of Eugenia's sudden death. I will miss seeing her gentle, smiling face every Sunday across the church. She was the first person I always thought of when anyone said the word "volunteer." What the parish will do without her, I can't imagine. And your own loss is, of course, immeasurably greater.

當我聽說尤吉娜突如其來的死亡消息時，感到非常難過。我會想念每個週日在教堂裡看到她溫柔的笑臉。當有人說出「志工」一詞時，她是我第一個想到的人。沒有她，這一個教區該怎麼辦，我無法想像。當然，你所失去的更是無法估量。

I was so sorry to hear about your wife's death. She was one of those truly gracious individuals who make life so much more pleasant for everyone around her. You will miss her very much, I know.

我很遺憾聽到你妻子的死訊。她是如此的親切，讓身邊每個人的生活都更加愉快。我知道，你會非常想念她。

We felt so bad when we heard about the burglary. Something similar happened to us, and it affected me much more deeply and took longer to get over than I would ever have expected. I hope you are not too undone. May we lend you anything? Help put things back in order? Type up an inventory of what's missing? I'll stop by to see what you need.

當我們聽到你們家遭竊時，覺得很遺憾。類似的事也曾發生在我們身上，它的影響程度與時間比我預期的更為深遠。希望你不會感到太心煩。我們能借給你什麼嗎？是否需要協助整理？列出失竊物品的清單？我會經過看看你需要什麼。

This will acknowledge your letter of the 16th. Unfortunately, Mr. Newman is vacationing in a wilderness area this week, but I know he will be most distressed to learn of your brother's death when he returns. Please accept my sympathy on your loss—Mr. de Bellegarde visited here only once, but he left behind the memory of a charming, generous man.

您於十六日的來信已經收到。不幸的是，紐曼先生本週正在野外度假，但是我知道，當他回來得知您兄弟的死訊，他會深感痛心。請接受我對您的慰問。德貝佳先生只來過這裡一次，但他留下了一個迷人、慷慨的身影。

Dear Mrs. Miller,

Saturday is the first anniversary of Daisy's death, and I couldn't let the day go by without writing to see how you are getting along and to tell you that all of Daisy's friends here in Switzerland miss her as much as ever. Her beauty, innocence, and enthusiasm will always live in our hearts.

With warmest regards and renewed sympathy, I am

Sincerely yours,

米勒太太您好：

星期六是黛西去世一年的忌日，我不能就這麼讓這天過去，我必須寫信問您過得如何，並且告訴您，黛西在瑞士的朋友都一如從前思念著她。她的美麗、純真與熱情永遠活在我們心中。

在此致上最溫暖的問候和再一次的慰問。

〇〇敬上

Dear Rollo,

I felt so bad when Mother called to say Mary died this morning. I know how happy the two of you have been these past years, despite health problems for both of you. I never saw a couple who traveled as much and were as involved in so many organizations as you two. Your love and respect for each other was obvious to all who knew you. I know that life will be very lonely for you without this splendid companion.

My memories of Mary go back forty years to the doughnuts and apple cider she made for us in your big farm kitchen after a hayride.

I will visit the next time I'm back in Iowa. Until then, dear Rollo, you will be in my thoughts. I am also thinking of your "boys" (all grown up now, and I still call them boys) and their families. This is a very sad time for all of you.

Affectionately,

親愛的羅洛：

當母親打電話說瑪麗今天早上去世的時候，我感到非常難過。儘管過去幾年你們兩人都有健康問題，但我知道你們過得相當開心。我從來沒有見過一對夫婦這麼常旅行、參與了這麼多的組織。所有認識你們的人，都明白你們對彼此的愛和尊重。我知道如果沒有這個好夥伴，你的生活將會非常寂寞。

我對瑪麗的記憶回到了四十年前，當時我們夜遊之後，她在你們的大農場廚房裡為我們製作甜甜圈和蘋果酒。

下次我回到愛荷華州時，我會過去拜訪你。在此之前，親愛的羅洛，我會惦記著你。我也在想著你們的「男孩」（現在都是大人了，但我仍叫他們男孩）與他們的家人。對你們大家來說，這是一個非常難過的時刻。

愛你的〇〇上

Dear Adam,

Please accept my sincerest sympathy on the death of your mother. Although I never had the pleasure of meeting her, I know how much she meant to you. I also know she left behind a great many friends in the accounting department from her years of excellent work there.

My thoughts are with you and your father on this sad occasion.

Sincerely,

親愛的亞當：

請接受我對令慈去世的真心慰問。雖然我從沒有見過她，但我知道她對你有多重要。我也知道，當年她在會計部門的優秀工作表現，讓她在那裡有許多朋友。

在這個悲傷的時刻，我會惦記著你和令尊。

○○上

Dear Ms. Abinger:

I was sorry to hear of the recent flooding you've had at the Corner Stores. It is one of those horror stories that haunt the dreams of self-employed businesspeople everywhere. I wish you all good luck in getting things back to normal as quickly as possible.

I wanted to assure you that although I will temporarily order my supplies elsewhere, I will be bringing my business back to you as soon as you are ready. I appreciate our long association and am looking forward to doing business with you again.

Sincerely,

45
慰問信

艾賓格女士您好：

我很遺憾聽說街角商店最近淹水。這對每位自營商人來說，都是如惡夢般的恐怖故事。祝福您們能盡快恢復正常。

我想向您保證，雖然我會暫時在其他地方訂購用品，但一旦您準備好了，我會立即把生意帶回來給您。我很喜歡我們一直以來的長期合作，並期待再次與您合作。

○○敬上

✉ 參見：03 回應、04 遲回的信、12 致謝函、14 收件通知、15 公告通知、44 早日康復信

Chapter 46

情書
Love Letters

> 若情人像一場溫柔細雨，
> 情書便如熱帶風暴那樣難以預測，且無所不能。
>
> ——珍妮佛・威廉斯

情書是最難寫、最容易引發挫折感的信，因為我們都希望情書能盡善盡美，能絕妙、難忘、感人、扣人心弦、機智、溫柔、聰明，還有（我們提過了嗎？）完美。

為了所愛之人，做得再好都不為過。我們拿起筆，想像著這封信能說出我們所有的心聲、會為我們做到任何事。但是，我們的文筆是否跟我們的愛一樣偉大美好呢？似乎不是。

情書有兩種。一種是寫給也愛著你的人，這種情書幾乎一定會成功，因為你的讀者覺得你做什麼都很棒。在這個章節，儘管你已經握有王牌，但你可以再學起來幾項高招。

另一種情書是寫給你追求的人，你希望贏得對方的愛。在「特殊狀況」的段落，你可以找到幫助你寫出這種信的方法。

✉ PART 1 說明篇

寫情書給誰？

| 男人 | 女人 |

該怎麼說？

1. 以簡單的句子開場，寫出這封信的主要目的，例如 Dearest Leslie, I miss you. 親愛的雷思莉，我想你。」；Dear Jack, This has been the longest week of my life!「親愛的傑克，這真是我人生中最長的一週！」

2. 繼續講述你對於對方的想法與感受。

3. 回想過去一起度過的快樂時光，並提到未來你們兩個都會參與的計畫。

4. 告訴對方你最近在做些什麼、想些什麼、感受到了什麼。對方是極度想知道你的消息的。主動分享關於自己的事情很棒，對方也會分享有關的事情。I have never told you this, but...「我從沒跟你說過這個，不過……」；When I was little,

I always dreamed that...「當我小時候，我總是夢想著……」；One thing I'm really looking forward to (besides seeing you again!) is...「讓我真的很期待的一件事情（除了再次與你見面！）是……」；My favorite way of spending a Sunday afternoon is...「我最喜歡度過週日下午的方式是……」。

5. 偶而用對方的名字。沒有什麼比看到戀人手寫（或打出）自己的名字更美好的事情了。

6. 把這句話說出口：「我愛你」。這句話怎樣都不嫌多，而戀人，尤其是剛相戀的情侶，都渴望得到這樣的保證，來撫平心中的恐懼與不安。

什麼不該說？

- 不要太簡短。美國編劇家茱蒂絲·維奧斯特（Judith Viorst）說過：「簡潔或許是智慧的展現，但說『我愛你』時便是另一回事了。」對方希望的是你不停地講、寫，或說出他有多麼美好，所以可別太吝嗇。

- 別使用對你而言不自然的句子。儘管你很想用華麗、浮誇的詞藻裝飾情書，但會讓這封信看起來不像你寫的，而你，才是你的讀者所愛之人。

- 別寫出讓你必須在最後加註「讀完立刻銷毀」的內容。收信人很少會這麼做。如果你只是害羞，那麼撕毀與否並沒有太大差別；但要是這封信落到錯誤的人手中，那你可會後悔寫這封信了。

- 不要叫別人幫你先看過情書。只有你與你愛的人才能體會這封信的美好。美國小說家梅朵·里德（Myrtle Reed）曾寫道：「一封真正的情書，對每個人來說都很荒謬，只有寫信人與收信人除外。」這點迄今依然不變。

寫作訣竅

- 下筆前，先列出能引導你寫出句子或段落的想法：戀愛有何特別或意外之處？對方有什麼討人喜愛的地方？對方什麼地方讓你心動？你最想念的對方的什麼地方？如果對方現在走進房間，你會怎麼做？你最常想起對方的哪一點？什麼會讓你想起他？如果你無所不能，你會給對方什麼？你為什麼欣賞他？要具體明確，舉一些讓你心中充滿愛意的例子。

- 從心出發，情書最重要的特色就在於真摯。

- 寫作的時候，心中要一直想著對方。試著想像他正在想什麼、感受到什麼、做什麼，之後再想像他讀著你的信的模樣。

- 若想為你的信增色，可以附上簡報、漫畫、乾燥花或葉、書籤、相片、完成一半讓對方繼續填完的填字遊戲。

- 要是表達自己對你來說很困難，你可以買市售的情人卡片，但要仔細挑選上面的文字。加上一兩行手寫的內容，如 This is exactly how I feel.「這完全表達出我的感受。」；I can hardly wait to see you Friday.「我等不及星期五見到你了。」可以畫插圖或加上結語。雖然卡片比不上信，但能帶來一些變化，作為信與信之間的一個中場休息。

- 在每封信都寫上不同的「我愛你」的理由。

- 如果你要寫的不只是幾封情書而已，那你可以買本戀人絮語集，為你帶來靈感，並幫助你用語句表達情感。有些語錄很適合拿來和對方討論：Do you agree with Antoine de Saint-Exupéry that 'love does not consist in gazing at each other but in looking outward together in the same direction'?「你是否同意安東尼‧聖修伯里所言：『愛不是凝視對方，而是朝著同一方向一起往外看』？」貝絲‧史崔特‧艾迪許（Bess Streeter Aldrich）曾寫道：「愛是你用以看見的光。」艾迪許應該不會介意你這麼寫：「You are the light that I see by.」（你是我得以看見的光），接著你便能解釋原因。

- 需要靈感時，可以看看知名的情書集：

(1) 表達如火的熱情時，可以讀法國女演員茱麗葉‧德魯埃（Juliette Drouet）寫給雨果的信（出自《The Love Letters of Juliette Drouet to Victor Hugo》）：

"A fire that no longer blazes is quickly smothered in ashes. Only a love that scorches and dazzles is worthy of the name. Mine is like that."

「不再燃燒的火焰很快便化為塵埃。只有灼熱閃耀的愛才值得稱為愛，而我的愛就是如此。」

"I see only you, think only of you, speak only to you, touch only you, breathe you, desire you, dream of you; in a word, I love you!"

「我只看著你、只想著你、只對你說話、只碰觸你、只呼吸著你、只渴望你、只夢見你；簡而言之，我愛你！」

"I love you because I love you, because it would be impossible for me not to love you. I love you without question, without calculation, without reason good or bad, faithfully, with all my heart and soul, and every faculty."

「我愛你,因為我愛你,因為我不可能不愛你。我愛你,沒有質疑、沒有計算、無論好壞,忠實獻上我的全心與靈魂與所有感官。」

"When I am dead, I am certain that the imprint of my love will be found on my heart. It is impossible to worship as I do without leaving some visible trace behind when life is over."

「當我死去,我確信人們會發現我的愛刻在我的心上。在生命逝去時,若無法留下明顯的印記,便不可能像我那樣愛慕。」

(2) 若要表達真摯含蓄的情感,可以看美國詩人奧格登・納許(Ogden Nash)給老婆法蘭西絲・雷德・李奧納德(Frances Rider Leonard)的情書(出自《Loving Letters From Ogden Nash: A Family Album》):

"I couldn't go to bed without telling you how particularly marvelous you were today. You don't seem to have any idea of your own loveliness and sweetness; that can't go on, and I shall see that it doesn't."

「在沒有告訴妳今天的妳是如何特別美好之前,我無法入眠。妳對妳的可愛甜美似乎沒有自覺。不能再這樣下去了,我必須讓妳知道才行。」

"Both your letters arrived this morning. Thank you. I had sunk pretty low in the eyes of the elevator man, to whom I have been handing a letter to mail nearly every night and who has evidently noticed that I have been getting nothing in return. I could sense his thinking, 'You have no charm, sir.' But now it's all right again—his attitude today is as respectful and reverent as I could wish."

「我在今天早上收到了妳的兩封信,謝謝妳。這陣子電梯員想必很看不起我,我幾乎每個晚上都交給他一封信,但他一定有注意到我沒收到任何回信。我可以感覺到他正想著:『先生,你毫無魅力』。但現在一切都沒事了,今天他的態度就如我希冀的一樣恭敬。」

"I've been living all day on your letter.... Have I ever told you that I love you? Because I do. I even loved you yesterday when I didn't get any letter and thought you hated me for trying to rush things. It ought to worry me to think that no matter what you ever do to me that is dreadful I will still have to keep on loving you; but it doesn't, and I will."

「我一整天都在寫要給妳的信……我曾經告訴妳我愛妳嗎?因為我確實愛妳。即便是昨天沒收到妳的任何一封信,還以為妳因為我性子太急而討厭我,我也一樣愛妳。我真應該要憂慮,因為不管妳對我做了什麼可怕的事,我還是會繼續愛妳;但我並不憂慮,我會繼續愛妳。」

"I've been reading your letter over all day, it's so dear.... Haven't you a photograph or even a snapshot of yourself? I want to look at and touch it, as I read and touch your letters; it helps bring you a little closer."

「我一整天都在讀著妳的信；它真是珍貴……妳有沒有獨照，或甚至是快照也行？像我讀著、摸著妳的信那樣，我想要看著、觸摸著妳的照片；這能讓妳更靠近我一些。」

"Do you know what is the most delightful sound in the world? I'm sorry that you'll never be able to hear it. It's when I'm sitting in your library, and hear you cross the floor of your room and open the door; then your footsteps in the hall and on the stairs. In four days now—."

「妳知道，這世界上最令人開心的聲音是什麼嗎？很抱歉妳永遠都無法聽到。當我坐在妳的圖書室裡時，我會聽到妳走過房間的地板並打開門，然後妳的腳步聲從門廳與樓梯上傳來。至今已有四天……」

(3) 若是關於長期維持且歷久彌新的愛，可以讀英國宰相邱吉爾與妻子克萊門汀寫給彼此的信（出自《Clementine Churchill: The Biography of a Marriage》）：

邱吉爾給克萊門汀：

"I love you so much and thought so much about you last night and all your courage and sweetness."

「我好愛妳，昨晚想了妳好多的事、妳的勇氣與甜美。」

"You cannot write to me too often or too long—my dearest and sweetest. The beauty and strength of your character and the sagacity of your judgment are more realized by me every day."

「我最親愛、最可愛的，妳不能太常寫信給我，或是寫得太長。我每天都更加能體會妳字裡行間的美麗與力道，而妳的判斷是多麼睿智。」

"The most precious thing I have in life is your love for me."

「妳給我的愛，便是我此生最珍貴之物。」

"Do cable every few days, just to let me know all is well and that you are happy when you think of me."

「每隔幾天就給我發電報，讓我知道妳一切都好，而且妳在想著我時會感到開心。」

"This is just a line to tell you how I love you and how sorry I am you are not here."

「這封電報只是要告訴妳，我有多愛妳，而妳不在這裡我多麼遺憾。」

"Darling, you can write anything but war secrets and it reaches me in a few hours. So send me a letter from your dear hand."

「親愛的，除了跟戰爭有關的祕密外，妳可以寫任何事情，我幾個小時內就會收到了。所以務必親筆寫信給我。」

"Tender love my darling, I miss you very much. I am lonely amid this throng. Your ever-loving husband W."

「我親愛的、溫柔的愛人，我好想妳。在這人群中我感到好孤單。永遠愛妳的丈夫 W 上。」

"My darling one, I think always of you. ... With all my love and constant kisses, I remain ever your devoted husband W."

「我親愛的，我永遠都惦記著妳……我全心全意愛妳、不斷親吻妳，我是一直奉獻於妳的丈夫 W。」

"Another week of toil is over and I am off to Chartwell in an hour. How I wish I was going to find you there! I feel a sense of loneliness and miss you often and would like to feel you near. I love you very much, my dear sweet Clemmie."

「艱難的一週又結束了，我在一小時內就會出發前往查特韋爾莊園。我真希望能在那裡見到妳！我感到孤單，常常想妳，希望能藉此感受到妳在我身邊。我好愛妳，我親愛又可愛的克萊門汀。」

克萊門汀給邱吉爾：

"I miss you terribly—I ache to see you."

「我瘋狂地想著你，心痛般想見到你。」

"I feel there is no room for anyone but you in my heart—you fill every corner."

「我的心再容不下任何人，只裝得了你；你填滿了每個角落。」

"My beloved Winston, This is a long separation. Think of your Pussy now and then with indulgence and love. Your own, Clemmie."

「我摯愛的丈夫，這次的分離很長，想想你的小貓，然後盡情地想著她、愛她。屬於你的克萊門汀上。」

"My darling. My thoughts are with you nearly all the time and though basking in lovely sunshine and blue seas I miss you and home terribly. Tender love, Clemmie."

「親愛的，我幾乎無時無刻不想著你，儘管我正在湛藍海邊曬著暖和的陽光，我依舊非常想念你與家。你溫柔的愛人克萊門汀上。」

"I'm thinking so much of you and how you have enriched my life. I have loved you very much but I wish I had been a more amusing wife to you. How nice it would be if we were both young again."

「我正非常想念你，你豐富了我的生命。我一直非常愛你，但我希望對你來說我是個更有趣的太太。要是我們都能再次年輕，該有多好。」

特殊狀況

- **寫信給欲追求的對象時**，信要簡短，不要太長。保留一些情感上的距離。你可以說一個工作上的有趣事件，但不要提到對你有重大意義的兒時故事。不要急著邀請對方去露營，先問問他是否曾經露營，以及對露營的想法。不要在信中一直說著「你」與「我」（尤其不要說「你和我」，好像你們已經是情侶一樣），請保持中立。其實跟寫申請信一樣，只是你瞄準的不是職位，而是得到面試機會。你要呈現一個溫暖、陽光、好笑、有趣的自己，才能維持對方對你的興趣，直到你以追求者的身分展現自己。

格式

- 任何格式都可以。你的選擇（信紙類型、信封、郵票、鋼筆、簽字筆、電腦、電子郵件、甚至是傳真）展現了你的特質。你可以寫在有劃線的信紙上、有香味的信紙，或是咖啡廳收據背面。你可以每次都使用一樣的筆、墨水與信紙，這樣你的信便有了容易辨識的外觀，即使隔了一段時間也認得出來。你也可以適時變換，運用不同質感的信紙，或有時打字、有時在寫在卡片上。你可以在信封上使用色彩鮮艷的郵票與橡皮印章；也可以使用端莊、保守的十號信封，但在信中寫上瘋狂的內容。

- 用電子郵件寄發的情書，還算是情書嗎？有時是如此。不過，電子郵件中再浪漫的文字，都比不上實體信裡浪漫文字的影響力。實體信是直接從戀人手裡寫出來的，很私人、有實體、像手工藝品一樣。即使將電子情書列印出來，感受還是不大相同。用電子郵件寄送「我正想著你」之類的簡短訊息就好。

單字

attractive *(a.)* 有魅力的	fascinating *(a.)* 令人著迷的	inspiring *(a.)* 鼓舞人心的	promise *(n.)* & *(v.)* 約定
bliss *(n.)* 極大的幸福	fate *(n.)* 命運	intensely *(adv.)* 強烈地	remember *(v.)* 記得
boundless *(a.)* 無邊際的	feeling *(n.)* 感受	lasting *(a.)* 持久的	soulmate *(n.)* 靈魂伴侶
charming *(a.)* 迷人的	fiercely *(adv.)* 炙熱濃烈地	lonesome *(a.)* 寂寞的	sweetest *(a.)* 最甜美的
cherish *(v.)* 珍惜	forever *(adv.)* 永遠地	lovable *(a.)* 可人的	tenderness *(n.)* 溫柔
dearest *(a.)* 最親愛的	handsome *(a.)* 帥氣的	lucky *(a.)* 幸運的	treasure *(n.)* & *(v.)* 寶物；珍藏
delight *(n.)* 愉悅	happy *(a.)* 開心的	memories *(n.)* 回憶	unceasing *(a.)* 不停的
desire *(n.)* & *(v.)* 渴望	heart *(n.)* 心	miracle *(n.)* 奇蹟	undying *(a.)* 不朽的
dream *(n.)* & *(v.)* 夢想	heaven *(n.)* 天堂	paradise *(n.)* 樂園	unforgettable *(a.)* 難忘的
endless *(a.)* 無盡的	immeasurable *(a.)* 無可計量的	passionately *(adv.)* 熱情地	unique *(a.)* 獨特的
eternal *(a.)* 永恆的	incomparable *(a.)* 無可比擬的	pleasure *(n.)* 樂趣	

46

情書

from the first moment
從第一刻起

only love of my life
我人生的唯一摯愛

hardly wait for the day when
等不及……的那一天

on my mind
在我心頭

how I long to
我多麼渴望

remember the time
記得那時候

how much you mean to me
你對我有多麼重要

reread your letter
重讀你的信

if I had only one wish
如果我只能許一個願

so happy to get your letter
真開心收到你的信

in my heart
在我心中

wait for the mail every day
每天都等著信件寄達

I often think of
我時常想起

want to hold you
想要抱你

make life worth living
讓一切都值得

whenever I think of you
每當我想起你

memories that keep me going
讓我繼續向前的回憶

when we're apart
當我們分離

miss you so much
好想念你

without you, I feel
沒有你，我覺得

one of the happiest moments of my life
我人生中最快樂的時刻之一

you make me feel
你讓我覺得

if only you knew
但願你知道

句子

I couldn't sleep last night—and you know why.
我昨晚睡不著覺,而你知道為什麼。

I'd give anything to be able to touch you right now.
要是現在能馬上觸摸到你,我願意付出任何代價。

I had to tell you how much I enjoyed being with you yesterday.
我必須告訴你,昨天我有多麼享受與你在一起的時光。

I'll never forget the first time I saw you.
我永遠不會忘記我第一次見到你的那一刻。

It's too lonely without you!
沒有你實在太孤單了!

I've been carrying your last letter with me everywhere and it's getting limp—will you write me another one?
我走到哪都帶著你最後一次寫給我的信,所以它變得破爛了,你可以再寫一封信給我嗎?

Just when I think I know everything about you, there's a new and wonderful surprise.
每當我覺得我已經了解你的一切,你便又帶給我新穎、美好的驚喜。

Two more days until I see you—I'm not sure I can wait.
再兩天才能見到你,我不知道我還等不等得下去。

We're some of the lucky ones—our love is forever.
我們屬於幸運的那一群人,因為我們的愛是永恆的。

You are my whole world.
你是我的全世界。

You're the answer to my prayers and my dreams.
我祈禱,我夢想,而你就是賜給我的應許。

段落

You are the first thing I think of in the morning. You are the last thing I think of at night. And guess who's on my mind every minute in between!

你是我早上睜開眼想到的第一件事；你是我晚上入睡前想的最後一件事。那麼猜猜看，在早晚之間是誰佔據了我每分每秒的心思！

There is nothing I want more to do and feel less able to do than write you a beautiful love letter. When I try to write, I'm wordless. I've been sitting here, pen in hand, for half an hour trying to express what you mean to me.

我想寫給你一封美麗的情書，但再也沒有比這更讓我想做卻心力不足的事情了。我試著寫信，但一個字也寫不出來。我已經坐在這裡，手拿著筆，長達半個小時，試圖表達你對我的重要性。你是否能接受我借用別人的話呢？

46

情書

Will you accept some borrowed words? Jeremy Taylor once said, "Love is friendship set on fire." I feel them both, the fire and the friendship. Bless you for bringing them into my life.

傑瑞米·泰勒曾說：「愛是著了火的友情」。我確實兩者都感受到了，火與友情。謝謝你把這兩者帶進我的生命。

Why do I love you? It's going to take the rest of my life to tell you, so I'd better get started now. For one thing, your unswerving calm is both soothing and exciting to me. For another, with your smile we could enter you in the Smile Olympics—and win! For another...

我為什麼愛你？我必須用餘生的時間才說得完理由，所以我最好現在就開始。一方面，你一如既往的從容不迫，總是撫慰我又令我興奮；另一方面，你的笑容，一定能讓你進入微笑奧林匹克大賽並拿下勝利！此外……

I feel more intensely alive, more intensely real, more intensely myself since I met you. As if a dimming filter had been removed, the world suddenly shouts with bright colors, sharply outlined shapes, evocative scents, intriguing textures, music, laughter, flashes of joy. You.

在遇見你之後，我更加覺得自己更有活力、更真實存在、更能做我自己。這就像是移除昏暗的濾鏡一樣，這世界突然間變得鮮豔而立體，充滿著回憶的氣味、有趣的紋理、音樂、笑聲、愉悅的光芒，還有你。

Dear Nance,

Because of you, I find myself filled with love for the whole world. Ruth Rendell wrote in one of her mysteries, "It is not so much true that all the world loves a lover as that a lover loves all the world."

Yes! I do! I now pat grubby children on their grubby little heads. I no longer kill mosquitoes. I straighten up crumpled weeds in the sidewalk cracks. I let dogs sniff my ankles (and, well, you know). I line up the bars of soap on the shelves at K-Mart. The world is mine, and I am its, and I love it. Maybe this is a way of saying that I love you a whole world's worth!

Kisses from me

親愛的南西：

因為你，我感到我擁有了給全世界的愛。露絲・藍黛兒在她其中一本推理小說中曾寫道：「這世界愛一個戀人的程度，並不如一名戀人愛這世界的程度」。

沒錯！我就是這樣！現在的我會拍拍髒兮兮的孩子的髒兮兮的頭；我不再殺死蚊子；我會把人行道裂縫中彎曲的野草拉直；我讓狗兒在我的腳踝聞來聞去（然後，嗯，你知道的）；我在凱馬特超市把架子上的肥皂排整齊。這世界是我的，而我屬於這個世界，我深愛它。也許這也是一種方法，讓你知道我對你的愛值得全世界！

獻上我的吻

46

情書

Dearest Oliver,

There's only time for a quick postcard between flights, but I wanted to tell you how I treasure my last sight of you waving at the window. All I have to do is shut my eyes and I see you again.

Three more days and I won't need to shut my eyes! Until then, all my love!

最親愛的奧立佛：

我只有在航班間快速寄一張明信片的時間，但我想要告訴你，我非常珍惜最後看著你對窗戶揮手的那一刻。我要做的就是閉上我的眼，然後再度見到你。

再過三天，我就不需要再閉上眼了！到時見了，致上我全心的愛！

Dear Sophy,

Scientists seem unable to measure love. I—you will not be surprised to discover this, knowing how talented I am!—have found a way to do it.

When you go to your seminar in Denver next week, I am going to keep Traddles for you. Now you know that I am not, and have never been, a dog person. If I were a dog person, my tastes would not run to Mexican hairless dogs with bat-like ears, rat-like tails, wrinkled snouts, and, in this case, a cast on its leg.

Not only will I keep Traddles (we haven't taken the full measure of this love yet!), but I will let her sleep in my bed, I will be faithful to her finicky feeding schedule, and I will even—once or twice a day—kiss her on the lips. Or near the lips anyway. I will pet her, I will let her watch football with me and follow me around. I will take her for her daily walks, even though everyone who sees us will look at her cast, then look at me and think, "Ah, a man who abuses dogs!"

And all this because I love you. So, what do you think? Have I found a way to measure love?

Tom

親愛的蘇菲：

科學家似乎無法丈量愛情，但我找到了一個方法。當你聽完之後，想必不會太驚訝，因為你早已明白我多有才華！

等你下週去丹佛參加研討會時，我會幫你照顧崔多。現在你知道我並不是也從來不是個愛狗人士；要是我是個愛狗人士，我就不會喜歡一隻有蝙蝠似的耳朵、老鼠似的尾巴、滿是皺紋又有個大鼻子的墨西哥無毛狗，腿上還打了石膏。

我不只會照顧崔多（我們還沒說完丈量這份愛情的方法呢！）還會讓她睡在我的床上、好好按照她講究的時間表餵食，我甚至會親吻她的嘴巴，一天一到兩次，或至少親在嘴巴附近。我會寵愛她，讓她跟我一起看足球賽、跟著我走來走去。我會每天帶她去散步，儘管看到我們的每一個人都會盯著她的石膏，然後看著我心想：「啊，這男的虐狗！」

這一切都是因為我愛你。所以，你覺得如何呢？我是否找到了丈量愛情的方法？

湯姆

Dear Carol,

Today I found one more reason to be grateful for you.

You don't want to hear the whole sorry tale but my day involved things like oversleeping and then running into Mr. Valborg while trying to sneak into the office; losing irreplaceable data to the computer gremlins; dripping spaghetti sauce on my white shirt (while having lunch with, of course, Mr. Valborg); having to deal with two incredibly irate clients; and finding, when I finally left the office, that my battery was dead.

Thinking about you was the only pleasant thing in my life today! Thank you for being so wonderful that all by yourself you make up for everything that goes wrong.

Love,
Will

親愛的卡蘿：

今天我又發現一個感謝你的理由。

你不會想聽完整個悲慘的故事，但我在一天之內發生了睡過頭、偷溜進辦公室時撞見華伯格先生、因電腦小精靈而弄丟無法回復的數據、把義大利麵醬汁滴到白襯衫上（當然，是與華伯格先生吃午餐時）、對付兩位怒氣沖沖的客戶、好不容易離開辦公室時卻發現電池沒電。

在今天，我生命中唯一值得高興的事情，就只有想著你！謝謝你的如此美好，只需你一人，就能彌補出錯的一切。

愛你的威爾

✉ 參見：11 表揚信、47 給親友的信

Chapter 47

給親友的信
Letters to Family and Friends

務必讓我知道你的消息，
即便只是封二十頁的信。

──美國喜劇演員格魯喬‧馬克思

儘管便宜的視訊電話已經是親朋好友之間聯絡的主要方式，每年仍然有上百萬封寄給親朋好友的信，而電子郵件更是大大增加了親友間的通信量。

當你和朋友講到收到信是多麼愉悅時，便會聊到家庭的年度總結信（family round-robin letter）；說起將多年信件歸還給孩子與孫子的祖母；說起結婚紀念日時，大聲念出對方寫的第一封情書的夫妻；或說到把信保存了二十五年的高中同學。

其中也不乏有嚴肅的信：有個男子每次在接受化療前，都會從朋友那收到雪花般的來信；有個年輕未婚女子讀著許多夫婦的來信，決定讓誰領養她的孩子；一個高齡九十歲的爺爺，耳朵已經聽不見，卻可以開心讀著每週收到的信。

作家莉莉安‧華森曾說：「無論何時何地，人們都在殷殷盼著從家鄉來的信！他們在傷感中一次次問著那古老而熟悉的問題：『有給我的信嗎？』」

PART 1 說明篇

給親朋好友的信包括哪些？

父親節、母親節	節日問候	與親友的聯絡	情書
	參見：08 佳節問候信		參見：46 情書

給孩子的信		特殊事件	
生日、恭賀達成目標、離家	筆友信	參見：07 恭賀信、08 佳節問候信、18 慰問信、50 婚禮相關信	歡迎新的家族成員 參見：10 歡迎信

該怎麼說？

1. 以開心的口吻開場，告訴對方你很開心能寫信給他。

2. 詢問對方的生活近況，但不要聽起來像個面試官。

3. 分享自己的近況。聊看過的書、看過的電影或舞臺劇；參加或出席過的運動活動；近期關心的政治議題；共同朋友的消息；讓你大笑的某件事；剛買的東西；夏天、秋天或明年的計畫；天氣狀況；工作上的改變；寵物、嗜好或收集品。也可以選一則最近發生的事件（不必是非常重要的大事），然後像說故事一樣描述它。

4. 結尾時，表達關心或愛意，並告訴對方期盼能相見或聽到對方的消息。

什麼不該說？

- 信的開頭必須歡快、正面、有趣。別一開始就說「我不知道我在寫什麼，因為我沒有什麼想說的」；「你知道我有多討厭寫信」或「很抱歉沒有早一點寫信」，除非你可以用詼諧、有創意的方式表達。

- 別只問問題，或只回應對方在上一封來信提到的事（「你新裝修的廚房聽起來棒呆了！」；「新車聽起來很讚」；「你的派對想必很有趣」；「我打賭你很為希瑟莉驕傲」）。普立茲詩歌獎得主馬克·范多倫（Mark Van Doren）曾說：「只是回應另一封信的信，算不上是信。」心理學家佛洛伊德則說：「我認為，寫好信的規則應該是：別說那些收件者已經知道的事情，反倒可以說些……從未聽聞的新鮮事。」英國作家勞倫斯（D. H. Lawrence）也說：「我最愛能寫下一張又一張私事的人，這是很慷慨的舉動。」

- 別抱怨或負面思考，除非你可以用好笑的方式寫出來。歡快正面的信才受歡迎。不過，要是你或你的收件人正處於困難，那便是例外。

- 別以「我讓你無聊夠久了」或「我最好在你睡著之前停筆」收尾。反之，要讓對方知道，你很喜歡聽到他們的消息，或是很想念他們，或再次重述你很為他們的好消息開心。

47
給親友的信

寫作訣竅

- 動筆時機：當你覺得寫信是件開心的事情，而不是件苦差事的時候。有人說，給親朋好友的信最好是短而頻繁，而不要長而稀有。不過這其實是個性問題，能收到私人信件就足以令人開心，收件人不會在意太短或太少寄，或太長或太頻繁。

- 如果信件往返之間已間隔數月，把這期間發生的種種都寫進信裡一定會累壞我們跟讀者。只提那些你現在正在做的事、讀的書或喜歡的東西。這樣信會比較短，對方也較能跟你產生共鳴。

- 請記得寫作老師不斷強調的「要闡述！闡述！」不要只是講你去了露營，而是要講個故事，或描述所見到的事情，這樣對方才能想像你說的情景。

- 可加入漫畫、剪報、快照、書籤等材料，讓收到的人更滿足，也讓信件更有分量。

- 沒時間寫信時，明信片是個好幫手。在書桌上準備一疊色彩繽紛、有趣或復古的明信片，然後養成一週寄出幾張明信片的習慣。這會幫你維持關係，你也不會因沒有回信而產生罪惡感。

- 如果不知從何下筆，可以先用引言表達心情，再往下寫。舉例來說，桃樂絲‧湯普森（Dorothy Thompson）曾寫道：「孩子天生就希望父親像一座大山做他們的後盾，而就像我們崇敬大山一般，我們也崇敬父親。」（Children want to feel instinctively that their father is behind them as solid as a mountain, but, like a mountain, is something to look up to.）並以親身經驗描述父親是個有責任感的父親，以及你崇敬他的理由。如果你與父親在運動上有共同興趣，或你們會一起做某些事情，那你可以引用索樂‧佛斯特（Solar Forst）的「好爸爸永遠都有些孩子氣。」（The good father never stops being a child.）並回憶你與他在一起的美好時光。其他引言：

My heart is happy, my mind is free
I had a father who talked with me.
我心愉悅，我思飛揚
我的父親，與我說話。

——希爾達‧畢格洛（Hilda Bigelow）

I am many things besides, but I am daddy's girl too and so I will remain—all the way to the old folks' home.
我有很多其他身分，但我也是爹地的小女孩，一直都會是，直到我去了養老院。

——寶拉‧魏德格（Paula Weideger）

When Father smiled, it was like the sun coming out, and spring and summer in your heart.
父親微笑時，就像太陽探出了頭，我的心中便有了春夏。

——葛萊迪‧泰伯（Gladys Taber）

All the feeling which my father could not put into words was in his hand—any dog, child or horse would recognize the kindness of it.

父親無法以言語道出的那些感受，都展現在他的手裡；無論是狗兒、孩童或馬，都能察覺他手裡的慈愛。

——弗雷婭・史塔克（Freya Stark）

A daughter's love for a kind father... is mixed with the careless happiness of childhood, which can never come again.

女兒對於父親的愛，夾雜著童年那無憂無慮的幸福，而童年一去不復返。

——康斯坦絲・芬妮默・沃爾森（Constance Fenimore Woolson）

特殊狀況

- 家人之間有種信件是最寶貴的，而且不需要貼上郵票就能傳遞，那可以是放在孩子午餐盒上的字條或圖畫，另一半放在行李箱上的字條，給努力念書的孩子的鼓勵信，或是夾在床罩上寫著「我愛你」的簡單字條。這些信在促進家庭和諧方面，可比它們本身的重量多了好幾倍。

- **利用母親節與父親節**，表達平常覺得不自在或太肉麻的話。無論是寫信，或是在市售卡片上加上幾句話，都要納入至少一則你們之間的有趣事件、美好回憶或是讚美，像是 I love it when you tear an article out of the newspaper that you think will interest me.「我很喜歡你總是把報紙上的文章剪下來，因為你覺得我會感興趣。」；I'll never forget your Sunday morning pancakes.「我永遠都不會忘記你在週日早上做的鬆餅。」；I wouldn't have gotten into basketball if it hadn't been for you.「如果不是你的話，我不會踏入籃球界。」；I like the way you discuss your work with me as if I actually knew what you were talking about!「我好喜歡你跟我討論你的工作，好像我真的知道你在說什麼一樣！。」

沒有靈感的話，可以試著用以下開頭想出句子：I'll never forget when you...「我永遠不會忘記那一天……」；You were so funny when you...「當你……時，真是太好笑了」；Thanks for the time you...「謝謝那時候你……」；One of my best memories is...「我最棒的回憶是……」；I like watching you get excited about...「我喜歡看著你因為……而興高采烈的樣子」；I've never forgotten what you once told me...「我從來都沒有忘記你曾經告訴我……」。表達感受時，簡單就好。I love you.「我愛你。」；I say 'thank you' for you every day.「我每天都想跟你說『謝謝』。」；I've looked up to you all my life.「你是我這輩子一直看齊的人。」；Thank you for all you've done for me and given me and been to me.「謝謝你為我做的一切、給我的一切以及為我展現的一切。」一個擁有八名子女的母親在過世前，從孩子那

裡收到的卡片、信件與照片，塞滿了一個大箱子，而在每一封信上，她都以鉛筆寫上日期以及她對於那個孩子的愛。

在母親節或父親節時，你也可以寄信給曾經待你如父母的人，如祖父母、老友、老師、鄰居。

- **將孩子暫交其他大人或機構照顧時**，必須提供一封授權緊急醫療協助的委託信給對方。如果是參加夏令營或是去托兒所，通常須填寫這類的表格。要是你是在週末將孩子委託給某人，你可以這麼寫：I [name] give permission to [name of person caring for your children] to authorize any necessary medical emergency care for [name of child or children] from [date] to [date].「本人〔姓名〕同意委託〔孩子照顧者〕，於〔起始日〕至〔結束日〕期間，若〔孩童姓名〕有任何接受緊急醫療照護之必要，可全權處理。」最後在信上簽名、註明日期，並提供能聯絡到你的電話號碼。

- 若一對情侶已訂婚，**雙方家人尚未見面之前**，雙方通常會交換信件，來表達兒女訂婚的喜悅，同時也可以藉此機會邀請對方來訪。一種既有禮貌又優雅的回應是，在拜訪對方前，由未來的女婿或媳婦寫一封短信，在信中感謝對方的邀請，並表示很高興即將能去拜訪。

- 儘管寫信給牢裡的陌生人通常不是個好主意，但是**寫信給在拘留所或監獄的家人朋友**（以及那些與你關係親近的親朋好友），是很好的想法。他們喜歡收到信。一開始的幾封信可能有些尷尬，但你可以講一些中性的主題（書籍、興趣、嗜好、共同朋友、社會議題），隨著時間與練習，會越來越上手。

- 處理強烈的情感時，寫信很有用。當人與人之間有了距離，人與問題之間也有了距離，才有時間能理清思緒，才有辦法將想法寫到紙上。不過，信也可能讓問題惡化。在盛怒之下寫出的文字，並不像說出來的話那麼容易忘記，而且懷恨在心的人還可以不斷重讀這封信。文字沒有手勢或微笑，也沒有抱歉的神情輔助，顯得更冷淡、不容改變。要仔細考慮收信人的脾氣，找到一個對方會願意「聆聽」的方法。不要在情緒最激烈的狀態下寫信。你可以先寫出來，但不要寄。用幾天的時間多次重讀改寫你的信。

- **寫信給兒童時**，以正楷書寫或打字，這樣比較容易讀。加入令人興奮、有挑戰或引發好奇心的話，提及一些瑣事、動腦問題、字謎、趣聞軼事。孩子很喜歡參與大人的世界；你可以告訴他對你重要的事情，如工作問題、你的花園、或下次選舉的事。分享你的見解、討論想法、問他問題。避免使用「kid」（小傢伙）這個字。為了方便讓兒童回信，你可以附上幾張明信片，或已寫好地址的信封加上一張還沒貼上的郵票（如果他們沒有回覆，郵票就不會浪費了）。或者，你也可以製作一張孩子可以直接回覆的信件，上面各種寫「好消息」跟勾選的空格，讓孩子可以直接作勾選。這種方法能確保你會收到至少一次回信。

孩童很喜歡信件，儘管他們根本不認識字，你可以在孩子的名字（很多幼兒很早就認識自己的名字）旁邊貼上剪下來的照片貼紙。在信中附上色彩繽紛的圖畫，你的照片，一支很炫的鉛筆、或一個小型玩具。請記得他的父母會大聲唸出你的信，而這會讓事情變得很不一樣。

- **寫信給第一次離家自立的孩子時**，你可以簡短告訴他「我們想你！」，不要太過強調家中變得空蕩蕩，有些孩子會覺得自己必須為父母的感受負責。不必詳述家中的每個人在做什麼，因為那也可能會讓孩子難過。反之，你可以提出問題，讓孩子在回信中有內容可寫：你什麼時候起床？你早餐通常吃什麼？你有游泳課嗎？還有誰住在你的小木屋裡？那裡有任何動物嗎？你去滑過獨木舟了沒？你最喜歡的活動是什麼？你的指導老師是誰？你有交到新朋友嗎？

- **想幫助孩子寫信時**，讓他們自己收信。給他們行距較寬的小紙張，以及有趣的筆。在他們寫出前二十封短字條時，和他們一起寫，對他們來說，跟你一起寫信也是樂趣的一部分。規定孩子在收到對方寄來的禮物後，必須寫一張感謝字條，但讓他們用自己的步調去寫。有機會時，可以為此開個小派對，同時你自己也寫一張感謝函。

- 雖然 pen pal（筆友）一詞聽起來只適用於年輕人，但成千上萬的成年人也喜歡交筆友，或許用「pen friend」會是更好的用詞。剛開始**和筆友通信時**，要謹慎給予個人資料；先從多數人都知道的事實開始聊，把比較隱私的細節留到之後再講。

  當筆友的主要原則是做自己。有人很討厭新筆友寄來長達十頁的信，但也有人會因此開心；有些人喜歡別人以自我為中心只講自己的事，有些人則會感到無聊；遇到從不提任何私事的筆友，有些人覺得這是謹慎，有些人則認為過於矜持。當你做自己，你最終會遇到喜歡你做自己的筆友。

格式

- 寫信給親朋好友時，可使用任何你喜歡的格式。若是寫給普通朋友，情況便有一點不同；與對方的交情越淺，信件或字條就得看起來越正式（使用私人信紙、手寫）。

PART 2 應用篇

單字

activity (n.) 活動	vacation (n.) 假期	busy (a.) 忙碌的	proud (a.) 驕傲的
event (n.) 事件	weather (n.) 天氣	funny (a.) 好笑的	satisfying (a.) 令人滿意的
friendship (n.) 友誼	announce (v.) 宣布	happy (a.) 開心的	affectionately (adv.) 深情地
going-on (n.) 發生的事情	tell (v.) 告訴	healthy (a.) 健康的	recently (adv.) 最近
news (n.) 新消息	pleased (a.) 愉悅的		

詞組

a warm hello 溫暖的問候	missing you 想念著你
did you know 你知不知道	remember the time 記得當時
good to hear from you 很高興聽到你的消息	sympathize with 與……同感
have you ever thought about 你是否曾經想過	thinking of you 正想到你
have you heard 你是否聽說	we were so happy to hear that 我們真是高興能夠聽到
how did you manage to 你是怎麼辦到	we wondered if 我們想知道是否

I enjoyed hearing about
我很喜歡聽到關於……的消息

I hope that by now
我希望目前

I meant to tell you
我想要告訴你

in your last letter you didn't mention
在上一封信中你沒有提到

I thought you might like to know
我想你可能有興趣知道

what did you think of
你想到了什麼

what ever happened to
無論……發生了什麼

what would you say to
你會對……說什麼

when are you going to
你什麼時候要去

句子

Are you planning to travel this summer?
你是否正計劃這個夏天要去旅行？

Have you read any good books lately?
你最近是否讀了什麼好書呢？

I can't tell you how much I appreciated your letter.
我難以描述我有多感謝你的來信。

I'll be counting the minutes till I see you.
我會不斷期待著見到你的那一天。

I'm wondering how your finals went.
我想知道你的期末考考得如何。

I think of you every day/so often.
我每天／時常都想到你。

I've never written to anyone I didn't know before, so let's see how this goes!
我之前從來沒有寫信給陌生人過，所以就讓我們看看會怎麼樣吧！

I was so glad to see your handwriting again.
我真開心能再次讀到你親筆寫的字。

Please write and tell me all the news.
請寫信給我，告訴我所有消息。

We'd love to see pictures of the new house.
我們想要看看新房子的照片。

We thoroughly enjoy your letters—you can't write often enough for us.
我們非常享受你的來信，你真的常常寫信給我們。

What a dear letter!
真是封可愛的信！

Write when you have time, will you?
有空就寫信給我，好嗎？

You must send the quickest of moral support notes to me because I'm having an absolutely dreadful time at the office.
你必須馬上寄信給我撫慰我的心靈，因為我現在在辦公室真是過得糟透了。

You're in my thoughts every minute of the day.
每分每秒我都想著你。

Your last letter was priceless/delightful/a pleasure to receive.
你上次寄來的那封信，真是無價之寶／令人開心／讓人愉悅。

Your letters always brighten my day.
你的信總是帶給我光明。

Your letter was such fun to read—thanks!
你的信讀起來真是有趣，謝啦！

段落

Hello! My name is Henry Earlforward and in addition to being your new pen friend I'm a bookseller by vocation and a bibliophile by avocation. I hope you like books as much as I do.

哈囉！我叫亨利·厄弗沃，我除了是你的新筆友之外，也是一名書商，業餘愛好則是收藏書本。我希望你就像我一樣愛書。

I can hardly wait for summer to get here. What's that you say? Summer has come and gone? The kids are back in school? But... but... I really don't know where the time goes.

我真希望夏天趕緊來到這裡。你是怎麼說的？夏天已經來了又走？孩子都回到學校了？可是……可是……我還真不知道時間溜去了哪裡。

Please say hello to everyone and tell Audrey thanks again for taking us out. We had a great time! Your family is so warm and fun to be around—so much energy and self-assurance! I miss you all!

請向每個人說聲哈囉，並幫我再次感謝奧黛莉帶我們出去玩。我們度過了很棒的時光！你的家人相處起來好溫暖又有趣，真是精力充沛又有自信！我很想念你們所有人！

I'm sorry about this one-size-fits-all letter, but my negligence in corresponding with all of you finally got so oppressive that I had to take immediate steps. These immediate steps have taken me almost three weeks. Meanwhile, my brand-new personal computer was crying out, "Use me! Use me!" Then... Poof! Voilà! Eureka! Hoover!... this letter was conceived and executed.

我很抱歉寄給你們這封制式信，但我之前太過疏忽，未能回覆你們每個人，這讓我壓力沉重，我不得不馬上採取以下行動，而這些行動花了我將近三週時間。與此同時，我全新的私人電腦向我吶喊：「使用我吧！使用我吧！」於是……呼！瞧！我知道了！敲敲鍵盤！……這封信便成形、完成了。

Will wonders never cease? Hannah is finally sprouting some teeth—believe it or don't. I mean she's only seventeen months old! I was beginning to wonder if kids need teeth to get into first grade. Well, those teeth may have been slow in coming but at least they brought out the monster in her for four months. Actually she's been pretty good considering how sore her mouth must be.

真不可思議，不是嗎？漢娜終於開始長牙齒了，信不信由你。我的意思是，她「才」十七個月大呀！我之前還在想，小朋友上一年級時需不需要牙齒。嗯，這些牙齒也許是出現得比較晚，但還是足以讓她在過去四個月變成小怪獸。老實說，她算是表現得不錯了，畢竟她的嘴巴一定癢死了。

示範信

Dear Angela and Tom,

Parlez-vous français? That means "Sorry I haven't written lately." It all started when I ran out of lined paper at my office. I hate trying to write on this blank stuff, it's like trying to drive on a snow-covered road, only a little safer.

So how's the world treating you these days? We are winding down from another busy summer and hoping for a beautiful and serene fall. Whoever coined the phrase "lazy days of summer" ought to have their vital signs checked. I mean, who are we kidding here?

Both Kalli and Lauren are taking a gymnastics class, so we spend a lot of after-dinner time in the yard practicing what they are learning, with me as their "equipment." But it's fun, at least until the mosquitoes begin setting up their derricks.

I had a busy summer at the office, but September is slow as usual. The kids are back in school, the farmers are busy, and bow-hunting season is here. It's actually a nice pace although hard on the budget. I think I would enjoy dentistry a lot more if I didn't have to make money at it.

I'm manager of our softball team this season. It's one of those things that doesn't sound like much, and shouldn't be, but is. I'd rate it about a 9.8 on the headache scale (of 10). We are winning at 11-3 and tied for first in our twelve-team league, but, honestly, the manager has nothing to do with that. Now if we were losing, then it would be my fault. The hardest part is collecting money from people for various things and making a lot of phone calls.

Well, that's all for now. Say hello to the kids for me.

With love,

親愛的安琪拉與湯姆：

你會說法語嗎？這句話的意思是「抱歉我最近沒寫信」。這一切開始於我用完辦公室的橫格線信紙的那一天。我很討厭用這種空白玩意兒寫信，很像是在滿覆白雪的路上開車，只是比較安全一點而已。

那麼，這個世界最近待你如何呢？忙碌的夏天過去，我們終於能漸漸放鬆下來，期盼一個美好、寧靜的秋季。發明「慵懶夏日」這個詞的人，應該要去檢查他的生命跡象才是。拜託，他想騙誰啊？

卡莉與勞倫都在上體操課，所以晚餐後，我們花很多時間在院子裡練習他們學到的動作，並把我當成「器材」。但真的很好玩，至少在蚊子伸出牠們的長喙之前是如此。

夏天的辦公室非常忙碌，但秋天則像之前一樣步調緩慢。孩子們回到了學校、農夫們忙了起來、弓箭狩獵的季節開始。這種步調其實很不錯，但經濟上便變得拮据。如果我不必靠當牙醫賺錢，我想我會更喜歡做一名牙醫。

我是我們壘球隊這一季的經理。這件差事聽起來不怎麼累，也不該太累，卻真的很累人。在頭痛指數上，我會給它 9.8 分（滿分 10 分）。我們以十一比三贏得比賽，並在共十二隊的聯賽中拿到第一；但是，老實說，經理跟這些一點關係也沒有。如果當時是我們輸了的話，那就是我的錯。最難的部分是為了各種事情向人們收錢，還有要打非常多通電話。

嗯，目前就這些事了。幫我向孩子們說聲哈囉。

愛你的○○

Dear Mrs. K.,

It was so nice to hear from you. I wish we could have had a longer visit at Easter. This semester has gone by so quickly—there are only three weeks left. Maybe we can get together when I come home for the summer.

I know you don't watch TV, so I'll tell you what Oprah Winfrey said. The average cost of a wedding is $13,000. Can you believe that? Mom tried to break the news to Daddy. He guessed the average wedding cost was $700 to $1,000. Poor Daddy.

Because there is going to be a wedding! We think next year. Can you believe I've written a whole page and haven't mentioned the love of my life? Jeff is fine, and sends his love too.

With a hug,

47

給親友的信

親愛的 K 太太：

很開心能知道你的消息。真希望復活節那時我們能再多待一些時間。這個學期過得很快，現在只剩下三週了。等我夏天回家時，也許我們能聚聚。

我知道你不看電視，所以我要告訴你歐普拉（Oprah Winfrey）說了什麼。婚禮的平均花費是 13,000 元，你能相信嗎？媽試著要把這個壞消息告訴爸爸，他還以為婚禮平均只要花 700 到 1,000 元呢。可憐的爹。

這是因為我要結婚了！我們打算明年舉行婚禮。我已經寫了一整頁，竟然都還沒提到我的人生摯愛，很誇張吧？傑夫很好，他也向你致意。

○○獻上擁抱

✉ 參見：07 恭賀信、08 佳節問候信、10 歡迎信、12 致謝函、13 致歉信、23 建議、43 紀念日、44 早日康復信、45 慰問信、46 情書、50 婚禮相關信

Chapter 48

給鄰居的信
Letters to Neighbors

過去在邊疆，敦親睦鄰的精神相當重要，因為鄰居非常少；
但現在，這種精神更是重要，因為我們有太多鄰居。

——小瓢蟲詹森夫人（Lady Bird Johnson）

我們追求鄰里和睦，就跟人類社會的歷史一樣長久，而人們對此事總有源源不絕的建議。於一九〇二年出版的《The Correct Thing》（暫譯：正確的事）是一本許多人都曾查閱的禮儀書，作者佛羅倫斯·霍·浩爾（Florence Howe Hall）在其中寫道：「當鄰居文明地告訴你，他希望你的孩子別再打破他家窗戶時，我們若因而感到被冒犯，便是不正確的。」當然！我們怎麼會不知道這點？

發生在鄰居間的麻煩事，大多都可以用常識與善意解決。茱蒂絲·馬丁曾經提到：「禮節的難處，並不在於對別人展現善意，而是當你面對他人的不良舉止時，不去模仿對方。」

 PART 1　說明篇

何時需要寫信給鄰居？

傳達社區發生的問題	宣布個人或商務消息	恭喜或表達感激
介紹你在社區做的生意	邀請參與社區活動	有怨言

提供協助	寄送祝福	感謝合作或協助

該怎麼說？

1. 先確認寫信是適當的方法。如果數次面對面或電話討論都徒勞無功，那麼寫信或許是個辦法。面對面處理問題時，問題看起來比較小；一旦討論升級到書面上，情況會變得比較複雜。

2. 陳述想講的話，如「謝謝你」、「恭喜」、「我們邀請你」、「你聽說了嗎」。如果你想提出要求，請務必具體明確：遠離我們的新草皮、修剪延伸到我們家的樹枝、一起分攤修理公共籬笆的費用。

3. 若合適的話，可以提議給予某種回報，或以某種間接的方式表達你希望當一個好鄰居。

4. 以客套話、讚美或表達對未來的期待結尾。

什麼不該說？

- 不要指責對方，這會讓鄰居心生戒備，一旦對方產生戒備，就不會道歉或做出改變。使用間接的措詞。不要說「你從來不曾把垃圾桶上的蓋子蓋好，難怪垃圾最後都跑來了這裡！」，而要說「我每週四都會在小徑上發現垃圾」。不要說「你的風鈴快把我搞瘋了」，而要說「因為風鈴，我們晚上很難入睡」。

- 不要以偏概全，如「你總是（always）把車停在我們的房子前面」或「你從來都不（never）把走道的雪鏟除」。這會削弱你的立場，並激怒對方，因為他們記得自己常常在走道上鏟雪。

寫作訣竅

- 如果你有寫信給鄰居致謝、表揚、恭賀或說聲「我正在想著你」的習慣，那麼你便建立了良好基礎，未來若有突發問題也會好處理許多。

特殊狀況

- **住在公寓或大樓容易有許多問題**，因為有屋主，還有人數眾多的鄰居。若要針對問題寫信，請參見：25 抱怨與客訴。

- **吵鬧、有攻擊性或愛亂闖的寵物**是相當常見的鄰里問題。除非是非常過分的事件（例如虐待動物），否則無法從警察或其他官方單位獲得太多幫助。你從一開始與寵物主人的交涉情況，就會影響問題是否能順利解決。在訴諸衝突之前，先試著以軟性的訴求交涉。
- **沒規矩、沒人照看或有人管教卻依然令人頭痛的孩子**，在鄰里中總是存在。編輯海倫·凱瑟（Helen Castle）曾說：「給鄰居孩子一點空間，他們便會佔領整個院子。」只有當你已經對孩子好言相勸，或在勸說無效後與家長談過，才能動用寫信這一招。在信中描述你眼中的情況；以「我」為主語，而不要以「你」為主語，例如「你讓她玩瘋了」。如果可能的話，你可以表示願意幫忙解決問題，或展現出願意妥協的態度。
- **發生爭執時**，試著從你鄰居的角度去看待問題。當你越了解對方的視角，你便越能找出有效的論點，讓你的鄰居也能獲益或有臺階下，藉此開通解決問題的管道。
- **邀請鄰里參加社區派對**、野餐或冰淇淋聚會，藉此打造社區向心力。預防鄰里問題可是比解決鄰里問題有趣多了。

格式

- 手寫或打字皆可，可以親手遞送或郵寄，也可以透過電子郵件寄發。

✉ PART 2 應用篇

單字

admire *(v.)* 欣賞	concerned *(a.)* 關心的	helpful *(a.)* 有幫助的	share *(v.)* 分享
agreement *(n.)* 協議	considerate *(a.)* 體貼的	kindness *(n.)* 好意	socialize *(v.)* 社交
appreciate *(v.)* 感激、表揚	cooperation *(n.)* 合作	neighborly *(a.)* 和睦的	solution *(n.)* 解決方法
attention *(n.)* 注意力	coordinate *(v.)* 協調	respect *(v.) & (n.)* 尊重	troubling *(a.)* 令人煩惱的
careful *(a.)* 小心的	generous *(a.)* 慷慨的	responsibility *(n.)* 責任	upkeep *(v.)* 維修保養

詞組

affecting the neighborhood 影響社區	did you know 你知道……嗎
ask your help/cooperation 請你協助／合作	get together to discuss 聚集討論
block watch 街區守望隊	happy to help with 樂意協助
combined action 聯合行動	hope you are willing to 希望你願意
community council 社區委員會	important to all of us 對我們都很重要
coordinate our efforts 同心協力	inform you that 通知你

48

給鄰居的信

not really my business but 不完全與我相干，但是	wanted you to be aware that 希望你知道
on behalf of the neighbors opposite you 代表住在你對面的鄰居	what would you think of 你會想起什麼
reluctant to write 很不想寫	would you consider 你會不會考慮

句子

Could you speak to the tenants on the first floor about the strollers, bicycles, and skateboards they keep in the entryway?
你能不能跟租房的房客講講他們放在一樓門廊的嬰兒車、腳踏車與滑板？

Here is a key to our back door— I'd really appreciate your keeping a copy in case I get locked out again.
這是我們後門的鑰匙，若你能幫我保管一把備用鑰匙，以免我再次把自己鎖在外面的話，我會非常感激的。

I am going to be the "Safe House" this year, for children walking to and from school, and I wanted to explain how it works.
今年我家會作為孩子走路上下學時的「安全屋」，而我想解釋一下這如何運作。

Thanks so much for taking care of things while we were away—we look forward to doing the same for you.
真是謝謝你在我們外出時幫忙照看一切，我們也期待能為你做同樣的事。

Would you have time to come over some evening for coffee and dessert—and to discuss what kind of a common fence we all might like?
你是否有空在某個傍晚前來喝個咖啡、吃個點心，並一起討論我們都會喜歡的公共籬笆樣式？

Your daughter is the most dependable newspaper carrier we've ever had—I'm writing her a note, but I also wanted you to know what a delight we think she is.
你的女兒是我們雇用過最可靠的送報員；我會寫信告訴她，但我也想讓你知道我們有多喜歡她。

段落

Hi, Neighbors! We have corn coming out of our ears (and, oddly enough, ears coming out of our corn)—if you can use some, please help yourselves.

嗨，鄰居們！我們的玉米從穗中長出來了（奇怪的是，也有穗從玉米中跑出來），如果你們會用到的話，請自行取用。

As you know, the fire last week at Alice and Roddy Wicklow's was pretty destructive. Their most urgent needs right now are warm school clothes for the kids, blankets and bedding, and kitchen utensils. If you have anything you think would be useful, give me a call—I have a list of their sizes as well as a sense of what they most need.

如你所知，上禮拜在艾莉絲與羅迪‧維克洛家發生的火災很嚴重。現在他們最緊急需要的是給孩子上學穿的暖和衣服、床單與寢具、以及廚房用品。如果你覺得你有能用上的東西，請打電話給我，我有一張清單列有他們的尺寸，也了解他們最需要的是什麼。

This is to let you all know that Ajax is having a graduation party for about twenty of his friends Friday night. Bill and I will be home all evening, but if it gets too loud for you give us a call (I'm hoping you won't need to do that).

這封信是為了告知你們，艾杰克斯在這週五晚上會舉辦畢業派對，大約有二十個朋友會來參加。比爾跟我整個晚上都會在家，但要是你真的覺得太吵了，請打電話給我們（我希望你不會需要這麼做）。

I've just heard that Rosa Klebb is in the hospital with a broken hip. Would the seven families on this block want to buy a plant for her—perhaps something she could later plant in her garden? I'll be glad to buy it and take it to the hospital. I'll stop by tomorrow to see what you think and to have you sign the card.

我剛聽說羅莎‧克勒普因髖部骨折住院。這個街區的七戶人家要不要一起買盆植物送她，或許她以後能種在她的花園？我很樂意去購買並帶去醫院。我明天會經過詢問你們的想法，也讓你們在卡片上簽名。

48

給鄰居的信

I wonder if you're aware of zoning regulations prohibiting small businesses in this area. I'm guessing it wouldn't be a problem for the neighbors if your students didn't take up all the street parking three nights a week.

我不知道你們曉不曉得都市分區規定這個區域禁止設立小型企業。就我的猜測，要是你的學生沒有一週三晚佔據街上所有的停車位，這個社區也不會出現這個擾鄰的問題。

示範信

Dear Jeremy and Alice,

We've been so delighted to have you for neighbors that it's difficult to write this letter. It's because we do value your friendship that we're hoping to settle something that's become a problem for us. In a word, Cleo.

This probably comes as no surprise to you since we've called several times about Cleo's early morning, dinnertime, and late evening barking. We understand that she has to be put outside sometime, but it is difficult to understand why she barks every minute she's outside. The early morning barking has been disturbing as we are often up all night with the baby. I can't imagine all the neighbors are up by 5:30 so it must waken some of them too. Cleo tends to bark an average of six hours a day, which is really too much given how close together the houses are.

We appreciate your apologies and goodwill, but we are hoping that this time you can figure out some way of actually solving the problem.

On behalf of my family and several of the neighbors, I am writing to ask you to make other arrangements for Cleo when you are at work during the day. As I have mentioned several times on the telephone, when you leave Cleo on a leash in the backyard she barks and howls almost without interruption all day long. Knowing what a good neighbor you are in other respects, I felt that you would want to resolve this without us having to resort to more official means of restoring peace and quiet to the neighborhood during the day.

Cordially,

親愛的傑瑞米與艾莉絲：

我們一直很高興有你們當我們的鄰居，因此真的很難下筆寫這封信。正因我們重視與你們的友誼，所以我們希望能夠解決這件讓我們困擾的問題。簡而言之，是關於克里歐。

也許你們並不驚訝，畢竟我們已多次因克里歐早上、晚餐時間與深夜的叫聲打過電話。我們明白有時候她必須待在室外，但實在很難理解為何她在室外時要不停吠叫。一大早的叫聲讓我們很煩惱，因為我們時常整晚照顧嬰兒而沒闔眼。我很難想像所有的鄰居都是五點半就起床，所以想必她的叫聲也吵醒了其他的一些人。克里歐平均一天要叫六小時，這真的太多了，尤其我們的房子都很靠近。

我們很感激你的道歉與善意，但這一次，我們希望你們可以想辦法真正解決這個問題。

我代表我的家人與幾戶鄰居，在此寫信請你們於白天上班時為克里歐另做安排。一如我之前數次在電話中提到的，當你們將克里歐用繩子拴在後院時，她便會一直吠叫、哀號，幾乎一整天不停斷。我知道你們在其他方面都是很棒的鄰居，因此我認為你們也會想解決這個問題，而不會讓我們必須採取更正式的途徑，來找回這個社區白天的平靜。

〇〇敬上

Dear Friends,

Samson and I feel so bad about Dan cutting your flowers. It seems somehow worse that his goal was a Mother's Day bouquet for me.

By the time you get this, Dan should have been to see you with his own apology, four-year-old style. We have thoroughly explained to him how wrong this was, and why. I just wanted you to know that we take this seriously, that he has been spoken to, and that I would be surprised if he ever touched anything on your property again. I think he has learned something, but I'm sorry it was at your expense.

Mali

親愛的朋友：

丹剪了你們的花，這使山姆森與我真的很過意不去。而他這麼做竟是為了送我母親節花束，這從某方面來說讓我覺得更糟。

當你們收到這封信時，丹應該已經去親自向你們道歉了，用他四歲的風格。我們已經清楚向他解釋這是非常不對的事情，也跟他說明原因。我只是想讓你們知道，我們很重視這件事，而且我們已經找他談過，如果他日後還敢再次亂碰你們的東西，我會很驚訝。我想他這次學到了教訓，但我很抱歉是你們付出了代價。

馬莉

Dear Mr. Tsi-Puff,

I've been asked to approach you about your nightly routine of riding your exercise bike while watching videos. It appears that in order to hear the movie over the noise of the bike, you have to turn the volume way up.

You're popular with the other tenants, so nobody wanted to complain, but apparently the problem is severe, especially for those who retire early, for renters on either side of you, and for those one floor up and one floor down. The general thinking is that you do not realize how loud the sound is.

Nobody wants to curtail your admirable exercise program, but there is a simple solution: headphones.

Let me know what you think of this. I'm particularly eager to see if this works because the sense I got was that a number of your neighbors were quite taken with the idea of exercise bikes and old movies!

茨波福先生你好：

　　有人請我來找你談談你每晚固定騎健身腳踏車並看影片的習慣。你似乎為了能在健身車的吵雜聲中聽見電影內容，把音量開得太大了。

　　你是個受到大家喜歡的房客，所以沒有人想對你抱怨，但顯然這個問題很嚴重，尤其對那些早早就寢、住在你兩側與上下的房客。大家基本上覺得你根本不知道音量有那麼大。

　　我們不希望限制你有個良好的健身習慣，所以有一個很簡單的解決辦法：戴耳機。

　　請讓我知道你對此的看法如何。我特別想知道這麼做有沒有效果，因為就我看來，你的很多鄰居都覺得一邊騎健身車一邊看老電影是個好主意！

Dear Polly,

　　Thanks for your comments on our new sod last week—it's about time we did something about the yard!

　　I have a small sod-related problem. I need to water it almost constantly these first few weeks, so I've got the sprinklers going most of the time. Johnny and Emma have discovered how much fun it is on these hot days to ride their bikes through the sprinklers. However, that means they are riding on the new sod, which can't take the activity.

　　By the time I get outside, they're off and away, and anyway I hate to be the Bad Guy here, so I was wondering if you could say a word or two to them about how fragile new sod is.

　　Thanks!

親愛的波莉：

　　謝謝你上週對我們的草皮的建議，確實是該為我們的院子做點事了！

　　我有一個關於草皮的小問題。在一開始幾週，我必須不停斷地澆水，所以我大部分的時間都開著灑水器。強尼與艾瑪發現在這種大熱天騎腳踏車穿過灑水器非常好玩；但這表示他們是在新草皮上騎車，而新草皮還無法承受這種活動。

　　當我走到外面時，他們早已騎完跑走了，而且我也不想扮黑臉。所以，我在想你能不能跟他們說一下，讓他們知道新草皮很脆弱。

　　謝謝你！

Hello Neighbor!

　　The Darnel-Greaves Community Council (District 14) is celebrating its 10th anniversary in the green space Saturday, July 15, from 1 p.m. to 4 p.m. We invite you not only to enjoy the refreshments and some good conversation with your neighbors but to consider joining us in making our neighborhood a better place to live. (The only "cost" of belonging is to attend monthly meetings when you can.)

　　In the last ten years the Darnel-Greaves Community Council has organized a recycling program, offered free radon checks of your home, bought bulk quantities of longlife light bulbs, lobbied for three new "Stop" signs, AND saved the green space from development!

　　See you Saturday!

48

給鄰居的信

哈囉，鄰居！

　　丹諾－葛利夫社區委員會（第十四區）即將慶祝十週年紀念日，於七月十五日星期六下午一至四時在綠地舉行。我們邀請你一同前來，不僅享用茶點、與鄰居暢聊，還能考慮加入我們，讓這個社區更適宜人居。（加入後的唯一「花費」，只有在有空時出席每月一次的會議。）

　　在過去十年，丹諾－葛利夫社區委員會設立了資源回收計畫、提供各家免費的氡氣檢測、大量購買長效型燈泡、爭取到三個新的「停止」標誌，而且拯救了綠地，使其不受開發！

　　週六見了！

✉ 參見：05 敏感信件、07 恭賀信、12 致謝函、13 致歉信、18 邀請函、20 請求與詢問、43 紀念日

Chapter 49

旅遊相關信
Travel

當你承受不了目前所承受的事情時，
就去旅行吧。

——亞德蓮・安斯沃（Adeline Ainsworth）

今日多數的旅遊安排（預訂機票、汽車與飯店；索取旅遊、護照、健康相關資訊；取消旅程）都是透過電話、電子郵件或網路進行。不過，有些時候，信或傳真仍是我們呈現複雜計畫、確認預約、處理特殊問題或申訴的最好選擇。

旅遊業者寄給顧客的任何一封信（即便上面只用了一句話來回應索取資料的請求）都是銷售信或商譽信，必須有禮貌、積極正向而體面。

 PART 1 說明篇

可以寫旅遊信給誰？

大眾運輸	設備租賃業者	住宿業者
航空公司、客運、鐵路、郵輪	如租車或租露營車	飯店、民宿、汽車旅館等
遊客諮詢中心	**觀光局**	**國家公園**
旅行社	**遊樂中心**	
或代辦業者	主題公園、營地、度假村、溫泉浴場、觀光農場等	

預計旅遊的客群	親朋好友	公司雇主
		報銷旅費用

該怎麼說？

1. 以欲詢問的問題或業務起頭。
2. 列出相關細節：日期；住宿天數、人數、房間數、住宿類型、所需額外服務、確認路線、游泳池、有線電視、娛樂設施；車的種類、天數、取車與歸還地點；系統紀錄、內容確認或編碼序號；信用卡號；你的住宿地址與電話號碼；旅客姓名。
3. 提醒對方隨信已附上的訂金或優惠券。
4. 再次提到在電話上提過的條款或資訊。
5. 索取確認號碼。
6. 以禮貌的口氣收尾。

什麼不該說？

• 若對方沒有詢問，勿列出不必要的個人資訊。
• 不要在信裡寫出完整的信用卡號，除非你跟對方公司很熟。
• 不要假設。不確定的細節請直接詢問。

寫作訣竅

• 除了標準的禮貌用語，如 Thank you for your assistance/attention.「謝謝你的協助／關注。」，其餘關於旅遊安排的部分須盡量簡短。
• 以簡明方式分行陳列各項資訊，如：

compact car	小型汽車
standard transmission	手排車
airconditioning	有冷氣
3 days, May 11-14	三天，五月十一至十四日
pickup: New York York—JFK	取車：紐約到甘迺迪國際機場
drop-off: Boston—Logan	還車：波士頓到洛根國際機場

• 如果要訂國外的飯店或度假村，或是國外旅行社要求確認信或回應，可以附上國際回信郵票券（可在郵局購得），確保能得到回覆。如果沒有國際回信券，可建議對方用電子郵件或傳真回信。

- 請帶著預訂與確認信的副本記錄。
- 如果想在旅途中寫信給親朋好友，可以讀讀以下幾本好書：
  (1)《俄羅斯紀行》（*A Russian Journal*），作者：約翰‧史坦貝克（John Steinbeck）
  (2)《旅行開麥拉》（*Travels*），作者：麥可‧克萊頓（Michael Crichton）
  (3)《Letters from a Traveller》，作者：Pierre Teilhard de Chardin
  (4)《Letters of Travel》，作者：Rudyard Kipling
  (5)《Letters of Travel》，作者：Phillip Brooks
  (6)《Persian Pictures》，作者：Gertrude Bell
  (7)《Baghdad Sketches》，作者：Freya Stark
  (8)《When You Look Like Your Passport Photo, It's Time to Go Home》，作者：Erma Bombeck

特殊狀況

- 預約飯店時，納入以下資訊：人數、房間數、單人或雙人床、到達時間、離開時間及額外需求（嬰兒床、泳池邊的房間、連通房型、加床、禁菸房）。請對方寄給你預約確認信，並指明如何付款，以及你是否享有折扣。
- 取消旅行計畫時，請重述你在原信中提供的資訊。務必取消預訂，這不只是一種禮貌，要是你忘記取消，對方可能會從你的信用卡收取第一晚的費用。
- 提到「旅行」就會想到「明信片」。若你用心挑選了明信片，那你便有可以寫的內容了，如 Our hotel is right by this canal.「我們的飯店就在這條運河的旁邊。」；We toured this castle yesterday.「我們昨天參觀了這棟城堡。」；We went to the top of this mountain in a funicular.「我們搭纜車到這座山的山頂。」明信片讓收件人能看見鮮豔、有趣、不熟悉的景物。可以寫出你當下的愉悅（沒有人希望聽到你遇上了麻煩），告訴對方你最喜歡什麼、你第一次吃到的食物、關於當地的有趣事實或歷史，以及這趟旅程帶給你的意義。

格式

- 除了明信片以及寫給親朋好友的信，其餘的旅遊相關信件都須以電腦打字，以避免錯誤。
- 傳真與電子郵件時常用於安排旅行。

單字

accommodation *(n.)* 住宿	deposit *(v.) & (n.)* 支付訂金；訂金	nonrefundable *(a.)* 不可退費的	schedule *(v.) & (n.)* 安排時程；行程表
arrangement *(n.)* 安排	directions *(n.)* 交通路線	register *(v.)* 登記	sightseeing *(n.)* 觀光
availability *(n.)* 空房、空位	discount *(n.) & (v.)* 折扣	reimburse *(v.)*（費用）報銷	tour *(n.) & (v.)* 觀光遊覽
booked *(a.)* 已預訂的	excursion *(n.)* 遠足	rental *(a.)* 租金；出租	visa *(n.)* 簽證
cancel *(v.)* 取消	fare *(n.)* 交通費用	reservation *(n.)* 預約	voyage *(n.)* 航行、旅行
charter *(n.)* 許可證	lodging *(n.)* 借宿	roundtrip *(n.)* 往返旅程	

詞組

activities for children 專屬兒童的活動	hold for late arrival 會稍微晚到，煩請保留房間
advance purchase requirements 預購優惠價條件	map of the area 該地區的地圖
areas of interest 感興趣的種類	nearby horseback riding 周邊的騎馬活動
bed and breakfast (B&B) 提供住宿和早餐民宿或小旅館	sightseeing/tour package 觀光／遊覽套裝行程
discount for those over 55 五十五歲以上旅客享有折扣	sports facilities 運動設施
eighteen-hole golf course 十八洞高爾夫球場	travel insurance 旅遊保險

especially interested in
對……特別感興趣

youth hostel
青年旅舍

flexible schedule
彈性的時程

句子

Attached is a completed form about the luggage lost November 8 on flight #78 as well as photos and descriptions of the missing luggage.
附件是關於十一月八日在 78 號航班上遺失行李的完整表格，以及該行李的照片和描述。

Enclosed are the reimbursable hotel, meal, and car rental receipts from my trip to Miami February 10–14.
隨信附上二月十日至十四日邁阿密出差的酒店、餐飲與租車收據，皆可報銷。

Is your resort fully accessible to someone who uses a wheelchair?
對於使用輪椅的人來說，您的度假村是完全無障礙空間嗎？

I would like to dispute the $150 charge for changing the return date on my ticket.
我更改機票回程日期而被收取了 150 元費用，對此我想提出質疑。

Please send a brochure and rates for the Kokua Family Resort.
請寄一份柯庫瓦家庭度假村的介紹手冊與價格給我。

Sweeting-Nunnely Telecommunications is considering holding its annual shareholders' meeting in your area and would appreciate your sending us information on your convention center, hotels, area attractions, and any other material that would be helpful in making our decision.
史維廷－南利電信公司正考慮在貴區舉行年度股東大會，請寄給我們相關資訊，包括會議中心、飯店、地區景點以及任何其他有助我們做出決定的資料。

This will confirm the cancellation of our reservation at the Doddington Dude Ranch.
跟您確認，我們將取消在道汀頓觀光牧場的預約。

We will be spending the month of July in Sundering-on-Sea and would appreciate receiving a map of the area, train schedules, a calendar of local events, and anything else that would help acquaint us with your area.
我們七月將在桑德林濱海小鎮度過，希望能收到該地區的地圖、火車時刻表、當地活動一覽表，以及其他能幫助我們認識這地區的資料。

段落

We spent the night camped at a remote campground in Badlands National Park. The stars were stunning, and there were buffalo everywhere—we had to drive through a herd to get to our campsite. Right now we're in Wall Drug eating breakfast. I wish you were here with us.

我們在遙遠的巴德蘭國家公園露營一晚。滿天星星很驚人，而且到處都是水牛，我們必須開車穿過牛群才能到達我們的營地。現在我們正在沃爾藥店商場吃早餐。真希望你也跟我們一起在這裡。

I am interested in flying from Denver to Hong Kong sometime after June 7 and returning to Denver from Hong Kong approximately three weeks later. I will need two roundtrip tickets Denver–Hong Kong, and I am hoping you can find the most inexpensive seats available. I understand that if I purchase tickets by March 1, there will be a discount. My plans are fairly flexible as to departure and return dates if that helps obtain lower-priced tickets. Please call me as soon as you have some information.

我想在六月七日後某天從丹佛飛到香港，並於大約三週後從香港返回丹佛。我需要兩張丹佛至香港的來回機票，希望你能找到最便宜的座位。我知道在三月一日前購買機票會有折扣。我的去回程時間其實很有彈性，希望這有助購得較便宜的機票。若你有什麼消息，請盡快打電話給我。

I would like to reserve a single, nonsmoking room on one of the lower floors for July 7–17. I will be arriving late on the evening of the 7th so please hold the room for my arrival.

七月七日至十七日，我想在較低的樓層預訂一間禁菸的單人房。七日晚上我較晚才能抵達，煩請保留我的房間。

You asked about transportation between the airport and the hotel. We operate a free shuttle service that leaves the airport every half-hour between the hours of 7 a.m. and midnight from the Ground Transportation area. Look for the Crossley Hotels logo on the bus.

您詢問機場與酒店間的交通問題，我們有提供免費接駁車服務，每天早上七點至午夜之間，每半小時從機場的地面運輸區發車。請尋找車身上有克羅斯利飯店標誌的巴士。

Your room will be billed on the group account for the convention so you do not have a confirmation number. However, at check-in give your name and say you are with Gammon, Quirk & Co.

您的房間將會以會議的團體帳戶結算，所以您沒有訂房確認號碼。但是，在辦理入住手續時，請提供您的姓名，並告知您屬於珈蒙奎克公司。

示範信

TO: P. Bottome
FROM: Amelie von Rohn
DATE: April 3, 2018
RE: Travel arrangements
Phyllis,

Johan Roth, Freya Breitner, and I will represent the Department at the XVI International Meteorological Conference in Tokyo. Convention dates are October 14–18. We'd like to arrive in time to get a good night's sleep, and it would help if the flight home would also allow us to get a night's sleep before returning to work. But do what you can.

Can you arrange for the three of us:
 roundtrip airline tickets
 hotel reservations (see attached Convention brochure)
 a rental car to be picked up and dropped off at the airport
 the current allowable travel cash times 3 (in yen)
Thanks!

              Amelie

收件人：P・波特姆
寄件人：愛蜜莉・范羅恩
日期：二○一八年四月三日
關於：旅行安排
菲莉絲：

約翰・羅斯、芙雷雅・布萊納與我，將代表部門出席在東京舉辦的第十六屆國際氣象大會。大會日期是十月十四日至十八日。我們希望能及時到達睡個好覺，最好回程時間也能讓我們在回來上班前好好睡一覺。但是，盡你所能就可以了。

請幫我們三個人安排：
 來回機票
 酒店預訂（見附件的大會手冊）
 一輛在機場取車、還車的租賃汽車
 三份旅遊零用金，現金（日幣）
謝謝！

              愛蜜莉

Dear Mr. Dallas,

Vivian Grey Hotels International is pleased to learn that you are considering the Burnsley area for your August family reunion. We look forward to an opportunity to extend our warm hospitality to your group for this special event. Although we are not currently holding space for your group, we have accommodations available at this time that meet your needs. Please call or fax your reservations to us as soon as possible.

達拉斯先生您好：

維維安格雷酒店國際集團很高興得知，您正考慮八月時在伯斯利區舉辦家庭聚會。我們期待能有機會在此特別活動中熱情款待您的團隊。雖然我們目前沒有空房，但我們在那段時間有符合您需求的住宿房數。請盡快以電話或傳真預訂。

Signor Gian-Luca Boselli,

I would like to make reservations for October 31 (1 night). We will need 2 rooms for 4 people (each room must have 2 beds).

May we please have rooms with a view of the Temple of the Concord? The last time we had rooms #6 and #15, and they were perfect.

Below is my credit card number to hold the rooms.

I am looking forward to enjoying your lovely hotel once again.

吉安－盧卡・博塞利先生您好：

我想預訂十月三十一日（一晚）。我們總共四人，需要兩間房間（每間房間必須有兩張床）。

我們可否預訂能看到協和神廟的客房呢？上次我們住在六號和十五號房，這兩間都很完美。

以下是我用來預訂房間的信用卡號碼。

期待再次入住您們這間可愛的旅館。

Re: Rental agreement #AI9946X, dated May 18, 2018

Before returning this car to the rental car return area at the Cairo Airport on June 3, I stopped at a gas station one block away and filled the tank to the brim. My bill indicates that I am being charged for 17 liters of gasoline in addition to the penalty charge for returning a car without a full tank of gas. Please look into this, and refund the inappropriate charges. Thank you.

關於：租賃協議 AI9946X，簽約日期二〇一八年五月十八日

我在六月三日將這輛車歸還開羅機場的還車區之前，在一個街區外的一間加油站停下，將油箱加滿。但我的帳單顯示，除了因未加滿油箱還車而遭罰款外，我還必須支付十七公升的汽油費用。煩請調查此事，並退還不合理的收費，謝謝。

✉ 參見：02 傳真信、14 收件通知、20 請求與詢問、25 抱怨與客訴、32 備忘錄、37 客訴處理信

Chapter 50

婚禮相關信
Wedding Correspondence

我加入社區的單身社團。
有一天,社長打電話跟我說:
「歡迎加入社團。我想知道你希望舉辦什麼活動。」
我回答:「婚禮。」

──電影監製琳恩‧哈里斯(Lynn Harris)

婚禮及婚禮相關信件,只需遵守以下原則:有禮、合宜、符合常識。以下的指南融合了傳統與現代的慣例,你可以以此為基礎,再根據自己的品味與狀況做調整。

 PART 1 說明篇

婚禮相關信件包括哪些?

婚前雙方家屬通信	預告婚禮日期通知	結婚通知
寄發喜帖	回應喜帖	確認婚禮相關安排
延期或取消婚禮	告知前夫或前妻再婚	事後的致謝函
收禮後的收件通知	婚前派對 邀請與致謝	尋找婚禮招待人員 伴郎伴娘、主持人、演奏

- **訂婚的消息**，可透過以下四種方式宣布：

  (1) 親筆寫信給親朋好友，內容包含：結婚對象的名字；婚禮日期（若已知）；如果你想要的話，簡述與對方相識的過程與時間；用幾句話表達喜悅；針對收信人量身打造的話。

  (2) 在報紙上刊登訂婚通知，內容包括：你的全名；家鄉；父母的姓名與家鄉；學歷與工作地點；婚禮日期，若未定，可提大概的計畫，如 A spring wedding is planned.「計劃春季舉行婚禮。」有些報紙設有訂婚宣告的刊登條件與截止日期，有些則只能在訂婚與結婚消息中擇一刊登，不能兩種都刊登，所以請事先查詢。

  (3) 寄發正式印製的喜帖：Maria and Ernest Rockage announce the engagement of their daughter Phyllis to Stephen Newmark. An August wedding is planned.「瑪莉亞與厄尼斯特・羅凱傑宣布他們的女兒菲莉絲與史蒂芬・紐馬克訂婚，計劃於八月舉辦婚禮。」

  (4) 邀請親朋好友參加晚餐派對或其他活動時，在活動中宣布。

- 先前訂婚時如果未發出正式通知，**破局的訂婚約定**就不必特地宣布。要是你已經寫信給家人朋友告知訂婚消息，只需再寫一封私人信件，告訴他們訂婚已經取消，不必解釋原因。

- **寫信詢問擔任伴郎、伴娘或工作人員的意願時**，告知對方你希望他們做什麼，以及各自須支付的項目。給對方一個能優雅拒絕的方法，他們才不會感到壓力。表達你對於這份友誼的感謝。

- **安排婚禮時**，很多事情都是透過電話聯絡，但還是有必須寫信確認的時候，如確認儀式場地；給主持人、教堂司事，與婚禮演奏者；給伴郎伴娘與招待人員；給攝影師；給花店、珠寶店、糕點店；寫給飯店安排蜜月；請餐飲負責人安排接待茶會；寫信訂購給工作人員的禮物、走道地毯、蠟燭、緞帶等裝飾。這些不同的信件有三個共通的必要條件：(1) 盡可能提供所有細節資訊；(2) 從一開始就把該知道的一切問清楚；(3) 保留通訊紀錄。

- **辦婚前派對時**，可寄發親筆寫的邀請函或市售邀請卡，內容包含：主要貴賓姓名（準新娘、準新郎、準夫妻）；偏好的禮物種類（廚房、工具、洗浴、花園、食譜、家用品）；時間、日期、地點；請對方回覆，或不參加才須回覆；負責的姓名、地址與電話號碼。收禮人需在派對上感謝送禮人，事後也須寄致謝函給每個送禮人。也需要送給負責人一個小禮物，以及一張特別的感謝函。

- **喜帖**可以是印製或手寫。婚禮越正式，喜帖也必須越正式。

  正式婚禮喜帖會有兩個信封，外層信封會密封以供郵寄，上面寫著寄件人地址，且收件人的地址須用手寫。內層的信封則裝著喜帖（信封打開時，喜帖正面朝上），不必封口，信封正面有受邀人的姓名。信封中也可以裝入保護用的薄紙，或附上寫有可拜訪日期的聯絡拜訪卡（at-home card）、宴會卡（reception card）、大型婚禮的帶位卡（pew card）、標示結婚儀式或宴會地點的地圖、入場卡（如果儀式是辦在公共場所）。回覆卡會放入寫好你的地

址、貼好回郵的信封中，再插入內層信封。為了減少紙張的浪費，有些人會省去內層信封，或使用再生紙來製作喜帖。回覆卡的信封大小至少必須為 5X3.5 吋，才符合郵寄規定。若你不使用回覆卡，則在「RSVP」下面列出地址或電話號碼，賓客才知道如何回覆。

較不正式的小型婚禮，可使用黑色墨水，親筆寫在品質好的白色或米白色紙上或折頁卡片上。以第一人稱撰寫，就像任何非正式的邀請函一樣。小型婚禮通常不會使用印製卡片。

喜帖內容包括：新娘與新郎的姓名；日期、時間、地點；婚禮結束後的招待活動；表達能與賓客慶祝的喜悅。無論正式與否，代表寄發喜帖的人可以是新人、雙方父母、女方父母、男方父母、親戚或家屬的友人；簡而言之，只要是主辦活動或身分最適宜的人，都可以作為代表寄發喜帖。已故的父母不會作為喜帖的發信人出現在喜帖中，但如果喜帖是由新郎與新娘代表寄發，便可加入已故父母的姓名，如 Jean Lucas, daughter of Martha Lucas and the late George Lucas, and Bruce Wetheral, son of Mr. and Mrs. John Henry Wetheral, request the honor of your presence...「琴・盧卡斯，瑪莎・盧卡斯與已故喬治・盧卡斯之女，以及布魯斯・威瑟洛，約翰・亨利・威瑟洛先生與夫人之子，敬邀您參加……」。

- **在信封上寫地址**是一門藝術。外層信封要寫出收件人的全名與地址，盡可能不要使用縮寫。內層信封只須寫出姓氏，如 Mr. and Mrs. Hollingrake「侯林葛夫婦」。外層信封不必列出收件人小孩的姓名，但在內層信封則須將小孩的名字寫在父母姓名之下，絕不要只寫「and family」（及其家人）。年紀較大的孩子（十三至十八歲）應收到他們自己的邀請函。

  如果收件人是未婚同居的情侶，可以在邀請函上寫上兩人的全名。寄件人地址應寫在左上角，除非你使用的是有浮雕的信封，此時寄件人地址便須寫在信封背後的蓋口上。（請注意，郵局並不鼓勵將寄件人地址寫在背後蓋口。）用一支高品質的鋼筆、簽字筆或尖頭沾水筆來寫地址。

- **婚禮取消**的通知，會使用與喜帖類似的風格與格式。如果喜帖是正式的，則取消通知也是正式的；不必像喜帖本身那樣講究，但質感要大致差不多。內容很簡單：Marjorie Corder and Theodore Honey announce that their marriage on the twenty-first of April, two thousand and eighteen, will not take place.「瑪潔莉・柯朵與席爾多・哈尼宣布他們於二〇一八年四月二十一日的婚禮將不會舉行。」

- **結婚通知**可以根據喜帖的樣子做類似設計，可印製或手寫，用來寄給未受邀參加婚禮的人。使用與喜帖相同的信紙以及類似的措詞。若喜帖是正式的，則結婚通知也是正式的；若是喜帖用手寫，那麼結婚通知亦用手寫。郵寄的時間越接近婚禮越好（最好提前寫好地址），並可附上聯絡拜訪卡。結婚通知可由新娘的家庭負責寄發，如 Mr. and Mrs. Raymond Gray announce the marriage of their daughter Polly to...「雷蒙・葛雷先生與夫人宣布他們的女兒波莉與……結婚」；也可由結婚的新人自己寄出，如 Camilla Christy and Matthew Haslam announce their marriage on Saturday, the fifth of June...「卡蜜拉・克莉絲堤與馬修・哈斯蘭宣布他們於六月五日星期六結婚……」；或是由雙方家長代為寄發，如 Evelyn and Peter

Gresham and Bridget and Henry Derricks announce the marriage of their daughter and son, Audrey Gresham and George Derricks, on Friday, the third of April, two thousand and eight, Emmanuel Lutheran Church, Golding, Nebraska.「愛芙琳與彼得・葛斯漢，以及布莉姬與亨利・德里克，宣布他們的女兒與兒子奧黛莉・葛斯漢與喬治・德里克於二〇〇八年四月三日星期五在內布拉斯加州戈爾汀郡的艾曼紐路德教會結婚。」

- 喜帖一定要回覆。可以使用寄來的喜帖中的回覆卡，如果沒有附的話，則用與喜帖相同的措詞與正式程度來 accept with pleasure（愉悅接受邀請）或 decline with regret（遺憾拒絕）。即便用不正式的方式回應正式的喜帖，也不會不適當，重點在於一定要回覆。如果你只受邀參加結婚儀式，便不必回應（在國外，結婚儀式與婚宴〔wedding reception，就是吃吃喝喝的派對〕是分開的）。

  只有受邀參加婚宴的人才能參加婚宴。倘若邀請函上沒有你孩子的名字，表示他們未受邀，把他們帶去婚宴是非常不適宜的。同理，如果信封上沒有寫「and guest」（與客人），請不要攜伴。

- **收到結婚禮物的致謝函**，務必以親筆信回覆，即便已經親口表達謝意，或每天都見到對方也一樣。夫妻都有寫致謝函的責任；無論是由誰執筆，都必須提及另一人，如 Mae and I appreciate...「梅與我感謝……」；Hugh joins me in...「休與我一起……」。

  傳統上，婚禮後的一個月內都可以寄發感謝函，在三個月內完成即可，無論如何，最遲也要在蜜月後寄出。很多夫妻從三個月拖到半年，又拖到一年，而後他們開始覺得尷尬、否定現實，最終只好抱著罪惡感忘了這件事。現代人都很忙碌，送你禮物的人也都是特地為你抽空的大忙人，所以你實在沒有藉口可以拖延致謝函的寄發。

- 每封致謝函都應包含以下內容：具體描述禮物，如「the silver bread tray」（銀色麵包盤），而不要只寫「你送的可愛禮物」；表達喜悅；告訴對方你會如何使用、你喜歡的原因、你有多麼需要這個禮物；用一兩句話說說與禮物無關的事情，如 so good to see you at the wedding「真開心在婚禮上見到你」或 hope you will come see our new home「希望你能來看看我們的新家」。若收到的禮物是錢，不要在致謝函中提及金額，但要告訴對方你會如何使用這些錢。對於合送禮物的朋友，也應單獨寄感謝函給每個人，除非禮物是來自一個大團體，例如同事。如果你想使用市售的致謝折頁卡片或小卡，請選擇素雅的設計。當結婚禮物不符合你的品味時，你只須在信裡強調對方的好意，而不必聚焦在禮物上。若想知道更多撰寫致謝函的建議，請參見：12 致謝函。

- 當你**無法立刻或在時限內寫好致謝函**（因為禮物太多、蜜月延長或生病），可以先以卡片或手寫方式寄出收件通知，對方便知道禮物已安然抵達，並向對方保證你會盡快寫致謝函給每一個人。收件通知絕對不能取代致謝函，寄發收件通知後，須盡快寄出致謝函。

- 在正式的喜帖與結婚通知中，不要使用任何縮寫，稱呼頭衛（Mr.、Mrs.、Ms. 與 Jr.）與軍階是唯一例外。「Doctor」要完整寫出，除非後面接的姓名過長。遇到名字字母縮寫，你可以寫出那些字母所代表的名字，或乾脆省略這些縮寫。在姓名後完整寫出「Second」與「Third」，或使用羅馬數字，如「Caspar Goodwood II」，姓名與羅馬數字之間不需逗點。州的名字也要完整寫出來（寫「Alabama」，而非 Ala. 或 AL），日期與時間亦然，如「November third」（十一月三日），以及「half past eight o'clock」（八時三十分）與「half past five o'clock」（五時三十分）。所有小於一百的數字都要完整拼出來。除了星期之後的逗點（Saturday, the sixteenth of June「六月十六日星期六」）以及稱呼頭衛中的句點外，不要使用任何標點符號。只有人名、地名、星期與月份會出現大寫。喜帖上年份不必列出，但結婚通知一般都會寫出來。
- 為結婚禮物寫致謝函時，不要為了換貨而詢問購買地點。如果禮物重複了，也不要提到。

寫作訣竅

- 傳統而言，the honor of your presence（敬請光臨）指的是有宗教儀式的婚禮，而 the pleasure of your company（敬邀參加）則會用於沒有宗教儀式的婚禮，或是結婚儀式之後的宴會。
- 在喜帖、結婚通知及其他婚禮相關通信中，對兩位準新人的稱呼必須一致，如 the marriage of Adela Polperro to Mr. Lucian Gildersleeve「艾德拉・波佩洛與路西安・蓋德史里夫先生結婚」。不是在兩人姓名前都加上敬稱（如 Ms. 與 Mr.），不然就都不要加（多數人偏好都不加）。不要寫「man and wife」，而要寫「husband and wife」或「man and woman」。
- 抓準時機寄出相關婚禮安排信件：確定婚期後，立刻詢問朋友擔任招待人員的意願；至少在婚禮前三個月就訂製喜帖（信封可以比喜帖早領取）；大約在婚禮前三至六週，郵寄出所有喜帖。
- 如果喜帖中附有回覆卡，受邀人便知道該如何回覆。若你不這麼做，則在「RSVP」下方註明地址或電話號碼，他們才知道該如何回覆。
- 在瑪莉・歐文・克勞瑟於一九四一年出版的書中，她告訴讀者：「不要使用兩張一分錢的郵票來取代一張兩分錢的郵票；出於某些原因，一分錢的郵票被認為不夠高貴。」儘管她的建議已經過時，但你必須考慮郵票貼上去的樣子。多數的喜帖與結婚通知都會使用好看或有意義的紀念郵票。

- 收到訂婚或結婚通知時，你沒有義務要寄禮物，但要寫恭賀信。你可以從以下兩種祝福中擇一寫進信裡：congratulations（恭喜）或 best wishes（祝賀）。（以前這兩種祝福詞是跟性別有關的，一個只能用於女性，一個則只能用於男性。）

- 如果你延誤了寫恭賀信的時間，還是要寄出去。大多數的人都能理解，並會因為你仍然記得而高興。你只須簡短地為延遲道歉。

- 在伴隨禮物寄達的簽名小卡背面，可以簡單描述你送的結婚禮物。很多新婚夫妻都認為這麼做很有幫助，他們才有辦法找到每個神祕禮物的來源。

特殊狀況

- 現代人生活繁忙，很多準新人會在舉行婚禮的一年或更久之前，就先以郵寄或電子郵件的方式寄出**預告婚禮日期通知**（save-the-date notice）給親朋好友。

- **喜帖的寄發**則是按照一般習慣，在婚禮前六週寄出。當親朋好友都住在同一地區、知道彼此消息時，六週當然可算是很充足的時間；但在今天，若你得訂機票、安排休假日期或讓婚禮當天沒有其他工作日程的話，六週便太短了。

- **在報紙上刊登結婚通知時**，盡量把以下幾點寫進去：兩位新人全名；婚禮的日期、時間、地點；主婚人或主持人的姓名；結婚派對參加者的姓名（以及與新人的關係）；雙方父母（有時也可能提到祖父母）的姓名、家鄉、職業或成就；新人的學歷及職業；描述花朵、音樂與結婚派對的服裝；宴會的舉行地點；婚後住址。如果女性保留原姓氏，或夫妻採用中間以連字號相連的姓氏，那麼這會是你向大家宣布的好機會：Marian Belthem and Augustus F. G. Richmond will be living at 1871 Meredith.「瑪莉安‧貝瑟與奧古斯都‧F‧G‧里奇蒙未來會住在梅瑞迪斯 1871 號。」避免使用綽號與縮寫。提前打電話給報社，了解刊登結婚通知的注意事項。有些報社只會刊登有新聞價值的婚禮資訊，有些則會收費；有些只允許訂婚或結婚通知擇一，不能兩種都登上版面；還有些報社不願刊登已成「舊聞」的結婚通知，亦即比婚禮晚了好幾週的通知。有些報社希望你在婚禮三週前就提供資訊，這樣他們才能在婚禮後隔天刊登消息。你也可以把結婚通知寄給公司內部報紙、校友報或其他所屬機構的出版物。

- **如果新娘、新郎或兩人都是軍人的話**，在喜帖與結婚通知上會列出他們的軍階，除非他們不是軍官，而是士官或士兵，那就可以省略。

- 如果家庭成員能寫一封親切的**歡迎信給未來女婿或媳婦**，他們會很感激的。

- 如果你**邀請的人當中只有一小部分的人參加結婚儀式，而不出席宴會**，在喜帖上只需要提到結婚儀式就好。另外製作一張小卡（約是 3×4 吋大小，設計風格與喜帖相同）作為宴會邀請函，放入有受邀出席宴會的賓客喜帖中，內容則是喜帖的縮減版本：Nora Hopper and George Trimmins request the pleasure of your company at their wedding reception [or: a reception following their wedding], on Saturday, the twelfth of June, Walter Village Inn, 55 North Walter Street. RSVP.「諾拉‧霍伯與喬治‧楚明斯敬邀您參加他們的婚禮接待宴會〔或：儀式後的接待宴會〕，於六月十二日星期六，沃特村飯店，沃特北街 55 號。敬請賜覆。」如果所有賓客都受邀參與儀式與接待宴會，那你可以直接在喜帖上的婚禮地點後加上：Reception immediately following「隨後立即舉行接待宴會」；and afterward at...「隨後移駕至……」；followed by a reception at...「隨後在……舉行接待宴會」。

- 如果賓客提到他們會帶朋友或小孩一同參加，但**你並沒有邀請其朋友與小孩**，此時你可以回信告訴對方你很高興他能參加婚禮，但接待宴會只限受邀者參加，因為空間不足，或因為只邀請成人。如果你邀請的朋友可能不認識接待宴會上的其他人，你可以打電話詢問他同伴的姓名（這樣你便可以寄一封喜帖給同伴）或在他們的喜帖上加上「and Guest」（與客人）。

- 若要**通知婚後住址**，可在喜帖或結婚通知中附上一張聯絡拜訪卡，這張小卡的風格通常跟喜帖相同，大小約為 2.75X4 吋，上面可以寫一段帶有婚後住址的一句話：Linda Condon and Arnaud Hallet will be at home after the sixth of June at 1918 Hergesheimer Road, Waunakee, Wisconsin 53597.「琳達‧柯登與阿諾‧哈雷在六月六日之後會在家，地址為 53597 威斯康辛州沃納奇村赫格海默路 1918 號。」

- 若要**讓親朋友好知道女方會保留原本的姓氏**，或你們夫妻將採用以連字號相連的姓氏或一個全新的姓氏，可以在喜帖或結婚通知中附上一張印製的小卡（風格同喜帖）：After their marriage, Clarissa Graham and Charles Belton will use the surname Belton-Graham.「婚後，克萊麗莎‧葛雷漢與查爾斯‧貝爾頓將會使用貝爾頓－葛雷漢為姓氏。」；Clarissa Graham wishes to announce that following her marriage she will retain her birth name.「克萊麗莎‧葛雷漢在此宣布她在婚後會保留原姓氏。」

格式

- 寄給報社的訂婚或結婚通知，請以打字方式呈現，並使用雙倍行距。若會附上照片，請在照片背面標註姓名，以免照片與通知分開。（不要直接寫在照片背面，使用寫有寄件地址的標籤或黏一張紙在上面。）

- 喜帖與結婚通知可以是印刷或手寫。根據婚禮的類型做選擇，婚禮越正式，喜帖與結婚通知也要越正式。你可以一次買好相同風格的姓名卡、致謝函、非正式信紙、便箋紙或其他信紙。

- 決定信封大小與紙張重量之前，建議查詢郵局對信封大小與重量與價格規定。

- 若要回應沒有附上回覆卡的喜帖，請使用正式的信紙或折頁卡片。如果你有名片，可以在名片的姓名下方寫上「accepts with pleasure」（愉悅接受）或「declines with regret」（遺憾拒絕），並重述活動內容與日期。

PART 2 應用篇

單字

acknowledge (v.) 告知收到	ceremony (n.) 典禮	marriage (n.) 婚姻	ritual (n.) 儀式
announce (v.) 宣布	congratulations (n.) 恭喜	matrimony (n.) 婚姻生活	union (n.) 結合、結婚
bless (v.) 祝福	happiness (n.) 幸福	nuptials (n.) 婚禮	vow (v.) & (n.) 立誓；誓約
celebrate (v.) 慶祝	joy (n.) 喜悅	pleasure (n.) 愉悅	wishes (n.) 祝福

詞組

acknowledges with thanks the receipt of 抱著感謝告知收到	rehearsal dinner 婚禮綵排晚宴
groom's dinner 新郎晚宴	request the honor of your presence 敬請你的光臨
happy to announce/to invite you to 很高興宣布／邀請你參加	request the pleasure of your company 敬邀你參加
help us celebrate our wedding 幫助我們慶祝我們的婚禮	share in the joy 分享快樂
invite you to celebrate with us 邀請你和我們一起慶祝	united in wedlock 結為連理
joined in holy matrimony 加入神聖的婚姻生活	wedding party 婚禮派對
our fondest congratulations 我們最誠摯的祝賀	we would be honored to 我們將很榮幸
witness our marriage 見證我們的婚姻	wish to acknowledge the receipt of 希望確認收到

句子

Aurelia and I were greatly touched by the beautiful family tea service you gave us for our wedding—we feel we're now connected to all the family that's gone before and all that is yet to come.

在我們的婚禮上，你為我們準備了美好的家庭倒茶活動，讓我和奧蕾莉亞都深受感動。我們覺得我現在已跟以前與未來的所有家人緊密連在一起了。

Best wishes on your wedding day!

為你的婚禮獻上最好的祝福！

Jane Vallens and Andrew Satchel gratefully acknowledge the receipt of your beautiful wedding gift and look forward to writing you a personal note of thanks at an early date.

珍‧瓦倫斯和安德魯‧薩契爾已收到你美麗的結婚禮物，十分感謝，期待能盡快寫好給你的致謝信。

Jesse joins me in thanking you for the oil painting you did especially for us—it is our first piece of original art!

傑西和我一起感謝你為我們特別畫的油畫，這是我們的第一件原創藝術品！

Mary Llewellyn and Martin Hallam request the pleasure of your company at the marriage of their daughter Mary Frances.

瑪麗‧盧埃林與馬汀‧哈藍敬邀您參加他們女兒瑪麗‧弗朗西斯的婚禮。

Our very best wishes to you both for many years of happiness, health, and prosperity.

我們衷心祝福你們擁有多年的幸福、健康，子孫滿堂。

Please join us in celebrating the marriage of our daughter Sally to William Carter.

請與我們一同慶祝我們的女兒莎莉與威廉‧卡特結婚。

Thank you for your generous check, which will go a long way toward helping us buy the piano we have our eye on!

感謝您慷慨寄來支票，這將會大大幫助我們購買想要的鋼琴！

The ceremony will take place at 1:30 p.m., and a reception at the house will follow.

儀式將於下午一時三十分舉行，隨後將於屋內舉辦接待茶會。

We're sorry, but we are limited in the number of guests we can have at the reception—we hope you'll still be able to come and that we can meet your cousin some other time.

我們很抱歉，但接待宴會上我們能招待的客人數量有限；我們希望您仍然可以參加，並期待未來某日見到您的表弟。

We were delighted to hear of your engagement—Anita is an intelligent, beautiful, and kind young woman, and the two of you are beautifully matched!

我們很高興聽到你訂婚的消息。安妮塔是個聰明、美麗、善良的年輕女子，你們兩人真是相配！

We wish you every happiness as you celebrate the love you have for each other.

在你們慶祝彼此的愛情的這天，我們祝你們一切幸福。

段落

Mr. and Mrs. Solomon Darke accept with pleasure Mr. and Mrs. Charles Heath's invitation to the marriage of their daughter Margaret to Rupert Johnson on Saturday, the twelfth of June.

所羅門‧達克先生與夫人很樂意接受查爾斯‧希思先生與夫人的邀請，參加他們的女兒瑪格麗特於六月十二日星期六與魯伯特‧強森的婚禮。

Congratulations and best wishes to both of you on this, your wedding day. May you take with you into the years ahead some beautiful memories of those who love you and of your shining love for each other.

在這一天，你們的婚禮當天，獻上祝賀與祝福。願你們在未來能一直記得愛著你們的人，以及你們對彼此的閃耀愛情。

We would like to make an appointment with you to discuss the music for our wedding, which is scheduled for June 16 at 1 p.m. We have some ideas (and will bring some music with us), but we would appreciate some suggestions from you.

我們想和你約個時間討論我們婚禮上的音樂，婚禮將於六月十六日下午一點舉行。我們有一些想法（並會帶上一些音樂），但如果你能提供一些建議，我們將不勝感激。

Julia and I will be married at our apartment on Saturday, June eighteenth at 5:30 p.m. It would mean a great deal to us if you would join us for the ceremony and for dinner afterwards.

茱莉亞與我將於六月十八日星期六下午五點三十分在我們的公寓結婚。如果你能參加我們的儀式及隨後的晚餐，對我們來說意義重大。

Bernice and I are absolutely delighted with the electric blanket. You must have been poor students yourselves once, living on the third floor of an old brownstone, hoping that perhaps today the heat might make it all the way upstairs. It's a beautiful, thoughtful, practical gift, and we're grateful.

伯尼斯和我對電熱毯非常滿意。你想必也當過窮學生，住在古老的褐砂牆樓房三樓，希望今天的暖氣可以一路到達樓上。這是一個美好、貼心、實用的禮物，我們很感激。

50 婚禮相關信

Mr. and Mrs. David Herries
announce that the marriage of
their daughter Dorothy
to Arthur Bellairs
on Saturday, the tenth of May
will not take place.
Mr. Edmund Roundelay
regrets that owing to
the recent death of
Evelyn Ferguson Roundelay
the invitations to the marriage
of their daughter Crystal
to Maxwell Dunston
must be recalled

大衛‧赫里斯先生與夫人
宣布
他們的女兒桃樂絲
與亞瑟‧貝萊爾
於五月十日星期六的婚禮
將不會舉行
愛德蒙‧朗德利先生
遺憾宣布
由於艾芙林‧弗格森‧朗德利
最近去世
他們的女兒克莉絲塔
與麥斯威爾‧唐斯頓
的婚禮喜帖
必須撤回

The honor of your presence
is requested at the marriage of
Sybil Anstey Herbert
to
Harry Jardine
on Saturday, the tenth of October
at one o'clock
Lehmann Methodist Church

50
婚禮相關信

and afterward at
The New Lehmann Inn

RSVP
Sybil Anstey Herbert
20 Ianthe Court
Lehmann, OH 45042

敬邀您光臨
希碧兒‧安斯泰‧赫伯特
與
哈利‧夏汀
的婚禮
於十月十日星期六
一點整
在萊曼衛理公會教堂舉行
隨後至
新萊曼酒店

敬請賜覆
希碧兒‧安斯泰‧赫伯特
45042 俄亥俄州萊曼市
易安思巷二十號

Dear Lucy and Fred,

Christopher and I are so pleased you will be able to attend our wedding celebration. I'm afraid there's been a misunderstanding, however. You know how much we enjoy Freddy, Elsa, and Charles, but we are not planning on having any children at the reception. I hope you can find a babysitter so you can still come. Thanks for understanding.

Love,

親愛的露西和弗雷：

克里斯多福與我很高興你們能參加我們的婚禮。但恐怕你們有些誤會。你們知道我們有多喜歡弗萊迪、艾莎和查爾斯，但我們不打算讓接待茶會中有任何小孩。我希望你們能找到褓姆，這樣你們才能參加我們的婚禮。謝謝你們的理解。

愛你們的○○

Miss Laetitia Prism
regrets that she is unable to accept
the kind invitation of
Mr. and Mrs. Oscar Fairfax
to the marriage of their daughter

Gwendolyn Fairfax
Saturday, the sixth of June
two thousand eighteen
at half past seven o'clock

蕾蒂莎・普里森小姐
很遺憾她無法接受
奧斯卡・菲爾法斯先生與夫人
的好意邀請
參加他們的女兒
關多琳・菲爾法斯
於二〇一八年
六月六日星期六
七時三十分舉行的婚禮

Dear Grace and Harold,

Our dear Stella and Stanley Kowalski are being married on Saturday, September 4, at 3 p.m. in an informal ceremony at our house.

We'd love to have you celebrate with us, and stay after the ceremony for a small reception. Let me know if you can join us.

Fondly,

親愛的葛蕾絲和哈洛：

我們親愛的史黛拉與史丹利・柯瓦斯基將於九月四日星期六下午三點結婚，會在我們家進行一場非正式的儀式。

我們很希望你們能與我們一同慶祝，並且留下參加儀式後的一個小小接待茶會。請讓我知道你們是否可以參加。

愛你們的〇〇

✉ 參見：03 回應、04 遲回的信、07 恭賀信、12 致謝函、14 收件通知、15 公告通知、18 邀請函、20 請求與詢問、21 接受、22 拒絕

50
婚禮相關信

附錄一　書信格式

附錄一討論信件的格式，包含信件應具備的元素，美國郵政總局所規範的寄件規範與常用郵政縮寫表。

信件應含括的項目

私人信件

- **日期**：將日期寫在頁面的右上端。如果對方不知道你的地址，而你也沒有使用有署名地址的信紙時，先在右上角以地址開頭（通常寫成兩行），再寫出日期，並將這三行齊頭對齊。
- **信首稱謂**（salutation）：接著空幾行之後，從頁面左側寫下信首稱謂，並加上逗號，如 Dear John,。不用像寫商務信件一樣在信首稱謂上方放上對方的地址。
- **正文**：每個段落開頭要縮格，如果是打字，空五格半型空格；手寫大約空出四分之三英吋（約 1.9 公分）。
- **結尾**：正文結束後，空一行後書寫**結尾祝頌詞**（complimentary close，如 Love, 或 Sincerely,），靠頁面右邊書寫，讓結尾祝頌詞對齊日期左端。在結尾祝頌詞下一行簽上名字。如果信件超過一頁長，單面書寫或打字即可。

備忘錄

- **標題欄**：備忘錄的最上方是標題欄，包含 To（收件者）、From（寄件者）、Date（寄件日期）與 Subject line（主旨列），標題欄取代了私人信件中的信首稱謂。最常見的標題欄如下：

To:	Paul Rayley	Date:	April 23, 2018
From:	Minta Doyle	Re:	Lighthouse repairs

收件者：保羅萊利	日期：2018 年 4 月 23 日
寄件者：明塔多莉	主旨：燈塔修繕

To: Martin Fenner	收件者：馬丁芬諾
From: Owen Kettle	寄件者：歐文凱朵
Date: July 14, 2018	日期：2018 年 7 月 14 日
Subject: Series on tuberculosis	主旨：肺結核序列

- **正文**：備忘錄的正文並沒有嚴格的行距規範，不過一般都會在標題欄與正文之間空二到三個單行間距的距離，每一段都從左側開始書寫，段落之間空一行距離。
- **備註欄**：附件（Enc.）或轉寄（cc:）資訊的書寫方式同一般信件，從左側開始書寫。

商務信件

- **回郵住址**：如果你使用的是沒有信頭的信紙，請在日期上方用兩行書寫你的地址，包含門牌號碼、街道名、城市、居住州名、郵遞區號(註)。除了非常正式的信件外，可以使用縮寫（Rd.「路」、Apt.「公寓」、NY「紐約州（或市）」）。
- **日期**：使用以下格式：October 12, 2010（二〇一〇年十月十二日）。月份不使用縮寫，日期用阿拉伯數字書寫，日期的序數字尾（st, nd, rd）不用寫出來。**寄到國外或是給政府的信件**，可以寫 12 October 2010。如果你需要親自寫下或打出回郵住址，直接將日期寫在回郵住址下方，否則在有信頭的信紙上書寫日期時，須和回郵住址之間空六行距離。
- **在備忘錄上使用簡短的日期**（10/12/2010）時，記住這樣的縮寫方式只用於美國，在其他國家，第一個數字是日期，第二個數字才是月份。
- **「機密」（Confidential）或「私人」（Personal）標示**：將這類標示放在日期行與信內地址之間，靠左對齊。
- **信內地址（inside address）**：日期一行與信內地址之間的行距數依信件總長度決定。平衡信件中的元素，避免信內地址上方與最後一行下方有太多空白。信內住址一律靠左對齊書寫，單行行距。如果放成一行太長，可分成二行，第二行縮格二到三個半型空格。收件人姓

註：此為英文住址書寫順序，中文的地址書寫順序則與英文相反。

名放在第一行，後方放上簡短的職稱，中間以逗點隔開；或是將職稱放在第二行。如果信件文字太多放不下，可省略職稱。如果收件者是兩人以上，以首字母排序，放成一行。公司名稱放在下一行，部門或分部名稱放在更下一行（如果放不下，可省略）。其他如幾號房、幾樓或哪間公寓也須另起一行，除非街道名稱夠短，則可和街道名放同一行。過去信內地址的標準寫法是單字須拼寫出來（不使用縮寫），不過州名請使用兩個字母的縮寫。如果是非正式的信件，其他縮寫（如 Ave.「大道」）也可以使用。放在街道名前的羅盤方位（compass direction）須拼寫出來，但放在街道名之後的羅盤方位可使用縮寫，如 14 North Cedar 或 14 Cedar N.W.「席達路北 14 號」。

- **經辦人欄（Attention Line）**：當你不知道該收信人是誰，或是不知道該寄給哪位可以解決你需求的人，就在信內地址下方空一行後，寫出經辦人職稱，如 ATTN: Customer Service Representative「經辦人：顧客服務代表」。你也可以將經辦人欄放在信內地址的第一行或第二行（公司名稱之後）。

- **信首稱謂**：信內地址下空一行再書寫信首稱謂，後方加上逗點或冒號。

- **主旨列**：請在信首稱謂與信內地址之間寫出 Subject: 或 Re:，後方寫出簡短的主旨，如 Subject: block and brick work「主旨：砌磚工程」或 Re: vacation dates「回覆：假期日期」。在非個人信件或是收件人無具名的信件中，許多人會直接用主旨欄代替信首稱謂。一大疊的信件當中有主旨欄的信件相當受到歡迎，因為你能靠瀏覽主旨欄確定每封信的目的。不過，如果信件中陳述多種目的，就不建議寫出主旨列。

- **參考資料列**：當信件提及訂單號碼或是某個參考文件號碼時，跟處理主旨列的方式一樣，將參考資料列放在信內地址與信首稱謂之間，或是信首稱謂與正文之間（前後請各空一行）。也可以放在日期列與信內地址之間。

- **正文**：信首稱謂（或主旨欄）下空一行之後再開始書寫正文。一般來說，正文行距使用單行間距，段與段之間空一行。不過，如果你的信很短，可以使用兩行或是一點五行間距。也可以調整左側邊界距離平衡頁面，如短信就使用寬邊界距離，長信則使用窄的邊界距離（邊界距離最窄不要小於 11/4）。段落須縮格，空五到十格半型空格。

  勿動到右側邊界距離。

  如果你的信有兩頁，請在第二頁上方依序標註收件人姓名、日期與頁碼（大約佔用六行寬度）。如果你的收信人有兩位，將名字放在左側，一行放一個名字。接著空兩行，在右側寫上日期與頁碼。接著，空三到五行再開始書寫正文。第二頁結末處應至少留三行空白與足夠放下手寫簽名的位置。

- **結尾祝頌詞**：在正文之後空一行，寫上結尾祝頌詞（如 Yours truly,）。

- **署名**：在結尾祝頌詞下方簽上簽名，手寫簽名下方加一行以打字方式列出姓名與職稱（見下點）。

- **姓名與職稱**：在結尾祝頌詞下方空四行供手寫簽名（如果你的手寫簽名較大，可空多行一些），在第五行用打字方式列出名字，名字首字母對齊結尾祝頌詞的首字母。如果你要列出職稱，列在名字下一行，職稱首字母同樣對齊結尾祝頌詞首字母。如果信頭已經出現過職稱，這裡就可省略。

- **身分欄**（identification line）：姓名與職稱之後空一行，接著從左邊以大寫字母寫出署名者姓名的首字母，加上斜線號或是冒號，之後以小寫字母列出打字員姓名首字母，如 DCK/jp 或 IN:pjm。因為署名者的姓名顯而易見，通常會省略署名者姓名首字母縮寫，只列出打字員的首字母縮寫。本欄現在幾乎不使用了。

- **附件欄**（enclosure line）：在身分欄或姓名與職稱欄之後空一行，從左邊寫上 Enc.:「附件是：」，接著，依照附件在正文出現的順序，列出所有附在信封裡的附件，一個一行。當附件不只一個時，你可以將附件編號，如 Encl. (1) 或 Enclosures (4)。

- **副本收件人欄**（copies line）：前方文字後空一行，從左邊寫上 cc:「副本給：」（cc 是 carbon copy 的縮寫[註]），後方以字母順序列出所有會收到信件副本的人，一個一行。所有人名格式需一致，可以是寫出全名，或是只寫姓與名，或是只列出姓氏與職稱。住址視情況也可加上。

  如果你不想讓收件人知道你將信件轉寄給誰，請寫 bcc:「密本副本給：」（bcc 為 blind carbon copy 縮寫），後方只列出收到正本（office copy）的人。

- **補充說明**（postscript）：補充說明列以「P.S.,」起頭，將補充說明列放在由下數來第 3 行位置。

- **郵遞方式**（mailing notation）：此行說明郵遞方式，如 Special Delivery, Overnight Express「特殊郵遞方式：隔夜快捷」，在過去僅註明於信件影本上，正本中不註明。本欄現今已經鮮少使用。

註：以前只有紙本郵件的時代，會在信紙下方墊上複寫紙，同時將信件寫給很多人，因而有 carbon copy「複寫本」一詞，演變為今日的副本。

商務信件示範信：

信頭 •────────── CHANNING FURNITURE RENTAL

1927 James Avenue

Huntly, WI 53597

日期 •────────── March 15, 2018

機密標示 •────────── Confidential

信內地址 •────────── Yorke Furniture Rental
ATTN: Constance Yorke
1862 Wood Street
Huntly, WI 53597

信首稱謂 •────────── Dear Constance Yorke:

主旨列 •────────── Re: bad checks

正文 •────────── We spoke at the Huntly Business Association meeting last month about exchanging lists of customers who have written at least three unbankable checks. Enclosed is my list.

結尾祝賀詞 •────────── Yours truly,

署名 •────────── [signature]

姓名與職稱 •────────── Hamish Channing

President

附件欄 •────────── Enc.: list

補充說明 •────────── P.S. I don't feel too bad about passing these names along because I keep this same list posted by my cash register.

常寧家具租借

詹仕大道 1927 號

53597 威斯康辛州杭特力

二〇一八年三月十五日

機密

約克家具租借

經辦人：康士坦斯・約克

伍德街 1862 號

53597 威斯康辛州杭特力

親愛的康士坦斯・約克：

主旨：無效帳戶

上個月我們在杭特力商會聯盟會議上談到交換客戶名單一事，其中至少有三名客戶帳戶是無法兌現的，附件是詳細名單。

[簽名處]

總裁

漢米許・常寧致上

附件：名單

附註：這些名單就直接給你無妨，因為我這裡已經用自己的現金帳戶把名單記錄下來。

✉ 美國郵政指南

美國郵政署（United States Postal Service，USPS）提供許多便民小冊子、使用手冊與出版刊物，可在線上免費取得（www.usps.com/publications）。美國郵政署亦提供如線上或隨郵郵票販售服務，電話諮詢，郵遞區號列表，與線上指導影片。

以下是美國郵政建議可加速郵件遞送的幾點說明：

- 確保你的郵件是光學字元辨識系統（Optical Character Recognition，OCR，一種電子裝置，用來自動篩選郵件以加速寄件速度）可辨識讀取的：使用標準（長方形）信封；僅使用純白色、象牙色或郵政信封；避免使用少見特殊的信封規格，如太亮的紙張；收件地址一律放在信封右下方，以大寫字母書寫，字與字之間以一到兩個半形空格區分開來，不使用標點符號（除了郵遞區號中可使用短破折號）。
- 勿使用釘書針；釘書針會使郵件分類機卡住。
- 信封上需寫出寄件地址，很多人都會漏放。
- 州名一律使用兩個字縮寫（見下方郵政用美國州名縮寫表），並使用增加號碼後的美國郵遞區號（ZIP+4）。
- 將信件條碼化。使用 ZIP+4 與條碼能讓享有最多郵資折扣，也能協助郵政添購的掃條碼機回本。
- 隨時注意美國郵政最新出版品、計畫、郵資費率與服務。

郵政縮寫表

美國州名、外島與大洋洲國家

縮寫	全名	縮寫	全名
AL	Alabama 阿拉巴馬州	MT	Montana 蒙大拿州
AK	Alaska 阿拉斯加	NE	Nebraska 內布拉斯加州
AS	America Samoa	NV	Nevada 內華達州
AZ	Arizona 亞利桑那州	NH	New Hampshire 新罕布什爾州
AR	Arkansas 阿肯色州	NJ	New Jersey 紐澤西州
CA	California 加州	NM	New Mexico 新墨西哥州
CO	Coronado 科羅拉多州	NY	New York 紐約州
CT	Connecticut 康乃迪克州	NC	North Carolina 北卡羅萊納州
DE	Delaware 德拉瓦州	ND	North Dakota 北達科他州
DC	District of Columbia 華盛頓哥倫比亞特區	MP	Northern Mariana Islands 北馬里亞納群島
FM	Federated States of Micronesia 密克羅尼西亞聯邦	OH	Ohio 俄亥俄州
FL	Florida 佛羅里達州	OK	Oklahoma 奧克拉荷馬州
GA	Georgia 喬治亞州	OR	Oregon 奧勒岡州
GU	Guam 關島	PW	Palau 帛琉
HI	Hawaii 夏威夷州	PA	Pennsylvania 賓州
IL	Illinois 伊利諾州	PR	Puerto Rico 波多黎各
IN	Indiana 印第安那州	RI	Rhode Island 羅德島
IA	Iowa 愛荷華州	SC	South Carolina 南卡羅萊納州
KS	Kansas 堪薩斯州	SD	South Dakota 南達科他州
KY	Kentucky 肯塔基州	TN	Tennessee 田納西州
LA	Louisiana 路易斯安那州	TX	Texas 德州
ME	Maine 緬因州	UT	Utah 猶他州
MH	Marshall Islands 馬邵爾群島	VT	Vermont 佛蒙特州
MD	Maryland 馬里蘭州	VA	Virginia 維吉尼亞州
MA	Massachusetts 麻州	VI	Virgin Islands 維爾京群島
MI	Michigan 密西根州	WA	Washington 華盛頓州
MN	Minnesota 明尼蘇打州	WV	West Virginia 西維吉尼亞州
MS	Mississippi 密西西比州	WI	Wisconsin 威斯康辛州
MO	Missouri 密蘇里州	WY	Wyoming 懷俄明州

其他常用縮寫

縮寫	全名	縮寫	全名
APT	Apartment 公寓	HDQTRS	Headquarters 總部
ATTN	Attention 致	HOSP	Hospital 醫院
BLDG	Building 大樓	INST	Institute 機構
CTR	Center 中心	NATL	National 國立
CO	Company 公司	PKWY	Parkway 公園大道
CORP	Corporation 集團公司	PO BOX	Post Office Box 郵政信箱
DEPT	Department 部門	RM	Room 室
DIV	Division 部門	RR	Rural Route 鄉道
FLR	Floor 樓	STE	Suite 房
GOVT	Government 政府		

附錄二　書信內容

附錄一討論信件格式，附錄二則是說明信件內容的基本注意事項，包括撰寫信件的基本原則、撰寫制式信的原則、標點符號用法，與避免偏見的文字。

✉ 撰寫信件的基本原則

以下指南主要適用於**商務信件**。商務信重視簡單扼要。寫給家人的信，不必像寫商務信一樣在第一句就點出主旨，但商務信的讀者則希望立刻知道你想說什麼。以下建議能幫你提升整體商務信件。

- 動筆前，釐清寫信目的（收到退款、安排會議、寄發邀請）。收集需要的資訊。想想你的讀者，你越了解收信人，越能為對方量身打造一封信。
- 在第一或第二個句子點出主旨。
- 要簡短。作曲家喬治・伯恩斯（George Burns）對於布道的建議，同樣適用於信件：「好的開頭與好的結尾……兩者間的距離越近越好。」解釋、說明與理由簡單扼要即可。
- 要具體。沒有什麼比具體細節更能為寫作帶來力量了；這些細節能夠取代模稜兩可的單字與詞彙。讀者想要知道價錢多少、顏色為何、日期是哪天、幾點幾分、尺寸多大、尺寸多小。重讀你的信，然後質疑每一個形容詞：這個詞是否盡職？還可以更具體嗎？
- 要愉悅、有禮、正面、給人希望。呈現樂觀態度能帶來驚人的效益。
- 商務信要實事求是，避免顯露情緒（在私人信件裡則可以展露出來，對方甚至喜歡這樣）。你的讀者並不在乎你的感受，他們想要的是事實、結果、成效或原因。不要誇大，以免讀者不信任你寫的內容。最好稍微講得保守一點，讓讀者覺得是自己發現了其中的美好。
- 在整封信中，要時常使用第二人稱「you」（但不要過度），尤其是開頭前幾句。最重要的寫信規則，便是「想著讀者」。遣詞用字要符合讀者興趣，需求與期待。使用 you 能讓讀者有參與感。關於 you 的使用，唯一例外是抱怨信與反對信，因為 you 讓內容更像控訴、更有敵意。此時，請改用第一人稱「I」來表達。
- 使用主動句，如 I received your letter last week.「我上週收到你的信。」而非被動句，如 Your letter was received last week.「你的信上週已收到。」使用有力直接的動作動詞（「is/are」、「do」與「make」並不包括在內）。當某些字太常出現時，利用同義字字典查找其他更強而有力（避免冷僻、陌生、拗口的字）的替代字。

- 用生動、像在交談的語氣大聲唸出信件內容，有助找出彆扭的地方。

- 為你的信選擇一個適合的調性，全篇保持一致。正式或非正式；冷靜或溫暖；嚴肅或輕鬆；活潑或和緩；簡單或複雜；優雅或平易近人。無論選了哪種，都要前後一致。

- 避免太常使用像 very（非常）與 basically（基本上）這樣的詞。這些詞沒有意義，反而讓讀者厭煩。

- 避免俚語、術語、陳腔濫調、流行語、法律用語、菁英用語，或像 I shall「我應當」這類生硬做作的用法。不要選冷僻字，要選大家熟悉的字詞。

- 寫信給外國人時，使用簡單的句子與句法。

  (1) 避免俚語、術語、譬喻、與文化有關的典故、被動句與複雜的結構。使用現在式與過去簡單式就好。不要說 If we had only known...「要是我們知道……」，改說 We did not know...「我們不知道……」。

  (2) 在日期中使用數字時，請用「日／月／年」的格式，而不要用「月／日／年」。

  (3) 如果你對對方的語言有所了解，可使用讀者語言中的敬稱，如「Madame」（法文的夫人）、「Signore」（義大利文的先生）、「Herr」（德文的先生）、「Señora」（西班牙文的夫人）。

  (4) 使用對方給你的地址，完全照著寫，才最有可能寄達目的地。

  (5) 來自其他國家的信件，通常結尾都有固定的禮貌用語；參考與你通信的人是怎麼寫的，並用同樣的方式回應。

- 讓通信人方便回信：附上已貼郵資的信封，或是已寫上地址且貼好回郵的信封。

✉ 制式信的基本指南

有了制式信這類的信件，人們便不必一遍又一遍打著相同的信，在銷售信與例行商務信件（業務確認、收件通知、封面信、拒絕）中，制式信是必要的。

作者約瑟夫・海勒（Joseph Heller）在《第二十二條軍規》（*Catch-22*）中曾這樣取笑制式信：「親愛的丹尼卡夫人、先生、小姐或夫婦：當我聽說您的丈夫、兒子、父親或兄弟遭到殺害、受傷或失蹤時，我感到深切的哀痛，言語無法形容。」

為了避免寫出這樣的制式信，必須針對讀者設計內容。這並不是指在制式的句子空格中填上對

方姓名而已，對方也不會把這種信件視為真正的親近。

若想讓制式信看起來像是為對方量身打造，可以多使用第二人稱「you」，並將制式信的內容根據不同目標族群做不同措詞。你可以先將郵件通訊錄以不同目標族群做分類。如此，當你的目標讀者是園藝家，或是家庭主婦，你便知道該如何措詞。

重要的郵件須使用高品質信紙，並且要親筆簽名（有些人拆開信的第一件事就是看簽名是不是真的，藉此決定要繼續讀或把信丟掉），以限時郵件寄出。

✉ 英文標點符號與大小寫注意事項

- **句點（.）**：在句末用句點。句點也會出現在縮寫之後。使用刪節號時，在句中是三點（...），在句末則是四點（....）。
- **逗號（,）** 用來將一連串的事項分開。列舉數個項目時，and 的前面可以加逗號（如 milk, butter, and eggs），也可不加（milk, butter and eggs），唯一原則是保持一致。如果你不知道何時該使用逗號，可以大聲念出句子，當你念完一串詞組停頓了下來，此處可能就是要用逗號的地方。在 etc. 前後、日期年份的前後，如 On May 27, 1678, the sun rose...「一六七八年三月二十七日，太陽升起」，以及學位前後放上逗號。姓名前面也必須有逗號，如你要寫 Are you eating, Jim?「你在吃飯嗎，吉姆？」，而非 Are you eating Jim?「你正在吃吉姆嗎？」
- **問號（?）**：在間接問句與祈使句之後，不要使用問號，如 He asked what went wrong.「他問發生什麼事了。」以及 Please sweep up here after yourself.「如廁之後請自打掃完畢。」在類似 "Do you like it?" she asked.「她問：『你喜歡嗎？』」的情況下，要省略問號後面的逗號。
- **驚嘆號（!）**：商務信不需要也不應該出現驚嘆號（!），只有銷售信例外。私人信件中也應少用驚嘆號。J・L・巴斯福（J. L. Basford）認為，「常使用句號的人是哲學家；常使用問句的是學生；常使用驚嘆號的是狂熱分子」。驚嘆號會讓你的信看起來過度激動，好像你正因自己的笑話而大笑似的。一開始移除驚嘆號時，你會不禁心痛；但不久之後，你就會欣喜地發現，你沒有它們也能過得很好。
- **引號（""）** 用來引用文字，或標示雜誌文章標題及電視與廣標節目名稱。所有的標點符號都應出現在引號之內，如 "What?"、"Egads!"、"I won't," he said. 但在一些少見的例外中，則需要用常識來判斷，例如 How many times have you heard a child say "But I'm not tired"?「你聽到多少次孩子說『我還不累』？」

- **括號（（））**：在主要思路（主要句子）之外插入題外話時使用。當題外話是不完整的思緒（不完整的句子）時，通常會放在一般句子的中間，這種狀況下，第一個字母不必大寫，也不放任何標點符號。不過，當題外話是完整的思緒（完整句）時，句首字母便須大寫，也會有句末的標點符號。在句子裡使用括號時，所有的標點符號都放在括號之外，如：Please order more ribbons, paper (30#), and file folders.「請訂購更多的緞帶、（30號）紙張與資料夾。」

- **連字號（-）**用來讓一組詞語形成一個容易閱讀的單位。以 ly 結尾的詞不必加連字號（如 newly appointed「新預定的」），放在名詞之後的形容詞詞組也不必加連字號，所以 well-known telecaster「有名的 Fender 吉他型號」要加，而 she was well known「她很有名」則不必。目前趨勢是直接將兩字結合成一個字，取代用連字號或分成兩個字（使用 headlight，而非 head-light 或 head light）。查字典能確保你在多數情況下使用正確的形式。

- **撇號（'）**來取代縮寫的字母（如 isn't 等於 is not）或顯示所有格（如 Simon's）。最常用錯撇號的例子是 its（它的）與 it's（it is 的縮寫）。區分方法是，可以用 it is 替代的便得加上撇號；如果你難以分辨這兩種形式，那就只使用 it is 與 its，直到你能輕易辨別其中的差異。要是所有格擁有者超過一人，則在 s 後面加上撇號，以表示複數的所有格，如 union members' votes「工會成員的票數」或 the parents' recommendations「家長的推薦」。
  若是一串數字或一串字母組成的單字形成複數形，則省略撇號，如：PhDs、the 1990s、the 2000s、the '50s、three 100s、IBMs。

- **冒號（:）**時常用在一串清單或一段引言之前，如 We carry the following brand names: ...「我們代理以下的品牌：……」。若無必要，勿使用冒號將句子斷開，例如在 Your kit contains: a lifetime supply of glue, four colors of paint, and a set of two brushes.「您的工具包含：無限量供應的膠水、四罐油漆、與兩組刷具。」一句中，應移除冒號。冒號也會用在商業信件開頭或正式敬稱之後，如 Mr. President:「總統先生您好：」。

- **分號（;）**會讓你的信看起來一本正經又老派。不過，偶爾還是非常有用。當你列出一長串的清單，且清單中的各個項目皆標有標點符號，此時你必須用分號隔開各項目。你也可以用分號隔開一個句子中的兩個子句。

- **破折號（—）**：過度使用破折號，文章會變得破碎草率（英文中，破折號稱為 dash，有匆忙之意）。如果你是個常使用破折號的人，請檢查有沒有其他標點符號可以取代。破折號是會繁殖的，一旦養成了使用破折號的習慣，它就會在頁面上越長越多，使你的信好似一直在向前衝，令人喘不過氣。

- 英文書名與電影標題要**加底線或使用斜體**；其他類型的標題則應放入引號內。

- 專有名詞與特定地點的首字母應**大寫**。若想知道一個名詞應小寫（dad）或大寫（Dad），

你必須先決定這個名詞指的是一種類別（如：父母）還是名字或稱號（如 Hi, Dad.）。當你說 My father is great. 時，你的口氣便跟 My piano is great. 沒什麼兩樣。但要是 Dad 的作用就如同他的名字，就應該大寫，如 Thanks, Leo. 跟 Thanks, Dad.。

✉ 與人有關的話題

帶有成見的言論，忽視了每個人都是獨立個體的事實；排外的言論，則是忽視了某些人。當你邀請顧客參加招待會，卻忘了告知這個活動設有無障礙空間，此時你便忽視了殘障人士。當你用「Dear Sirs」為信件起頭，你便忘了收信人也有可能是女性。當你提起「猶太基督教倫理觀」，你便排除了一大群高度重視倫理的非猶太、非基督教人士。文字可用來排外、展現偏見與歧視別人，無論是關於性別、年齡、種族、身心障礙、社經地位、性傾向或宗教。

若想知道更多與尊重他人有關的用語，可參見我的其他著作《Talking About People》與《Unspinning the Spin》。

放下成見在做生意上是非常重要的，如果你排除某些人或對他們抱有成見，你便永遠無法把東西賣給他們，或從他們身上獲得資訊與幫助。以下提供一些基本原則：

- **我們首先是人，而後才是有殘疾的人**、六十五歲以上的人、去浸信會教會的人，或是芬蘭裔美國人。寫信時，先決定是否需要區別出性別、年齡、種族、宗教、經濟地位、殘疾等類別。大多時候並不需要。若有疑慮，省略這些類別。不要用部分的特徵來指稱一個人。如果瑪德蓮患有下身麻痺，那當你稱呼她「半身不遂者」時，你便是用部分特徵來形容她整個人。人們並不是「受困於輪椅」，而是使用輪椅。

- **檢查平行結構**：你是否只提到其中一人的婚姻狀態，卻未提及另一人的？只提到一人的種族，而非其他人？僅指出某些人是同性戀，卻不說其他人是異性戀？她是威廉‧葛斯翠夫人，他卻是雷‧帕克？或他是雷‧帕克，而她卻是雪拉？

- **不要用帶有男性意識的 man 或 mankind 來指稱大家**，而要使用能把全部人都包含進來的字詞，如 people（人們）、we（我們）、us（我們）、humanity（人類）、human beings（人類）、individuals（個體）、human society（人類社會）nature（自然、本質）、planet earth（地球）、the world（世界）。當你指的是「he or she」時，不要只寫 he。把 A mail carrier has his work cut out for him today. 改成複數形式：Mail carriers have their work cut out for them today.「郵差今天遇上了艱鉅任務。」你也可以用 you 或 we 改寫這個句子。避免寫「his or her」或「she or he」，這看起來很奇怪。

- 用「they」指稱單數名詞（如 to each their own）是行之有年的做法，本書也一直這麼使用。多數的語言專家都接受或支持這種寫法，包括：《牛津英語詞典》（*Oxford English Dictionary*）；《芝加哥論文寫作格式》（*Chicago Manual of Style*）第十五版；《American Heritage Dictionary of the English Language》第四版；《American Heritage Book of English Usage》；《the National Council of Teachers of English》；《Random House Dictionary II》；《韋氏第三版新國際字典》（*Webster's Third New International Dictionary*）；藍道夫・奎克（Randolph Quirk）等人所著之《A Grammar of Contemporary English》。

- 以 -person 為結尾的詞大多看起來很不自然，僅有少數是例外（例如 layperson「普通教徒；門外漢」），請用其他字替代。用 chair（主席）取代 chairperson，前者不僅使用較久也更為乾脆。我們也常使用 head（這裡指的是「領導」之意，如 the head of the department「部門主管」；She headed the organization.「她帶領組織。」），而不擔心會被認成一顆沒有身體的頭顱；同理，也沒有人會將委員會主席認成一張椅子。

 # 姓名

書寫姓名只有一項原則：使用收信人偏好的形式。注意事項包括：

- **正確拼寫**收信人的姓名。這絕對值得你花幾分鐘的時間與長途電話的費用，詢問寫信對象的正確姓名與目前職稱。

- **在某些狀況下你可以直呼對方的名字**，但在確認這麼做是可行之前，最好寫 Dear Mr. Cokeson（社交頭銜加上姓氏），不要寫 Dear Bob（僅寫名字）。禮貌小姐曾說，為了避免別人在未經同意下直呼她的名字，她的預防措施便是不取名字。每當陌生人稱呼她的名字，以為可以拉近距離時，她總是感到為難，而她不會是唯一這麼想的人。若你不確定應該用多正式的格式，請採取比較正式的做法。

- **訂製商務用或社交用名片時**，使用全名。像 Mr.、Ms.、Mrs.、Miss 這類的社交頭銜（social title），亦稱禮儀稱謂（courtesy title）或尊稱（honorific），過去會置於姓名之前，但現在大多都已省略。醫療界的人士會在社交名片使用 Dr. 或 Doctor，如 Doctor Christopher Bembridge（專業稱謂加上全名）。在商務名片上則會使用 M.D.、D.O.、D.D.S.、O.D.，如 Muriel Eden, D.D.S.（全名加上詳細職稱）。

  名字中的二世、三世等，可以用 Joseph Farr Jr.（縮寫）或 Joseph Farr II（羅馬數字）表示。若要在律師姓名後面使用 Esq.（Esquire 的縮寫，為先生、士紳之意，在美國用來代表律師），如 Marian Beltham, Esq.，則省略其他擺在姓名之前的頭銜（Mr.、Ms.、Mrs.、

Miss）。

- **寫信給女性時**，要使用對方所使用的社交頭銜。你可以參考她最近一封來信的簽名，或打電話親自確認：Do you prefer Miss, Mrs., or Ms.?「你偏好被稱為小姐、夫人或女士？」。如果你不清楚對方的婚姻狀態（對於男性，我們從來不需擔心這種問題），則使用全名，不加任何社交頭銜，或是使用較中性的社交頭銜 Ms. 加上姓氏。

  商務信件往來上，已婚女性會使用婚前姓氏。在一般社交，有些已婚女性則會使用丈夫的姓氏。傳統而言，已婚或喪偶的女性使用丈夫的姓氏，而離婚的女性則用婚前姓氏或前夫姓氏，或兩種姓氏都使用。單身女性可使用 Miss，也可以不用，端看對方喜好。這種針對女性婚姻狀態的稱謂系統，在現代已不常使用。

- **稱呼夫妻時**，使用他們稱呼自己的方式：Mr. and Mrs. Walter Evson（丈夫全名前加上雙方的社交頭銜）；Adela and George Norrington（妻與夫的名字，最後加上夫姓）；Dr. Guy and Mrs. Elizabeth Phillips 或 Dr. Linda and Mr. Arnaud Hallet（夫妻一方使用全名，另一方寫出名字，頭銜任意不需對稱）；Katherine Halstead and Frank Luttrell（各自寫婚前全名）。書寫信封或信內地址上的收件人姓名時，若是兩個名字都很長，可按照字母順序將姓名分行寫出。

- **寫信給一人以上的對象時**，使用每個人的全名，或是用社交頭銜加上每個人的姓氏。若寫信對象的性別都相同，你可以用 Mesdames（或 Mmes.）稱呼女性，或以 Messieurs（Messrs.）稱呼男性，不過這種稱呼看起來比較過時。這些稱呼後面只須加上姓氏。若寫信對象有女有男，則採用能包含兩者的敬稱，如 Dear Friends、Dear Cochairs、Dear Committee Members，或是 To:（列出姓名，每行一個姓名，按字母順序排列）。

✉ 信首稱謂、結尾祝頌詞與署名

信首稱謂

- 信首稱謂會最先出現在左方。**信首稱謂的第一個字要首字母大寫，但接在之後的形容詞不用**，如「My very dear Joanna」中的 very 與 dear 不用大寫。**社交頭銜與姓名都要首字母大寫**。用縮寫表示社交頭銜（Ms.、Mr.、Mrs.、Dr.），但其他的宗教、軍事與專業頭銜要完整拼寫出來，如 Father（神父）、Sister（姊妹）、Major（少校）、Colonel（上校）、Professor（教授）。在私人或非正式信函中，敬稱以逗號結尾；在商務信件中，則用冒號或逗號結尾。

- **最好找到最適合收信的人**，並確認對方的姓名正確拼法與目前職稱。有需要可以打電話到公司確認。

- **如果你知道收信人的名字**，可以寫 Dear Neil A. McTodd（全名、無頭銜），或是 Dear Ms. Lee、Dear Captain Crowe、Dear Inspector Hopkins 或 Dear Senator Burnside（頭銜加上姓氏）。如果不知道收信人性別，或不清楚對方習慣使用的社交頭銜時，使用第一種方法。若對方有專業或學術頭銜，如 Dr.、Representative，則以此頭銜為準，不使用社交頭銜 Mr.、Miss。

- **若你不知道收信人的姓名**，或者當你寫制式信時，還是可以用 Dear 開頭，後面接上名詞，如 Neighbor（鄰居）、Subscriber（訂閱人）、Friend（朋友）、Motorist（駕駛）、Reader（讀者）、Colleague（同仁）、Student（學生）、Customer（顧客）、Gardener（園藝家）、Client（客戶）、Employee（員工）、Potential Employee（職缺候選人）、Parishioner（教區居民）、Collector（催款人）、Cardholder（持卡人）、Concerned Parent（關心的家長）、Initiate-Elect（入選的新成員）、Handgun Control Supporter（槍枝管制支持者）、Member（會員）、Homeowner（屋主）、Supplier（供應商）、Executive（業務主管）、Aquarist（水族館館長）、Equestrian（馬術家）、Do-It-Yourselfer（DIY 愛好者）。或者也可以用工作職稱：Dentist（牙醫）、Copywriter（文案撰稿人）、Electrician（電氣技師）、Metallurgist（冶金學家）、Customer Service Manager（顧客服務經理）。或是接公司名稱：Poulengay Upholsterers、Elliot-Lewis Stationers、Handford Lawn Care。

- 也**可使用問候語取代信首稱謂**，如 Good morning!「早安！」、Hello!「哈囉！」、Greetings!「您好！」最佳的解決方式，是將信首稱謂換成主旨列。

結尾祝頌詞

- 結尾祝頌詞放在正文後方，之間隔一行空行。以大寫字母起頭，並以逗號收尾。最常見且**適用各種情況的結尾祝頌詞包括：**

Sincerely yours	Very sincerely yours
Yours truly	Very sincerely
Sincerely	Very truly yours

（約四分之三的信件都是使用 Sincerely）

使用以上的祝頌詞絕不會出錯。禮貌小姐曾說，商務信件應以 Yours truly 為祝頌詞；不過，「在還活著的人當中，禮貌小姐或許是唯一知道這件事的人」。

- **與外交、司法或教會有關的極正式信函**，應使用 Respectfully yours 或 Respectfully。這些領域的非正式信函，則用 Very respectfully yours、Yours respectfully 或 Sincerely yours。

- **正式信件的結尾祝頌詞包括：**

Sincerely	Truly yours
Sincerely yours	Yours truly
Yours sincerely	Very truly yours
Very sincerely yours	Yours very truly
Very sincerely	Very cordially yours

- **非正式的結尾祝頌詞則包括：**

Love	Faithfully yours
With all my love	Yours faithfully
Lovingly	As ever
Lovingly yours	As always
Fondly	Devotedly
Affectionately	Yours
Yours affectionately	Best regards
Sincerely	Kindest regards
Sincerely yours	Warmest regards
Cordially	Cheers
Cordially yours	Your friend
Yours cordially	Be well
Faithfully	Until next time

- **介於正式與非正式之間的祝頌詞**則有：

With all kind regards	With all best wishes
Warm regards	Cordially
Best regards	Sincerely
Best	All the very best
Best wishes	With every good wish
With best wishes	Warm personal regards

你可以從上面列表中，各選一到兩個適合寫作風格的結尾祝頌詞。不必為每一封信都特別選一個祝頌詞，這並不值得你花費太多心思。

簽名處

- 雖然過去署名的規定很多，但今日原則已變得相當簡單：**你希望收件人怎麼稱呼你，就用那個姓名格式簽名**。若有任何不明確之處（如對方不知道你的全名，只知道你的筆名、出生時的姓名，婚後姓名或工作上的姓名），可以在簽名下面以打字方式呈現對方較容易認出你的姓名，並用括號圈起。一般來說，簽名不會簽上頭銜，所以請省去（不過，你可以在簽名下方的姓名列中打出社交頭銜）。

- **私人信件**只需要簽名就好。在**商務信件**中，簽名下方須以打字方式列出姓名與職稱（可放於同一行或分行，取決於文字長度）。姓名及職稱應與結尾祝頌詞相隔四行空行供簽名。如果你的簽名特別瀟灑，可空更多行。要是信紙的信頭就已經包含你的姓名與職稱，便可以在簽名下方省略這一部分。

- **代表他人簽名時**，將你的姓名字首字母列於簽名的正右下方，前面加上一道斜線（/）。如果你是代表他人寫信，則簽上你自己的姓名，並在下方姓名列中寫出你與委託你寫信的人的關係，如 Son of Christina Light「克麗緹娜‧萊特之子」或 Secretary to Cavaliere Giacosa「卡瓦利埃‧伽克薩的祕書」。

- **如果你在信首稱謂中以名字稱呼對方**，簽名時也簽上名字即可（但在商務信件中，你的全名與職稱仍會列在簽名下方）。倘若信首稱謂與署名的名稱沒有相對應，可能會讓對方感到被羞辱與厭惡。如果你開頭寫 Dear Fred，最後卻署名 Dr. Francis Etherington，表示你自認地位較高；反之，則表示你自認雙方關係親近，但或許並非如此。信首稱謂與簽名必須完全相對應，例如：Dear Rosa, 和 Love, Judy；Dear Thomas Eustick, 和 Sincerely, Margaret Kraft。

日月文化集團
HELIOPOLIS
CULTURE GROUP

感謝您購買 英文溝通寫作全技藝

為提供完整服務與快速資訊，請詳細填寫以下資料，傳真至02-2708-6157或免貼郵票寄回，我們將不定期提供您最新資訊及最新優惠。

1. 姓名：＿＿＿＿＿＿＿＿＿＿＿＿　　性別：□男　　　□女

2. 生日：＿＿＿＿年＿＿＿＿月＿＿＿＿日　　職業：＿＿＿＿＿

3. 電話：（請務必填寫一種聯絡方式）

　（日）＿＿＿＿＿＿＿＿（夜）＿＿＿＿＿＿＿＿（手機）＿＿＿＿＿＿

4. 地址：□□□＿＿＿＿＿＿＿＿＿＿＿＿＿＿＿＿＿＿＿＿＿＿

5. 電子信箱：＿＿＿＿＿＿＿＿＿＿＿＿＿＿＿＿＿＿＿＿＿＿

6. 您從何處購買此書？□＿＿＿＿＿＿＿縣/市＿＿＿＿＿＿＿書店/量販超商

　□＿＿＿＿＿＿＿網路書店　□書展　□郵購　□其他

7. 您何時購買此書？　　年　　月　　日

8. 您購買此書的原因：（可複選）

　□對書的主題有興趣　□作者　□出版社　□工作所需　□生活所需
　□資訊豐富　　　　□價格合理（若不合理，您覺得合理價格應為＿＿＿＿＿）
　□封面/版面編排　□其他＿＿＿＿＿＿＿＿＿＿＿＿＿＿＿

9. 您從何處得知這本書的消息：　□書店　□網路／電子報　□量販超商　□報紙
　□雜誌　□廣播　□電視　□他人推薦　□其他

10. 您對本書的評價：（1.非常滿意 2.滿意 3.普通 4.不滿意 5.非常不滿意）

　書名＿＿＿＿　內容＿＿＿＿　封面設計＿＿＿＿　版面編排＿＿＿＿　文/譯筆＿＿＿＿

11. 您通常以何種方式購書？□書店　□網路　□傳真訂購　□郵政劃撥　□其他

12. 您最喜歡在何處買書？

　□＿＿＿＿＿＿＿縣/市＿＿＿＿＿＿＿書店/量販超商　　□網路書店

13. 您希望我們未來出版何種主題的書？＿＿＿＿＿＿＿＿＿＿＿＿＿＿＿

14. 您認為本書還須改進的地方？提供我們的建議？

＿＿＿＿＿＿＿＿＿＿＿＿＿＿＿＿＿＿＿＿＿＿＿＿＿＿＿＿＿

＿＿＿＿＿＿＿＿＿＿＿＿＿＿＿＿＿＿＿＿＿＿＿＿＿＿＿＿＿

＿＿＿＿＿＿＿＿＿＿＿＿＿＿＿＿＿＿＿＿＿＿＿＿＿＿＿＿＿

＿＿＿＿＿＿＿＿＿＿＿＿＿＿＿＿＿＿＿＿＿＿＿＿＿＿＿＿＿

EZ TALK

英文溝通寫作全技藝

求職、行銷、情書、慰問⋯50 種工作與生活情境，面面俱到的英文書信寫作要點

How to Say It: Choice Words, Phrases, Sentences, and Paragraphs for Every Situation

作　　者：Rosalie Maggio 羅莎莉‧瑪吉歐
譯　　者：鄒詠婷
審　　訂：李佳勳
責任編輯：鄭莉璇
封面設計：白日設計
內頁設計：管仕豪
內頁排版：張靜怡

發 行 人：洪祺祥
副總經理：洪偉傑
副總編輯：曹仲堯
法律顧問：建大法律事務所
財務顧問：高威會計事務所

出　　版：日月文化出版股份有限公司
製　　作：EZ 叢書館
地　　址：臺北市信義路三段 151 號 8 樓
電　　話：(02) 2708-5509
傳　　真：(02) 2708-6157
網　　址：www.heliopolis.com.tw
郵撥帳號：19716071 日月文化出版股份有限公司

總 經 銷：聯合發行股份有限公司
電　　話：(02) 2917-8022
傳　　真：(02) 2915-7212
印　　刷：中原造像股份有限公司
初　　版：2018 年 8 月
初版10刷：2023 年 4 月
定　　價：650 元
Ｉ Ｓ Ｂ Ｎ：978-986-248-735-8

英文溝通寫作全技藝：求職、行銷、情書、慰問⋯50 種工作與生活情境，面面俱到的英文書信寫作要點／羅莎莉‧瑪吉歐（Rosalie Maggio）著；鄒詠婷譯. -- 初版. -- 臺北市：日月文化, 2018.08
608 面；16.7×23 公分（EZ Talk）
譯自：How to say it : choice words, phrases, sentences & paragraphs for every situation
ISBN 978-986-248-735-8（平裝附光碟片）
1. 英語　2. 寫作法
805.17　　　　　　　　　　107008361

How to Say It: Choice Words, Phrases, Sentences, and Paragraphs for Every Situation, 3rd edition
This edition published by arrangement with TarcherPerigee, an imprint of Penguin Publishing Group,
a division of Penguin Random House LLC.
through Bardon Chinese Media Agency
Complex Chinese translation copyright © 2018 Heliopolis Culture Group Co., Ltd
ALL RIGHTS RESERVED